RAVES FOR THE NOVELS OF
JUDITH GOULD

"The perfect beach read."   —*Library Journal*

"Just the thing to chase away the blues."
—*Chicago Tribune*

"A romp! A smash success."
—*New York Daily News*

"Superb . . . Fantastic reading . . . put this one at the top of your must-read list."
—*Rendezvous*

"GOULD IS A MASTER."   —*Kirkus Reviews*

Don't miss any of Judith Gould's sinfully scintillating tales:

The Love Makers, Dazzle,
Never Too Rich, Texas Born, Forever,
and, her latest, *Too Damn Rich*

SINS

JUDITH GOULD

A SIGNET BOOK

SIGNET
Published by the Penguin Group
Penguin Books USA Inc., 375 Hudson Street,
New York, New York 10014, U.S.A.
Penguin Books Ltd, 27 Wrights Lane,
London W8 5TZ, England
Penguin Books Australia Ltd, Ringwood,
Victoria, Australia
Penguin Books Canada Ltd, 10 Alcorn Avenue,
Toronto, Ontario, Canada M4V 3B2
Penguin Books (N.Z.) Ltd, 182–190 Wairau Road,
Auckland 10, New Zealand

Penguin Books Ltd, Registered Offices:
Harmondsworth, Middlesex, England

First published by Signet, an imprint of Dutton Signet,
a division of Penguin Books USA Inc.

First Printing, November, 1982
25 24 23 22 21 20 19

 REGISTERED TRADEMARK—MARCA REGISTRADA

Printed in the United States of America

PUBLISHER'S NOTE
This is a work of fiction. Names, characters, places, and incidents either are the
product of the author's imagination or are used fictitiously, and any resemblance
to actual persons, living or dead, events, or locales is entirely coincidental.

BOOKS ARE AVAILABLE AT QUANTITY DISCOUNTS WHEN USED TO PROMOTE PROD-
UCTS OR SERVICES. FOR INFORMATION PLEASE WRITE TO PREMIUM MARKETING DIVI-
SION, PENGUIN BOOKS USA INC., 375 HUDSON STREET, NEW YORK, NEW YORK 10014.

ACKNOWLEDGMENTS

No book is the result of the author's efforts alone, and grateful acknowledgment to the many people who have unstintingly given of their time, expertise, experiences, and suggestions is due:

For starting the whole creative process—Gladys Allison.

The team at NAL—Alison Husting, Angela Rinaldi, Elaine Koster, and Mary Anne Wilson.

For his fine-tooth-comb copy-editing—Raymond Phillips.

For his initial commitment—Evan Marshall.

For her enthusiasm and continued support—Maria Carvainis.

For research, anecdotes, and generous support—Lucy Gaston, Lynn Contrucci, Janice Resnick, Lola Peters, Maria and Albert Gardini, Annette Bodzin, Virginia Martin, Florence Pybus, John M. Severt, Jr., Harold B. Eisner, Helmut Schmidt, Rhea and Kathryn Gallaher, Gunther and Erna Bienes, and Alberto Silveira, who said: "You do a little bit at a time, and before you know it . . ."

And, of course, Gala, who lay patiently at my feet for thousands of hours. Here's a steak, little darlin', before Momma sits back down for another few years.

**To
Thomas E. Hill,
who helped make it possible**

Of what is't fools make such vain keeping?
Sin their conception, their birth, weeping:
Their life, a general mist of error,
Their death, a hideous storm of terror.

—John Webster, Duchess of Malfi, Act IV

TODAY

Tuesday, January 9

1

Through the porthole of the jet she could see the double strands of lights shimmering through the swirling mist as the plane touched down on the solitary runway. She was seated alone in the small passenger section, anxious for her signal to disembark.

The man was waiting for her at the end of the runway. For as long as he could remember, there was only one thing he had ever wanted that had eluded him, and that was the woman who was stepping off the jet. She could be as soft as creamery butter, as fragrant as wildflowers, yet as hard as nails. For years he had waited patiently for her. She had called him less than an hour earlier.

And now she was at the bottom of the stairs, her lithe body bathed in the lights. She broke into a run and headed toward him, her high heels clicking on the concrete. He ran forward to meet her, and halfway, they suddenly collided into each other's arms. Closing his eyes as she fiercely gripped him, he felt her shift slightly as she pulled away from him.

"Darling," he said softly. "I jumped in the car as soon as you called. How long do we have?"

"I've already lost an hour with this detour. Another hour and I've got to be off again."

"It's that bad?"

She nodded slowly.

Together they walked toward the car. When they reached it, he held the passenger door open for her and she slid inside, carefully smoothing her skirt over her knees. He walked to the driver's side and slipped in beside her, while he wordlessly reached into his breast pocket and took out a folded slip of paper. It was a cashier's check for eleven million dollars.

A veil seemed to drop over her eyes. "No," she said under her breath. "This isn't why I interrupted the flight."

"Please let someone help you for once. Take it," he gently urged.

Apologetically she smiled. "I'm sorry, I can't." She turned away and stared out the windshield, her eyes focused in the distance on something only she could see.

"If you change your mind . . ." He pursed his lips, sighed, and put the check on the dashboard within her reach. Fifteen yards away, the wing- and taillights of the jet blinked on and off, and the round portholes were ghostly circles of yellow light.

An hour later, he sat in the car alone, hearing the high-pitched whine of jet engines as the plane swept up off the ground and was once again lost to the black night.

Long after the runway lights clicked off, he still sat there staring up into the dark. Even in the hour of her greatest need, all she had wanted was to be near him.

The check was still on the dashboard.

2

In his luxurious apartment at the Hotel Pierre, Karl von Eiderfeld glanced at his seven-thousand-dollar Piaget wristwatch. One minute past eight, the thin gold-and-lapis dial read. A little less than five hours to go, he thought grimly. He sat in a French chair, tapping his fingers up and down its graceful arms. It was very unlike him to be nervous. Everyone who knew him said that Karl von Eiderfeld was always in control of his own destiny, as well as the destinies of others.

Emaciated and tall, von Eiderfeld carried his air of haughty aristocracy to perfection: people almost tended to forget that he was an albino. His flesh was cadaverous, and his head, crowned with thinning white hair, was narrow and skull-like in shape. His eerie pink eyes and strange coloring could not detract from his imperious posture, his aquiline nose with its long, thin nostrils, or his arched white eyebrows. But then, neither could his steel mills, his fleet of oil tankers, his refineries, and his many millions.

Karl von Eiderfeld had founded and forged his industrial empire out of the ashes of postwar Germany. The Reich that was to rule for a thousand years had collapsed. The spirit of his country had been spent. Tank treads crisscrossed the land once walked by a proud Barbarossa. The cities were smoldering. Germany was one vast ruin.

But von Eiderfeld had not been unhappy. He didn't believe in the bitter taste of defeat. Besides, vast sums of money were pouring in from America under the Marshall Plan. . . . Yes, he recognized it as a golden opportunity for those who would have a hand in rebuilding the vanquished Fatherland. And it was an even greater opportunity for those with foresight, imagination, and daring—for those who *knew* things. Little things. Little things such as where certain desperately needed items could be obtained. Items people were willing to pay for. Dearly.

Yes, he had known where forgotten stockpiles of much-needed propane gas were stored. By cover of night he quietly dug up the cylinders from their secret depots and transported them in horse-drawn wagons to a deserted winery on the Moselle River. It took him two months, but that winter it paid off. Nature was on his side and brought the coldest winter in ten years. Fuel was in short supply. He sold the propane, found his fortune, and financed his first steel mill.

In 1946 Karl von Eiderfeld emerged as one of the architects of the postwar industrial boom. In no time at all, his steel mills were helping rebuild the burned cities and bombed railroad tracks by pouring girders and rails. His refineries processed the oil that was needed to keep the railroad and construction machinery running. And his ships brought that oil to Hamburg, Bremen, and Bremerhaven. Soon nothing was beyond his reach. And he was making a most pleasant discovery. The more he accumulated, the quicker everything seemed to multiply. It was magic. Money indeed made money.

By 1949 he was a millionaire. By 1960 his companies had reached out and expanded into an enviable worldwide network with seventeen foreign branches. And now? Now his position as one of the three wealthiest and most powerful men in the entire Ruhr Gebiet was secure.

His piercing gaze swept around the dim, luxuriously furnished living room. It was on the fifteenth floor of the Hotel Pierre and had six windows facing Fifth Avenue. The view of Central Park was spectacular, but he never saw it. The heavy damask draperies were always kept drawn. Without the natural protection of pigmentation, his delicate eyes were painfully sensitive to light.

There was nothing remotely Germanic about von Eiderfeld's New York apartment. In style it looked as if it had been transplanted from Versailles. The walls of the living room were covered with authentic Régence paneling that had been carefully dismantled from a château in France and shipped to New York. It had been installed under the fastidious eyes of both a decorator and an art historian. From the ceiling hung a splendid pair of Venetian-glass chandeliers; over the marble mantel, a Venetian mirror flashed silvery. Scattered all about were Louis XVI settees and chairs, all genuine and upholstered in ancient blue damask. Like the chairs, the fabric was genuine eighteenth-century: worn thin, faded, and tattered. On the walls hung three gilt-framed Monets, two Goyas, and a small Fragonard.

His inspection over, von Eiderfeld rose from the chair with a thoughtful expression on his face and slowly paced the length of the room. Today was the day for which he had waited all these years.

By all rights I should be feeling triumphant, he was thinking, just like all those other times when I exacted my revenge. But this time was different. Vengeance somehow has a way of tasting bitter when you have to wait too long.

He sighed and shook his head. He had always destroyed his enemies as neatly and swiftly as an avenging angel. With the power of the mighty Von Eiderfeld Industrien G.m.b.H. behind him, that never posed any sort of problem. But to every rule there is an exception. His exception was Hélène Junot. Opposing her, he was as powerless as Goliath against David. Her weapon was, however, one he could well appreciate: she knew things. Just as he had once known things. But her knowledge had not become obsolete over the years. Instead, it seemed to increase in importance as time went by. It had brought her control—over people. And she had used him. He had been coerced into becoming one of the shareholders in her publishing firm. He had wanted no part of it. But he had given in. It was either that or . . . No, he still didn't want to consider the alternative. She had made that only too clear. It still loomed over his head like Damocles' sword. And he knew she wasn't bluffing. He knew it only too well.

Yes, he thought, Hélène Junot, founder of Hélène Junot International, Inc., and publisher of *Les Modes,* the world's most successful fashion magazine, was more than just a woman. Far from it. She was a beautiful, iron-willed, erotic, blackmailing *monster.* In short, dangerous. She had the power to destroy him. She had almost used it once, and he could remember it only too well. It had been a far-too-close shave.

He had no illusions. It could happen again.

The familiar hatred prickled hotly behind his ears. Gott im Himmel! How he despised her!

But today he and the others were finally prepared to wage war. Her time had finally come.

It was forty minutes past eight EST and Marcello d'Itri picked at his first-class, yet still bland Alitalia breakfast. Leaning back in his seat, he held out his empty champagne glass to the stewardess for a refill.

"Right away, sir," she said with a smile.

He smiled back at her as she filled his glass with more Piper Heidsieck. An extraordinarily lovely girl, he thought. He took an appreciative sip of his champagne. Ah, yes, *everything* was lovely today. The muted, steady roar of the Boeing engines coming from the rear pleased him. He couldn't remember when the thick sea of clouds far below had seemed more beautiful, and for once he didn't mind the blinding sunlight that poured in through the little square window. He wasn't going to pull the shade down. Not today, he wouldn't. Even the tasteless eggs he decried on every flight were a special joy.

Because in two hours he would land at Kennedy Airport and then, finally, all the little wheels he had so meticulously arranged would be set into motion.

A warm glow of satisfaction spread through his body.

Marcello d'Itri was forty-two years old, olive-complexioned, and of medium height. His hair was graying black, thick, and looked perpetually—almost calculatedly—unkempt. His cheeks had a constant blue-green tint from his thick beard that no amount of shaving could erase. He was dressed in a stylish gray velvet jacket, pleated gray trousers, a red-plaid shirt, and a thin gray tie. Other than his disheveled hair, he was superbly groomed; his fingernails were manicured, his hand-sewn loafers gleamed, and the thin belt around his small waist was fashioned from cobra skin and fastened with an eighteen-carat gold buckle. The gray leather briefcase beneath his seat sported a pattern of continuous diagonal initials—*Md'I . . . Md'I . . . Md'I*. He was quite content carrying the same "signature" luggage as thousands of other travelers. Especially since the initials were his.

Although he was now accepted as *the* leading Italian fashion designer of the past decade, d'Itri's chances of even moderate success had in the beginning been very slim. His fantastic, sometimes outlandish designs, as well as his humble peasant origins, had horrified both the industry and customers alike. In an age of aristocratic couturiers—when the titles Prince, Princess, Count, and Countess were expected on every fashion label—his simple "Marcello d'Itri" was enough to send customers scurrying.

But a fairy godmother had come to his aid. Hélène Junot had seen his designs and liked his potential. Enough overexposure in her fashion magazines had single-handedly put him firmly on the fashion map, even ahead of that other darling of society women, Valentino. But the setup, d'Itri discovered much later, was costly. Hélène had infiltrated his business like an elegant octopus whose tentacles were everywhere. She ended up controlling not only Marcello d'Itri fashions but also Marcello d'Itri himself.

He sighed, thinking back. Ah, well, it could have been worse. At least the success she had created for him had one wonderful compensation. Money. And so, little by little and very quietly, under the cover of various dummy corporations, Marcello had used his growing fortune to buy into Hélène Junot International, Inc. Before Hélène knew what was happening he was sitting on the board.

Now, after all these years of suffering at Hélène's beautiful hands, it would come to an end.

Her creation was going to help destroy her.

In the exclusive enclave of Manhattan's Sutton Place, Z.Z. Bavier gloated as she looked thoughtfully out at the East River through the giant beveled-glass French doors of her seventeenth-floor penthouse apartment. Outside, the icicle-draped yew bushes sat in their frozen, sun-drenched tubs on the terrace. Below, traffic on both levels of the Fifty-ninth

Street Bridge looked miniaturized, and sunlight flashed off chrome.

Z.Z. stood there, her Dunhill cigarette curling acrid smoke upward past the violet moiré draperies. She had just replaced the receiver of her ivory telephone after a short but highly satisfactory conversation. Hélène Junot was already back in town, ahead of schedule, the caller had informed her. Hélène Junot, that beautiful, ill-bred, high-fashion whore was smelling trouble through those pretty nostrils of hers, no doubt. Probably running scared, Z.Z. thought with sadistic pleasure. Oh, that was so delicious. And what a reception she'd get! After nearly ten years, the showdown was at hand at last.

Simply delicious!

Z.Z. Bavier was thirty-eight years old, spiteful, bone-thin, and deceptively short. She wore a puce-and-violet Pucci caftan, a gold necklace fashioned from ancient Byzantine coins, and gold sandals. Her hair was honey-colored and starched stiff from too much spray, her predatory nose had a sharp upward tilt, and her lynx eyes were small, green, and alert. She breathed the very elegance she had dedicated years to achieve. Of all her far-flung social contacts, none knew what her first name actually was, nor even what the letters Z.Z. stood for. Z.Z. delighted in the speculation.

She turned around from the window and stalked the length of the generously scaled living room, the Byzantine coins around her neck clunking softly against one another.

She snorted as she thought back to how it had all begun almost ten years ago. Ten long years ago when she had been Mrs. Siegfried Bavier, the lovely wife of the legendary financier who had had a celebrated nose for sniffing out sound investments and whose effortless wealth seemed to grow in leaps and bounds.

Then, in 1965, everything fell apart. Her darling Sigi had forced her into divorce. He didn't seem to care that she was pregnant at the time. His only concern was for Hélène Junot. Well, Z.Z. had let him have her, believing that it wouldn't be long before he'd come crawling back on his knees, begging for forgiveness. She was as certain of that as she was of receiving an invitation to Earl Blackwell's next party, being listed in the *Celebrity Register*, or having her latest wardrobe described by Suzie. And when Sigi came crawling back, what then? Well, she would punish him for a suitable time and then finally relent. It had happened before, but not to the point of divorce. She would simply wait patiently until this fling was over. And of course she had received a handsome settlement by any standards. Seven million dollars, the co-op apartment on Sutton Place and the house in Easthampton, two Picassos and one Braque, a collection of Georgia O'Keeffes, and a trust fund for the unborn baby.

But the unthinkable had happened. Her Sigi never came back. The day after their divorce was final, Sigi and that Hélène woman exchanged vows in a civil ceremony downtown. Two months later, he dropped dead on the floor of the stock exchange, leaving Hélène with fifteen million dollars, leaving Z.Z. to give premature birth to his son.

How desperately she had wanted to have their baby! She had banked on its bringing Siegfried back. They would be closer than ever; surely fatherhood would force him to stop his philandering and settle down. She had even decided on a name. Carla if it was a girl. Wilfred if it was a boy.

But when the Jamaican nurse had brought her face to face with the baby boy, her hands had flown up to her face to cover her eyes. In one glance she had seen enough of that horrible, distorted little creature. She had caught sight of the little pink face with the wide-set eyes, an inheritance from her, the little red mouth lolling open, the expression of utter helplessness. She had caught sight of that face scrunching up into hideous distortions. Her baby had survived his early birth, but he had suffered irreversible brain damage.

"Mine?" Her hoarse whisper seemed to echo from the green-and-white walls.

The nurse nodded solemnly.

Z.Z.'s eyes widened in horror. "It can't be," she wailed in a shocked voice, shaking her head. "It's *not* mine! It can't be! It *can't* be!" She had shrunk against the metal headboard, sobbing violently.

She couldn't believe it. She had given birth to a monster! The realization brought on a nervous breakdown.

When she recovered, Z.Z. told all her inquiring friends that the baby had been stillborn. And she had accepted their apologies and condolences and clucking ministrations for that which she wished so badly could only have been.

She was never able to erase Wilfred from her mind. Her rejection of him haunted her day and night. Did he ever wonder about his mother? she asked herself over and over. And what was he like now?

She shut her eyes and shivered. Always that same thought came back to her: *What was he like now?* But she had always been afraid to find out.

Hélène would pay for this, Z.Z. had sworn. Oh, yes, she would pay. It was all that whore's fault. If it hadn't been for Hélène, she would have inherited twenty-two million dollars instead of the paltry seven she'd had to settle for. And above all, she wouldn't have had to be alone while giving birth to Sigi's . . . She swallowed. Sigi's . . . *child*. She wouldn't have had to carry all by herself the horrible burden, the hidden stigma, of bringing a malformed child into the world. Sigi would have been there to share the anguish, and it would have seemed less.

And so, as it had become available, Z.Z. found herself buying three million dollars' worth of stock in Hélène Junot International, Inc.

She felt it was worth every penny. It was very satisfying to sit on the board, countering every move made by that woman she hated with all her being.

But *that* had only been petty warfare. The real offensive was just beginning.

The big Mercedes limousine fought its way through the dense morning traffic. Seated on the plush gray velour was a single passenger, the Comte de Léger. He was on his way from his fashionable brownstone on East Sixty-eighth Street to the Junot Building, the Fifth Avenue headquarters of Hélène Junot International, Inc.

A banker, a wine grower, and second cousin to the prime minister of France, the Comte was a member of the board of Hélène Junot, as well as an alcoholic. A sour, red-faced Frenchman with the handsomely cruel features that women tended to find irresistible, he had a flat stomach and stood six feet, two inches tall. His eyes were coal black and hard, and his abundant graying hair was swept back as if to offer less wind resistance. He was elegantly dressed in a blue suit that had been custom-tailored on Savile Row, highlighted by a black raw-silk tie. His cufflinks were engraved with the de Léger crest, a lion and a salamander supporting a shield between them. They were a family heirloom, passed down from one comte to the next. They had been fashioned from ancient gold earrings that had been a gift to the first Comtesse de Léger by King François I in 1546. The lion and the salamander symbolized the alliance of the de Légers to the French throne.

At the moment, the Comte was oblivious of the start-and-stop traffic, and he felt sick. He was oblivious of the traffic because he had more important things on his mind. He felt sick because he had spent a sleepless night drinking heavily. In the middle of the night he had received a telephone call from Paris. Hélène Junot had chartered a Lear jet and left Orly Airport in a tearing hurry, the faint crackling voice had informed him.

The significance of the Lear jet was not lost on the Comte. Obviously she hadn't taken the company's lavishly decorated Grumman Gulfstream II because she didn't want to alert anyone to her unexpected return.

She didn't want anyone to have time to prepare. He smiled. As if there was anything she could do now. Didn't she realize it was too late?

How naive she was to think that she could outsmart them! Especially when they had all waited so patiently and for so long.

Well, he was nobody's fool. He had expected a sudden move on her part, and he'd been prepared. She had been shadowed to Orly, and before the Lear jet had received flight clearance he had already known about it. And when the jet landed at Kennedy Airport a mere fifteen minutes ago, he had known that, too. The only thing that surprised him was that it had taken this long for her to make a move.

Ah, it felt so good to be on top of it all. Poor Hélène. She thought she was a queen when she was, in reality, only a pawn. His pawn.

She had been a fool. Somewhere along the way she had been lulled into a false sense of security. It was so easy to feel omnipotent just because of a few items in a lawyer's vault. He smiled secretly. Even the most secure vaults have a way of opening.

He felt the limousine lurch to another stop. The queasiness in his stomach returned. Better have another drink to dull that feeling, he told himself.

He opened the door of the built-in bar cabinet and splashed a generous portion of Armagnac into one of the Baccarat snifters. He drained it in one greedy gulp.

Ah, that felt good, he thought as the warm glow of the

brandy spread through him like a much-needed caress. Then he poured himself another.

Suddenly his lips compressed angrily as he slammed a fist into the velour seat. "Je suis bête!" he exclaimed. How stupid to have overlooked the obvious. He should have noticed it before.

Two hours were unaccounted for. He hadn't realized it at first, but Hélène's flight had taken 140 minutes more than the usual flight time. He had been notified upon both takeoff and landing. But what had she done during those two unaccountable hours? Surely she hadn't flown circles over the middle of the Atlantic. A Lear jet didn't carry enough fuel for that.

Yes, she must have interrupted the flight. She had landed somewhere. But where? And whatever for?

He picked up the limousine's mobile telephone. Someone would have to talk to the pilot and find out.

The Comte's black limousine was nearing the Junot Building just as James Cortland Gore III placed another syrup-drenched pancake into his mouth. Gore sat in the breakfast room of his baronial mansion in Greenwich, Connecticut, a mere forty-five-minute drive from mid-Manhattan. The small bright room was covered with a green fern-patterned wallpaper, and the floor was laid with dark gray flagstones. Sitting across the wrought-iron-and-glass table, his wife was silently looking out the big bay window. It was a moment of fantasy. The morning sunshine was throwing elongated shadows of trees across the blinding snow, making the lawn look like a zebra-skin rug.

Then she glanced back at her husband.

Gore was a short, porcine man of sixty-one with sagging jowls, pursed red lips, and innumerable chins. He had a bald head, and the beady gray eyes peering out of the sagging pouches beneath his stiff salt-and-pepper eyebrows were focused on the front page of *The Wall Street Journal* spread out beside him. His pinstriped suit reflected his position. As a successful banker he had a $150,000-a-year salary, generous expense accounts, and memberships in the exclusive clubs that cater to working gentlemen. He was at the pinnacle of his career.

Gore lifted his eyes from the newspaper and peered across the table.

One look at Geraldine left no doubt but that she was a

pampered woman. She was fifty-seven years old but looked no more than thirty-nine. Painfully thin, she had striking Indian-like cheekbones and her skin was dark with the unmistakable Palm Beach tan from weekends spent in Florida. Her lemon gown trimmed with matching ostrich feathers had come from Martha's in Bal Harbour. Her ash-blond hair was bleached almost white by the sun and hung thinly to her shoulders. It was styled each Thursday afternoon at Susumu's salon on Fifth Avenue before her Friday flights to Palm Beach. Her nose was thin and delicate. More than fifteen years earlier it had been "redone" in an exclusive clinic outside Lausanne. A sparkling canary-diamond bracelet hung from her bony wrist. She'd picked it out at Bulgari a week ago, and since then it hadn't left her wrist for a moment.

Gore cleared his throat. "By the way, dear, there's some bad news." His chins quivered as he spoke.

"Bad news?"

"I'll have to work late tonight."

"Oh, no, darling," she said with a moan. "Don't tell me! You . . . you can't! Not tonight. You *promised* nothing would interfere with tonight. We're invited to the Asburys' for dinner, remember?"

Gore was annoyed. Remember? How could he forget? "Sorry, dear," he said calmly. "You'd better call them up and cancel."

"Oh, d-a-m-n!" Another fine evening spoiled by his work. And she'd been so looking forward to this one. The Asburys had houseguests from France, and Geraldine was dying to show off her half-forgotten Sorbonne French and the taffeta Grès gown she'd bought in Paris last year. It was gorgeous, in geranium, port, and bottle green. There was no doubt about it—the Grès was a masterpiece. It hugged her body where it was supposed to, but not too tightly; rather it . . . yes, it *caressed* her.

Now the evening was ruined. She couldn't go to the Asburys' unescorted. It just wasn't *done*. S-h-i-t, she spelled out in her mind. Careful, she told herself. Simmer down. Be dignified. She glanced at her husband.

Across the table, Gore, not content with one helping of pancakes, was engrossed in sating his unusually limitless appetite. He was, however, genuinely sorry for ruining Geraldine's plans. Nobody knew better than he how much

14

she'd been looking forward to dinner with the Asburys and their French guests. He didn't enjoy disappointing her. But tonight he had other plans. Tonight he was going to make one of the most important decisions of his life.

Just three days were left, he thought. *Just three more days and the Junot bank loan would be due. If it could not be repaid on time, then it would be up to the bank—up to him—to decide the fate of the collateral: 20 percent of the entire stock of Hélène Junot International, Inc. A juicy 20 percent of Hélène Junot's personal 51 percent of the corporation, for it had been a personal loan. And members of the board of Hélène Junot International, Inc., had approached him—discreetly at his clubs, openly through associates and attorneys, and even secretly with mysterious telephone calls. There were whispered offers of what he would receive. One million dollars, tax-free, as long as Hélène did not get an extension and the bank decided to distribute the shares to the other stockholders for their market value.*

Like greedy vultures, they were all waiting to pounce on her. For one reason or another, each of them seemed determined to have her out of the way.

Oh, what a million dollars couldn't solve. There had never been a time he needed it more. He enjoyed living comfortably, and Geraldine demanded a life-style that . . . well, that had practically gone out of style. There was the mansion in Greenwich and the house in Palm Beach, both so very necessary socially, and both so prohibitive financially. Both were mortgaged to the hilt. On the landing strip outside town sat the Beechcraft Bonanza that they used each weekend to commute to Palm Beach. The honey-gold-and-champagne Bentley sat in the heated garage between the brand-new Cadillac Seville and the late-model Lincoln Continental. Then there were the shopping sprees in Paris, where Madame Gore was becoming an increasingly well-known fixture. The red carpet was already being rolled out for her at the couturiers' and she was even getting front-row seating during the shows. And finally there was the sixty-foot Chris Craft yacht Geraldine was determined he buy for her. After all, she reasoned with typical rationale, the house in Palm Beach looked stark naked with an empty dock. His suggestion that they tear out the dock had not been met with disapproval. It had been met with horror.

And then, two months ago, the most expensive habit of all had surfaced. "Picking up trinkets" at Harry Winston or Bulgari. He glanced at the diamonds sparkling on her wrist and winced.

All that was so difficult to manage on $150,000 a year. Geraldine didn't know it, and God knows he couldn't bear to break her pretty heart by telling her, but his finances were looking very bleak.

Already he had "borrowed" from the bank, discreetly giving himself loans from time to time. He always planned on repaying them when he had a windfall, or sometime when Geraldine wasn't costing him so much.

Damn her! he thought angrily. It was so hard to say no.

The million dollars offered for throwing Hélène Junot's shares in the other stockholders' directions was irresistible. An answered prayer.

And best of all, no one need ever know.

He tossed the newspaper aside. It was far more pleasurable to think about a million dollars than to scour the news.

That was how he missed a three-column headline on page two. It read: "SHAKE-UP AT JUNOT PUBLICATIONS?"

The icy wind stung bitterly at his face as the Chameleon snapped the phone-booth door shut behind him. Frowning, he inserted a dime in the phone and punched out the number of another pay phone somewhere across town. He listened to the soft rings. Once. Twice. Three times. He replaced the receiver on the cradle and his dime jingled back into the return slot. He fished it out and waited twenty seconds. All around him he heard the noisy turmoil of Times Square.

Paper and garbage flew in the wind while neon flashed gaudy advertisements. The record and shoe shops weren't open yet. The porno theaters were quiet. No one dashed in and out of massage parlors. It was too early. Altogether, Times Square looked seedy, an ancient dowager turned bag lady. Still, it wasn't too bad, the Chameleon thought to himself. Times Square never looked too bad at nine-thirty A.M. But at nine-thirty at night it was a whole different story.

Last night it had looked like a Babylonian carnival. Rows of movie marquees were festooned with cutouts of voluptuous nudes. Peep-show parlors promised a glimpse of Sodom for a quarter. Hookers in rabbit coats paraded around with bare, frozen thighs. Drag queens strutted on shaky heels, their

16

coats open wide to show off rock-hard, expensive breasts. Hungry-eyed boys in tight Levi's were posed to accentuate their firm round bottoms. All available, for a price.

At Forty-fourth Street a Puerto Rican girl had stepped out of the shadows. She wore white plastic boots and a short skirt. Her long bare legs were red from the cold.

"You give me light?" she asked softly. Shiny black eyes looked at him over her cigarette.

He fished in his pocket for his lighter. As the flame flared up, he caught a glimpse of tawny skin and wet red lips. Her cheeks were powdered but gray, the shivering fingers holding the cigarette too thick, too masculine.

He shook his head and continued walking. Another drag queen. He liked real pussy, not a queer prick tucked out of sight. He sighed. Weren't there any women working these streets anymore?

At a red light he set his suitcase down on the sidewalk and lit a cigarette. Then he looked for a hotel.

On Forty-eighth Street, just off Broadway, he found one. He stared up at it. A real fleabag. Eight stories high, bricks painted an ugly gray. There was an alley beside it that led to a parking lot in the rear. Around the corner he could see an elaborate fire escape that led down to it. "HOTEL ZANZIBAR," the flashing red neon on the front announced. "Rooms $5.00 and up. Permanents and Transients Welcome," a rusty sign read.

It was the type of place that offered total anonymity, where no one asked any questions. Pay for your flop in advance, and then come and go as you like.

Perfect.

He tossed his cigarette into the gutter and watched it land with a shower of sparks. Then, whistling softly, he went up the concrete steps, opened the door, and walked into the lobby.

The lobby was something else. It was tiled and looked like a cross between a Turkish bath and a 1920's theater lobby. The sconces along the walls were of surprisingly good quality, but dented and rusty and missing their shades. The tear-shaped bulbs glared harshly. From one of the rooms down the hall a radio was on full blast. It was loud, tinny salsa, distorted and painful to the ears. Steam radiators hissed and clanged like snorting locomotives.

To the right, just inside the door, was a glass-and-wood

17

booth. It almost hid the short, tired-looking blond who sat behind it reading a confession magazine.

He cleared his throat.

Reluctantly she put the magazine down on the counter and her pale face looked up at him. "Yeah?" she rasped unenthusiastically.

He set his suitcase down. "I want a room," he said softly.

"Well, there's not much choice," she answered in a hoarse voice. "All I got's one." She snapped her bubble gum. "Rest's full up."

"Does it face the street?"

She shook her head. "Nope, out back. Looks down on the parking lot. Third floor. Real quiet."

"How much?"

"Twenty bucks a night."

"Twenty bucks a. . . ? But the sign outside says five!"

"Yeah," she said wearily, "I know. It's an old sign. Take it or leave it." Her voice sounded annoyed. She wanted to get back to the confession magazine.

He sighed. "All right, I'll take it."

"How long you want it for?"

He considered. "Oh . . . make it a week."

She shoved the registration book toward him and watched him bend over and sign in. "A. Samuels," the legible script read, from Washington, D.C. A change, she thought, from all the illegible John Smiths that filled the ledger. She turned around and took a key from one of the cubbyholes behind the desk. He reached out for it.

"Uh-uh," she said with a shake of her head. "That'll be a hundred and forty bucks. In advance."

He reached for his wallet and counted out three fifty dollar bills.

"Room's number three-oh-four," she said, slapping a ten and the key down on the linoleum counter. "That's on the third floor. Elevator's over there, on your right." She nodded vaguely in the direction. "And leave the key here at the desk whenever you go out. The management don't like their guests takin' off with their keys."

"Sure," he said, picking up his suitcase. Then he walked to the elevator.

Room 304 was everything he had expected. It was small and shabby, the paper-stiff sheets on the bed hiding a stained, lumpy mattress. In the bathroom, a leaky faucet endlessly dripped into the green-stained sink. Rough voices and rock music filtered through the thin wall from the room next door.

He pushed aside the faded curtains and peered out into the darkness. He couldn't have chosen a better place. All around were the backs of old office buildings. At this hour of the night they were empty. Below, the parking lot was dark and deserted, strewn with garbage. And right outside his window, the fire escape led down to that parking lot. A grimy private staircase. He would be able to come and go up and down that fire escape anytime after nightfall. If he was cautious, maybe even during the day. And best of all, the Hotel Zanzibar was far removed from that glittering world of high society he'd have to come into contact with. He might end up getting bitten by bed bugs, but at least he wouldn't be connected with the job. When it was done, the police would scour among the Beautiful People, not the city's cheap hotels for an anonymous stranger. Anyway, by that time he planned to be long gone.

He drew the curtains, turned away from the window, and went over to the bed. He placed the suitcase on it and unlocked it. So far, everything was going according to plan. In the bus terminal he'd found the key and the suitcase in two separate lockers.

The suitcase was neatly packed with stiffly folded clothes. Unceremoniously he dumped them on the floor. Taking out a pocketknife, he slashed apart the lining inside the lid. Then he slid his hand between the lining and the vinyl shell.

The Chameleon smiled. His fingers felt paper. "Oh, baby," he whispered to the suitcase. "Sweet, sweet baby. I could come all over you."

He pulled twenty-six envelopes out from behind the lining. First he tore open the twenty-five thick ones. Each was filled with crisp new hundred-dollar bills. He stacked them neatly in a pile. Then, wetting his finger, he quickly counted. The amount checked out: $50,000.

The down payment on a murder.

Finally he tore open the twenty-sixth envelope. It felt empty. But inside was a single newspaper clipping, neatly folded. Slowly he unfolded it.

He let out a low whistle and blinked. Then he sat down on the edge of the bed and stared at the photo of the first female target he'd ever had. Such a pity, he thought. God, she was a beautiful dame. She didn't stand a chance. Not against him.

The Chameleon was the best contract killer in the business. He lit a cigarette and glanced again at the photo with its simple caption: *Hélène Junot.*

3

The Junot Building was located on the northeast corner of Fifth Avenue and Twelfth Street. In the midst of that sedate old neighborhood it stuck out like a dazzling, blinding diamond. Hélène had hired Kevin Roche, John Dinkeloo, and Associates to design the nineteen-story structure.

"I want something spectacular," she had told the architects. "Something dazzling and chic, yet something with panache and *guts.*"

And that, exactly, was what she got. It literally stopped traffic. A small-scale forerunner of their spectacular U.N. Plaza Hotel, Roche, Dinkeloo, and Associates had designed an award-winning structure of angular walls of mirrored glass. In the morning light the Junot Building looked frosty and ice-cube-cold. During the day it caught movement and activity and seemed alive. At night it was almost as if a million candles shimmered inside the facade. But at sundown it was at its most spectacular. It faced west, and the dying sun turned its faceted mirror walls to fire.

The building's facade loomed cold and silvery at nine-thirty when Hélène emerged from her white Rolls-Royce Silver Cloud, New York license plate HJII. The mirrors threw reflections of the car all over the building as the gray-liveried chauffeur held the door open for her. On the sidewalk, several passersby looked at her. Hélène was the type of woman who naturally made heads turn. Wherever she went, she was noticed. This was due in part to her celebrity status, in part to her extraordinary beauty.

Anyone who did not know her would have laid odds that she was under thirty and a fashion model. Actually she was thirty-eight and owned the controlling shares of Hélène Junot

International, Inc., the publishing empire that bore her name. She had founded and forged the corporation that printed the world's most influential and widely read fashion magazines. She was slender, stood five feet, ten inches tall in her stocking feet, and held herself with regal poise and grace. Her exquisitely pale oval face was as delicate as a Dresden figurine's, and she had the most strikingly violet eyes. Set in her face like radiantly rare jewels, their exact coloring was dependent on the lighting around her. Fluctuating somewhere between smoky amethyst and translucent violet, they were speckled with the tiniest flecks of sapphire. Her luxuriant hair was raven black. Drawn back into a chignon, its severity only emphasized the delicate cheekbones that were as pronounced as a Bolshoi ballerina's. Her lips were full and sensual and her teeth had the gleam of new porcelain. The collar of her lush Blackglama mink coat was turned up and hid her long, graceful neck.

She glanced down Fifth Avenue toward Washington Square. This was basically a residential area: the sidewalks were nearly deserted. At the foot of the avenue the arch gleamed white in the sunlight. In front of it the giant Christmas tree was still up. Her lips tightened when she saw it.

Merry Christmas, she thought, shaking her head unhappily. Such a sad holiday, so sad because it is always what others seem to celebrate. Others, all those secure, nameless families snowbound in quaint little houses with creaking rocking chairs and colorful quilts and wonderful relatives with whom they can share the holidays.

I had a wonderful family once.

She felt a shiver, but it was not from the cold. Instinctively she drew the mink lapels closer to her throat and held them there.

"Madame?" a voice said gently from behind her.

She came out of her reverie and turned around. The chauffeur was still holding the car door open, unable to close it. She was in the way.

"Oh! I'm sorry, Jimmy," she said in her throaty, French-accented voice. Her breath made little white clouds of vapor in front of her face. Quickly she moved aside.

He shut the door. "Shall you be needing the car for lunch, madame?"

She considered. "No . . . five-thirty will do."

"Very well, madame. Will you be needing anything else?"

She shook her head. "No. Thank you, Jimmy. Just drop the luggage off at the apartment." She could not help smiling faintly as he clicked his heels together, Prussian fashion, giving a slight bow while touching his visored cap with his fingertips. A moment later the Rolls-Royce engine purred and the big car slid silently down Fifth Avenue.

Nothing had changed in the week she had been gone. Except for the Junot Building, nothing on the block had changed for decades. Across Fifth Avenue, the massive gray hulk of the Forbes headquarters squatted with the invincibility expected of a financial soothsayer. It amused her that the solid, classical temple had to face her building. The Junot Building did not fit in with Malcolm Forbes's pillared tabernacle to the almighty dollar. Nor did it fit in with the haughty elegance of the prewar apartment buildings that lined the avenue down to the arch.

But the location fit. After all, her empire was to the fashion world what Forbes's was to economics. Her name had become just as synonymous with haute couture as the Fairchild empire housed in the squat, ugly factorylike building next door. Fairchild, the downtown publisher of *Women's Wear Daily* and *W*, was not a Junot competitor like snooty uptown Condé Nast was with *Vogue*, or Hearst was with *Harper's Bazaar*. Regardless, jokes abounded about two fashion publishers rubbing elbows on the same block.

Smiling faintly, she pivoted on her heel and walked to the entrance of her building. The blatant snobbery of New York's "glamour" industries never failed to amuse her; they always insisted on being associated with the posh Upper East Side. After all, where was Condé Nast? Where were all the modeling agencies? But she showed them. She alone had been responsible for shifting glamour's axis back downtown. When she'd decided on the tranquil Twelfth Street location for the building, the whole boardroom had been in shock.

Would the ridiculous snobs never learn? If uptown was always pictured as being so very fashionable, what, then, was *more* fashionable than fashionable lower Fifth Avenue? What could compare with the peaceful elegance reminiscent of Paris, and the stateliness associated with London?

The glass doors of the Junot Building slid open electronically, and she entered the warm, cavernous lobby. Nodding to the receptionist seated behind the marble desk, she crossed the lobby to her private elevator. Though she had entered its doors countless times, she still looked around with pride. This was her world, the world she had created, the world over which she alone reigned. Employees on errands rushed around purposefully, their brisk footsteps echoing on the black marble floor. Voices became part of the low murmur that drifted to the ceiling, and occasional coughs rang out like the dull tolls of a cracked bell. Faintly she could hear the relentless ringings of telephones in the distance. This was the way she liked it. Her world was alive and well.

She glanced up at the enormous silver block letters on the lobby wall above her. "HJII," they read. And underneath, smaller letters translated: "Hélène Junot International, Incorporated." It was a ritual with her to always check those letters. Just to be sure she wasn't dreaming.

"Good mornin', Miz Junot," a cheerful voice said from behind her. She turned. Henry, the uniformed daytime guard, was following her. His wizened black face wore a wide, toothy grin. "Happy New Year," he said.

Hélène smiled. "And a very Happy New Year to you, too, Henry," she answered.

"Thank *you*, ma'am."

They had reached her private elevator. He punched the button outside it, and the door slid silently open. Courteously he held it aside for her.

"Have a real nice day, Miz Junot," he said, meaning it.

"Thank you, Henry, I will," she replied in spite of what she knew. She stepped into the small walnut-paneled elevator and pressed the button marked nineteen.

The nineteenth floor was the executive floor. The windowless reception area was dim, spacious, and lavishly appointed. Here the dollar-and-cents value of the empire was translated into tangibles for all to see. No expense had been spared. Even the blond receptionist behind the enormous ellipsoid marble desk was gorgeous, chicly dressed in a peach-colored designer shift. The floors were carpeted in thick mahogany pile which ran all the way up the walls to the acoustic-tile ceiling. Suede-upholstered conversation pits—by Brueton, $24,000 per sofa—were scattered all around, with brass tables holding neat stacks of the latest Junot magazines. The magazines were not listed on a roster by name. Instead, all around on the walls they were represented by the covers of their most recent issues. Lit by all but invisible lights, the shadow-boxed blowups hung at evenly spaced eye-level intervals like twelve small movie screens. Without fail, they were changed each month at the exact moment the issues hit the newsstands.

Hélène's imperious gaze swept over them. She had seen each cover hundreds of times, and had the final say on each one, had helped choose the layout and the color, style and size of the typeset, and still she felt a thrill of maternal pride coursing through her. Her babies, and she was their proud mother. Each one of them called by the name she had baptized it:

Les Modes	Les Modes
(American edition)	(English edition)
Les Modes	La Moda
(French edition)	(Italian edition)
Mode	Les Modes Homme
(German edition)	(French edition)
La Moda Uomo	Glamorous Miss
(Italian edition)	Ladies' Bazaar
Bride's World	Yachting and Boating
Beauté	

All beautiful slicks with a combined monthly circulation of almost twenty-eight million copies. Worldwide. All part of a publishing empire that spawned new vogues and changed life-styles around the globe.

The cover girl behind the reception desk glanced up with visible surprise. "Miss Junot!" she said quickly. "We . . . we hadn't expected you back so soon. Not until this afternoon . . ."

Hélène began to unbutton her mink. "I decided to come back early, Maggie."

Maggie glanced around suspiciously, and her voice dropped to a conspiratorial whisper. "The Comte de Léger is already here. He came in twenty minutes ago. Almost as if he knew you were arriving this morning instead of this afternoon."

Hélène stopped unbuttoning her coat. Hubert de Léger? As usual he was too well-informed. She had left no word that she was coming back early. There was only one way he could have known: he probably had someone in Paris watching her Île St.-Louis apartment. Spying on her. So it had come to this. She had suspected that sooner or later it would. "And he's the only one?" she asked.

Maggie nodded. "So far. But the grapevine's on Red Alert. Rumor has it the whole board will be here by this afternoon."

This came as no surprise. She herself had scheduled the board meeting more than a month ago. For those not in the know, it was a routine formality. For those in the know . . . She felt a strange tightening of her throat. In a faraway voice she murmured, "Yes, they'll all soon be here."

Maggie gave her a strange look. "Are you all right, Miss Junot?"

Hélène managed a smile and nodded. "Yes. Thank you, Maggie."

The reception phone rang and Maggie picked up the receiver. Hélène turned and walked down the long, plushy carpeted corridor to her office. Vaguely she could hear snatches of Maggie's conversation drifting after her. "Yes . . . she's already here . . . just came in . . ." But Hélène wasn't paying attention. Over and over she kept thinking: It's another winter, another one of those cold, dreadful winters.

"Miss Junot!"

She stopped and turned around. Albert Lourie, her executive secretary, was running to catch up with her. He was a thin, pasty-complexioned man in his thirties with mousy brown hair. In one hand he clutched a folded newspaper.

"Why, Albert!" Hélène said. "You *are* in a hurry!"

"Thank *God* I caught you," he said breathlessly. His face was flushed. "Maggie just told me you came in. There's something I think you ought to see right away."

From his discomfiture, Hélène could tell it was something serious. Albert was not one to sound false alarms. "Well?" she asked.

"Not out here." He gestured to a small conference room off the corridor.

Hélène nodded. They went into the walnut-paneled room, closed the door, and sat opposite each other on rich brown leather Tucroma chairs. "Now," she said, "what is this matter of life and death?"

"This." Morosely Albert tapped the newspaper in his hand. "Today's *Wall Street Journal*. Have you seen it yet?"

"I haven't had a chance. And. . . ?"

Without answering, he handed her the paper and jabbed an accusing finger at an article on page two. Hélène stared at it.

The three column headline seemed to scream at her: "SHAKE-UP AT JUNOT PUBLICATIONS?"

Her lips went dry as she read the second bank of headlines: *"Publishing Giant in Serious Trouble?"* Stunned, she read on:

A formal, but unannounced meeting of the board of directors of Hélène Junot International, Inc., is expected to commence today. A reliable source who wished to remain anonymous disclosed that the meeting will focus on what seems to be a secret power struggle for control of HJII. It is no secret, however, that Miss Junot is overextended with loans, and that *You!*, Junot's new magazine oriented toward the working woman, has been a commercial failure, with a loss of millions. Observers in the publishing industry and on Wall Street speculate that a power struggle at this time could conceivably harm HJII's financial footing and already tenuous stock value.

The power behind the publishing giant has always been Hélène Junot, the legendary French publisher who began the magazine *Les Modes* in 1957 in Paris and who built it into a worldwide publishing conglomerate noted for its ability to set fashion trends and arbitrate taste.

Two years ago, Miss Junot used a large portion of her personal shares in HJII as collateral for a massive loan to finance Junot Publications, a separate corporate entity held exclusively by Miss Junot. That note reportedly is shortly due. If Miss Junot is unable to meet her commitments on time, the huge bloc of HJII voting shares may become property of the ManhattanBank N.A., which can then, in turn, sell them as it sees fit. This would leave the founder and president of HJII, Miss Junot, with only a minor portion of voting stock, barely enough to exercise a veto concerning a public offering of HJII stock....

There was the crunching of newspaper as Hélène flung the paper aside. Her face was grim. She knew what this article meant. Someone on the board of HJII had deliberately leaked the story to the press, determined to undermine her position as president of the corporation and to weaken her standing with the banks. It was a sneaky tactic designed to throw doubt on her ability to lead. Also, it was a way to publicize her steadfast refusals to allow the company to go public, and thereby pressure her to reconsider. While the other members of the board would realize an enormous profit if she agreed to it, none would gain as much as she. But the thought of unknown investors invading the company she had fought in countless ways and against innumerable odds to create, only to speculate for higher and higher profits, terrified her. In the search for the corporate dollar, quality would undoubtedly slip. To Hélène that was unthinkable. After all, what was HJII but a trend-setter of quality? HJII had a handful of stockholders, and that was the way she wanted it to remain.

Albert squirmed nervously in his chair. "I . . . I'm awfully sorry, Miss Junot," he stammered. "I just thought you should see it before . . ." Helplessly he spread his hands apart.

She looked at him. "Yes. Thank you, Albert," she said in her throaty voice. "I appreciate it. Really."

Then she got up, clapped a weary hand on his shoulder, left the conference room, and walked slowly down the corridor to her office. I've been betrayed, she thought miserably. And not for the first time, either. The only thing that doesn't change is the dirty taste it leaves in your mouth.

Of course HJII had problems, she admitted to herself. What company didn't? But to leak such problems under the guise of "news" to *The Wall Street Journal* was despicable and inexcusable. Who was the culprit? De Léger? She wouldn't put it past him. Still, she couldn't be sure; the others were not much better.

She could be absolutely certain of only one thing. The leakage to *The Wall Street Journal* was not a warning shot across the bow. It was an open declaration of war. And long or short, she knew it would be a bitter conflict. One or all of the board wanted control of Hélène Junot International, Inc. They had for years. And she knew why. Not because they cared for a single share of their Junot stock. Not even because they cared an iota for money or fashion or publishing. But because they hated her enough to try to take from her the only thing she'd ever loved and cared for—her corporation.

She made a left turn at the end of the corridor and stopped in front of a polished teak door. At eye level, the small gold letters spelled a single word: "President." It looked so alien. So weighty. She wished her title would read "Founder and Artistic Director" instead. That was what she was proudest of.

She put her hand on the knob and opened the door. The steady droning of a typewriter greeted her as she stepped into the outer office. Julie, her secretary, was busy attacking a pile of letters that had accumulated over the holidays. Throughout the building and behind her back Julie was known as "The Sphinx." Her reputation for guarding the entrance to Hélène's inner office was legend.

At the sound of the door opening, Julie glanced up suspiciously, her fingers never leaving the keyboard. Her dark brown eyes fluttered with surprise. "Why, Miss Junot!" she exclaimed. Abruptly she stopped typing, her fingers poised in midair.

Hélène smiled. "Good morning, Julie."

"You're back early! There wasn't even notification that the plane . . ."

"Yes, I know," Hélène answered. "I thought I'd rush back very quietly, so I chartered a Lear jet." She paused and said slowly, "Not quietly enough, it seems. I hear the Comte is waiting."

Julie made a face. "Inside," she said. Then she frowned, leaned forward, and placed an ear beside the intercom on her desk.

Hélène looked at her strangely. "What in—?"

Julie put a finger to her lips to silence her. Then she straightened with satisfaction and pointed at the intercom. Hélène understood. She nodded, leaned close, and listened carefully. She could hear a faint humming sound. Hubert de Léger had switched it on from the inside office. He was eavesdropping.

Hélène shook her head. This didn't surprise her in the least. She knew the Comte better than anyone else did. He was sly and brash and managed to force his way in wherever it pleased him to do so. Even the Sphinx's determination was no match for his will. Nothing short of armed guards could have kept him out. Hélène shrugged. "Any messages?"

"These." Julie handed her a sheaf of small pink message memos. "Also, your brother called. He wants to see you privately before the board meeting this afternoon. He says it's very important."

Hélène nodded. She would see Edmond as soon as she got rid of the Comte. "Thank you, Julie," she said. "And please make certain we're not disturbed. Hold all calls."

Julie nodded and went back to her typing. Hélène walked

over to the inner office door and began to turn the knob, but stopped and waited. She closed her eyes for a few seconds as she steeled herself for the confrontation with de Léger. Then she entered her office.

It was a corner office that actually consisted of four rooms—office, kitchenette, bedroom, and bath. All the rest of the offices and corridors in the Junot Building had been decorated by an expensive design firm, but Hélène had warned them about touching her office. "Hands off this one!" she had told the aging decorator whose firm she had chosen. He had been horrified. "You try to touch this suite and I'll have your head on a platter!" she warned.

In the large room which served as her office, the two outside walls were floor-to-ceiling windows. One faced the solemn Forbes Building; the other looked down Fifth Avenue to the stately arch guarding the entrance to Washington Square Park. She had chosen this corner for her office expressly for that view. The arch reminded her of the Arc de Triomphe in her beloved Paris.

The inside walls were an innocuous white and the floor covering was nubby beige wall-to-wall wool carpet. In these respects it looked like any other corner office in New York. However, Hélène had used her personal stamp of good taste, style, and memories to create her own luxurious yet eminently comfortable environment.

The walls were hung with framed fashion sketches, her favorites from past issues of *Les Modes*. The furniture was her own, lovingly hunted-down pieces of ancient French furniture whose meticulous restoration she had personally directed. Whether she was in town or not, a vase of fresh flowers always sat on her desk.

One glance told Hélène that the Comte had made himself at home in her sanctuary. He sat in the delicately carved French chair behind her Louis Quinze desk. The vase of fresh flowers had been moved aside, and both of his damp patent-leather loafers rested informally on the highly polished marquetry top. In one red hand he held a glass of Napoleon brandy that he had served himself from the bar behind her desk, in the other a cigarette with an enormous ash cocked on its end.

Hubert de Léger blew a stream of smoke skyward and looked at Hélène. Amusement glinted in his jet-black eyes. "Entrez!" he slurred. The ash fell away from the cigarette and landed on the spotless beige carpet. "My beautiful Hélène," he said in French. "I have been expecting you. Please. Come in. I do not bite. And even if I did, I am not suffering from rabies at the moment." He broke into a series of thin, hollow laughs.

Hélène closed the door quietly behind her. For a moment she looked at him; then she turned her face away. There was repulsion in her eyes. She knew he drank heavily. But my God, she thought, not to this extent at nine-thirty in the morning.

"Can I offer my beautiful Hélène a drink?" he asked mockingly as he hoisted his glass. "The bar in this office is most superbly stocked."

"Thank you, no," she replied coldly.

"Hmm. C'est dommage." He made a childish face.

For an instant she remembered how he had once looked with his youthful, dashing good looks, his raven-black hair, his stiff posture, his lean, athletic physique, his sober black eyes and determined cleft chin. Now his jaw had slackened, his hair was gray, and his once-sober eyes were glassy from drink. Could this be the same man she had known since childhood? Was this the Hubert de Léger who had at one time wooed her so ardently?

Tightening her lips, she crossed the room and wordlessly looked down at his feet. Anger surged through her. He was playing games, seeing just how much he could get away with. Suddenly she grabbed his feet and pushed them off.

He heaved a sigh and let them drop heavily to the carpet. "My dear, that was not very nice of you," he said reprimandingly.

"Hubert," she said in a peculiar warning tone, "you take far too many liberties."

He raised his eyebrows, but she didn't notice. She was moving the vase back to the spot where it always stood, and then slipped out of her mink. Haphazardly she flung it over the back of one of the two little Louis Quinze chairs facing her desk. Both were upholstered in ancient cracked green leather. Then she walked over beside his chair and stood there for a moment looking down at him. He stared back up at her with a pretended lack of understanding.

"Hubert? Must you be reminded?" she finally asked. "This is *my* office."

He looked at her with a blank expression. Then he slapped

the palm of his hand against his forehead in mock forgetfulness. "How thoughtless of me!" he said. "Of course, it still is, isn't it? How silly of me." He frowned ostentatiously, peered deep into his brandy, and said slowly, "Well, we might as well be truthful. It *still* is your office. And it will be, at least until this week is up."

"At least," she said, her voice curt and razor-sharp. "My chair, Hubert . . ."

"Your . . ."

"Chair. If you insist on plaguing me with your company, I'm afraid you shall have to do it from there." She pointed to the empty chair in front of her desk.

He raised his glass in a silent, airy toast and took his time getting to his feet. His lips were twisted into an ugly smile. After making a courteous, if ungenuine display of helping her into her seat, he sat where she'd specified.

"Charming office . . . such a marvelous view," he said approvingly. "But the place needs some changes. Too feminine for my tastes . . . too many curlicued French touches."

Hélène stiffly folded her hands and stared down at them. If she said nothing, perhaps he would burn himself out.

"You know," he said, "by next Monday I may have to call up a design firm and have them redecorate this place. 'Tear it all out!' I'll demand. 'Make it sleek and masculine.' "

She was only half-listening; her mind was racing over the possibilities of how to get him out of the office. Some way that was quick, yet wouldn't give him a chance to create a scene.

He stubbed out his cigarette in a crystal ashtray. Then, pretending to notice her mink for the first time, he reached over to the chair beside him and hoisted up one of the sleeves. "The famous Blackglama?" he asked.

"Yes," Hélène said quietly.

He laughed. "How marvelous! Every woman in this city would commit arson to get one. But you? All *you* have to do is model one coat for Richard Avedon and . . . presto! You're a living Blackglama 'legend.' Ergo, Hélène Junot, who by the way has whole closets full of furs, gets another one for free. And not only that, but the title 'legend' as well!" He leered at her. "You've always wanted a title, eh, Hélène?"

Hélène looked at him steadily. "I don't think you came here to discuss the coat, Hubert," she said dryly.

He let the sleeve drop. "As a matter of fact, I didn't."

31

"Then why *did* you come?"

"Our mutual business interests," he replied. "Hélène Junot, of course. The corporation *and* the woman."

She stiffened, her violet eyes flashing warily. "In that case, I'm afraid we have nothing to discuss."

"Nothing?"

"Nothing whatsoever. As you're only too well aware, the board meeting is this afternoon. I suggest you discuss any pertinent complaints you have regarding my publishing policies—or me—openly at that time."

"Bring the dirty laundry out into the open and it disappears, eh?" He clucked his tongue. "My, but such a display of courage. But then, you were never a quitter, were you, Hélène? You've always gotten everything you set that iron heart of yours on, haven't you?"

"Hubert," she said wearily, "please get to the point."

He lit another cigarette. "Ah, but you see, I'm getting there. I've come to warn you. I want you to be prepared before you set foot in that boardroom."

"Prepared? Whatever for?"

"Corporate slaughter, my dear."

YESTERDAY

I

MURDER

1

Paris, 1944

It was after three o'clock, and Hélène was playing in the park. The January afternoon was cold and windy and the narrow streets were nearly deserted. It was very quiet. Overhead, the sky was clear blue and the sun was shining. Completely surrounded by buildings, the little park was in deep shadow.

Across the street was her house. It was almost identical to the other grim, crooked houses that sagged against one another like rows of tired dominoes, each dependent on the next for support. But her house stood out proudly from the others. The windows on the ground floor were covered over with thick iron bars twisted into fanciful curlicues, and the front door was painted bright yellow. *Canary* yellow, Maman called it. And above the snow-covered rooftop she could glimpse the white dome and cupolas of Sacré Coeur gleaming in the sunshine.

She thought she heard something. She stopped playing with Antoinette, her porcelain doll, and listened carefully. It was a rumbling noise, still far away. But it was coming closer. A truck is headed this way, she thought with surprise.

She waited in anticipation. Motorized traffic in this working-class section of Paris was rare. There were no taxis or private automobiles. Parisians rode bicycles everywhere. Only the Boches and their collaborators experienced the luxury of traveling in cars and trucks. The streets of Montmartre were old and crooked, many of them too narrow to accommodate even the smallest automobiles.

The noise of the truck engine grew louder, and she put her lips close to Antoinette's ear. "Watch, Antoinette," she instructed the doll in a soft whisper. "Watch and you'll soon see your first truck!" She straightened the yellowed lace of

Antoinette's gown. After all, Antoinette was a lady, and ladies must look their best when they are seen in public.

Two minutes later a gray truck came roaring around the corner from the rue Durantin.

As she watched, it switched into low gear and rattled uphill, coming closer. The snow chains clattered and the gray tarpaulin stretched over the back flapped in the wind. Plainly she could see the swastika stenciled on the sides of the cab. Even as a child she already knew what it meant.

In a moment, the truck had passed by. She wrinkled her nose at the offensive stench of gasoline fumes. Curiously she stared after it. She wondered what it was doing in Montmartre. Then there was the sound of grinding gears as it turned a corner and disappeared. The noise of the motor slowly died away. A minute later there was silence. But a cloud of gray exhaust still hung heavy in the air.

She looked around to see if she was being watched. She wasn't. Then she did what she had seen other people do many times. She spat in the street. She was only seven years old, but she had already picked up the habits of older Parisians. One could not spit directly at the Boches. That was too dangerous. But one could spit after him when his back was turned.

It was almost half an hour after the truck had gone by that she had the feeling something was wrong. She had been building miniature snowmen on the slats of the park bench for Antoinette. Suddenly, somehow, she just *knew*.

She felt a sudden prickling of her spine.

Something was wrong.

She glanced across the street at her house. Everything appeared normal and peaceful. Nothing seemed amiss. Nothing . . . except the front door was open a crack and a woman was standing outside it. Hélène couldn't see her face underneath the black wool scarf, but she thought she recognized Madame Courbet, the wife of a switchboard operator at the Prefecture of Police. Still, she couldn't be certain. Whoever it was gestured frantically to someone inside, all the while throwing furtive glances over her shoulder. Then the woman hurried off. Hélène still wasn't able to see her face. The scarf was pulled too far forward, and the woman's face was in shadow.

Hélène would never know what gave her that feeling, but the moment she felt the prickling along her spine, she knew

Maman needed her. She didn't waste any time. She picked up Antoinette and ran across the street and up the three steps to the canary-yellow door.

It opened before she even reached it.

"Quickly!" Michelle, Maman's huge, plump servant, hissed at her. Michelle didn't even wait for Hélène to stomp the show off her shoes. Roughly the thick fingers of her hands grabbed hold of the girl and pulled her inside. She slammed the door shut behind her and bolted it. The foyer was dark. The curtains were drawn, and between them, a chink of light showed.

Hélène looked up into Michelle's tense red moon face. "What's the matter?" she asked.

Michelle shrugged and brusquely turned away. Perhaps she was moody because it was so cold in the house, the week's coal rations already depleted. Despite her size, Michelle didn't take well to the cold.

Michelle had big peasant bones and enormous breasts. She was the maid, housckccper, and nanny all rolled into one. Like a member of the family, she was devoted beyond endearment. Hélène knew that Maman couldn't afford to pay Michelle wages anymore, not with Papa gone all the time. Yet Michelle stayed on.

Hélène glanced around the little foyer. Maman was standing at one of the foyer windows, with her back turned. She was anxiously peering out through a crack in the drawn curtains, nervously wringing her slim hands. Hélène noticed that her belly looked larger than ever, and she knew why. Recently Maman had explained to her that a little brother or sister was on the way.

Maman was tall and bone-thin. Hélène remembered when her face had been unlined, her blond hair untouched by gray, and her eyes clear and lively. Suddenly, almost overnight, they looked tired. Still, she was a thoroughly elegant woman. Even the lean Occupation years could not put a dent in her poise.

And a working mother. She had held her job as a seamstress for Madeleine de Rauch ever since 1939. That was when Chanel, for whom she used to work, closed her doors.

Oh, and could Maman sew! Like an angel, she spun out one creation after another at her archaic pedal-operated machine, or even by hand. And after her long hours at

Madeleine de Rauch's salon, sewing for the fat German women she despised, Maman would bring work home. Sometimes she even did small jobs for neighbors as well—neighbors who could pay with precious rations instead of money.

Now Maman stopped peering out the window. If she noticed Hélène, she didn't let on. Instead she nervously paced back and forth in the foyer. "Mon dieu!" she said breathlessly. "Catherine is still not coming. Those acting lessons should be over by now."

"Then we must leave without her," Michelle said flatly. "If she wants to become the new Sarah Bernhardt so badly that she spends all her time at that theater—"

"Leave without Catherine?" Maman looked at Michelle in horror. "We *must* wait for her."

Michelle made clucking noises and threw her fat red hands up in despair. "There is no time! You heard what Madame Courbet said. She risked her life coming here to warn us. We haven't a moment to lose. We *cannot* wait!"

"We *must* wait," Maman said through clenched teeth. "You'll see. She'll be here any minute."

"Minute!" Michelle shouted. Her voice was shrill. "We don't have minutes. Seconds count!"

Maman wrung her hands. "Michelle. We have to wait. Can't you understand that? Catherine is my daughter!"

"And she is like mine also!" Michelle retorted.

"See, then you understand," Maman said without logic.

Michelle let out a frustrated growl. "There is no getting through to you," she snapped. "I might as well get whatever is in the pantry. If anything. We'll need food. It's a long journey."

Maman nodded absently and moved toward Hélène.

"Edmond!" Michelle called out. She hurried to the kitchen faster than Hélène had ever seen her move before.

Maman looked down at Hélène through tired eyes. Then she stooped over and wrapped her thin arms around the child. She held her very tight, too tight, and it hurt. Hélène felt frightened. More than ever, she knew something was terribly wrong.

"Edmond!" Michelle's voice came from the kitchen at a dangerously high pitch. "Give me a hand, you lazy good-for-nothing!"

"I'm coming, I'm coming!" Hélène's eleven-year-old

brother came down the stairs wearing his warmest winter clothes.

"Maman?" Hélène said, looking up at her.

"Yes, ma petite?"

"Is Papa coming home soon?"

Maman didn't answer. Her eyes looked moist and she wiped them with the back of her hand. From the nursery upstairs, little Marie began crying. She was hungry or lonely or wet.

Gently Maman pushed Hélène away. "Go upstairs," she said, her voice soft. "Go and put some warm clothes on Marie. The blue wool suit and the warm coat. Then bring her right down. And hurry!"

"Are we going somewhere, Maman?"

She nodded. "We're going on a journey."

Hélène's eyes sparkled. A journey? That sounded like fun. She loved journeys. "Can we take the train, Maman?" she pleaded. "Oh, please, let's do take the train. I love the train."

"Yes, ma petite," Maman whispered. "We'll take the train. But you must hurry. Otherwise we might miss it."

Hélène wrapped her arms around Maman and hugged her tightly. "I'll hurry!" she promised.

Maman smiled a strained little smile and tousled Hélène's hair affectionately. Hélène ran upstairs. From the top of the landing she looked down. Maman was at the window again, anxiously peering out through the crack in the curtains. Her lips weren't smiling anymore. Maman looked very frightened.

Hélène ran down the hall and entered the nursery. Marie stopped crying as soon as she saw her, and her tiny pink face broke into laughter. Her eyes were wide, luminous, and blue, like Maman's.

Hélène sat Antoinette down on top of the dresser and took Marie's blue wool suit and tiny winter coat out of a drawer. Then, carefully but quickly, she dressed her. Marie giggled and squirmed playfully as she put her into the clothes and buttoned them. Usually Marie's laughter would bring Hélène laughter. Not today. Today something was terribly wrong. Hélène didn't know what, but that only made her all the more uneasy.

Carefully Hélène took Marie into her arms and carried her downstairs. Maman was still pacing the foyer. She had put on her thick brown winter coat. Michelle and Edmond stood silently to one side. Each carried a string bag filled with rutabagas. Inwardly Hélène groaned. She hated rutabagas. It seemed that fried rutabagas were all there ever was to eat anymore, and there were never enough of those.

Once again Maman parted the curtains a crack and peered out. This time she let out a sharp little cry. "She's coming!" she exclaimed. "Catherine is coming!"

"Well, then, tell her to hurry!" Michelle snapped.

Maman ignored her, unbolted the door and let Catherine in, then threw the bolt back into place.

Hélène's sister Catherine was thirteen years old but looked older. Already she'd lost most of her baby fat. She had large brown eyes, shoulder-length brown hair which she wore pinned up, and she was growing into a stunning-looking young woman. Hélène knew this was true because of the special looks men gave Catherine on the street. Hélène had no doubt but that Catherine would become an actress when she grew up.

At the moment, Catherine stared at everyone in silence. A puzzled look come over her face. "Are you going someplace?" she asked.

"*We* are! We all are!" Michelle cried hysterically. Her big bosom rose and fell excitedly. "Now, run and put your warmest clothes on. We haven't a moment to lose!"

"What's the matter?" Catherine asked. "What has happened?"

Michelle's eyes flashed dangerously. "Never mind what's happened!" she snapped. "Just do as I say. Get dressed warmly! Now!" There was no mistaking the authority in her voice.

Catherine shot a questioning look at Maman, who nodded gravely. Without another sound, Catherine turned and went upstairs to change. Gently Maman took Marie out of Hélène's arms and held her close. Her hands were shaking.

Two minutes later, they were all set to leave.

"Hurry!" Michelle, who was clearly in charge, urged. "We're going out the back way—through the garden!"

At the kitchen door, Hélène suddenly remembered that she had forgotten something. She stopped and turned to Edmond. "Antoinette," she said. "I forgot Antoinette."

"Forget it," Edmond said roughly. "She's only a doll."

"She is not!" Hélène retorted angrily. "She's my friend."

Maman touched Hélène gently on the shoulder. "There is

no time, ma petite," she said. "We'll have to come back and get her later."

Hélène stood where she was, resolutely refusing to budge. "I want to get Antoinette. I want her now! I won't leave until I have her!"

Michelle rolled her eyes and let out a murderous sound. If looks could have killed, hers would have mowed Hélène down right on the spot. Then Michelle glanced at Maman.

Maman's mouth tightened. She sighed. "Oh, very well," she said. "But hurry!"

Hélène smiled as she ran upstairs to the nursery. No, she wouldn't leave Antoinette behind. Not for anything in the world. Maman had given her the doll for her birthday. She was the first doll that was really hers. All the others had once belonged to Catherine.

Antoinette was sitting on top of the dresser where Hélène had left her. She picked her up and hugged her tightly. As she was going out the door, she heard an ear-shattering roar outside on the street. She rushed to the window, pushed the lace curtains aside, and looked down.

Led by a motorcycle escort, a long, shiny black Daimler and several gray trucks pulled to a halt outside the door. Pennants were affixed to both front fenders of the car. Hélène recognized those flags. Who wouldn't have? They flew all over Paris, a constant, hated reminder of subjugation and defeat.

Her heart skipped a beat and she shivered. The Boches.

A sudden dread came over her. They want me! she thought. Because I spit in the street after their truck had gone by.

As she watched, the tailboards of the trucks dropped with a crash and soldiers spilled out and scrambled to line up alongside the curb. Their heavy, cleated boots clattered loudly on the cobblestones. Within seconds they snapped to attention in a precise straight line. Their chests were thrust out like pigeons' and their rifles were affixed with bayonets. Some of them were dressed in gray, others in black. It was the ones in gray who wore the coal-scuttle helmets and who were lined up. They had hopped down from the backs of the trucks. Hélène started to count them but stopped. There were at least twenty. The ones in black silver-trimmed uniforms, riding breeches, peaked caps, and highly polished boots stood casually to one side of the stiff formation. There were three

41

of them. By a sudden barked order, the ones in gray broke out of line and half of them rushed the door. With a noisy clatter, the other half double-timed it down the street and turned the corner, disappearing out of sight.

"Hélène!" Maman was calling. "Quickly! Quickly!" Her voice quivered with fear.

Hélène left the window and started for the stairs. She looked down at Maman. Her face had gone white and she was pacing the foyer, Marie in her arms.

Michelle stood at the foot of the stairs. "Get down here!" she screamed hysterically. "*Now,* you little ingrate!" There was panic in her voice. Apparently Hélène still wasn't moving fast enough for her, because she took a deep breath and began to charge up the stairs. Her face glared at Hélène and her huge breasts rose and fell with the effort of the climb. As soon as she reached the girl, Michelle grabbed her arm roughly with one hand and pulled her along, all the while muttering prayers under her breath.

A moment later there were thuds at the front door. Maman let out a gasp and froze. The door shook but held fast. They hadn't bothered to knock. Instead, they were hurling all their weight against the door.

"Come *on,*" Michelle wailed at Maman. "Quickly! We haven't a second to lose! Or did you forget about the little ones?"

Maman came out of her terror and found her feet. Hélène shot a last frightened look back as they rushed into the kitchen. Behind them, the front door was quivering. Wood creaked each time there was a thud. Suddenly Hélène wished she hadn't gone back for Antoinette.

Maman solemnly handed Marie over to Catherine. Then she slowly opened the kitchen door a crack and peered out. It led out to a courtyard where the neighboring buildings shared vegetable gardens.

Maman let out a gasp, slammed the door shut, and shot the bolt in place. There were soldiers out back too.

A hunted look crossed Maman's face. She closed her eyes and shrank back against the kitchen wall. "The Boches!" she whispered.

Michelle looked at her in horror and let go of the string bag. It hit the floor with a dull thump and precious rutabagas spilled out, rolling in all directions across the linoleum. Nobody took any notice of them.

"The children!" Maman whispered. "Where are we going to hide the children?"

"I don't know," Michelle replied. "Where in all France can one hide anything from the Boches?"

Suddenly there was a terrible crash at the kitchen door, accompanied by a heavy cracking noise that sounded like thunder. Michelle let out a shriek and crossed herself. Marie began to wail. They all backed away from the door.

"Sssssh, little one," Catherine said softly as she rocked Marie back and forth in her arms. "Sssssh."

Maman looked around in desperation. "There must be someplace . . ." Her voice trailed off.

They backed into the dining room. Hélène lost her grip on Antoinette and dropped her. She knew better than to try to retrieve her. Not now.

"Why, of course!" Michelle suddenly cried out. "The dumbwaiter!" Her plump red hands lost no time in shoving the children toward it. Then she pulled at the old oak doors that were set in the wall and slid them apart. They rattled like a warped window that had not been opened for ages.

So we're going to play games, Hélène thought. She, Edmond, and Catherine had used the dumbwaiter many times playing hide-and-seek.

She remembered when Michelle had once caught them at it. She had boxed their ears mercilessly.

"You imbeciles!" she had ranted. "Are you trying to kill yourselves? That thing is as old as the revolution! The wood's rotted, most likely. Or God forbid the cable should break! You want you should fall and die at the bottom of the shaft?"

And now she was trying to shove them into the very dumbwaiter she had fought so hard to keep them out of in the past. Hélène's mind was in a whirl. Had Michelle gone completely crazy? Had the world?

"Get in there!" Michelle ordered. "All of you!"

From her voice they knew they'd better do exactly as she said. She held the double doors open. Catherine handed Marie to Maman and then climbed in. Edmond and Hélène followed. The floor of the dumbwaiter shook as Maman handed Marie back to Catherine,

"And not a sound!" Michelle warned. Her dark eyes looked oddly hostile as she waved her fist threateningly. "If I hear as much as a single peep, I'll come and wallop all four of you, but good!"

Hélène shrank back, frightened.

Maman leaned forward into the dumbwaiter and her hand shook slightly as she touched each of them gently on the forehead, her thumb sketching the sign of the cross upon them. Maman was not a religious woman, but somehow a great strength had come to her at this moment. Her face was no longer haunted by terror. Instead, her pale blue eyes were composed and brave and her lips were set in a sad but gentle smile.

"Edmond," Maman said softly, "you are forced to become a man much sooner than nature intended. My son, be strong like your father, whose place you must now take. And you, Catherine. You are the oldest. You will take my place. Together the two of you must take care of Hélène and little Marie. Do so with your lives! Then, if you have the chance, forget everything, and when it's safe . . . run. Your Tante Janine is a good Christian woman. She lives in Saint-Nazaire—that's at the mouth of the Loire, on the Bay of Biscay. I don't know how you'll do it, but get to Tante Janine's. God will forgive you for what you may have to do in order to get there! It won't be easy, but take heart. Soon the British and the Americans will land there. Then you will be safe forever. They are not pigs like the Boches. You'll see, another year and they'll drive the pig Boche out of France and back to his pigsty across the Rhine!"

Ca-rack! The doorjamb at the front door gave way and crashed into the foyer with a piercing sound. Hélène jumped with fright. Maman shot a glance behind her.

"It is now time to say good-bye, my children. Never forget, my darlings, that your Maman loves you more dearly than you'll ever be able to know."

"Yes, Maman," Catherine whispered gravely in a very grown-up voice. She reached for Maman's hand and kissed it. "We love you, too."

Maman suddenly snatched her hand back and fumbled with her fingers. The children watched her silently. She was pulling off her gold wedding ring. Awkwardly she pressed it into Edmond's hands. "Take this, my son," she whispered. "It is all I can give you. Use it to bargain with."

His hands closed over it.

"Go with God, my children," Maman whispered. "May he

love and protect you." She wasn't crying, but her pale eyes were moist and sorrowful.

Edmond had to turn his face away. He was ashamed of the tears in his eyes.

"Remember what I told you!" Michelle warned in a thick wavering voice. "Not a sound!" She sniffed and wiped her red nose with the back of her hand. Her eyes were glassy, too, just like Maman's. Gently she pulled Maman away and slammed the dumbwaiter doors shut. They banged together like the jaws of a toothless whale and the children were enveloped in darkness. The thuds and crashes were now muted.

From their games in the dumbwaiter, Hélène had learned where to peek out without being detected. There was a hole in the wood on her side. It had once been a knothole that had since been punched out. Soon her eyes adjusted to the darkness, and the hole in the wood stood out clearly. It let a thin stream of light through, in which danced a million tiny dust motes.

The cracking and banging noises at the door continued, this time followed by a horrible splintering noise. Something else had given. Hélène reached for Catherine's hand and held it tight as the thuds grew louder and louder. Catherine's hands was clammy and trembling.

Suddenly there was an ear-splitting crash. It sounded like the whole roof had caved in. The dumbwaiter shook and Hélène let out a cry. Marie began wailing, and Catherine rocked her back and forth, sticking a thumb in her mouth. Hungrily Marie began sucking on it.

"The roof," Hélène whispered to Catherine. "The roof has fallen in."

"No," she whispered back. "It's the door."

"But Maman—"

"Keep quiet!" Edmond hissed.

Boots thudded inside the house now, and sharp orders were barked in German. Hélène placed her ear against the knothole to listen, but she couldn't understand a word. She knew only a few random words of German. Then she peered out.

Her view was restricted to a small portion of the room and all she could see were headless figures. The knothole was located too far down to see anything taller than a child. She did see starched uniforms and shiny black boots. Then she recognized Maman's gray-woolen-stockinged legs and old worn shoes. They were a sad contrast to her dress and coat. "Thank goodness I can sew," she used to joke. "Unfortunately, even I can't sew shoes or weave silk stockings."

Hélène didn't need to see her head to recognize Michelle. Her unmistakable tublike shape was backed against the wall beside the kitchen door. Hélène was puzzled by something, and then it came to her. Uncharacteristically, Michelle's hands were folded behind her back. Michelle always had her hands at her hips, never behind her back.

Hélène shifted her gaze to the right. She caught sight of Antoinette lying on the floor. As she watched, a shiny boot stepped on her. She winced as the porcelain face so dear to her shattered with a crunch. Then the boot kicked at the pieces, scattering them.

Suddenly Hélène heard a stilted Boche voice speaking awkward French, so she moved again to peer out in Maman's direction. She was speaking to one of the Germans dressed in black, but her voice was too low to carry. Suddenly there was a resounding slap. Maman's torso jerked as she screamed out in pain.

Edmond recognized Maman's scream. With a strangled cry of rage he started to reach for the dumbwaiter doors to jump out and protect her.

Catherine sucked in her breath and dug her fingernails deep into his arm. "Didn't you hear what Maman and Michelle said?" she hissed at him. "We're to take care of the little ones! Or do you want to have all of us killed?"

He settled back stiffly and let out an angry sigh. Catherine was right. Maman and Michelle had given explicit orders.

The Nazi asked something else, again in French. His accent was so bad Hélène had to strain her ears to understand.

"Jacqueline Junot," she heard Maman reply.

"What?" the sharp voice snapped. "I can't hear you. Louder!"

"Jacqueline Junot!" Maman yelled back at him. "Jacqueline Junot!"

"Don't you *dare* raise your voice at an officer of the Reich!" the Boche barked. There was a crack as another slap rang out. Maman's cry for help was lost in her scream.

"What did you say?" the Boche asked.

"N-nothing," Maman said in a trembling voice.

"So . . ." The Nazi voice took on a tone of satisfaction. "Now are you ready to talk?"

"Yes," Maman said in a hoarse whisper. "Yes."

"Then where is the transmitter?"

"Transmitter?" Maman asked. "I don't know what you mean. What on earth——"

Smack! Yet another resounding slap rang out, this time much harder and louder. Maman moaned and tumbled to the floor, not more than four feet in front of the dumbwaiter. Hélène could see all of her now. She was doubled over on her knees, her head touching the floor. Hélène knew she was in great pain. Her face was flushed. She coughed and vomited, her nose and mouth pouring blood. In shame she turned her face away from the dumbwaiter. Hélène's stomach wrenched in sorrow for her. Above all, Maman would never have wanted her children to witness her humiliation.

The Boche moved toward Maman where she cowered. From Hélène's vantage point all she could see were boots and black breeches standing over her. He made a production of clearing his throat. "About this transmitter . . ."

"I don't know what you're talking about!" Maman cried, her voice gurgling from the blood in her mouth. "I swear I don't *know*!"

"Liar!" One of the boots flashed as it kicked out at her, catching her in the belly. An agonized, bile-filled scream reverberated around the room and into the confines of the dumbwaiter. Edmond covered his ears with his hands. He was sobbing quietly.

Hélène closed her eyes. She couldn't bear looking at Maman any more. Maman had drawn herself up as tightly as she could, her arms wrapped protectively around her swollen belly, around the baby boy or baby girl who was shortly to arrive.

"Maman," Hélène whispered painfully without making a sound. "What are they going to do to you, Maman?"

A Boche issued a command. Curious, Hélène opened her eyes. Instantly the soldiers in gray split into four groups. The thuds of their boots echoed clearly as they stomped up the stairs and down into the cellar. Hélène heard doors banging, and then there was a crash as glass shattered. Their voices were muffled as they smashed furniture and tore the house apart. A tremendous crash from above shook the whole house.

"We're going to die," Hélène whimpered.

"Keep quiet!" Catherine whispered.

It seemed to go on forever. Then someone yelled from the top of the stairs. The Nazi who stood over Maman squatted, grabbed her by the hair, and pulled her head up a foot.

"You fool!" he laughed at her. "They've already found it. Was it worth it to hold out on the Gestapo? Was it?"

Maman drew back and winced. Then he spat in her face. Hélène saw her grimace and blink as the spittle hit her and ran down her cheek. He let go of her hair and her head dropped back onto the carpet. But not before Hélène caught a glimpse of his face under the visor of his peaked cap.

She stared at him incredulously. His face was as lean and narrow as a skull, with lips that were thin and cruel and bloodless. A tiny crescent-shaped scar stood out on his cleft chin. But it was his coloring that left her in shock. His skin was as pale as a corpse's, while his eyes were hideously pink. If he'd had horns, he would have looked like the devil himself.

He got to his feet, straightened his tunic, and went upstairs. Hélène felt a wave of relief when he had gone. Somehow she was more terrified of his ugliness than of his cruelty. Two soldiers in gray came and stood guard over Maman. Each time she moved as much as a finger they swiftly delivered her a vicious kick.

Hélène shifted position and peered toward Michelle. She hadn't moved from the kitchen door. There was a grim expression on her moon face, and her arms were still behind her back.

She heard the thuds of many boots coming down the stairs. They were all returning to the dining room. Apparently they had found what they'd been looking for. One of the soldiers carried it downstairs. It was a bulky, complicated-looking metal box covered with little dials and switches. Hélène had never seen it before.

The sinister, white-faced Boche gestured to the men standing guard over Maman. "Show her how we punish liars and traitors," he said in an authoritative voice. "And when you're through, take her to headquarters!" Then he left the room, the back of one gloved hand tucked into the small of his erect back.

The guards clicked their heels. "Zu befehl!" they chorused. Then they glanced down at Maman. She was silent, but her eyes were wary. Two of the soldiers bent over and pulled her to her feet. She stood swaying unsteadily. As Hélène watched, one of the Boches in black approached her and made a fist. Suddenly he slammed it into her belly.

"Traitor!" he shouted.

Maman let out a wrenching scream and collapsed. "My baby!" she screamed. "I'm losing my baby!" Tears were pouring down her cheeks.

Again the fist punched into her belly. Again she screamed. Hélène was filled with a murderous hatred.

Suddenly she noticed movement by the kitchen door. With the stealth of a huge cat, Michelle crept forward toward the soldiers. One of her fat red hands moved slowly from behind her back, and Hélène's eyes caught something flashing—a kitchen knife. It was the longest and sharpest one in the house.

With a cry Michelle dived forward upon the nearest Boche and plunged the knife into his back. He let out a howl and sank to his knees. Blood spewed from his gaping mouth and his eyes widened as if in surprise. Then they froze in a glassy, unseeing expression. He pitched forward, and Hélène saw that the knife was buried in his spine. The dark brown haft still quivered.

The others faced Michelle with a mixture of shock and surprise. One of them pointed his rifle at her. Instinctively she raised her hands out in front of her. There was an orange flash and the room seemed to explode. Michelle was jerked backward against the kitchen wall. Then, like a limp puppet, she slid downward into a ludicrous sitting position. In her lap, a large red spot was forming. Her glazed eyes seemed to stare straight through the knothole at Hélène.

Angry Nazi hands clawed at Maman and dragged her outside to the trucks. She was hunched over, her face smeared with blood. Suddenly Hélène noticed that her gray-stockinged legs were stained with blood too. Twice she tripped and fell to her knees, and each time she was pulled along and kicked.

"Vive la France!" Maman shouted with a last surge of strength. "Vive la République!" The brave words echoed gloriously into the street like a forbidden song. Even in the confines of the dumbwaiter, the cowering children heard it clearly. Then there was a moment's heavy silence before the motors of the car and trucks roared to life and drove off.

Two soldiers, however, still remained in the room to guard the house and wait for a detail to clear away the bodies.

49

They had taken off their helmets and leaned their rifles against the kitchen doorframe beside Michelle.

One of them struck a match and lit a cigarette. The other was talking in moody tones. Cursing, he kicked at a chair and it overturned.

It was then that Marie started crying.

The soldier who had kicked the chair turned and listened. Then he walked over to the dumbwaiter. Hélène's view from the knothole went dark. Suddenly the doors flew open with a clatter and blinding light streamed in.

2

They blinked in the sudden light.

"Ach, seh' mal was ich hier gefunden habe!" the soldier called out. His face was a shadow against the bright room behind him. He turned toward his partner and gestured him over.

Edmond and Hélène huddled closer to Catherine. They clung together like frightened puppies who had been abandoned. Hélène could feel Catherine's shivers. Eyes downcast, she was holding Marie tightly against her breast. Marie's cries were louder now, and Hélène could see her squirm fitfully.

The second soldier came over and peered in for a moment. Then he grunted, and there was the scraping of a match. In the flickering light Hélène saw both of the Boches' faces clearly, their lips spread in hungry grins. Their eyes ignored her, Edmond, and Marie, staring greedily at Catherine with the same look Hélène had seen on children eyeing the cakes in the windows of the neighborhood pâtisserie. Catherine, though the oldest of them, suddenly looked the most helpless and frightened. Her lips were tense, her brown eyes wide and wary.

"You," the second soldier said to her in bad French. "You come out from in there."

Catherine looked up at him but did not move. She stayed

cowering as the children clutched each other tighter than ever.

"You!" the soldier said in a cold voice. "Do I have to pull you out?"

Trembling, Catherine solemnly handed Marie over to Hélène. Then without a word she pushed Edmond aside and slid slowly out of the dumbwaiter. Clumsily she stumbled onto her knees.

"Ah-hah!" the Boche exclaimed, leering at her with appreciation while, like a shark, he slowly circled his prey.

The other soldier threw the remains of his cigarette on the carpet, carelessly ground it out with the heel of his boot, and looked at his comrade with a hard expression. "Ich gehe zuerst," he announced with finality. For emphasis he poked a thumb toward his chest.

The other one vehemently shook his head. "Nein! Ich habe Sie von dort 'raus gebracht!" He gestured toward the dumbwaiter.

Still on her knees, Catherine stole a glance over her shoulder. Her eyes met Hélène's. Her lips were pressed tightly together and her body had gone limp. Hélène had seen that look far too often on the streets—the look of defeat.

Ashamed, Catherine turned away from her and looked toward the stiff, awkwardly seated Michelle. Hélène looked too. The blood that stained the front of Michelle's dress with a huge maroon splotch had already coagulated. A horrible nausea swept over Hélène and she looked quickly away.

The Boches' arguing had now turned to grumbling. One fished in his pocket and took out a leather change purse. He unzipped it, poked through it, and extracted a coin. Going through a weird ritual, he rubbed it, kissed it, and tossed it high into the air. It spun and flashed and then fell. Expertly he caught it with a swift downward motion of his hand and slapped it onto his wrist.

They both peered closely at it. The Boche who had won Catherine grinned widely. The other one mumbled sourly.

The victor carefully replaced the coin in his change purse and put it back in his pocket. Then he bent down and grabbed Catherine by the shoulders of her coat. With one swift movement he jerked her to her feet.

"A pretty young thing," he said in his bad French. "Well, we will soon see just how pretty you really are. Probably too

51

skinny." He made a face. "All French are too skinny." He patted one of her cheeks with his big hand.

Instinctively Catherine flinched and pulled away.

Amusement glinted in his eyes. "She's a virgin," he said to the other Boche. "I can always tell. A nice sweet virgin. Really nothing like it."

The other shrugged. "I've had virgins," he replied in equally weak French. "No big deal."

Hélène exchanged glances with Edmond. "What are they going to do?"

Edmond's eyes were cold as he looked at her. "Do not be afraid," he whispered in a voice far more mature than his years.

She nodded solemnly. "I'll try not to be."

There was a shout from across the room. "Silence!"

Hélène jumped. Edmond gave her hand a reassuring squeeze and smiled. But she noticed that his eyes were not smiling.

At the other side of the room, the Boche had stuck his face close to Catherine's. "It is not every day a man finds for himself a virgin, is it?" he taunted in a loud voice.

Suddenly he let out a shriek, spun Catherine around, and threw her away from him. With a thud she landed against the edge of the dining-room table. Her hair was hanging over her face and she was gasping for air.

The Boche cursed and gingerly touched his lower lip. It was bleeding. He glanced at his finger, grunted, and wiped the blood on his thigh.

The other Boche giggled hysterically. "Mensch," he called out. "Kannst Du nicht einmal ein Mädchen handeln?"

The bitten one glared at him. "Halt's maul!" he snarled. Then he lunged savagely at Catherine. His hands tore at her coat and pulled it off.

"No!" Catherine screamed. "Oh, please God, no!"

The Boche grinned and licked his lips. Catherine backed against the table, her steepled fingers held pleadingly out in front of her as if in prayer. Hélène could hear fabric ripping as he tore the dress Maman had sewn for her. Buttons popped and bounced on the tabletop. The dress fell around Catherine's ankles.

"Please," Catherine whimpered. "Please . . ."

Something else ripped; her brassiere. Desperately she held

on to it, but it was torn out of her grasp. Protectively her hands flew up to cover her small breasts.

"Please . . . please don't," she begged in a low voice.

"Quiet!" There was a sharp report as he slapped her across the face. She recoiled as if stung. Then she curled her fingers into claws, and with a cry of rage she fiercely swiped his cheeks with her nails. Almost instantly four red streaks seeped to the surface.

"Verdammt!" Hélène heard him curse under his breath. Then more slaps rang out as he flung her onto the tabletop. Catherine kicked and squirmed as he pulled her wool stockings and panties down to her ankles. She was naked now, her tears streaming. He grabbed her and yanked her off the table. She struggled to get her footing, tripped on the garments collected around her ankles, and fell headfirst to the carpet. Not wasting a second, the Boche loosened his pants and pounced on her.

3

A searing rage tore at Hélène's stomach. She had never known hatred, but she had her first taste of it that afternoon as her sister was spread-eagled to the floor, a Nazi pinning her down. Nausea rose from her churning stomach to her throat like gaseous fire, and it took everything in her to swallow and hold it down.

"No," Catherine gasped. "No!" Her firm, boyish breasts rose and fell with each terrified breath.

"Let her go!" Hélène suddenly screamed.

Amused, the soldiers glanced toward the dumbwaiter and grinned. Then the one holding Catherine down by the wrists glanced at her groin. She tried to raise her hands, but her strength was no match for his. Her wrists were held down firmly, and her arms only reddened and trembled uselessly under the pressure. She bit her lips in pain.

"Mensch, mach's schnell!" the watching soldier snapped impatiently.

The Boche atop Catherine ignored him.

Edmond almost imperceptibly nudged Hélène and slowly glanced toward the kitchen door. She followed his gaze. Surely Edmond didn't expect her to stare at Michelle. No, there must be something else. Something very important . . . Then she understood. Beside Michelle, the soldiers' rifles were propped against the doorframe. She glanced back toward her brother. Their eyes met grimly, and she nodded ever so slightly. Even without speaking she knew what they had to do. Carefully she set Marie down on the dumbwaiter floor. Then they awaited their opportunity.

The Boche pinioning Catherine to the floor placed his groin close to her and with one vicious thrust of his body entered her. Catherine's drawn-out scream seemed to hang in the air forever. For one long, agonized moment her back arched and Hélène was certain her sister was going to throw him off, but after a moment Catherine slumped back wearily, horrible sobbing sounds escaping through her teeth.

Hélène shared in Catherine's humiliation and pain. So did Edmond. He sucked in his breath sharply. "Soon," his lips mouthed soundlessly. "Soon."

Hélène answered with a blink.

Flesh slapped obscenely against flesh while Catherine tossed her head from side to side in agony, horrible grimaces deeply etched on her face. The eyes of the other soldier were fixed on the rape taking place at his feet. He undid his belt and let his pants drop around his boots in anticipation of his own turn.

Edmond nudged Hélène. It was time. She watched as he hopped soundlessly out of the dumbwaiter. He waited a second and glanced cautiously at the men. They were too intent on Catherine to notice. Like a crab, Edmond scuttled behind the dining-room table and motioned Hélène to follow.

Trying to imitate his ease and nonchalance, she followed, joining him behind the table. She had reached it unseen. He gave her hand a reassuring squeeze.

"For God's sake, *stop* it!" Catherine's voice rang out.

Hélène glanced around the edge of the tablecloth, but Edmond grabbed her arm and pointed toward the kitchen door. He wanted her to follow on his heels. She nodded. From across the room, the noises rose and fell.

"Oh God!" Catherine was crying. "Oh God, *where are you?*"

Edmond nodded. Together he and Hélène began to crawl slowly and cautiously toward the stiff body of their beloved Michelle. Toward the rifles.

"*Aghhhhh . . .*" the soldier hammering at Catherine bellowed.

Edmond and Hélène were halfway between the table and Michelle. Fascinated, they stole another glance backward. The soldier was thrashing against her much faster now. Sweat poured from his flushed forehead, and the purple veins on his temples protruded so far Hélène thought they would burst.

"*Aghhhhh! Aghhhhh! Aghhhhh . . .*" Spasms racked his body.

Edmond prodded Hélène to move on. She hastily crawled after him, and they didn't look back until they had reached Michelle. By that time the soldier, eyes squeezed shut, was beginning to catch his breath. Catherine was sobbing softly. Hélène felt another wave of nausea rising in her throat, but she didn't need to do much to stifle it. The German did it for her. He was staring straight toward her and Edmond. "Verdammte Scheiss Kinder!" he roared abruptly. He pointed an angrily shaking finger.

Marie began to wail again, her cries sounding hollow coming from inside the dumbwaiter.

"Quickly!" Edmond shouted. "Quickly—get behind me!"

Hélène was frozen to the spot. "I . . . I can't move!" she whispered.

Edmond grabbed her arm and yanked her toward the kitchen door. Wasting no time, he took advantage of the soldiers' surprise. He picked up the rifle nearest him and swung it straight out in front of him, narrowly missing Michelle's head. The barrel glistened blue-black and oily. It was heavy. A man can hold such a rifle steady. In the hands of a child it wavers. But hatred makes adrenaline flow freely, so it was hatred that held up that rifle, not Edmond Junot.

Edmond squinted as he peered along the barrel the way he had seen actors do in cowboy films. But cinemas do not teach a boy how to shoot. Tanks and rifles had been common in Paris for years now, and Edmond and his friends had studied them from close and afar, exchanged notes on the mechanics of them. Thus it was that Edmond, a mere eleven-year-old child, knew where the safety catch was. And now he released it.

The Germans didn't miss this action. Both stiffened perceptibly. There was hatred in their eyes. That and something else that hadn't been there a few moments earlier. Fear.

"Runter, du verdammtes Schwein!" the Boche on top of Catherine yelled, too unnerved to search his mind for the elusive French words. With his hands he motioned Edmond to lower the rifle and put it down. The other soldier bent over and pulled his pants up, but his angry eyes never left them, not even while fastening his belt. He took a step in Edmond's direction.

Hélène was terribly afraid. "Now!" she cried. "*Now*, Edmond. Shoot!"

Frowning, her brother hesitated. The heavy rifle swung back and forth in an arc in his trembling hands.

The soldier slowly stepped closer. His angry face was flushed, and his dark eyes flashed. "Come on. Hand it over," he coaxed in bad French.

Edmond stared at him dully.

"Come on, put it down." His voice was gentler now. "Nothing's going to happen, boy."

Hélène knew it was a trick to get the rifle out of Edmond's hands. And if that happened, then what? Would they all be killed? All she knew was that Edmond mustn't hand the rifle over.

"Come on," the soldier said in a calculating soft voice. "Be a good boy and lay it down."

Oh, how Hélène despised that deceptive voice. And now the German was attempting a benign smile. Her heart was pounding wildly. Oh, Edmond please do something. Don't be fooled! Do something quickly . . . while there's still time.

The Boche was closer now. His left hand reached out for the rifle. He approached slowly, like a man nearing a cobra, with infinite caution. "Lay it down," he said in a soft whisper. "Nothing's going to happen." His voice was seductive. You have a chance, it seemed to say. A chance not to do anything monstrous you'll be sorry for later.

Instinctively Edmond took a step backward toward Hélène.

"Edmond," she warned between clenched teeth. "Edmond . . ."

The Nazi's eyes flashed angrily upon her. He was afraid

her pleas might influence her brother. The other soldier was staring with a grim expression on his face. Marie was quiet.

The Boche's hand had almost reached the barrel. It was trembling. "Come on. Steady," the voice said softly. "That's right. Steady, boy . . ."

"Edmond!" Catherine screamed as she tried to sit up and push the other soldier away. Hélène looked over at her. Catherine's eyes were frightened ovals. "Edmond!" she screamed. "For God's sake—"

"Halt's maul!" the soldier screamed suddenly, and backhanded her viciously. She fell back with a screech of pain as her head hit the carpet with a dull thud.

A strangled cry of rage issued forth from the depths of Edmond's throat, and he pulled the trigger. There was a flash. Simultaneously, a blast shook the room. Maman's good china in the armoire rattled. From the dumbwaiter Marie let out a high-pitched wail. And then, as suddenly as the room had seemed to explode, it was so quiet that Hélène dared not breathe. She was afraid it would intrude on the silence. Even Marie suddenly quieted down. The acrid odor of cordite passed over them like a curse. For the first time that afternoon Hélène noticed the steady, persistent ticking of the grandfather clock by the front door. Then she glanced at Edmond and sucked in her breath.

He still held the rifle out in front of him, but his face was dull, dazed. He didn't seem to realize that he was hurt. A stream of blood ran down his neck from his mouth, and he was missing two front teeth. When he had squeezed the trigger, the butt of the rifle had hit him squarely in the jaw as the recoil threw him back against Hélène. But he had managed to retain his footing, and he still squinted along the barrel.

The soldier in front of Edmond was no more. At pointblank range, he'd had no chance. The bullet had smashed into his chest, and his ribs and lungs had shattered into a million flying fragments that slammed haphazardly against the wall as he'd been flung backward. Bits of bone and bloodied flesh were embedded in the wallpaper.

There was one less Nazi on French soil. He was a Boche no more. Just like Michelle was no more.

I never even screamed, Hélène thought.

The other Boche stared at Edmond with stone-cold eyes.

Edmond gestured at him with the rifle. "Pull up your pants," he said in a hollow voice.

There was a moment of quiet tension. Then the Boche started to bend forward.

"Very slowly," Edmond warned. "Otherwise . . ." Unspoken, the threat hung heavy in the air.

Slowly the Boche pulled up his pants and tucked in his shirt. His face was expressionless, but Hélène saw that his eyes were wary. They never left Edmond, not for a fleeting instant. When he finished buckling his belt he let his hands drop alongside his thighs. His fingers were splayed and rigid. Instinctively Hélène knew why. He was waiting for an opportunity to pounce.

Edmond lowered the rifle slightly and looked toward Catherine. "Get up," he told her gently.

She turned her tear-streaked face toward him. With the palms of her hands she wiped her eyes.

"Go and fetch some clothes," Edmond said. His voice was thick with emotion. "Go. Get dressed."

Catherine nodded. Eyes downcast, she managed to stagger to her feet. Feebly her hands covered her pubis. She looks so haggard, Hélène thought. So . . . so *ashamed*. A hot, prickling humiliation began to spread through Hélène. Then with a shock she noticed that Catherine's thighs were smeared with blood. Quickly she averted her eyes.

Suddenly the Boche made his move. Hélène's eyes caught the blur of movement, and her heart jumped. In vain she tried to cry out a warning. Her throat was frozen with terror.

She heard Edmond's gasp. He saw too, but it was too late. For one split second he had taken his eye off the Boche, and that instant was all it took.

With split-second timing the Boche dived at Catherine and tackled her legs. She toppled back to the floor and grunted as the wind was knocked out of her. Then, pulling her up in front of him, using her limp body as a shield, the Boche got to his feet. He had one arm wrapped around her neck and something flashed in his hand. A pocketknife, the point of it pressed against her throat. Not hard enough to puncture, but enough to depress the soft skin where the point of the blade rested. Her eyes were wide with terror; her mouth was open and gasping for air.

"Drop the rifle or I'll slit her throat," the Boche said quietly. His eyes were narrowed and he looked at Edmond with contempt.

Hélène stared at the Boche. There was no mistaking that

he meant every word. Edmond didn't move. His somber face was wet. He had broken out in a cold sweat. There was nothing he could do now, but still he held the rifle in front of him.

The knife point pressed harder against Catherine's throat. Then a bead of blood appeared and slid slowly down her neck.

"Drop that rifle," the Boche repeated.

Helpless, Edmond let go of the rifle. With a clatter it fell at his feet.

The Boche's lips spread into a thin cruel smile. He eased the pressure of the knife but still held it close to Catherine's throat. Clumsily he stepped forward.

He was face to face with Edmond now. With one swift movement he kicked the rifle behind him, toward the foyer. "You fools," he hissed. Hélène could smell the garlic on his breath.

She felt the shiver of gooseflesh and slowly let her eyes roam toward the door. Something told her that they were not the only ones in the house anymore. She had heard nothing, but she sensed someone else's presence. She was right. She saw a man slip stealthily from the shadows of the foyer into the dining room. This was no Boche. She stared at him in recognition. Could it be? Her heartbeat quickened. Yes, it was Monsieur Laval, Papa's friend. Hélène's eyes met his. He paused and held a finger to his lips, not five feet from the Boche, when a floorboard creaked. Startled, the Boche let go of Catherine and spun around. He cursed and his arm shot out in a wide arc. Hélène heard the knife whistle through the air. Monsieur Laval ducked low, but the blade grazed his winter coat, slicing open the thick wool down to the lining. Hélène shuddered. Beside him, swaying dizzily, stood Catherine.

"Catherine!" Hélène screamed. "Catherine!"

Catherine stared at her with blank eyes. She was lost in some fog only she was aware of.

"Catherine!" Hélène screamed again. "Move away from them!"

Now her words penetrated the fog. Catherine snapped out of it and scrambled out of the way. Hélène took her ice-cold hand.

Once again the knife sliced through the air. Hélène could hear it before she saw it. Monsieur Laval flung himself to one side, brought up his knee, and slammed it into the Boche's groin. The Boche let out a scream of pain and doubled over. The knife fell from his grasp and his face turned a sickly gray. Then he slumped to the floor. He lay on one side in a fetal position, hands pressed against his groin.

Monsieur Laval took a handkerchief out of his coat pocket and wiped his forehead. He was still breathing rapidly from the exertion of the fight. He was no longer a young man.

"Monsieur Laval!" Hélène said suddenly. Fiercely she tugged at his coat. "They've taken Maman away! The Nazis have taken Maman!"

As he looked down at her she saw the compassion in his tired brown eyes. He put his hands on her shoulders and pressed her close to him, the way Maman always did. But his belly wasn't warm like hers, or soft like Michelle's. His coat was cold and rough. Hélène didn't like the scratchy feel of it. It didn't comfort her at all. For the first time that afternoon she began sobbing.

Gently Monsieur Laval pushed her away and squatted down until both their faces were level. He looked deep into her eyes. "Yes, Hélène," he said quietly. "They took your Maman. But we mustn't let them take you, must we?"

She shook her head silently.

"Good. Then you be a brave girl and wipe your eyes."

She sniffed and nodded and did as she was told.

"There. That's better." He forced a smile with his lips. "Now, I want you to listen carefully. Will you do that?"

"Yes." Hélène's wavering voice was thick.

"You have to leave this house right now," he said, "It isn't safe for you here. Do you understand?"

Again she nodded her head.

"Good. I will take you someplace where you will be safe." Monsieur Laval got to his feet and glanced toward Catherine. For the first time he noticed her bloodied thighs. He stared at her in shock. "You poor girl," he murmured, shaking his head. "They are worse than animals!"

Catherine turned her face away in shame.

"Don't!" Monsieur Laval said sharply. "Don't be ashamed! Ever! You have done nothing wrong. You must remember that!"

"Yes." Catherine's voice was a whisper. "Yes. I'll remember."

"Now, run upstairs and put some clothes on," he told her. "But don't wash up. There isn't time."

Catherine nodded and dashed from the room.

Monsieur Laval looked at the Boche, then at Edmond. "I'll need a towel and a sturdy rope."

"Will a laundry line do?" Edmond looked at him questioningly.

Monsieur Laval nodded. "A laundry line will do just fine."

Without another word, Edmond left. Hélène heard him rummaging in the kitchen. A minute later he came back out, holding the towel and a length of white rope. Monsieur Laval kicked the Boche over on his belly, then bent down and with the rope began to truss him expertly. That done, he gagged him with the towel. The Boche whimpered with fright. So he wasn't that brave after all, Hélène thought with satisfaction.

Catherine came back downstairs already dressed. Without looking at anyone, she headed straight for the dumbwaiter, picked up Marie, and held her close.

Monsieur Laval looked around. "Everyone ready?" he asked.

In silence the children nodded. They didn't waste another moment going through the kitchen and out the back door. Behind them, a single gong from the grandfather clock announced that it was three-thirty. Less than a half-hour had passed since Hélène was playing in the park with Antoinette. Less than a half-hour, and her life had changed. Forever.

With Monsieur Laval in the lead, they ran across the brittle, crusty snow lying frozen on the ground of the courtyard. It crunched beneath their feet. They passed the rusty old barrel that was used to collect rainwater for the garden. It was covered with ice. Something deep inside Hélène told her she would never see it again. High above their heads, the familiar laundry lines crisscrossed the courtyard. Laundry hung stiffly in the biting wind. Then they ran through the dark, tunnellike passageway of the building across from theirs.

They were on the run. For their lives.

4

The house was located at the end of a short, dark alley that
branched off the one they traveled. Monsieur Laval halted in
front of the door of 17 rue Jules Talet and hit the buzzer
three times in quick succession.

The building was ancient and dingy and gray. Like all the
other houses in the district, it looked like the tenants had always lived in a near-poverty level. There was a mailbox next
to the door, but it didn't have any name tags on it. Hélène
looked up. All the windows were dark,

Just when she thought no one was home, the door opened
abruptly and a flood of yellow light poured out into the alley.
A bald, heavyset Negro giant was silhouetted dimly against
the light. His massive black arms were folded in front of his
chest.

Monsieur Laval took off his beret and murmured something under his breath.

The giant turned toward the children, his eyes hard and
appraising. Then he stepped aside and motioned them to enter. Silently they slipped past him into the hallway. The heavy
door shut behind them.

Hélène glanced at Edmond. His eyes had widened as much
as hers. Outside, the house had looked old and dilapidated.
Inside, it was luxurious to a fault. The first thing Hélène noticed was how warm it was. Their own home had always been
cold and drafty; this one was practically a blast furnace. The
furnishings were antiques. There were crystal chandeliers, fine
blue-and-white Oriental vases, and thick rugs. The walls were
covered with rich red fabric, and to either side of a pair of
handsome double doors stood massive bronze torchères.
These torchères were in the shape of muscular Moors. Each
held a many-branched candelabrum aloft.

The giant motioned them to wait. He walked toward the
big doors, knocked once, and entered. For a moment Hélène

could hear the hum of conversation and the clear tinkling of a woman's laughter suspended in the air. Then the doors closed behind him and there was silence.

Hélène glanced around the hallway. Catherine was leaning wearily against the wall. After a half-hour of carrying Marie, her arms seemed to sag under the weight. Edmond was gingerly touching one of the torchères. He behaved as if it might suddenly come to life and bite him. Monsieur Laval was standing back to back with him, his lower lip jutting out slightly and his squinting eyes thoughtful. His beret was clutched limply in his hands.

A moment later the doors opened and the giant came back out. He was followed by a tiny lady who walked with slow, delicate steps. She was Oriental. Hélène stared in rapt fascination. Never before had she seen anyone so exotic. There were the murmur and scent of faraway places, of orchids and water lilies and unspoken taboos. Her skin was pale and her hair was jet black. Worn loose, it hung all the way to her waist. Her eyes shone brightly in the lights of the torchères. They were slanted, black and shrewd. Her red gown was of shiny silk and fit snugly, cut low to emphasize her figure. Though she was very slim, her breasts were large. From around her neck a platinum chain dangled a huge marquise-cut diamond into the cleft of her bosom. In the winter of 1944 that sparkle was obscene.

The giant hovered at a discreet distance, but the woman made no move to dismiss him. Nor did she give any indication that she noticed Catherine, Edmond, or Hélène. She came straight toward Monsieur Laval and held out a hand as delicate and white as new porcelain.

Hélène watched as Monsieur Laval shook her hand. He held it gently, with a grace Hélène was unprepared for.

The woman was very short and had to look up to him. "Monsieur," she said. Her singsong voice was high-pitched but clear. It was then that Hélène realized that the crystalline laughter she had heard was hers.

Politely Monsieur Laval inclined his head. "Madame Chang," he said in a respectful voice, "it is good of you to see me."

She bowed her head. Without prologue she said, "Monsieur, I know you are here because you are in trouble. Do not misunderstand me; I will help you if I can. However, I want to know absolutely nothing about this trouble." Her voice was still soft and delicate, but her tone was now brusque and businesslike. It was almost as if a chill wind had touched upon the most delicate of blossoms. "Do we understand each other?"

"Perfectly, madame. Your discretion is both wise and highly appreciated."

She looked up into his eyes. "Now. What is it that you wish me to do?"

Monsieur Laval gestured toward the children. "They need a safe place in which to stay."

Madame Chang's face was impassive. "That is not such an unusual request. But you realize, Monsieur, that I cannot be expected to close my establishment for the night. Not because of four children."

"I realize that," he said.

"Good. Then we understand each other." Her almond eyes bore into his. "How long do they need to remain here?"

"Until tomorrow sometime. I shall return and take them elsewhere."

She nodded. "It is settled, then. But remember. I shall expect you to pick them up no later than three o'clock in the afternoon."

Monsieur Laval practically prostrated himself with a profusion of thanks. "Madame is too kind," he began. "An—"

Madame Chang held up a hand to silence him. Hélène noticed that her fingernails were long and lacquered red. "I must have one guarantee," she said.

They all stared wordlessly at the woman.

"They must keep very quiet," she said. "The older ones are capable of keeping the baby silenced?" She looked questioningly at Catherine.

Catherine nodded gravely.

"Very well, then." Madame Chang turned to the giant. "Take them upstairs to Gisèle's room."

Wordlessly the giant bowed. With his hands he motioned the children to follow.

Hélène hesitated and glanced beseechingly at Monsieur Laval. He was the only familiar face in these strange surroundings, and the thought of being separated from him terrified her.

He noticed her reluctance. "What are you waiting for?" he asked. "Go . . . go along with him. I will pick you up tomorrow afternoon."

She looked at him skeptically. "Is that a promise?"

He nodded. "I promise. Now, do not worry. Everything will be all right."

On an impulse, Hélène flung her arms around Monsieur Laval and gave him a massive hug. Then, just as suddenly, she disengaged herself from him and followed the giant. Edmond and Catherine walked behind her.

Catherine was feeding Marie from a makeshift bottle when Edmond spoke to Hélène. "You better be careful. You could fall out the window."

She ignored him. Gisèle's room was in the attic and had a dormer window. By standing tiptoe on her bed Hélène could look out over the jagged rooftops. Night had fallen and it was almost pitch black out.

"Have it your way, then," Edmond said. "See if I'll help if you start to fall."

"Children," Gisèle warned. "Keep quiet! Madame Chang doesn't want you to make a sound!" She glanced at Edmond and patted the mattress.

He made a face but sat down obediently beside her on the edge of the bed. Hélène could feel the mattress shift under his weight. It had good springs.

After a few minutes she left the window and joined them. It was too dark out to see anything anyway. From below she could hear a piano playing, and several times there were shrieks of high-pitched laughter. It sounded like a party going on.

Gisèle said she was one of twenty girls in the house. Right now she would normally have been sitting downstairs with the others, waiting for clients to arrive. But she was having her "delicate condition," and Madame Chang wouldn't hear of her girls working during those times.

Gisèle was tall and full-breasted. She just missed being pretty. Her misfortune, she lamented, was her torso. It was too short-waisted for her to ever hope for a lean, elegant figure. She would forever seem to be slightly dumpy. Her large breasts made her look more like a woman in her early twenties than the seventeen-year-old girl she actually was. A year ago she had come to Paris from the suburb of Auteuil. Ever since then she had worked for Madame Chang.

There were certain advantages for the girls who worked at Madame Chang's. The pay was good and, unlike the rest of

Paris, which was starving, there was always enough food in the larder here. But best of all, a girl who worked here could afford a pretty wardrobe. That was an almost unheard-of luxury.

Some of the other, more beautiful girls had luxurious high-ceilinged rooms and clothes designed by the most expensive couturiers. Jocelyne, Gisèle said, almost reverently, was the most ravishing and highest-priced of them all. Men who could afford her claimed she was the most sensational creature in all of Paris. But to afford her, a man had to be able to part with six thousand francs for one hour. A fortune.

"I'm getting bored," Edmond grumbled. Gisèle's story did not interest him.

Hélène nodded. "Me too. I hate just sitting around here doing nothing."

Gisèle thought for a moment. Then her face brightened. "I know what!" she said. "I'll sketch all of you! Would you like that?"

Edmond made a sour face.

"I'm quite good, actually," Gisèle said quickly. "That is, as long as you promise to sit still. Let me get my sketchpad." She hurried over to the dresser, where she kept her pad and a supply of blue-leaded pencils. Then she made a production out of moving one of the chairs to just the precise spot she wanted. Finally satisfied, she sat down in it and faced them. With a frown she studied the children one by one. Then she motioned Hélène to sit still. With deft strokes of the pencil, Gisèle began to draw.

Hélène sat in self-conscious silence and watched Gisèle's hands. They were small, the fingers too stubby. They were capable-looking hands, but a far cry from Madame Chang's exquisitely lacquered claws. Hélène wondered if all short-waisted people had little hands.

Edmond cleared his throat, and Hélène glanced at him. The moment their eyes met, he began to make funny faces. Hélène started to giggle.

Gisèle shot her a warning look. "Sit still!" she said angrily.

It took Gisèle a half-hour to draw all four. Then, with a sudden fanfare, she held up the sketches. "What do you think?" she asked eagerly.

Hélène studied them closely. They were quite good, and she recognized Catherine instantly; it was her spitting image. She was disappointed by the way she herself had turned out, though. She thought Gisèle had drawn her too young and sweet, and it wasn't at all what she saw when she looked at herself in the mirror. Edmond's was a pretty good likeness, but then again, it didn't *really* look like him. The nose was all wrong and the eyes were set too close together.

Gisèle looked at Hélène. "Well?" she asked.

Before Hèléne had a chance to voice her opinion they heard footsteps in the corridor and then a knock on the door. Catherine jumped and turned toward it, a frightened-animal look in her eyes.

Gisèle smiled gently and patted Catherine's hand. "Don't worry. It's only Roland." She got up, put the sketchpad back in the dresser, and unlocked the door.

The black giant came inside carrying a tray. On it were several domed lids with steam escaping from under them. He set the tray down on the dresser and left.

"He's not very friendly, is he?" Hélène asked when he was gone.

"Why do you say that?" Gisèle asked.

"Well, for one thing, he never says a word."

"That's because he's a mute," Gisèle said. "He cannot talk."

"Oh." Hélène was curious. "How come?"

Gisèle shrugged. "I do not know."

"But he can hear us and understand us?"

She nodded, walked over to the dresser, and lifted the domed lids off the tray. Billowing clouds of steam rose from the big platters as the delicious aroma reached Hélène's nostrils. Her mouth fell open. It had been a long time since she smelled anything so mouth-watering. Suddenly she forgot all about Roland the giant and his lack of speech. She was ravenous.

Gisèle spooned the food onto gilt-trimmed china plates. Hélène stared at her helping with wide-eyed wonder. On her plate she had thick slabs of beef with a mushroom sauce, steamed green vegetables, and potatoes. She looked over at Catherine's and Edmond's helpings. Figuring that they were older and had bigger appetites, Gisèle had piled their plates even higher. And as if all this were not enough, a plate of petit fours had been included for dessert. For a moment Hélène closed her eyes and savored the aromas of the food. Then she wasted no time in attacking it.

* * *

Hélène was wide-awake. Groggily she looked around, trying to figure out what had awakened her. She listened carefully. Then she heard it again. Someone was gently tapping on Gisèle's door.

Slowly her night vision adjusted to the darkness. She glanced over to the bed and could make out Gisèle as a sound-asleep shadow. On the comforter spread out on the floor, Catherine, Edmond, and Marie were still curled up, fast asleep.

Again Hélène heard the tapping, a little louder this time. She wondered whether she should answer the door, but Gisèle had reprimanded her when she tried to go out and use the toilet and had made her use the chamber pot behind a screen. The door had to stay locked at all times. The order had been emphatic.

Hélène turned to Edmond. For a moment she hesitated, then shook him awake.

He sat bolt upright. "What the—"

Hélène clapped a hand over his mouth. "Sssssh!" she whispered. "There's someone at the door."

He cocked his head to listen.

Again the tapping. This time it must have reached through Gisèle's shroud of sleep. She moaned and lifted her head off the pillow. "Go away," she called out in a sleepy voice.

"Gisèle!" a woman's hoarse voice called softly. "It's me! Jocelyne. Open up! I need to talk to you!"

Gisèle moaned again and sat up. "Oh, all right," she said grumpily. She stretched wearily and rubbed her eyes. Then Hélène heard the bedsprings creak as Gisèle swung her legs over the side.

Edmond and Hélène lay back down as Gisèle stumbled over to the door. By the time the key turned in the lock, the children's eyes were closed in pretended sleep.

The door creaked open and weak, flickering yellow light shone into the room. Whoever was standing out in the hallway was holding a candle.

"Jocelyne," Gisèle said in a whisper. "What are you doing out there? What time is it anyway?"

"Almost four o'clock," the throaty voice replied.

Gisèle shook her head. "What do you want at this unearthly hour?"

"Sssssh." There was a pause. "Are they asleep?"

"How do you know about them?" Gisèle's voice was guarded.

"Simple. I saw two of them going up the stairs yesterday afternoon. I know that there must be more. There were far too many little footsteps. Besides, I saw the dinner tray being brought up." Hélène saw her trying to peer into the room over Gisèle's shoulder. In the shimmering candlelight she caught sight of the most extraordinarily beautiful woman she had ever seen. She was tall and blond, and under the voluminous pale blue chiffon of her peignoir, her figure was voluptuous but slender. "Come on, Gisèle," Jocelyne coaxed. "Let me in for a moment. I have to see them."

Gisèle shook her head in exasperation. "Why? There must be a reason."

"All right, all right. I'll tell you." Jocelyne looked around conspiratorially and her voice dropped an octave. "There may be money in it for both of us."

"Money?" Gisèle's voice sounded explosive in the night.

"Sssssh!" Jocelyne hissed. "Don't wake them up! Just let me in to see them. I'll tell you about it later."

Gisèle placed her hands on her hips. "Suppose you tell me now."

"Oh, all right. One of my visitors tonight was that Standartenführer who's so crazy about me."

"Yes, yes. The bald regular. I know the one."

"Well, he told me they're scouring Paris for four kids."

"*Four* kids?"

Four kids. Hélène felt a shiver slither down her back. Beside her, Edmond stiffened.

"Yes, four. An older boy and a girl, and a little one of seven or eight. Plus a baby."

"But why should the SS be out looking for children?" Gisèle asked.

"They're killers."

Gisèle laughed. "Killers? Those sweet little darlings?"

"Don't be fooled." Jocelyne's voice was serious. "They're killers, all right. They shot a Boche yesterday. There were two of them, but only one came out of it alive. He told the story, and now there's a reward out for information leading to their capture."

"A reward?"

Jocelyne nodded her head vigorously.

"How much?" Gisèle's eyes flashed greedily as she glanced toward the children.

Jocelyne was silent for a moment. "Half a million francs."

"Half a mil . . ." Gisèle sucked in her breath. "Good God! That's a *fortune!*"

"And half of it would be yours," Jocelyne said quickly. "Just think! A quarter of a million francs apiece. We could go out and get three, maybe four dresses at the couturiers'. . . . Now, are you going to let me in or not?"

Gisèle still hesitated. "But Madame Chang—"

"Madame Chang need never know. Trust me. I can arrange that."

"But—"

"But nothing." Jocelyne smiled faintly. Gently she reached up and touched Gisèle's face with slender, tapered fingers. "And another thing, darling. I've seen the special way in which you constantly watch me. I can tell, you know. You don't want the men. You prefer the women." The smile was wider now. "But that's no crime. I myself am sometimes attracted to other women. Maybe I will even let you come down to my room." The air was heavy with promises.

Gisèle's voice was a choked whisper. "Come to your room. . . ?"

Jocelyne nodded. Slowly she parted the front of her peignoir. Her breasts were as firm and perfectly shaped as a Greek statue's. Hélène heard Gisèle gasp.

"And not only that," Jocelyne continued in a lilting voice. "I will let you do whatever you want." She paused. "I will even part my legs for you so that you may eat my écu."

With trembling hands Gisèle pulled the door wide open and stepped aside. "Come in," she whispered.

Jocelyne swept into the room. Edmond poked Hélène. They both closed their eyes simultaneously and he began breathing regularly, as if in a deep sleep. Hélène copied him and snored gently. A moment later she could feel the women's presence as they came close and shone the candlelight over them. She could smell Jocelyne. Lavender.

"Is that them, do you think?" she heard Gisèle whisper.

"They seem to match the descriptions, all right," Jocelyne whispered back. "I'm certain it's them."

Then Hélène heard them move away, and she ventured to open her eyes. The women were back at the door.

"Jocelyne . . ." Gisèle's voice was a tremor.

"Yes?"

"I want to come with you down to your room. Now."

Jocelyne looked at her in surprise. Then she smiled and took Gisèle in her arms. Noisily she kissed her on the lips. "Come along, then. But you'd better come back up here in an hour to check up on them. Besides, I have to get *some* sleep. I have to go and see the Standartenführer first thing in the morning." She shuddered. "He'll probably *insist* that I lunch with him at that horrible café on the Champs-Élysées."

Then the door snapped closed behind them. Once again the room was in total darkness. Hélène waited for the key to turn in the lock, but in her haste Gisèle must have forgotten about it.

Edmond didn't speak until their footsteps receded in the hallway. Then he sat up straight as a board. "Wake up Catherine," he ordered grimly. "Then get dressed."

Hélène sat up. "A half million francs!" she said. "Imagine! There cannot be so much money in the world."

"Hurry!" Edmond hissed at her. There was no mistaking his tone; obedience was called for.

He was on his feet already, tiptoeing over to Gisèle's nightstand. After fumbling around in the darkness, he found what he was looking for. Hélène heard the scratch of a match and then saw the flame leap up. By the time he had the nightstand candle lit, she had already shaken Catherine awake.

5

Their progress was tedious. The alley was unlit, and several times they slipped on the treacherous ice. There were no streetlights; electricity was too precious a luxury. Paris got only one-half hour of it each evening.

Hélène shivered from the cold and pulled the collar of her winter coat up around her chin. The temperature had plummeted during the night and her coat was not thick enough. Her ears stung from the cold and she needed a cap.

On her left, Catherine trudged along in stony silence. In her arms, Marie was a small, quiet bundle. The sudden exposure to the cold couldn't be doing her any good, Hélène thought. It was dangerous to expose a baby to sudden cold.

It was even more dangerous to be caught out on the streets after the midnight curfew. They had heard enough stories from Michelle to know what happened to curfew violators. Any Frenchman caught by the night patrols was taken to the Feldgendarmarie headquarters. There, either of two things happened. If they were lucky and it was a peaceful night, the curfew violators would spend the night polishing the Boche's boots. If they were not so lucky and the Resistance killed a German during the night, the curfew violators were the reprisal victims. They would be shot by a firing squad.

Yesterday afternoon, Edmond had killed a Boche. Now with a heavy heart Hélène wondered what innocent Frenchmen—unknown and faceless—would end up paying for that deed. For someone would surely have to pay. The Boche always saw to that.

Bitterly she wondered which was the harsher fine—the loss of their own lives if they were caught, or the subsequent attack on their consciences if they were to live. Instinctively she knew that somehow they would all eventually have to pay. If they were to be delivered from danger now, they would probably be guilt-ridden for the rest of their lives. How else could they ever begin to do penance for those who substituted for them—those who would suffer such a brutal, final solution in their place?

Still, it is survival—not sacrifice—that is the foremost of human instincts. The fight for survival was now on—consciously and subconsciously. Their first move was only too clear. As quickly as they could, they had to get out of Paris. That was their only hope for survival. They had to follow Maman's instructions and try to reach the safety that beckoned to them from Tante Janine's house in faraway Saint-Nazaire.

Saint-Nazaire. Oh, but how distant it sounded! And Hélène had never been farther from Paris than Rambouillet. Then she frowned, and the magic in the name crumbled like ashes in the wind. Travel took money.

"We don't have any money," she found herself worrying aloud. "Why, we can't even get on the métro. How will we ever get out of Paris?"

"We have money," Edmond said softly.

"We do?" Catherine asked. There was surprise in her voice.

"Yes," Edmond said. "We have Maman's wedding ring, along with a pile of francs. Over two thousand."

"Two thousand francs!" Catherine whispered. Then her voice turned suspicious. "Where did you get it?"

"From Gisèle's nightstand, of course. Where else?"

"But . . . but that's *stealing*," Catherine said.

Edmond didn't bother answering. Hélène could imagine him shrugging his shoulders. Then she spoke up in his defense. "I'm glad he did it," she whispered to Catherine. "Gisèle was a monster! She deserved it! She wanted to sell us to the Boche!"

"But still, stealing—"

Edmond cut Catherine off. "What do you want?" he hissed savagely. "To stay in Paris and get caught? Have them repeat what they did to you? Is that what you want?"

His words had the effect of a slap across her face. She recoiled and fell silent. All Hélène could hear were Catherine's quick footsteps in the darkness. Then she heard another sound, and it hurt her to hear it. Catherine was crying softly.

Edmond heard, too. He was helpless against tears. "I'm sorry," he told her gently. "I . . . I didn't mean to hurt you. God knows, you've suffered more than enough. But please try to understand. If we're to reach Saint-Nazaire at all, we'll need that money. That and more. *Believe* me."

Catherine sniffed, and they walked on in silence.

6

Her feet were sore, her legs were sore, even her back and neck were sore. She couldn't tell whether it was because of the cold or all the walking they'd done. It was days now since they had left Paris. Edmond had bribed a vélo-taxi driver to take them out of the city, but the danger hadn't ended there.

Now they had to battle the Boche-infested countryside. Instead of the roads, they had stayed on the dirt paths that crisscrossed the fields. By doing this, they not only managed to avoid any traffic—namely the Boches—but also skirted most of the villages along the way. The earth must have been soggy just before winter set in; the paths all had deep wheel ruts frozen into the dirt. As a result, walking was treacherous.

It was Edmond's turn to carry Marie. He held her in such a way that she could look backward over his shoulder. He was singing softly to her.

Suddenly Hélène stopped walking. "I have to take a short rest," she announced wearily.

Edmond turned to her. "We'll rest for five minutes," he said. "But then we'll have to move on again."

"Thank heaven," Catherine murmured gratefully. "For the last half-hour I thought my legs were going to give out on me."

Keeping her hands in her pockets, Hélène looked out across the endless barren fields and past the villages that dotted the landscape up ahead. Way in the distance, where the earth met the sky, thin twin spires poked up out of the horizon.

"Hey . . . what's that over there?" she asked.

Edmond looked around. "What's what?" he asked.

"In the distance," Hélène said, pointing toward the spires. "See? Those two little things."

Edmond squinted. Then he shrugged. "Looks like a church or something," he answered.

Catherine shook her head excitedly. "It's got to be Chartres! Michelle once told me that after Ablis, you can already see the cathedral. Well, we've just passed through Ablis."

Ablis was one town they hadn't managed to bypass, but they had stayed near the outskirts to avoid being seen by too many people.

Edmond nodded thoughtfully. "If Michelle was right, that has to be Chartres," he said slowly. "There's no other cathedral around here that I've ever heard of."

Once again Hélène glanced at the distant spires. "Do you think it's far to Chartres?" she asked.

He smiled. "On foot, everything is far."

She poked him angrily. "I meant in kilometers."

He frowned. "I don't know. But it could be ten, maybe fifteen kilometers."

To Hélène, fifteen kilometers sounded a world away. "I hope it isn't as far again to Saint-Nazaire as it is from here to Chartres," she murmured. "I don't think my feet could stand it."

Weakly Edmond smiled down at her.

Suddenly Hélène had an inspiration. She gripped his arm. "Couldn't we take the train the rest of the way?" she asked eagerly.

He shook his head. "I'm afraid not. We'd need travel permits and money to do that. We don't have either."

"Oh." Her face fell. "But I thought we had money."

"It's all gone. I paid the vélo-taxi driver with it."

"But we still have Maman's ring," Hélène pointed out. "Can't we use that instead of money?"

Edmond tapped the pocket where he kept it, just to make sure he hadn't lost it. "We're not going to touch the ring if we can help it," he said flatly. "It's the only thing Maman could give us. It's . . . well, it's like an . . . an heirloom."

"Couldn't you steal some more money, then?" she asked.

Catherine shot Edmond a triumphant look. "Fine things she picks up from you. Before we know it, she'll become a pickpocket."

An expression of hurt crossed his face. Hélène glanced sharply at Catherine. "What's a pickpocket?" she demanded.

"Someone who reaches into other people's pockets and steals their money," she said harshly.

Hélène shook her head. "No, I don't think I'd like that," she said thoughtfully. "It doesn't sound very nice." Then she looked at Edmond curiously. "You weren't a pickpocket when you took Gisèle's money, were you? I mean, it wasn't actually in her *pocket*."

Edmond put a hand on her shoulder. "Just remember one thing, Hélène," he said quietly. "Whether you lift something from a person's pocket or from a nightstand or a chicken coop, it amounts to the same thing. Stealing is stealing, no matter how—or why—you do it. It's wrong, and nothing can ever make it right." He glanced sharply at Catherine. Her face reddened and she turned away in shame.

Hélène took Edmond's hand and squeezed it. "But if it's wrong, then why did you. . . ?" Her words trailed off uncomfortably.

He smiled sadly. "Because I had no choice. Remember what Maman said. She told us that God would forgive us for what we might have to do. But that still doesn't make it right."

Hélène digested this in silence.

Suddenly Edmond clapped his hands. "All right," he said gruffly. "Five minutes is up! It's time to get moving again."

"Already?" Catherine moaned.

"Already," he said with finality. "We still have far to go." He looked up at the sky. Hélène's eyes followed his. The sun was starting to go down and the sky was graying again. She knew that as soon as the sun dropped down, so did the temperature. Another couple of hours and it would get dark. And much colder.

They hadn't continued walking for five minutes when Catherine cried out sharply. Startled, Edmond and Hélène stopped and looked over at her. She was bending down, rubbing her left ankle with her hand.

Swiftly Edmond lowered Marie into Hélène's arms; then he touched Catherine gently on the back. "What's the matter?" His voice was concerned.

She looked at him sideways, her hair falling down over her face. Between strands of hair, Hélène could see her eyes. They were glazed over in pain. "It's my ankle," she moaned. "I . . . I twisted it in that rut."

Edmond knelt on the ground, his fingers gently probing around her ankle. Hélène could hear her sucking in her breath in pain.

He stood back up, placed a hand under Catherine's armpit, and pulled her to an upright position. "Do you think you can walk?" he asked.

She took a few tentative steps and nodded her head. "I'll be all right," she said.

Edmond looked thoughtfully across the fields, his eyes roving to the distant road. "We'll get off the path and stick to the road," he said with finality. "That way, walking will be a lot easier for you."

"The road?" Catherine said in a worried voice. "Do you think it's safe?"

"Right now it's a lot safer for you than the path. You could have a sprain, and these ruts won't help it any. Besides, I doubt that anyone's out here searching for us. The Boches may be looking for us in Paris, but they can't scour all of France. Not for us, anyway. We're not that important."

Catherine nodded. What he said made sense.

"Come on," he said. "Hélène can carry Marie for a while. You just hold on to me, and I'll help support you. That way we'll take some of the weight off your leg."

Even though they switched over to the smooth asphalt road, their progress had now slowed considerably. But Hélène had to credit Catherine with having guts. She tried to make light of her pain, although she limped noticeably, and much as they wanted to, she wouldn't hear of stopping so she could rest. And she was right. They had to keep on going. Already it was about time to look for a place to spend the night. So far, they hadn't come across a single shelter that looked suitable.

It was almost half an hour before they encountered any traffic. Then they heard the lonely drone of a car somewhere in the distance.

Hélène glanced at Edmond and pointed questioningly at the ditch. "Do you think we should. . . ?"

He shook his head. "I don't think that's necessary. But in case anyone asks, your names are Sara and Denise. Mine is Jacques. We live in Ablis and we're on our way to visit our sick grandmère in Chartres. Got that?"

Catherine and Hélène nodded in unison. Quickly they decided that Catherine was Sara and Hélène would be Denise.

It was just as well that they had the story prepared. Less than a minute later, a black car coming from the direction of Ablis pulled to a halt alongside them. A plump, red-faced Boche in a field uniform rolled down the window and leaned out, gesturing for them to come over.

Hélène glanced at Edmond hesitantly. He nodded, and they drew toward the car. Then, while he and Catherine talked with the driver, Hélène stood on tiptoe and peered curiously in through the back window. She was surprised to see that there were no passengers. Only a big bundle, wrapped up with brown wrapping paper and tied with a string, was on the backseat.

"Where are you headed?" she heard the driver ask in surprisingly fluent French.

Catherine tossed her head brusquely. "Our grandmère is sick," she said in a cold voice. "We are on our way to visit her."

The driver's mouth curved into a faint smile as he stared at Catherine longer than was necessary. "Where does she live?"

Catherine pointed in the direction of the distant spires. "Chartres."

"I noticed you were limping."

"I twisted my ankle," Catherine said with a shrug. "It's nothing."

"Even without a twisted ankle it's a long walk to Chartres," the Boche said. Suddenly his smile widened. "I tell you what. I shall drive you there." He leaned sideways and opened the front passenger door from inside. "Get in."

It sounded more like an order than an offer. Catherine didn't move. "What about my brother and sisters?" she asked stiffly.

"They can get in the back."

Once again Hélène looked at Edmond. Grudgingly he nodded his head, and she stood aside as he opened the back door. He shoved the package against the far side and let her climb in first.

Hélène glanced around excitedly. This was all new to her. She had never been in a car before. The seats were soft and bouncy and smelled faintly of leather; the dashboard was paneled with polished wood. She felt very important to be riding in such style.

After they piled in, the Boche expertly put the car in gear and drove off smoothly. While driving, he kept glancing sideways at Catherine. She didn't mask her distrust for Germans. She leaned against the door, as far from his reach as she could get. In frosty silence she stared out the windshield at the lifeless flat scenery up ahead.

"What is your name?" the Boche asked finally.

"Sara," Catherine answered softly. She didn't bother to look at him.

"My name is Kurt," he said. "I am from the Rhineland. From Koblenz. Where do you live?"

"In Ablis."

With curiosity Hélène inspected the wrapped bundle on the seat beside her. The brown paper crunched when she touched it. "What's in here?" she asked loudly.

The driver's eyes glanced back at her through the rearview mirror. "Newspapers. Every day I have to drive to Paris and pick up the *Pariser Zeitung, Paris-Soir,* and *Le Petit Parisien* for the general staff in Chartres."

"Oh!" The package might as well have been a snake; instinctively Hélène withdrew her hand. Even she knew what those newspapers were. Every kiosk in Paris sold them. The *Pariser Zeitung* was Paris' daily German newspaper. The others were French collaborator papers.

Good Parisians didn't read them.

"You can look at them if you like," the driver said. "You have plenty of time. Chartres is still a long way off. Over twenty kilometers."

"No, thank you," Hélène declined politely.

He chose not to hear her. He took one hand off the wheel, reached for a folded newspaper on the seat beside him, and handed it back over his shoulder. "If you don't want to tear the package open, here's a loose copy."

She had no choice but to take it. She murmured her thanks, and since she didn't want it, she handed it to Edmond. He started unfolding it.

Suddenly he let the paper drop facedown on his lap. He stared out the window thoughtfully.

Puzzled by this reaction, Hélène decided to find out what had triggered it. She lifted the newspaper and saw that it was a copy of *Paris-Soir*. The headlines screamed at her: "A MOTHER'S ANGUISH." Smaller headlines underneath it read: "Countrywide Search on for Kidnapped Children—One-Million-Franc Reward Offered." There was a blurred photo of a fat woman whom Hélène had never seen before. And below that, three pencil sketches.

Nausea rose up in her throat. The drawings had been reduced in size, but how well she recognized them! *They were Gisèle's sketches!* And Catherine's likeness was incredibly accurate, unmistakably recognizable. . . .

A series of chills swept through Hélène. The tactics were clear. The Boches were after them—but good. And in their search, they were even trying to enlist the aid of the unsuspecting French populace. Had it been spelled out that they were wanted for murdering a Boche, they'd be overnight heroes. Any good Frenchman would have welcomed—and helped—them with open arms. But instead, they had been "kidnapped," and their tearful "mother" was anxiously awaiting their return. The romantically inclined French loved children. They would go out of their way to reunite them with their "mother." Hélène had no doubt that whoever recognized them now would quite innocently head for the nearest police station and report seeing them.

And their "mother" in the photo? She would probably turn out to be a Gestapo agent.

Suddenly the Boches were no longer all they had to fear. Now every Frenchman was their potential enemy too.

Now they couldn't trust anyone. Under any circumstances.

Edmond turned away from the window. His face wore a grim expression. Carefully he laid the paper on his lap and turned it to face the front seat. He tried to make his voice light. "Look, Sara," he said. "Isn't this interesting?"

It took Catherine a moment to respond: she wasn't quite used to her new name yet. Then she twisted around in her seat.

Edmond pointed at the pictures.

Catherine's expression didn't change, but her face went white. Slowly she turned back around and stared blankly out the windshield.

There was a little more traffic on the road now. They passed a platoon of soldiers marching in the direction of Chartres. The sight of them only increased Hélène's dread. She couldn't help wondering what would happen if the driver recognized them. But she already knew the answer to that. He would turn them in—without giving it a second thought. In fact, at this very moment he might already be driving, not to Chartres, but to the nearest police station. Or worse, Gestapo headquarters.

The driver glanced over at Catherine again and frowned. "You know," he said slowly, "you look familiar. Somehow I can't get over the feeling that I've seen you somewhere before."

"I don't think that's possible," Catherine replied quickly.

"No, I'm sure of it. Maybe it was in Ablis. I often drive through there."

"Of course!" Catherine lied. "I remember now! I've seen you before too!"

Suddenly he hit the brakes. With a tremendous jolt, the car screeched to a halt. "Ach du lieber Himmel!" the driver exclaimed. He twisted around in his seat and snatched the newspaper off Edmond's lap. Then he peered closely at the drawings on the front page and rattled the paper. "You . . . you're the kidnapped children! The ones the whole country is being searched for!" He stared at Catherine.

Suddenly she began to laugh. It was a laugh Hélène had heard her practice over and over in her room at home. Perhaps her acting lessons would now pay off, after all.

"What is so funny?" the driver asked.

Catherine pretended to be out of breath. "Don't you see?" she gasped. "We weren't kidnapped. We ran away from home!"

He hesitated. "But . . . why?"

Catherine's face took on a spiteful look. "Because Maman is a monster!" she spit out vehemently. "We had to get away from her. She beats us till we're black and blue."

"But why are you going to Chartres?"

She took a deep breath. "A friend of mine named Yves happens to live there. It's the only place we have to go."

"But . . . the newspapers," the driver said with disbelief. "They wrote that you were kidnapped. Newspapers don't tell lies."

Catherine laughed bitterly. "Don't they?" She looked into his eyes.

"But why?"

"Simple. Maman's a very clever woman. She must have felt that people would look harder for us if they thought we were kidnapped."

He nodded slowly. "How could she arrange all this publicity?"

Catherine smiled. "For a year now she has been seeing a high-ranking German. He's head over heels in love with her, and she can make him do anything." She tapped the newspaper in his hand. "Even arrange for things like that."

He shook his head slowly. "It sounds so farfetched. Yet I believe you. But much as I hate to do it, I'll have to report you to the authorities. That's my sworn duty."

"I know," Catherine said. Suddenly she lowered her eyes. "I'm too old to let Maman run my life," she said in a whisper. "I've grown up so quickly that she never even noticed my needs. She only seeks gratification for her own."

The driver's interest quickened. "Needs?" he asked. "What needs?" Hélène caught a glimpse of his eyes. They shone brightly.

"Oh, you know." Catherine shrugged. "Being a woman and not being able to do anything about it."

He sat up straight. "Don't you have any other friends? I mean, men friends who will . . ."

"Other than Yves?" Catherine shook her head and sighed painfully. "Not really. You see, most men I've met aren't really men. They're all simply terrified of Maman. Only Yves has ever had the courage to face up to her." She paused suddenly and stared at him intently. "Would you stand up to her?"

"I . . . I think so," he stammered.

She smiled and reached out slowly, her fingers gently exploring his crotch.

"No," he said. "You must not do that. I have to drop you off at a police station. We shouldn't lose any time."

She smiled at him again and unbuttoned her coat. Then she took his hand and placed it on her breast. "I am not a child," she said. "I am a woman."

Nervously he pulled his hand back and drove on again. He wasn't paying much attention to the road now.

"Do I excite you?" Catherine asked.

His voice was a whisper. "Yes."

Once again, Catherine's hand began to explore. "You're getting hard," she said in an admiring tone. "My, but it's big."

"Bigger than your boyfriend's?"

"Much bigger."

The driver preened visibly. "Then why don't you undo my fly and get down on it?"

She smiled promisingly. "No, it's much too big to do just that. I want it . . . *inside* me."

The car swerved.

She glanced quickly out the windshield. On the right, a small forest of evergreens was coming up.

"I tell you what," she said. "See those trees up ahead? We can pull in there for a few minutes. Nobody will see the car if you drive in far enough."

He hesitated. "They could send me to the Russian front if they found out."

"Don't worry, they won't. Who is there to tell them? Certainly not those little monsters in the backseat."

Hélène was getting a bit annoyed. Catherine was pushing it a little too far. Monsters, indeed!

"Come on, it won't take long," Catherine said. "Afterward you can drop us off at the police station. But first I want you to treat me like the woman that I am."

The Boche's face broke into a smile. Suddenly he hit the

brakes and made a sharp turn onto a dirt road that branched off into the forest. Dipping evergreen branches brushed the sides of the car. It was darker here among the trees. They blotted out a lot of light.

After about ten meters, they pulled into a clearing. It was a log-splitting area; chopped yellow firewood was stacked up in neat piles. Between the graceful boughs of the pines they could catch glimpses of the road, but for anyone to see them, they would have to draw quite a bit of attention to themselves.

The Boche switched off the engine. "Do you want to send the kids out for a walk?" he asked.

Catherine shook her head. "It's too cold. Besides, this is nothing new for them. They've seen it before."

"Whatever you say." He lifted his hips off the seat and undid his fly.

Hélène felt a hand on her arm. She glanced over at Edmond. His eyes were expressionless. He was motioning for her to slip the string off the bundle on the seat beside her.

"It's even bigger when it's out!" Catherine's voice sounded impressed. "So big and red and swollen."

Hélène had the string off now. Impatiently Edmond snatched it away from her. Grimly he wrapped some of it around his hands, then stretched the remainder of it taut. At first Hélène thought he was going to play cat's cradle. Then suddenly she realized what he was going to do, why Catherine had lured the Boche into this secluded clearing. She held her breath and waited.

"First take it in your mouth," the driver was saying. "It will get even harder that way."

With a cry, Edmond pounced forward. He brought the string down in front of the driver's neck and pulled back hard, choking him.

The Boche's face began to get beet red. He made horrible gasping noises and his hands flew up to his throat, fingers clawing at the string. Catherine let out a shriek. She shrank into the corner of her seat. Then she leaned down and groped under the seat for something to club him with. She came up with a heavy flashlight. Savagely she began pounding him over the head with it. But the Boche could take a lot of punishment. With a sudden surge of strength he managed to tear the string loose. He shook his head, trying to clear it. In a rage, he lunged at Catherine.

Edmond immediately jumped out of the car. Hélène followed right behind him. There were pieces of firewood lying around on the ground. Without hesitation, he picked up the nearest piece and yanked the driver's door open.

The Boche had his big hands clamped around Catherine's throat. Her mouth hung open, desperately gasping for air, her body slumped in the seat. She was suffocating.

With the log, Edmond began to pound the Boche on the back of the neck. The Boche turned around with a snarl, but his hands wouldn't leave Catherine's throat.

Hélène looked around in desperation. Then she saw a metal tool lying next to a stack of chopped wood. It was a spike, the kind used for splitting logs. The point looked very sharp. She tried to pick it up, but it was too heavy. She tugged at Edmond's arm. "Use this!" she screamed. "Use this!"

Edmond threw down his piece of wood. He grabbed hold of the spike with both hands. Once again he flung himself on the Boche. This time, he was armed with a weapon that could destroy. Swiftly he plunged the spike into the Boche's belly.

The Boche screamed. His hands left Catherine's throat and his eyes moved down to his belly. In shock he stared at the protruding spike. Then came the blood.

But he wasn't dead yet.

At that moment Hélène heard the steady footfalls of marching feet coming from the road. Her heart began thumping even faster. That sound could mean only one thing. The platoon they had passed earlier would soon be upon them.

The Boche must have heard it too, for suddenly he rallied his strength and tried to cry out. Quickly Catherine pressed her hands over his mouth to muffle the cries. She winced as he sank his teeth into her fingers, but she held on. Then, struggling fiercely like some wounded animal, he tried to crawl out of the car. "His legs!" Edmond hissed at Catherine. "Grab his legs!"

She let go of his mouth and grabbed his pants, trying to pull him back into the car.

Hélène glanced toward the road. Between the pine boughs she could see the platoon. It was just passing by. And when she looked back at the car, she could see something else. The Boche was trying to reach for the center of the steering wheel. *For the horn!*

Catherine let go of his legs and tugged at his arm. Each time she pulled it away from the horn, he managed to reach for it again. And again. And again.

Grimly Edmond grabbed the driver by the hair. He pulled his head halfway out of the car and began slamming the door shut on it. The Boche grimaced and groaned, but he didn't cry out. Hélène could hear one sickening thud after another as Edmond pounded the door against his skull. The fifth time, there was a horrible crunching sound and the blood began pouring from the head. And slowly the Boche gave up the fight. His body went limp.

Finally he was dead.

The platoon was gone now, the sounds of marching receding into the distance. The road was clear.

Fatigued, Edmond threw himself to the ground. He sat there, a weary expression on his face. Right beside him, the Boche's head hung out of the car. From the backseat, Hélène could hear Marie's whimpers starting up. Incredibly, she had slept through the entire incident.

Catherine stumbled out of the car. She had to hold onto the car to steady herself as she came around it. She took one look at the driver, then bent over and vomited.

"The newspapers," Edmond said in a whisper. He was still breathing heavily. "We'll have to . . . carry them . . . a distance away. Burn them. Or bury them. They mustn't get to Chartres."

Catherine nodded wearily and dropped to the ground beside him.

They rested for fifteen minutes. By then Edmond and Catherine had some of their strength back. Hélène helped them lug the newspapers to a spot about fifty meters from the car and burn them. To hide the evidence of a fire, they covered up the charred remains with pieces of wood and pine boughs.

7

It was pitch dark by the time they found shelter for the night. They had discovered it by accident. They had walked more than three kilometers along the road to Chartres when they saw a car's yellow headlights bobbing in the distance.

"Quick!" Edmond said. "Into the ditch!"

They scrambled off the road, and there it was, right in front of them. A large round culvert that connected the ditches that ran along both sides of the road. Here, directly under the road, they would be well hidden. The bottom was filled with water, but it had long since turned to ice. Although cold, they would at least be safe.

After the car passed by overhead, they set out to make the shelter as comfortable as possible. Edmond had them pull out shrubs from the roadside. He figured that they could stuff them at each end of the pipe, thereby blocking out some of the wind. But the shrubs were stubborn: their roots were frozen into the ground. All they managed to collect were some bare branches. These they spread out over the ice. Then they lay down on top of them.

They slept curled up together, cold and hungry, using their body heat to try to warm each other, to try to draw some comfort from their closeness. But Hélène didn't sleep well; Marie cried a lot that night. And when dawn finally came, Hélène awoke shivering, her teeth chattering noisily. Even before she opened her eyes, she sensed that Edmond was gone.

An hour later, he returned. He had been to loot a house in a nearby village, and he brought back some milk, small slabs of cheese, two thin sausages, and a little sugar. The sugar was still in its blue-and-white ceramic bowl. He had also come across a bottle of brandy. He pulled out the cork, and taking turns, they each took a swig. It tasted bitter and burned all the way down their throats, but then they would feel a comforting warm glow spreading through them. They even wet Marie's lips with a little taste of it. To their surprise, it quieted her down.

"The brandy seems to silence her," Edmond said. "We'll give her some whenever we need to keep her quiet."

After they finished eating, they moved on. They headed southwest across yet more barren fields and then through forests which lacked underbrush. Over the centuries, the bushes and brambles had been cleared away, and Hélène imagined that in summer the earth would be carpeted with moss. Right now it was covered with yellowed pine needles and fallen cones. Overhead, the sky was thick and gray, looking like snow.

In the afternoon, it began to sleet.

It caught them unawares, while they were still in the middle of the forest. Numb with cold and soaked to the skin, they finally found a shelter. It was a deserted woodcutter's cabin, and it even had a fireplace. Stacks of chopped wood were piled up along the outside walls, and they carried some into the cabin. Edmond built a fire. Wet wood doesn't burn well, and the cabin got very smoky. It made their eyes water, but they were grateful for the warmth.

Realizing that they might be snowed in for days, they ate sparingly in order to stretch their rations. And when there was no more milk, they fed Marie a mixture of sugar and warm water.

It looked like the storm would continue for some time, so they took the opportunity to wash Marie's diaper. It must have suited her well, for that night she slept soundly.

But getting soaked hadn't done them any good. Catherine and Hélène came down with colds. They both sneezed and coughed a lot, and Catherine got laryngitis on top of it. That night, the sleet turned to snow.

Two days later, the weather cleared. They stepped outside the cabin and gazed around in wonder. The temperature had plunged even lower, but the air was crystalline and pure. The sky overhead was of the palest blue, and everything was covered with a blanket of thick, glistening snow. Even the branches of the trees looked as if someone had piled cotton on top of them. To a young girl it was a fairyland.

"Isn't it beautiful?" Hélène said to Edmond.

He nodded. "Yes, it is very beautiful," he agreed. But beauty, apparently, didn't weigh heavily on his mind right now. There were more important things to think of. He turned to Catherine. "Is there any sugar left?"

"A little." Her voice was a hoarse croak.

"Mix whatever there is in some warm water and give it to Marie," he said. "Then, when she's done eating, prepare her for the cold. We shall be moving on shortly."

Catherine nodded obediently and went inside the cabin to wake Marie. A moment later, she rushed back outside.

Edmond stared at her. "Is something wrong?"

"It's Marie," Catherine said huskily. "She's burning up. I think she has a fever!"

Edmond pushed her aside and entered the cabin. Swiftly he crossed over to where Marie was lying and touched her little forehead with his hand. "I'm afraid you're right," he told Catherine grimly. "She really is sick."

Hélène did as he had done and laid her hand on Marie's forehead. It was wet with perspiration, but ice cold. "What are we going to do?" she asked.

Edmond stared down at Marie. "What we must do," he murmured. "Find a doctor for her."

Catherine looked at him. "No doctor will come here."

"Then we must go to him," he replied simply.

Catherine took him firmly by the arms and shook him. "But it's too cold!" she said sharply. "It's dangerous to take her outside in her condition!"

Edmond began to strip off his coat. Hélène watched as he gently wrapped Marie in it. "This will keep her warm," he said.

"But what about you?" Catherine asked. "What are you going to wear?"

He shrugged. "I'll be all right. I don't have the fever."

Catherine stared at him. "Have some sense! You'll freeze to death!"

"Maybe," he said. "But that can't be helped." Then he raised his voice. "Enough of this. Hurry up and get ready. We'll leave right away."

Catherine threw up her hands in exasperation. Then she stomped around the cabin gathering up their few belongings.

As Hélène buttoned her coat she looked at Edmond. "Don't doctors cost money?" she asked.

He nodded.

"Does that mean you'll steal some?" she whispered hopefully.

"No, I will not," he said sharply.

"Oh." She frowned. "Then how are we going to pay the doctor?"

He patted his breast pocket. "We'll have to use Maman's ring. Although I hate to part with it, I think Maman would understand."

Hélène nodded. He was right. Under these circumstances, Maman would.

Each time they neared a village, Edmond had them wait out of sight while he took Marie and went off to find a doctor. Doctors, it turned out, were a scarcity in the country. It was only after a few hours that he finally found one. He left Marie there and hurried back to where Catherine and Hélène waited. Once again, he was wearing his coat. "Come along," he said. "The doctor's house is nice and warm. A little heat won't hurt us."

Catherine looked at him with apprehension. "Do you think the doctor can be trusted?" she asked.

"I hope so," he answered. "Anyway, we have little choice. I left Marie with him."

"Is the doctor in the village?" Hélène asked, pointing at the sleepy clusters of houses in the distance. "Or is he in one of the farmhouses?"

"In the village. Come along." Their footsteps crunched on the snow as he led the way up the peaceful main street. At the last house, he opened a gate into a small front yard, and then they waited on the steps while he knocked on the door. It was opened by a heavyset middle-aged woman. She recognized Edmond. "Come in, come in," she said, herding them inside with her hands. "The doctor is upstairs with the little one."

They stepped into a dark, narrow hallway. After the woman closed the door behind them, she gestured at their feet. "Take off your shoes, they're probably soaked through. Leave them by the door. Then come along with me."

They followed her down the hallway. She opened a door with opaque glass panels set into the frame. This was the kitchen. There was a huge enamel-and-tile stove in the corner, and a lot of heat radiated from it. Quickly the children drew around it, holding out their hands over the glowing top, trying to warm them.

"Sit down," the woman said, gesturing at the table. "You look like you could do with some food. I was just preparing a hot lunch."

"But Marie—" Edmond began.

"The little one is fine," a man's voice said from the doorway.

The children turned and looked across the room at him. He was elderly and white-haired, with deep wrinkles etched into his face. He wore silver-rimmed glasses and a thick wool sweater. "She's upstairs, asleep."

"Is it anything serious?" Edmond asked anxiously.

The doctor looked at Edmond. "She is but a baby," he replied. "At her age anything is potentially serious. The little ones have very little resistance." Then he smiled reassuringly. "But I think she will be all right. What she needs right now is to stay out of the cold. Let's hope the fever breaks soon. If it does, I don't think it should take more than a few days until she can travel again."

"A few days!" Edmond exclaimed. "We don't have that long, doctor. We . . . we've got to be on our way soon."

The doctor frowned. "You're not from anywhere around here, otherwise I'd have recognized you. That means you must still have far to go. Am I right?"

Silently Edmond nodded.

The doctor sat at the kitchen table and gestured for them to sit down. "You can trust me," he said with compassion. "Would you like to tell me about it?"

Edmond looked at him in silence. After a moment's hesitation he nodded. Seated around the table, and over steaming cups of cocoa, he told the doctor everything that had happened, beginning with Maman and Michelle and the Boche banging the canary-yellow door down. . . .

Four days later, Marie was fit to travel. The children were well rested; the stay had done them good. Hélène's cold was gone, and so was Catherine's laryngitis.

When it was time to say good-bye, tears filled Hélène's eyes. The doctor and his housekeeper had both gone out of their way to be kind, and she hated to leave. They had made them feel welcome and at home, when they had no right to expect it, and now it suddenly felt as if they were saying good-bye to close friends.

Hélène buried her face in the woman's big soft bosom and gave her an enormous hug. "I'll miss you," she whispered.

"And I will miss you, too," the woman said quietly, looking down at her. "Take care of yourself, and may God bless you."

Edmond took the doctor aside. He reached into his pocket for Maman's ring. "We owe you so much," he said. "This is all we can pay you with."

The doctor shook his head. "I can accept nothing."

"But you saved Marie's life," Edmond insisted.

"It was my duty—as a Frenchman and as a doctor."

Edmond nodded. "Thank you," he said softly. "And for the new clothes, too."

The doctor shook his head. "No, it is we who must thank you. Although they are a small minority, there are those who collaborate with the invaders of our country and blacken our pride. Yet you—mere children—have the courage to fight the Boche. You are an inspiration. We are grateful to you."

Carefully the housekeeper lifted Marie, bundled up in a thick new blanket, into Catherine's arms. "Take care of the little angel," she told Catherine.

Catherine smiled. "I will."

The woman wiped her moist eyes and sniffed. "Sometime, when all this is over, let us know how your journey went. Even if it is years from now." She hugged Edmond tightly and then fumbled with the silver chain that hung around her neck. Attached to it was a little religious medallion. Solemnly she fastened it around his neck. "You have our blessings. We shall pray for you." Then she reached up to the table and handed Edmond a heavy basket which she had filled with the choicest foods from the larder. "For your journey," she said simply.

Edmond stood on tiptoe and kissed her cheek. "Thank you," he whispered.

Suddenly they heard the ringing of bells coming from outside. "What's that?" Hélène asked, rushing to the window. Her eyes widened. A big sleigh pulled by two chestnut drays had slid to a halt on the snowy street in front of the house.

"That will be Claude Sorel," the doctor said. "He's a poor farmer who owes me a favor. Last year I saved his wife's life. He couldn't afford to pay me, so now I am letting him work off his debt. I arranged it so that you will spend the night on his farm. Tomorrow he will drive you in his sleigh to

Châteaudun. Once there, head south for sixty kilometers. Then you will be at the Loire. Follow the river westward until you reach the sea. There you will find Saint-Nazaire."

8

When they reached his farm, Claude Sorel pulled up in front of the house and turned around in the driver's seat. "We're here," he said, his deep-set, penetrating eyes looking down at the children.

Without another word, he hopped to the ground and waited as they climbed out of the sleigh. They stretched their legs. They had been riding for well over an hour, and they were numb with cold despite the thick old lap blanket that they had pulled up around them. Sorel didn't bother unhitching the horses. He tethered them to a post, where they stood twitching their tails and snorting noisily. Their chestnut bodies heaved from exertion and gleamed with sweat. He had been driving them mercilessly, flaying them when they weren't flying fast enough across the softly powdered fields.

"Come along," he said tersely.

They started toward the front door, and Hélène looked up at the house. It was large and cheerless, a drab rambling blight on the fairytale landscape. Like most of the buildings in the province, it was ancient. Roughly built and picturesque in its very neglect, at each end rickety wooden lean-tos—obvious afterthoughts—sagged against the stone walls for support. The small square windows punctuating the thick walls were few and far between, lending the building the look of a forbidding fortress. Each of the windows had weathered wooden shutters; some of them were pulled closed, a few were loose and banged in the wind. The solitary chimney gave the only evidence of habitation. Out of it trailed a meager wisp of smoke.

On the doorstep they stopped to stomp the snow off their

shoes. Then Sorel grunted, pushed open the door, and they entered.

Inside the dim hall, the ceilings were so low that Sorel had to duck through the doorways. The walls were whitewashed with chalky paint that rubbed off on your fingers if you touched them.

They went through another door and found themselves in the kitchen. Like the hall, it was dimly lit. The floor of roughly hewn boards was bleached almost white from decades of scrubbing. Some antlers and stuffed deer heads hung on the walls. The deer were half in shadow, but their eyes caught the light coming in from the window and glinted malevolently. Hélène couldn't understand why people wanted to decorate their walls with such frightful objects.

"Hey, woman!" Sorel called out in a loud, abrasive voice.

They heard a door opening and closing. Then a woman shuffled listlessly in from a room in the back. "Yes?" she mumbled. Her speech sounded slurred; then Hélène saw why. Her lip was swollen.

Hélène stared at her. She was much shorter than her husband, her face red and tired-looking. Her thick, frizzy hair was plaited. Somberly dressed, she wore a heavy black skirt, a thick black sweater with sleeves that were too long, and a faded blue apron. There was something about the way her shoulders sagged that reminded Hélène of an animal whose spirit had been broken.

"Can't you see that we've got visitors, you lazy woman?" Sorel shouted. "Don't just stand there stupidly! Hurry up and put some food on. Then fix them a place to sleep!"

"Yes, Claude," she said dutifully. Hélène noticed that the woman's face had reddened. Hers would have too, if she were treated like that in front of strangers.

The woman glanced at them and gestured that they sit around the rough-hewn table. It was only then that Hélène realized how young the woman really was. Young and worn out.

"Make sure you put 'em to bed early," Sorel grumbled. "Tomorrow I'm supposed to drive them to Châteaudun. We got to get an early start."

She looked at him over her shoulder. "Yes, Claude."

He grunted again, lifted an earthenware jug down off a shelf, uncorked it, and took a swig. Hélène could smell the cider as it spilled down his chin. He wiped it off with his

93

sleeve, brought the jug over to the table, and set it down with a bang. He scraped a chair back and sat down, putting his boots up on the spotless table.

Hélène could see the disapproval flickering in the woman's eyes, but she kept prudently silent.

Sorel took another swig of cider and pushed his chair back heavily. He got to his feet. "I'll be back later," he growled. "Make sure they're bedded down early."

"Where are you going?" the woman asked. Hélène could recognize the fear in her voice.

"To the village."

She turned to him, nervously twisting a corner of the apron between her fingers. "Claude, please, no," she begged. "You just went there last night and came back . . ." He scowled at her and she fell silent.

"Shut up, woman!" He waved his warm threateningly. "You want a shiner to match your lip?"

"No, Claude," she said wearily. With a sigh of resignation she turned back to the stove as he stomped out.

"I don't like these people," Catherine said.

Edmond nodded in reply. He was sitting on one of the hard lumpy mattresses. Occasionally he would bounce Marie up and down on the creaky springs. Each time he did, she squealed with delight while thick clouds of dust rose up in the air around them. They all wore their coats. The upstairs of the house was unheated. Once in bed, under the ancient feather quilts and moth-eaten blankets, they'd be nice and warm, but not until then. The room was in shadows, gloomily lit by a solitary oil lamp.

Hélène got to her feet and went over to the tiny window. It was barely big enough for a pigeon to squeeze through, but it was at one of the gable ends of the house, and when she stood on tiptoe she could look down to the farmyard, two stories below. The moon was out. White and almost full, it bathed the landscape and cast long night shadows across the snow.

Edmond settled back against the splintery headboard. "It's the farmer," he said. "His wife isn't too bad, but she's terrified of him. Did you see her lip? He must have punched her real good."

"I can't understand why the doctor has anything to do with

them," Catherine said with a toss of her head. "Doesn't he know that the farmer is . . . well, not quite right?"

"Maybe he feels sorry for the wife. Or maybe the husband doesn't show his real feelings in front of him," Edmond said thoughtfully. "Don't you remember how he smiled when we got into the sleigh, and how friendly he was to the doctor?"

Catherine nodded slowly. "Yes, it must have been an act."

Hélène balanced herself on her toes and looked out the window again. All she could see were dim yellow fields of snow, and then the darkness that stretched beyond. Somewhere out in that darkness was the village where the kind doctor lived . . . and his housekeeper with the warm bosom. And even farther out, somewhere way to the south, was the Loire. The river of kings, they called it, lined with massive castles and majestic white châteaus. All they'd have to do was to follow the meandering riverbed, and eventually they'd end up in Saint-Nazaire, where they would find Tante Janine, an aunt they'd never even met, and wait with her for the Boche to be driven out of France, for Maman and Papa to come and get them and take them back to Paris.

Suddenly she heard the faint jingling of bells. She peered out in all directions. Far in the distance she could see the sleigh. She watched as it came closer and pulled up out front. This time, instead of jumping, the farmer climbed unsteadily down from the seat. He didn't bother tying the horses to the post. He stumbled, straightened, and then reeled into the house. From the floor below came a sudden deafening crash.

Catherine jumped. "What was *that?*"

"It's the farmer," Hélène said, turning away from the window. "He just came back. He must have fallen over something." She giggled. "I think he's drunk."

"I sure hope he's sober enough by morning to drive us to Châteaudun," Edmond mumbled. He cocked his head to one side and listened. The farmer was coming heavily up the rickety stairs. When he reached the landing, he lumbered toward the door. There was a moment's silence before he stumbled on down the narrow corridor, his footsteps fading. Finally a door slammed.

Then they heard his voice through the walls. "Woman, are you in bed already!"

A conversation followed, but it sounded one-sided; only his words were spoken loud enough for the children to catch.

There were banging noises, and the sounds of drawers being opened and slammed shut.

Finally they heard the wife's voice adding to the commotion. "Claude, don't!" she shrieked in rising hysteria. The door down the hall was flung open, and once again his footsteps echoed out in the hall. Hélène could hear the woman as she ran after him. "No, Claude, don't! Please, I beg of you!"

"Get your hands off me!" he snarled. There were the sounds of a scuffle. Hélène winced as a sharp slap rang out. The woman moaned. She must have tumbled to the floor, because it suddenly shook. "You fool woman!" he spit out. "What do you want? For us to be poor the rest of our lives?"

"No, Claude," she sobbed. "That's *not* what I want. But I don't want blood money, either!"

"Shut your mouth, bitch!"

There was a short silence, after which he approached the children's door. Hélène held her breath. For a moment she was afraid that he was going to come in and beat on her, too. But instead he inserted a key in the lock.

She stared at the door in horror. Somehow, this was even more terrifying than if he'd tried to attack. She flinched when she heard the key turn. Then she saw the door handle lowering as it was tested from the outside.

A sudden dread knowledge came over her. The worst possible thing had happened.

They had become prisoners.

"There—they're locked in," the farmer said with gruff satisfaction. "They can't go anywhere now."

Hélène stared first at Catherine, then at Edmond. "What are we going to do?" she whispered.

"Sssssh!" hissed Edmond. "Be quiet!"

The farmer grunted. "Get up, woman! Go and get dressed. I want you to be presentable when the Germans arrive. They'll soon be here." He paused. When he spoke again, it was with awe in his voice. "Just imagine—a million and a half francs! Me, Claude Sorel, a millionaire!"

Hélène shook her head in despair. So the reward for our capture had gone up once again, she thought. At Madame Chang's, it had been half a million francs; in the newspapers six days ago, a million. Now it had been increased by yet another half-million. If, somehow, they did manage to get out of here—and that seemed a remote possibility at best—the reward would soon be so astronomical that anyone, perhaps even Tante Janine, could be induced to turn them over to the Boche.

"But you don't even know it's them," the woman wailed.

Claude Sorel laughed. "There was a newspaper in the tavern. Sure as hay, the pictures were theirs. Especially the older girl's. The paper claimed that they'd been kidnapped. Isn't that funny?" He laughed again. "If it hadn't been for the doctor telling us otherwise, I'd have believed that story myself. Anyway, it's a good thing I went out drinking. If I'd listened to you and stayed home, I would never have found out about the reward. That's how fortunes are made, by being in the right place at the right time. Good thing the gendarme was there, too. He let me use his telephone."

The woman's voice was barely a whisper. "Who did you call?"

"Since I knew who was really searching for them, the Gestapo, of course. Going through the Feldgendarme might take days. I wanted to make sure there'd be no delay with the reward. You know how long paperwork takes to process."

The woman was sobbing uncontrollably now. Hélène could imagine her red face getting even redder. "How could you?" she screamed. "We're *Frenchmen*! And the doctor is a friend! He *trusted* us! And we're in his debt!"

"You mean *you're* in his debt. Anyway, *he's* not about to give us one and a half million francs, is he?" Sorel rationalized. "Well, it's none of his business, then. So stop worrying and wipe your eyes. I can't stand it when they're all bloodshot and puffy. You're ugly enough as it is!"

It was with an empty feeling that Hélène heard their footsteps receding. She had hoped the woman would stay behind. Perhaps she could have been cajoled into stealing the key from her husband and unlocking the door.

Edmond put Marie down and rose from the bed. "We have to get out of here," he said softly.

Catherine nodded. "But how? We're locked in." She looked over at Hélène. "Can that window be opened?"

Hélène nodded. "Yes, but it's too small. Even Marie couldn't squeeze through it."

Edmond picked up the oil lamp and walked around the room, shining the light into the dark corners, feeling along the walls with his fingers, staring in thoughtful silence around the ceiling, down at the floor. But there were no other exits except for the door—no trapdoors to the roof, no forgotten blocked-up doorways behind the moldy wallpaper. Even a mouse would have had a difficult time of it escaping.

"Well?" Catherine asked. Her large brown eyes were watching Edmond intently.

He shook his head glumly. "I'm afraid we'll have to choose between the frying pan and the fire. There's only one way we can get out of here."

Catherine raised her eyebrows questioningly.

He glanced at her and sighed. "We'll have to set the place on fire."

She stared at him. Then she slowly nodded. "And hope they'll come and unlock the door in time?"

He didn't answer. "We'd better get started," he said. He snapped his fingers. "Help me drag the mattresses over toward the window."

He set the lamp down on a crate and they began to tug at the mattresses. Stuffed with horsehair, they were stiff and heavy. When they were all piled against the wall, Edmond made sure they wouldn't fall as soon as they started to burn. Then he wiped his dusty hands on his trouser legs. Catherine picked up Marie.

"Cover her face with her blanket," he said. "That way, she won't inhale too much smoke."

Catherine nodded. She kissed Marie's forehead and gently tucked the soft cover up around her tiny pink head. "There, baby," she whispered soothingly. "Don't be frightened."

"Now, back up against the door and stay put," Edmond ordered.

He grabbed a blanket and draped it over Hélène's and Catherine's shoulders.

"Pull this over your heads and hold it there. It should shield us from some of the heat." He glanced questioningly first at Catherine, then at Hélène. Nothing needed to be said. They understood.

Edmond held the lamp high. Hélène watched as he gracefully tossed it toward the window. The glass globe shattered against the wall and fell to the pile of mattresses, soaking them with oil. Instantly a pillar of furiously crackling flames shot up to the ceiling.

From that moment on, instinct took over. They began stomping on the floor and banging on the door with their fists.

"Fire!" Hélène screamed abruptly. "Fire!" There was genuine terror in her voice.

Catherine's eyes were wild with fear. "Help!" she shouted. "Fire!" From the pitch of her voice, Hélène knew that Catherine's terror was no less real than her own.

She glanced backward. The mattresses were all ablaze now. As she watched, the quilts caught, too. Within seconds the whole far side of the room was a roaring sheet of flame. The stench of burning hair and feathers was nauseating. Then suddenly she couldn't breathe. It was as if the fire were sucking all the air out of the room. Her eyes burned and teared. She began to hammer even more furiously on the door, and screamed again.

"Fire!"

"Help! Help!"

Now the smoke was like a thick black screen. It burned raw in their lungs and they couldn't see a thing. Then they heard quick footsteps outside in the hallway. The farmer was cursing.

The woman let out a shriek. "Smoke!" she screamed. "Pouring out from under the door! Claude, *do* something! The house will burn down!"

Once again they could hear the key turning in the lock. Then the cylinder clicked. There was a rush of sudden fresh air as the door opened.

Choking and coughing, the children stumbled blindly out into the hall. Claude Sorel pushed past them and ran into the inferno. He tore off his jacket and began beating the flames with it. It was futile. On all sides, the wallpaper was a solid wall of flame, and already tongues of fire licked up from the dry wooden floor. The noise was awesome: the fire roared.

The woman was in hysterics. She held her arm up in front of her face to shield it from the heat. "Claude!" she kept screaming. "Put it out!"

And then the children rushed down the rickety stairs, almost falling over themselves in the process. There was a dull crash from upstairs as something gave way and fell. The woman shrieked and drew back. Hélène looked up and saw that a massive blazing beam had burned itself loose from the ceiling. One end of it was poking crazily out into the hall; the other still slanted up to the ceiling inside the room. Now it was only a matter of moments before the hall would be engulfed in fire too. And the stairs.

Less than a minute later, they were outside in the clear, icy night. Never had fresh air felt so good. Hélène took deep lungfuls of it and wiped the perspiration off her forehead; her whole body was soaked with sweat.

For a moment they stood there in the snow, staring up at the house. The tiny window at the end of the gable flashed brightly, and the snow on the roof had begun to melt from the heat. Water was pouring down off the eaves. Then suddenly a huge tongue of fire leaped up through the snowy roof into the black sky, licking at the white moon and sending showers of sparks high into the night. Everything around was now yellow, flickering as though it were alive. The house. The barn. The snow. Hélène felt a tug at her sleeve.

"Come on!" Edmond hissed. He was starting off across the snow.

"Wait," Hélène cried, pointing. "The sleigh! Can't we take that?"

He nodded. "You two hop in," he said. "I'll drive."

They hurried toward it, but just then part of the roof caved in with a crash. Terrified, the horses reared and neighed. They broke into a gallop and shot off into the night, pulling the empty sleigh. Edmond ran after them, but in vain. They were halfway across the fields already. He made a gesture of defeat and sprinted back, panting and out of breath.

Once again the children headed across the fields on foot. Only this time they left clear tracks in the snow. Like Hansel and Gretel and their trail of bread crumbs, Hélène thought. Only with us, the birds won't come to peck at them and erase our path.

Edmond seemed to read her thoughts. "I wish it would start snowing again," he murmured. "At least then our footprints would be covered." He glanced hopefully up at the sky, but it was obvious that there would be no snow coming.

After they had gone about a hundred meters, Hélène turned around and glanced back at the house. The fire completely engulfed the downstairs now, and two little figures—one shorter than the other—were silhouetted against the blaze, rushing around frantically. For a moment Hélène thought about the woman's immaculately scrubbed floors, brushed almost white by her and generations of women before her. Now blazing like kindling. But this was no time for pity. Already she could see the bobbing headlights of vehicles in the distance. We have less time than we thought, Hélène said to herself.

The Boches were fast approaching.

This time, they had dogs.

They could hear them baying in the distance. Hélène's lungs were burning and raw from all the running, but she didn't dare to stop and rest for an instant. Whenever she looked back, she could see tiny flashlight beams cutting through the night.

In their hurry, they had no time to waste choosing the best, safest, or easiest routes. They crashed through scratchy winter foliage, stumbled over frozen fields, and plunged past barren orchards. The dark and the snow were enemies, too, hiding obstacles in their path—rocks, stumps, tree trunks, and fallen branches. Often they fell, but the snow, the culprit that hid the dangerous traps, ironically lent them a helping hand in the process, providing a soft cushion each time they fell.

Every minute, it seemed, the baying of the dogs drew closer. Whenever they glanced back, the waving flashlights had definitely gained on them.

When they reached a narrow, frozen creek with two long boards stretching across it as a kind of bridge, Edmond had them stop for a brief moment so that they could catch their breath. Gratefully they took deep lungfuls of air. Marie was crying, but there no longer was any brandy to silence her with. It was in the burning house, along with the basket of food the doctor's housekeeper had given them. From where they stood, they could still see the fire. The whole sky to the north was tinted with a rosy glow. All of a sudden the glow flared.

"It must be the barn," Edmond said. "It must have gone up too. The sparks probably carried over from the house."

Catherine spit in the snow. "Serves them right," she said.

Edmond stared at the plank bridge in the moonlight. "Listen," he said excitedly. "I've got an idea."

Hélène turned to him. "What is it?"

"We'll split up."

Catherine stared at him. "Split up? But—"

"No buts," he said roughly. "We must, especially since they have dogs. Besides, two of us won't be as easily recognized as four. Four children are what they're looking for."

Hélène was trembling. "I don't think I like this," she whined. "We should all stick together."

"We can't," Edmond said with finality. He took a deep breath. "Catherine, you take Marie. You cross the creek. Once you're over, Hélène and I will remove the planks. That way, the dogs won't follow you. We'll head south along the creek, throwing them off your track."

Hélène had a sudden sinking feeling. "No!" she cried. "I want us to stay together."

"Shut up!" Edmond hissed. He looked at Catherine.

Her face was pale in the moonlight. She nodded solemnly. "I'll take good care of Marie," she promised quietly.

"Take care of yourself, too," Edmond said. "We'll meet at Tante Janine's."

A veil dropped over Catherine's eyes; even in the moonlight Hélène could see it. "Yes, we'll meet at Tante Janine's," Catherine said softly.

Quickly they kissed each other good-bye. For a moment Catherine clung to Edmond, her eyes staring into his. "I'm sorry," she said.

"What for?" he asked.

"For being such a fool. About the stealing. I had no right."

He dug his foot in a pile of snow and looked down. "Forget it," he said. "Once we meet in Saint-Nazaire, we'll be able to exchange notes on who stole what."

She smiled. "Yes. We'll do that. Good-bye, Edmond. Good-bye, Hélène."

Suddenly Edmond reached into his pocket and pressed something into Catherine's hand. "Maman's ring," he whispered. "You may need it more than us."

She nodded. Then, tears in her eyes, and gently holding Marie against her breast, she carefully crossed over the plank bridge. Once she got to the other side, she stood on a mound of snow watching as Edmond and Hélène knocked the planks loose. Edmond lifted them up and tossed them to the other side. With a fallen branch he brushed snow over where the bridge had been.

It was no longer possible to tell that it had ever been there. Edmond's tracks, and Hélène's, would head along the creek, throwing off the pursuers. For the time being, Catherine and Marie would be safe. It was a small comfort, but at least they had a good head start.

Edmond straightened up and tossed away the branch. For

a moment he and Hélène stared over at Catherine. She looked like a forlorn Madonna holding her child. Hélène lifted her arm in a wave. Gravely, Catherine waved back. Then Hélène and Edmond headed south, quickly running along the creek.

Hélène sniffed and wiped her nose with her hand. Her vision was blurred by tears. She wondered if she would ever see Catherine and Marie again.

9

It was half an hour later when they realized they'd lost their pursuers. Hélène could no longer hear the baying of the dogs. When she looked back, the night was black and peculiarly silent. The flashlight beams had vanished. It was clear the Boche weren't following. She tapped Edmond's arm excitedly. "They're gone!" she exclaimed. "Look behind us!"

He stopped and turned around. "So they are," he said in surprise.

She took what she thought was a well-deserved rest and flung herself down on a felled log. She looked up at Edmond. "Perhaps they gave up?" she said hopefully.

He turned to her and shook his head. "Fat chance," he said soberly. "They don't give up *that* easily. Especially not after all the trouble they went through to try to capture us in the first place."

A terrible thought suddenly took shape in Hélène's mind. Unconsciously she got to her feet. She stared at him. "You don't think they . . ." Her words trailed off. She couldn't get herself to finish the sentence; it was too horrible to put into words.

Edmond's face clouded over. "You're wondering whether they've managed to follow Catherine instead of us," he said heavily.

She nodded.

"I can't answer that. All I know is that she should be safe. I thought we covered her tracks rather well."

"Maybe they got suspicious," Hélène said. "They followed three sets of tracks from the farmhouse, and one set petered out at the stream. Don't you think they might have decided to have a look around?"

"I suppose it's possible," Edmond said softly. He kicked the log with the tip of his shoe. "Maybe they went back to get horses. If they decided to do that, they may have knocked off for the night. After all, they can continue the search in the morning and still catch up with us. Our tracks won't disappear overnight." He smiled grimly. "They'll be here for days to come."

She nodded. "So what do we do?"

"We trick them. We won't leave any tracks for them, nor any scent for their dogs."

She looked at him suspiciously. "How?"

"We keep following this creek and hope that it joins up with an even bigger stream. One that's faster moving, and not covered with ice. Then we'll wade through the water. They should be completely thrown off."

"Brrr . . ." The mere thought of it made her shiver. "But won't the water be too cold?"

"It will be freezing," he replied. "But it's our best bet." He punched her playfully. "We better get moving."

They trudged on. They came across several creeks, but it was only after about three hours that they found an angrily moving stream that was free of ice except at the very edges. Fearfully Hélène stared at this dark caldron boiling angrily over a bed of rocks and boulders.

Ever resourceful, Edmond grabbed a stick and tested the depth of the water. It proved to be pretty shallow. Then he threw the stick in. Quickly it was swept downstream.

He nodded to himself and took Hélène by the hand. "The current's strong," he cautioned. "I want you to hold on to me. If you don't, it might sweep you downstream."

She nodded. "I'll be careful," she said.

Slowly he stepped into the water, and she followed gingerly. She winced, and it took everything for her not to cry out. The water came up to her knees. It was so cold that she thought a knife had suddenly cut off her legs. A second later, she could no longer feel them. She supposed that in a way it was a kind of blessing.

Edmond sensed her distress. "Bear with it," he said. "We're not going to stay in here any longer than we have to."

But it seemed to her that they waded through that tricky current forever. Several times she lost her footing or a loose rock in the riverbed gave way under her feet. Then only her hold on Edmond saved her from being swept away.

When they reached a low wooden bridge, Edmond drew to a halt underneath it. "Hold on to something," he warned. "I'm going to let go of you. I want to have a look."

Hélène wrapped her arms securely around an ice-encrusted piling. She watched as he knocked some icicles loose from the edge of the bridge, grabbed hold of it, and pulled himself up. After he had a quick look, he lowered himself back down into the water. She looked at him questioningly.

He smiled. "It's a little road," he said. "It's been traveled on quite a bit lately. Which is good, because our tracks won't be the only ones. Come on."

They got out of the water, and Edmond climbed up the steep, snow-covered embankment. She followed him, her numb fingers clutching at dead clumps of weeds. When she nearly reached the top, he grabbed hold of her arm and pulled her up the rest of the way.

She was glad to be out of the stream, but strangely enough, she felt even colder now. She guessed it was because some of the feeling was returning to her legs. She looked down. Her stockings and shoes were dripping water. She could hear her teeth chattering.

Edmond's eyes roved over the dark countryside. Thank God for the moonlight, Hélène thought. Once again it had turned into an ally. Without it, they wouldn't be able to see a thing.

"We mustn't lose any time," Edmond said. "We've got to find a place where we can get warm. Someplace where our clothes can dry. Otherwise we're sure to come down with pneumonia."

10

It happened seven days after they had fled the blazing farmhouse. The sky was pale with the first light of dawn. The crystalline air was freezing. It was the kind of cold that turned the mucus inside Hélène's nose to frost and made her ears feel like chunks of ice ready to break off. They never even heard the Boches. Suddenly they were just there. The fir branches rustled as the rifle-wielding figures swept soundlessly out from behind the trees and formed a circle around them. Mechanically, one of them stepped forward and checked them for weapons. Then he grunted and drew back.

Hélène was confused and frightened. She glanced at Edmond. He nodded his head, warning her to keep quiet and do as she was told.

Swiftly they were marched uphill to the nearest road. Here four tarpaulin-covered trucks were parked on the shoulder. The Boches pushed them toward the back of the third one. They climbed inside. A couple of armed guards followed behind them.

The truck had two rows of wooden benches facing each other. They sat down on one side, the guards on the opposite. It was much colder now that they weren't moving. Hélène wrapped her arms around herself, briskly rubbing herself with her hands, trying to keep warm.

The truck engine wheezed, coughed, and backfired. There was a sudden lurch as the truck began moving. The road was full of potholes, and they bounced around on the bench.

Hélène looked at Edmond. "Do you think—" she began.

He cut her off by nudging her roughly. "They may understand French!" he hissed. "Watch what you say!"

"*Silence!*" one of the guards said harshly.

Edmond smiled bleakly. But Hélène could tell he was satisfied that he'd at least managed to say this much. He looked sort of funny with his short, ragged hair. She supposed she looked pretty strange, too. They'd had to cut each other's hair because of lice.

After they'd ridden for a few kilometers, Edmond leaned over and put his head between his knees. Hélène could hear him singing softly to himself. The roar of the engine and the rattling of the truck was so noisy she could barely hear him. At first she didn't pay any attention. Then suddenly she concentrated carefully. Because he wasn't singing to himself. He was singing to her!

It was a tune she knew well, but he was substituting words of his own:

We're just simple peasant children from the town of Saumur.
We have never been to Paris, and no farther than Tours.
Just stick to that story, and even if they know better,
You must stick to what I'm telling you, right to the letter.
Our Papa grew champignons in a cave before he died,
And our dear, sweet Maman she is dead, buried at his side.
Not a brother or sister have we, we are all alone.
Your name will be Eloise and mine is Henri Goyon.
In case they force the issue, maybe get nasty, or what,
Act crazy, have tantrums, do anything to throw them off.
Should they show us the pictures of our sister, remember:
Do not flick an eyebrow, get nervous, or recognize her.
So whatever will happen, little sister, Eloise,
If you understand what I'm saying, won't you poke me, please?

She gave Edmond a poke with her elbow. He stopped singing and sat back up. They exchanged glances and she gave him a little smile.

Yes, she understood. She was Eloise Goyon, and he was her brother, Henri. Catherine and Marie were alien to them. Both Papa and Maman were dead. Papa grew champignons (in a cave like the one they'd spent last night in, no doubt). And if the Boches got violent (like they had with poor Maman), Hélène was to act crazy or childish. That should not be too difficult, she thought. Michelle had often been exasperated by her fits and tantrums.

They stared out the open back of the truck, but their view was restricted to the truck that followed behind theirs and the skeletal trees that lined the road. Once in a while, when they turned corners, she caught glimpses of a frozen-over river. By its size she could tell that it was not the Loire. It was one of the smaller tributaries. Then suddenly they arrived at the Boche headquarters. She was surprised at the beauty of the building. But of course, she thought; the Boches always appropriated the best of everything. So too with their headquarters. It was located in a breathtaking old château that had been built right over the willow-lined river.

Built of pale white stone, it rose in splendor above the iced-over water, which, she assumed, served as a sort of reflecting pool in warmer weather. There were four corner turrets, massive cornices and machicolations and large double-mullioned windows. The green mansard roofs sported decorative dormers and fairly bristled with chimneys.

It would have been a beautiful château at any given time, and still was, but the imprint of the Boches was unmistakable. Part of the Italian gardens had been bulldozed flat in order to make a dirt parking lot. The entrance steps were flanked by stiff, gray-uniformed guards. Two huge flags hung from poles extending out from the machicolations. One was the ubiquitous swastika banner. The other sported twin Z-shaped S's.

Hélène had yet to discover what the S's stood for.

The tailgate of the truck dropped with a clatter and one of the guards prodded them with his rifle. Edmond and Hélène hopped down onto the parking lot. Then they were hurried up the wide, imposing steps and through the heroically carved double doors. Hélène was wide-eyed. Never before had she seen such luxury. But it was cold luxury. There was no central heating, only the enormous, inefficient fireplaces.

They stopped in the long, high-ceilinged hallway. She looked around in fascination. Here were painted wooden beams, massive tapestries, elegant silk-upholstered bergères, and gleaming parquet. All this beauty was marred by the ugly, functional pieces necessary to the bureaucracy. Metal filing cabinets and masses of telephone cables incongruously vied for attention with a magnificent ormolu desk.

The soldier escorts drew themselves up and stiffly saluted a bald, monocled officer who sat behind it. There was an exchange of words, but it was all in German so Hélène couldn't understand any of it. Finally the monocled officer nodded. He picked up his telephone receiver and spoke softly into it. A moment later a young, fair-haired Boche arrived.

Papers were signed and exchanged, and the Boches who had brought them here drew themselves up again and thrust out their right arms.

"Heil Hitler!" they chorused.

Wearily the officer returned a haphazard salute. "Heil Hitler," he murmured dryly. Snappily the two Boches turned on their heels and strode off.

Now the fair-haired young guard was in charge. He led Edmond and Hélène through the château. They passed an elegant, balustraded staircase, turned right into a gloomy corridor, and then descended a steep flight of much less elegant steps to what was obviously the cellar of the château.

The basement room was round, probably located in one of the turrets on the shore side. It was damp, cold, and windowless. It smelled of mildew. Indeed, in the garish glare of the solitary bulb that was screwed into the ceiling, they could see that the stone walls were white with mold.

The worst thing of all was the waiting. She and Edmond must have been kept in that room for half a day. They were seated on a hard wooden bench that faced a long trestle table and a comfortable-looking tapestry-covered chair. Hélène had to pee badly. Each time she told the Boche, he gave her a blank stare. She thought he didn't understand French.

Whenever she heard footsteps out in the corridor, she would look up with a mixture of hope and dread. Hope that perhaps someone would come to release them. Dread that it could just as easily be their executioner. But always the footsteps passed by, and then she would hear a door opening and closing.

For what must have been the hundredth time, she looked up. Once again she could hear voices and footsteps outside in the corridor. Then suddenly the door flew open with a clap and the guard snapped to attention. Two more gray-uniformed Boches marched into the room. Behind them was a fat, red-faced sergeant. And behind *him* . . .

Hélène's eyes widened in shock and she began to tremble. She could feel Edmond jabbing her with his elbow, warning her to keep her composure. She tried to keep from shaking, to make her face look natural. But how could she? She was sick.

Sick, because the German in the elegant black breeches and gleaming knee boots was all too familiar. His face was cruel, narrow, and skull-shaped, his chin was cleft, his lips bloodless. His skin was white and colorless, and the polished visor of his peaked cap was pulled down low over his eyes. Still, she could glimpse those eyes. Those pinkish, satanic eyes that seemed to glow evilly from within when the light lit them.

He was the one who had spit into Maman's face.

He was the one who had barked: "Show her how we punish liars and traitors."

He was the Evil One himself.

When he entered the room, he had one gloved hand tucked in the small of his back. Suddenly he looked away, as if to shield his eyes. He made a rapid gesture at the bulb on the ceiling.

The fat sergeant puffed his belly out importantly. "Zu befehl, Herr Obersturmbannführer!" he shouted. Without needing to be told, his plump red fingers hit the light switch and the room was plunged into darkness.

Now the only light came from out in the corridor. Against it, the Boches were demon silhouettes throwing grotesque shadows across the floor. It was easy to imagine that the eerie yellow light was the glow of hell's fires.

The sergeant hurried off down the hall and disappeared, his heels clicking swiftly on the stone floor. A few minutes later he returned carrying a lamp. It must have been the only lamp he could get his hands on quickly. The base was ormolu and sprouted into a large onyx ostrich egg. The shade was silk. Promptly this lamp was set down on the trestle table and plugged into an outlet. The silk shade glowed delicately. In that dismal room it was an anachronism of luxury.

While the others stood stiffly against the wall, the white-faced Boche sat down in the tapestry-covered chair and crossed his legs. Once again he made a rapid gesture with his hand. Instantly the sergeant stepped forward and produced a sheet of paper.

The Boche held up the paper and studied it intently. It was illuminated from behind by the lamp, and Hélène could see through it. She held her breath. Printed on the other side were three sketches. *Gisèle's sketches.*

Edmond noticed them too. He pressed his leg against hers, trying to ease her fears.

The pink eyes flickered between the pictures on the paper

110

and the children. The white face showed dissatisfaction, unsureness.

The Boche twisted around and looked up at the sergeant. "Es könnte diese Kinder sein," he said. "Ich weiss nicht. Jeder der Ihnen gesehen hat, hatte bei diese Gleichnisse geschworen. Aber"—he rattled the paper ominously—"Ich bin nicht zufrieden." He glanced sharply at the sergeant. "Schmidt! Bringen Sie mir das Mädchen!"

"Jawohl, Herr Obersturmbannführer!" The sergeant clicked his heels together and once again hurried off.

Schmidt, Hélène thought. That must be the sergeant's name.

The white-faced Boche stared coldly at her. Then he pointed a gloved finger at Edmond. "What is your name?" he demanded in the same badly accented French Hélène remembered hearing when they hid in the dumbwaiter.

"Henri Goyon," Edmond replied. His voice sounded calm enough, but Hélène could feel his leg twitching spastically against hers.

Swiftly the Boche's finger switched directions. The pink eyes were on Hélène now. "What is *your* name?"

"Eloise Goyon," she said with dignity.

The Boche leaned back in his chair and steepled his gloved fingers. He regarded Hélène thoughtfully. "And where do you live, Eloise Goyon?" he asked coldly.

"In Saumur."

"Where is your mother?"

She sniffed and wiped her nose. "Maman is dead."

"And your father?"

"Dead, too."

"What did he do for a living?"

"He worked under the ground."

The Boche looked at her sharply. "He was in the underground?"

"No, monsieur," Edmond cut in quickly. "He worked in a cave."

The pink eyes narrowed suspiciously, and Hélène could almost feel their malevolent heat. "A cave?"

"Yes, monsieur," she said. "Papa grew champignons. See?" On an impulse, she reached into her pocket for one of the mushrooms they'd picked two days ago and held it out toward him.

He wrinkled his nose in distaste and motioned for her to

111

put it away. Then he turned and glared up at the Germans who had led him to this room. Both of them seemed to shrink against the wall. They knew he was displeased. Hélène hoped it was because he thought he was wasting his time. That she and Edmond had convinced him they were not the children he was looking for. After all, Gisèle's sketches of Edmond and her didn't really look like them. Especially not after they had to cut each other's hair.

Now she could hear two sets of footsteps coming down the hall. The sergeant must be returning with someone, she thought. She wondered who it could be.

The footfalls got louder as they approached. "Mach's schnell!" the sergeant snapped impatiently.

"All right, all right, I'm hurrying," a low voice replied.

Hélène's heart began to thump wildly. How well she recognized that voice.

It was Catherine's.

So she, too, had been captured by the Boches. Then Hélène froze, realizing the enormity of Catherine's presence. The Boches were going to use her to help identify Edmond and herself. And unsuspectingly, Catherine would come into the room and throw her arms around them. It would be the kiss of Judas in all sincerity. In all innocence.

Faintly, so very faintly that even she could barely hear it, Edmond began to hum a tune. It was the same tune he had sung in the truck.

He was trying to tell Hélène something. But what? Her mind raced. Then the words of his song came back to her:

Should they show us the picture of our sister, remember:
Do not flick an eyebrow, get nervous, or recognize her.

Suddenly she understood. He was telling her that they must turn their backs on Catherine. That she mustn't give any indication of knowing her. Hélène looked hesitantly at the door, and her soul was in torment. She must treat her sister like a stranger.

It was an agonizing position to be put in. Hélène wanted to rush out into the hall and throw her arms around Catherine. Yet the situation demanded her to denounce her, to deny the fact that she was her flesh and blood. But even if she did that, what was the use? Whether they pretended to know her or not, Catherine would still recognize them.

Hélène couldn't ponder the situation any further, because the footsteps had reached the door. The sergeant gave Catherine a push and she stumbled into the room ahead of him.

11

Hélène mustered a blank expression and looked up at her sister. It was Catherine, all right, but she had changed. The gaunt, stringy-haired girl who stood there clutching a baby against her breast looked haggard and broken. Spiritless. Her eyes were without life, and her body seemed to sag. Hélène noticed that Maman's ring gleamed on her finger.

"Look!" the white-faced Boche said tauntingly. "We have found your brother and sister!"

Catherine turned her head and looked at Hélène. Hélène thought her eyes flickered for a moment, but it was so brief that she couldn't be sure. "Who are they?" Catherine murmured listlessly.

"You don't recognize them?" he asked.

Catherine shook her head slowly. "No," she whispered hoarsely. "Should I?"

"You mean you've never seen them before?"

She shook her head again.

The pink eyes narrowed. "If we find out that you're lying, you are going to die. Do you know that?"

"Yes," she said quietly.

"And it's not them?"

Catherine's face was expressionless. "No. I already told you that."

"I don't believe you!" he accused.

She shrugged sadly. "Believe what you want," she said wearily. "It doesn't make any difference."

The Boche sighed. Slowly he pushed himself to his feet and came around the table toward Hélène. His hand shot out and caught her by the collar and pulled her to her feet. He shook her roughly. "Is she your sister?"

Hélène looked over at Catherine and shook her head. Then all at once he lashed Hélène across the face. She grunted as the pain shot through her, and she tottered toward the table. Her hand flew up to her nose. Her fingers touched something wet. Blood.

He looked at Catherine. "You still don't recognize them?" he shouted.

"No," Catherine persisted.

He hit Hélène again. This time she tumbled to the floor. For a moment she lay there crying softly. When he turned away from her, Edmond squatted down, helping her back up.

The Boche reached into one of his pockets and selected a cigarette from a gold case. Deliberately he tapped the end of it on the case. The sergeant leaped forward to light it.

The Boche inhaled deeply, staring thoughtfully at Catherine. "Put the baby down," he ordered.

Catherine looked around for a place to put Marie.

"On the table."

She hesitated. Then gently she carried Marie over to it and laid her down. She whispered softly, soothingly stroking her little head.

"Now step back."

Reluctantly Catherine obeyed. There was a knowing look of fear in her eyes.

The Boche handed the cigarette to the sergeant and pointed to Marie. Noisily Catherine drew in her breath. "No!" she cried. "Don't! *Please!*" She reached for the Boche's sleeve and tugged it desperately. "I beg of you!"

He threw her loose and slapped her. Instantly her cheek turned white, his handprint standing out clearly. Grimly he turned and then faced Edmond and Hélène in turn, his bleak eyes gleaming evilly. There was a crooked smile on his face. Then he spun back around and faced the sergeant. "Jetzt!" he commanded.

In horror Hélène watched the sergeant unbuttoning Marie's little suit. Slowly he brought the glowing end of the cigarette down on her belly and held it there. Marie let out a terrible shriek and began to kick her little legs frantically. Her screaming seemed to go on and on. The two Boches standing against the wall looked away. Catherine's face was pale, and tears rolled down her cheeks.

And it was then that Hélène swore it. Someday, she thought. Someday, if they managed to get out of here, she would make those horrible creatures pay for what they were doing. She would make them pay and pay and pay. She didn't know how. She didn't know when. She didn't know much, but at least she knew the sergeant's name. That was a start.

"Please!" Catherine begged. "Leave the baby alone!"

The cruel smile was frozen on the bloodless lips. "Well? Are you ready to admit that these children are your brother and sister?"

Hélène held her breath and watched Catherine. She seemed to slump in agony, but her voice was calm. "How many times do I have to tell you? It's not them."

Angrily he brought his fist down on the table. Marie shrieked again as the lamp toppled over. The shade cushioned the bulb from the fall, but now it glared in the Boche's eyes.

He turned away from the table and motioned for the sergeant to draw back. Then he faced the other two. "Release them," he spat out in French, pointing at Edmond and Hélène.

Hélène glanced at her sister. For a moment a triumphant look glinted deep within Catherine's eyes. Then it was gone.

The Boche's voice rose. "As for the idiots who brought them here, I want to see them immediately. They are going to be sent to the Russian front!"

Schmidt cleared his throat and pointed questioningly at Catherine.

"The girl and the baby get the usual treatment." The Boche made an irritable gesture. "Arrange for their transportation to Poland."

Catherine's expression didn't change, but her body no longer seemed to sag. She held herself with a kind of quiet dignity. It was the same kind of pride Hélène had often seen in Maman's bearing. Maman would have been proud of Catherine.

Then angrily, as if he didn't want to waste another precious second, the white-faced Boche strode out of the room.

Schmidt stayed behind. He grabbed Catherine by the arm. She nodded wordlessly.

Hélène was the only one who noticed that Catherine had worked Maman's ring loose from her finger. When she bent down to pick Marie back up, she quickly slipped the ring under the lampshade.

For a moment the two sisters' eyes met. "Take the ring," Catherine's expression seemed to say. Hélène nodded imperceptibly.

Then Catherine was gone.

Once again Edmond and Hélène were on their way. The wind had picked up, and they pulled their coats tightly around them. They didn't know where they were. The surrounding countryside was hilly, densely forested, silent, and dark. Though they knew they must still be somewhere near the Loire, they couldn't see the river anywhere. It was late afternoon, and soon night would fall. Already the patches of light between the trees were no longer blue. They'd have to find shelter fast.

Only one thing gave Hélène strength. Hate. Already, so young, she was becoming consumed with destroying those who had separated her from her family. Those who had tortured first Maman, and now Marie. Yes, she was going to exact a heavy vengeance. Even if it took years. After all, she was young. She could afford to wait.

Schmidt, she thought once again. She mustn't forget that name, ever. A fat, red-faced sergeant named Schmidt. That was where she would begin, and by the time she was through, she would cut down the sinister white-faced Boche. But she would do it slowly. That way he would suffer.

These thoughts of revenge were sweet. At the moment, they were the only way she could fight the Boche, the only way she could vent her fury and hatred.

When the doors of the château banged shut behind her and Edmond, she had waited until they were out of earshot before she gave Edmond Maman's ring. She explained to him how Catherine had slipped it under the lampshade, and how she had managed to snatch it up without being seen. He clenched his hand fiercely around the little band of gold, and then he slowly opened his fingers one by one, looking down at the ring as if it might disappear at any moment. On a sudden impulse he brought it to his lips and kissed it reverently.

Then his face darkened. His arm was trembling as he raised it and flung it high into the air. The ring flashed once before it disappeared in a distant clump of bushes.

Slowly Edmond dropped to his knees. He pressed his cheek

against the frozen ground, and his body heaved with pain as he wept aloud. Hélène stood there helplessly, unable to comfort him. She could feel the tears running down her cheeks. She wondered what she had done wrong.

Just as the last light of day faded, they came upon a clearing. It was like a narrow, dark valley cut out between the pine trees, and a pair of gleaming railroad tracks ran along it. They followed the tracks for a while and spent the night alongside them in an unheated tool shed. Edmond managed to jimmy the door open and they sat down on pieces of equipment, leaning back against the walls of the shed as they ate the rest of their champignons. They were ice cold and the chill hurt Hélène's teeth, but once she chewed them well, they seemed somehow warmer. At least they soothed the gnawing emptiness in her belly. Then they cleared a bit of floor space, made a makeshift bed out of pieces of tarpaulin, and curled up together to go to sleep.

But it was an uneasy sleep. As soon as she shut her eyes, the bad dreams began. She dreamed of Paris, but it was not the Paris she knew. This was a grotesque, nightmarish world of distortion in which Sacré Coeur was stretched out of shape into an evil black minaret, the Seine was like an ocean, and all the bridges were gone. The wide-open Place Vendôme was threateningly cramped and dark, like some medieval alley, and the Bois was filled with treacherous cliffs and monstrous trees that had massive gnarled roots. Then Saint-Nazaire entered the dream, and that was strange, because it looked exactly like the beautiful Paris she remembered. And then there was a terrible noise. The earth shook, the buildings trembled, and Saint-Nazaire tumbled to the ground. She awoke suddenly, sweating profusely.

It was the middle of the night and a train was roaring past outside. *So that was why I dreamed of an earthquake,* she thought with relief. The entire shed was shaking. She got to her feet, stumbled over to the door, opened it a crack, and peered out. A blast of icy air rushed past her. The night was pitch black, and the locomotive spewed showers of reddish sparks high into the sky. This hellish spectacle frightened her so much that she quickly shut the door, huddled close against Edmond's warmth, and closed her eyes. Before she knew it, she was asleep again. And the dreams continued.

This time she was in a pitch-black wide-open space. All around her she could see sparks glowing in the distance. Then she realized that they were slowly moving . . . steadily approaching her. As they got closer, she saw that she had been mistaken. The sparks were actually white-faced Boches brandishing cigarettes. In horror she watched as they closed in on her. The nearer they got, the hotter the heat of the cigarettes felt. She tried to draw back, but she was surrounded. They pressed closer. Closer.

And suddenly they lunged forward, their cigarettes searing her skin and burning deep into her flesh.

She began to scream and scream and scream, and Edmond was saying: "Hélène! Wake up! Wake up!" Then she felt his hands shaking her awake. "Wake up!" he said. "Wake *up!* You're having a bad dream."

She opened her eyes and clung to him tightly, still trembling with fear. He stroked her head reassuringly. It was morning already. Outside, the light was soft and gray.

After she calmed down, they ate some more champignons. Then they continued walking westward along the railroad tracks. They still had no idea where they were. Only that they had to head west. Always west. Every so often they would hear a train approaching, and whenever they did, they quickly fled out of sight and stayed behind the trees, waiting until it chugged past. Hélène noticed that most of them were freight trains, long serpentines of boxcars and flatcars loaded down with heavy machinery.

In the afternoon, the tracks brought them to a railway freight yard on the outskirts of a large town. There were quite a few signs around with the name of the town printed on them. At least now they knew where they were. Angers.

The signal tower was built in the middle of the yard. It was thin and ugly and had huge windows at the top that went all the way around, giving a 360-degree view. Occasionally Hélène would catch glimpses of figures sitting behind the glass. Those were the controllers, directing the traffic.

When they reached the far perimeter of the yard, where the maze of rails once again funneled into two solitary tracks, Edmond put a restraining hand on her arm.

She stopped and looked at him.

"What do you say we take a train?" he asked slowly.

"You mean . . . actually ride on one?"

"Yes. All we have to do is catch one heading west and hop aboard. A lot of them seem to stop up ahead, waiting for the signal to change. See?" He pointed to where a long freight train was halted, the locomotive looking like it was floating on a cloud of steam. As they watched, the signal changed and the locomotive chugged, wearily starting to pull its burden.

Hélène looked back at Edmond. "Would a train take us all the way to Saint-Nazaire?" she asked hopefully.

He shrugged. "I don't know. But they're sure to go part of the way, at least."

"And if they turn off somewhere and start going in the wrong direction? What then?"

"Then we'll have to jump off."

Less than half an hour later they sat in a big boxcar half-filled with bulky crates, with the sliding door cracked partly open and the countryside flashing by outside. In the late afternoon they were shunted onto a siding somewhere and the train stopped. Hélène could see cranes swinging enormous tapered cylinders onto the flatcars at the rear of the train. These cylinders were of dark gray metal and sprouted sleek sharklike fins at the bottom. Edmond told her they were rocket bombs. The place was swarming with uniformed Boches. Some of them were slowly making their way from the rear of the train to the front, sliding open the doors of the boxcars and inspecting them.

"They're headed this way," Edmond whispered. "Quick, we have to get off before they find us."

He pushed open the sliding door on the other side of the car and looked out. The coast was clear. On this side of the train there was no activity: a steep shrub-covered hill sloped up from the edge of the tracks. Silently he and Hélène hopped down off the train and scuttled uphill. For a while they walked along a plateau. Then abruptly they drew to a halt. They could go no farther. A sheer abyss plunged a hundred meters down to a dry, boulder-strewn riverbed. There was no way that they could climb down it, cross the riverbed, and then get back up the sheer cliff on the other side. They would have to find another way to cross it. A quarter of a kilometer to their left, a strange structure bridged the abyss. The top was level with the plateau, and trees and bushes grew up out of it, giving it a bizarre, almost theatrical look.

Hélène pointed at it. "What's that thing?" she asked.

"An aqueduct," Edmond replied. "The Romans built them in order to channel water across valleys."

"It leads westward," she noted.

They headed toward it. When they got there, she froze. From far away it had looked delicate but sturdy. Close up, it looked ready to collapse. Stones were missing, the edges were crumbling, and there was no railing of any kind, just a low curb that barely came up to her ankles. The channel where water had once flowed was now filled in with dirt, and here the trees and bushes had taken root.

Fearlessly Edmond stepped onto the narrow aqueduct and started across. Hélène hung back, staring at it in apprehension. The aqueduct seemed to hang in space before her, devoid of any visible support. She turned sideways and looked down at the dry riverbed. That was a mistake. Quickly she averted her eyes.

It was a long drop.

Edmond turned around. "Well?" he demanded. "What are you waiting for?"

"It . . . it looks awfully dangerous," Hélène stammered in embarrassment.

He stared at her for a moment. Finally he spoke. "It's safe," he said gently. "It's probably stood here for over a thousand years. It's not likely to come tumbling down now." He gestured for her to follow him. "Come on."

Reluctantly she took a few steps. She realized immediately that it was even worse than she'd imagined. They had to pick their way carefully around the tree trunks and bushes, sometimes forced to stand at the very edge of the parapet.

Suddenly she stopped in her tracks. Her head was spinning crazily. It was impossible for her to go on. She would never get across this way. Not with her sanity intact.

Edmond turned around again. "For God's sake, Hélène!" he called over his shoulder. "Come *on*. Don't you want to get to Saint-Nazaire?"

That did it. She forced herself to look her fears in the face. Slowly she began to follow him again. Her hands were clammy and she found herself breaking out in a sweat. "Just don't look down," she kept repeating over and over to herself. "It'll be all right as long as you don't look down!"

So she kept her eyes on Edmond's back. She emulated his every move. When he skirted deep holes where the aqueduct had begun to cave in, she skirted them in exactly the same manner. When he climbed over piles of rubble, so did she.

The wind was strong now. It buffeted them as it howled

by, sometimes almost throwing them off balance. It got so strong that after a while they prudently dropped to their knees and crawled on all fours. Once her fingers dislodged a stone and it fell over the edge. For what seemed an eternity, she heard nothing. Then finally a faraway clatter. Slowly she crawled on.

When they were halfway across, she could hear a train in the distance. She had to squint against the wind as she glanced over at the railroad bridge. From here it looked tiny, like a pattern of rusty toothpicks. As she watched, the front of the locomotive came into view. Slowly it chugged westward across the bridge. It must have been the very train they had abandoned earlier. It had boxcars followed by flatcars loaded with evil-looking cylinders. When the locomotive reached the middle of the bridge, some of the cars were still out of sight. It was a long train indeed.

She stared at it wistfully, wishing she was still aboard. She'd have much preferred crossing the abyss in the shelter of a boxcar to having to crawl over the aqueduct.

A moment later she took back her wish.

It began with a droning in the skies above. She looked up. An airplane had broken out of the cloud cover and came swooping down toward the bridge. Suddenly tiny figures appeared to be swarming all over the train; it must have taken on a battalion of Boches. She heard the sharp cracking of gunfire and the chattering of machine guns. Then there was a shrill, ominous whistle.

"Duck!" Edmond screamed. "Lie flat and keep your head down!"

Hélène did as she was told, but she kept her face turned sideways, toward the bridge. She saw that something had fallen out of the belly of the plane. Whatever it was seemed to float lazily through the air. It wasn't until a moment later that she realized it was a bomb.

It missed the bridge and landed on the floor of the abyss. Suddenly the earth shook and there was a massive explosion. Debris and fire and smoke and destruction blew high into the air. Hélène let out a shriek. In the reverberation of the blast she could feel the aqueduct shaking. The stones under her actually lifted up and shifted. Then they finally settled back into place with an audible sigh. Before her eyes, a row of curbstones crumbled away and fell down out of sight.

When the smoke cleared, she saw that the distant bridge

was still standing, and the train continued to chug steadily across it. When they had seen the bomb coming, some of the Boches had hit the roof of the cars; now they were getting back on their feet. She could see one Boche hanging on to a girder of the bridge, his tiny legs futilely kicking air. As she watched, he lost his grip and fell down into the abyss, his body doing a wild spiral.

Another airplane droned and broke through the clouds. She started to pray hysterically, but it didn't help. This plane, too, dived at the bridge, spit fire, and then dropped its bomb. There was another terrible whistling noise, and then the earth shook again. And again. And again. Debris was raining down all around her, and with each explosion the stones of the aqueduct did their terrible dance, rippling like a swift tide from one end to the other before settling back down.

And then one of the bombs hit its mark. In a single frozen, blinding split second, the bridge broke in half. The train buckled gently like a snake in midair, and then it plunged headlong down into the abyss. Now came the worst explosions imaginable. One after the other, the rocket bombs went off.

The aqueduct shook spastically. The stones rattled like millions of chattering teeth. Rocks and earth and pieces of the train rained down all around them. A section of twisted track shrieked through the air, landed not five meters away from Hélène on top of the aqueduct, and impaled itself on the stones like an angry, quivering piece of sculpture.

Suddenly Hélène caught the smell of burned hair. It was a moment before she realized what she was smelling. Her own hair, singed by the distant holocaust.

Then there was silence, an intense, shell-shocked silence the likes of which she had never heard before. Slowly she turned her head and looked around. The spot the bridge had spanned was now three times the width it had been. Neither bridge nor train was anywhere in sight. What hadn't been blasted to pieces or scattered was buried under tons of rock and rubble.

This was one shipment of rocket bombs that would never reach the coast, would never fall on the place called London.

And then she began to whimper. Softly at first, increasingly louder, until finally her body shook uncontrollably and she started to weep. She wept for herself, for Catherine and

122

Marie, for Maman. She wept for the bridge. For Paris. For all of France.

Edmond crawled toward her. "Are you all right?" he asked softly.

She raised her head and looked at him through tear-streaked eyes. "Yes," she managed to croak. "And you?"

He nodded and shrugged. "I've a few scratches, nothing serious."

It was a miracle. They had come through unscathed. Not very pretty, with most of their hair singed off and their faces beet red, but their hair would grow back and they weren't badly burned. Just superficially. Yes, it was a miracle.

She stopped weeping long enough to dry her eyes and said a silent prayer of thanks. Then they lost no time crawling across the rest of the way. Now she didn't give the aqueduct a second thought. Her fear of heights was a small thing compared to what they'd just lived through.

Five minutes later they stood on the far side of the abyss. For a long moment they looked around in silence. Then they continued walking.

They had gone only a few meters when they were surrounded by a motley group of men pointing rifles at them. Hélène counted a dozen of them.

Not again, she thought with a sinking feeling. Not the Boches again. Not after what they'd been through already.

She didn't see the men lowering their rifles. She didn't notice the ragged clothing they wore or the strange assortment of weapons they wielded. All she knew was her hatred and her fear. It had been walled up deep inside her for too long. Now it burst like a boil. She flung herself upon the nearest man. She clenched her fists and furiously hammered him in the stomach. She kicked and clawed and bit. He stood there stonily, staring down at her in silence.

"My God!" one of the others exclaimed in the soft speech of Touraine. "She's a savage! An animal!"

Savage? Animal? She whirled around. What did that idiot know? And why was he speaking such good French? And then it hit her. He must be a collaborator. She spat. Collaborators were even worse pigs than the Boches. Then she attacked him in a fury, beating him until she was ready to drop from exhaustion. When she looked up, she saw that he was looking down at her, not with pain, but in surprise.

I'll make you hurt, you pig, she thought. I'll make you hurt good! She bent down, grabbed a big rock, staggered up, and began to raise it over her head. She was going to smash him with it. Smash him like a bug!

Effortlessly the man reached out, took the stone out of her hands, and tossed it away.

Suddenly she began to tremble. What was the use of fighting any longer? she asked herself. They were captured once again. And now she had no more energy, no more fight left in her. She was surrendering, and it hurt her more than she could bear. Especially with Catherine's and Marie's sacrifices having been in vain.

Numbly she slid down into a sitting position. Tears streamed down her cheeks. She found herself howling like a mortally wounded animal.

"We're your friends," the stony-faced man said gently. He squatted down in front of her and looked her in the eyes. "Where are you from?"

She looked away in silence. They wouldn't get a word out of her. Not a single word. Even if they tortured her. Even if they burned her like they had burned Marie.

"What about you?" she heard the man ask.

"Paris," Edmond answered. His voice sounded foggy and far away, as if in a dream. Things were becoming unfocused, focused, unfocused again.

"Paris!" the man exclaimed. "And you came all this way? Alone? What's your name?"

"Edmond Junot."

"And hers?" He pointed at Hélène, but she couldn't see it. She was slipping into the unfocused zone again.

"She's my sister Hélène. My other two sisters and our mother were carted off by the Boches. The Boches are looking for us everywhere. They claimed that we were kidnapped. We weren't! We killed some Boche, and now they want to kill us! Maman had a transmitter hidden in our house. That's how it all started. It was the right thing to do, having a transmitter, wasn't it?"

"Indeed it was," the stony-faced man said. "Your mother fought for France. You have much to be proud of."

Maman! Suddenly Hélène could see her blurry shape standing in front of her. She tried to reach out and touch her, but her arms felt like lead. Then everything came into focus again. It wasn't Maman . . . it was the stony-faced man.

And Edmond was speaking with him. She was becoming very confused.

"So you're the so-called kidnapped children," the man said thoughtfully. "And you managed to hide all this time?"

Hélène saw Edmond nodding. "We're going to our aunt's."

"Where is that?"

"Saint-Nazaire."

The blurry men exchanged glances. "That's still a long way off," one of them said finally.

Then Hélène blacked out. The last thing she remembered was being lifted up by the stony-faced man. He smelled strongly of sweat, and somehow that was comforting. "Come with us, Little French Girl," he whispered softly. "We will see to it that you get safely to Saint-Nazaire."

TODAY

Wednesday, January 10

1

It was ten-fifteen in the morning when Hélène walked into the conference room and shut the door softly behind her. She wore a champagne Chanel suit and her hair was pulled back in the ubiquitous no-nonsense chignon. Her only piece of jewelry was a large gold brooch pinned to her lapel.

The board members were already seated around the table, waiting. Before she came in she had heard the buzz of their conversations, but now the room had suddenly fallen silent. Smiling tightly, she came around to her place at the head of the table. She remained standing, her fingertips poised on the oiled teak, her violet eyes alert and appraising.

They were all in their usual places. Wearing dark sunglasses, von Eiderfeld nevertheless sat with his chair pushed away from the table, which was flooded with light from the overhead tracks. Next to him was the Comte, who looked up at Hélène, red-faced and mocking. She noticed that his hands were trembling. Beside him, like an elegant black widow, sat Z.Z. She was dressed in a black silk shantung suit, long leather gloves, and a little hat with a veil half-covering her face. She smiled and chain-smoked malevolently, the smoke picked out by the lights like swirling veils. Opposite her, d'Itri was doodling on a piece of paper, a bored expression on his face.

The Sphinx was present to transcribe the meeting. She was in the far corner of the room, legs crossed, steno pad on her lap, pen poised.

The door opened abruptly and Edmond walked in briskly. Wordlessly he crossed the room, pulled up a chair beside Julie, and sat down.

Hélène looked at him. Almost imperceptibly he shook his head from side to side. She looked thoughtful, masking her emotions. He had just returned from a meeting at ManhattanBank. The day after tomorrow, the ten-million-dollar loan was due. He had gone to fight for a desperate last-ditch extension.

The shake of his head told her all she needed to know. There would be no extension. Unless some sort of miracle happened, the bank would seize her collateral—20 percent of HJII stock—and throw it to the vultures. Or perhaps even to some higher bidder she did not know of. Either way, the outcome would be the same. She would lose control over HJII. The others would end up owning 69 percent of the total voting stock and her remaining 31 percent wouldn't amount to a hill of beans. Out of hatred and revenge, they would continue to band against her, this time armed with enough power to topple her. Almost certainly they would elect a new president. It was a grim prospect, but one she had to face. After all, Hubert had gone so far as to spell that out.

The idea of him—or one of the others—sitting in her office, running HJII, was revolting. She felt like a mother must feel when her baby is about to be snatched away from her. After all, HJII *was* her baby.

But this was no time to show her feelings. She had to be impassive. Composed.

Like an actress about to make an entrance, she took a deep breath. "Good morning," she began. Her crystalline voice rang out clearly, impersonally. Without a hint of her inner turmoil. "The board of directors' meeting is called to order.

"I know that time is a precious commodity for each one of us. Therefore, I strongly suggest we stick to the subjects listed on today's agenda. Let's try not to stray from them as we did the last time. However"—she looked down at Hubert, who was grinning up at her with amusement—"I do want you to know that I have noted the criticisms you voiced over how I run this corporation. I'm afraid I can do little about those complaints that dealt with my personality. But when I have the time, I will review those that directly affect HJII's publishing policies.

"Now, to the first item on the agenda. In front of each of you is a bound copy of this year's projected plans. If you would be so kind as to open them, we can then discuss the items, one by one." Hélène sat down, reached for her copy, and opened it to the first page.

They all stared down at their reports, but not one of them made a move to pick them up.

Z.Z. smiled slowly. Then she reached out and pushed hers

aside. "I realize that these plans are most important," she said craftily. "However, I feel that I *must* move that we drop the subjects on today's agenda so that we may discuss something far more important to HJII's future."

Hélène folded her hands and looked wearily at Z.Z. This move came as no surprise; she had expected something of this sort to happen. "Such as?" she asked calmly.

Z.Z.'s smile broadened. She lifted her little black veil and slowly pushed it over the top of her hat. "Something that concerns each and every one of us." She paused. "Leadership."

"All right," Hélène said with resignation. "Say what you have to say."

Z.Z. rose to her feet. Hélène could detect the excitement flashing in her narrowed green eyes. She knew that look only too well. It would be another day of cat-and-mouse games.

"Last night," Z.Z. purred, "the gentlemen sitting around this table and I had a private . . . chitchat, you might call it. We all agreed that for the past few years HJII has been faring quite well. However, separate though it may be from HJII, the disaster produced by that new magazine you insisted on publishing puts everything in a different . . . *perspective.* We're quite concerned about the fact that you are having personal financial difficulties. Of course, under ordinary circumstances that would be none of our business. However, the fact that you used twenty percent of HJII stock as collateral for a loan you will not possibly be able to repay affects us immensely."

Hélène stared at Z.Z. numbly. *Not be able to repay!* Those vultures were disgustingly well-informed. They knew things they had no business knowing. Yesterday's *Wall Street Journal* article speculated on her inability to pay back the loan; today it was known for certain that she could not. She wondered if someone at the bank had been shooting his mouth off. Gore, perhaps?

"After all," Z.Z. continued self-righteously, "what would happen if ManhattanBank sells those shares to someone none of us knows? If some outside stranger would buy them and just walk right in? It could be disastrous, that's what! After all, they'd be owning one-fifth of this corporation.

"So we discussed it, the gentlemen and I. And we've come to an agreement." Z.Z. stopped and smiled sweetly at Hélène. "We hereby offer to help you weather the storm. We are

131

willing to buy twenty percent of your HJII shares for eleven million dollars. That's ten million plus the million interest. In that way, you could pay off ManhattanBank, your collateral would be returned, and we wouldn't have to worry about having an outsider sitting on the board. This way we'd *all* benefit."

Sure, *you'd* benefit, Hélène thought. You'd get your claws into the business without my putting up a fight.

"If you were to sell us twenty percent of HJII," Z.Z. continued, "we would certainly have to look upon that action as a gesture of goodwill. It would ease our fears of outside . . . invasion. It would also boost our confidence in your leadership ability." She turned to the others and smiled shrewdly. "Am I correct, gentlemen?"

"That you are," Hubert said heartily.

Z.Z. spread her hands apart. "So you see?" she said sweetly. "It's as simple as that." She sank down into her seat.

Hélène cleared her throat and chose her words carefully. "It seems that 'outside invasion' of HJII weighs heavily on your minds. Let me try to put your fears to rest.

"In my opinion, you would all be best off to wait and see *if*—and I stress the word 'if'—the bank does indeed seize my collateral shares. Should that occur, I believe you have nothing to worry about. As I understand it, you would be in a position to bid for them." She glanced across the room at Edmond. "Am I correct in assuming that?"

"Yes," Edmond agreed in an expressionless voice.

"There is your answer," Hélène said with finality. "No matter what happens, you'd have your chance to block 'outside invasion' of HJII. And if you did that, you would also be in a position to elect a new president. Then my leadership abilities wouldn't need to concern you." She looked around. "I believe that for the time being, at least, this closes the discussion brought up by Mrs. Bavier. Now, as far as this year's projected plans are concerned—"

"Not so fast, my dear," Hubert chimed in quickly. "I move that we suspend *all* the items on today's agenda and adjourn this meeting until Monday morning." He smiled. "That way, we'll all be wiser as to the future of HJII. After all, anything we might discuss today could be a waste of time. As you pointed out, we may be in a position to elect a new president on Monday. If we do that, all of HJII's policies would have to change."

Hélène forced her face to remain expressionless. His tactic was clear. The loan was due on Friday; the following banking day was Monday. If they had already convinced the bank to sell them the shares—and she wouldn't put that past them—it would not take more than a few minutes for the transaction to take place. Then the buyer could rush back uptown for the meeting and use the shares for a showdown vote. Cutting her out. *Throwing* her out of HJII. She would be nothing more than a minority shareholder with her hands tied.

As for the board of directors, she wondered which of them actually planned to buy the shares. Von Eiderfeld and Hubert were both filthy rich. Either one could afford it.

Z.Z. and d'Itri were worth quite a lot of money, but they didn't have eleven million dollars to squander. Perhaps they would all chip in; that way, they would get what they wanted and not even notice the dent in their pocketbooks.

Hélène rose to her feet suddenly. "All right," she said. "The meeting is adjourned until Monday morning at ten." Swiftly she strode out of the conference room. Her eyes had hardened. She knew what she had to do. She would set up her own meeting with Hubert and von Eiderfeld. She couldn't do anything about Z.Z., and d'Itri was a small fry; without Hubert and von Eiderfeld, they'd disband like third-rate criminals. But Hubert and von Eiderfeld . . . Yes, she just might be able to do something about them.

Much as she hated to, she'd use her hold over them for one last time. It shouldn't be too difficult.

After all, it had worked in the past.

An hour later, Hélène had Jimmy bring the Rolls around and she and Edmond rode uptown and had lunch at 21. The restaurant was already crowded when the captain led them to her usual table. On the way, they nodded and greeted many acquaintances.

To anyone who saw her, she never looked more beautiful and relaxed. But Edmond knew better. She was composed, yes. But she was very tense. He thought of the enormous pressures she was under and wished he could do something about them. For the past year she'd been working herself half to death. It seemed that each time she managed to win a round, something else popped up from behind her and knocked her back down. "How about a drink?" he asked.

She shook her head. "I could use one, but I think I'll stick to club soda. Today I decided that the best remedy for a lousy day would be to act like a woman." She smiled. "So I'll have my hair done. I called up Susumu's, and they'll squeeze me in after lunch."

He nodded and ordered soda for her and a martini for himself. When the captain left, Edmond lit a cigarette and leaned over the table. He kept his voice low. "I know you won't want to hear what I've got to say, but as your lawyer and brother, I think I owe it to you."

She nodded. "You're going to try to convince me to go public," she predicted calmly.

His voice dropped an octave. "Yes. I know you hate having to do it, but it's the only way you can keep control of HJII. This morning, after the bank turned down the request for an extension, I took the liberty of asking if they'd consider it were you to go public. They will, but only on that condition, because then they'll be virtually guaranteed that you will make a fortune. I must say that the well-fed Mr. Gore was quite beside himself when I brought the subject up. For some reason, he doesn't seem anxious for that to happen." Edmond frowned. "I really don't like that man. Never have. There's something odd about him. Something sneaky."

"I don't trust him, either." She looked thoughtful. "Perhaps Hubert or one of the others got to him."

Edmond shrugged. "I wouldn't put it past them."

She started to say something but fell silent as their drinks arrived. She sipped her soda slowly. "I talked to von Eiderfeld and Hubert," she said. "I'm going to go and see them this evening. I may be able to get them off my back."

"Yes, but it still won't raise the money," Edmond pointed out. "If you can't do that, they'll be able to walk right in and take HJII over. And you can't let that happen. Take my word for it, Hélène. Go public. Otherwise everything you've worked for will go down the drain."

She nodded soberly. "How long do I have before I need to come to a decision?"

"Tomorrow afternoon at the latest."

She looked down at her glass. That wasn't much time. Still . . . Suddenly she looked back up. "All right," she said, "I'll give you my answer at noon tomorrow. I'll seriously consider it."

"Please do." He reached across the table abruptly and covered her hand with his, his eyes pleading. "The way I see it, you stand to make an enormous profit by selling public stock. Forty million dollars. Perhaps more. And, Hélène, you really wouldn't be losing anything. You'd be chairman of the board. You'll still own fifty-one percent of the corporation."

She sighed wearily. "Yes, Edmond. We've been through that before. Remember?"

He nodded. "I remember," he said.

He did, too. Ever since he had first brought it up, she had been dead set against it. In a way, he could understand her reasoning. But one thing didn't make sense. If she felt so strongly about keeping HJII "private," why had she ever let the vultures in?

"Don't forget," he said. "Things are different now than they were a year ago. Going public's your only chance."

She shook her head slowly. "No, it isn't. I have another choice that nobody knows of. Even you."

He gave her a strange look. "What on earth are you talking about?"

Her voice was soft. "Nigel offered to lend me the money."

Suddenly he sat up straight. This news changed everything. Nigel Somerset, the Duke of Farquharshire, was the third-richest man in England.

"Why didn't you tell me this before?" Edmond asked.

She toyed with her glass. "Because I don't know if I should accept his help."

"Why? Because he loves you?"

"No," she said gently. "Because I'm in love with him." She paused and looked Edmond in the eye. "He's asked me to marry him again."

"And?"

"I still haven't given him an answer. I told him I'd have to think about it."

"But *why*? You said it yourself—you love the man!"

"Because I don't want to get married before the problems at HJII are sorted out. Somehow it wouldn't be . . . right."

Edmond rolled his eyes. "Oh, my God! Don't tell me! You don't want him to think you're marrying him because of the money. Is that it?"

She shook her head. "No . . . because *I* want to make certain I'm not."

2

Susumu's Fifth Avenue salon is reputed to be one of the finest beauty parlors in the world. It was here that Hélène had her hair done in a private room on the eighth floor. She watched in the mirror as the slim, Japanese hairstylist expertly wrapped her head up in a soft, thick turban. On a stool beside her sat the manicurist, busily working on her nails.

"Could you please excuse me for a moment?" Hélène asked apologetically. "I would like to go to the powder room."

"Of course, madame," Susumu said. "I believe you know where it is."

Hélène nodded. The hairstylist helped her solicitously out of her chair and smiled. The manicurist smiled too. They were expensive smiles. Having your hair done at Susumu's cost a fortune, especially if Susumu did it personally.

She crossed the room to the door. The stylist got there first and held it open for her. Just as she was about to step out into the corridor, a woman was being led to one of the other rooms. Hélène waited in the doorway for her to pass.

The woman looked up at Hélène and stopped. "Why, Miss Junot," she bubbled. "It has been *ages!*"

Hélène looked confused. "Yes?" she said, wondering who in the world this emaciated, blond, deeply tanned caricature of a woman could be.

"We met last year, remember? I'm Geraldine Gore. My husband handles your accounts at ManhattanBank."

Hélène smiled. "Of course. How do you do?"

Geraldine Gore extended her bony hand, and Hélène couldn't help noticing the two bracelets encircling her wrist. Both were identical, except that one was made of canary diamonds while the other was of bloodred rubies. Both were unmistakably from Bulgari. Both were unmistakably expensive.

136

"Oh, what lovely bracelets," Hélène admired.

Geraldine held up her wrist and smiled contentedly. "They are, aren't they? I just picked the ruby bracelet out a few minutes ago. I've been feeling *so* depressed lately. I told myself that just having my hair done simply won't be enough to make me feel better. It's amazing, isn't it, how shopping for little trinkets always helps one get over a depression."

"Yes, it really is."

Geraldine suddenly made a face. "But I hate to have to face my husband. I think he'll commit suicide when he sees it." She glanced at her attendant, who waited a discreet distance away. "Well, I'd better be going or else they'll never get finished with me on time. Usually I come in on Thursdays, but I'm flying to Palm Beach a day early this week. Virginia Simonsen is going to hold the most marvelous masked ball!" She sighed heavily. "I do so love masked balls, don't you?"

"Yes, I do," Hélène, who had never been to one, answered politely.

"Well, I *must* be going. It was so *nice* to run into you. Ta!" Then Geraldine started down the corridor after her attendant.

Hélène stared after her. What an abominable, name-dropping woman, she thought. But she did credit Geraldine with having one thing. Exquisite—if expensive—taste.

Vaguely Hélène wondered how the Gores could afford such high living.

Politely Karl von Eiderfeld took the Comte's hat and coat, hung them in the hallway closet, and led him into the living room. Even though it was already dark outside, the heavy damask curtains were still drawn tightly. Only two very dim lamps were lit.

Von Eiderfeld waved his guest into a faded French chair. "Sit, my dear Comte. It should not be long before our *friend* arrives. Meanwhile, would you care for a drink?"

"Armagnac, if you have it," the Comte said.

"I do." Von Eiderfeld crossed the room to the massive armoire. When he opened the double doors, Hubert saw that the inside had been converted into a bar, complete with refrigerator and sink. Von Eiderfeld brought the drink over. "You have the envelopes?" he asked.

Hubert nodded and snapped open his briefcase. He took

out a large manila envelope and placed it on the Directoire table beside him. "They arrived by courier from Paris less than an hour ago."

"You think they are what she is coming to see us about?" von Eiderfeld asked.

Hubert looked thoughtful. "It's possible," he said. "But I rather think she doesn't even know they're missing yet. I hired the best safecracker available. He stole only what I paid him to steal. Then he locked the vault shut again. There was no evidence of a break-in."

Von Eiderfeld smiled with satisfaction. "I commend you on your good work. She will have no hold over us now. Did you manage to discover where she stopped off yesterday when she interrupted her flight?"

"I did." The Comte took a big swallow of Armagnac. "She landed at a private airstrip in England. Our sweet Hélène travels in some very high circles. The airstrip in question belongs to Nigel Somerset."

Von Eiderfeld started. "She's still seeing him?"

"I believe so."

Von Eiderfeld digested this piece of information thoughtfully. "That is not very welcome news, I'm afraid. Somerset is one of the richest men in England. What if he comes up with the eleven million dollars for her? Then we'll have lost the battle."

"I don't think that will happen," Hubert said confidently. "Otherwise, it would already have been arranged. You don't know Hélène as I do. She wouldn't wait until the last possible moment—she would have arranged everything long ago. Besides, her ethics would never permit her to accept charity, even in the form of a loan. No, my friend. She's squirming right now. She'll never be able to raise the money."

Von Eiderfeld looked gloomy. "I hope to God you're right."

At that moment, the telephone began to ring. Von Eiderfeld crossed over to the Directoire table and picked up the receiver. "Yes?" He looked at Hubert and nodded. "Have her come right up." He replaced the receiver and smiled grimly. "That was the desk. She's on her way up."

A few minutes later, Hélène arrived. She hadn't had time to change. She wore her Blackglama coat open, and the champagne Chanel suit still showed underneath it. Her hair was no longer in a chignon. It hung thickly to her shoulders, casually cut, yet eminently elegant, framing her face in lustrous waves. "Hello," she said stiffly.

Awkwardly von Eiderfeld motioned for her to come in. "Please. The Comte is already here. Can I take your coat?"

She shook her head. "I don't think I'll be staying that long."

Von Eiderfeld shrugged and led her into the living room, where Hubert was comfortably sprawled in his chair. He made no move to get up. "Ah," he said with a wicked grin. "So the president has stooped to socializing with mere stockholders. Do have a seat." He leaned sideways and patted the chair next to his.

"No, thank you," she said coldly. "I prefer to stand."

"As you wish. Now, what did you want to see us about?"

Hélène chose her words carefully. "I have come by in order to remind you that you would both find it more . . . agreeable, let's say . . . to stop fighting me. To stop playing cat and mouse. As you may recall, we've had this kind of discussion once before."

Hubert smiled and rose to his feet. He walked over to the fireplace, where a log and kindling sat on the grate. He squatted down and carefully lit it. Slowly the kindling started to burn, and after a few minutes the log caught fire. The blaze threw flickering yellow light around the dim room. Hubert made a noise of satisfaction and got to his feet. "I suppose you're referring to the 'hold' you have over us?" he asked.

"Yes," Hélène said.

Hubert smiled. "Take my advice, my dear. Go home and forget all about it. You see, we're no longer quaking with fear."

"I think you should take this matter more seriously," Hélène warned. "I could ruin you both." She turned and fixed a glacial stare on von Eiderfeld. "I could have you charged for war crimes. You would be hung." Then she turned back to Hubert. "And you. You, too, would be hung. For murder."

Hubert began to laugh. "That's preposterous! Who would believe you? You'd need proof to make these slanderous accusations stick!"

Her eyes narrowed. "Stop playing games, Hubert! You

know very well that I have the proof. The evidence is locked in a lawyer's vault."

He laughed again and went over to the Directoire table. He picked up the manila envelope and tore it open. Reaching inside it, he extracted a smaller white envelope.

"Do you recognize this?" he asked, holding it up. Scrawled across the sealed flap was her signature.

They could hear her sharp intake of breath. "Yes," she whispered. "Where did you get it?"

"Let's just say it's found its way here from a lawyer's vault in Paris. Don't blame your solicitor. It wasn't his fault. In fact, he doesn't even know that anything is missing yet." Hubert tore the white envelope open and pulled out some old, yellowed documents. He unfolded them and held them dramatically up in the air. "Evidence of war crimes," he announced in a loud voice. He handed the papers to von Eiderfeld. "Will you do the honors, my friend?" he asked softly.

Hélène watched in horror as von Eiderfeld accepted them gravely, walked toward the mantel, and tossed them into the fire. Greedily the flames sprang up and licked at them; then they blackened and curled.

"And now, this!" With a flourish Hubert produced a second white envelope, this one bulkier than the first. It, too, was sealed, the unbroken flap signed with Hélène's signature. "And do you recognize *this*?" he asked, taunting.

For a moment she shut her eyes. This can't be happening, she thought. *It can't be.* She opened her eyes. But it was.

Hubert tore open the second envelope.

Inside it was a reel of recording tape. He held it high. "Evidence for murder?" he called out laughingly. Then he clucked his tongue in mock sympathy. "Really, my dear. You should have known better than to resort to *blackmail*."

He walked slowly toward the fireplace and with a motion of disgust threw the reel into the flames. A portion of the tape unwound and snaked out onto the carpet. With his foot, he kicked it into the hearth. Then he turned to Hélène.

Her face was white. She was staring into the fire, mesmerized. As she watched, the recording tape began to melt, exuding a stench of burning plastic.

"See, my dear?" Hubert said pleasantly. "You no longer

have a hold over us. The past is gone and forgotten." He snapped his fingers. "Just like *that*."

She stared numbly into the flames. No, it wasn't. For her, the past would never be gone. Could never be forgotten.

YESTERDAY

II
RAPE

1

Saint-Nazaire, 1950

Tante Janine lived on the outskirts of Saint-Nazaire and made a modest livelihood off her plant nursery. Her house was on a raised piece of property a quarter of a kilometer from the sea. It was built of weathered gray stone, was two stories high, and had a steeply sloping roof. On a clear day you could even see down to where the Loire emptied into the sea. That was two kilometers to the south.

The nursery surrounded the house on all sides. Every square centimeter of space was put to good use. There were four big hothouses and dozens of long, glass-covered pits in which Tante Janine grew the seedlings which the townspeople would buy in the spring to plant in their own gardens. All around these odd structures, the earth was tilled and used for planting seasonal vegetables and flowers. There wasn't a patch of useless grass to be seen. Wooden planks served as paths between the flowerbeds and the vegetable patches.

Two additional structures were situated quite some distance from the house—a smelly three-sided bunker used for storing manure and compost, and a shed where the gardening tools were kept and in which they made wreaths or floral arrangements for funerals or an occasional wedding. For a long time, funerals had outnumbered weddings by ten to one.

A stone wall surrounded the property. Attached to it was a big wooden sign that faced the road. It read: "JANINE JUNOT." The black-and-white paint was peeling and blistered.

During Edmond's and Hélène's first winter there, things had not gone well at the nursery. At that time, Saint-Nazaire was considered to be of extreme strategic importance by both the Allies and the Nazis.

First, there were the German installations—namely the U-boat base. Many of the U-boat wolf packs that infested the

145

Atlantic originated from here. They depended on the Saint-Nazaire base for supplies, servicing, and repairs. It was the ideal spot, since much of the equipment they needed was already there from before the war. Saint-Nazaire had been known for its shipyards since the nineteenth century.

Second, and more important, the town was part of what the Allies called the Saint-Nazaire Pocket. This was considered to be the chief infiltration point into France from the Atlantic coast. As a result, Saint-Nazaire was nearly devastated.

Each time the British and the Americans pounded the installations, Tante Janine would burst into tears. Not that she was sorry about the U-boat base being demolished. But the nearby explosions reverberated all the way to her nursery and shattered the glass that covered her hothouses and pits. When that happened, the vegetables she had been nurturing so diligently would be in danger of exposure to the cold. For a while she managed to patch up everything as best as she could. Then came a particularly heavy bombing and the glass was shattered beyond repair. In a single night, every last seedling had frozen and died. When spring came, there was nothing to sell. It was a very lean year.

But 1944 did bring a moment of jubilation. On August 26, General de Gaulle marched triumphantly down the Champs-Élysées. At last, Paris was liberated. Frenchmen were in tears. The war was as good as over. Just like Maman had predicted, the Boches were being driven out of France and pushed back across the Rhine.

Like everyone else, Edmond and Hélène had greeted this news with joy. Now it would not be long before the family was reunited. But as month after month crept by with still no word from Maman, Papa, Catherine, or Marie, they slowly began to lose all hope of ever seeing them again. From the grown-ups, terrible fragments of stories about the Germans filtered down to them. Stories that were beyond their comprehension. Stories that just couldn't be true. Stories about what happened to those who were carted off by the Nazis. Stories about the camps.

In the beginning, Tante Janine had been relatively friendly. Then in May 1945 she "turned." Perhaps the realization that Edmond and Hélène were now solely her responsibility finally dawned on her. One thing was only too clear. She was stuck with two hungry mouths to feed. Two growing bodies to clothe. And times were bad. As a result, she began to strike out at the "cause" of her frustrations. The children.

Hélène would never forget the first time she and Edmond were subjected to Tante Janine's fury. It was on the fifteenth of May, a day that had started out smoothly enough. The afternoon sun was still shining strongly, and there was a sharp nip in the air. In the distance, Hélène could see the fishing boats bobbing out in the bay. Their bows bit into the waves and their gray patched sails billowed in the wind. Trouble seemed far away.

Instead of playing by herself, Hélène decided to help Edmond repair a section of the shattered hothouses, so they went out scavenging for pieces of broken glass. These would be cut into smaller squares, which would then be inserted into the hothouse frames. Luck was with them that afternoon. They found a large piece—big enough to cut into at least six squares. Carefully they carried it back to the nursery, and everything went fine until Edmond tried to cut it. For one reason or another, the piece splintered into shards.

Tante Janine threw a fit. Viciously her hand slashed across Edmond's face. Then she yanked his hair so hard that she tore out a fistful.

That was the beginning. For over a year, this kind of abuse continued. There was no telling what might trigger it. Edmond and Hélène were helpless. Their only relief came when Tante Janine made one of her sudden, unexplained trips to Paris. There was nothing they could do but suffer these rages in silence, and usually it was Edmond who had to take the brunt of them. Perhaps because he was the elder. Perhaps because he had the bigger appetite. Every night Hélène prayed fervently, begging God to have Maman and Papa come to rescue them from Tante Janine. But God turned a deaf ear.

Then, a year later, everything came to a head. Weeding among tiny lettuce seedlings, Hélène accidentally mistook some of them for weeds.

"Which of you idiots pulled these?" Tante Janine demanded.

"I did," Edmond lied. He knew that a beating was imminent and that his body could absorb the blows much more easily than Hélène's.

"You idiot!" Tante Janine raged. "You good-for-nothing!" She reached down, snatched up a slat of wood that was lying there, and angrily began to beat him across the back with it. Hélène screamed for her to stop it, while Edmond took the blows in silence. When it was over, he got to his feet, swayed unsteadily, and stumbled into the house.

Hélène ran after him. There were only two bedrooms. Tante Janine slept in one; they shared the other. When Hélène got upstairs, Edmond was already throwing his few belongings together.

"What are you doing?" Hélène asked in sudden panic.

He laughed mirthlessly. "What does it look like? I'm packing."

"But, Edmond!" Her voice was desperate. "Why?"

"I'm leaving, that's why! I can't stand living here any longer."

"I'm sorry, Edmond!" she pleaded. "I'll make it up to you. It was all my fault!"

He shook his head. "No, it wasn't your fault. It's that woman. She's a bitch!"

"Please don't talk like that."

Savagely he turned to her. "Well, she is! And I'm not going to stay here waiting to be beaten half to death. Anyway, I'm tired of slaving away for her."

"But where are you going to go?"

"I'm joining up with the fishing fleet. Let the old bitch look after her own stinking weeds!"

Hélène's eyes glistened with tears. "And me?" she asked softly. "What about me, Edmond?"

He came close and took her in his arms. He was wet from perspiration and smelled strongly of sweat. "Little French Girl," he said gently, "until I can arrange otherwise, you're going to have to stay here."

"But I can't!" she sobbed. "Not without you!"

"You can and must. To get away from here will take money. I swear I'll save every penny I earn. Then we can go away together." Gently he extricated himself from her and stuffed his belongings into a pillowcase. "Now, wipe your tears."

She nodded solemnly. Sniffing, she wiped her eyes. "Edmond . . ."

He looked up. "Yes?"

For a moment she didn't speak. Then she clutched him in sudden desperation. "You won't leave me here for good with her, will you?"

He looked at her. The fear and loneliness in her violet eyes tugged at his heart. "No, Little French Girl. All we have is each other. Nobody can ever separate us. Not after what we've gone through together. Neither the Boches nor that bitch can keep us apart."

Fearfully she looked up into his eyes. "And the sea?" she asked softly. "What if the sea separates us?"

Suddenly he grinned. He looked very sure of himself. "Even the sea won't be able to do that."

2

Hélène sat in the back of the classroom. Mademoiselle Gribius always put her best-behaved pupils there. This way the troublemakers would be in the front where she could keep her eye on them. The bell sounded. The girls automatically glanced toward the door. From out in the hall came the noises of slamming doors and the stampeding of feet. Restlessly they looked back at Mademoiselle. They were anxious to be dismissed. Home economics was the last class of the day.

Mademoiselle slowly got out of her chair and walked around to the front of her desk. Her hawklike eyes searched the room through the thick lenses of her eyeglasses. There was a look of approval on her thin lips. Not one girl had moved a muscle. Their eyes, yes. But that was all. They knew better. If one of them made an attempt to gather up her things before class was dismissed, they would all be kept behind for an extra five minutes.

"Ecoutez!" Mademoiselle's sharp, clipped voice carried to the back of the room.

The girls sat in tense misery, trying their best to look attentive.

Mademoiselle was not to be hurried. "By now most of you should have *some* inkling of how to sew. As you all know, there are only ten more periods of this class until the summer recess. Every year at this time it is traditional that my classes show me what they have learned."

There was a collective groan from the girls. Their faces fell. They knew what was coming. Mademoiselle's pet project.

Most of the girls hated to sew. The needles pricked their fingers, the threads got tangled, and Mademoiselle was ever unsatisfied. She complained endlessly about their buckling hems, their sloppy stitches. More often than once, each of them had experienced the humiliation of Mademoiselle's wrath: with her tiny scissors she tore out whole rows of stitches, and the tearful girl would have to start over from scratch.

Mademoiselle continued. "You are each assigned to sew a dress. The dress shall be something utilitarian. Something simple. You will design and cut out your own patterns. You will supply your own fabric. You will sew it without help. All work shall be done in this classroom. What you sew, and how well you do it, will determine your final grade." She paused. "Do I make myself clear?"

"Oui, mademoiselle," the girls chorused.

Mademoiselle raised her chin. "Girls!"

They all sat stiffly at attention.

"Class is dismissed!"

There was much scraping of chairs, a stampede out the door. On the other side of the building the boys would be waiting.

Usually Hélène was the last one out. She had nowhere to rush except home to Tante Janine. But today she sailed happily out the door with the rest of them. Her heart pounded. Of all the girls in the class, she was the only one who greeted the news of the sewing project with delight.

"What's with *her*?" Jeanne-Marie Berty asked loudly, staring after Hélène. "I've never seen her in a hurry before."

Jeanne-Marie's friend Edith Loiseau said something in a whisper, and the girls glanced at Hélène, giggling noisily.

Hélène could feel her face flushing, but she ignored them. Jeanne-Marie and Edith thought they were better than everyone else. Monsieur Berty owned a shipyard and Monsieur Loiseau was the head of the local fish cannery. They were the wealthiest families in town and the two girls were vain, stuck-up, and vicious. They got their jollies making fun of other people. Hélène always went out of her way to avoid them. But often their loud wisecracks followed her and caught her off guard.

Today she didn't care. Let them snicker, she thought. She'd show them! Her heart did another joyous leap. She had not only a talent for sewing but also a secret passion for it. Perhaps it was a legacy from Maman.

She smiled to herself. She would have ten classes—ten Saturdays—on which to work on her project. And eleven Saturdays from now was the annual Feux de St.-Jean festival. For that the townswomen would don their traditional costumes with the fantastic starched lace caps and celebrate proudly. But she? She would celebrate *beautifully*.

Hélène stopped hurrying for a moment in order to catch her breath. She leaned against a stone wall and shut her eyes. Yes, she could see it already. At the festival she would wear a beautiful dress. Something besides the humiliating hand-me-downs that Tante Janine collected from neighbors on whose children Hélène had seen the same shapeless outfits a year or two before. Yes, for once she would dazzle. She would be Cinderella, the festival her ball.

It wouldn't be difficult. She had the talent and she had a little money. For the past few years she had squirreled away a few francs that people had given her when she ran errands for them. A few francs Tante Janine didn't know about.

Hélène smiled again. On the way home she would stop at Madame Dupré's shop. Madame Dupré was the local seamstress. But she didn't only sew. She sold fabrics by the bolt or by the meter. Most of them were simple, inexpensive fabrics. But a few—ah, a few were fabulous!

And best of all, Madame Dupré had back issues of fashion magazines—copies of *Paris Vogue* and *Elle* and *L'Officiel*. Hélène would flip through them, carefully selecting a style for the dress she was going to sew.

She skipped along the steep cobblestoned streets, past the stone houses that had turned pale gray under the onslaught of the salt winds. Within a few minutes she would pass Madame Dupré's and peek in the window. And on Monday, right after school, she would march in armed with her precious francs.

3

On the following Monday, Hélène stood paralyzed in front of the door to Madame Dupré's. In the window was a breathtaking dress on a headless wooden dummy, and underneath it a photo clipped from one of the Parisian fashion magazines. Hélène saw that the dress was a copy of the one in the picture. Only the fabric was different.

She was enthralled.

Slowly she opened her hand and looked down in her palm to make certain that the money was still there. It was. Then she fortified herself with a deep breath, opened the door of the shop, and went in.

The shop was dim. Through an open door she could see the brightly lit workroom in the back. There were two girls sitting there. One was sewing meticulously by hand; the other sat facing a machine, pedaling with her feet and spinning a large wheel with one hand.

But what caught Hélène's eye was the long counter in front of her. Displayed on it were bolts of beautiful cloth. She stared at them but didn't dare touch them. One fabric in particular fascinated her. It was gray and had tiny nubs, like imperfections, scattered all over it. Instinctively she realized that they were not imperfections; they were indigenous to the fabric.

"May I help you?" a cultured voice said from behind her.

Startled, she turned around and looked up in awe. Madame Dupré herself was standing there. She was a tall, imposing woman. Hélène thought she was the most elegant woman in the world. She wore a striped silk blouse with a delicate lace bow at the collar. Her eyes were brown and gentle, her hair elegantly gray, and she smelled faintly of perfume. Next to her, Hélène felt extremely shabby and awkward. For a moment, a feeling of panic seized her. She wanted to turn and run right back out. But something gave her courage. Perhaps it was the way Madame Dupré looked at her.

"Bonjour, madame," Hélène said meekly.

"Bonjour, mademoiselle," Madame Dupré returned with extreme politeness. "May I be of assistance?"

Hélène took a deep breath and clutched her handful of francs tighter. "I would like to buy some beautiful fabric."

Madame Dupré smiled wisely. "All fabrics are beautiful," she said. "It depends on how they are sewn. What is it that you would like? I have cottons, woolens, linens, silks and satins, velvets . . ."

"Oh!" Hélène looked a bit deflated. Then she composed herself. "Something like that"—she pointed a trembling finger at the nubby gray material—"how much would that cost?"

"You have good taste, mademoiselle," Madame Dupré said with approval. "That is raw silk, from the Orient. It is the only bolt I have. It is very expensive. But oh, so fine." She looked at Hélène warmly. There was something about the way the girl took to the fabric that reminded her of herself when she was young. Having an eye for fabrics was a rare gift. And the girl had it. She smiled. "Would you like to feel it?"

Hélène's eyes lit up. "May I?"

"But of course, mademoiselle."

Madame Dupré watched Hélène as she reached out and reverently stroked the fabric. Then she held a corner of it between her fingers and caressed it. The woman nodded to herself. The girl was getting the feel.

To Hélène the cloth seemed to have a lifeblood of its own. She could feel it coursing between her fingertips. The texture was luxurious to the touch. The sheen was soft, like subtle moonlight on a tranquil sea.

"It would make a beautiful gown, n'est-ce pas?" Madame Dupré said.

Hélène was breathless. "Oh, yes! How much is it?"

"Ah." Madame Dupré looked at her shrewdly and wagged her finger. "You must not think that raw silk is all there is. The woolens are sturdy, coarse and warm, or they can be soft and subtle. The linens are crisp. The velvets are like the deep colors of the night. And the cottons are cool. Each fabric has its own personality and characteristic. You yourself must judge what fabric will suit your needs best. Royal fabrics like silk and velvet must never be used to make aprons or housedresses. But a ball gown—yes! Linens and cottons are for the summer. Woolens for the winter. There are fabrics for every season of the year. For every function in the world!"

Hélène's eyes shone with rapture. The door to a whole new world was opening before her. And she was dazzled.

There was the sound of someone coming into the shop. Madame Dupré turned around automatically. Discreetly Hélène examined a bolt of navy-blue linen, comparing its texture to the raw silk.

"Bonjour," Madame Dupré said.

"We need fabric," an all-too-familiar voice said loudly.

"Yes, something simply extravagant!" a second voice chimed in.

"For mademoiselle's annual sewing project, no doubt," Madame Dupré said dryly.

"Oui." Suddenly there was a shriek. "Jeanne-Marie! Look who got here ahead of us!"

Hélène glanced sideways at Edith and Jeanne-Marie. The two girls put their heads together and started whispering and giggling. Hélène clenched her fists. It was as if a dark cloud blotted out the sunshine. Those two malicious creatures didn't deserve to be here, she thought. Not among all these bolts of beautiful cloth.

Edith looked at Hélène. "Which fabric are you going to buy?" she called over.

"I . . . I don't know yet," Hélène murmured.

The girls whispered and giggled again. Madame Dupré glanced at them sternly. She felt sorry for Hélène, but she didn't dare chase the two other girls out. Their mothers were her best customers; most of their dresses were sewn at the shop. That was how Madame Dupré really made her money. Selling fabric was only a sideline. No, to chase them out was impossible, but she would try to get rid of them quickly.

"Could you excuse me for a moment?" she asked Hélène.

Hélène nodded and withdrew to a corner. Silently she stood there and waited. She watched in horror as Edith immediately homed in on a bolt of bottle-green velvet, pawing it like a bundle of rags. Jeanne-Marie was in no hurry. Slowly she examined each bolt, all the while watching Hélène out of the corner of her eye. When she reached the gray raw silk, she saw Hélène stiffen.

Jeanne-Marie smiled triumphantly and looked up at

Madame Dupré. "I'll take six meters of this," she said sweetly.

Hélène's heart sank. In panic she looked pleadingly at Madame Dupré.

The woman looked at her stoically. Then she turned to Jeanne-Marie. "That's a very expensive fabric," she told her. "Perhaps—"

"The cost doesn't matter," Jeanne-Marie said firmly. "Maman said I was to choose whatever I want. You're to put it on her bill."

"Very well," Madame Dupré said with a sigh. The sight of Hélène tugged at her heart. The girl stood trembling in the corner, clutching her coins pathetically.

A few minutes later the two girls left, their noses in the air. Their fabrics were wrapped up in brown paper parcels and tucked under their arms. They were chattering happily, grandiosely planning their dresses. Edith had the bottle-green velvet; Jeanne-Marie walked away with the raw silk.

"I thought those two would never leave," Madame Dupré murmured wearily after the door closed behind them. "Ill-mannered girls! What they both need is a good spanking!" Then she turned to Hélène. "Now, mademoiselle," she said gently, "let me teach you something."

Hélène didn't speak. She remained in the corner, staring up at her. There was deep hurt in her eyes.

"Come, come," the woman said knowingly. "This is not as tragic as you think. The raw silk and the velvet are all wrong. They are not for dresses. They are for gowns or beautiful suits. And gray does not become Mademoiselle Berty at all. Not with her terrible pallor. It will make her look all washed out. Neither does green suit the other one. Her skin is much too dark."

Hélène nodded slowly. She thought she understood what Madame Dupré was trying to say. "But . . . it's just . . ."

"Never mind, my dear." Madame Dupré made a gesture that looked as if she were waving away an irritating fly. "Let them make fools of themselves. They have no taste. You are smarter, non?"

Hélène gave a tentative nod. She felt a little better. Not much, but enough. Still, the excitement was gone from her eyes. Her pleasure had turned sour.

Madame Dupré touched Hélène on the shoulder. "Fortunately I have no fittings scheduled this afternoon. Come upstairs to my apartment with me. We will have some tea and I will teach you a lesson that you should never forget. Danielle!"

The sewing machine in the back of the shop stopped chattering. The skinny girl who operated it came out front. "Madame?"

"I am going upstairs, Danielle. You're in charge of the shop while I am gone."

Hélène looked up at the elegant wall clock. It was three o'clock. They had been talking for almost two hours.

Madame Dupré rose from her chintz-upholstered chair. "That's enough of a lesson for one day," she said, smoothing her skirt. "Now, go home and digest what you have learned. Don't forget what I told you—that there are two approaches to design. The first?" She looked questioningly at Hélène.

Hélène took a deep breath. "Designing the pattern and then finding a fabric to suit it."

"Bon. And the second?"

"Designing the dress around the fabric."

"Correct. And which will you do?"

Hélène did not hesitate. "I shall design a dress that will look good on me. Then I'll use whatever fabric best suits it *and* me."

Madame Dupré looked at her with respect. The girl learned fast. With the right tutoring, she might even get someplace.

4

It was ten Saturdays later that Mademoiselle Gribius came around from behind her desk. She clapped her hands sharply, bringing the class to order.

The girls sat erect, nervously looking up at her. On the table in front of each of them was a neatly folded garment.

Mademoiselle cleared her throat. Her face was impenetrable and her voice was emotionless and dry. "As you all know, this is the last class until September. I have tried to teach you well. Now we shall see what you have absorbed during the past year."

She was silent for a moment. Her sharp eyes swept through the room. "You will all change into the outfits you have sewn. You will remain dressed in them for the remainder of the day. However, you will not wear them home. Upon dismissal you will change back into your school uniforms."

She frowned. "I think this is prudent, since it will spare you much embarrassment. I have been watching you while you were sewing, and it saddens me to realize how little some of you have learned. I do not think your parents would appreciate the humiliation of your looking like clowns on the way home."

She paused. "All right, girls! Change into your dresses!"

Hélène's heart began to hammer. She took a deep breath. Slowly she reached for her dress and began unfolding it. For a moment, the rest of the class slipped out of her consciousness. All she had eyes for was her new dress.

During the past ten weeks, Mademoiselle had indeed kept her eye on the girls' progress. However, she offered no advice or comments. No approval or disapproval. Not one girl knew what she thought. Mademoiselle never smiled. Her stern face gave nothing away.

Edith had the most trouble. Her constant "ouches" and muttered curses were greeted with muffled giggles from the rest of the class. She found it very difficult to sew and drape the green velvet. The fabric was thick and difficult to handle. Somehow or other, it got so much wear and tear that the nap was already beginning to wear off in a lot of places. Each Saturday, Edith was ready to burst into tears.

Jeanne-Marie had no fewer problems, but she attacked them with gusto, if only to spare herself ridicule. Each time she stuck herself with her needle she refrained from cursing or crying out. But her sharp intakes of breath were enough. The hisses carried to the back of the classroom. She was discovering—too late—that the raw silk she had bought out from under Hélène was no easier to sew than the velvet, for silk has its own characteristics. It "crawls" right out from under the needle. A beautifully fluid fabric, it also tends to show off flaws in workmanship more easily than "everyday" cloths such as cotton or linen.

Adding to their misery were their designs. Mademoiselle's instructions for a "simple" dress were interpreted differently by each girl. But no interpretations were as ambitious—or bizarre—as Edith's and Jeanne-Marie's. Clearly both of them got carried away. They tried to create updates of lavish eighteenth-century court dresses. This process required repeated visits to Madame Dupré's. Almost daily they bought multicolored ribbons and frothy white or gold lace. Each time they saw a new item, they would pounce on it. Madame Dupré was no help. Knowing that they would return, she shrewdly put all her ribbons, laces, and bows out on display. It was too much for Edith and Jeanne-Marie. They knew no restraint. They had to have everything. And everything was destined to go on their dresses.

Hélène was grateful for Madame Dupré's tutelage. She took what she'd learned to heart and designed the simplest dress imaginable. She had gotten the idea for it from a picture she saw in *L'Officiel*. It had an unadorned bodice and a modest skirt and was supposed to be the latest rage in Paris. The sleeves were short, and the neckline, although low, was not low enough to be scandalous. For fabric, she'd chosen a lightweight cotton that was itself simple and easy to work with. The rich shade of burgundy would go dramatically with her raven hair. For adornment she sewed a belt out of the same fabric and used the beautiful buckle Madame Dupré had given her as a gift.

The pure simplicity of the dress gave it its elegance.

Slowly the girls began to change into their dresses. Most of them did it with trepidation.

"Hurry up!" Mademoiselle snapped. "We haven't got all day."

Unhappily, they hurried. Then Mademoiselle instructed them to walk around the room one by one. When they reached the front of her desk, they had to do a pirouette before returning to their seats. The girls sitting up front went first.

When Edith got up, a burst of laughter reverberated through the room. She stood there blushing helplessly. Her dress was a disaster. One sleeve was longer and fuller than the other, the hemline was crooked, and she'd pleated so much velvet at the waist that it made her look pregnant. All the trimmings she had applied were a horror. It looked as though a dozen bakers—none of them talented—had frosted the same cake over and over. Even Jeanne-Marie couldn't help giggling. But the laughter soon died in her throat. She was next.

Slowly Jeanne-Marie got to her feet. For once her poise and assurance deserted her. She walked meekly around the room. From a distance the raw silk did not look too bad. Close up, it was a nightmare of loose threads, bunched-up fabric, and sloppy seams. There was something so pathetic about her serious demeanor that no one laughed. But when she did her pirouette, everyone noticed something odd about her back. The dress buckled terribly, making her look hunchbacked. The class erupted in gales of laughter. Even Mademoiselle's lips held the hint of a smile.

Hélène was last. When Mademoiselle called out her name, a feeling of dread passed through her. She froze. Heads turned, looking back at her. Mademoiselle called her again. She forced herself to get up.

She walked slowly, self-consciously. Every step was an effort, and she felt as if her feet didn't belong to her. She held herself stiffly and her hands were clenched awkwardly. She could feel the perspiration breaking out on her forehead and under her arms. She kept thinking: This dress is new and now I'm going to soil the armpits.

When she finally reached the front of the room, she stood there while insecurity bombarded her. Her temples were throbbing.

Finally she did her pirouette. The girls gaped at her. Their mouths hung open. A sudden, spontaneous "ah" filled the classroom. It was a moment before she realized what it meant. Slowly her eyes began to glow with pride. Her dress was a success.

For the first time she was drunk with excitement.

She had found her métier. Fashion.

5

When school was dismissed, the girls all clustered around Hélène. They wanted to know about the dress, begged to have a close look at it, asked a million questions. Where did she get the idea for it? How could such a common fabric look so beautiful? How could such a simple cut be so dazzling?

Hélène had never been happier. Suddenly she found herself in the midst of an admiring crowd. The dress had shot her to popularity. Even Edith and Jeanne-Marie grudgingly came over.

Jeanne-Marie looked hesitantly at Hélène. "Could you design and sew a dress for me?" she asked. "For money, of course."

Hélène had never felt the warmth of adulation before. Tante Janine kept her from making friends by clamping down on her socializing. There was Mass to attend, the nursery to be worked in. There was time for nothing else. But now she basked in the sweetness of acceptance.

When Hélène came out of the big school door, she squinted in the sunlight. She was clutching the string bag in which she carried the dress. She was still surrounded by the chattering girls.

Suddenly a deep voice whispered into her ear from behind. "Hello, Little French Girl."

Hélène spun around. Edmond was standing there, his grin white against his deeply tanned face. His smile was marred only by the two missing top teeth which had been knocked out so long ago by the recoil of a rifle in Paris. For a moment she just looked at him. Then she flung her arms around him, and effortlessly he lifted her high into the air. "Edmond!" she shrieked. "Oh, Edmond!"

The fishing fleet had just come in. He hadn't bothered to take the time to wash up. His cheeks felt scratchy from his beard. He stank of fish. But she didn't care. At the moment it was the best smell in the world.

When he finally put her down, she looked proudly up at him. It had been almost two months since she'd seen him last. His chin looked stronger, and he seemed to have grown taller. He looked more ruggedly handsome than ever. His shoulders were broader. There was a weather-beaten, outdoor quality about him. The manual labor was packing hard muscle onto his body. She could feel it through his shirt.

Suddenly she put her face against his chest and started to cry.

He looked down at her in surprise. "What's the matter?" he asked softly.

She smiled through her tears. "I know it sounds silly. But . . . oh, Edmond, Edmond! I'm so happy to see you." She sniffed and wiped her eyes.

He grinned widely. "Tell you what. I just got paid. Come on, I'll buy you a meal in the best restaurant in town. I'll eat anything as long as it's not fish. And we can have a long talk."

"Don't you want to come . . . home with me? We can talk there."

His expression darkened and he shook his head. "No!" he said vehemently. "I don't want to see that bitch."

She nodded soberly. His attitude hadn't softened. He still didn't want to see Tante Janine, didn't care if he never saw her again. When he was in port he rented a room in a boardinghouse near the waterfront.

They walked in silence for a while. Then he took her hand suddenly. "I've got ten days' leave till we go back out to sea."

She smiled contentedly. "Then you're going to take me to the Feux de St.-Jean festival?"

"You bet. You'll be the second-prettiest girl there."

She stopped walking. She stared at him dumbly. "Second!" she said bewilderingly. "Who's the first?"

"Someone you'll meet at the restaurant."

Suddenly a strange fear passed through her. "Is . . . is it a . . . a girlfriend?" she asked weakly.

He nodded slowly. "I met her last time we were in port." He saw the look of pain in her eyes. "Oh, come on. Jeanne is special. But she can never take your place." He smiled. "You're my Little French Girl."

She smiled back, but her smile was tight. Some of her happiness had died. She wasn't the only girl in his life any longer. He had a girlfriend. She had wondered how long it would take. He was too handsome not to have one. No, she hadn't wondered. She had worried.

Suddenly she knew what she felt. Jealousy.

The restaurant was called Au Petit Caporal. Hélène had passed it often but she'd never been inside. They had to go down two steps from the sidewalk and pass through an old but clean kitchen to the dining room in the back. It was almost empty. It had a low vaulted ceiling, white stone walls, and a flagstone floor.

They sat down on cane chairs at a round table covered with a checkered tablecloth. Beside them was a small window. Geraniums grew in the flower boxes, and beyond that were rows of moored fishing boats. The sunlight reflected the squirming water on their hulls.

Hélène recognized Edmond's girlfriend instantly: she could tell by the way the young waitress looked at him. Hélène stared at her disapprovingly, comparing the girl's looks with her own. She was Edmond's age, almost eighteen. Her hair was brown, almost mousy, but her face was kind and her brown eyes were soulfully gentle. She looked very pretty when she smiled.

Edmond got to his feet and kissed her cheek. Once again Hélène could feel a stab of jealousy. She looked away.

"Hello, Jeanne," she heard him say. There was a peculiar warmth in his voice that she had never heard before. "This is my sister, Hélène. Hélène, my . . . Jeanne."

Hélène looked up. "Hello," she said awkwardly.

Jeanne smiled. "How do you do," she said warmly. She sensed that Hélène felt threatened by her presence. She pulled up a chair and sat down. Then she reached out, took Hélène's hand, and looked earnestly into her eyes. "I like Edmond very much," she said honestly. "And I know how much you love him. He's told me. If you'll let me, I . . . I want us to be close friends."

Somehow Hélène felt immediately better. She looked at Jeanne with respect. "I would like that," she said. "I've never had a good friend before."

The day of the Feux de St.-Jean festival dawned warm and clear. The sun shone brilliantly and there wasn't a cloud in

162

the sky. Tante Janine even closed down the nursery for the festivities.

Early in the morning, Hélène filled the big kitchen pots with water and put them on the stove. When it boiled, she washed herself carefully, scrubbing the gardening earth out from beneath her fingernails, shampooing her hair and combing it out. She took infinite care with her appearance. Today she would wear her new dress. She hadn't shown it to anyone yet. Not Tante Janine, Madame Dupré, or Edmond. She would surprise them all! Especially Edmond. He and Jeanne would be waiting for her outside the nursery gate at exactly twelve o'clock.

"It's time you got dressed," Tante Janine snapped at eleven-thirty. She was already wearing her long traditional black dress with the white lace collar. Her gray braid was wrapped around her head and the high, stiffly starched lace cap was pinned to it. It made her look somehow invincible, bigger than life.

Hélène nodded obediently and went upstairs to her bedroom. She wasn't about to tell Tante Janine that she was planning to leave without her. Nor did she dare mention Edmond's name. Tante Janine would fly into one of her rages.

No, Hélène had a better plan. When her back was turned, she'd simply slip out of the house.

She dressed carefully. The burgundy cotton felt good and new against her clean skin. She had gotten up in the middle of the night, heated a brick in the oven, and put it inside the iron. Then she had surreptitiously pressed the dress. It didn't have a single crease or wrinkle.

Happily she did a pirouette, watching the fabric swirl around her hips. She wished she had a mirror so she could see what she looked like. But Tante Janine didn't believe in mirrors. They were a sign of weakness. Of vanity.

She parted the flimsy curtains and looked down. She could already see Edmond and Jeanne waiting for her at the gate. Edmond was leaning against one of the posts, smoking a cigarette. She waved to him. He saw her and waved back.

Quickly she smoothed the dress, ran a hand through her hair, and opened the door a crack. Tante Janine was nowhere in sight. She took a deep breath. Quietly, gritting her teeth against each creaky step, she descended to the kitchen.

Hélène had never looked lovelier. The dress seemed to

163

have a life of its own. It even made her skin tone look warmer. In the excitement of the occasion, her violet eyes glittered like jewels. She felt truly beautiful.

She tiptoed across the room to the door. When her hand touched the handle, a staccato voice froze her in her tracks. "Where do you think you're going!"

Hélène turned around slowly. Tante Janine was standing near the wardrobe. Her eyes were wide and her hands rested on her gaunt hips.

Hélène gestured to the door. "Edmond is waiting for me at the gate."

Tante Janine approached her with the crafty stealth of a spider. "Running out to see your brother, are you?" she spat contemptuously.

"Yes," Hélène said coldly.

Tante Janine laughed shrilly. "All dolled up, too." Then her lip curled. "Where did you get that dress?"

"I made it."

"Don't lie to me!"

"I did make it! It was Mademoiselle's year-end project."

"And the fabric? Where did you get that sinful color? Red is the color of the devil!"

"It's not sinful!" Hélène said. "Even the Abbé wears red robes sometimes!"

Suddenly Tante Janine flew at her. "You wicked, cursed beast! How dare you equate that lascivious garment with the Holy Church!" Her hand slashed out to slap Hélène, but Hélène effectively blocked it with her forearm. Tante Janine sucked in her breath in pain. Then suddenly she grabbed hold of the bodice of Hélène's dress. She jerked downward with all the strength her bony fingers could summon.

There was a terrible ripping sound as the bodice tore. Hélène let out a cry and looked down in despair. Her dress—her dazzling Cinderella dress—was ruined! The bodice hung in shreds around her waist. Her white slip was all that covered her small breasts.

"I hate you!" Hélène cried out. "I despise you!"

"Get dressed into something decent," Tante Janine snapped. "You're going to confession."

"I am not," Hélène said quietly. Then she drew herself up. Her eyes flashed. "I'll tell the Abbé what a wicked woman you are! How you . . . you . . ." Hélène lifted up the sagging bodice and smiled suddenly. "How you attacked me so that you could see me naked!"

"You wouldn't dare tell a lie like that!" Tante Janine whispered. "God would punish you like he punishes all sinners! You'll see!" Then she turned, her black dress rustling as she stormed out the door.

6

Summer passed, autumn came, and winter followed. Then once again the seasons slipped into their perpetual cycles. Spring, summer, autumn, winter. On the sixth of January 1952, Hélène turned fifteen. She was invited to spend the Sunday afternoon with Edmond and Jeanne.

When she arrived at Jeanne's gray apartment house, Jeanne answered the door. "Hello." She smiled. "Edmond's here already. Come in."

Hélène was led to the familiar kitchen. It was off the narrow hallway, separated by a door that had wavy, opaque panels of glass set into it. Edmond was sitting at the table. When Hélène came in he got up and kissed her.

"Now my two favorite girls are here," he said, smiling.

Hélène slid down beside him on the wooden banquette while Jeanne crossed the room and disappeared into the pantry. She came out holding a bottle of white wine. She took three glasses from the credence. Carefully she filled them and set one down in front of each of them. Then she slipped into the banquette on Edmond's other side. She raised her glass. "To Hélène," she announced. "Who in another year will be graduated from school."

Edmond raised his glass. "À votre santé," he said.

Hélène smiled. "À votre santé."

By the time she sipped her second glass of wine, Hélène felt a warm glow settle over her. The wine made her relaxed and content. Her favorite hours were those idly spent in this little apartment that Jeanne's mother had "inherited" after her grandmother died. It was cozy, warm, and cheerful. Edmond still rented his room at the boardinghouse whenever he was in port. But he spent most of his days here, going back to his room only at night.

For a while they exchanged small talk and gossip. Then Jeanne took Edmond's hand. Her face was serious as she looked at Hélène. "We have something to tell you," she said hesitantly. She glanced at Edmond and squeezed his hand, signaling for him to do the talking.

He nodded and she looked away. "Jeanne and I . . ." He paused and took a deep breath, his brown eyes flickering nervously. "We're going to get married."

For a brief moment Hélène stared at them openmouthed while she let the news sink in. When it did, she jumped to her feet. Her heart thumped and she was beaming. She bent down, grabbed hold of Edmond, and hugged him tightly. He looked up at her with surprise. Then she rushed around the table and hugged Jeanne. "Congratulations!" she cried with excitement. "When's the big day? Did you set a date? Just think!" She shook her head unbelievingly. "I'll have a sister-in-law! My present to you will be the wedding gown," she announced. "I will sew it myself!"

"Would you?" Jeanne looked pleased.

Hélène lifted her glass. "I propose a toast," she said.

Edmond and Jeanne reached for their glasses, and a blush came to Hélène's face. It was the first time she had ever proposed a toast.

"To my brother and sister-in-law," she said quietly. "Both of whom I love dearly."

She walked back to Tante Janine's alone. The town was quiet and there was no traffic on the dirt road that led to the nursery. The sky had grown dark and the fog rolled heavily along the ground. The wind had picked up. Icy gusts tugged at her clothes, but she didn't seem to notice. Her mind was in another world. The world of fashion. Of Paris. Of magazines.

Yes, when she graduated from school she would immediately get a job and scrimp and save; when she'd saved up enough, she would buy a one-way ticket to Paris. That was where fashion reigned supreme. Once there, she would be able to start along the road that would lead to the fulfillment of her dream. Her glossy dream. Her magazine. A magazine more beautiful than all the others she had looked through at

Madame Dupré's. More beautiful even than *Elle*. More glamorous than *L'Officiel*. More powerful than *Vogue*. The thought of it made her drunk with excitement. She loved designing and sewing dresses. But she didn't want to do that. She had talent, true, but she also instinctively knew that she didn't have *enough*. Not to compete with such geniuses as Madame Grès and Christian Dior and Hubert de Givenchy. Her talent lay elsewhere. In recognizing fine things. Fine fabrics. Fine jewelry. Fine design. She had what Madame Dupré called an "eye."

When she got to the house the lights were glowing weakly in the ground-floor windows. Now that she'd have to face Tante Janine her dreams evaporated. With this return to reality came the sudden knowledge that it was very cold, and she shivered.

She found Tante Janine sitting in the kitchen with a visitor. She recognized the man instantly. He was an unemployed riveter who had worked in the shipyard and now spent most of his time frequenting the waterfront taverns. Hélène didn't like him one bit. He was tall, dark-haired, dark-eyed, and had a crafty look. Several times when she'd passed him on the street he had directed lewd remarks at her. His name was Pierre Péguy.

"Come here, Hélène," Tante Janine said sternly.

Dutifully Hélène crossed the room toward the table.

"Sit down." With her bony hand Tante Janine indicated an empty chair.

Hélène was suspicious of this sudden hospitality. It was the first time Tante Janine had ever asked her to sit and join her. Slowly she pulled out the rickety wooden chair and sat down stiffly.

Tante Janine looked at her expressionlessly. "I think it is only fair that you should know something," she said in a flat voice. Her dark eyes glanced at the man beside her. "Monsieur Péguy has asked me to marry him."

Hélène was staggered. Her mouth hung open as she stared at Tante Janine, then at Pierre, then back at Tante Janine. Her mind was reeling. Tante Janine marrying? And a penniless, drunken dockworker for a bridegroom? Surely this was a bad joke! She looked deep into Tante Janine's eyes. No, this was no joke.

"I have given Monsieur Péguy my answer," Tante Janine said. "I have accepted his proposal."

Hélène looked at her in horror. Abruptly she got to her feet.

"Where are you going?" Tante Janine demanded. "I haven't dismissed you yet."

"I . . . I don't feel well, Tante Janine," she stammered.

She started to leave the room. In her hurry she overturned her chair. It fell on its side with a clatter. Quickly she bent over and righted it. When she rose, her eyes met Pierre's. He had been staring at her derrière. She shivered. She didn't like the look in his eyes.

It was the same look the Boche had given Catherine.

Hélène awoke sometime during the night of Tante Janine's marriage. The room was dark. Pierre and Tante Janine were still up. She could hear mumbled snatches of their conversation coming from the next room. She frowned sleepily. Somehow it did not sound like the type of things that were said on a wedding night.

"Of course there's a house," Tante Janine was saying.

"You're sure . . . this?" Pierre asked.

"Absolutely. In Mont . . ."

The conversation was lost on Hélène. They were talking about a house in Mont Something-or-other. Montluçon? Montlivault? She yawned and dismissed it from her mind. A moment later she turned over. She was fast asleep again.

When she awakened in the morning the sun shone brightly through the window. She sat up, yawned noisily, and stretched. Then quickly she got dressed and went downstairs. She paused at the foot of the stairs and looked around the kitchen. Pierre was sitting hunched over the table, sipping steaming coffee out of a big enamel mug. Monsieur Champagne, the cat, sat alertly on a cold portion of the big stove, intently watching Tante Janine scrambling eggs, his pink nose sniffing the air. The kitchen smelled deliciously of frying ham.

Hélène's mouth watered. Perhaps marriage had softened Tante Janine, she thought hopefully. She had certainly never cooked such lavish breakfasts before. Usually there was only bread, accompanied by the weak coffee into which they dipped pieces of it. Or, in especially cold weather, hot oatmeal. But today even the coffee smelled strong and delicious.

"Bonjour," Hélène said. She covered her mouth to stifle a yawn. "It smells good."

Tante Janine grunted but didn't turn around.

Hélène went over to the table and pulled out a chair. As she sat down, she stubbed her toe on something. She looked under the table. It was a suitcase. "Is someone traveling?" she asked in a surprised voice.

Pierre looked up at her for a long moment. "I am," he said hoarsely. Then his eyes fell back to his coffee.

"Where are you going?"

"Paris."

"Paris!" Hélène's eyes lit up.

"That's enough!" Tante Janine snapped. She turned around from the stove and flashed Pierre an angry look. "It's none of the girl's business!"

He shrugged and sipped noisily at his coffee. A moment later, Tante Janine put an enamel plate down in front of him. On it were eggs and ham and bread. Greedily he picked up his fork and began to eat.

"You get yours later," Tante Janine told Hélène. "He's got a train to catch."

Pierre returned from Paris on the afternoon train eight days later. Hélène and Tante Janine were hoeing the ground near the gate when a car pulled up. They stopped working and watched as Pierre stumbled out, paid the driver, and unsteadily lugged his suitcase toward the house.

Tante Janine sensed that something was wrong. Stiffly she put down her hoe and wiped a strand of hair away from her eyes. Then she walked up to him and gripped his arm. "Why didn't you walk from the station?" she hissed.

He looked at her with puffy red eyes. "I didn't feel like it," he growled. He laughed when he saw her expression. "Don't worry! We can afford it. We're rich now!"

"You've been drinking!" she accused contemptuously. "I should never have allowed you to go by yourself!"

He jerked his arm free from her grip. "Leave me alone, woman!" he growled.

Tante Janine glowered at him. "How dare you speak to me like that!" For the first time she noticed his clothes. "That suit!" she shrieked. "Where did you get it?"

"I bought it."

"In Paris, no doubt." She drew herself up. "That sinful city! Thank God, now that the house is gone there's no more need to go there!"

Hélène frowned. House gone? In Paris? What house?

Suddenly it dawned on her. There was only one house she knew of in Paris. A shudder passed through her. Not Maman's house, she thought. Oh, God, no! Not the house in . . . Montmartre! Suddenly she remembered the conversation she'd overheard the night of Tante Janine's wedding. The "Mont" meant Montmartre, of course! Why hadn't she thought of it? She closed her eyes. That was the house, all right. She could still see it in her mind. The canary-yellow door and the curlicued window bars and the white domes of Sacré Coeur rising in the distance. The little park across the street. Oh, God, no. She had never given any thought as to whether Maman had rented or owned it.

Another wave of dread passed through her. If it had been owned, it would have been hers! And Edmond's! A place where she could have lived in Paris! Why hadn't she thought of it before? Perhaps she'd blocked the house from her memory because of the bad things that had happened there.

Slowly she approached Tante Janine and Pierre. "What are you talking about?" she asked in a whisper.

Tante Janine glowered at her. "It is none of your business! Get back to work!"

Hélène stood her ground. "It was Maman's house, wasn't it?" she said with sudden knowledge.

Tante Janine looked away. "What if it was?"

"You had no right to sell it!" Hélène cried. "It belonged to Edmond and me!"

Tante Janine whirled around and stabbed a finger at her. "You ungrateful child! Who took care of you for all these years! Who fed you and clothed you? Who took you in?"

Yes, Hélène thought dully. Who indeed? Who went around collecting castoff clothes for her? Who fed her the cheapest, starchiest foods money could buy? Who made her slave away in the nursery? Who indeed?

"Edmond's not going to like this," Hélène said between clenched teeth.

"Is that supposed to frighten me?" Tante Janine asked shrilly.

"Who's Edmond?" Pierre asked drunkenly.

Tante Janine glared at him. "Her brother."

"Yes," Hélène said. "My brother. Tante Janine knows what he's capable of. Don't you, Tante Janine?" Hélène looked at her tauntingly. "When he was eleven he murdered

170

the Boche who raped Catherine! I wonder what he'll do to
the thieves who stole Maman's house."

Pierre's eyes flashed and dimmed.

"I don't want to hear any more!" Tante Janine snapped in
a wavering voice. "Get back to work!"

7

Hélène felt Jeanne's hand on her arm. She turned and looked
at her future sister-in-law. Jeanne's eyes were reassuring and
her gentle touch gave Hélène courage. Together they went
into Monsieur Lefèvre's dim, musty-smelling office.

Hélène was nervous. She had been to the lawyer's only
once before. That must have been more than six years ago.
She could still remember the day. Tante Janine had made
sure that she and Edmond were scrubbed pink and clean, and
then she dressed them in their Sunday clothes. Even then, this
office had smelled musty and oppressive. But what she
remembered most was that an interminably long and boring
discussion that she couldn't understand had taken place. It
seemed that she and Edmond had to sit stiffly for hours,
well-behaved and confused, while vague things about their future were being discussed. Hélène remembered that her legs
hadn't quite touched the floor when she sat in the chair.

Now she was back in this office because she had told
Jeanne about Maman's house having been sold out from under them.

Monsieur Lefèvre heard the complaints, pursed his pink
lips, and went over to an old wooden filing cabinet. Slowly he
dug through a stuffed drawer. Finally he pulled out a worn
folder. "Here it is," he said. "Junot, Edmond and Hélène."
He went around behind his desk, sat down, and slowly
flipped through the pages, humming softly to himself as he
read.

Hélène glanced at Jeanne. Jeanne nodded and smiled encouragingly.

Monsieur Lefèvre finally closed the file, folded his fat hands on the desktop, and looked at Hélène. "The paperwork was filed between 1945 and 1946. In April 1946 your aunt, Janine Junot, filed for formal adoption of you and your brother. For some reason or other, she never followed through with it. She was, however, appointed your legal guardian."

"Which means?"

"Which means, quite simply, that she was considered legally fit and competent for raising you and your brother and looking out for your best interests."

Hélène leaned forward suddenly. "Tell me, Monsieur Lefèvre," she said in an oddly quiet voice. "Was the adoption procedure abandoned before she was appointed our guardian or after?"

He looked at her with respect. She certainly caught on fast. "After," he replied.

Hélène nodded slowly. So Tante Janine had been ready to adopt her and Edmond until she found out that it wasn't really necessary. She'd have complete control over them anyway.

"What about the property my father and mother owned?" Hélène asked. "Is Tante Janine free to dispose of it?"

"Property such as what?"

"There was a house in Paris. Tante Janine and my . . ."—Hélène swallowed—"my new uncle just sold it. Don't my brother and I have any claim to it?"

The lawyer sighed heavily. "I'm afraid not. You see, your aunt was placed in a position of trust. As long as it is related to your welfare, any decisions regarding you and your property can be made as she sees fit until you are twenty-one."

As the weeks wore on, Hélène found excuses to spend less and less time at home. Pierre's drunkenness—worse since the sale of Maman's house—had made life there increasingly unpleasant for her. For days at a time Pierre would go off on drunken binges or sit sullenly in the kitchen with his bottles of wine. Tante Janine would stare venomously at her husband, but instead of doing something about it, she let her anger fester. When it exploded, it was vented on Hélène.

Hélène retaliated by purposely flunking a series of mathematics and history exams. As usual, this ensured her staying late after school. Then, defying Tante Janine's orders to head straight home, she would go to Jeanne's apartment and wait there until Jeanne got home from work.

A close friendship had developed between the two young women. Jeanne was the first real friend Hélène had ever known. She helped Hélène to open up, to gain self-confidence, and it was from Jeanne that Hélène learned about the intricacies of womanhood. Like an older sister, Jeanne was always there when she was needed. And she was needed more and more as Hélène's home situation deteriorated.

"Where is Tante Janine?" Hélène asked. Pierre was sitting alone in the kitchen with a half-empty bottle of wine in front of him.

He took a swig out of the bottle and laughed. "Out," he said drunkenly. He staggered to his feet and came toward her. She drew back. His hot breath smelled sour from the wine, he hadn't shaved, and his face was purplish-red. "You're sort of pretty, you know," he said, lurching forward.

Adroitly Hélène sidestepped him and he stumbled against the table.

"I can make you feel real good," he whispered. "You got meat on you. Not like that bag of bones I married."

"Stop it!" Hélène whispered. She was becoming frightened. "Stop it!"

He leered at her. "Don't you want to feel good? Pierre knows how to make a woman feel like a woman!"

Hélène turned to go upstairs, but he caught her arm and pulled her toward him. Suddenly he pressed his scratchy face against hers, sloppily trying to kiss her. His mouth missed her lips and he ended up kissing her nose. She grimaced and pushed him away. With her sleeve she wiped his saliva off her face. "You pig!" she hissed. "If you ever touch me again, you're finished! I'll tell Tante Janine and she'll throw you out of the house!"

He laughed. "No she won't!" he cackled. He looked at her craftily. "She'll blame you! I'll tell her that you led me on."

Suddenly she was furious. Without warning she slapped him across the face. "You wouldn't dare!" Then she turned and ran upstairs. But even when she closed the door of her room she could still hear his drunken laugh.

That night she wedged her chair against the door handle before going to sleep. It wouldn't keep him out, but if he tried to come in, it would fall over. The noise would wake her. At least she would be warned.

Despite her preparation, she lay awake for hours, expecting to see the door handle moving in the pale moonlight that filtered in through the thin curtains. Finally she decided that he must have passed out in the kitchen, and she allowed herself to fall asleep. It was an uneasy sleep. She kept waking up, expecting to find him standing at the foot of the bed. But he didn't try to come into her room that night. When she was awakened in the morning, it was by a different sound. The cacophony of trucks.

Curious, she got out of bed, found her slippers, and went over to the window. She pushed the curtains aside, swung the window wide, and leaned out. The morning air felt brisk and cool. She watched as a small convoy of construction vehicles ground to a halt outside the nursery gate. She counted a bulldozer, a big cement-mixing machine on a flatbed truck, and two dump trucks. The big engines idled noisily and the air was filled with the odor of gasoline.

She leaned farther out to get a better view. Men were jumping down off the vehicles. Then she saw Tante Janine striding purposefully toward the gate. She was pointing to the left and the right, shouting instructions Hélène couldn't hear over the din of the idling motors.

Quickly she closed the window, got dressed, moved the chair away from the door, and ran down the stairs two at a time. A few seconds later she was outside. She found Tante Janine standing in the midst of a group of workmen. Hélène went over to her and touched her arm. "What's going on?" she asked.

Tante Janine looked at her with irritation. "They're going to do some work around here," she said tersely. Then she went on talking to the men.

Hélène then wandered around trying to piece together bits of information she overheard. She had no idea what—or how much—work was going to be done. Not until she stopped to listen to two of the men.

One of them was lighting a cigarette. "She bought two hectares of adjoining land," he said as he extinguished the match by waving it in the air. "All with cash. I know because my sister sold it to her."

The other one was impressed. He let out a whistle. "What did she do? Win the lottery?"

"Either that or she robbed a bank." He laughed at his own joke. "She's got fifteen giant hothouses going up."

Hélène stood there with a stunned expression on her face. She couldn't believe what she had just overheard. Suddenly she turned and ran into the house.

Tante Janine was expanding the nursery. Hélène didn't need to ask where the money had come from. She already knew.

From the sale of Maman's house.

She knew if she stayed with Tante Janine much longer she would go crazy. She had to get out. The time had come to break free. She would go see Madame Dupré the next day.

8

"Bonjour, madame," Hélène said politely.

Madame Dupré came around from behind the counter and smiled warmly. "It's a pleasure to see you again. It has been too long."

Hélène nodded. "I was afraid of bothering you, madame."

"Nonsense!" Madame Dupré said reprovingly. "You are never a bother. You should know better!"

For the first time, Madame Dupré looked closely at Hélène. The girl had changed, she suddenly realized. She had grown taller. But that wasn't all. She looked older. And she was certainly turning into a remarkable-looking young woman. Especially with those eyes. Strange, she'd never really noticed how vividly violet they were. All Hélène needed to do was lose some of her baby fat.

"I beg your pardon?" Madame Dupré said. "My mind was wandering." She smiled apologetically at Hélène. "I must be getting senile."

Hélène swallowed nervously, her throat tight and dry. "I was asking . . ." Suddenly she seemed to have lost her voice. Somehow she felt undignified, like a beggar. "A job, Madame Dupré!" she finally blurted out desperately.

Madame Dupré looked at her in surprise. "But aren't you still going to school?"

"Oui, madame. But I'm going to quit."

Madame Dupré frowned. She went over to the window and looked out thoughtfully. There was something pathetic about Hélène's lack of composure. The girl wasn't asking for a job because of her love for fabrics and her talent for sewing. There was another, more desperate reason. She could see it written all over her face. Yet underneath, she somehow knew there still lurked a cold ambition.

Madame Dupré hesitated, but only for a moment. She knew that Hélène's talent was exceptional. Something—instinct, perhaps—told her that she should hire Hélène. Anyway, she rationalized, Danielle, the girl who operated the sewing machine, wouldn't be working for much longer. She would soon be getting married. Hélène would learn very quickly at the machine.

Madame Dupré turned and looked at Hélène. The girl was tense, clearly preparing herself for a refusal. Madame Dupré smiled. "You have yourself a job," she said.

The desperation suddenly vanished from Hélène's face. She looked young again and her eyes shone joyfully. She wanted to fling her arms around Madame Dupré and show her how happy she was, but she stopped herself just in time. It wouldn't do to embrace one's employer.

"Don't be too excited," Madame Dupré warned. "The hours are long and the wages are low."

"I don't care," Hélène whispered. She took a deep breath. "When can I start?"

"Whenever you wish."

"Tomorrow?" Hélène asked eagerly.

Madame Dupré nodded. "Tomorrow morning, then."

For a moment Hélène shut her eyes. This was too good to be true! Not only was she getting away from Pierre and Tante Janine, but also she was taking the first step—the first *concrete* step—toward going back to Paris. Only there could she pursue her dream.

"You *what*?" Tante Janine said. Her voice was quivering with rage.

"I found a job," Hélène said quietly.

"I gave you no permission to go and look for one," Tante Janine snapped. "Besides, you're still going to school."

"I'm going to work," Hélène said firmly. "And nobody's going to stop me."

"What about the nursery?" Tante Janine asked. "I thought you were going to work here once school was out."

Hélène was silent.

"Well? Where are you going to live now that you're such a big shot?"

"I thought I would live here until I can afford to move."

Tante Janine's lips were compressed in a tight, ugly smile. "Why don't you move out of here right this minute, then?" Her voice had an ugly, cutting edge to it.

Hélène recognized the taunt that lay behind her words. Tante Janine was trying to pressure her to stay and work in the nursery, or leave and be done with. Either way, she would make it look like it had been Hélène's choice.

Hélène clenched her fists. She wasn't about to fall into the trap that easily. Much as she wanted to, she couldn't just pack up her things and go. She had no money. She still needed a place to live. Jeanne's? she thought suddenly. She squashed that thought immediately. No, it wasn't fair to Jeanne. What she had to do was to make Tante Janine see reason. And assert her own position, making it clear that she was no pushover.

"And if I decide to go to work and still live here?" Hélène asked. "What then?"

"I'll throw you out."

"You can't do that."

Tante Janine smiled tightly. "Try me. It's your choice. The nursery or your job," she said.

"I'm going to stay here until I can afford to move. And I'm going to work," Hélène said.

She looked at Tante Janine for a long moment. What she said next was going to be a gamble. She wasn't sure just how far she could go, but she'd push it.

"According to Monsieur Lefèvre," Hélène said in a quiet voice, "you are my guardian—and Edmond's, too—until we are both twenty-one. Only under the power of guardianship, *which you would relinquish by throwing me out*, are you allowed to dispose of our property." Hélène forced herself to smile triumphantly. "If you throw me out, you'd no longer be my guardian, would you, Tante Janine? I could even take you to court and win Maman's house back. Of course, it isn't there anymore. There's just the new nursery. Since my

177

money—and Edmond's—was used to build it, we might end up owning it. Then you'd have competition right next door." She paused. "Would you like that, Tante Janine?" she asked softly.

Hélène had to say one thing for her aunt. Tante Janine knew when she was beaten. Pale-faced and angry, she marched stiffly out of the room.

9

Slowly life for Hélène became sweeter. Her world revolved around the shop. She went to work early every morning and left late at night. The wages were low but Madame Dupré had told her confidentially, "Danielle will be leaving in three months. You will get a small raise then."

In the meantime, Danielle was in charge of her. She taught Hélène how to use the pedal-operated sewing machine and the exact way to stitch and hem to Madame's satisfaction (Madame was far more demanding and exacting than Mademoiselle Gribius had ever been). Hélène caught on to the thousands of little jobs that Madame found it necessary to farm out to the girls. And she learned quickly. By the time a week had passed, she was more adept at the sewing machine than Danielle had ever been. Her eager mind soaked up the craft like a sponge.

But her favorite hours were after closing time. When everyone left the shop, she would stay behind, turn out all but one of the lights, and sit on the floor beside the counter. With her knees drawn up to her chin and a studious expression on her face, she would leaf through the precious back issues of Madame Dupré's fashion magazines. That was when Hélène would enter what she considered the "real" world, the world of style and fashion and international vitality that transcended national borders and natural boundaries. In silence she would study each page of each magazine. Each layout, each advertisement, each model, each dress, each pose, each photograph. Nothing escaped her sharp eye. She learned to detect the subtle differences among the designers. There were the greats—Odile Joly, Schiaparelli, Dior, Madame Grès, and Chanel—and a crop of talented young hopefuls. (She decided that when she had *her* magazine, she would devote one feature in each issue to new talent.) She became aware of each designer's "mark," each one's *style*. It was by this unique style that she was able to recognize their garments as easily as she could recognize persons by their faces, their walks, their mannerisms. She even became adept at predicting what Madame Grès might do next, and what Dior would definitely *not* do. (Although she couldn't in her wildest imagination have foreseen that Chanel would come out with *costume* jewelry.) She was, however, able to understand the subtle differences between Chanel's classical simplicity and Schiaparelli's boldness; Dior's elegance and Madame Grès's daring. And above all, there was the great Odile Joly, the grande dame of fashion, who reigned supreme among even the high chieftains of fashion. Somehow, she always managed to melt all the differences of the competition into a single fluid style. Her style was so distinctive, so different, and yet so elegantly subtle that it transcended pure magic and astounded all the other magicians of design.

Hélène absorbed and absorbed until she could absorb no more. And still she studied the magazines again and again until she found a tiny something she had overlooked—and then she absorbed that, too. Her favorite days were those when the postman delivered new issues of *Elle* or *L'Officiel* or *Paris Vogue*. Madame Dupré understood Hélène's excitement and let her have the first look at them.

With trembling fingers Hélène would rapidly tear off the brown wrapping paper and stare at the colorful, glossy covers with awe. Always she felt the thick paper with the palm of her hand before turning the pages. She loved feeling the luxurious, slick texture against her fingers.

Finally the day came when Hélène looked at a photograph and frowned. She said to herself: "I could do that better. I would have placed the model differently. I would have had her wear the Grès gown in the other photo instead of the Schiaparelli. I would have had the camera focus upward, from below, instead of just head-on." That was the moment she knew she was learning.

Madame Dupré watched Hélène's progress with interest.

There was no doubt in her mind: Hélène was a natural. A natural seamstress, a natural learner, a natural barometer of taste. Instinctively she could differentiate between the good and the bad. And under Madame Dupré's subtle tutelage—making Hélène think she was actually discovering everything by herself instead of being taught—Hélène learned to tell the difference between the good and the exceptional. Between the exceptional and the sublime.

One day Madame Dupré stopped at the sewing machine and silently watched Hélène at work. The girl had a deftness, a professional assurance in handling fabric, that usually came only from years of experience.

Hélène stopped sewing and looked up at her.

"Come upstairs to my apartment, Hélène. I would like to have a private talk with you."

Hélène nodded. "Oui, madame." Quickly she took the dress she was sewing out from under the needle, carefully folded it, and followed Madame Dupré upstairs. Nervously she wondered what she had done wrong.

When they got to the little apartment above the shop, Madame Dupré switched on the parlor lights and directed Hélène to one of the floral-chintz-covered chairs.

Hélène uncomfortably folded her hands in her lap and watched as her employer sat in the chair opposite and elegantly crossed her legs.

Madame Dupré hesitated a moment. "How long have you been working here now?" she asked.

Hélène looked at her dumbly. "I . . . I'm not sure, madame. A month?"

Madame Dupré smiled and shook her head. "*Three* months to the day," she corrected her.

Hélène's mouth hung open. "It . . . it doesn't seem possible!"

Madame Dupré smiled. "It does. When you become my age, the weeks can drag by like years."

Hélène nodded. How strange, she thought. Every minute she spent at Tante Janine's was an eternity, and yet months here seemed mere minutes.

"In two weeks, Danielle will be leaving. On that day you will take over her job completely."

Hélène's lips broke into a smile. "Oui, madame," she said.

Madame Dupré raised an eyebrow. The girl showed no

nervousness about the added responsibility. She was confident that she could do the job well.

"It appears that you like your job," Madame Dupré said slowly.

"Oui, madame. I have never been happier."

Madame Dupré looked at her shrewdly. "And yet you are not satisfied." It was a statement, not a question.

Hélène hesitated a moment. Then she nodded. "I am satisfied for right now, madame," she said carefully. "And I'm very grateful for the opportunity you've given me."

"Ah. But it's not what you really want to do, is it?"

Hélène shook her head. "Not really."

Madame Dupré leaned forward. Her eyes met Hélène's evenly. "Tell me about it. What is it that you want to do?"

Hélène started to say something, then stopped. She got up and walked over to the window, parted the lace curtains and looked down at the cobblestoned street and the row of stone houses. She turned to face Madame Dupré. "I can sew and stitch well, madame. I can even design clothes adequately. But I'll never be very good at it. I borrow too much from other people's work. But . . ." She paused and then continued in a low, earnest voice. "But I can *see* what's good. Instinctively I know how to put things together."

Madame Dupré nodded. The girl was wise beyond her years. "Go on," she said gently.

Hélène took a deep breath. "I want to return to Paris," she said fervently. "I want to start my own . . . fashion magazine."

Madame Dupré did not look surprised. She had felt the currents of Hélène's ambition and yearning stirring restlessly beneath the surface. Lately she had felt the current gathering strength. She sighed. Yes, she too once had a similar ambition. But now it was too late. Somehow she had become too entrenched in her comfortable life-style. Perhaps her ambition hadn't burned strongly enough. But Hélène's did.

"I wanted to move to Paris once," Madame Dupré said. There was a faraway look in her eyes.

Hélène looked surprised. "Why didn't you?"

Madame Dupré shrugged her shoulders elegantly. "One falls into a trap. One is too comfortable. One is afraid of adventure. Of starting anew." She paused. Suddenly her voice was very quiet. "Or one doesn't have enough talent."

Hélène stared at her. She had always thought Madame

Dupré was strong-willed and extremely talented. She didn't think there was anything she couldn't do, once set on it. Suddenly she remembered the first time she had gone into the shop, and the beautiful dress that was displayed in the window. The *copy* in the window, she corrected herself. Now she knew what it had been. A Grès.

Madame Dupré rose to her feet suddenly. "Come with me," she said.

Hélène got up and followed her into an elegant little bedroom. The walls were papered with a forget-me-not pattern; there were a pale blue dresser with a mirror and two big wardrobes.

Madame Dupré motioned for Hélène to sit down. "I want to show you something," she said softly. "I visited Paris once and brought something back." She opened one of the wardrobe doors and took out a wooden clothes hanger draped with a long sheet. She flung the sheet away.

Hélène let out a gasp. The gown had to be a Dior. It was the most beautiful garment she had ever seen. Even on the hanger it had a life of its own. The pale satin shimmered with a luminosity that came from within.

"It is beautiful, non?"

Hélène was speechless. She was barely capable of nodding. Then slowly, delicately, she reached out to touch the gown. She laid it carefully out on the bed and examined the design, the workmanship, the fabric. It was a culmination of everything that was genius. Slowly, reverently, she lifted a corner of it to her lips and kissed it.

Madame Dupré watched her. "Now do you understand that I am a . . . a failure?" she asked.

Hélène looked at her compassionately.

"Never would I be capable of creating something like that," Madame Dupré said in a whisper. "But oh, how I *longed* to. Now I've learned to accept my shortcomings. My lack of genius. But I learned it too late. After too much hungering. Strange, how every so often something reminds me of my failed ambition." She smiled painfully. "This time it was you."

Hélène nodded solemnly.

Suddenly Madame Dupré grasped Hélène's hands in her own. "Leave Saint-Nazaire!" she whispered. "As soon as you can! You are lucky. You know your ambitions. Your limitations. Leave and become successful with your magazine!"

Hélène swallowed. "Yes, madame. As soon as I can, I will."

Carefully Madame Dupré covered the gown with the sheet and hung it back inside the wardrobe. She snapped the door shut and they went out to the parlor. For a moment, neither of them spoke.

"I have promised you a raise," Madame Dupré said finally. She crossed the little room to a delicate desk and opened the top. She took a thin booklet out of a pigeonhole and handed it to Hélène.

"What's this?" She looked at it curiously. "It's . . . a bankbook!"

"In your name. I have taken the liberty of depositing the first month's difference between your salary and your raise. Bank it every month from now on." She looked into Hélène's eyes. "For Paris," she said softly.

"Yes . . ." Hélène whispered. "For Paris!"

The night was dark and cool as she walked home. The road to the nursery was treacherous because it was hard to see the ruts and bumps without any moonlight. But Hélène liked the quiet solitude of the night and the distant, reassuring rumbling of the surf. It gave her time to think. To plan. Madame Dupré was right—she would have to leave Saint-Nazaire soon. There was no future here. Sadly she recalled Madame Dupré's own shattered dreams and lost hopes, a lesson to remember. She mustn't fall into the same trap. She must keep her ambition burning.

She rounded a familiar bend more by instinct than by sight. In the distance she could see the lights glowing in the Brocqs' house. She put her hands in the pockets of her coat. Yes, she thought, she'd learned a lot today. She smiled to herself. She was judging each day by what she had learned.

"There's my pretty!" a voice hissed out of the darkness.

Hélène suddenly froze and her heart pounded against her ribs. Pierre! In terror, her eyes searched the darkness around her, but she couldn't see anything. What was he doing out here? It was still a good kilometer till she'd be home. Suddenly she knew what he was doing here. Lying in wait. Setting his trap. For her.

The whisper came again. *"My pretty. Pierre is waiting!"*

Hélène whirled around. "Where are you?" she cried out.

The foliage on the trees to her left suddenly rustled. She turned to face them. But it was only the wind.

"I'm over here, my pretty!" Now the voice seemed to come from her right. She whirled in that direction.

"No, no, no. Pretty mustn't run! Pierre is in front of you!"

She drew back instinctively—right into his arms. He clamped them around her.

He hadn't been in front of her! He'd tricked her! He'd been behind her all along!

She started to scream, but a cold hand covered her mouth.

"Pretty better not scream," he whispered, his breath hot against her neck.

She let out a muffled wail. Her mind raced. She had to do something. Anything. For a moment she sagged in his arms. He loosened his grip in surprise, and suddenly she dived out of his grasp. He tried to grab her again, but she twisted around and brought her knee up in his groin. She could hear him grunt. Then, as fast as her legs could carry her, she started off across the dark fields. She plunged past trees whose branches tore at her dress and scratched her face. Every branch held a special terror. To Hélène they seemed like fingers, as she ran out of their reach. She tripped over a rock and fell, and for a fleeting instant she thought Pierre had tripped her. With a grunt she struggled back to her feet and continued running, never stopping to listen to see if he was following. She had lost all sense of direction.

After a while she felt as if her lungs were going to burst. For a moment she stopped running, her breasts heaving as she swallowed mouthfuls of air. Her heart hammered like it had gone out of control.

"Pierre's waiting!"

"No!" she screamed, and covered her ears. "No no no no no *no!*"

And suddenly she felt herself slipping into nothingness. For a moment she swayed unsteadily, and then she could feel herself falling. She was aware that he was very near, but she wasn't quite sure where. She thought she could feel his thighs clamping around her face. It was all so . . . so dreamlike. So unreal. In the distance she heard breathing. It sounded shallow and faraway.

After a while things slowly focused again. She felt drops of warm liquid falling on her face. Had it begun to rain? she wondered in surprise. Then the pressure left the sides of her face and she heard a noise moving away in the underbrush.

She moaned and lay there without moving. He was gone. She shook her head to clear it and realized that there was liquid on her lips, too. For a moment she caught the taste of it. It was strangely salty.

Suddenly she knew what it was. Semen. In disgust, she started to wipe it away with her wrist. But she never finished. The nausea rose instantly. Before she could bend over, she threw up.

When the lights in the shop went on, Hélène looked up and blinked. Madame Dupré was standing in the doorway, a coat over her nightgown, her hair in metal curlers. Her eyes were red and swollen; she looked like she'd just awakened. "What are you doing here?" she asked. "It's after midnight!" Then she sucked in her breath. "What's happened to you? Your face—it's got scratches all over it!"

Hélène trembled. She looked away. "I couldn't stay at home, madame. So I came here. I tried to let myself in quietly. I'm sorry. I didn't mean to wake you."

"That's all right. I heard noises and came down to investigate." Madame Dupré came close and examined Hélène's face. Her elegant features suddenly contorted with rage. Her voice was sharp. "Who did this to you? You look as if you were beaten!"

"Please . . ." Hélène begged. "Don't make any trouble."

"Trouble!" Madame Dupré snorted. "Somebody certainly made trouble, but it wasn't I!" She looked at Hélène. "Well?" she demanded. "Was it one of the boys?"

Hélène shook her head slowly.

Suddenly Madame Dupré's eyes widened. "Don't tell me it happened at home!"

Hélène nodded.

Madame Dupré frowned crossly. "Was it your aunt?"

"Please . . ." Hélène's voice was a small, timid whisper.

"All right, we won't talk about it, then." Madame Dupré shook her head. "But tell me—is this why you wanted the job so badly? To get away?"

Hélène nodded again. "I had to get away from home, madame. I was trying to save up to get my own apartment."

Madame Dupré wrapped her arms around Hélène. "You poor girl! Don't worry, you won't have to go back. And you won't have to spend your money on an apartment, either. You must use it to get to Paris!"

Hélène nodded. "But where will I live?"

"I know just the place."

Hélène looked at her questioningly.

Madame Dupré smiled and pointed at the ceiling. "Upstairs, in the garret. There's an old iron bed up there and a few sticks of old furniture. It will be your own room."

Hélène brightened. "Really, madame?"

Madame Dupré nodded. "Come with me. I'll get you some sheets and pillowcases. Tomorrow you can go back to your aunt's and get your things." She wagged a warning finger. "But don't you go alone!" she said sternly.

"Non, madame. I'll have my brother's fiancée come with me."

"Bon. It is settled, then. Come along. Let us see how you like your new room."

They went up two flights of stairs. The garret was on the third floor, right under the beams of the eaves. The roof was steep, and they could stand up only in the center of the room. It smelled musty and the air was full of dust. Clotheslines crisscrossed it from one end to the other.

"You'll have to clean it up a bit," Madame Dupré said as she threw open one of the little dormer windows. "But it should be comfortable enough."

Hélène nodded. "I don't know how to thank you."

Madame Dupré shrugged. "It's nothing. Just try to get a good night's sleep. And take tomorrow off." She clapped the dust off her hands and walked over to the door. "Good night, Hélène."

"Good night, madame."

Hélène waited until Madame Dupré's footsteps disappeared down the stairs. Then she walked over to the open window and looked out. Over the rooftops she could see down to the dimly lit quay where the fishing boats tied up. Right now, it was strangely deserted, with barely a boat in sight. Beyond it, the bay was dark, melting into an equally dark sky. She smiled to herself. From up here she would be able to see Edmond's ship when the fleet came in.

Jeanne flapped the dust rag out the window and made a face. She coughed and turned to Hélène. "Sprinkle the floor with some more water before you go on sweeping. Otherwise we'll be choking to death!"

They were dressed almost identically, in Jeanne's old housedresses, with scarves tied around their heads.

Jeanne shook her head and giggled. "If we don't look like two housewives."

Hélène smiled and bent down as she carefully swept out a corner with the horsehair broom. "Once it's cleaned up, it should look rather nice."

Jeanne looked around the garret. "It's certainly big enough for one person," she said in an impressed voice. "And just think! It's a place of your own." Her voice suddenly became angry. "At least you'll never have to go back to those horrible people anymore!"

Hélène sighed and sank down into a broken chair. "I can't tell Edmond the truth though, Jeanne. That hurts me, because we've never kept any secrets from each other. But I'm scared . . ."

Jeanne looked over at her. "I know. You don't have to worry about me—I won't breathe a word. But what *are* you going to tell him?"

"Part of the truth, at least. That I couldn't bear living with Tante Janine any longer. That this place is very convenient, since I only have to go downstairs to go to work. That I'm just biding my time till I go to Paris."

"Good. Then our stories will match."

Suddenly Hélène came over to Jeanne and embraced her. "When we first met, you told me that you wanted us to be friends," she said softly. "Well, I want you to know how happy I am that we are."

"I know," Jeanne replied. She gave Hélène a squeeze. "But we'd better get working. Edmond will be back on shore this weekend. We want him to be impressed when he sees this place, don't we?"

Hélène nodded. She was studying Jeanne.

"What are you staring at?" Jeanne asked.

Hélène smiled and turned away. "Nothing," she said vaguely.

But that wasn't quite true. She had been studying Jeanne's height and build and figure. Her seamstress mind instinctively appraised it and sized it. Tonight, after Jeanne left, she would begin designing her wedding dress. After all, the wedding was only four months off.

There was a knock at the door.

Hélène turned toward it. "Come in," she called.

Madame Dupré came in carrying a wooden tray covered with a napkin. "I thought you both might use some lunch," she said with an apologetic smile. "I took the liberty of making you a little something." She set the tray down on the bed. Then she looked around. "Good gracious! I never thought this place would clean up so well!"

"We've barely started," Hélène said.

"Perhaps you should take up interior decoration instead of fashion."

Hélène smiled. "That's stretching it a bit, I'm afraid. But I have a feeling about this place." She gave the room a proprietorial look. "I guess everybody does about the first place of their own."

"Yes," Madame Dupré said. "I'll never forget mine. A small room with peeling wallpaper. Chinese flowers . . ." She made a limp gesture with her hand. "Anyway, I'm sure you have better things to do than listen to an old woman rambling on. I'll leave you two in peace." When she reached the door she turned around. "Oh, Hélène . . ."

"Oui, madame?"

"I got a letter from the Comtesse de Léger this morning, confirming her fittings. I don't believe I told you."

"No, madame."

Madame Dupré sighed. "Every year the Comtesse goes to Paris and orders an entire wardrobe from the couturiers. Unknown to everyone but me, she never wears her good clothes except for special occasions. She has me make a copy of each of the garments she buys. This way she has an identical—cheaper—wardrobe to 'wear around the house.' This project usually takes me four weeks. I close the shop for the duration, since the work is done at the de Léger château." She paused. "I always take my best seamstress with me. I am planning to take you."

Hélène's eyes shone. "I'd love to go, madame. When is it?"

"The entire month of September."

Hélène's face fell.

"What's the matter? I thought you'd be pleased."

"I am. It's just that Jeanne and Edmond . . ." Hélène turned around and looked desperately at Jeanne. "They're getting married then, and—"

Jeanne interrupted. "Hélène, I want you to go," she said

firmly. "Edmond and I will postpone our plans. We'll marry in December instead."

"But—"

"Quiet! This is the opportunity of a lifetime. You've never been in a château, have you?"

Hélène didn't answer. She didn't want to remember back that far, not to a Nazi-occupied château on the Loire, and Catherine and Marie . . .

"Besides, who knows?" Jeanne said lightly. "You might meet a handsome Comte." She glanced at Madame Dupré. "There is one, isn't there?"

"Oh . . . yes. But he's married to the Comtesse. However, he does have a rather handsome young son, the future Comte. His name is Hubert, I believe. Yes, Hubert de Léger." She looked thoughtfully at Hélène. "Actually, he's only a year to two older than you are."

10

The sky was cloudy and looked like rain when Hélène and Madame Dupré got off the train in Bordeaux. They were met on the platform by an elderly white-haired man in a dark blue uniform with brass buttons, gleaming high boots, and a visored cap. He recognized Madame Dupré instantly and clicked his heels smartly, giving a low bow. He gestured to her luggage.

Madame Dupré smiled. "Bonjour, André. Yes, those are ours."

Quickly the suitcases were loaded onto a trolley and André led the way out to the parking lot, where an old black Citroën limousine was waiting. André held the rear doors open for them, stowed the luggage in the trunk, and then got in behind the wheel. As they drove off, Hélène pressed the velour seat with her hand. It was firm but soft. She smiled to herself. This was luxury indeed.

They rode slowly through the narrow streets of the town.

Hélène pressed her nose against the window. Bordeaux was much larger than Saint-Nazaire. In a way, it seemed part of a different country. The stone houses were large and ornate. Some of them even had balconies. There were many shops and cars. They passed a bustling open-air marketplace where bright umbrellas and awnings had been set up over tables piled high with cheeses, breads, fruits, and vegetables. She could see intricately braided heads of garlic hanging from the vegetable stalls.

They drove through the dark tunnellike arch of the Great Clock Tower. This was a bizarre building. On its facade, high above the arch, was a big square clock. And even higher up, in another arch flanked by stone turrets, hung the big bell, proudly silent after its morning's cry that harvesttime had come once again to the vineyards of Bordeaux. When they drove back out into the daylight, Hélène twisted around in her seat and looked out the rear window. After a moment, she could see the clock on this side. Its giant gold-colored hands read five-thirty.

Soon they left the town behind and headed north. Green pastures, vast pine forests, and timeless villages flew past in a blur. They had to slow down whenever the road cut through the villages, and then Hélène would catch sight of ancient stone houses and window boxes overflowing with pale pink impatiens and deep red geraniums. Often the countryside opened up into gently sloping hills that looked as if someone had run a comb through them. These were the vineyards that were the heart and soul of Gascony. After they had traveled a while longer, Hélène turned to Madame Dupré. "How much farther is it?"

Madame Dupré patted her hand. "Another hour and a half. So you just relax. The de Léger châteaux are in the Médoc."

Hélène perked up. Her voice was incredulous. "*Are*? You mean there is more than one?"

"There are two." Madame Dupré settled back comfortably. "There are the Château Hautecloque-de Léger and the Château Loustalot-de Léger."

"And both of them are real castles?"

Madame Dupré nodded. "Both of them, and each with its own vineyard. But the Comte and the Comtesse live in the Château Hautecloque. It's the larger and by far more luxurious one." She smiled slightly. "Also, it's the more prestigious."

An hour later, they arrived at the edge of the de Léger estates and Madame Dupré pointed out the sights. These vineyards were by far the biggest they'd yet come across. The gently sloping hills seemed to stretch from horizon to horizon.

"It's the single biggest vineyard in all of France," Madame Dupré said.

Hélène nodded. She was speechless. Never had she seen so many furrowed slopes in her life.

"Look quickly! There on your left!" Madame Dupré pointed to the window on Hélène's side of the car.

Hélène turned her head and gazed out. All around, workers were swarming through the chest-high rows of vines, bending over and picking grapes, looking up at the ever-darkening sky with worried eyes. She noticed that a complex maze of paved roads crisscrossed the vineyard. And in the distance, bathed by the tranquil waters of a large moat, was a sprawling château. Medieval stone turrets and crumbling retaining walls merged nicely with the elegant additions of the Renaissance.

"That is the Château Loustalot-de Léger," Madame Dupré said. "What you see all around it are more than two thousand acres of grapes."

"It's so . . . so enormous!" Hélène said.

Madame Dupré nodded. "Two years ago the château produced almost two million bottles of wine. Can you imagine!"

Hélène shook her head in awe. "The de Légers must be very rich," she said.

Madame Dupré smiled but said nothing. Yes, she thought. They were very rich indeed. But the Comtesse had inherited the typical shrewd frugality of the French. Instead of spending an additional ten thousand francs at the couturiers' for a second wardrobe, she was having copies made for three thousand. It was unbelievable. A woman worth multimillions went out of her way to save seven thousand francs!

"And the Château Hautecloque-de Léger?" Hélène asked. "What about it?"

"It is a little farther to the north. It covers only two hundred and thirty acres. We'll be there soon."

Just as they got there, heavy splatters of raindrops were starting to fall. André grunted and mumbled something about the grapes. He slowed the big car down and they drove through the gates of the château.

Hélène leaned down and peered up through the arcs of glass that the thumping windshield wipers were clearing. She caught a blurry glimpse of a large stone plaque on top of the gate. Carved in relief were a lion and a salamander supporting a crest between them. The crest of the de Légers.

They rode down a long poplar-lined drive. To either side of it was the vast park attributed to Le Nôtre, the landscape architect who had designed the gardens of Versailles. Even through the heavy sheets of rain Hélène could see the Château Hautecloque-de Léger. She took a deep breath. It was unlike any château she had ever imagined. There were no towers, no turrets. This was an elegantly noble building, and yet there was a haughty coldness about its perfect symmetry. It consisted of a narrow pavilion flanked by two wings that had larger pavilions at each end. It was three stories high, its steep dark roofs rounded off to support lanterns. In the center was a sweeping marble staircase.

They drove around the building and pulled up to a small door in the back. André produced a huge black umbrella, hurried out, held their doors open, and kept them covered as they ran to the building.

A fat red-faced woman dressed in white flung the door open and they rushed inside. André hurried back to the car.

Hélène looked around. They were in a massive kitchen. Copper and steel pots and pans hung from the walls and ceiling. At a wooden table, a young girl with her sleeves rolled up was expertly kneading dough. Hélène couldn't help but feel a certain disappointment that they hadn't pulled up to the majestic staircase in the front.

The fat woman was obviously a cook. After she closed the door, her face broke into a cheerful smile and she wiped her large hands on her apron. "Bonjour, madame," she said in a friendly voice. "Did you have a pleasant journey?"

Madame Dupré returned her smile and brushed some raindrops off her sleeves. "Bonjour, Thérèse. Yes, the journey was fine until the rain began."

Thérèse lifted her red hands in despair. "This weather! We have had such a dry summer, and now all this rain! It is not good for the poor grapes." She shrugged her shoulders philosophically and sighed. "I suppose you cannot hope for every year to be good."

192

"I suppose not," Madame Dupré said.

"The Comtesse has instructed me to put you in your usual room," Thérèse said. "Is that all right with you?"

Madame Dupré smiled. "That will be fine, merci."

"Then I will take you upstairs at once. I'm sure you're anxious to wash up and change."

Madame Dupré looked at Hélène. "Come along. Our luggage will be brought to us."

Hélène followed them up a steep staircase to the servants' quarters. They were located on the top floor of the château, under the gently rounded roof. Their rooms were identical, connected through an adjoining door.

Hélène sat down heavily on her bed and looked around miserably; the plaster walls were cracked and the furniture was comfortable but plain. There was one circular window so low to the floor that she would have to bend down in order to look out.

Once again Hélène couldn't help but feel a bit resentful. She had expected a stately suite with a canopied bed and rich furnishings. She bit down on her lip. She must be careful to say nothing. The chauffeured limousine aside, it was obvious that they were considered slightly superior to the rest of the servants but far below the lordly station of the de Légers.

Late the next afternoon the Comtesse summoned them to the Embroidered Room. A liveried manservant led them through the house and down a stone staircase. This staircase, unlike the servants', was delicately carved with fruits and flowers. Hélène saw that the interior of the château was lordly indeed. The rich architecture was well-preserved, looked almost fresh and new. Everywhere there were seventeenth- and eighteenth-century paintings, Flemish tapestries, Chinese lacquered commodes, and Aubusson carpets. The exquisite furnishings were of the Louis XV style. "All genuine!" Madame Dupré whispered.

Hélène let out a cry as the manservant opened the giant double doors of the Embroidered Room. The walls were covered in red-and-gold-painted moldings set with the fanciful needlework panels that gave the room its name. Again, the furnishings were Louis XV bergères and fauteuils. But there were no paintings in the Embroidered Room. Instead, Chinese and Japanese porcelains were everywhere. There were blanc-de-chine figurines, covered vases, and mandarin dolls. A delicate table held a lavish arrangement of flowers. Seated on an embroidered settee behind it was the Comtesse de La Brissac et de Léger.

The Comtesse could trace her genealogy all the way back through the Brissac-Orléans; one of her far-distant ancestors was Anne de Bretagne, the wife of King Louis XII. The Comtesse was thin and elegant, as haughty-looking, Hélène thought, as the facade of the château. Her hair was uniformly gray and immaculately set. Her pale skin was almost porcelain-toned, but her hands, in which she held a small Maltese spaniel, attested to her years. They were spotted with a faint sprinkling of age spots. She had a very distinguished Roman nose, a perpetual frown, and a network of tiny wrinkles in the corners of her cool, stony dark eyes. She sat stiffly erect and wore a simple white silk blouse and a beautiful pale yellow suit. A Chanel, Hélène thought.

Madame Dupré curtsied politely. "Bonjour, Comtesse," she said formally.

"Bonjour, madame." The Comtesse's clipped voice was loud and clear. She pronounced each syllable precisely.

"May I introduce my new seamstress, Hélène Junot." Madame Dupré gestured gracefully to Hélène.

Hélène curtsied as Madame Dupré had instructed her to, but her movements were somewhat awkward. She could feel a blush coming over her face. "Bonjour, Comtesse," she whispered nervously.

The cool dark eyes swept imperiously over Hélène. "But she is very young!" the Comtesse said with surprise.

"Oui, Comtesse," Madame Dupré said quickly. "She is the most talented seamstress I have ever had. She will go far."

"Is that so?" Once again the Comtesse's dark eyes looked at Hélène, this time with keen interest. "She is rather an attractive young lady."

Hélène could feel another flush of embarrassment coloring her face. She rarely received compliments, and when she did, she didn't know how to accept them graciously, so she remained silent. From the Comtesse's pleased expression, Hélène knew that her silence had been misinterpreted as modesty.

The Comtesse pulled a bell rope that hung beside the settee. A moment later a young maid in black uniform appeared soundlessly.

"Lise, I want you to give Madame Dupré and her associate all the assistance they may require."

"Oui, Comtesse."

"Bon. You may take them upstairs to the sewing room. Then I want you to bring them the clothes that have arrived from the couturiers. Everything except for the gowns."

"Oui, Comtesse."

"That is all." The Comtesse made an imperious gesture of dismissal.

Madame Dupré glanced at Hélène. Once again they curtsied, then followed Lise out of the room.

The sewing room was on the second floor of the northeastern wing. At one time it must have been a sumptuous bedroom. There were high carved ceilings, boiserie-paneled walls, and big mullioned windows that allowed maximum light. Sheet-draped objects stood around the room like ghostly white sculptures. The room was cold and dusty and needed airing. Hélène went over to the windows and threw them open. A blast of fresh air and a sprinkling of raindrops came blowing in. For a moment she stood there looking out at the sweeping view of Le Nôtre's park.

With a snapping motion of her wrist Madame Dupré went around the room pulling off the white sheets. Hélène saw that they had draped the sewing machine, a big paper-covered table, the dressmaker's dummy, a coatrack in the corner, a three-paneled screen (behind which the Comtesse could dress or undress with delicacy), and a tall three-paneled gilt-framed mirror. Then Madame Dupré crossed the room to the carved wardrobes and threw open the doors. Inside were bolts of fabric, threads, needles, pincushions, shears, trimmings, and all other tools of the dressmaker's trade.

"The Comtesse insists on many fittings," Madame Dupré told Hélène in a low voice. "That is why the sewing room is not in the servants' quarters!"

Hélène pushed her plate away. "I'm full," she announced.

Madame Dupré looked at her sharply and wagged her finger. "A lady never says 'I'm full,'" she said sternly. "In society a lady says 'I've had plenty, thank you.' You must not underestimate the importance of these social graces. Once you get to Paris, they can make the difference between success and failure."

Hélène nodded and filed this bit of information. They were

195

having dinner on the little table in Madame Dupré's room. This arrangement was the result of a bizarre etiquette that placed them in a no-man's-land: their social status was far below the de Légers' but somewhat above the servants', so they could dine with neither. Madame Dupré explained to Hélène that if there had been a governess in the house, she would have been an acceptable dinner companion for them, but since there were no small children there was no governess, and thus they had to eat alone in Madame Dupré's room. Hélène was somewhat annoyed at such intricacies of the social ladder and wondered how many rungs there could possibly be.

Carefully Madame Dupré placed her fork and knife in an X on her plate, signifying that she, too, was finished. Delicately she dabbed her lips with her napkin.

"Thérèse will bring us coffee and dessert later," she said. "She knows I like it a few hours after dinner."

Hélène nodded, sipping delicately at her wine. "I can't wait until tomorrow," she said. "The dresses are so beautiful! And the Chanel suits—I can't believe their quality. I'd have never thought of sewing tiny chains into the hems to make them fall better."

Madame Dupré nodded. "Chanel is a genius," she said simply. She rose and walked over to the little round window. She bent down, parted the filmy curtains, and looked out. She let the curtains drop back in place and turned to Hélène. "It has stopped raining. Shall we take a walk?"

Hélène pushed back her chair and got to her feet. "I'd love some fresh air. Let me get my coat."

They went downstairs and walked out through the kitchen door. It was still daylight, but dusk would soon begin to fall. The rain had made the dull autumn lawn appear green and springlike. A fine mist had settled over the countryside. The clouds overhead were thinning and looked like a gray watercolor wash. All at once they parted and a glimmer of weak sunshine broke through.

Madame Dupré glanced at the sky and smiled. "Perhaps there is hope for the tender grapes after all," she said. "Let's take a look around."

When they had walked for some minutes, the sprawling stables suddenly came into view. Hélène marveled at their size. "The de Légers must have a lot of horses to need so many stables."

Madame Dupré smiled. "They do. The de Légers pride themselves on horsemanship. They hold fox hunts and even race horses." She stopped talking as they both heard the approach of pounding hoofbeats. They turned around.

Hélène let out a shriek and threw herself at Madame Dupré. A magnificent black Arabian stallion was charging across the grass toward them. It looked as if the equestrian had lost control, but at the last moment he expertly drew in the reins and the big horse whinnied and skidded to a halt barely a meter away from them. Bits of earth flew up all around. Hélène could feel the animal's heat. It must have been galloping for some time.

The shadow of the rider fell across Hélène and she looked up. He was undeniably handsome, with dark hair, a determined cleft chin, and deep, flashing eyes. They were the same eyes as the Comtesse's, but whereas hers were cold, his were mischievous. Under the serge riding habit she could sense a wiry, athletic physique, and his bearing bespoke an aristocratic heritage. This had to be the Comtesse's son.

Hubert de Léger grinned suddenly and touched the little visor of his cap with his riding crop. "Ah, Madame Dupré," he said.

Madame Dupré gave a curt little nod. "You scared us half to death," she said with quiet fury.

He ignored her and nodded his chin at Hélène. "Who are you?"

Hélène could feel his dark eyes boring through her. There was something virile and powerful about him that made her suddenly afraid. She felt paralyzed. "Hélène Junot," she murmured softly, and looked away.

"You're a lot better-looking than that woman Madame Dupré brought with her last year." He looked at Madame Dupré and smiled disarmingly. "Isn't she?"

"I think it's all a matter of personal taste," Madame Dupré replied stiffly. "I wouldn't know."

Hubert de Léger threw back his head and laughed heartily, showing strong white teeth. Then his expression became serious as he looked at Hélène. "Do you ride?"

Hélène looked confused. "You mean . . . horses?"

He grinned easily. "What else is there?"

"I . . . I've never tried."

"It's easy to learn." He kept his hands on the reins; the stallion was restless.

"I'm not sure I like horses," she said quickly.

"You will," he said confidently. "You'd cut a fine figure on a horse. We have many in the stables. Some of them are quite gentle. Perhaps I should teach you to ride." He paused. "You should be flattered."

Hélène looked flustered. She fidgeted with her hands and turned her face away. "Maybe some other day," she murmured.

"Tomorrow?" he said quickly.

"No, I'm afraid I've work to do tomorrow," she said firmly, then looked at Madame Dupré, clearly wanting the woman's backup.

Madame Dupré took her cue. "I'm afraid your mother would be very displeased if her garments weren't finished on time."

He grinned slyly and bowed to Madame Dupré. "But I know better. You never work after six o'clock, madame." Then he looked at Hélène. "We'll have the lesson here tomorrow at half-past."

Before Hélène could refuse again, he neatly smacked the stallion with his crop and dug in his spurs. Instantly horse and rider went flying across the lawn, hooves pounding and kicking up pieces of earth. Soon he disappeared.

Hélène turned to Madame Dupré. "What do I do now?" she moaned.

Madame Dupré shrugged. "Hubert does not easily take no for an answer. He has inherited the determination of the Brissac-Orléans."

Hélène looked uncomfortable. "Perhaps I should go and speak with him later."

Madame Dupré shook her head. "That would be a waste of time. He is charming but evasive. You can search everywhere, but you'll never find him until six-thirty tomorrow afternoon. I'm afraid you'll just have to go."

11

A little after six o'clock the next afternoon, Madame Dupré chaperoned Hélène as far as the stables and helped her into one of the riding habits that were kept on hand for guests. When Hélène was fully dressed, Madame Dupré stood back to study the effect. She frowned thoughtfully. "It's a little big in the bust, but otherwise it suits you quite handsomely." She stepped closer to rearrange the wisps of veil that hung off the top hat. "Yes, *quite* handsomely," she repeated with satisfaction.

Hélène walked over to the tilted dressing-room mirror and stood in front of it awkwardly. She stared at her reflection. The outfit *was* beautiful. The long black skirt was just short enough to show off the gleaming boots that had been murder to pull on and that didn't quite fit. They were too narrow in the ankles—"A lady really needs custom-made boots," Madame Dupré had growled as she helped Hélène struggle into them. The black coat and white blouse were slightly too big, but elegantly cut, and the black bow tie was a dressy touch. Still, Hélène felt ill-at-ease, as if wearing a costume she didn't belong in.

They went out into the pine-paneled saddle room, fragrant with the smells of leather and wood. A glass-fronted vitrine was filled with racing trophies and dressage ribbons, and the walls were hung with tack, saddles, brass hunting horns, and framed engravings of horses that the de Légers had raced at Chantilly and Longchamps.

Hélène took one look at the paraphernalia and turned to go back into the dressing room. "Maybe I'd just better—"

Madame Dupré caught her arm. "Oh, no, you don't! You are going to have to go through with it."

"But—"

"Silence!" Madame Dupré gestured in agitation. "Just be yourself! Right now you're too stiff and self-conscious. Relax!

199

Don't give anything a second thought." Then her voice softened. "Remember, you look lovely."

"I'm hungry."

Madame Dupré rolled her eyes. "A little dieting won't hurt," she said between clenched teeth. "You can stand to lose a few pounds."

Just then they heard approaching hoofbeats outside.

"Out you go," Madame Dupré said firmly. She pushed Hélène toward the door. "There's nothing to be afraid of. Have fun and . . . be careful." She gave Hélène an obscure look.

Hélène blushed. Silently she cursed herself. She was blushing all the time lately. She'd have to find some way to bring it under control. It wouldn't do to walk around with a red face half the time. But what had Madame Dupré meant about being careful? Careful of what? The horse or . . . Hubert?

When he saw her, Hubert de Léger expertly swung down off his saddle and strode toward her, leading his Arabian by the reins. "You look marvelous in that getup, but of course, I *knew* you would."

"Thank you," she said coldly. Her lips trembled angrily at his arrogant self-confidence.

"Come," he said. "I will tie up Sheik here and have a boy bring your horse around. We'll stay in the corral for a while."

She nodded nervously and he called out to one of the stableboys. A few minutes later, her horse was led out. It was a huge chestnut mare with a sidesaddle. Hélène looked up at it and cringed. "It . . . it looks so high."

"You'll manage."

"If you say so," she said doubtfully.

For the next half-hour he taught her only to mount and dismount. She had the sneaking suspicion that this exercise was being practiced so diligently because it gave him the opportunity to put his arms around her, hold her by the hips, and "accidentally" brush against her as he lifted her up. With surprise, she found that she rather liked the feel of his body against hers. She sensed a certain rough power in him, a cruel streak perhaps, but to her he was gentle and polite. Several times his face was close to hers, and for a few seconds they would stare at each other. Then she would look quickly away and he would continue with the lessons as if nothing had happened.

200

He was playing a game, she thought, smiling to herself. Two could play such a game. She would simply alter the rules and play a game of her own—learning quickly how to mount and dismount. She was strangely pleased when she saw his disappointment over her quick progress. Hélène one, the hungry lion zero, she thought.

"Now we ride," Hubert said at last. "Just a slow trot around the corral for practice, and then once around the park." He reached into his pocket for a lump of sugar and held it out to the mare. She nuzzled his hand as she took the sugar gently from him.

Hélène practiced riding around the corral. Then slowly she was graduated to the park. She had to admit that she enjoyed it immensely. It took concentration and skill, and she was catching on quickly. For a moment she even brought the mare to a canter, and the wind felt exhilarating against her face.

When they returned to the stables, Hubert told Hélène to stay put. Then he leaned low over the Arabian's neck, dug in his spurs, and headed toward a fence. Hélène drew in her breath. He was going to try to jump the fence! She saw that there was a series of hurdles in varying heights inside the en- closure.

Neatly the Arabian leaped over the fence and Hubert took it through its paces over the hurdles. The horse cleared each one. Hélène shook her head unbelievingly. Hubert was showing off for her, she knew, and dangerously so. Yet it was a beautiful, graceful demonstration of the unity of man and beast.

The hurdles completed, he headed the stallion back over the fence and galloped toward Hélène. When he drew up alongside her, he looked at her questioningly. She said noth- ing, but she thawed with a smile. Apparently satisfied with that reaction, he hopped to the ground and motioned for her to dismount. They handed their reins to two stableboys.

Hubert looked at Hélène. "Are you tired?"

She nodded. "Yes, but it's a rather thrilling tiredness."

He nodded. "I know what you mean. Feel sore from the saddle?"

She looked at him challengingly. "Not a bit."

He grinned. "You will tomorrow."

Together they walked across the park back to the château. Dusk was at hand and the sky was turning deep purple. For a few minutes they were silent. He still carried his riding crop and kept slapping it against his boot.

"I made you miss dinner," he said finally. "You may have it with me."

She looked at him. "I'm not hungry."

He smiled. "I won't take no for an answer."

"But . . . I'd have to get changed." She gestured at her riding skirt.

"Then get changed."

She paused. "No," she said firmly. "I'm afraid I can't." She shook her head. "It wouldn't be right."

He looked at her queerly and stopped tapping his boot with the crop. "What wouldn't?"

"My having dinner with you."

"Why?" He looked at her with amusement. "Because I'm a de Léger?"

She flushed. "Yes," she said softly.

But he was very persuasive. She could have countered him if he had ordered her to dine with him. But he hadn't. Instead, he threw himself at her mercy and begged. Finally she laughed. It was impossible to refuse. She suspected that he knew this was the only way she'd agree to it. But she no longer really cared. Too much virility and a potential cruel streak aside, he was very charming.

When they reached the house, they parted company for an hour. She ran upstairs, waited for one of the maids to come out of the bathroom they shared (what took her so long!) and quickly drew a bath. For several minutes she luxuriated in the tub, then hurried to her room and dressed with care. When she was finished, she looked in the mirror approvingly. The dress was black and plain, almost severe, but it was acceptable for anything from taking a walk to attending a funeral. At any rate, it was the only decent thing she owned. In her excitement she'd forgotten to close the connecting door between her room and Madame Dupré's. With a start she realized that Madame Dupré was watching her with amusement from the doorway.

"Do I . . . look all right?" Hélène asked hesitantly.

"That depends on where you are going."

"Downstairs. Hubert has asked me to dine with him."

"In that case, you look beautiful," Madame Dupré said. She frowned slightly. "But a bit severe."

Hélène looked at her in panic. "What do you mean?"

"We'll have to break up the gloominess of all that black. Black is elegant, but not by itself." Madame Dupré reached behind her neck and unfastened one of the thin gold chains she wore. "Here, I'll lend you this."

Hélène shook her head. "I couldn't."

Madame Dupré smiled. "Don't worry. You won't break it."

Hélène nodded. "I'll be very careful with it."

Madame Dupré smiled and fastened the chain around Hélène's neck. Hélène had never looked better. There was a color in her face that did not come just from riding. It was a flush of happiness and excitement. Love? she thought suddenly. She hoped not. Hubert de Léger was too wild. Too youthful and playful for a sensitive girl like Hélène.

The same manservant who had taken them to see the Comtesse arrived to escort Hélène downstairs. Suddenly Madame Dupré reached out, grabbed Hélène's hand, and squeezed it. "Enjoy yourself," she said. Then her voice dropped to a whisper. "Remember your manners."

Eagerly Hélène nodded. "I will," she replied quietly. Then she was gone.

Hubert was waiting for her in the Salon de la Rotonde on the first floor. He crossed the Savonnerie carpet and looked at her appreciatively. "We'll have to wait a few minutes. My mother and father will be right down."

Hélène's pulse seemed to stop. "You mean . . . they haven't eaten yet, either?"

He shook his head. "No. We usually dine late." He smiled. "Don't worry. They do not bite."

Nervously Hélène fingered Madame Dupré's necklace. She had counted on dining alone with Hubert, not with the Comte and the Comtesse. She hadn't even met the Comte yet, but the Comtesse had unnerved her enough. She was too imperious, too studiously elegant and refined. Her cold dark eyes frightened Hélène. For an instant she was tempted to murmur her excuses and flee. Instead, in a voice that sounded as if it belonged to someone else she said, "What a lovely painting," and gestured to one of the gilt-framed canvases on the pale blue moiré-covered walls.

"Let's go closer and take a look," Hubert said. He touched her arm to lead her around the room.

A faint flush came over her face as he touched her, and it gave her skin a beautifully rosy glow. She looked at him and smiled nervously. He let his hand drop and stood back watching her as she went from painting to painting. For a long time she lingered in front of a small canvas over one of the couches. It was very old, and she could see that the paint had developed a network of fine cracks. It depicted a young boy with a beatific smile and half-closed eyes. "This is the most beautiful one of all," she said softly.

"You have good taste, mademoiselle. That is a Raphael," a woman's voice said.

Hélène stiffened and turned around slowly. She knew that clipped voice, with its precise pronunciations, only too well. Swiftly she curtsied. She was surprised that it came off so gracefully. "Good evening, Comtesse," she said politely.

"Good evening, mademoiselle." The Comtesse smiled coolly and came toward her. "The Comte will be down shortly." Her dark eyes looked at Hélène curiously. "I had no idea you appreciated fine art. Sometime, perhaps, I must show you around. The château has many fine examples of Italian and French paintings. It is said that we have the largest collection of Claude Lorraines in Europe. One of my ancestors was a devoted romantic."

Hélène nodded politely. "I would like very much to see them, Comtesse."

The Comtesse turned to Hubert. "Did you ride today?" she asked.

He grinned. "Yes, as a matter of fact I rode with Mademoiselle Junot."

The Comtesse's eyebrows lifted a fraction. "She rides, also?"

"I . . . I'm just learning," Hélène said quickly.

"Every young lady should learn to ride," the Comtesse said flatly. "When I was young, I won many ribbons and trophies in dressage."

"Really?" Hélène asked. She had no idea what dressage was, but she looked at the Comtesse with surprise. The elegant woman hadn't struck her as an equestrienne.

A moment later, Hélène saw the Comte enter the room. She curtsied, once again surprising herself with her own grace. It was from him, she realized at once, that Hubert had inherited his stature and physique. But Hubert's face, with its dark eyes and cleft chin, clearly came from the Comtesse, for the Comte's eyes were bright blue. His graying hair still showed streaks of its natural blondness, and he was, Hélène decided, very distinguished-looking.

"Shall we?" he asked, hooking his arm into the Comtesse's. The Comtesse nodded. Hubert touched Hélène's elbow, and she started. It was as if a spark of electricity crackled in his touch. She could feel it coursing down to her groin and erupting into an exquisite pain. Why does he do this to me? she wondered.

Then they went into the dining salon.

The dining salon was rich in elegant woods. It had gleaming dark parquet-de-Versailles flooring, lustrous Régence boiserie walls, a marble mantel, an antique Waterford chandelier over the table, and shiny caned French chairs. The sterling candelabra with their slim beeswax tapers, the heavy silverware, the fine Limoges plates, and the Baccarat crystal were set directly on the polished wood table. There was no tablecloth.

Hélène saw four table settings with baffling rows of forks, spoons, and knives laid out with military precision. A liveried footman stood behind each of their chairs. Hélène had never imagined splendor such as this.

Solicitously the footmen held their chairs away from the table. Hélène waited until the Comte and the Comtesse were seated before she sat down. She followed Madame Dupré's instructions: "If you're in doubt about anything—any fork or glass or finger bowl—watch to see what the others do. Just follow their example and you can't go wrong." Hélène glanced at the Comtesse. She was delicately unfolding her linen napkin and placing it on her lap. Hélène did likewise.

The dinner was long; most of the conversation was dull. But to Hélène it was the most exciting evening of her life. She felt pleased that she had been invited. She knew that she had not succeeded in breaking down any impermeable social barriers, but she had been invited, and that was a minor victory in itself. It proved that entrance to the upper stratum could be gained. It was a matter of meeting the "right" people. Staying in the class was a different story. By being beautiful and charming, by having exquisite manners and developing her wit, it could probably be accomplished.

Mentally Hélène thanked Madame Dupré when a footman held the soup tureen filled with crayfish consommé out to her for a second helping. "I've had plenty, thank you," she murmured politely despite the fact that she was ravenous. She knew she had been right in declining when she saw that no one else took a second helping.

Hélène was dazzled by the food. It looked even more delicious than it tasted. After the consommé came a course of sherbet. At first she thought this was dessert. It wasn't. It was served merely to clear the palate. Then a sterling platter was carried from person to person. On it was a whole pike stuffed with scallop mousse. The fish's back was artfully draped with lettuce leaves lined with little florets. All around the big fish, the platter was decorated with mushroom caps. This course was served with a white butter sauce and was accompanied by a bottle of Pouilly-Fuissé. It had been sitting uncorked on a sideboard to give it time to "breathe." Hélène raised her glass and savored the bouquet of the wine. The Comtesse once against raised her fine eyebrows. Delicately Hélène sipped at the wine. She couldn't believe how delicious it tasted. Her only wish was that she could have shared this moment with Madame Dupré.

Most of the conversation eluded Hélène. It centered around vintages, antique cars, politics, and a piece of gossip about a certain Baronne de Savonnières and her beautiful daughter, Mirielle. Hélène listened in silence, content just to be there hearing these things discussed in her presence. She was surprised to find that the gossip wasn't whispered. It was told amusingly and straightforwardly but with the deadly wit of a rapier.

Then the subject changed to one she could appreciate. Apparently a fancy-dress ball would be held at the château the night before she and Madame Dupré were to return to Saint-Nazaire.

The Comte flashed a quick look at his wife. "Did you invite the Baronne de Savonnières?" he asked.

"But of course," the Comtesse replied as if it was the most natural thing in the world.

He raised an eyebrow and his voice took on a worried tone. "But don't you think that with this recent scandal it would have been wise not to?"

The Comtesse's lips curved into a faintly malicious smile. "Au contraire, Philippe. Everyone will love me for it! You know how I adore throwing people together—especially enemies!" She wrinkled her Roman nose in delight. "It makes for such delicious stories afterward."

For a while, no one spoke. The silence was broken only by the sounds of silverware scraping on china. Hélène's eyes glowed with excitement. The round window in her room looked down over the front drive. From it she would be able to see the guests arrive. She wondered how she might recognize the notorious Baronne de Savonnières and her beautiful daughter.

Dessert was served: enormous velvety peaches on Limoges plates. Hélène was about to pick the fruit up with her fingers, but caution intervened. Discreetly she glanced at the others for guidance. They were picking up their dessert cutlery. Carefully she followed suit. She had never imagined that there were people who ate fruit with knife and fork. It proved that she had a lot to learn.

Hubert smiled across the table at her. "You're invited to come, of course," he said. "As my guest."

Hélène stared at him blankly. She had been too engrossed with watching the Comtesse slice her peach to pay attention. Now she was puzzled. Invited? To what? "I beg your pardon?" she asked politely.

"The ball, of course," he said matter-of-factly. "You shall come as my guest."

Suddenly a thrill of excitement coursed through her. The ball! She hadn't dared hope for an invitation, but now Hubert had asked her. And right in front of the Comte and the Comtesse! Quickly she looked at them, expecting some sort of negative reaction, an imperceptible shake of the head perhaps, or a widening of the eyes, or a faint arching of the brows. But she saw none of these.

Modestly Hélène lowered her eyes. "I . . . I don't know," she said softly.

"Why not?" he demanded. But as soon as the words tumbled out of his mouth, he cursed himself. He knew why. For the same reason she had tried to turn down the dinner invitation. Because he was a de Léger and she would feel out of place. "You'll be quite at ease," he assured her quickly. "Believe me, you will be a success."

"Thank you," Hélène said, fighting to keep her voice level. "I will think it over and let you know."

Satisfied that her reply was as good as an acceptance, he continued eating his dessert.

Hélène suddenly felt sick. She cut off a tiny piece of her peach and chewed it dumbly. Would Hubert never understand her dilemma? She *wanted* to go to the ball. Oh, but *how* she was dying to go. She wasn't frightened any longer. She wasn't even worried about being out of place. But she had nothing to wear to a fancy-dress ball. The severe black dress she had on certainly wouldn't do. And that was the best one she had. The feeling of disappointment was like a dull ache that spread outward from her heart and extended to her limbs until even her fingertips were numb. She sighed to herself. There was nothing she could do. She would just have to make the best of it.

After dinner they went back to the Salon de la Rotonde for coffee and brandies. Hélène sipped her coffee but declined brandy. She was not used to liquor, and the wine had already made her feel peculiarly light-headed.

Carefully the Comte lit a cigar. He and Hubert sat facing each other in chairs at the far side of the salon, discussing business and politics. The Comtesse was sitting beside Hélène on a couch, pointing out some of the paintings in the room and reciting the history behind each one. She seemed to enjoy having a captive audience. As she talked, her cold dark pupils flashed with excitement, as if each historical detail was unfolding right before her eyes. Hélène fell under the spell. It seemed that centuries of de Légers had had their fingers in many pies—in government, in wine, in art. She was fascinated with the Comtesse's copious knowledge, and flattered that the woman was so open with her. Greedily she filed away everything she learned.

Finally the Comte rose to his feet. Then he and the Comtesse excused themselves and retired. A footman closed the door softly behind them. Hubert smiled at Hélène. "Did we bore you?" he asked in an amused voice.

"On the contrary!" she countered. "I found it fascinating."

He changed the subject. "How about going for a ride?"

She shook her head. "I'd have to change again. Besides, you warned me about getting saddle sore."

He laughed. "Not a horseback ride. I meant in a car. To the village. I know—we could go to Chez Gaston for a nightcap! There's music there."

"I'm not sure I should," she said quickly.

He looked at her challengingly. "Do I detect fear in your voice?"

She looked at him sharply. "Of course not."

"Then get your coat. I'll see about a car. I'll pick you up in front, at the entrance."

For a moment she couldn't believe her ears. She stared at him. "Up front?" she asked slowly. "You mean . . . at the big marble staircase?"

"Of course. That's the entrance, isn't it?"

Is it? she thought uncharitably. Maybe for you it is, Hubert de Léger. But for Madame Dupré, Thérèse, the rest of the servants, and me, the entrance is the kitchen door. But she said none of these things. Instead, she found herself saying: "I'll be there in five minutes."

He smiled. "Make that ten. I'll have to gas up the car first."

She hurried up the servants' staircase and rapidly entered her room. The connecting door to Madame Dupré's room was still open. When the woman heard her come in, she put down the book she was reading and came to the door. "You look excited," she observed shrewdly.

Hélène nodded breathlessly. "Hubert de Léger is taking me to the village."

Madame Dupré stared at her. "He's certainly rolling out the red carpet," she remarked dryly. "He seems quite taken with you."

Hélène caught the undercurrent in Madame Dupré's voice. She looked at her hesitantly. "You think I shouldn't go?" she asked.

Madame Dupré smiled weakly. "You go," she said, wagging an admonishing finger at Hélène. "Just be careful. Hubert de Léger is a headstrong womanizer. He usually ends up with what he sets out to get."

"I'll be careful," Hélène promised. On an impulse, she hurried across the room and kissed Madame Dupré lightly on the cheek. Then she grabbed her coat and rushed back out, leaving the door slightly ajar.

Chez Gaston wasn't in the next village. It was located in Saint-Médard, ten kilometers north of Bordeaux, in the cellar of an old building. The stone walls had been whitewashed; the place was dark and noisy and the air was blue with smoke. The music was American, played on a scratchy, blaring phonograph.

Hélène surprised herself. She was a very good dancer. Per-

209

haps it was because she gave herself over to Hubert and let him lead her. His arms were around her and she responded naturally, holding on to him, her head resting on his chest. She thought she could smell the animallike manliness of him. For a while she closed her eyes and let herself go, feeling the delicious strength of him as he moved her gracefully around the floor.

When the slow dance stopped, she opened her eyes and smiled tiredly up at Hubert. He took her hand and led the way back to their little table. Her steps were slow and she walked very carefully, as if she was not sure in which direction her feet were taking her. He helped her into the rush-seated chair and then sat down across from her. He lifted the champagne bottle out of the ice bucket to refill their glasses.

She covered her glass with her hand and shook her head. "I think I've had enough," she said thickly. She frowned. It seemed to take a lot of effort to form the words.

"Come on," he coaxed. "A little more won't hurt you. Besides, it will loosen you up."

She met his eyes. "Do you think I need loosening up?" she asked softly.

He grinned and made a gesture with his thumb and forefinger. "Just a little."

She looked at his other hand. He was still holding the bottle over her glass. Or was it the second bottle? She pursed her lips thoughtfully. Then she shrugged and threw caution to the wind. She removed her hand and he filled both their glasses to the brim. "À votre santé," he said.

"À votre santé," she repeated. She drained half the glass in one long swallow. She hadn't realized she was so thirsty. It must be the dancing and all the smoke.

He fixed his eyes on her and reached across the table. Again a thrill coursed through her body. "You're very beautiful," he said. "Do you know that?"

A red flush rose up her face. She was suddenly grateful for the dim lighting. At least it hid her constant blushes.

"Do I make you nervous?" he asked softly.

She nodded slowly. "Yes."

He smiled. Then his eyes fell to her breasts and lingered there. She forced herself not to look down at herself. What's the matter? she thought. Is the dress torn? Did I spill champagne on myself? What *is* it? But suddenly, instinctively, she knew what it was. Abruptly she pushed her chair back and got unsteadily to her feet. "I . . . I think we'd better dance," she said in a serious voice.

He sensed her discomfiture and nodded. He followed her to the dance floor. For a moment she stopped and looked down at her feet. They felt strangely light, as if she were walking on cushions of air.

When they got to the floor, the music changed to a slow dance. She wrapped her arms around his neck and he embraced her. Slowly she moved her body in rhythm with his. She closed her eyes, once again smiling contentedly. Now she felt safe. Here on the floor, he didn't look at her with longing or say things that made her feel uncomfortable. Here it was just him and the music, the firmness of his body, the grace with which he led her. Again she caught that peculiar male smell. Or was it just sweat? Or her imagination?

His hand moved down to the small of her back and he pressed her tightly toward him. Suddenly she was aware of his groin pushing against her hips. She took a deep breath. The familiar, exquisite pain was growing inside her again. Fiercely she tried to push it out of her mind, but the harder she tried, the more painful and insistent it became. Suddenly she could feel a strange moistness between her legs.

He lowered his head so that his lips were at her ear. "I want to make love to you," he whispered.

Slowly she opened her eyes and looked up at him. "I think I'm drunk," she said slowly.

"That doesn't matter," he said quickly. "It won't change the way I feel about you."

Her eyes held a questioning look. "How do you feel about me?" she asked softly.

"I want you."

She turned away, suddenly disappointed. Her voice was tight. "Is that all?"

He shook his head. Then he pressed her face against his chest. He stared over her head at the dance floor and grimaced. His voice was bored, but she didn't seem to notice. All she heard was the whispery echo of his words, and they were the words she wanted to hear.

"I love you," he said.

12

They left the noise of Chez Gaston and went out into the quiet of the moonlit night. The air was cold and smelled clean and fresh after the stuffy, smoke-filled cellar. Hélène breathed deeply and clung tightly to Hubert's arm. Their heels made sharp slapping sounds on the cobbled street.

He helped her into the car, banged her door shut, and got in on the driver's side. He smiled over at her. Her face looked pale in the moonlight, and she was huddled against the door. Suddenly he leaned toward her and took her in his arms. He kissed her deeply with moist, hungry lips. Her hands clung to him fiercely.

Slowly he pulled himself away from her and started the car.

"Where are we going?" she asked in a weak voice.

"I thought we'd go to a hotel."

She reached out and touched his arm. "Not a hotel, Hubert," she said in a small voice. "Someplace romantic."

He tapped his hands on the steering wheel, thinking quickly. Then he made a grunting sound, switched on the headlights, and put the car into gear. "I know just the place."

"Where?" she asked.

He grinned. "You'll see soon enough."

The roads were deserted and he drove swiftly. The reflecting markers on the roadside picked up the glare of the headlights and flashed past in a blur.

Less than half an hour later they approached the Château Loustalot-de Léger. From a distance it looked like a brooding black shadow against the dark sky. As if on cue, the moon came out from behind some clouds and washed the battlements, the fat, medieval turrets, and the newer, more elegant Renaissance additions in a magical pale white light. The moat looked like liquid silver. Hélène gasped at the drama of the scene.

"Is this romantic enough?" he asked.

She nodded. "Yes," she said softly. "It's beautiful."

Hubert threaded the car through the dark web of roads that crisscrossed the vineyards of Loustalot. Several times the hills sloped up in front of them or the road made a turn and they lost sight of the château. Then it would appear again, looming in front of them, always larger than before.

Finally they drew to a halt alongside the moat. From here the Renaissance additions could not be seen, only the towering rock walls of the Middle Ages. In the moonlight these battlements and turrets looked mighty and impregnable.

Hubert placed his arm around her waist and led her to the entrance, a permanent stone bridge that had long since replaced the drawbridge.

"What if someone sees us?" Hélène whispered. She glanced up at him out of the corners of her eyes.

He laughed, and his teeth gleamed in the moonlight. "Don't worry," he told her. "I am a de Léger, not a thief. Anyway, we keep only a handful of servants here. We'll never even see them. I've been known to come and go at odd hours."

Suddenly she froze in her tracks. "With . . . women?" she asked. What a stupid question! she thought angrily. Whom was she trying to fool? Of course Hubert came here with other women! What was it Madame Dupré had called him? A womanizer. A veil dropped down over Hélène's eyes. Before Hubert could reply, she drew herself up with dignity.

"Take me back, Hubert," she said firmly. "To Hautecloque."

They drove back in silence. Hubert was angry, and he kept the accelerator pressed down to the floorboard. Hélène was afraid to speak. Afraid to beg him to slow down. She sat white-faced in her seat as the dark vineyards flew past. We're going to have an accident, she thought as fear constricted her throat, clamped her chest like a vise. We'll both be killed.

When he stopped to let her out at the marble steps, she looked at him and hesitated. She wanted to say something—beg him not to be angry with her, explain how she felt. But the situation was too awkward. She fumbled with the door handle (this time he didn't treat her like a lady and hold it open for her), got out of the car, and closed the door. It didn't shut the first time and she had to close it a second time more firmly. Then he gunned the engine, turned the car around, and sped back down the poplar-lined drive toward the road. Back to Saint-Médard? she wondered. Back to Chez Gaston? Back to some woman he'd once had who would welcome him with open arms and hungry lips?

She stared up at the white marble steps. Suddenly they looked too imposing, too cold and regal. She shuddered. Quickly she began to walk around the château, finally letting herself in through the kitchen door.

She was angry with Hubert. And the more she thought about it, the angrier she became. He had plied her with champagne, probably suspecting her low resistance to alcohol. And after doing that, he had tried to trick her into going to bed with him.

But she was even angrier with herself. She should have known better than to go out with him in the first place.

She didn't see Hubert anymore, nor did he try to contact her. Clearly their friendship was over. He was either as elusive as Madame Dupré had said he could be whenever he didn't want to be found, or else it was she who was elusive. At any rate, they had few opportunities to run into each other. He was in the lavish parts of the château; she was in the servants' quarters. Most of her day was spent in her room or in the sewing room. She did her best to stay indoors. The rare times she went outside were when she took walks with Madame Dupré. Hélène had never told her what had happened, and Madame Dupré was sensitive enough not to bring up the subject.

The day of the ball drew near. Hélène no longer had any desire to attend. In fact, she wished she didn't have to be in the same house where it was being held. Everything had been soured by the . . . the misunderstanding with Hubert, as she thought of it. And the ball would only be a painful reminder.

The day before the ball, Madame Dupré sent word to the Comtesse that her wardrobe was completed. Despite the flurry the household was in, the Comtesse's manservant came to announce the Comtesse's arrival in half an hour.

"She will try on all the outfits," Madame Dupré said. "Let's hope she will be pleased."

Hélène looked at her. "I don't feel well," she stammered. "Could I be excused?"

Madame Dupré frowned. "Sit down," she said, gesturing to one of the chairs.

Hélène sat down nervously and looked up at her.

Madame Dupré's eyes narrowed. "I don't know what did or did not occur between you and Hubert de Léger," she said. "However, that is between you and him. I do assume that the Comtesse is in no way involved?" She arched her eyebrows questioningly.

Hélène was silent for a moment. Then she shook her head. "No," she said finally.

"In that case, I think it is your duty to be here. After all, you worked very hard on her wardrobe, and you are partially responsible for its success or failure. If the Comtesse has any praise or criticism, you should also hear it."

Hélène looked away. "But I . . . I don't feel well," she said weakly.

Madame Dupré shook her head. "I believe you feel fine," she said firmly. "I insist that you stay."

Hélène nodded morosely.

The Comtesse was punctual. Exactly half an hour later, there was a knock on the tall door. A footman threw it open and stepped aside as the Comtesse swept in. She was dressed in a flowing, belted robe of an Oriental fabric. Her silvery hair was carefully coiffed and gleamed like the silver thread embroidered into her robe.

Madame Dupré flashed Hélène a quick look. Both of them curtsied gracefully. Immediately the footman withdrew and closed the door. The Comtesse crossed the room and went behind the three-paneled screen while Madame Dupré brought her one outfit at a time. They were on satin-covered hangers. The sleeves of each garment were carefully stuffed with lengths of tissue paper, the tops of the hangers padded with a "neck" of more tissue paper so that the collars of each garment would fall naturally.

First Madame Dupré brought out the copy of the Comtesse's pale yellow Chanel suit. This was followed by two more Chanels—one in pale blue, the other in a tweed. Then came a startling red Schiaparelli dress and two Balenciagas—one white, one black. Finally there were three Givenchys—two suits and one dress—in varying earth tones.

Each one fit the Comtesse to perfection. Madame Dupré eyed them with satisfaction. Even a professionally trained eye would find it difficult to distinguish the copy from the original, she thought.

The Comtesse stood in front of the three-paneled gilt-framed mirror in each garment. She carefully scrutinized herself from all angles, moving her arms, twisting her thin body. Finally, after trying on the last Givenchy, she nodded approval. "You have done well, madame," she told Madame Dupré.

Madame Dupré looked pleased. "It was a pleasure, Comtesse," she replied modestly.

The Comtesse nodded and went back behind the screen. When she reappeared in her Oriental robe, she said, "I will have Lise collect the clothes in a few minutes."

Madame Dupré nodded.

The Comtesse turned her dark eyes on Hélène. "I had hoped we would see more of you, mademoiselle," she said reproachfully.

Hélène felt herself flushing. "Oui, Comtesse," she murmured. "I had hoped so also."

"I recall that my son invited you to the ball tomorrow. You *are* coming?"

Madame Dupré started. This was news indeed! Quickly she looked at Hélène. The girl's eyes seemed to dull; the violet pupils turned to smoky amethyst.

"I'm afraid I won't be able to accept your kind invitation, Comtesse," Hélène said. "I hope you will excuse me."

Madame Dupré gasped and the Comtesse looked at Hélène in surprise. "But that is not possible! My son will be very upset if you do not appear. He has asked me to tell you personally that he will expect you in the Salon de la Rotonde at eight o'clock tomorrow evening."

Hélène's heart gave a joyous leap. Did Hubert really say that? Was it possible that he still wanted to see her? Was he no longer angry with her? The sudden news made her curiously light-headed. But she couldn't go to the ball. She had nothing to wear. She would have to make up some excuse.

"I'm sorry," Hélène said. "I thought he . . . I . . . ." She looked helplessly at Madame Dupré, her eyes begging for help. Almost imperceptibly Madame Dupré shook her head sideways.

The Comtesse reached out, touched Hélène's chin with her elegant fingers, and gently turned her face toward her. "I do not know whether you are very dumb or very clever, mademoiselle," she said softly. "My son was extremely agitated by your behavior."

"I . . . I'm sorry."

"Do not be. Apparently you are the first woman who has ever dared to refuse him." For a moment the dark eyes flashed with amusement. "He was very hurt, but strangely enough, he respects you for it. As do I." She smiled. "You will be in the Salon de la Rotonde at eight?"

"I'm sorry, Comtesse." Hélène made a helpless gesture with her hands. "It is such short notice. I thought I wouldn't be welcome, so I didn't prepare anything to . . ." Her eyes fell. ". . . to wear."

The Comtesse frowned thoughtfully. Then she glanced at Madame Dupré. "Could you quickly sew something for her, madame?"

Madame Dupré bowed her head. "Of course, Comtesse. But there is the matter of fabrics."

"There are still some in the wardrobes, non?" The Comtesse gestured toward them.

"Oui, Comtesse. But they are mostly fine white silks."

The Comtesse smiled. "Use as much as you want, but make it beautiful. You shall be paid extra for it."

"Oui, Comtesse." Suddenly Madame Dupré looked at the Comtesse with inspiration. "I know it is asking too much, Comtesse, but the greenhouses . . ."

"Yes?" The Comtesse looked at Madame Dupré quizzically.

"Some flowers. For decorating the dress. Might I have the gardener bring me some?"

"Fresh flowers for a dress?" The Comtesse frowned. "That sounds rather bizarre. But as long as it is beautiful, take all the flowers you want."

"Thank you, Comtesse," Madame Dupré said.

The Comtesse started toward the door. Quickly Hélène and Madame Dupré curtsied. Suddenly the Comtesse turned around in the doorway. She gazed at Hélène. "Eight o'clock tomorrow, then. In the Salon de la Rotonde."

And the tall door closed.

Hélène let out a painful sound and sank into a chair. She pushed her fingers through her hair. "What do I do?" she wailed.

Madame Dupré looked at her with delight. "I know what *I* shall do. For once, I am going to design and sew a dress that

217

truly inspires me!" Her eyes flashed with excitement. She made an agitated gesture with her hands. "Quickly—get undressed! I shall measure you immediately! We have no time to lose!"

Madame Dupré ate no lunch or dinner. "There is no time!" she cried. "I have a gown to sew—overnight!"

Hélène began to feel an excitement growing within her as she watched the woman deftly attacking the bolt of silk with her shears. The fabric parted smoothly in two as the sharp blades slid through it. Hélène reached out and touched the silk. It was soft and white and fluid. It seemed to shimmer with the radiance of sunshine on new snow.

Madame Dupré's pace never flagged. She seemed to know exactly what effect she was striving for. What style the gown would be. How much fabric to use. She worked without a pattern and with a speed and surety Hélène had never seen before. Madame Dupré seemed to have burst out of the shackles that had bound her creativity. She was creating a garment that was totally original, that would be spectacular. There would be no "borrowing" from Givenchy, Balenciaga, Odile Joly, or Dior.

As the hours passed, the gown slowly began to take on a shape. Hélène could see that it would have a square, low-cut neckline and an enormous full skirt. There would be no sleeves, only loose over-the-shoulder straps.

From time to time Madame Dupré would pin the pieces of silk around Hélène. Then she would step back, her mouth full of pins, and study the effect with a critical frown. She would make a quick tuck here, a swift chalk line there. Then everything would be spread back out on the paper-covered table.

Madame Dupré did everything by hand. Hélène was astonished. It seemed that the woman was quicker with the needle than the machine. Her fingers flew.

When it was nearly midnight, Hélène could no longer hold her eyes open. She fell asleep in her chair. Madame Dupré glanced at her and smiled. Hélène's legs were stretched out, her feet crossed, and her hands were folded in her lap. Her head was tilted sideways against one shoulder, her black hair tumbling down over her face. Ah, the sleep of the young, Madame Dupré thought. How peaceful and rejuvenating it was. Well, Hélène would need every wink she could get. Attending a ball was going to be exhausting.

When morning came, Madame Dupré was still at work. Strangely enough, she didn't feel a bit tired. It was as if the thrill of her creativity superseded her need for sleep.

Hélène suddenly stirred. She opened her eyes and blinked. She yawned noisily, and with her fingers she rubbed the sleep from her eyes. Sunlight was already streaming in through the big windows. She looked over at Madame Dupré with surprise. "Why . . . it's morning!"

Madame Dupré smiled. "It is, and a beautiful morning at that!"

Hélène let out a gasp. She had seen the gown lying on the table. Slowly she got to her feet and came toward it. Already it looked finished. As the sunlight hit its whiteness, the silk seemed to dazzle and threw blinding light back at her. She had to squint.

"It's beautiful!" she breathed.

Madame Dupré smiled and glanced at Hélène out of the corner of her eye. "It shall be, but that will be many hours from now. Did you sleep well?"

Hélène nodded, rubbing her shoulder briskly; it felt sore from sleeping in the chair. "Yes, well enough. But you didn't get a wink!"

"I will once this gown is finished. Now I need you to try it on quickly before I continue. Then I want you to eat a very light breakfast and a tiny lunch. The emptier your stomach, the better you will look. We must make you appear to be *very* slim."

Hélène nodded. "And I'll need to take a bath and wash my hair and do something with it—"

"Don't do anything with your hair except wash it!" Madame Dupré said sharply.

"Why not?"

Madame Dupré smiled secretly and got to her feet. "You'll see. Now, stand over here and we'll have a fitting."

Quickly Hélène slipped out of her clothes and Madame Dupré helped her into the gown. The low-cut bodice fit snugly, and Hélène noticed that it pushed her small, firm breasts upward, making them appear larger and more shapely than they actually were. The skirt was huge and magnificent—kilometers of soft, voluminous silk billowing like a cloud. On an impulse, she walked over to the three-paneled mirror and whirled around. She caught sight of her reflection. The skirt shimmered as it sailed around her legs, and she could hear the soft rustling of the silk.

"It . . . it's lovely!" Hélène said. She whirled around again, and a look of despair suddenly marred the excited look on her face. Her body seemed to slump. She had seen her shoes. They were the only pair she owned and certainly couldn't be worn with the gown. Her heart sank. It was an impossible situation.

"What's the matter?" Madame Dupré asked, instantly catching her dismay.

Wordlessly Hélène lifted the skirt to display her shoes.

Madame Dupré smiled. "I know that," she said soothingly. "So don't worry, I have already thought of it."

Hélène looked relieved. She posed in front of the mirror, watching the folds of silk shift and fall. The gown seemed to have a lifeblood of its own. Then she turned questioningly to Madame Dupré. "What have you thought of for shoes?"

"I shall sew silk slippers with soft leather bottoms. They will tie around your ankles with white silk ribbons, rather like ballet slippers."

Hélène beamed. On an impulse she hugged Madame Dupré. "You're a genius!" she said happily.

Madame Dupre looked pleased, but her voice was gruff. "Careful!" she said. "You're crushing the dress! Now, off with it! I want to finish it on time. We have less than ten hours until the ball." She helped Hélène to undress. "You go and eat. Before you take your bath, look in my nightstand. I have some scented bath seeds. Pour a handful into the tub."

By four o'clock Hélène had completed her grooming. She had bathed twice and carefully washed her hair. When it was dry, she did what Madame Dupré had told her to do—winding it as tightly as possible around her head and pinning it in place. Then she went back down to the sewing room.

The gown was nearly finished. Hélène just stood there staring at it, transfixed. She shook her head in disbelief. She had never seen anything quite so lovely. It lay on the table, and Madame Dupré was deftly sewing a surfilage along the hem. The surfilage wasn't necessary, but it was an added luxurious touch. Hélène knew that only the finest garments had this finishing touch that would keep the hem from fraying. Not that the gown would be worn enough to fray. But she knew that Madame Dupré wanted it to stand up to the most lavish designer gowns at the ball.

"There. Fini." Madame Dupré sighed with approval and let the hem fall back down on the table. "Try it on once more," she said. "I've got to see if it needs any last-minute adjustments."

Eagerly Hélène slipped into it. Her eyes glowed and her breath came in short, excited gasps. The gown was spectacular indeed. Its very simplicity gave it a style of its own. Madame Dupré stepped back to study the effect. She nodded with satisfaction.

"It's more beautiful than anything I've ever seen in *Vogue*," Hélène said in a hushed voice.

Madame Dupré nodded. "It fits perfectly. Thank God, no adjustments are needed. Now, slip out of it and hang it up on one of the hangers. I'm going to work on the slippers now. In the meantime, I want you to go and see the gardener. Tell him the Comtesse said it was all right to deliver enormous bunches of baby's breath to me immediately."

Hélène frowned. She had forgotten all about the flowers. She wondered what on earth they were for.

At seven-thirty she got dressed. Madame Dupré was like a fussing, clucking mother hen. First the slippers. Hélène slipped into them and tied the silk ribbons around her ankles. She tried walking around the room in them. It was like walking on air. They let her move with a grace she'd never known she had. Then the gown. After Madame Dupré approved the way it fell, she reached for a matching silk turban she had sewn and slipped in over Hélène's head. It covered her skull tightly, hiding her ears and framing her face. It made her forehead look elegantly peaked.

Then came the crowning touch. The flowers. Madame Dupré picked up a cluster of baby's breath she had tied together with almost invisible wires and pinned it to the back of the turban. The flowers looked like a lacy halo growing up out of the silk. Then she reached for an enormous thick boa of more baby's breath. This, too, she had wired carefully together. She draped it around Hélène's shoulders and bodice. Then she got out her needle and deftly stitched it on.

Hélène let out a gasp when she looked at herself in the mirror. It was a fairy-tale gown. The lacelike flowers were far more elegant and beautiful than jewels could ever be.

Madame Dupré glanced at her watch. It was five minutes until eight. She stood back and smiled with satisfaction. She knew that for the first time in her life she had sewn a masterpiece. A masterpiece that was not a copy, that had not been inspired by anyone except herself. Suddenly she felt very tired. Soon she would be able to rest.

"You look beautiful!" she told Hélène proudly.

Hélène's eyes were moist with tears. "I don't know how I can ever thank you."

Madame Dupré's eyes narrowed. She said hoarsely, "Wipe away those tears! You don't want to have puffy red eyes, do you?"

Vehemently Hélène shook her head and wiped her eyes.

Madame Dupré took her hand and squeezed it affectionately. "Enjoy yourself."

And then there was a knock at the door. A footman in red satin livery had come to escort Hélène downstairs.

The guests were already arriving as Hélène swept down the carved stone staircase behind the footman, and she could hear the faint sounds of an orchestra somewhere within the château. She tried not to show her nervousness. Delicately she lifted the skirt of her gown so that she wouldn't trip on the hem. She caught sight of herself in an ornate pier glass and gasped. She still couldn't quite believe that the reflection she saw there was hers.

Several guests were milling about at the foot of the stairs, the men in hand-sewn tuxedos, the women in lavish gowns and elaborate jewels. Hélène's eyes caught the flashing of diamond chandelier earrings, the sparkle of weblike necklaces of diamonds and emeralds, the deep fiery flashes of rubies, the cool moonglow of sapphires. She could see the expressions on the guests' faces as they looked curiously up at her. They were all stunned.

They stepped aside for her as the footman led her through the open double doors of the Salon de la Rotonde. The room was crowded with guests. The Comte and the Comtesse were standing inside the door, greeting the guests as they arrived. Hélène could see Hubert at the far end of the room. He was impatiently pacing up and down, looking at his gold pocket watch. With a quick motion he snapped it shut. He looked very handsome in black tuxedo and white silk shirt and bow tie.

Suddenly all conversation in the room stopped. For a moment Hélène wondered why. Then she knew. She could feel all their eyes upon her.

For a moment she hesitated. Then gracefully she dropped a curtsy in front of the Comte and Comtesse. When she got back up, Hubert was suddenly beside her, touching her arm.

The Comtesse smiled at Hélène. "Extraordinary," she murmured. "You are quite lovely. And Madame Dupré is a genius. You must tell her for me."

"Thank you, Comtesse. I shall do that."

The Comte smiled at Hélène, his blue eyes looking at her with quickening interest. Then Hubert led her aside. A manservant presented a silver tray with glasses of champagne. Hélène took a glass and sipped delicately, looking at Hubert over the rim. But she drank very slowly. She had decided to have no more than two glasses all night long. She would be above reproach.

"Who *is* she?" she heard a young woman in an apricot Dior gown ask an older one.

"I do not know, chérie. But I'm going to have to find out where that gown came from."

Hubert smiled at Hélène. "You are quite a sensation. I had no idea you were so beautiful."

She smiled, genuinely pleased.

"Would you like to go to the ballroom?" he asked.

She nodded, and he took her arm and led her down a long hall. She gasped in amazement. The hall was lined with linen-draped tables. Spread out on them were lavish hors d'oeuvres: bright red "trees" of crayfish; silver tubs filled with escargots; platters of scallops, mussels, oysters, and clams; tiny quail eggs on beds of Iranian caviar. There was an abundance of everything, all artfully arranged around a dazzling ice sculpture. Predictably, it depicted the familiar lion and salamander holding the crest of the de Légers.

Hélène was even more dazzled when they entered the ballroom. For a moment she could only stand there staring. She had never seen anything so festive. The room was enormous, with a high, fanciful trompe l'oeil ceiling and columned walls. All around the room were palms from the hothouses. Concealed among the graceful branches were flowerpots whose orchids gave the appearance of growing among the palm fronds. Overhead, the crystal chandeliers sprouted forests of slender white candles, and the walls danced with flickering light. At the far end, on a small stage, an orchestra was playing waltzes.

"Would you care to dance?" Hubert asked, executing a solemn little bow.

Hélène looked out across the shiny floor. It was still early. No one was dancing yet. She nodded, handed her champagne glass to a passing footman, and let Hubert pull her into his arms. Soundlessly he swept her across the room. Her gown rustled and billowed like a graceful white cloud, and the baby's breath looked like hundreds of snowflakes frozen around her.

When the waltz ended, another one started up. A few more couples were whirling around them now, moving across the floor with the grace of lithe swans. One waltz melted into another. And another. And another. Hélène had no idea how many they danced. "I think I need a rest," she said finally.

Hubert hooked his arm into hers and led her away from the swirling guests. She saw that the Comte and Comtesse were now standing at the edge of the dance floor. The guests must have all arrived, she thought.

The Comte made a little bow to Hubert and smiled at Hélène. She could feel his penetrating blue eyes upon her. She felt herself flushing.

"May I have the pleasure of this dance?" he asked.

Then she felt his hand on her arm. She started. Whatever she had felt at Chez Gaston with Hubert was nothing compared to the powerful surge that now coursed through her body. Was she to feel this with every man who touched her? she wondered.

"You look lovely," the Comte told her softly as they swirled around the floor. "May I compliment you on your gown?"

"Thank you," Hélène murmured politely. "You are too kind."

"White suits you so much better than black," he declared. "You should wear white always."

Her heart pounded and she looked up at him. He remembered what she'd worn at the dinner three weeks ago! Was it possible? They hadn't exchanged two sentences. He had hardly looked at her.

When the music stopped, he led her back to Hubert. The Comtesse smiled. For the first time, Hélène noticed the Comtesse's jewelry. She wore nothing but gold earrings. They were large and looked very old. Raised in relief on them were the salamander, the lion, and the crest of the de Légers. Hélène realized that the Comtesse must own much fine jewelry, but since she chose to wear these, they must be quite precious.

"My dear Comtesse," a fawning, woman's voice said from behind.

They all turned. "Why, Baronne, how delightful that you could come," the Comtesse said smoothly. "For a while I didn't think you were going to make it."

The Baronne laughed a high, brittle laugh. "I'm afraid I'm always late."

Hélène stared at the Baronne. She was in her mid-thirties, red-haired, sharp-eyed, and bony. She wore a Balmain gown of scarlet satin and her neck was draped with blood-colored rubies. A palsied, very old gray-haired man stood on one side of her, a beautiful young woman in green on the other. The young woman wore an emerald necklace and matching earrings and held herself with cool self-confidence.

Curiously Hélène wondered if the red-haired woman could be the Baronne de Savonnières. She glanced at the poised beauty. Was that Mirielle? Were they the ones the Comtesse had gossiped about during the dinner, so delighted that she'd invited them?

The Comtesse smiled and introduced Hélène. So it *was* the Baronne de Savonnières and Mirielle. And the old man was the Baron.

Mirielle gave Hubert a reproachful look and touched him on the arm. Her face was close to his. "I haven't seen you for ages," she said in a husky voice.

He smiled uncomfortably at her. "I'm afraid I have been kept very busy. I must apologize for the neglect."

The Baronne's eyes flashed and she smiled like a shark. Her teeth were long and pointed. "Aren't you going to ask her to dance?" she said slowly.

Hubert knew when he was cornered. He bowed to Hélène. "Please pardon me for a few minutes," he said. She watched as he dutifully hooked his arm into Mirielle's and led her across the floor.

"They make a charming couple, don't you think?" the Baronne said approvingly.

The Comtesse nodded wordlessly. Smoothly she changed

the subject and brought Hélène into the conversation. After one dance, Hubert returned with Mirielle.

"What is the matter?" the Baronne asked with undisguised acidity. "Only one dance? Don't tell me you have become stingy!" She flashed Hubert a disapproving look.

Hubert smiled politely and gestured to Hélène. "I have invited Mademoiselle Junot to the ball. I'm afraid it is my duty as her escort to show her some attention." Before the Baronne could reply, he bowed to Hélène. "May I have the pleasure?"

Hélène couldn't help smiling at Mirielle's vitriolic look as they waltzed away.

"Who is *she*?" the Baronne asked angrily, watching Hélène.

"A friend of the family's," the Comtesse replied vaguely. "A very charming young lady."

"Yes . . ." The Baronne's voice trailed off as she gazed sharply around the room. "Come, Mirielle. I see some Rothschilds over there . . ." She pointed a splintery finger to a cluster of people standing at the far side. Immediately they hurried toward them, the old man limping along behind. The Rothschilds saw them coming and fled onto the dance floor, waltzing in the opposite direction.

"What a dreadful woman," the Comte said when the Baronne had left. "I can't understand why you always invite her."

The Comtesse smiled wisely. "To add spice to the party, of course. People love tension, and the Baronne supplies it naturally." She looked over the dance floor with satisfaction. So far, the ball was a huge success. Her eyes caught sight of Hélène. "Hubert and the girl look well together, don't you think?"

The Comte nodded. "They certainly do," he said slowly. "She is very beautiful. And she dances well."

"Yes," the Comtesse said with a sigh. "It is a pity that she has no title." She glanced up at her husband. "Well, Philippe. Aren't you going to ask me to dance?"

He turned away from the dancing couple. "Of course," he said. He bowed gallantly and waltzed the Comtesse across the floor. She moved very elegantly but with an economy of movement that precluded natural grace. Every now and then he would catch a glimpse of Hubert and Hélène. Yes, the girl was quite stunning, he thought with sudden longing. And she moved well. Like an angel. Somehow, she made you know that she was a woman and you were a man.

Hélène left the ball at one o'clock. Hubert caught her arm. "Where are you going?"

She smiled. "Upstairs. I have a long journey ahead of me tomorrow. I'll need my rest."

"You're leaving, then." His voice was flat.

She nodded. "Yes. Our work here is over."

"But don't you want to stay?"

She looked into his eyes. There was a painful shadow within the black pupils. "I'd like to stay, but I can't, Hubert. There are things that I must do."

"What kind of things?"

She was silent for a moment. How could he ever understand what she had to do? How could she explain to him that her dreams were glossy pieces of paper glued together to become a magazine? She was certain that he would never understand her need to create something. For him, life was glittering parties, beautiful women, fragile grapes. "I have to go, Hubert," she said firmly. "I'm sorry."

He looked at her sullenly. "I thought you loved me," he said.

Silently she looked out across the crowded dance floor. She saw the beautifully dressed couples moving elegantly in time to the music. She saw the jewels of the women glittering around their patrician throats like the chandeliers high above their heads. She saw the self-assurance of these women, the bearing and style and confidence that could come only from a high-placed birth. That was the type of woman Hubert needed. Someone elegant and cultured and composed. Someone who knew how to make small talk, which wines to serve with dinner, what types of people to invite in order to make a party a success.

"I thought I loved you, too, Hubert," she said softly. "But I'm not ready for love. And I'm not right for you."

He reached out and grasped her hand. "We could get married!" he said quickly. "I am the future Comte. You would be the future Comtesse. We could live in the Château Loustalot while my parents are alive. Then we'd move in here." He squeezed her hand in desperation. "In time, you would learn to love me."

227

She stared at him. For a moment she didn't know what to say.

Then she smiled sadly. She shook her head. "It wouldn't work, Hubert," said gently. "I'm sorry."

When she got to the servants' quarters she could no longer hear the sounds of the ball. Although the connecting door to Madame Dupré's room was shut, Hélène was very quiet. She knew that the woman must be exhausted, and she was afraid of waking her up.

Slowly Hélène took off her turban, slipped out of her gown, and hung it carefully on a clothes hanger. In the morning she would remove all the baby's breath and then carefully pack the gown. Cinderella's ball had not lasted long. Five beautiful, exciting hours. Now she was a seamstress again. Suddenly she realized that she was tired and that her feet were aching from all the dancing.

She sat down on the edge of the bed and unlaced her slippers. At last she had time to think. Thoughtfully she massaged her feet, kneading her ankles with her hands. Had Hubert been serious about his proposal? she wondered. Probably. But there were two things she believed a successful marriage needed. Love, and acceptance from the family. She knew that she did not love Hubert enough to become his wife. She was not sure that he loved her. Perhaps he had mistaken infatuation for love. And acceptance from the family? She had no family to speak of, but he did. Would the Comte and Comtesse have allowed a marriage between their heir and a seamstress? She couldn't be certain, but she believed they wouldn't.

Abruptly she got to her feet and walked over to the round window. She bent down, parted the curtains a crack, and looked out. The night was dark and misty. In the light of the gaslights, one after the other, she saw chauffeured limousines pulling up to the marble steps. The guests were departing. The ball was over. For everyone. But not as much as for her.

13

"I want to hear everything!" Jeanne said excitedly when Hélène returned to Saint-Nazaire. "Did you see the Comte? Was his son handsome?"

Hélène looked across the kitchen table at Jeanne and smiled weakly. She cupped her hands around the warm coffee mug and looked quietly down into it. "Yes," she said slowly. "He was very handsome."

"Did you fall madly in love with him?"

It was supposed to be a joke, but Hélène couldn't laugh. She shook her head. "At first, I thought I did. I'm afraid he was more taken with me than I was with him."

Jeanne stared at her. "You mean he . . . ?"

Hélène nodded. "He asked me to marry him."

"You're not serious!" Jeanne gave Hélène an appraising look. Then her voice took on a quiet respect. "You *are* serious."

Hélène nodded.

Jeanne looked sharply at Hélène. "Don't tell me you turned him down!"

Hélène smiled. "I did."

"Well, that does it! Now I have to hear every last detail!"

They talked far into the night. Hélène didn't omit a thing. When she got to the part about the ball, Jeanne shook her head. She couldn't believe it. It all sounded too lavish for this world.

"You'll have to see my gown," Hélène said wistfully. "It was the most beautiful one there."

Jeanne's eyes brightened. "I can't wait to see it."

Suddenly Hélène smiled. She reached across the table and put her hand on top of Jeanne's. "Tell you what. I'll give it to you. It'll need a little taking in since you're so skinny, but it will make the perfect wedding gown."

229

Jeanne shook her head. "I could never accept it," she said in a tight voice. "It . . . it means too much to you."

Hélène smiled. "You must accept it. I wanted to make a dress for you, but this one is just perfect. I want you to look beautiful. After all, you get married only once, right?" She waited for Jeanne's nod. "And you want to look beautiful for Edmond, don't you?"

"Yes, but . . . you might need to wear it someplace . . ."

Hélène shook her head. "I'll never have the opportunity to wear it again."

Jeanne looked doubtful. "But what about when you get to Paris?"

Hélène sighed. "That's still a long way off, I'm afraid. Madame Dupré gave me a generous bonus, and I've saved quite a bit of money already, but it's not enough. Not for Paris." Suddenly her face broke into a smile. "How is Edmond?"

"He was here for only two days," Jeanne said. "He decided we could use the extra money, so instead of taking his month's vacation, he went back out to sea. It seems that your ambition is rubbing off on him."

"What do you mean?"

Jeanne suddenly clapped a hand over her mouth. "Oh-oh. Now I've let the cat out of the bag."

Hélène's eyes narrowed. She leaned across the table. "Out with it," she demanded.

"I'm not supposed to tell you," Jeanne said hesitantly. "Edmond wanted to tell you himself."

Hélène chuckled. "You told me this much; now I might as well hear the rest."

Jeanne sighed and shook her head. Then her voice dropped an octave. "We're saving up so that Edmond can go to school."

Hélène's eyes widened in surprise. This was news, indeed. "School," she repeated aloud, rolling the word on her tongue. A sudden keen intuition came over her. Edmond was right. An education would serve him well.

Jeanne's eyes burned with earnestness, but when she spoke, it was in a curiously soft voice. "Edmond wants more out of life than just being a fisherman, Hélène. He wants a future. He wants to be somebody. And when we have children, he wants them to be somebody, too. So he's thinking of going into law." She paused. "Just like you, he decided that in order to do it, he needs to return to Paris."

"Paris!" Hélène's eyes lit up and she could feel her heart beginning to pound. "That's *wonderful!*" she said.

Breathlessly Jeanne plunged on. "We've got it all worked out. For the next two years we'll scrimp and save. Then, as soon as we can afford it, we'll follow you to the city. They say there are many jobs there, so I shouldn't have any trouble finding work as a waitress. That way, I can help pay his way while he's going to the university!" She looked at Hélène proudly.

It's too bad that we no longer have Maman's house in Montmartre, Hélène thought bitterly. Then none of us would have to wait to get to Paris. But instead of voicing these thoughts, she asked brightly, "When's the fleet due in?"

"Next Friday. And the wedding is on the following day. Just think, Edmond's getting a whole week off!"

Hélène grinned. "Good. There'll be enough time for two celebrations, then."

Jeanne frowned. "Two?"

"Of course. One for your marriage, the other for your future." Suddenly Hélène sprang to her feet and began to pace thoughtfully up and down the kitchen. She tapped an index finger against her lips. "Let me see, now . . . there's the wedding. Are all the preparations made?"

Jeanne nodded.

"Good. And we'll have to plan a big dinner and . . . Good Lord! There's still so much to be done. We have no time to lose! You'd better come by my place this Sunday. I'll have to do the alterations on the gown immediately! And if I can find the right fabric by then, I'll sew your veil, also."

Jeanne stared at her. Suddenly she started to laugh.

Hélène stopped pacing and looked at her. "What's so funny?"

"You look so nervous, everyone would think you're the bride!"

14

The wedding was beautiful and Jeanne was the picture of the
bride that all women dream they will be one day. Hélène
sighed. This was a fairy-tale dream that happened once in
your life. And Edmond was waiting for his lady, understand-
ably nervous, yet visibly anxious for her arrival, for their
hands to be joined forever.

Now it was over and Hélène realized that her time had
come—not to meet her love, but finally to return to her beloved Paris to pursue her own dream.

She was ready.

Carefully she stepped over two sets of railroad tracks to
the third platform. Edmond set her cardboard suitcase down
at her feet. She turned around and looked at the small party
of well-wishers who followed her. The only friends she had
were here. Jeanne, Edmond, and Madame Dupré. And now
she would be separated from them. Tears stung at her eyes.
How long would it be until she saw them all again? she wondered.

She could hear the faint chugging of a locomotive. She
glanced down the tracks. In the distance, a plume of white
smoke marked the approaching train.

"It's coming," Jeanne murmured.

Hélène held her breath. She nodded with apprehension.

Madame Dupré gave Hélène a small package. "I've made
you some sandwiches," she said.

Hélène nodded gratefully.

"Wait a second, there's one more thing." Madame Dupré
reached into her pocketbook, took out an envelope, and
pressed it into Hélène's hand.

Hélène looked at it curiously. "What is this?"

"A little something that might come in handy," Madame
Dupré said vaguely.

232

Slowly Hélène lifted the flap of the envelope. She could see money inside. "No," she said firmly.

"You'll need it," Madame Dupré said, pushing Hélène's hand aside. "There isn't much. I didn't have a chance to go to the bank. It was all there was in the cash drawer."

Hélène embraced Madame Dupré. For a moment she couldn't speak. "Thank you," she said finally, her voice husky. "For everything. I'll never forget all you've done for me."

Madame Dupré's eyes were moist. "You just become successful!" she whispered. "You just take Paris by storm!"

"I will," Hélène promised. She turned to Jeanne. "Good-bye, friend."

Jeanne's lips quivered. Then she drew Hélène wordlessly toward her.

"You'll take care of Edmond?" Hélène asked softly.

Jeanne nodded. She looked ready to burst into tears.

Hélène turned to Edmond.

"Well, it looks like you're finally on your way, Little French Girl," he said softly.

Hélène found herself sniffling. She threw herself into his arms. He wrapped them around her, and she could feel his gentle strength. "I'm frightened, Edmond," she whispered.

He looked at her in surprise. "What of?"

"Paris."

"Don't be," he said solemnly.

"I don't like to be all alone."

"Don't worry. We'll join you there as soon as it's possible. And Jeanne will write to you every week."

Hélène nodded and looked up at him. She smiled through her tears. "If I'm rich before you, I'll send for you and put you through school."

"And if I get through school before you're rich, Little French Girl, I'll start a magazine for you."

The train rolled in with a metallic screech and then crawled to a stop with a mighty hiss and a jolt. Hélène looked up at the rows of grimy green cars. Then she glanced at her friends. There was nothing more to be said.

"Off you go," Edmond said cheerfully, extricating himself from her arms. "To Paris."

A lump rose up in her throat. "To Paris," she repeated softly.

TODAY

Thursday, January 11

1

It was after ten o'clock in the morning when James Cortland Gore III spun his swivel chair around to face his office window. It overlooked New York harbor to the right and the East River to the left. Idly he switched his gaze directly downward. Twenty-one stories below, he could see the tourists already swarming around on the decks of the antique tall ships that were docked at the South Street Seaport.

He spun back around to face his desk and pulled open the top drawer, where he kept his cigars. Opening the wooden box, he selected one, sniffed it, held it to his ear, and carefully rattled it. Satisfied, he trimmed the end off, leaned back, and lit it slowly. He folded his hands over his ample stomach as the expensive aroma of the Havana filled the office. Contentedly he puffed at it.

Things were certainly looking up, he thought with satisfaction. In fact, in a few days he might even surprise Geraldine by ordering the half-million-dollar Chris Craft Roamer she had been hungering after. He thought about it for a moment. Yes, a yacht might be very nice indeed. After all, there would be nothing to do on board but eat and drink, and he loved to do both. Best of all, it would even be affordable. Because only last night he had received another telephone call. . . .

He had been at home going over some documents in the big paneled study, a redolent pine fire sparkling in the fireplace when the call came.

"Do you know who this is?" the familiar voice asked softly.

His heart had begun to pound wildly and he looked around to make sure he was alone in the room. Geraldine had an unnerving habit of entering a room quiet as a mouse, and you'd never even know she was there. "Yes," he whispered into the receiver as if the walls might overhear.

"Well? Have you come to a decision?"

He took the silk handkerchief out of the breast pocket of his red silk smoking jacket and mopped his forehead. He had broken out in a sweat.

"Yes," he finally answered. "I have decided."

"And your answer?" the voice demanded.

He hesitated, but only fractionally. "I'll do it," he whispered. "She will not get an extension. I will arrange it so that you will get her shares."

"Good." The voice sounded satisfied. "The moment we sign the papers, you will receive a briefcase containing one million dollars."

"Consider it done."

The phone clicked and went dead, and it took him a moment to realize that the caller had hung up. His chins were quivering as he replaced the receiver. He felt relief. Yes, and at the same time, he was very nervous. As nervous as he was each time he "wrote" himself a loan. . . .

The intercom on his desk buzzed. He leaned forward and pressed the button. "Yes, Alice?"

"Mr. Gore, there are two men from accounting here to see you."

He stared at the intercom, his face going pale. Men? From accounting? Once again he began to break out in a sweat. Good God, not the auditors, he prayed. Not at a time like this. Not when he'd be able to replace all his "borrowings" in less than a week's time. Dear, sweet, merciful God, no. Then he put the brakes on this ridiculous train of thought. He was just feeling guilty and panicky. There really was nothing to fear. After all, it was part of his job to deal with the accounting department. It would not do to panic each time he had to talk things over with them. That thought made him feel better, but one thing was certain. As soon as he got his hands on the million, he'd lose no time in replacing the missing funds.

After a long moment he cleared his throat. "Send them in," he said.

Seconds later, Alice opened the door and ushered them into his office. His heart began to thump and he thought he was going to be sick. Instantly he realized that he had reason to panic. These were not just two men from accounting. He recognized them. The short, stocky one was Paluzzi, the tall blond one O'Rourke. They were part of the bank's internal auditing team.

Gore's mind began to race. If he didn't think fast, he'd find his whole world, his dreams, indeed his whole life come crashing down all around him. Somehow he'd have to stall them; somehow he'd have to find a way to gain a week in order to dig himself out of this mess. Above all, he must conceal his fears. His guilt.

"Gentlemen," he said with a forced smile. "Won't you have a seat?"

They nodded expressionlessly and sat down in the two overstuffed chairs that faced his desk.

Gore quietly folded his hands on the polished mahogany surface. It did not surprise him to find that his hands were shaking. Trying to keep his voice natural, he favored the men with the friendliest look he could muster. "What can I do for you?"

Paluzzi looked curiously at him. A sturdy Italian with thick black hair and extremely broad shoulders, he looked more like a weight lifter than an accountant. But looks can deceive. Gore knew that Paluzzi's reputation at ManhattanBank was secure. He was the best auditor they had.

"Mr. Gore," Paluzzi said softly, "we've been going over your accounts dating back over the last five years. The first forty-three months are in order. But beginning seventeen months ago, we've found some discrepancies."

"Discrepancies?" Gore could feel his blood pressure rise. "What kind of discrepancies?"

Paluzzi's dark eyes were steady. "I think you already know, Mr. Gore."

This can't be happening, he told himself over and over. It's only a nightmare. A *nightmare*. It'll be over when I wake up.

Now O'Rourke spoke up. "Don't you want to know the amount of the discrepancy, Mr. Gore?"

No! He didn't want to hear another word. He couldn't bear it any longer. But in a faraway voice he found himself murmuring, "How much?"

"Exactly five hundred thousand, ninety-five dollars," Paluzzi said. "All of it missing from your accounts."

Gore forced a thin laugh. The moment it came out, he realized how unconvincing it sounded. "You must be mistaken," he said. "You have the ledgers?"

"In our office. They are correct."

Gore pushed back his chair and rose to his feet. "I would like to go over them with you, if it won't be inconvenient. Could you wait outside for me? I would like to make a tele-

239

phone call first." He caught them exchanging glances. He puffed his chest out with dignity. "No, gentlemen," he assured them, "I'm not going to call a lawyer. I have no need for one."

O'Rourke looked questioningly at Paluzzi. The shorter man shrugged. Then both got up and went back into the outer office, closing the door softly behind them.

Gore covered his face with his hands. It was over. He didn't stand a chance now. He would be branded a thief, put in jail, ostracized from his clubs, never find another job. At least not in another bank. No bank in the world would ever touch him again. He was a thief.

One more week, and everything would have turned out differently. But now? Now it was too late. Suddenly he wondered what Geraldine would think. He smiled bitterly. She'd probably be mad as all hell that after all her years of working so hard at being a social item, it would be gone down the drain in one fell swoop. She would despise him.

Geraldine didn't like losers.

Slowly he walked toward the door, then stopped and turned around to stare out the window. From here, all he could see was the sky. Like a siren, it seemed to beckon sweetly.

Suddenly he knew what he had to do. It was the only way out.

He took a deep breath. Then, before he could change his mind, he charged forward, holding his hands out in front of him. They smashed through the plate glass, his knees caught on the thigh-high air-conditioning and heating ducts, and as he plunged through the window, his body did a grotesque, graceless somersault.

The sudden rush of cold air felt strangely exhilarating. He let out one short scream, and then it was all over.

Geraldine had been right. Her husband did kill himself. If not because of the Bulgari bracelet, then because of some others.

2

Hélène was standing behind her desk, her back to the windows. She looked down at the artboards that completely hid the beautifully inlaid marquetry. There was a thoughtful expression on her face. The artboards were all mock-ups of Junot magazine covers. The tissue paper protecting each picture had been carefully folded back behind each board, and a sea of glossy faces stared coldly up at her. She studied each one closely.

There was *La Moda,* with a fiercely scowling super-model; French *Les Modes* showing a tart with glossy, pouting lips; the German *Mode* cover girl, almost in too aggressive a pose; and a sweet-faced, airbrushed blond for American *Les Modes.*

It was funny, Hélène thought, that the average American woman preferred the sweet-looking girl-next-door-type model to the angular Amazonian Venus the Europeans adored. Her eyes roved on.

The English edition of *Les Modes* showed a full figure in a billowing summer dress by Halston, and *Yachting and Boating* had a photo of two "New Wave" girls in blue suede bikinis at the helm of an outrageously expensive Riva speedboat.

All the covers were fantastic, and she knew it. Yet there was something about each one that didn't quite suit her. At first she couldn't put her finger on what it was, but then it dawned on her: they were the covers for the June issues, and outside it was still midwinter. Even after years of preparing the magazines four to six months ahead of their issue dates, she still hadn't learned to get used to seeing bathing suits and chiffons in winter, wools and furs in summer. There was something oddly obscene about it. It made her feel like a clairvoyant when the issues—and clothes—finally came out, and it was a rather creepy feeling. Each season confronted her with this peculiar sense of *déjà vu.*

She heard the door opening and looked up. It was Edmond. He hadn't bothered to knock. He was the only person permitted to walk in unannounced, but usually he did not exercise this prerogative. As a matter of courtesy to Julie and herself, he always let himself be announced. The fact that he hadn't bothered with formalities aroused Hélène's misgivings. Something very important must have happened. She could remember only two times before that he had rushed in like that. Both times had been emergencies.

He walked briskly toward her and didn't wait for her to ask what had happened. "You've just gained a week's extension!" he said excitedly. "ManhattanBank has decided it won't call in the loan tomorrow."

She frowned in silence, digesting this unexpected turn of events. Stretching the deadline by a week wouldn't help her in the long run. Still, it was a nonrenewable note. As such, the extension *was* significant. "I don't understand," she said.

"Why don't you have a seat and I'll explain it to you."

She nodded and they sat down in the fragile French chairs that faced her desk. She crossed her legs and waited while he lit a cigarette.

"I just found out that Gore is no longer handling your accounts," he said. "Whoever is appointed to replace him will have to acquaint himself with them, review your financial predicament, and come to a decision. He'll need a week—maybe more—to catch up on it."

Hélène gave him an odd look. "But why? Has Gore quit his job?" she asked curiously. She couldn't imagine the well-fed banker doing anything of the sort.

Edmond shook his head and watched her closely. His voice was soft. "He committed suicide. Jumped out of his office window."

Hélène went pale. An uncontrollable chill rushed through her. "I think someone just walked over my grave," she said quietly.

"What do you mean?"

Hélène looked down at her hands. "Only yesterday, I ran into his wife at Susumu's. She showed me a bracelet she'd just bought at Bulgari, and do you know what she said?" Edmond shook his head in silence. "She said: 'My husband will probably kill himself when he sees it.' Those were her exact words!"

Edmond stared at her. "That's too bad," he said sympathetically. "I only hope the poor woman won't blame herself for it." He paused. "But mercenary as it may sound, Gore's done you an enormous favor. It's gotten you an extension. Even if it is only for a week or so."

She nodded slowly. At least now she'd have more time to think everything over carefully, to weigh the alternatives and arrive at the right decision. But there was still one thing she couldn't understand. "Edmond, *why* did he do it?"

He shrugged and took a deep drag on his cigarette. "I'm not certain, but the rumors are flying. ManhattanBank tried to put a lid on them, but word's leaked out anyway. They say he's embezzled a lot of money. Apparently he must have thought death was the only way out."

Hubert de Léger waited in his upstairs library until the house phone rang. "Monsieur le Comte," the soft-spoken butler said in French, "they are all here."

"Very well, Eduard," the Comte said. "I'll be down shortly. See that they're made comfortable. Serve them drinks."

"I already have, sir."

"Good." The Comte replaced the receiver and finished the letter he was reading. He was in no hurry. Let them wait, he thought with a smirk. It would only add to their suspense. He had hastily summoned them little more than half an hour ago, and each one had pointedly inquired about the reason for the urgent meeting. He had been purposely mysterious, and none of them had lost any time in getting here. Now he would let them speculate.

He made some notes on a pad, wrote out a telex, finished his inevitable Armagnac, and finally got to his feet. By now they would be bursting with impatience.

He took the small suede-lined elevator down to the foyer. At the living-room doors he hesitated. Then he flung them aside and strode in.

Slowly he looked around the big, Empire-furnished room. Seated on chairs with sphinx heads for arms and on couches with gilt claws for legs were Z.Z. Bavier, Karl von Eiderfeld, and Marcello d'Itri. A look of satisfaction showed in the Comte's eyes. No, not one of Hélène's enemies had wasted a second getting here. All of them had drinks in their hands.

The Comte could feel the hostility in his guests' eyes, and his lips spread into a sudden smile. "My friends," he announced with a quick nod of his head, "I am pleased to see that you could all come so quickly. Especially on such short notice."

Z.Z.'s lynx eyes narrowed. "Is that why you kept us waiting for so long?" she hissed in annoyance.

The Comte smiled easily. "Of course not, my dear Z.Z. I was delayed by a most urgent call." He came toward her, bent down, kissed her cheek. "My heartfelt apologies."

She looked at him doubtfully. Suspicious bitch, he thought to himself. He crossed the room to the bar, poured himself a glass of Armagnac, and leaned against the marble fireplace. Since they were all seated, he preferred to remain standing. It gave him a certain feeling of dominance.

"Well?" Z.Z. demanded. "Would you mind explaining what is so urgent that we had to drop everything and rush over here?"

The Comte sipped his Armagnac. "An unexpected development has come up. It requires that we revise our plans."

Z.Z. looked at him sharply. "An unexpected development? What the hell has happened?"

"Gore," he answered softly. "The banker."

D'Itri exchanged glances with Z.Z. "What about the banker?" the Italian designer asked. "Has he had a change of mind? Won't he sell us her collateral?"

The Comte looked at d'Itri. "It's not that he won't sell it. It's that he *can't*."

D'Itri looked puzzled. "I don't see any difference between 'won't' and 'can't.'"

"Ah, but there *is* a subtle distinction," the Comte said.

"You mean she's actually managed to pay it all *back*?" Z.Z.'s voice was incredulous.

All at once d'Itri and von Eiderfeld began to talk excitedly.

The Comte raised a hand to silence them. "No, she hasn't paid it back. But she's gotten a week's extension."

"An extension!" Z.Z. wailed. "*How*! It's a nonrenewable loan!"

The Comte smiled grimly. "At ten-forty-five this morning, Mr. Gore made a rather untimely departure from this life. He committed suicide."

"Verdammt!" Von Eiderfeld slammed his palm down on one of the sphinx heads of his chair. "I knew we should not have trusted that man!"

D'Itri stared sullenly at the Comte. "So what do we do now?"

"What *can* we do!" Z.Z. shrieked. She stared accusingly at the Comte. "You assured us that it was all arranged! That nothing could go wrong!" With trembling fingers she lit a Dunhill.

The Comte was calm. He wasn't about to be goaded into an argument. "This was beyond even my control," he said patiently. "I like it as little as you do. It seems that Gore had been embezzling money. It just so happens that he got caught at the worst possible moment."

"Oh, Christ!" Z.Z. swore. She drained her drink in one long swallow.

"Now that Gore is gone," von Eiderfeld murmured thoughtfully, "where does that leave us?"

The Comte shrugged. "Someone else will have to take Gore's place. We'll just wait patiently and see who it is. Then we'll approach him."

"And if he can't be bribed?" d'Itri snapped. "What then?"

"My dear Marcello." The Comte's tone was cold. "Everyone has his price. You should know that better than anyone."

D'Itri flushed. "Just what do you mean by that?" he demanded angrily.

The Comte smiled. "All I mean to say is that of all of us, you are the one with the scantiest excuse for hating Hélène. Without her, you'd be nothing. Oh, maybe you'd have a third-rate dress shop somewhere. But face it—she made you. She set you up, and now you don't like the price." He paused. "Marcello, you're biting the hand that feeds you."

D'Itri's hands shot up to cover his ears. "Shut up!" he screamed. "Shut up!" Angrily he jumped to his feet. "What about you?" He pointed an accusing finger at each one of them in turn. "And you? And *you?*"

The Comte smiled benignly. "We have other reasons, Marcello. Better reasons. With us it's not a simple matter of turning our backs on a debt."

"Well, fuck you!" With his hands, d'Itri made an obscene gesture and left, slamming the door behind him.

For a moment the others sat in stunned silence. Then Z.Z. began to laugh. "My, my! Such a vulgar outburst!"

The Comte crossed the room and poured himself another glass of Armagnac. "Marcello is a peasant," he said derisively. "He may have money, but in the end, class always tells. There is nothing worse than the nouveau riche." He looked at von Eiderfeld and smiled apologetically. "Excepting yourself, of course. I do not consider you to be in that category."

"I should hope not," the industrialist said with dignity. He rose to his feet. "As soon as you contact the new banker, you will let us know?"

The Comte nodded. "Of course."

"Good. And now I must regretfully be going. I have an important appointment, and I am already late." Von Eiderfeld stiffly shook hands with the Comte, and the butler showed him out.

When they were alone, Z.Z. shook her head. "Von Eiderfeld never fails to give me the creeps," she said. There was a note of disgust in her voice. "All that dreadfully white skin and those bloodless eyes. He reminds me of something out of a monster movie." She shuddered.

The Comte was silent, and she took it as a cue.

"Well, I suppose it's time for me to go also," she said with a sigh. "After all this bad news, I might as well stop at Bendel's and buy a little something to cheer me up."

The butler came with her silver-fox coat and she took her time slipping into it. Then the Comte personally escorted her to the door, drink in hand.

In the foyer, she halted, turning to face him. Her lips formed a mocking smile, and there was a glint of wicked amusement in her eyes. "You never mentioned why *you* hate Hélène Junot so much, my dear Comte. Could it be too unladylike for my delicate ears to hear?"

He stared down at his glass. His face looked haggard with pain, and he couldn't help wincing. For an instant she felt genuinely sorry that she had brought up the subject.

When he spoke, his words came out so softly that she almost didn't catch them. "I . . . was in love with her once."

Z.Z. glanced at him sharply. Curiosity had replaced her momentary pity. "So? What happened?"

Suddenly he began to tremble, then gripped his glass so hard that the delicate crystal shattered in his hand. She stared at his fingers; they were starting to bleed, and pieces of jagged crystal were embedded in the flesh. She heard what sounded like a strangled sob in his throat.

"What *happened?*" he screamed. Then his hysterical laughter reverberated around the foyer.

YESTERDAY

III

ADULTERY

1

Paris, 1953

A lump came up in Hélène's throat as the train sped into Paris. She got to her feet, pushed down the window, and leaned her head out. She had to squint as the cold wind hit her face and rushed through her hair. She swallowed her first deep gulps of Parisian air and the tears sprang to her eyes. In the distance, through the tears, she could see the Eiffel Tower. For a while she stared out at it in rapt fascination. It seemed to spring triumphantly up from among the endless sea of gray and black rooftops like a welcoming beacon. Then it disappeared as the train began the drawn-out, grating screech that signaled its approach to the station.

When the train jolted to a halt, Hélène carefully stepped down onto the platform. Up front, clouds of steam billowed up from under the hissing locomotive. It sounded like a weary giant letting out a deep sigh. Overhead, the metal girders of the Gare Montparnasse soared up to the glass roof in apparent defiance of the laws of gravity. She put down her suitcase and looked around. The first thing that caught her eye was that the travelers looked fatter and healthier than the Parisians of her memory, and they were far better dressed. All around her was the vibrant air of life that the French called joie de vivre. Gone were the dark things that had left a smudge on her memory: the haunting silence, the frightened looks on people's faces and the constant furtive glances over their shoulders, the fumblings with those all-important documents—official, stamped papers. Missing, too, were the swastikas and the sharp-eyed, ever-present Boches. Paris was different. She could feel it, and it felt good.

An old porter came up to her. "Mademoiselle?" he asked. He looked at her questioningly.

Quickly she shook her head. "Non, merci," she said softly.

Porters cost money, and she didn't have as much as a sou to throw away on such an extravagance. She grabbed her old suitcase and lugged it out to the street. The sunlight was bright and hurt her eyes. She blinked, but not because of the sun. In front of the station was the most incredible sight she had ever seen. Rows of gleaming black taxis. She shook her head in wonder. Would miracles never cease? And the streets—it was the first time she had ever seen the streets of Paris so crowded. Gone were the horse-drawn wagons, the vélo-taxis, and the hordes of bicycles. Instead, there were cars of every shade of the rainbow. How different everything looked from the Occupation! If only Maman were here to see it, she thought with regret.

"Taxi, mademoiselle?" A driver with a mustache held the door of his Renault open.

Hélène hesitated and peered inside. The seats were thickly upholstered and looked inviting. For an instant she almost splurged and got in. It would be nice to celebrate her return and ride down the Champs-Élysées and through the narrow streets of the Right Bank in style. But like the porter, it was a waste of money. Quickly she tightened her grip on the suitcase and walked away. She would need every last precious sou she had. Her first priority would be to find an inexpensive place to live. And then to buy food.

Wearily Hélène climbed the four narrow flights to her apartment. Another useless day, she thought listlessly as she unlocked the door. She threw the key down on the rickety kitchen table, kicked the door shut behind her, and slipped out of her clothes. Then she flopped down on the bed. The mattress sagged under her weight. In silence she stared up at the cracked ceiling. She was bone-tired. When she first arrived, her hopes had known no ceiling. Anything was possible. Now reality was crushing her hopes slowly but inextricably.

Still no job, she thought miserably. For three weeks she'd been looking now, and still nothing. Meanwhile, all Paris was bustling while she was pounding the pavement. And today had been the worst day yet. She closed her eyes.

Today she had answered an advertisement for a brassiere manufacturer looking for models. It was not the kind of job she wanted, but in desperation she'd gone anyway. It had been a gross mistake. The "manufacturer" had turned out to be nothing more than a front for a low-class whorehouse. And the disgusting fat pig who ran the place took one look at her and chased her around the filthy "office." She shuddered in disgust. Luckily she had managed to outwit him, get to the door, and flee. Now what would she do?

She had less than fifty francs left to her name. There was nothing in the tiny cupboard but two eggs, plus the bottle of milk she kept out on the windowsill to stay cool. The rent was due in two days.

She sighed and opened her eyes. Then she sat up and looked around the apartment. It was unbelievable. One room in a crummy Montmartre garret. She shook her head. In the expansive letters she had sent Edmond and Madame Dupré, she had written that it was small but charming, and had a splendid view. So they wouldn't worry about her, she had even lied and written that she had several job possibilities lined up. And that she'd have to think each over carefully to choose the one she thought would best suit her future.

Future? What future? Job opportunities? Being chased around by a pervert who smelled of cheap wine? Was that a job possibility?

Suddenly she began to laugh.

Charming apartment? She began to laugh even harder. Sure it was charming, she thought. The walls were covered with dirty white paint, the linoleum floor was cracked, and three of the nine panes of glass in the one small window were broken and boarded over. And the view she had written home so warmly about? She was in gales of laughter now. The view was the window of an apartment across the courtyard. In it lived a shaggy young artist who masturbated with more frequency than he painted. When Hélène had discovered that, she lost no time in yanking the tattered tablecloth off the kitchen table and draping it across the window. She was only too happy to spare herself that view.

And the size of her apartment? Also laughable. It was a single room, twelve feet long and not quite nine feet wide. There wasn't even a closet. All her clothes were hanging from hooks on the wall that some previous tenant had put up. The toilet out in the hall was unheated. She shared it with three other tenants on the floor. There was no bath.

She despised the place.

Her eyes came to rest on a heap of fabric on the floor. It was the dress she had been wearing. Tonight she'd once again have to wash it out in the sink, hang it up to dry, and then borrow the concierge's iron. Tomorrow she'd have to wear it to go back out and pound the pavement again.

Suddenly her laughter turned to tears and she buried her face in the pillow. Violent sobs began to rack her body. Oh, what was the use? she asked herself. Surely this was the end of the road.

Just then there were heavy footsteps outside on the stairs, followed by a loud knock on the door. A frown crossed her face. She wasn't expecting anyone; so far, she knew no one in Paris. As she lifted her head from the pillow, a feeling of dread went through her. Perhaps it was the concierge. Could she already be coming around to collect the rent?

The thought sent a chill of terror through her. She didn't have enough money left to pay the rent. She hesitated and stared at the door. Perhaps if she kept really quiet the old hag would go back downstairs where she belonged.

The knocks came again, louder this time.

Hélène sighed. "Just a minute," she finally called out in a weary voice. She struggled up and swung her legs over the edge of the bed. She took her robe down off the hook, slipped into it, and quickly wiped her eyes dry with the palms of her hands. Clutching the front of her robe together, she went over to the door and opened it a crack.

She stood there and stared up at him in surprise, He was a tall man. Very tall. He must have stood at least six-feet-four, had unruly red hair, a red beard, an engaging smile, and she had never seen him before. His eyes were gentle and sky blue. In the crook of his arm he carried a half-full bottle of wine and a rolled-up newspaper with the tip of a loaf of bread sticking out.

She blinked. "Who are you?" she asked.

He grinned. "I'm Guy Barbeau," he said easily. "Artist and ne'er-do-well, by my own admission. I live across the hall." He held out his free hand.

"Oh. I'm Hélène Junot," she said awkwardly. They shook hands. When he let go of her hand she pointed vaguely behind her. "I . . . uh . . . I live here."

He laughed and peeked past her into the room. "I can't believe it!" His voice was incredulous.

She was confused. "Believe what?"

"You've got even more space than I've got!"

Despite herself, she laughed. "I can't believe anything could be more cramped than this pigeonhole."

"You'll be surprised. You should see my dump. May I come in?"

The request took her by surprise. She hesitated. Should she entertain a man in her room? Although she wasn't frightened, she wondered if it were proper. Then she pushed the thought out of her mind. She nodded and stepped aside. Guy Barbeau came in and set the wine and bread down on the kitchen table.

"Have you had your supper yet?" he asked.

"Have I . . . ?"

"I see you haven't." He acted very sure of himself. "We'll sup together, then. Have you got two glasses and a knife?"

She blushed. "I haven't got any glasses," she said shyly.

"Will two small milk bottles and a knife do?"

"Splendidly. The height of luxury. Thank God your kitchen is better equipped than mine." He scraped the table closer to the bed and unwrapped the newspaper. Besides the bread there was a chunk of Roquefort, a tin of sardines, and a length of hard salami. Expertly he opened the can of sardines, smoothed out the newspaper, and artfully arranged the food on it. When she finished rinsing out the bottles in the sink, he was already sitting down on the edge of the bed.

"It looks delicious," she said politely as she sat down beside him.

He laughed. "It's merely poverty food. Fuel for our bodies. Alas, not enough to nourish our souls." He poured a few fingers of wine into each milk bottle. "Santé."

"Santé."

She let the glass door of the boutique slam shut behind her. It was still raining out, and she pulled the collar of her coat up high around her neck. Another dead end, she thought morosely. She sighed deeply. Today the rent was due.

She turned right and headed toward the Boulevard St. Germain. She had applied for a job as a salesgirl in a smart new boutique opposite Sainte Clotilde. The owner, Madame d'Arbeuf, had interviewed her in a little office in the back of the store.

Madame d'Arbeuf held a lot of faith in first impressions. Through her elegant blue-framed glasses, her stern eyes had studied Hélène. What she saw did nothing to inspire her.

Even Hélène's best dress was a sad contrast—an embarrassment, actually—to the posh refinement of her shop. Worse, it had begun to rain and Hélène had gotten caught in it. She was soaked.

"What experience do you have in retail sales, mademoiselle?" Madame d'Arbeuf purred smoothly.

"I . . . I've worked in a dress shop," Hélène replied.

"Oh. Where was that?"

"In Saint-Nazaire."

Madame d'Arbeuf frowned. "Saint-Nazaire? Let me see, now, Saint-Nazaire . . ." She shook her head. "I can't seem to recall where that is. Is it near Cannes?"

Hélène couldn't help but smile. Saint-Nazaire might as well have been a million light-years from Cannes. "No, madame. It's on the Bay of Biscay."

"Oh." Madame d'Arbeuf rose to her feet. "Actually, we're looking for someone with more . . ." She smiled thinly. "More sophistication. More polish. You see, the Boutique Chat Blanc has an international clientele, mademoiselle. I'm afraid . . ."

Hélène's desperation was written all over her face. "But, madame! I'm very clever! I learn quickly! You'll see . . ."

Madame d'Arbeuf looked at her with distaste. "It's no use," she said sternly. "I'm sorry to have wasted your time."

2

Hélène's concierge was right at the foot of the stairs when she came in. There was no avoiding her. She was on her knees scrubbing the linoleum with a stiff brush. When she saw Hélène she struggled to her feet and wiped her red hands on her apron. "Mademoiselle! The rent is due today."

Hélène looked at her. "I'm sorry, Madame Guérin. I don't have it yet. Perhaps tomorrow."

"Tomorrow!" Madame Guérin stormed. "I have my orders to collect it the day it is due. That is today. That, too, was our agreement when you moved in."

"I know. Just give me a few days," Hélène begged. "Please. My brother will send it."

"I'm sorry, mademoiselle. In this building we collect the rent in advance. It's either pay now or move out now!"

Behind them the front door creaked open. The person entering evidently had second thoughts about coming in and started to leave again. Hélène turned and caught a glimpse of Guy Barbeau slinking away like the cat that caught the canary.

"Monsieur Barbeau!"

Madame Guérin's shrill voice froze Guy in his tracks.

"You also! Like I was telling Mademoiselle Junot, the rent is due!"

Sheepishly he came toward them, rain pouring off his overcoat. His soaked red hair was plastered against his head. Wearily he smiled at Hélène. "Hello again."

"Hello," she replied.

"Had any luck?" he asked.

She shook her head. "No," she said softly.

Madame Guérin placed her hands on her hips and looked up at him. "Do you have the money?" she demanded.

He sighed heavily and looked down at his feet. "Just a few days. Please."

"We've been through that often enough now. Go upstairs and start packing before I call the police."

"But my paintings! The canvases! It'll take days to move them." In desperation he looked at Hélène. "You wouldn't by any chance . . ."

She shook her head. "I'm being tossed out too, remember?"

All of a sudden he grabbed her by the arm and pulled her aside. "Listen," he whispered excitedly. "How much money have you got?"

She was puzzled. "About forty francs. Why?"

He did some quick calculations. "And I've got fifty!"

"So we're both broke. What good will that do us?"

"Don't you see? Your rent's seventy francs, right?"

She nodded.

"So we'll let my apartment go and move into yours! We'll be roommates."

She hesitated. "I don't know," she said slowly. "It'll be awfully cramped."

"It's either that or the streets for both of us."

It made sense. Slowly she nodded. "As long as it's strictly platonic," she stipulated.

He held up his right hand. "As God is my judge."

She smiled. "Monsieur Barbeau, we've just bought ourselves a month's reprieve."

Five minutes later, it was all arranged and they went upstairs to move his things into her apartment. At his door, Hélène's eyes opened wide. Leaning against one wall was an enormous canvas. It was almost the length of the room. She backed against the far wall and squinted at it. "It's extraordinary!" she exclaimed.

"It's my best work to date," Guy said. He moved a stack of small canvases aside and stood beside her. "I'm calling it *The Hyperbolic Ascension.* I've been working on it for nine months now. Another couple of days and it should be finished."

Hélène couldn't take her eyes off it. It depicted a surrealistic Madonna exploding in space, her body all in shards against a background of light. It looked as if someone had placed a charge of dynamite inside her and then frozen the picture in the midst of the explosion.

"As soon as it's finished, it'll go to the Lichtenstein Gallery," he explained. "André Lichtenstein himself came by to see it a couple of weeks ago. He's willing to handle it. He's big-time. They say he's the most important art dealer in Paris."

"That's wonderful!" Hélène said warmly.

He nodded. "Hopefully a buyer will think so, too."

She smiled. "I don't think you need to worry about that. I'm certain it'll be snatched up right away. And whoever gets it will be very lucky."

He looked at her curiously. "You really believe that, don't you?"

Without taking her eyes off the painting, she nodded her head. "It's more beautiful than most paintings I've seen in the Louvre. It reminds me of Raphael, only there's so much more depth." She shook her head. "It's really incredible."

On Saturday they ate a light breakfast of bread and fruit.

The bread was hard and stale. The loaf had been two days old, but as a result they had gotten it for next to nothing.

Hélène had cut up the fruit into little cubes and made a

salad out of it. It looked delicious. Actually, she had prepared it that way so it wouldn't look too depressing. The night before, Guy had scavenged among the crates of throwaways at Les Halles. Since each piece was partially spoiled, it called for surgery. She decided it was much more appetizing to eat a salad than fruit with big chunks pared out of it.

When they had finished eating, Guy picked up the table and set it down in the far corner out of the way. "Food for the muses," he murmured. "You didn't warn me that you could cook. Besides a roommate, I seem to have gained a first-class chef as well." He stifled a burp. "Well done. It was rather a nice change from biting into amputated apples."

She smiled. She was glad he appreciated her effort. "You're going to start painting now?" she asked.

He nodded.

"Good. Then I'm going to take a long walk. I've spent two weekends catching up on culture in the Louvre, and every weekday for three weeks chasing down dead-end jobs. Today I intend to walk around for the sheer joy of it." She reached behind *The Hyperbolic Ascension* and felt around for her brown wool skirt and heavy knitted sweater. She would wear the sweater outside, over the skirt, and then fasten her brown leather belt around it. Already she was picking up fashion pointers from chic Parisian women she saw in the streets. Perhaps she would even pin up her hair. The idea made her smile. She wondered how it would look.

"Want me to go outside while you change?" Guy asked.

She shook her head. "No, I'll use the toilet. At least there's a mirror in there."

He nodded, took the tablecloth down off the window, and opened it. The sun was shining and light flooded the room. A chill wind blasted in along with it.

"You better wear a coat or you'll catch cold," she suggested.

He nodded absently. Already he was in another world, his eyes searching the big canvas. He didn't even hear the door snap shut behind her.

She walked for hours. At first it was aimless wandering. She left the old streets of Montmartre behind and took one of the arched bridges over to the Left Bank. The sidewalks were crowded with Saturday shoppers and families out taking a stroll. Even some of the sidewalk cafés already had a few hardy customers braving the chill. Spring was not long off. In Paris, you could smell it coming.

Passing a lingerie shop, between the ghostly shapes of brassieres, she caught sight of herself in the glass. Could that be me? she asked herself. She stepped closer. It *was* her. She couldn't believe it. Pinning up her hair made all the difference in the world. She looked taller, more mature, but still youthful. And to her surprise, the past few weeks of fasting hadn't taken their toll. Instead, they had done the exact opposite. Gone forever was her baby fat. She was no longer slender; she was very thin. But not in the way malnourished people are emaciated. Rather, in the way that fashion models are slim, statuesque.

She looked closer. Her cheekbones, too, had gained new prominence, and her eyes seemed larger and oddly luminous. The belt around her sweater accentuated her tiny waist. She pivoted, checking the profile of her body. Satisfied, she made a mental note to remember to take in all her clothes at the waist.

As she continued walking, she found herself humming softly to herself. She felt suddenly more beautiful, more confident, more stylish. More like a real Parisienne. Now she had only to gain a little polish. She would study the elegant ladies. She would pick up their walks. Their mannerisms.

Each time she passed a shop window, she found herself sneaking quick glances at her shadowy reflection. Yes, it was really true. She had changed.

When she reached the Boulevard St. Germain, the jugglers were already out in full force. They were entertaining a pack of little children who shrieked and clapped their hands in delight. Smiling, Hélène stopped and watched them in idle amusement. But as she looked at the jugglers, she saw other jugglers from the past. The amusement in her eyes dimmed. Other jugglers, from years ago. Years ago, with Michelle.

Years ago . . .

Suddenly she found herself slipping back in time. Perhaps it was triggered by the mesmerizing effect of the little red balls that were being tossed and caught with such hypnotic repetition. Maybe it was the shrieks of the children. Or even the smell of spring in the air. Whatever it was, something had unlocked the long-shut door to the memories of her childhood and laid them bare for her to see. For a moment she felt a wave of nausea. It was like she was on a merry-go-round and the world was reeling all around her.

As if in a trance, she turned and began to walk on. This time it was not with the aimless pace of a Saturday-afternoon stroller but with purpose. It was almost as if some unexplainable power—some magnet—was drawing her toward a certain destination.

All the background noises of the city were now muffled. Behind her, the shrieks of the children were distorted whispers in the afternoon. Loud in her ears was the sound of her heels clacking faster and faster on the sidewalk. Each footstep seemed to reverberate louder than the last, like a distant roll of thunder that was fast approaching. Even the sidewalk seemed to warp, a ribbon of undulating waves.

Then the peal of thunder was upon her. She felt a sudden blast of heat and then began to fall. An iron lamppost was within reach, and she wrapped her arms around it to steady herself. For a moment she just hung on.

An old man stopped and looked at her. "Mademoiselle?" he asked in a concerned voice. "Are you all right?"

She took a deep breath and slowly nodded. The man moved on. Was she all right? No, she wasn't all right. But there was nothing anyone could do to help.

For the next half-hour she walked briskly, without stopping. The vertigo was gone, and in its place was new understanding. She knew her destination.

She had no trouble finding the flights of twisting stone steps that led up to the top of the Butte. It had been almost ten years, but it all came back to her as easily as if it had been yesterday.

Halfway up, she reached the little park. It was still there, and so was the bench where she used to play with Antoinette. So, too, were the acacia trees. They were bare, like the last time she had seen them. Only they were much bigger now. Acacia trees grow quickly.

And there, across the alley, stood the house. She looked at it curiously. It looked much smaller now that she was grown. But she could still recognize it, even if it did look seedier and more modest than the house of her memory. The front door was different; it was of varnished dark oak. Gone forever was the canary-yellow door. But the ground-floor windows were still covered with the curlicued bars, and above the rooftop, the domes of Sacré Coeur gleamed whitely. Odors of greasy food hung heavy in the air. Someone was cooking pork.

This was where she would be living now if Tante Janine hadn't sold the house out from under her, she thought bitterly. Rightfully the house had belonged to her and Edmond.

But it was no use harping on that now, she told herself savagely. Be practical. Be realistic. She and Edmond no longer had any claim to it. It had been stolen from them. Her lips tightened. *Stolen*.

She stared at the house. If . . . *if* it were still theirs, it would have solved so many of her problems. She would have lived on the ground floor and converted the dining room into a bedroom. Perhaps put up a cheerfully patterned wallpaper. There would have been a separate living room and kitchen as well as access to the garden out back. There would have been no need to share a claustrophobic closet with Guy Barbeau. She would even have been assured a steady income by renting out the upstairs. There would have been no financial woes, no pleading with dour concierges, no scavenging for rotten fruit . . .

Suddenly the vertigo started up again. Her head began to spin and she sank down onto the cold hard slats of the bench.

Like a series of slow-motion negatives, a chain of distorted pictures flashed through her mind. She saw Maman being punched mercilessly in the belly by the Boche. Even now she could still hear her screeches of pain echoing through the neighborhood. Once again she heard the ear-shattering blast of the gunshot that threw Michelle against the kitchen doorway and made her collapse like a limp sack of potatoes.

Abruptly Hélène got up and quickly began to walk away. Tears blurred her vision. Fiercely she wiped them away with her hands. She could deal with many things. This house was not one of them. She never wanted to see it again. Ever.

"It's just as well that that thief Pierre sold it," she said to herself as she stumbled along the cobblestones. "I could never live there. *Never*. It's no use trying to live in a house full of ugly ghosts."

She headed straight home, strangely glad that Guy would be there. His company would be a comfort.

The window was still open when she got back. The room was icy. Guy didn't speak. He was sitting on the floor with

260

his back against the wall. He looked exhausted. His eyes were on *The Hyperbolic Ascension*.

Hélène stepped over his palette and sat down on the floor beside him. She stared up at the canvas, which seemed to explode off the wall with a force of its own. She didn't need to be told. It was finished.

In silence she got to her feet and went back out. Ten minutes later she returned with a bottle of champagne. She had splurged recklessly. It had cost every last sou they had left. When she opened it, the cork flew across the room and out the open window. She heard it land in the courtyard below. Carefully she filled their drinking bottles and handed one over to him. They clunked the bottles together.

She looked into his eyes. "To your masterpiece," she toasted in a solemn whisper. "To your future."

He nodded. Even he couldn't help but admit that *The Hyperbolic Ascension* had turned out to be a masterpiece. And with André Lichtenstein at his side, even the impossible was possible. The art dealer was an acknowledged genius when it came to discovering new talent.

Guy smiled. Suddenly the road to his fame and fortune looked paved with promise. He would be not only a respected artiste but perhaps also even a member of the small, close-knit community of financially successful artists as well. Who could tell? He might even become another Picasso, another Dali. Anything seemed possible.

But it never happened.

3

Breathlessly Hélène dashed past a startled Madame Guérin and ran up the steep flights two steps at a time. When she flung open the door and burst into the room, sweat was pouring down her forehead and her breast was heaving from exertion. She had run all the way.

261

Guy was standing at the sink. He twisted around and looked at her red face in surprise. "Where's the fire?"

She took deep gulps of air and plopped herself down on the bed. "The news . . . I couldn't wait . . . to tell you . . . I ran . . ."

"First catch your breath," he said calmly. "Then tell me everything. Can I get you a glass of water?"

She nodded and waited impatiently while he went over to the sink and filled the bottle under the tap. Water dripped down on the floor as he carried it to her.

"Thanks." She held the bottle between her trembling hands and drank thirstily.

He sat down beside her. "Caught your breath?"

Excitedly she nodded her head. With the back of her hand she wiped the water from around her mouth. "We're rich!" she blurted out. "I got a job!"

His eyes widened. "What?" He hugged her tightly and then held her at arm's length by the shoulders. "Where? How?"

Her eyes shone. "I answered an ad. I didn't tell you about it because I didn't want to give you false hopes. I didn't really think for a moment that I would get it! But finally we'll have some money! Now we'll be able to buy food and even be able to cover the rent!"

Jumping to her feet, she raised her hands above her head and broke into a flamenco. Fiercely she snapped her fingers and stomped her heels. Her dress swirled around her. "We're rich!" she sang. "We're rich!"

From the floor below, someone began banging on the ceiling. Undaunted, Hélène danced on. Finally she collapsed on the bed. She was out of breath again.

"Well?" Guy demanded. "Are you going to dance all night? Or are you going to tell me about it? What kind of job is it? Where is it?"

"It's nothing, really. Just a hat-check job. But it's not far from here, and I'll be able to walk to work. Even in the rain. I think the very first thing I'll buy myself will be an umbrella." Her eyes were shining. "Then I'll go out every time it rains just to luxuriate under it. I'll never have to get wet again!"

"You'll be a hat-check girl?" he asked softly.

"That's what I said." She waved her hand deprecatingly. "Oh, I know. It's no big deal. But they told me the tips are good."

262

He looked at her questioningly. "Where is it?" he asked hesitantly.

"On the rue de la Tour-d'Auvergne."

He nodded slowly. "It wouldn't by any chance happen to be the Folies de Babylon?"

She looked at him in surprise. "You've been there!"

He shook his head, and their eyes met. "No, I haven't been there. But I've heard enough. It's not a good place, Hélène. It has a . . . reputation, let's say."

She turned at him angrily. "Not good? Reputation? What are you trying to say? That I shouldn't work there because it's a nightclub?"

"Not because it's a nightclub. Because it's where men go to pick up girls. Girls who aren't nice. You know what I mean."

"Prostitutes. Yes, I know," she said wearily. "I've been in Paris long enough to know that there is such a thing as prostitution. So what? I'm not a prostitute and I certainly don't intend to become one. I'm merely the hat-check girl."

He shrugged. "Have it your way, then. You won't last there anyway. They've got a fast employee turnover."

"Then I'll work twice as hard. Three times as hard. I'll make sure I keep my job."

He fell silent and got to his feet. He shoved his hands deep into his pants pockets and started to pace the room in annoyance.

She looked up at him for a while. Finally she spoke. "You don't want me to work there, do you?"

He stopped pacing. "I can't tell you what to do."

She reached out, grabbed his sleeve, and shook it. "We need the money, Guy. Can't you understand that? This is a chance! Another two weeks and the rent will be due again." She motioned around the room. "This is no way for human beings to live! We need money to live well. To eat well." She looked at him pleadingly. "Please understand me. I want to eat some good food for a change. I'm tired of going through garbage cans and chasing away the flies just to get at other people's leftovers!"

"Don't you understand?" he asked softly. "It's worse at the Folies de Babylon. There *you'll* become garbage."

"Then I'll become as rotten as the garbage I eat!" she declared angrily. "I know the taste well enough by now. Do you really think working in a trash bin is any different than eating out of one?"

263

He reached up and grabbed his coat off a hook on the wall. "I'm taking a walk." He looked at her in disgust. "I need the clean air."

She looked stunned as he stalked out. She was about to open the door and call after him when she had second thoughts. She sighed and turned away. No, it wouldn't be of any use. He was too stubborn to listen.

Suddenly she noticed that something about the room was different. Then she realized what it was. *The Hyperbolic Ascension* was no longer there. André Lichtenstein must have had it picked up while she was out. Now she understood. With the excitement of her pitiful job offer, she had stolen Guy's thunder. No wonder he felt so hurt.

She rushed over to the door and flung it open. "Guy!" she screamed. "Guy! Please wait!"

But it was too late. Her calls were answered by the angry slamming of the front door. Even four flights up, she could hear the panes of glass rattling in the frames.

"You fool!" Madame Guérin's shouts echoed shrilly in the stairwell. "Are you trying to tear the whole house apart?"

Slowly Hélène shut the door and slumped heavily against it. She let out a deep breath. She wished she had the time to sit down and relax, to get all the ill feeling out of her system. But she'd have to start getting ready soon. In less than two hours she would have to report to work.

Her lips twisted bitterly. This was a hell of a way to start off her first working day.

She got to the nightclub on the rue de la Tour-d'Auvergne half an hour before opening time. The night was dark but the tall red neons over the entrance hadn't been turned on yet.

For a moment she hesitated in front of the big glass double doors. They had been painted over with lilac paint so that people couldn't peek in without paying admission, but to her it only made it appear that much more ominous and foreboding. Already she was so nervous that her teeth were chattering like castanets. She had never before worked in the city, let alone in a nightclub, and she was filled with fears. Perhaps people would look down on her like Madame d'Arbeuf had, and think she was provincial. Or worse yet . . . Her heart began beating heavily. Perhaps the Folies de Babylon was an even worse fleshpot than Guy had let on. For an instant the impulse to flee seized her. Then she forced herself to stifle it. Think of the money, she told herself grimly. Or do you want to starve? She stared at the lilac doors. Then, fortifying herself with a deep breath, she pulled open the heavy doors and walked in. She tried her best to act casual, but her legs felt weak. They were trembling as if she had the ague.

The bright overhead lights inside the club were still on, and in the glare everything looked tawdry and cheap. She couldn't help wrinkling her nose at the odor of stale tobacco and spilled drinks that hung in the air. Passing the hat-check room, she paused to give it a brief inspection. Then she wove her way past the sea of tiny tables toward the stage that took up the entire front of the massive room. As she walked, she looked around the club.

Right away her worst fears began to vanish. She had half-expected to be met by a fire-breathing dragon, but instead it all looked rather amusingly threatrical. Whoever had decorated the place must have had two things in abundance, she thought. No end of bad taste and a fixation on lilac and pink. The walls were lilac and embedded with pink sequins, and so was the heavy curtain drawn across the stage. On each side of the stage, an enormous cutout of a turbaned Negro woman was attached to the wall. Except for the faces, these, too, were heavily decorated in lilac with pink sequins.

Squeezed into the room must have been a hundred tables. Each one was draped with a pink cloth and held a little pink-shaded lamp, a large pink card with a big black number printed on it, and a pink French-style telephone. Instinctively she knew what the phones were for. You could use them to call from one table to another just by dialing the number of the table you wanted. It was supposed to be a discreet way for people to contact each other. She was highly amused.

Behind the pink bar, two middle-aged, bored-looking Algerians were polishing glasses. In front of the bar a big Algerian bouncer was seated on a stool. He scowled across the room at her. He had been cleaning his fingernails with a pocketknife. Carefully he folded it up and snapped his thick fingers at her. She came over and looked at him questioningly. His dark eyes shone at her from under thick black eyebrows.

"Front door for customers only," he growled in bad French. "Employee door in side alley." He nodded to his left.

265

Hélène looked confused. "I'm sorry," she said. "They didn't tell me."

"Well, don't forget for future. This club belong to Monsieur Blond. Monsieur Blond don't like mistakes. Especially not from pretty ladies." He eyed her up and down. "Around here, you gotta do what Monsieur Blond says."

She nodded and smiled tightly. "I'll try to keep that in mind."

"You be smart girl and do that." He reached in his pocket for a cigarette and looked at her as he lit it. He took a deep drag and nodded to himself. She was fresh-looking and healthy, not like all those worn-out, pasty-faced showgirls and painted hookers. Yes, she really was quite beautiful. In fact, if Monsieur Blond didn't take a fancy to her, then perhaps . . . His face broke into a smile. "Now, be a good girl," he said in a friendlier voice. "Run along and go behind stage. Ask for Mother. She get you in costume and tell you what to do."

Costume? Hélène thought. What costume? Nobody had said anything about a costume. Then she shrugged. She turned around, skirted the bar, and climbed up the steps to the stage. She groped around the curtain for a while. Then she found an opening and slipped backstage.

From the look of things, there was a lot going on. The overhead lights were much brighter back here than out in the club, and they burned with a stifling heat. Hélène saw tall, long-legged showgirls in sequined bikinis and mountains of feathers, muscular showboys in sequined stretch tuxedos or obscene-looking loincloths. They all stood around looking bored, smoking cigarettes in groups. Close up, their makeup looked garish. Their skin underneath the greasy, powdered surface was pimply and uneven. With surprise, she noticed that even their bodies had makeup. The girls' breasts were rouged and the boys' washboard stomachs were outlined in brown greasepaint.

She noticed immediately that it was not the performers but the stagehands who were panic-stricken. They were rushing around seeing to this and that, screaming at the repairmen who were hammering away on a damaged set. In a corner, an ambivalent orchestra was tuning up. A clarinet squeaked.

Hélène was dazzled by the shabby glamour of it all. The set facing the curtains was big and garish and glittery. She looked up at it in awe. Prancing atop a wide, gold-painted

266

pyramid were three stuffed stallions with colorful plumes on their heads. Hélène gazed farther up, at the ceiling. There were more flat sets up there, suspended above the height of the stage, ready to be lowered at a moment's notice.

Suddenly the floor under her began to move. She looked down in horror. Then she realized that she was standing on a revolving stage. When it stopped moving she quickly hopped off the big platform. She found herself in the midst of a group of gossiping girls. Most of them wore pink bikinis and massive headdresses sprouting pink ostrich plumes. They held their heads curiously straight, afraid that their elaborate headgear would slip off.

"I can't stand wearing all this crap," one of the girls complained crossly. She was wearing a thick, arched ponytail on her rear and another atop her head. "Monsieur Blond's a sadist for making us get ready so early. My feet hurt and I want to sit down!" She snorted and stamped her feet. The tail bounced up and down, and it rather looked like the movements of a horse. Hélène couldn't help giggling.

The girl turned around, her heavily made-up eyes flickering up and down Hélène. She placed her hands on her bare hips. "Would you like to share the joke?" she demanded.

Hélène clapped a hand over her mouth and drew back. "N-no, mademoiselle," she stammered in embarrassment. "Excusez-moi, I wasn't laughing at you. It's just . . . I'm looking for Mother."

"Humph!" The girl's eyes narrowed. "You're new around here, huh?"

Hélène nodded. "I'm the new hat-check girl."

"Listen, honey, we've all been hat-check girls. Right, ladies?" She looked at the others and winked.

They all burst out laughing. Hélène felt a deep blush coming on.

One of the girls stepped forward. "Don't mind Angélique," she said gently. "She's just pissed off because she's pregnant and she'll have to foot the bill for the abortion herself. Come on, I'll take you to Mother." She took Hélène by the hand and scowled at Angélique. Then she looked back at Hélène and smiled. "My name is Denise."

Hélène smiled shyly. "Mine's Hélène."

They walked on farther back, through a dim, narrow corridor. "Don't mind the girls," Denise said. "They're not that bad, really. They just like to sound tough. And all these feathers get hot and heavy, believe me. It's amazing that tempers don't fly more often. Ah, here's Mother."

They had stopped at one of the dressing-room doors. It was open, and Hélène could see inside. An old, limp-wristed little man with short brown bangs and a ruffled white shirt was touching up one of the showgirls' makeup.

"I can't see through these eyelashes, Mother!" the girl wailed. "They feel like stiff brushes!"

The man gave a high-pitched cackle and tossed his wrist. "Don't worry, chérie. The worst they'll do is poke your eyes out." He made a minor adjustment on her eyes. "*There*." He stepped back to study the result and rubbed his hands together. "You look very chic."

Hélène glanced at Denise curiously. "*Th-that's* Mother?" she whispered incredulously, pointing at the man.

Denise nodded. "Except for his tongue, he's really quite harmless. If you're a girl, that is. The showboys don't like him, since he's constantly trying to grab them. The reason we call him Mother is because he's a pouf. Actually, he rather likes being called that, since it makes him feel he's one of us."

"One of us?"

"Sure. Us girls." Denise smiled. "Anyway, he mothers all of us. He's like an old hen, but we love him dearly."

Hélène shook her head. It was all so bizarre. Women with horses' tails. Stiff false eyelashes. A man called "Mother" who liked to grab the boys.

She watched as the showgirl bent close in to a mirror and blinked her eyes. "I'll probably be blind in five minutes," she wailed.

Mother put his hands between her bony shoulder blades and propelled her to the door. "Off you go, chérie." Suddenly he stopped in his tracks and stared at Hélène. He knocked his hand against his forehead. "I think I'm going to faint!" he shrieked. "Where did this wholesome creature come from? Mon Dieu! I'm supposed to make *her* look like a painted hooker? Yes, I think I *am* going to faint!"

"She's the new hat-check girl," Denise said.

Mother minced over to Hélène, looking her over. "How *do* you do? Hmmm. You do have lovely skin. Perhaps I'll give you the milkmaid outfit," he mused, a thoughtful pinkie resting on his lips.

Hélène looked perplexed. "The . . . milkmaid outfit?" she asked cautiously, glancing at Denise.

Denise narrowed her eyes. "He wouldn't dare! It's one of his peasant costumes. It's simply the ugliest thing we've ever laid eyes on. So far, all the girls have refused to wear it. It's got a low-cut bosom so that your tetons practically hang out, with a little lace edging and one of those god-awful Marie Antoinette peasant caps. Ugh!" She shuddered involuntarily.

Mother put an angry hand on his hip and snapped, "What do you mean 'ugh'? I designed it myself! Peasant top, net stockings, and all. It's very flattering."

"It's very disgusting," Denise snapped. "Have you got cataracts? Where's your taste? Can't you see that this girl's got class? Now, give her something decent so she won't look like a hooker. Otherwise, we'll all gang up on you and cut off your pecker!"

He let out a shrill scream. "You naughty girls! You wouldn't dare!"

It was six o'clock in the morning when the girls finally poured out through the employee door into the side alley. Already the blue light of dawn was in the sky. Hélène blinked. After the carnival atmosphere of the club, the big dark room with the pink-shaded lamps, the false energy onstage, the men's evening suits and the women's gowns, it was startling to be out in the fresh air and find that it was daylight.

Guy was waiting for her in the alley. As soon as she saw him, her heart lifted.

He grinned at her. "How'd it go?"

She smiled happily. "Come to think of it, not bad at all."

It was true. In a strange sort of way, she had actually enjoyed it. Perhaps it was because she was finally working. Or maybe it was the girls. Denise had been right. They really weren't a bad bunch.

"Good," he said. "I want to hear all about it."

Hélène felt a hand tugging on her arm. She turned around. It was Denise, her face pale and ordinary without all the makeup, her red hair hidden underneath a scarf. "See you tonight," she said. She glanced at Guy out of the corner of her eye and leaned forward, putting her lips to Hélène's ear. "That's some handsome man you got," she whispered. "And a gentleman, too. Imagine, waiting up this long just to escort you home! You'd better keep your claws in him and get a ring on your finger real fast!" Then her voice rose to normal. She raised her hand in a wave. "Bon nuit!" she sang.

Hélène laughed and returned the wave. "Bon nuit, Denise,"

Guy hooked his arm through Hélène's. "You look tired," he said, leading her home.

"I'm beat! I've never worked so hard in my life. I've been on my feet since nine o'clock. You know the first thing I'm going to do when I get home? I'm going to boil a big pot of water and soak my feet in it."

He grinned. "You're going to do nothing of the sort. You're going to sit down and I'll boil it for you."

They walked in silence for a few minutes. Then she stopped and looked up at him. "Listen, Guy," she said softly, "I'm sorry."

"What about?"

"This afternoon. In all my excitement I didn't even realize that the painting was gone."

He shrugged tolerantly. "Well, look at it this way. We've both managed to get something positive accomplished on the same day." He paused and looked ruefully into her face. "I'm sorry, too, about the way I talked to you. I had no right to say what I did. You'll never be trash, Hélène." He smiled gently. "You'll still come to the gallery for the show?"

"You can count on it. I wouldn't miss it for the world."

He looked pleased. "Of course, I'm not the only one who's going to be exhibited. You've got to have twenty or thirty paintings to have a show of your own. Still, it's a start. And Monsieur Lichtenstein thinks that the chances of fetching a decent price for my painting are good. As I told you, he only picks winners. Now, about you. How did it go?"

She fumbled in her pocket and held out a wad of money. "Look!"

"Good Lord! How much is there?"

She shoved the money back in her pocket and laughed. "I haven't even counted it yet. I get one-third of the tips. The house keeps a third and Yvette, the other hat-check girl, gets a third. Listen, what do you say we find a café that's open at this ungodly hour and celebrate with some breakfast?"

He frowned. "Do you think we should?"

"Certainly. It's only money."

"Spoken like a true millionairess."

Half an hour later they finished their coffee and croissants in a little hole-in-the-wall frequented by early risers of the working class. Hélène set her cup down on the tiny marble table. She looked at Guy as his laughter reverberated around the tiny room.

"Really, Guy!" she said. "I'm serious. I had no idea! I was assured that I wouldn't have to . . . put out, you know? With men. But anyway, this old white-haired man took a fancy to me. He wanted me to sit with him and have some champagne. I didn't want to, but Yvette told me I couldn't possibly refuse. So I left the hat-check room and went over to his table. He was very courteous and invited me to sit down. Then one of the waiters—they're *all* Algerians, you know—came over and said, 'Would you like a drink, mademoiselle?' And I said, 'Yes, please. I'll have a glass of mineral water.' Anyway, not three minutes had passed when the waiter returned with orders for me to see Monsieur Blond immediately. He's the boss, you know. Well, I thought he was going to insist I go to a hotel or someplace like that with the old man. On the way to the office, I started making up all sorts of excuses. But when I got there, I received the worst tongue-lashing of my life! 'Mademoiselle,' Monsieur Blond said in a cold, quiet voice"—she mimicked him, her own voice taking on a chilly, whispery tone—" 'I do not know what remote region of this country you hail from, but let me make something clear to you. Do you have any idea how we make our money?' I looked at him stupidly. 'From the cover charge?' I asked in confusion. 'No, mademoiselle. Off the house champagne. Anytime a customer wants to buy you a drink, you order champagne. Is that clear?' "

Guy was laughing so hard that the tears were rolling down his cheeks. It was contagious. She found herself laughing hysterically too.

"You know," he said, "if anybody can single-handedly destroy that place's reputation, it will be you!"

4

A week later, just past midnight, Jocelyne came into the Folies de Babylon. Casually she dropped her fur coat over the hat-check counter, took the plastic tag stamped 47, and floated after the maître d' to table 21. She was seemingly unaware that every male eye was hungrily following her. In her path she left behind the thick sweet scent of lavender.

Lavender. The bitch still wore lavender, Hélène thought as she clutched the counter and found herself slipping back in time, back to 1944 in Nazi-occupied Paris, to a luxurious bordello run by an elegant, diminutive Madame Chang. Back to the night they had spent hidden in Gisèle's room and she had been awakened by furtive taps on the door. Jocelyne had worn a peignoir of pale blue chiffon then, and her conversation with Gisèle had been a throaty whisper.

"But why should the SS be out looking for children?" Gisèle had whispered.

"They're killers," Jocelyne hissed.

Gisèle had laughed. "Killers? Those sweet little darlings?"

"They're killers, all right . . . they shot a Boche soldier yesterday . . . now there's a reward out for information leading to their capture . . . half a million francs . . . we could go and get three, maybe four dresses at the couturiers'!"

That was what the price had been. Four children delivered into Nazi hands in exchange for three, maybe four dresses. For Jocelyne and Gisèle, dresses were expensive, but life was cheap.

Hélène stared after Jocelyne. The initial shock was wearing off, and she could feel the chill of deadly hatred beginning to swell up inside her.

Yvette looked at Hélène. "Is something the matter?" she asked in a worried voice.

Grimly Hélène continued to stare out over the counter.

272

There was a faraway look in her eyes. "Nothing's the matter!" she said huskily.

"Well, hurry up and hang up the coat, then."

Hélène drew back from the fur as if it were covered with snakes.

"Pardon *me!*" Yvette glared at Hélène, grabbed Jocelyne's coat, and went to hang it up.

Hélène kept her eyes on Jocelyne all night long. Jocelyne had presence; she had to credit her with that. The moment she was in a room, everybody became aware of her. She was graceful and poised. Not once did she glance up at the tawdry show on the stage. It was as if she was the star of the Folies de Babylon. In a way, she was.

She was even dressed like a star. She wore a strapless red evening gown and white shoulder-length gloves. She still had that captivating beauty. That slender body that burst into voluptuousness at her breasts. That spun-gold hair, those thin gold eyebrows. Only the blue eyes had changed. They looked curiously vacant now.

So Jocelyne wasn't working in a high-class bordello anymore, Hélène thought to herself with satisfaction. She had become a common bar hustler. But she deserved far worse! That whore had blown the whistle on Edmond, Catherine, Marie, and her. She was a traitor. A collaborator.

Hélène's eyes narrowed. Jocelyne had been responsible for having Gisèle's sketches plastered all over the Boche newspapers. She was as responsible for Catherine's and Marie's fate as the Boches themselves. It was because of her that Marie had been burned with the cigarette. That Catherine and Marie had disappeared, never to return.

Yes, fate had been kind to Jocelyne. Much too kind.

For an hour Jocelyne sat at her table sipping champagne, chain-smoking cigarettes, and answering her pink telephone. But as time dragged on, she began losing her composure. She looked worried about something. Hélène wondered what. Certainly not about finding a man. Her phone was ringing off the hook.

Finally a tall dark man with a beard approached Jocelyne's table. Hélène perked up. He didn't sit down. He exchanged a few words with Jocelyne, discreetly put one of his hands into a pocket, and slipped her something. Jocelyne palmed it, and the man went away. Then she glanced around warily and rose to her feet. Hélène thought she was leaving. Instead, she headed for the powder room.

Hélène hesitated a moment, then turned to Yvette. "I have to go to the bathroom. Can you cover me?"

"Sure. Are you all right?"

Hélène nodded. "It's something I ate," she said quickly. Before Yvette could ask any more questions, she let herself out and followed the path Jocelyne had taken.

The powder room was located off a little corridor. When Hélène closed the door, she stood in the starkly illuminated room for a moment. It was relatively quiet in here. The sounds of the show were weak and distant. She glanced at the three doors leading to the toilet stalls. She knew that they had locks. She knew, too, that the locks were broken. The girls said it was because Monsieur Blond didn't like hanky-panky going on in the toilets. One of the hookers had once brought a john in there.

She crossed over to the first door and pulled it open. The stall was empty. The second was empty, too. Then she pulled open the third. She stifled a gasp.

Jocelyne was sitting on the toilet. Her eyes were closed, the long white glove on her left arm was rolled down, and a hypodermic needle was stuck in the crook of her arm.

Quickly Hélène closed the door. In her oblivious euphoria, Jocelyne hadn't even noticed her. Quickly she left the powder room and went back outside. For a moment she just stood there. Then she noticed the pay phone on the wall beside the powder-room door. She pursed her lips thoughtfully. Suddenly she knew what she had to do. But she needed small change. She rushed back to the hat-check room.

Yvette looked at her suspiciously. "What do you need change for?" she asked.

"Don't be so nosy. I've got a telephone call to make."

Reluctantly Yvette reached into the tip box and handed her a coin. "Make it fast. Monsieur Blond doesn't like to see his employees goofing off."

Hélène looked over her shoulder, but Jocelyne still hadn't come out of the powder room. "Thanks for the advice," she said dryly. Then she hurried off to call the police. One of the bouncers passed her while she was on the telephone. She stopped talking until he was out of earshot.

When she returned to the checkroom, Hélène kept her eyes peeled for the gendarmes. She had given them Jocelyne's description, the location of the powder room, her table number. Anxiously she turned to Yvette. "What time is it now?"

Yvette sighed and looked at her wrist. "Two minutes later than the last time you asked," she said wearily. She looked suspiciously at Hélène. "What's the matter? You waiting for somebody?"

Hélène shook her head. "No . . ." Suddenly she stiffened. Jocelyne was returning to her table. Hélène watched her sit down. The whore was no longer nervous. The heroin was doing its stuff. One of the waiters came over, took her champagne bottle out of the ice bucket, and refilled her glass. She smiled up at him. Then she answered her telephone, looked across the room, and smiled professionally. Her head bowed in a kind of little nod. A moment later Hélène saw a short fat man in an evening suit getting up from table 16. He waddled excitedly across the room toward Jocelyne, pulled up a chair, and leaned across the table, lighting her cigarette.

A few minutes later there was a commotion at the door. Hélène leaned out over the counter. Two uniformed gendarmes were pushing the bouncers aside. They looked around and walked straight over to Jocelyne's table. Jocelyne looked up in surprise. The short fat man shot to his feet, gesturing nervously. One of the gendarmes grabbed Jocelyne's purse, dumped its contents out on the table, and then pulled her to her feet. She let out a shriek. Roughly he yanked her gloves down. She stood there motionless, her shoulders sagging, her hair falling down over her face as she stared at the floor. Conversation in the club had come to a halt. Monsieur Blond and one of his bodyguards hastily approached the table. The club owner's dark suit and sunglasses contrasted with his yellow-dyed hair. He took one of the gendarmes aside. His face was devoid of expression as he tried to throw oil on the troubled waters. Onstage, the orchestra didn't skip a beat and the showgirls were doing their best to continue the performance. But no one was watching. Customers were signaling for their checks. The hookers were gathering up their purses.

"What's going on?" Yvette asked curiously. She pushed Hélène aside in order to get a better view.

"They're arresting somebody," Hélène said softly.

Yvette looked at her accusingly. "It was you, wasn't it? You called the police. That's why you needed the change for the telephone. That's why you were so nervous!"

Hélène looked down silently.

275

"You bitch!" Yvette hissed. "Don't you know that this place is already operating at the very fringes of the law! Do you want it to be closed down? Do you want all of us to lose our jobs?"

Hélène shook her head. "I'm sorry," she murmured. "I didn't think of that."

"You didn't think! For God's sake, where are your brains? If the others hear about this, they'll scratch your eyes out!"

"You won't tell them, will you?"

Yvette's face suddenly broke into a smile. "Not this time. Jocelyne's the nastiest cunt I've ever met."

After Jocelyne was taken away, the atmosphere in the club slowly returned to normal. Monsieur Blond quickly spoke to each departing customer; most of them were persuaded to stay. Then Hélène saw one of the bouncers whispering to Monsieur Blond and pointing toward her. It was the same bouncer who'd seen her use the telephone. Then Monsieur Blond nodded and went back to his office. The bouncer walked over to the hat-check room. He gestured at Hélène. "Monsieur Blond wants to see you," he said gruffly. "Now in his office."

Yvette shot Hélène a worried look. Hélène smiled tightly and followed the bouncer.

Monsieur Blond's office was located at the end of the same corridor where the powder room was located. When she was shown inside, Monsieur Blond was sitting behind his desk. He was still wearing his sunglasses. She had never seen him without them.

He looked up at her expressionlessly and pointed to the bouncer. His voice was thin and cold. "Houari tells me he saw you using the pay telephone in the hallway."

Hélène took a deep breath. It was useless to deny it. Any number of people might have seen her leave the hat-check room. "Yes," she said softly.

"And you called the police?"

Hélène nodded.

Monsieur Blond steepled his fingers. "Would you mind telling me why?"

Hélène looked down at the expensive carpet. It was an antique gold-colored Tabriz. Her eyes followed the intricate pattern. Finally she shook her head. "It's personal," she said softly.

276

"You are full of surprises, mademoiselle. It seems that you are intent on ruining us."

"I didn't mean to cause any trouble," she said hastily. Then she bit down on her lip. She felt like a fool. What could she say? That calling the police had been a personal vendetta? That she hadn't given the repercussions any thought?

"I'm afraid you leave me no choice, mademoiselle," Monsieur Blond said flatly. "As of this moment, you no longer work here."

Hélène looked up at the imposing stone building on the Faubourg St.-Honoré. It was Parisian architecture at its best. Solid, eighteenth-century neoclassical. It had a facade covered with columns and was crowned with a steep mansard roof. It looked more like a palace than a commercial building. The André Lichtenstein Gallery took up most of the ground floor.

"It looks rather awesome," Hélène said nervously.

Guy laughed. "Don't let all that grandeur intimidate you."

"I just feel somewhat out of place. I don't think I'm ready for high society."

"Who says they're ready for you? Come on, let's go in." He took her arm and led her to the big glass door. The doorman held it open for them.

The gallery was full of people. Most of them were in fancy dress. Hélène could tell the artists from the buyers. They were more poorly dressed and their hair was unruly. She noticed at once that *The Hyperbolic Ascension* had the place of honor. It was hanging high on the back wall of the main room, opposite a mezzanine, so that it could be appreciated from two levels.

A waiter circulated with a tray of glasses. Guy reached for two of them and handed one to Hélène. She smiled and clinked her glass against his. "To *The Hyperbolic Ascension*," she said.

"Amen."

André Lichtenstein made his way through the crowd toward them. He was a tall, distinguished-looking man in a perfectly tailored evening suit. He looked more like a stockbroker than an art dealer. But then, art was fetching a lot of money nowadays, Hélène thought. His hair was dark, his temples streaked with gray, and he wore small gold-rimmed glasses. "How's the genius?" he asked in a smooth voice.

Guy smiled nervously. "All right, I guess."

Lichtenstein turned to Hélène. "And who is your beautiful companion?"

"Mademoiselle Junot," Guy said. "Hélène, meet Monsieur Lichtenstein."

Hélène smiled, shifted the glass to her left hand, and extended her right. Lichtenstein surprised her by taking her hand, bowing over it, and kissing it. She could barely feel the breath of his lips. He straightened and smiled. "You are very beautiful, mademoiselle." Then he turned to Guy. "I want you to come and meet a couple who have expressed an interest in buying your painting."

Guy's mouth dropped open. "Already? Are they serious?"

Lichtenstein nodded. "They're serious," he said soberly.

Hélène looked at Guy. Her eyes were shining with eagerness. "Did you hear that?" her expression seemed to say.

Lichtenstein turned and looked around for a moment, his eyes searching the room. "They're probably still upstairs," he said. He put his hand on Hélène's elbow and led the way to the center of the room, where a circular Plexiglas staircase rose up to the mezzanine.

From the mezzanine, most of the main room could be seen and *The Hyperbolic Ascension* appeared to be exploding in midair, the multicolored shards of the virgin hanging in frozen suspension.

André Lichtenstein fell all over a middle-aged couple. He clicked his heels together and bowed. "Madame Vanel, I would like the pleasure of introducing to you the artist who painted *The Hyperbolic Ascension*, Guy Barbeau."

Monsieur and Madame Vanel belonged to that new, moneyed breed indigenous to the twentieth century, the nouveau riche. Monsieur Vanel had made his fortune quite by accident in the bakery business. He was short and plump, with a ruddy complexion and steel-gray hair. He was still perplexed by his sudden wealth, and although he was a millionaire, he looked like he still spent all day standing in front of an oven. Madame Vanel was another story entirely. She enjoyed the money with a vengeance. She was bone-thin and her hair was brown and stiff and carefully coiffed. She wore too much jewelry and too much makeup. Both her clothes and her voice were loud.

Guy smiled at Madame Vanel, his nervousness showing. "How do you do?" he said formally.

278

Madame Vanel held out her hand. He bent over it and kissed it awkwardly. She preened visibly.

Lichtenstein smiled at Monsieur Vanel. "Monsieur Barbeau is delighted to answer any questions you may have regarding the painting. Please feel free to discuss it with him. As soon as you have reached any decision, just have me paged."

Monsieur Vanel nodded absently. He reached for a glass of champagne from a passing waiter. Madame Vanel took Guy aside. Art was her territory. She didn't know what surrealism was, but she did know that the best homes had art that nobody understood hanging on the walls. It was a sign of culture, and she was determined to show that she had it. She was about to purchase one of those hideous, puzzling paintings. And she was socializing with a real artist. One whom André Lichtenstein had assured her was indeed a rising star. "Get him now while he's cheap," Lichtenstein had whispered to her in confidence. "In a few years his prices will skyrocket."

Lichtenstein smiled at Hélène and led her away. "Let's leave them to talk," he said. "The painting is as good as sold."

They halted abruptly as Lichtenstein made some small talk with a buyer. Not wishing to eavesdrop, Hélène looked around. Suddenly her heart began to pound. She recognized the old woman who was holding court in the midst of a small group. She had seen her photograph in all the fashion magazines. She was one of her idols. She was the living legend, Odile Joly, the most exalted couturière of the twentieth century. Hélène couldn't keep from staring at her.

Odile Joly was so tiny that she looked like a young girl. Actually she was seventy years old and bony as a starved bird. Her neck was thin and stringy, the cords standing out like taut wires. Her thick glasses were encased in tortoiseshell, and her bobbed black hair under the bowllike hat was a daring anachronism for her age. She was dressed in a suit of her own design. It was a pale pearl color, the fabric suggesting just the vaguest hint of gold. Stories circulated that it was the only suit she owned. When she smiled she looked like she was grinning from ear to ear, and her gestures were extremely emphasized. Her hands fluttered like an agitated bird learning to fly; for some reason or other—nervousness perhaps—she kept tugging at the hem of her jacket. She smoked incessantly, holding her cigarette with her elbow bent, her hand constantly at chin level. Her huge brown eyes darted about continuously. Although few people understood exactly what she was saying in her raspy voice, everyone listened raptly to her every word, absorbing them as if they were divine decree.

Suddenly Odile Joly looked up and caught sight of Hélène. The giant eyes flashed—studying, visualizing, deciding, all in one sweeping glance. Then she slowly stepped forward. The group surrounding her parted and let her through.

Hélène's heart began to pump even faster. Was it possible? Was Odile Joly approaching *her*?

"Always wear white, chérie," Odile Joly commanded imperiously, her cigarette hand sweeping dramatically through the air. "Never, never wear dark blue like you're wearing now." She frowned disapprovingly. "No, not even white. White is too startling. Too flashy. It *glares*. Wear champagne. Yes, that's it! *Champagne*." She rolled the word on her tongue, tasting the color with her lips.

Hélène was afraid to breathe. She cast a quick glance at the others. They were staring at her, digesting the great Odile's edict and nodding in agreement.

Finally she found her tongue. "I . . . I will wear champagne from now on," she stammered.

Odile Joly gave a birdlike nod. "Good. Champagne first and foremost, but anything very, very pale will do. But never, never wear pastels or sherbets. They are *non*colors. They are for cowards. For people who wish to look 'safe' and end up looking like ice-cream cones." Her eyes roved up and down Hélène. "You have a wonderful figure for clothes. A model's figure. Your proportions are fantastic. Tell me, chérie. Are you a fashion model?"

"N-no," Hélène managed to say. She could feel herself perspiring.

"Well, what is it you do, then?"

"Nothing at the moment, I'm afraid."

The huge, famous eyes glinted shrewdly. "You should be a model. If you're interested, come and see me at my atelier. The Maison d'Odile Joly. It's just up the street."

Hélène found herself nodding. This was the last thing in the world she would have dreamed could happen. She had heard about being in the right place at the right time, but who would have thought it was here? And to think that she hadn't even wanted to come to the gallery in the first place.

Not after losing her job and being without work for over a week. She had only come for Guy's sake. And what had happened? She had met the great Odile and been offered a job as a fashion model! Without a job interview, without any experience. It was too good to be true.

"Thank you," Hélène told Odile in a quivering voice, "I ... I shall be at the atelier on Monday."

Still shaking, Hélène stammered her excuses and retreated unobtrusively into a quiet corner. Although the crowds milling around her sounded like a thousand chattering magpies, she cut them from her mind completely. She needed time to mull over the extraordinary luck which had fallen her way. She had met the distinguished Odile Joly. Not only that, but the greatest couturière in the world—and the most formidable—had sought her out and offered her a job. Was it possible? Truly? She felt like pinching herself. It was more than she had ever dared hope for. When she had first arrived in Paris, she had been filled with naive dreams. Slowly they had evaporated. The truly successful, like the very rich, were part of a social orbit which was totally, hopelessly out of reach. Now, suddenly, not only was she mingling with an assortment of people she never thought she could meet but also she had met the one person she had idolized for years.

She had been alone in her corner no more than five minutes when a tall, attractive man came over to her. He smiled and handed her a glass of champagne. "I'm not intruding?" he asked politely in French. His French, she noticed, was heavily accented with the mellifluous tones of upper-class English.

"No, of course you're not intruding," she assured him quickly.

He smiled. "What do you say we mingle and look at the art? No one else seems to."

If we can see anything past the crowds, she thought. But aloud she said, "I'd love to."

He took her gently by the arm and guided her expertly around the pockets of people, pointing out various paintings here and sculptures there. She felt shy and as though she were dream-walking.

As they were standing in front of a faceless white Brancusi sculpture with only clean lines hinting at the features, she let her eyes dart sideways to have a good look at him. He was watching her with an expression of amusement.

Quickly she averted her eyes. I'm behaving like a schoolgirl, she chided herself.

"I don't even know your name," he said.

She looked at him again and swallowed. "Mademoiselle Junot."

He gave a little bow. "My name is Nigel."

"How do you do, Monsieur Nigel?" she said gravely.

He flung back his head and laughed.

She looked suddenly stricken. "Have I . . . have I said something wrong?"

"No, no. Not at all. You see, Nigel is my first name. Somerset is my last. You may call me Nigel."

Her heart began to beat faster. She felt suddenly drawn to him. What was happening? First Odile Joly, and now this intriguing stranger.

"Nigel . . ." she said slowly, as if to herself. "It's a very pretty name. Mine . . . mine is Hélène."

"Also very pretty. Stately, too."

She looked to see if he was joking; she was grateful to see that he wasn't.

"I hope I'm not too forward," he said, "but I was wondering if you would like—"

A scream suddenly reverberated around the high walls of the gallery. At once everyone stopped talking.

"Oh, my God, no," Hélène heard André Lichtenstein murmuring under his breath. Then she saw him quickly pushing his way through a crowd of well-dressed people.

"For Christ's sake!" a voice boomed out from the edge of the mezzanine. "Green! What are you, some kind of moron? Whoever heard of matching a painting to your living-room sofa!"

Hélène went pale. The voice was Guy's. What was he doing? Who was he screaming at? "I . . . I'm sorry," Hélène said quickly to Nigel. She handed him her champagne glass and started after Lichtenstein. They found Guy at the edge of the mezzanine, his face red, the veins on his temples popping out and throbbing. Madame Vanel was cowering against her husband, her eyes wide in fear.

"He's crazy!" Madame Vanel whispered in a frightened voice. "Crazy!"

Guy turned around to face the others. "This . . . this

woman"—he pointed a shaking finger at Madame Vanel—"wants me to change the colors in my painting. In *that* painting!" He whirled around, pointing at *The Hyperbolic Ascension.* "She wants me to prostitute my talent like a common whore!"

Lichtenstein reached Guy and took him by the arm. Angrily Guy threw him off.

Hélène came up beside Guy. "Come on, Guy," she said quietly. "I think it's time we went home."

He laughed derisively. "Home? What home? Some shitty rat hole? What's there? No one cares about art or how artists live. None of these people give a fuck about anything except their matched sofas and their bank accounts!"

She shook his arm. "Guy, come *on*," she whispered desperately.

He laughed again and pushed her away. There was a crazed look in his eyes. "Not without the painting, I won't! It's too good for these . . . these . . ." At a loss for words, he threw his fists high into the air. His body was trembling. Suddenly he rushed at the silent crowd. Frightened, they drew back. He ran down the Plexiglas stairs two at a time. Now everyone on the mezzanine crowded forward to see what was going on. Hélène grabbed hold of the steel railing and looked down. Guy was pushing through the crowd on the ground floor. Then he stood under the painting, staring up at it. He let out a cry of agony. "You're too good for this world!" he screamed at the painting. "You're too good! Do you hear that?"

The painting hung there in silence.

André Lichtenstein's face was stony. "He's finished!" he hissed under his breath. "I'll see to it that every gallery in this city will be closed to that maniac!"

Hélène closed her eyes. Why was Guy doing this? Everything had been going so well. The painting had been as good as sold! Why hadn't he just told Madame Vanel quietly that her request was impossible? Why create such a scandal? Why? *Why?*

Suddenly a gasp swept through the crowd. Hélène's eyes flew open. Guy was jumping up at the painting. He missed it the first time. On the second try, he managed to grab hold of the bottom edge of the frame. The painting was hanging away from the wall, and he hung suspended in midair, his feet off the ground. For a moment *The Hyperbolic Ascension* just swung sideways. Then one of the wires connecting it to the ceiling snapped abruptly. Guy lost his grip and fell, rolling across the carpet. The left corner of the frame missed him as it crashed to the floor, the big canvas wobbling under the impact. For a moment Guy looked stunned. Then he staggered to his feet. He picked up a chrome-and-leather bench and began attacking the painting, smashing the legs of the bench through the canvas. Once the holes were punched, he threw the bench aside. He grabbed hold of the canvas with both hands and began tugging at it.

The same fingers that had painted *The Hyperbolic Ascension* tore it to shreds.

5

With her forearm, Hélène wiped the perspiration off her brow. Then she put the paint roller back in the pan. She wiped her hands on a rag, placed them on her hips, and looked around the room. She was pleased. It was amazing what a can of paint could do. The old dirty-white room was transformed by a coat of bloodred paint that covered up the unevenness of the walls and all the little cracks in the plaster. Already the second coat was nearly dry.

The three-panel screen she'd bought at the flea market, which she'd also painted red, hid the sink and the little stove. With the fabric she had bought in a shop on the Right Bank, the transformation would be complete. The inexpensive bolt of red paisley had a pattern of deep blue and ivory. From part of it she had made a tablecloth that she would drape over the kitchen table. The square of glass she had bought would cover the top. Now that she had a little money to play with, she decided to buy a few things. A shaded lamp and the cracked old landscape in the gold frame she had seen at the flea market—no Rembrandt, mind you, but nice enough. She would be lavish with the paisley curtains, though. Skimpy curtains looked so cheap. For the bed she had sewn a cover of plain deep blue cotton, as well as some slipcovers for the cushions. They were of the same blue, and a few others were paisley. Now the bed would look nice and could double as a sort of couch. And very cleverly she'd suspended a rod over the far end of the room. It would hold a massive curtain of more paisley. She'd nailed all the hooks against this one wall, and now it would function as a makeshift closet. At least her clothes would be out of sight.

She looked down at the floor with distaste. Between the newspapers she had spread out, she could see hideous patches of yellow linoleum peering up at her. The next priority would be to put something over it. Perhaps she could find an inexpensive roll of glossy deep red linoleum somewhere. If she kept it waxed, it could look quite stunning.

She sat down on the edge of the bed. Now that she had finished painting, the room seemed awfully quiet. With Guy gone, she missed the incessant talk, the laughter, the humming while he painted. When he had stomped out of the gallery, he had gone off alone and gotten drunk. Then on Saturday morning he had returned sheepishly to the apartment and packed his things.

"Where are you going?" she had asked him.

He smiled grimly. "Back home."

"Not to Strasbourg!"

His gentle blue eyes were sad. "Yes, back to Strasbourg."

"But, Guy!" she protested. "You have so much talent!" Her voice took on a tone of sadness. "It would be such a pity to waste it."

He shook his head. "I can't paint anymore," he said quietly. "Not while the buyers are people like the Vanels."

Hélène sighed and got to her feet. She brought the roller, the paint pan, and the brush over to the sink and carefully rinsed them off. When they were spotless, she picked the newspapers up off the floor, got the apartment in order, and made herself a salad. She had to watch her weight and figure now that she was a model. After she cleared away the dishes, she sat down at the table to write some letters. Thoughtfully she chewed the eraser on the end of the pencil. She began to write:
Paris, July 30, 1953

Dearest Jeanne and Edmond,

I know I have been very lax in writing to you, and I feel

terribly guilty about it. Will you believe my excuse that I've been so busy I couldn't find the time?

I am a fashion model now. Not in the magazines but in a real couturière's atelier, the Maison d'Odile Joly. Sounds impressive. But until now I've only been a kind of dressmaker's dummy for Odile Joly. She designs all her clothes in the most peculiar manner. She uses live models instead of dummies, and some of the other girls and I have to stand there for hours, draped under tons of fabric, while the great Odile cuts the patterns with scissors and then pins them together.

Next week is the Big Event, the winter showing, and I've graduated from dummy to part-time runway model. It's going to be quite exciting. All the important buyers will be there, as well as the press and photographers from all over the world. Imagine me in the newspapers and magazines! If I can get hold of any of the pictures, I'll be sure to clip them and send them on to you.

I hope everything is going well for you both. I can't wait until you can come to Paris. It is so exciting here, and I'm sure you'll love it.

> All *my* love always,
> Your Little French Girl
> in Paris

Hélène read it over, folded it carefully, slipped it into an envelope, and kissed the seal before she licked it. Then she wrote another letter:

Paris, July 30, 1953

Dear Madame Dupré,

I know this is only my second letter, but I have been very busy working at odd jobs. Finally I have landed one I'm crazy about—I'm a fashion model in the Maison d'Odile Joly. Really! So I must tell you exactly what goes on there.

First of all, everybody always calls Odile Joly by both names—never just "Odile" and never "Madame Joly." On the other hand, according to those in the know, Jacques Fath is always called just "Jacques," Coco Chanel is plain "Chanel," Dior is "Christian," and Madame Grès is "Madame Grès." I'm becoming a storehouse of trivia.

Odile (to save words I'll call her just plain "Odile," woe

to my fate if she ever finds out) is very short and tiny. As you know, she is known mostly for her suits, although she designs dresses, gowns, and coats, too. You probably also know that she always wears funny little (or big) hats, and that she lives in an apartment in the Plaza Athénée. But did you know that she chain-smokes? Anyway, the atelier is on the Faubourg St.-Honoré, in one of those grand buildings Paris is so famous for. She owns the whole building, and the smaller one next door as well. One of the other models told me that over a thousand women work for Odile. Last year she sold more than thirty thousand garments—and you know how expensive they are! A poor family in Saint-Nazaire could live on one of those suits for a year. But this is not Saint-Nazaire. This is Paris!

So far, I have spent most of my time in the atelier. The atelier is everything but the showroom itself. There are many rooms where Odile creates her garments, and she'll work on a dozen different ones at the same time. Usually, though, she works in a big gray-linoleum-floored room. Here's her method. She'll drape yards and yards of shantung or wool or whatever around me and stand back, poke here and there with shears—snip, snip-snip, stand back, snip some more—put a pin here or there, have her whole mouth full of pins (and literally using her own sweater and skirt as pincushions, so that she'll constantly stick herself), and go scampering around the floor *on her knees, for heaven's sake,* trying to get a view from every angle. This is the way the originals are handled. Odile also has a ready-to-wear line which she exports (mainly to America). Can you imagine—over 500 midinettes copy and sew her garments day and night, day in, day out?

Last week was the first time I set foot in the showroom. That's because I was promoted. I'm still going to continue to be Odile's favorite dressmaker's dummy, I'm afraid—it kills your feet—but I'll be in the winter show as a runway model. Isn't that exciting? I've promised Jeanne and Edmond newspaper and magazine clippings if I'm in them, and I'll send you some, too.

If you want to know what's new on the fashion scene, I'm going to tell you. The favorite item I'm going to model in the show is one of Odile's suits. It's furry alpaca wool, champagne-colored. You wouldn't believe the finishing touches!

As soon as you come to Paris, I'll try to arrange for you to attend one of the shows. The showroom is actually five rooms, all connected by the runway. They are lavishly decorated, and remind me of Château Hautecloque. They are all carpeted, and the main room has a big staircase going up to one of Odile's workrooms. The staircase is supposed to be where the superimportant buyers and columnists sit during the shows. The walls of the rooms are white boiserie, and they have theater-type spotlights, crystal chandeliers, and wall sconces with silk shades.

At any rate, that's all the news I have right now. As soon as there's more, I promise to write.

Affectionately,
Hélène

She reread the letter carefully, wondering whether there was anything she should add in a postscript. Briefly she thought of mentioning the intriguing British gentleman she had met at the art gallery, but then thought better of it. She had thought of Nigel quite a bit since then, wishing that she had not had to run off after Guy, but it was too late now. It would be best if she just forgot him, chances being that she would never again run into him. She sighed, wrote out the envelope, and licked the flap shut. It felt good to be able to write the truth for once.

The unventilated dressing room behind the heavy velvet curtain was like an oven. The hot spell had hung over Paris for nearly two weeks now. All Parisians hoped for a cooling rain, but none as much as the models at Odile Joly's. The winter clothes were hot and heavy.

Nervously Hélène looked at her reflection in the three-paneled mirror. She watched as one of the dressers deftly buttoned up the back of her blouse. Then the fat, middle-aged woman stood back, frowned thoughtfully, stepped closer, and began to fuss with the collar. The heavy tweed jacket would be put on only at the last moment. All around the room, the other dressers were helping the models into their clothes. Lining the walls were metal garment racks on casters. On them hung Odile Joly's winter collection for 1953–1954.

For once, Odile Joly was not in the atelier. This was her moment of glory. She stood at the top of the famous circular staircase in the main showroom. From here she could watch everything. She could keep one eye on the models and the other on the most important buyers and the most powerful journalists. But she would watch no one as closely as the crème de la crème. They would be sitting at the places of honor—below her on the sweeping steps of the carpeted staircase.

Odile Joly's face had settled into an inscrutable expression. Despite the heat and the momentous occasion, she was relaxed and calm. Her work was finished, the Collection complete. She knew that it was good. For a moment she closed her eyes. She could feel the crackling excitement that hung in the air like invisible bolts of electricity in the summer skies. It was the same kind of excitement that can be felt in a theater before the curtain goes up. But she could not share in it. Her excitement derived from the pleasure of creating. From cutting. From pinning. From discovering a new style, creating a new pocket, designing a new button.

She looked down at the carpeted models' catwalk. It was laid out like a figure X. The center of the X was in the main room, and each end of the X extended into one of the four other rooms. But only the people in the main room counted. Those in the other rooms were yokels. Tourists whose hotel concierges had arranged for them to attend the show. Very minor journalists who insisted on covering the collection. People who were known never to buy anything.

Her large dark eyes darted around, absorbing what was going on. All the big French windows were open, trying in vain to catch a breeze that did not exist. Already the showrooms were filling up. The vendeuses were showing people to their seats. Right below her, the honored few started to take their coveted places on the staircase. There were two princes. The older one, Alfonse, was practically destitute. Odile Joly knew how he had fought against the Germans during the war, helping to preserve some of France's great national treasures from destruction, and she loved him for it. Ever since, she made certain the Prince and Princess were seated in the places of honor. Also, she insisted that the Princess was dressed at no charge.

There were two other princesses. One of them, ancient and stiffly coiffed, had been a Cleveland divorcée who had married a Danish prince. She was famous for never paying for anything in her life—not for a single lunch in the expensive restaurants she frequented, not for her lavish hotel suites, nor even for her clothes. Those bills of hers which *were* paid were footed by her "walker," the young American automobile heir who admired her and escorted her everywhere. The dotty old Prince did not mind. The young man in question was a known homosexual; thus the princess was in "safe" company. Odile Joly was one of the few on his list of creditors to be paid, as she refused to dress the Princess otherwise.

Odile smiled down at the wife of an exiled Far Eastern monarch. In the past three years, Sammyo Kittilongkhon had bought more than three hundred and fifty different outfits at the Maison d'Odile Joly. She was by far the best customer in the house.

Then there was a duchess, a German actress, and that American politician's wife, Barbara Sennett. The fabulously wealthy Mrs. Sennett, who had the irritating habit of squinting while perpetually grinning, had created a minor scandal the year before by altering her twenty-five-thousand-dollar sales slip from the Maison d'Odile Joly to read twenty-five hundred dollars. Her crude alteration had been caught by U.S. customs officials at Idlewild Airport. Then there were the truly powerful journalists.

Odile Joly's eyes roved over the gilt chairs that lined the models' catwalk ten chairs deep. Scattered among the rich social set were more journalists, their status decreed by the row in which they sat. First row was highly acceptable, last row was "Siberia." This hierarchy was strictly observed, closely watched, much gossiped about when someone gained or lost a row.

In the front row, Odile Joly saw Pauline Monnier, the society reporter from the *Couture Magazine*. Pauline deserved the back row, but she had come in with her inseparable companion, Daphne Epaminondas. Madame Epaminondas was the first wife of one of the world's wealthiest men, the Greek shipping tycoon Zeno Callicrates Skouri. She was worth thirty outfits a year. Also in the first row but on the opposite side of the catwalk was Cynthia Skouri, the tycoon's current American wife. And only two chairs away was Ariadne Cosindas, a renowned ballerina with a passion for haute couture. This seating arrangement would be talked about for a long time to come, because it was common knowledge that Ariadne Cosindas had been Zeno Callicrates Skouri's mistress through both his marriages. Now the three women who on different occasions had shared the bed of the same man were studiously avoiding each other's eyes.

Still in the main room but banished to the most inferior back-row seats were the representatives from *Women's Wear Daily's* Paris bureau—one reporter, one sketch artist, one photographer. *Women's Wear Daily* would ordinarily have been steered into one of the four other rooms, but Odile Joly had foresight. She predicted that within ten years *WWD* would be the most powerful fashion instrument in the world. But for now, even giving them the worst seats in the main room was being more than generous. As *WWD* progressed in stature, Odile Joly would begin moving them forward row by row.

Beside the *WWD* group sat the Comte and Comtesse de la Brissac et de Léger. Odile Joly's old face cracked into a malicious smile. The Comte and Comtesse had been relegated to these seats because of a photograph that she had seen of the Comtesse. There had been a local polo-pony tryout in Bordeaux. Although it would have gotten no press coverage under ordinary circumstances, the unexpected appearance of the Comte's first cousin—a former army colonel and now a rising politician—had made the event newsworthy. The Comtesse had been caught with her pants down, so to speak. Her full-page four-color photograph had appeared in *Paris Match,* and Odile Joly had seen it. Her eagle eyes had immediately recognized the Comtesse's "Odile Joly" suit as a copy. Since the Comtesse was a relatively steady buyer, and a social item at that, Odile Joly couldn't very well ostracize her from the main room. But she could—and did—kick the Comte and Comtesse from their usual second-row seats to the least important row in the back. This snub would be duly noted and reported and gossiped about. In the future, the Comtesse would be more careful. And more important, Odile Joly was certain that the Comtesse would now buy three times her usual amount of clothes to try to make up for her treachery and secure the usual second-row seats for the future. This gave Odile Joly a sense of satisfaction, a feeling of power.

Odile Joly's eyes swept down the catwalk into one of the adjoining rooms. She could see just a portion of it. Suddenly she stiffened. Someone looked all too familiar. She frowned, trying to place the face that went with the blond wig and the big glasses. Then the woman lit a cigarette. When she inhaled, she held it between her thumb and forefinger.

Quickly Odile Joly signaled for a vendeuse. The dark-haired woman in the black dress hurried over to the side of the staircase. Odile Joly leaned over the railing. "Room three, chair thirty-seven!" she whispered angrily. "How did she get in?"

The vendeuse turned around discreetly and glanced through the open doorway. The woman in chair thirty-seven wore large glasses, a wide-brimmed ocelot hat, and a silk blouse with a huge lace bow at the collar. The vendeuse turned and looked back up at Odile Joly. "The concierge at the Hotel Cusset called in her seat reservation. I don't see anything—"

"You fool!" Odile hissed. "That's Simone Doucet! Can't you tell?"

The vendeuse looked again. Her face suddenly paled. "By God, it is!" she said in a grief-stricken whisper. "I . . . I can't tell you how terribly sorry I am! I didn't recognize her in that getup."

Odile Joly snorted. "Getup indeed! You mean disguise. That lesbienne spy came sneaking in here dressed as a lady! Throw her out immediately!"

Quickly the vendeuse hurried off. Simone Doucet was on the design team of one of the lesser houses that thrived on stealing designs from the great couturiers. There was a strictly enforced rule in each maison de couture that the doors were shut to workers from all other houses. With satisfaction, Odile Joly watched the vendeuse dealing with the matter. Simone Doucet was being escorted to the door.

Odile Joly gave a little signal with her hand. Immediately the chandelier lights dimmed and the klieg lights clicked on. The show was ready to begin.

The dressing room was getting hotter by the minute. The models were sweating. They were lined up in order of appearance. The harried dressers, nervous despite years of experience, made last-minute adjustments to the models' hair or smoothed their hands over the skirts and jackets, dabbing the perspiration from their carefully made-up faces with tissues. Everything had been timed to the second. Within ninety seconds of leaving the dressing room, the first model would be back. Four others would be on the floor during that time. Each model had three minutes in which to get changed into the next outfit and be ready to go back out again. Each model had to make seven such changes of clothing.

Hélène was last in line. She watched nervously as the first model slipped out through the curtain. She could hear a smooth voice from outside explaining the garment. Four more models slipped out. Then the first model returned, quickly shed the outfit she was wearing, and was hurriedly dressed in the next.

Then there was only one other girl in front of her. The girl turned around. "Good luck," she whispered.

Hélène smiled faintly. "Thanks, Liane. Good luck to you, too."

And it was Hélène's turn. Her hands were shaking. Quickly she took a deep breath and slipped out through the curtain. She pretended that this was just a practice run. For the past week, all they had done each day was practice walking. Choreographing each step. From the audience's point of view it would all look effortless and natural. Only the models and Odile Joly knew how difficult it actually was. It had been planned so that four models would be on the catwalk at the same time, each on a different end of the X, but in precisely the same spot as the others. Then they would meet at the center of the X and switch lanes.

Graceful as a swan, she glided toward the main room, looking vacantly ahead, seemingly unaware of the hundreds of eyes that were upon her. There was scattered, polite applause. The popping flashbulbs from the cameras momentarily blinded her vision, but she did not falter. All the people were a blur. She felt Odile's eyes on her from atop the staircase and ignored them.

She pirouetted at the end of each catwalk, returned to the main room, took the branch-off into rooms one, two, three, and four, and finally returned to the dressing room.

The Comtesse de Léger recognized Hélène immediately. The cold patrician eyes narrowed, and the paper with which she was fanning herself stopped in midair. Quickly she recovered. It was a shock to see the girl here—the girl who knew about her copied garments. She wondered whether Hélène had tattled on her about Madame Dupré and the copied clothes. She glanced down at her lap. Or had it been that unexpected picture in *Paris Match*? She knew that the only person who could recognize one of Madame Dupré's expert copies of an Odile Joly suit—even from a distance or from a photograph—was Odile herself. Damn that photograph! Was that why Odile had put her and the Comte in these miserable seats this year? It was scandalous. Everyone would talk! The only thing she could do was to pretend it had never happened and to placate Odile Joly by placing an order for an enormous wardrobe.

Once again Hélène came back out from behind the curtain onto the runway. At the intersection of the X she passed Liane, who was floating gracefully back to the dressing room. Hélène was now wearing the alpaca suit. There was a spontaneous murmur of appreciation.

The Comte de Léger nudged his wife. "Isn't that the girl who was at the château?" he whispered.

The Comtesse nodded absently.

"What was her name?"

"Junot something or other. No, Hélène Junot." Irritably the Comtesse made a note on the paper with her pencil. She wanted the alpaca suit. In fact, if it would help regain her second-row seat, she was prepared to buy everything in sight. The miserable back-row seats rankled her.

When Hélène got back to the dressing room, there was a sudden commotion.

"Liane's fainted!" one of the models whispered.

A dresser came rushing over to the prostrate Liane.

"It's those lights!" another model hissed. "In this hot spell . . . they're too much!"

"Never mind!" the dresser snapped angrily. "One of you others is going to have to double for her." Quickly she glanced around. Her expert eyes rested on Hélène. "You're closest to Liane's size. It'll have to be you. Now you only have a minute and a half to change between each garment. You'll be out there twelve more times. The announcer will have to shuffle your sequence. Let's hope she can ad-lib. Now, quick! Up with your hands! There isn't a moment to lose!"

Hélène was dressed in Liane's outfit in record time. Two dressers helped her, Liane's and her own. One of them deftly pinned the sides of the dress to make it tighter. She felt herself perspiring enormously. Then she found herself pushed out through the curtain. Automatically, she smiled vacantly.

All at once, she was no longer nervous. Modeling was second nature already.

*   *   *

In the morning a delivery boy arrived at the atelier with a long slim box from a florist's on the Champs-Élysées. Puzzled, Hélène scratched a pen across the yellow delivery slip and took the box. When the boy left, she lifted the lid. A dozen long-stemmed red roses lay inside. She frowned.

"Any idea who they're from?" Liane asked from the doorway.

Hélène looked up and shook her head wordlessly. Then she reached down and picked up the small white envelope. She pulled out the card. It was engraved with an unmistakable coat of arms. The lion, the salamander, and the crest of the de Légers. She turned the card over. On the back, the blue ink read: "Tomorrow night at nine. Will expect you at Maxim's. Just ask for my table." It was signed simply "Philippe de Léger."

Hélène sank down into a rickety chair.

"Are you all right?" Liane asked.

Hélène nodded. "Yes," she said in a quivering voice. "You won't mind if . . . if I have a little while to myself?"

Liane shook her head. "No, of course not. I'm sorry to intrude. I'll talk to you later." She waved with her fingertips and closed the door softly behind her.

Thoughtfully Hélène turned the card over in her hand, alternately glancing at the crest on the front and the message on the back. She had been in Paris for more than six months now; she was no longer a naive child from the country. In Paris, you learned fast. In six months you knew all there was to know. And she knew that a man like Philippe de Léger didn't invite a girl to Maxim's just because she'd once been in his wife's employ or because he'd once danced with her. Then there was the matter of Maxim's itself.

Maxim's was a restaurant, not only a restaurant but one of the finest in the world. It was on the rue Royale. In the early years of the century the cocottes went there with their gentlemen; now it had turned into a highly respectable place. Everyone went there to see and be seen. The best of society. The tourists. You only had to be rich and not bat your eyelashes at the prices.

She puckered her lips thoughtfully, tapping the card in the palm of her hand. Perhaps a cocotte was what Philippe de Léger fancied, but on the other hand, she didn't necessarily need to become one. More important, the card had no address on it. He had given her no chance for declining.

Hélène smiled to herself. It was probably only a dinner, and here she was making a big fuss about nothing. Going to Maxim's was probably no more exciting for the Comte than going to the corner food market was for her. Keep things in perspective, she warned herself.

Tonight she would stop by the restaurant and wait outside to see what the women were wearing. She had a little money saved up. Not enough for a Dior or an Odile Joly, but enough to buy a simple black dress at Bon Marché or Au Printemps. The red linoleum she'd seen in a little shop on the rue Victor-Masse would have to wait.

Hélène purposely stayed late at the atelier. Before she left at seven-thirty, she put the roses back in the box, tucked it under her arm, and walked down the Faubourg St.-Honoré. When she came to the rue Royale she made a right turn, crossed the street, and stayed on the opposite side of the street so that when she got to Maxim's she could look over to the other side. She didn't want to stand right outside the door, looking obvious. Fifteen minutes later, she knew all there was to know. A plain black dress would be perfectly acceptable.

The next morning she got to the atelier at her regular time. By midmorning a series of delivery boys had arrived with boxes. All for Hélène Junot. "What is going on?" Liane asked.

Hélène looked confused. "I . . . I don't know."

Liane lit a cigarette and inhaled deeply. She gestured at the boxes. "Aren't you going to open them?"

Hélène glanced over at them. "I guess I'd better."

Liane smiled. "Don't tell me! You have a secret admirer! Yesterday roses, today . . ." She stopped in mid-sentence, her mouth suddenly hanging open.

Hélène looked distressed. "What's the matter?"

"You'd better not let Odile Joly see them."

"But why?"

"The top and bottom boxes. Don't you recognize them?"

"No. Should I?"

Liane smiled grimly. "Odile Joly would. They're from the competition. Those boxes are from the House of Dior."

Hélène nodded, and they went over to the boxes. They began with the one on top. Inside was a pair of elbow-length red silk gloves.

"They're beautiful!" Liane breathed. She held one up. Then she smiled sideways. "He isn't kinky by any chance, is he?"

"I don't think so," Hélène said good-humoredly.

Next was a box from Germaine Guérin. Hélène took out a red Moutin silk evening bag. The box underneath that one came from Charles Jourdan. In it was a pair of elegant red high heels. The next box held identical red shoes, a size larger. Altogether there were four different pairs, all in different sizes. Hélène began to laugh.

Slowly she lifted the lid off the big Dior box. She parted the soft tissue paper and let out a gasp.

"My God!" Liane said quietly. "It's the dinner suit!"

Carefully Hélène lifted the ruby-red silk dinner jacket out of the box. It was bloused and had flaring hips, huge elbow-length sleeves, narrow lapels, and a thin red belt. The matching skirt was narrow and calf-length.

Liane let out a whistle. "He must be enamored of you," she stated.

Hélène turned away and stared across the room. She was silent for a moment. "I don't know. It seems too much to accept."

"But you can't return it!" Liane said quickly. "It would break the poor man's heart." She looked at Hélène. "He must be very rich."

Hélène nodded. "He is."

Suddenly there was a knock at the door.

"Just a minute!" Hélène called out. Quickly she folded the dinner suit, placed it in the box, and put the lid back on. She looked around, spied a piece of cloth, and quickly draped it over the boxes. Then she wiped her brow and went over to the door.

"Another messenger," one of the old ladies who worked in the atelier said dryly, gesturing to the young man beside her.

Quickly Hélène signed another delivery slip, took a small package, and closed the door.

Liane looked up. "Where was he from?"

"I don't know," Hélène murmured. "I didn't think of looking at the slip."

Liane placed her hands on her hips. "Well, unwrap it!" she ordered.

Silently Hélène undid the ribbon and tore off the paper. She let out a gasp. The leather-covered little box was imprinted with gold letters: "Chaumet." With trembling fingers she lifted the lid.

Two diamond-and-ruby earrings in the shape of parrots shimmered against the velvet-lined box.

"Well . . ." Liane said in an impressed voice. "Now comes the jewelry."

6

Gracefully Hélène followed the maître d' through Maxim's. She walked slowly, her full champagne-colored Balmain gown sweeping the floor, her full-length Révillon mink touched with glistening drops of melting snowflakes. By order from Liane, her hair was in a chignon, offsetting her cheekbones. She wore the canary-diamond clips on her ears.

As she walked, she smiled at the people she knew. Twice she stopped at tables, exchanging cheerful greetings and gossip as the maître d' waited patiently.

"She's like one of the old time cocottes," one ancient woman said in a dry whisper, her voice like a wind sweeping across desert sands. She sighed wistfully as Hélène swept by. "This place used to be full of them. You could hear the satin rustling, I tell you! They wore the most exquisite gowns. That was the way you could tell a cocotte, you know—sweeping gowns, enormous hats. They were worn with pride. It was like the Chinese empress who never cut her fingernails. It showed that she was not a common laborer."

"I heard she works," the younger woman beside the ancient one said. "Although, granted, she doesn't need to."

"Yes, she's a fashion model. But still she's the closest thing to those darling cocottes. I'll never forget one night in here . . ." The ancient woman's face took on a faraway look. "It was 1913, I think. Or was it 1914? Anyway, one of the cocottes broke a bottle of wine and slashed her lover across the face with it. All because he was with another woman! Those were the exciting days!"

The Comte smiled as Hélène sank down into the red banquette and shrugged off her mink, letting it fall back off her shoulders. The strapless Balmain gown showed her figure off to perfection. He took her hand and brought it up to his lips. "You look more beautiful all the time," he said. She looked into his eyes. The bright blue pools held that intent look that she knew only too well. He lowered her hand and brought it down between his legs. His shaft was swollen hard.

She smiled and removed her hand as a bottle of champagne and a massive silver ice bucket were automatically brought to the table. They spent so much time at Maxim's that no one needed to ask what they would drink. Everyone who worked there knew that they always had champagne first, followed by a bottle of Château Hautecloque-de Léger with dinner (if they ate fish, they ordered Château Haut-Brion blanc instead), and after a café moka they had Cognac Prince Eugène. Hélène never had more than half a glass of wine and champagne, and only a few sips of the cognac.

"I'm sorry I couldn't meet you at the house," the Comte said smoothly. He gave an elegant shrug.

Hélène nodded. She knew what that shrug meant. The Comtesse had been in town. She took a sip of her champagne. The only times he mentioned the Comtesse were when he'd been detained by her visits. The Comte reached into his pocket, took out a long skinny box from Van Cleef, and handed it to Hélène. "Just so that you don't feel too left out, I brought you a little gift."

She smiled and opened the box. The cool sapphires surrounded by loops of diamonds flashed fire up at her. She took a deep breath. It was the most extravagant gift he'd given her to date.

"Like it?" he asked lightly.

She looked up. "I love it," she said softly. Immediately she removed her canary-diamond earrings and let him hang the sapphires around her throat. She reached up and felt their coldness with her fingers. She was glad to have them. Now the canary diamonds could be put to good use. To the same use as she had put the ruby-and-diamond parrot earrings. Then, the next time he gave her a jewel, she would "retire" the sapphire necklace. It would go where all the other jewels had gone.

Was it possible that seven pieces of jewelry had already gone that route? she asked herself. Could it be possible that she had been seeing the Comte for six months already? That she'd been going regularly to Maxim's ever since then? She would never forget the night she had first come here.

She had followed the maître d' to the Comte's table, walking her graceful model's walk and staring vacantly ahead. Silently she thanked Odile Joly for making her practice it over and over. Now it served her well. It covered up her nervousness, her trembling legs. It made her look self-confident. Aloof. Blasé.

She had been intimidated by Maxim's. The big rooms were all Art Nouveau. They had patinated murals of wine-sipping nymphs. Behind the banquettes were yellow fleur-de-lis lamps overlapping on the huge, swirling wood-and-beveled-glass mirrors. The dim overhead lights looked like inverted umbrellas. She walked past a spiral staircase, wood-edged pillars, black iron columns, and old brass that shone with newness. The tablecloths and napery were crisp and white, the silver flashed, the crystal gleamed. The women were elaborately gowned and decked out in expensive jewels. The men were in elegant dinner jackets and evening suits.

The murmur of conversation suddenly stopped as if someone had switched it off. Hélène could feel everyone's eyes watching her with curiosity. The people were leaning toward one another, whispering. It was almost too much to bear. She knew that the whispers were about her.

"Dior," she heard one woman whisper.

"She's beautiful!" another added. "Look at those cheekbones!"

It was a moment before Hélène understood. She laughed scornfully at herself. What a fool she had been to worry. It was *they* who were in awe of her!

Now she dared look around. She was glad that she had decided to wear the red dinner suit after all. Just one glance told her that she was the most beautifully dressed woman there. Suddenly she felt invincible. Good clothes gave her a confidence she hadn't known could exist.

The Comte rose to his feet, the maître d' held the table away, and Hélène sat down. The Comte ordered champagne. For a moment he and Hélène just looked at each other in silence.

"It was quite a shock to receive all the packages," she said haltingly. "I didn't want to embarrass you by coming here in rags, so I took the liberty of accepting the clothes."

"I'm glad you did. I knew that they would look stunning on you."

Hélène opened the evening bag. With trembling fingers she took out the little box from Chaumet. She put it on the table.

He was watching her with amusement.

"But I can't possibly accept these," she said quietly. "They're far too valuable."

He laughed suddenly. "You're being distressingly correct, mademoiselle."

She could feel one of her blushes working up. She looked down at the table. As suddenly as the blush had begun, it receded before it could rise to her face. She looked back up, steadily meeting his eyes. "I'm being dishonest," she said with sudden wisdom. "There is no difference between accepting clothes from Dior and jewels from Chaumet."

He looked at her in surprise. Then he nodded, reached for the case, and lifted the lid. The parrots caught the light from the fleur-de-lis lamps and beveled mirrors behind them and flashed red and white sparks. Slowly he picked up the earrings and put them gently on her ears. "They look as if they were made for you," he said, slowly withdrawing his fingers.

"And the payment for all this?" she asked in a quiet voice. "What is it that you want from me?"

For a moment he didn't speak. He leaned back against the velvet banquette and lit a cigarette. He waved out the match and tossed it into the ashtray. He watched her closely. "I'm not asking for repayment," he said finally. "However, I have a proposition to make. You may accept it or turn it down. I will give you all the time you need to make up your own mind."

She looked at him questioningly. Her lips were suddenly numb. She could feel that intense electricity she had felt when he had first touched her at Hautecloque, asking her to dance. Only this time he didn't need to touch her. She felt it all the same.

"And what is this proposition?" she whispered, knowing very well what it would be.

He didn't mince words. "I want you as my mistress," he said honestly.

She looked at him levelly. So she had been right. He wanted a cocotte. It didn't shock her. It didn't even surprise

301

her. She was only glad that he hadn't been evasive, that he hadn't tried to glamorize the possible relationship, that he didn't try to frost it up with sweet words of love. Besides, he *was* very attractive. She'd never be able to forget the thrill she had felt when he had taken her into his arms at the ball at Hautecloque. And now that same feeling had been reawakened in her. Who knows? she thought—what the Comte was suggesting could even turn out to be ... quite interesting.

For a moment her lips tightened. Then she smiled coolly. "And what would we both gain by such a ... relationship?"

He brought the cigarette to his lips and inhaled calmly. "I would gain a mistress," he said flatly. "I'm usually in Paris for two days each week. I would expect to spend those evenings with you. As for you, I am prepared to give you the use of a town house I own on the Boulevard Maillot. You would have a certain monthly income and charge accounts at the better shops. You would receive gifts every now and then."

"But I have a job," she said evenly. "I don't want to give that up. It gives me a sense of security."

He nodded. "You don't need to give up your job," he said.

For a long time she sat in silence, her eyes focused on nothing in particular. But her mind was racing. The Comte was offering her a town house in one of the best sections of Paris and charge accounts at God-only-knew what expensive shops. But most important, she could not only keep her job at Odile Joly's but also receive an extra income. Plus "gifts every now and then." Jewels, probably. It was the type of offer that any "nice" girl turned down immediately. Without second thoughts. Hélène knew that being kept by a man would categorize her as a "mistress" at best—and as a "whore" at worst. Yet there was another side to it, one she didn't dare overlook.

Long ago she had sworn to herself that she would seek out and find two Nazis—a sergeant named Schmidt and an albino with a thin, cruel face—perpetrators of senseless violence. She had sworn to bring to justice the animals who had made Maman, Catherine, and Marie suffer and disappear. Finding those monsters would be no easy task. It would take money. Much money.

She had sworn, too, that if she became successful before him, she would help Edmond. He and Jeanne were stuck in Saint-Nazaire with nothing but a bleak future looming in front of them. There would be no way for Edmond to escape

302

Saint-Nazaire. Not on his own. He would need help. Again, only one thing stood between her helping him and not. Money.

And last, but certainly not least, there was her own dream. Her magazine. Starting it would require more money than she could ever lay her hands on in the normal course of events.

She gave a painful inner sigh. Everything she wanted to accomplish took money. True, she had a decent job at Odile Joly's. But she wasn't earning nearly enough as a model to make a single one of her ambitions come true. Probably never would. And worst of all, models had a short, expendable lifespan. Once she began to show signs of aging—then what? Then her future would be as bleak as Edmond's and Jeanne's was right now. It was time to insure her future—time to think of her dream. Time to work fast. Time to make all her ambitions a viable reality.

The Comte's offer would be the first step toward it.

The champagne arrived. Hélène watched the waiter uncork the bottle and pour. When they were alone again, she sipped delicately. Her violet eyes looked at the Comte over the rim of her glass. She had come to a decision.

She would make a deal with the devil.

"Monsieur le Comte"—she smiled softly—"you have yourself a deal."

He had given her two more gifts that night. A ruby-and-diamond necklace to match the earrings and a solid gold key—the symbolic key to her new home. For practical use, he had also given her a regular key. After dinner they rode to the house in the black-and-burgundy Rolls. When they got there, the chauffeur held the rear door open. Hélène looked out at the house in awe. The old white building behind the small garden looked like a little palace. It was four stories high. Above the big double doors were balustraded balconies on the second and third floors. The top floor, with its mansard roof, had five small oval dormers. All the rest of the windows were big and mullioned.

"Do you find it agreeable?" the Comte asked.

Hélène turned to look at him. She was speechless. She didn't know what to say. Finally she managed to nod her head.

"Shall we go inside?" Without waiting for her reply, the Comte placed the palm of his hand on her elbow and led her through the garden and up the marble steps. She took out her key and unlocked the front doors of her new home for the first time. Unbelievingly she looked around the foyer. The marble floor gleamed and the walls were lined with pilasters. She was dying to explore the rest of the house, to go from room to room and acquaint herself with all that a new home has to offer. But that would have to wait until morning. Tonight she sensed that the Comte had something far more urgent on his mind.

Immediately they went upstairs to the huge, dimly lit bedroom overlooking the Bois de Boulogne. She watched as he went over to the window and pulled the heavy draperies together. She knew what was expected of her. Wordlessly she got undressed.

When he was naked, she stood there staring at him. His penis was erect and pulsing. Suddenly she was afraid. She went over to the giant bed, pulled down the cover, and lay stiffly on the Porthault sheets, watching him with frightened eyes.

Slowly he came over to her. He sat on the edge of the bed and reached down, tracing his fingertips across her nipples. At first she was tense. She refused to submit to her longings. Then suddenly she stopped resisting. She closed her eyes and gave herself up to the tingling sensation that swept through her body in little waves. Her breasts rose and fell with each breath, her nipples rising under his touch. After a while he rolled on top of her and their arms and legs intertwined. His face found hers and his tongue darted deep into her throat, probing, exploring, licking. She could feel his stiff penis rubbing against her legs. She moaned softly, her head making a slow pendulum motion on the pillow. A current of excitement surged through her body. She struggled to free her lips from his. "Love me," she whispered, giving herself over to him completely.

She felt him moving away from her, freeing her from his grasp. Then there was a delicious sensation between her legs. She looked down. His head was buried in her pubis, his tongue licking her clitoris. She shuddered, feeling the beginnings of her first orgasm. He waited for her excitement to ebb. Then in one savage thrust he entered her. She gripped him fiercely, relishing the sensation of his body against hers. Abruptly he pulled out of her.

"Don't stop!" she cried.

He grabbed her by the ankles and held her legs high in the air, over her head. Her buttocks were now off the bed. Without warning, he forced his penis up into her anus. Instinctively she clamped her sphincter tight. With one massive thrust he pushed deeper. Her hips jerked, her body shuddered. She writhed in agony. The pain was excruciating. A scream burst forth from her lips.

"Whore!" he hissed. His hand shot out and slapped her across the face. The sting of his slap erupted on her cheek. The scream died in her throat.

"Whore!" His voice was louder now, and he raised his hand to strike her again. She flinched and whipped her head sideways. Suddenly he let out a cry. A spasm shook his body and he emptied his juices into her. He let go of her legs and let them drop back down on the bed. He bent forward and buried his face in her breasts. "Mother!" he sobbed. "Mother!"

Hélène looked down at him and stroked his head gently. She could feel his tears rolling down the cleft of her breasts.

The uniformed maid knocked gently on the door. Then she entered the bedroom and crossed soundlessly over to the window. The curtains blocked out all the light. In two swift draws she yanked them aside and the faded winter sun came weakly into the room. Hélène stirred on the big bed and rolled over, burying her face in the pillow. The maid went over to the marble mantel and got to her knees, placed kindling in the grate, stacked some logs on top of it, and lit a fire. She fanned the flames until they burned evenly, then got back to her feet. She looked at Hélène. "It's time for your breakfast, mademoiselle."

Wearily Hélène sat up and blinked. She yawned and wiped her eyes. "What time is it, Marthe?"

"Eight-thirty, mademoiselle. You requested that I wake you, remember?"

Hélène nodded. Now she remembered. It was Saturday. Odile Joly had given her the day off, but she had an important errand to run. Quickly she looked over at the pillow beside hers. The Comte had left already; all that remained of his spending the night was the depressed shape of his head in the pillow.

Hélène sighed. "All right, Marthe. I'll have breakfast now."

Efficiently Marthe marched out. She returned a moment later with a wooden tray. She set it down on the nightstand, waited for Hélène to lean forward, and plumped the pillows up behind her. Carefully she placed the tray on Hélène's lap and poured a cup of coffee from the china pot into one of the delicate gold-bordered cups. Hélène took a sip and shuddered. She put the cup back down. She hated black coffee. She liked it sweet, with cream and sugar, but she had to watch her weight. She looked down at the plate. On it was a single flaky croissant, hot and steaming. On the tiny side plate was a minuscule dab of country butter and a teaspoon of red raspberry jam. It had been a long, exhausting night. The Comte had been insatiable. After sex, she always had an appetite. Now she was hungry as a horse. Perhaps if she ate very slowly the croissant would be enough to fill her. She sighed, broke the croissant in half, and began to butter it carefully.

"Is there anything else you need, mademoiselle?"

Hélène looked around the room. She saw the Balmain gown draped across the back of a French chair. "Send the gown to the cleaner's. Oh . . . and don't forget to change the bedsheets."

Marthe gave a little curtsy. "Oui, mademoiselle." She would have changed the sheets automatically anyway. After the Comte stayed overnight, Mademoiselle always insisted on fresh sheets.

"That's all, Marthe, thank you."

The maid picked up the Balmain, left the room, and gently shut the big carved door behind her.

Hélène took a bite out of the croissant and chewed it slowly. Then she looked at the rest of it and dropped it on the plate. Suddenly she didn't feel hungry anymore. There was too much to do today.

She lifted the tray, set it back on the nightstand, and threw off the covers. She walked across the soft carpet and went into the big marble bathroom. She leaned over the tub, spun the gold-plated faucets, and watched the steaming water crash down onto the smooth, contoured enamel bottom. She leaned over the tub for a moment, letting the clouds of steam rise up into her face. This was luxury, she thought. Hot running water. Not like the single ice-cold low-pressure tap at Tante Janine's or Jeanne's.

Humming softly, she poured a generous portion of scented bath oil into the water. She sat down on the edge of the tub, rolled up one sleeve of her peignoir, and reached down into the water, stirring the oil around with her hand. Then she rose and dried her hand. She slipped out of the peignoir and tossed it over the back of the vanity chair. Carefully she stepped into the tub. The water was hot and delicious. She spun the taps, and immediately the water stopped. She sank down into the tub and soaked for a few minutes. Then she began to lather herself with the almond cold-cream soap. She lathered her pubis well, rinsing it off with the shower attachment when she was done. Her private parts had gotten her to the Boulevard Maillot. They, too, might help make her dream come true. She smiled to herself. Her dream. Her magazine. It seemed more important than ever to start it soon.

When she finished dressing, she looked at herself in the mirror. She used very little makeup; with her complexion she didn't need to. Only her right cheek was thickly made-up. Every time the Comte approached orgasm, he called her a whore and slapped her across the face. Then he would become the repentant little boy, crying "Mother! Mother!" and fall asleep on her breasts, his face streaked with tears. Hélène shook her head. It was bizarre, and she didn't understand it. She only wished he didn't hit her so hard. Her cheek bruised easily, and only her artful mixing of four different shades of makeup covered up his handprint. What will be will be, she told herself. She bent close to the mirror. Even under the harshest lighting, neither the bruise nor the makeup would show.

She tore herself away from the mirror and crossed the room to where a gilt-framed painting hung on the wall. She felt along the frame, released a catch, and the painting swung forward on its hinges like a window. Behind it was a small wall safe. Deftly she spun the intricate combination. She heard the familiar click and pulled down on the iron handle and swung the heavy door open. She reached inside and felt for the Cartier box with the canary-diamond earrings.

"Good-bye, Cartier," she whispered.

*　　*　　*

307

Baghat Cheops picked up the loupe and held it close to his right eye. He closed his left eye and studied one of the canary-diamond earrings through the magnifying lens. Then he pushed the earring aside and reached for the second one. He studied it as closely as the first. Finally he replaced the loupe carefully in its velvet-lined case. His face was expressionless as he looked at Hélène. "They are not bad," he said.

Hélène's face was a mask. She knew what the dark little Egyptian was trying to do. Bring down the price. Start by offering her a fraction of what the stones were worth. He knew, and she knew, that they were flawless. Each earring had three diamonds, one three-carat, one two-carat, one half-carat. Cartier's asking price must have been enough to buy six Citroën limousines. Baghat Cheops would begin by offering her a sixteenth of their value. They would end up by agreeing on about a twelfth of their value. Then he would turn around and sell them for double or triple what he'd paid. Hélène's only consolation was Cheops' assurance that he would sell them only to transient foreigners. She knew that the jewelry was all recognizable, one-of-a-kind pieces. She couldn't afford to take them back to Cartier's. Even discreetly. They'd be right back on the market. That was too dangerous. The Comte might find out that she'd been selling the jewelry he was giving her, and he'd be furious.

Carefully Cheops laid the canary-diamond earrings side by side on a velvet cloth. He lined them up by tapping them with his nicotine-stained fingernail. They winked with yellow light. "Twelve thousand," he said, smiling. His gold tooth gleamed.

Hélène's face was impassive. It was the most ridiculous starting offer he'd ever made. Obviously the little Egyptian thought he'd found an easy touch. Someone who gambled. Or who had an expensive drug habit. Deliberately she reached out, took the earrings, and put them back in the box. Lazily she dropped it into her purse. "Good-bye, Monsieur Cheops," she said. "It is a pity we could not do business again." She started out of the room.

The Egyptian watched her shrewdly, calculating the chances of her seriously walking out of the shop. He smiled. Once at the door, she would have second thoughts. She would turn around. He had seen it happen often enough.

Hélène closed the door behind her, looked up and down the street, and began walking briskly down the sidewalk. At the next corner, a breathless Cheops grabbed her by the arm. He had been running all the way. It was her turn to smile.

"Twenty thousand," he said between gulps of air.

Marthe was on the telephone when Hélène let herself into the town house. "Un moment, Monsieur le Comte," the maid said quickly. "Mademoiselle has just come in." She held her hand over the mouthpiece. "It's the Comte!" she said in a flustered voice.

Hélène nodded, hurried over to Marthe, and took the receiver. "Philippe?" she said softly. "Where are you?"

As usual, the Comte was in a hurry. He spoke quickly. "I'm at Orly. My flight departs in a few minutes."

"Orly! Where are you going?"

"Scandinavia."

She stared at the receiver. This was news. He'd made no mention of it last night.

"Something's come up," he explained quickly. "I'll be there on business for a week."

Her heart leaped hopefully. This might give her the time she needed to put her plan into action. She made her voice sound disappointed. "Does that mean you won't be here on Tuesday?" she asked carefully.

"Yes," he said irritably. "I'll see you on Friday and Saturday instead. Keep both days open."

Hélène smiled to herself. Good. She would have Marthe call up the Maison d'Odile Joly on Monday and say she was sick. And as soon as the Comte hung up she would make a reservation for the train. Suddenly she spied the neat stack of mail lying next to the telephone. She picked it up and leafed idly through the envelopes. Bills from the electric company. From Hermès. From the telephone company. A letter. She tossed all the envelopes but this one back down. She recognized the handwriting instantly. Jeanne's.

"Are you there?" the Comte asked coldly.

"Yes, of course," Hélène said automatically. He was certainly being irritable today! she thought. In the background she could hear a tinny voice.

"They're announcing my flight," the Comte said, "I've got to go."

"Have a good trip," she said.

But he didn't hear it. Already he'd hung up. Hélène made a face at the receiver and put it back down in the cradle.

Quickly she tore open Jeanne's letter, reading it as she walked into the salon.

Saint-Nazaire
January 30, 1954

Dear Sister,

Here everything is so quiet, as Edmond is still at sea. He won't be back for a week. Things are always so hectic when he's around, so I thought I'd better quickly write to you now, before he returns. I pity him out there, especially in this cold. Every time he's gone I say prayers for him.

I have seen Madame Dupré quite a few times. She always asks about you. You can't imagine how proud she is of you! She has your clippings hanging up in the shop. For a while, she even had them in the shop window! Ours are on the doors of the kitchen credence. You are the most famous person in Saint-Nazaire, did you know that?

I saw your aunt in town once. She wouldn't speak to me. I never saw anyone giving me a more hateful look in my life.

I haven't had the chance to tell Edmond yet, since he is at sea, so you're the first person to hear the news. Hélène, I'm *pregnant*! I'm going to give Edmond a child! I know he'll be as delighted as I am. And I'll make certain that if it's a girl, she'll be named after you! I'm only worried that Edmond will treat me like an invalid when he finds out I'm carrying his baby. How I wish you could be here for the christening. Of course, here I am, already planning something that's still so far off!

Don't ever forget, we both love you dearly.

Your sister,
Jeanne

Hélène put down the letter and smiled. Was it possible? Jeanne a mother? Already? Suddenly she felt the tears pressing out of the corners of her eyes. Jeanne and Edmond were so lucky, she thought with a flash of jealousy. They had each other. They were sustained by love.

For the first time, she found herself feeling sorry for herself. What did she have to sustain her? Angrily she wiped her tears away. Plenty, she told herself. You have your dream, your ambition. Your magazine. You have your work and your vows. You want money and power. You have a lot to

310

look forward to. But love? And children? She looked blankly down at the letter on her lap.

She had never even given them any thought.

7

The black Gothic stone spires of the cathedral were menacingly poised against the angry gray wash of sky as Hélène came out of the train station. She put her suitcase down and pulled the collar of her mink coat tighter around her neck. She looked up at the cathedral. The wind was like ice. It swept in from the Rhine and battered the imperturbable flying buttresses that leaned heavily against the massive nave. "Köln," the signs on the train platform had read. Cologne. The cathedral in front of her had stood for centuries. It had accumulated the grime that blackened it through storms and pestilence and bombings.

The narrow streets were busy. It was rush hour. Soon it would be dark. She watched the old women who hobbled out of the cathedral, their heavy dark scarves tied firmly under their chins. She saw the young couples gathered around the lit store windows. She looked to see what was so fascinating. On display were shiny Grundig radios, Telefunken record players, Siemens appliances. She noticed that the best-dressed women wore Persian-lamb coats. Children walked quietly beside their parents, well-disciplined and neat. Everything was orderly, everyone was polite.

Once in the hotel she found the air less oppressive. Tourists and businessmen stood around the spotless lobby. There were the sounds of many languages, not just the guttural staccato German Hélène remembered that the occupiers of her country spoke. Somehow she hadn't expected Cologne to be so cosmopolitan. Then she understood. Bonn was the new capital. It was a small town, just downriver. Cologne was bound to catch some of the international overflow.

The pride of the German woman in postwar years was the

311

Persian-lamb coat. To everyone, it showed that the woman had wealth and status. But nothing impressed anyone as much as mink. The chief desk clerk took one look at Hélène's coat and fell over himself. "Darf ich—"

"Hélène Junot," she said coldly, and added in French: "I have a reservation."

"Oui, madame," he replied, smoothly slipping into French. "One moment, please." He consulted the ledger, his lacquered fingernail sweeping down the page. A veil fell over Hélène's eyes as she watched him. She couldn't help but wonder whether he had been in France during the war. He had been of age. He spoke French well enough. Had he learned it in Paris? Had he been in the Gestapo? Or had he been an ordinary Wehrmacht soldier? Stop it! she told herself harshly. You've been asking yourself that same question every time you've seen an adult German.

The clerk looked up and smiled professionally. "Here it is, Madame Junot. Five days, room seven forty-three." He reached for one of the keys hanging from the cubbyholes on the back wall. Wordlessly she opened her purse and handed him her passport. She scribbled her signature in the register. Then she pushed it back toward him.

"Your passport will be returned to you shortly, madame," he said.

She nodded. "Also, I would like to have something locked in the vault." She gave him a thick envelope. In it was money. A lot of money. Everything she had gotten from Baghat Cheops. Tomorrow, it would be deposited in a German bank.

Hélène paused in front of the frosted-glass door. The gold block letters outlined in black read: *"K. Häberle."* And underneath it: *"Privat Detektiv."*

It was the eleventh such office that she had been to in the last three days. For one reason or another, the other ten hadn't suited her. Before she could change her mind about this one, she pushed down on the brass handle and went inside.

She found herself in a secretary's office. A young blond was sitting behind the desk, a beige cardigan draped across her shoulders. She looked up at Hélène and smiled pleasantly. "Guten Morgen," she said.

Hélène forced a smile. "Parlez-vous français?" she asked.

The woman smiled and made a motion with her thumb and forefinger. "Un peu," she replied. "Won't you have a seat?" She gestured to the dark varnished wooden chair in front of the desk.

Hélène shook her head. She had learned that service tended to be swifter if you looked uncomfortable. "No, thank you," she said. "I prefer to stand. Is Herr Häberle in?"

The blond's smile broadened. "Yes, of course. One moment, please." She pushed her chair back, got up, and walked over to another frosted-glass door. She opened it and spoke to someone inside. Hélène could overhear the conversation but she couldn't understand any of it. She had never bothered to learn German.

The secretary gestured for her to come over. Quickly Hélène crossed the room and entered the inner office. The secretary closed the door behind her and stayed outside.

Behind a beat-up secondhand desk sat a slim young man with thick, prematurely gray hair. His blue eyes were gentle, but sharp and appraising. His suit was dark and loose; his white shirt, washed-out gray. The collar was unbuttoned, the tie was loosened. He got to his feet and held out his hand. "I am Karl Häberle," he said formally in French. "You must excuse my vocabulary and pronunciation. I'm afraid it has been a few years since I studied French."

Solicitously Häberle pulled up an upholstered chair and Hélène sat down. "Would you like a cup of coffee?" he asked.

She shook her head. "Thank you, no."

"You don't mind if I smoke?"

"Of course not."

Häberle went around his desk and sat down behind it. He reached for a pack of HB's, fished a cigarette out, and stuck it in his mouth. He struck a match and held it to the cigarette. Then he leaned comfortably back in his chair. He eyed her curiously. "Tell me, mademoiselle—it is mademoiselle?" Hélène nodded. "Why do you require the services of a private detective?"

She looked down at her lap as if the answer somehow lay there. For a moment she was silent. Then she looked back up and met his eyes squarely. "I wish to locate someone," she said quietly.

Karl Häberle nodded slowly through the blue cloud of smoke. "Who?"

313

"A man. A man who served in France during the war."

He gave her an obscure look. "A German."

"Yes," she replied softly. "A German."

He nodded to himself, his keen blue eyes boring through hers. "And why do you wish to find this man?"

She looked away. "Because he was kind to me. He . . . he saved my life."

Häberle shook his head. "You are lying, mademoiselle. You hate the man."

Hélène stared at him. Then suddenly she leaned forward. Her eyes blazed. "Yes!" Her voice was a whisper that echoed around the thick old walls. "I hate him!"

"And why is it that you want him found? To bring him to justice or in order to . . . exact vengeance?"

Hélène's voice was shaky. "He must pay for what he has done."

"I shall have to know what that is."

Painfully Hélène closed her eyes. Her voice grew dull and heavy, almost weary. "In 1944 I was seven years old," she said. "The Ger—I'm sorry, the Nazis—came to our house and broke down our doors. My mother was in the underground. She was pregnant at the time. Very pregnant. They found a radio transmitter hidden somewhere in the house. They beat my mother in the belly until . . . until . . ."

"One moment, mademoiselle."

Hélène started and her eyes blinked open. They were confused and startled, like a dreamer's who is suddenly awakened from a nightmare. Häberle was reaching into his desk. He brought out a bottle of schnapps and splashed some into a glass. He leaned across the desk and handed it to her. She nodded gratefully and drank it down. Her fingers were trembling.

"Please continue," he said gently.

Hélène nodded and swallowed. She put the glass down on the desktop. "My mother miscarried, Herr Häberle. I'll never forget seeing the blood running down her gray stockings. Then they took her away and she was never heard of again. Our maid, Michelle, was shot trying to protect her. My brother, my older sister, Catherine, my baby sister, Marie, and I managed to escape. We got separated. A few weeks later, the Nazis caught up with my brother and me. They took us to their headquarters. They had Catherine and Marie. Catherine pretended not to know us and my brother and I managed to get freed. They tortured Marie, though. Right in front of our eyes. What kind of men are those who torture a baby?"

Häberle was silent. There was nothing that he could say.

For a moment she could find no more words. "I never saw my sisters again," she said finally. "I think they were sent to Poland."

Häberle looked at her with compassion. "And you know who was responsible for these atrocities?"

Hélène nodded. "I will never forget him."

Häberle's voice was gentle. "It's possible that he may already have been convicted for war crimes. Or that he has been tried and acquitted. Have you given that any thought?"

"Yes. But deep inside I know that he *hasn't* been caught. That he's walking around free somewhere. In Berlin, or Munich, or Buenos Aires. Perhaps even here in Cologne. I can feel it!"

"You should also realize that many Germans served in France during the war, mademoiselle. Many of them were transferred elsewhere. Some to the Russian front, some back here to Germany, others to Italy, to Holland . . ." He shrugged. "And many died. There were also a lot of cases of the men's service records having been destroyed. It is difficult to trace the events and people in a time of chaos."

"I realize that," she said.

He looked at her closely. "You could go to the Americans or to the Jewish organizations," he said. "It would be much less expensive."

"No!" She shook her head vehemently and tried to keep her voice under control. "No," she repeated softly. "I don't want that. I don't want them to get hold of him. I want him for myself."

He ground out his cigarette in the kidney-shaped ashtray. "Do you have his name?"

"No."

"Do you know where he was from?"

"No."

Häberle heaved a sigh. "Then it will be very difficult."

Suddenly Hélène leaned forward. She reached for his arm and gripped it tightly. Her face was determined. "He must be found," she said grimly.

"As you wish. But I cannot promise you any results. And it will be very expensive. Personally, I recommend that you

do not go through with this. It may be a waste of money."
He looked at her sympathetically. "And emotions," he added
gently.

Hélène instinctively liked this young man. He was refreshingly honest. Not like the others, who she felt would have gouged her for everything they could get.

"I am prepared to pay whatever it costs," she said with finality. "I want you to give this case your undivided attention."

"It could take months," he warned. "Years, even."

Her voice took on the hard edge of a knife. "I have time," she said. She reached into her purse and took out a thick envelope. She tossed it on the desk. "Here is your retainer."

Idly he undid the flap and thrummed the stacks of money like a deck of cards.

"Twenty thousand deutsche marks," she said. "Cash. And if you find him, I am willing to pay you a bonus on top of your fee. Two hundred thousand marks have been deposited in a branch of the Dresdener Bank in anticipation of your finding him."

Häberle let out a whistle. "You must want this man very badly," he said.

"I do, Herr Häberle. And you? Do you want to take this case?" There was a challenging look in her eyes.

He grinned. "With wages such as you're offering, I would be a fool not to. Now, tell me everything you know about the man you want found."

Hélène nodded. "First, I know that he was acquainted with a sergeant named Schmidt. A fat man."

"There are hundreds of thousands of Schmidts all over this country. It is one of the most common German surnames. Can you describe him better?"

Hélène nodded. "I would say he was rather short. Dark hair. Red-faced. He looked large to me as a child, but then, all grown-ups do when you're so small." She smiled mirthlessly. "Also, he had a mole on his chin. About here." She put a finger on her own chin.

"Anything else?"

"I'm sorry. No."

"And the man you want?"

She gave an ugly laugh. "I know his rank, I know that he

was in the SS, and I can describe him very well. He is tall. His face is shaped like a skull." She paused. "He is very ugly, Herr Häberle. You see, he is an albino."

8

Politely the Comte helped Hélène slip out of her mink. He tossed it carelessly over the back of one of the velvet seats. She sat down carefully so as not to wrinkle her gown and leaned over the balcony of the Comte's private box.

She loved going to the opera. She enjoyed dressing up for it and seeing the other people in their finery. She felt a thrill whenever she climbed the magnificent great staircase. But above all, she loved losing herself in the musical world of make-believe drama that unfolded onstage. Somehow it was so unreal, and yet at the same time so very real. She had never sat through a single performance without constantly breaking out in gooseflesh.

Her eyes roved around the enormous theater. There was marble of all colors everywhere: the pale, stony shades of white and rose, the deeper, richer hues of green and red and blue. The gleaming chandelier hanging from the domed ceiling was enormous. It was said that it weighed six tons.

She looked down at her program as the Comte took his seat beside her. "*Alceste*," the title read. "Christoph Willibald Gluck." She opened the program and began reading it with quickening interest. She had never heard of this particular opera, and that made it twice as exciting.

The Comte leaned toward her. "Front row, orchestra center. Do you see the old man with the white hair?"

Hélène frowned and stretched her neck like a swan. She looked down at the front row and then back at the Comte. "Yes," she said. "Who is he?"

"Stanislaw Kowalsky, the pianist."

Hélène nodded without speaking. She didn't need to be told who Kowalsky was. Neither did half the schoolchildren in France. He was one of the world's finest concert pianists. For once, even the hard-boiled critics and enthusiastic audiences agreed: he was more accomplished than even Rubinstein and Horowitz.

The door in the back of the box suddenly opened. "Sorry," a deep voice said. "I didn't realize anyone was here."

Hélène and the Comte turned around in their seats. Behind the elegant velvet swags stood Hubert de Léger. Beside him was a young aristocratic lady in a pink gown. She appraised Hélène coldly.

For an instant Hélène locked eyes with Hubert. Then he turned to the girl beside him. "Lille, could you be an angel and wait outside for a moment?"

The girl looked confused. Then reluctantly she nodded and left, closing the door behind her.

Hubert stepped forward. "I thought Lille and I would go to the opera, since the family box is never used," he said quietly. "But I see that I was mistaken."

"Invite her back in," the Comte said easily. "There are enough seats."

Hubert gave a low laugh and looked at Hélène with a sudden knowledge in his eyes. "Don't tell me where you're living. On the Boulevard Maillot?"

She was silent.

"Father always lends that house to his current favorite. Did you know that?"

"I'll forget that remark, Hubert," the Comte said softly. "Now, I think you'd better apologize to Hélène and leave us be. Go back to the university. Your grades could stand your studying some more."

Hubert's face flushed. "Why are you trying to get rid of me? So you can be alone with your whore?"

Hélène rose to her feet. Her face was devoid of expression as she looked at the Comte. "I don't feel like the opera suddenly," she said quietly.

The Comte nodded and got up. He picked up her fur and draped it over her shoulders.

"Leaving won't help," Hubert said tightly. "It won't change a thing. A whore's a whore."

Hélène started for the door. She had almost reached it when Hubert caught her arm and spun her around. "Hélène," he said in a yearning voice. "Leave him. Come with me."

She turned away. "Let me go," she said dully.

"In a minute." He pulled her closer. "You sleep with him, don't you?" he demanded in a hissing whisper, glancing at the Comte, then back at her. "But you wouldn't sleep with me. What's the matter? Is it money you're after? I have a trust fund. Or do you naturally like old men?"

Angrily she tried to pull her arm free. His fingers dug deeper into her wrist. "You're hurting me," she said from between clenched teeth.

"Why did you turn me down?" he asked. "Just so you could turn around and rush off with him? Does his title turn you on?"

"Let her go," the Comte said in a whisper, the muscles twitching in his cheeks.

Hubert looked at him. "You like to steal my girls, don't you, father? That's what it takes to make you feel like a man, isn't it?"

Hélène's free hand suddenly lashed Hubert across the face. He let go of her arm and looked at her in surprise, his fingers gingerly touching his reddening cheek.

"I may be a whore," she whispered, "but you? You don't deserve your father. You don't even deserve me!" Then she pushed past him and started out of the box.

The thickly leafed chestnut trees in the Bois de Boulogne were turning yellow as the taxi pulled to a stop alongside the curb. "Here we are," Hélène said.

Madame Dupré started to reach into her purse. Hélène shook her head. She put a restraining hand on her friend's arm. "You are my guest," she said firmly.

Madame Dupré hesitated. Then she smiled. "All right. Thank you."

They got out of the taxi and watched the driver lifting Madame Dupré's valise out of the trunk. He set it down on the sidewalk. Quickly Hélène paid him and grabbed the valise by the handle.

"What a lovely house!" Madame Dupré said. She gazed up at it, shaking her head in amazement. "And in such a chic neighborhood, with the Bois right there."

"Yes, it is nice," Hélène said.

"I shall take many walks through the Bois." Madamé Dupre smiled. "I love autumn in Paris. I'd almost forgotten how beautiful it can be. There is nothing like Paris in the spring and the fall." She followed Hélène up the marble steps and waited for her to unlock the front door. Hélène held it open for her.

"After you," she said, gesturing inside with a flourish.

Madame Dupré stepped into the foyer. She looked around in surprise. "Why . . . I thought this was an apartment house!" she said. She turned to Hélène.

Hélène turned around and smiled wryly. "I never said it was." She started to close the door but stopped. A young man in uniform was coming up the steps. She waited until he was at the door.

"I have a telegram for Mademoiselle Junot," he said.

"I am she."

He handed her an envelope and she signed for it. He started to leave.

"Just a moment," she said. She fished in her purse for some coins and gave them to him.

"What was that?" Madame Dupré asked.

"A telegram," Hélène said thoughtfully. She frowned as she tore the envelope open. Then she pulled out a paper, unfolded it, and quickly read it:

LITTLE FRENCH GIRL STOP WE HAVE A DAUGHTER YOU HAVE A NIECE STOP JEANNE INSISTS CHRISTENING HER HELENE STOP SO WE DON'T CONFUSE YOU TWO SHE WILL BE PETITE HELENE STOP LOVE YOU STOP PROUD MOTHER AND FATHER JEANNE AND EDMOND

"Jeanne's just had her baby!" she cried excitedly. She thrust the telegram into Madame Dupré's hand.

Madame Dupré read it and shook her head. "She must have been born while I was on the train!"

Hélène grinned. "Imagine me—an aunt!" Then softly she said, "Petite Hélène. It's got a nice ring to it, doesn't it?"

Madame Dupré nodded. "It certainly does. And I know she must be a beautiful baby," she said warmly. "Jeanne must be very happy."

Hélène nodded solemnly. "She'll make a wonderful mother." Then she smiled. "Well, I'd better show you to your room. I know the trip must have been exhausting. You'll want to wash up and maybe take a nap. You'll need all the rest you can get. I've got the next few days all planned out, and it'll be a grueling schedule. Tomorrow I've got to work, but I've reserved a seat for you at Odile Joly's for the show. It's only the daily showing, and not at all as exciting as the big summer and winter shows, I'm afraid. But you'll get to see all the clothes." Hélène hugged Madame Dupré fiercely. "I'm so happy you could come and visit!" she said. "Even if it is only for five days."

Madame Dupré smiled. "And I am happy, too."

"Come, let's go upstairs."

Madame Dupré started to reach for her valise.

"Just leave that there for now," Hélène said. "Marthe will bring it up later."

"Marthe?"

"She's the maid," Hélène said with embarrassment.

Madame Dupré nodded wordlessly. Then she followed Hélène upstairs. When they got to the guest room, Hélène flung the door open and stepped aside. "Voilà!"

Madame Dupré stepped into the room. The draperies had been pushed aside, and the room was filled with the autumn air. She looked out at the Bois and around the cream-colored room. Against one wall was a big four-poster bed draped with kilometers of cream-colored satin. "It's beautiful!" she said.

Hélène smiled and led the way. She flung open some doors. "This is the closet, this is the bathroom. Soap, towels, it's all here. You can get washed up even before Marthe brings up the valise."

Madame Dupré nodded. "Such luxury," she said with a smile. Then her smile faded as she spied the thick white bath towels. Woven into them was a familiar crest. The crest of the de Légers.

Hélène saw the look on Madame Dupré's face. "Back to square one, right?" she joked quietly. "Only this time it isn't the servants' quarters."

Madame Dupré came closer and held Hélène's hand. Within her brown eyes was a sad and worried look. "Be careful," she said softly. "When a woman is in a position . . . What I mean is . . ." She hesitated, clearly embarrassed.

"I know," Hélène said, forcing her voice to sound light. "I'm a kept woman who could be thrown out at any moment."

Madame Dupré turned away. "It's not that that worries me. We French are very forgiving. We know all about affairs of the heart. Just remember . . ." She shook her head. "I'm sorry. It's none of my business. I will say no more."

Hélène's face was expressionless. "No. Go ahead."

Madame Dupré made an agitated gesture and turned to face her. "Hubert is . . . well, like I warned you at Hautecloque, he's a womanizer. He doesn't believe in being faithful to one woman. He doesn't even believe in having just a wife and one mistress like his father. He's a playboy. He loves *all* women. Now that he's got you, I'm afraid that his interest will wane. I'm afraid for you, Hélène. I don't want to see you hurt."

Hélène suddenly began to laugh. She sat down on the edge of the bed and looked down at her feet.

"What's so funny?" Madame Dupré asked.

The laughter subsided and Hélène's face grew serious. She looked up into Madame Dupré's eyes. "I am not seeing Hubert," she said softly. "I'm the Comte's mistress."

Punctually at seven o'clock they had dinner in the big dining room. Hélène had had a hand in everything, and it showed.

"It looks lovely," Madame Dupré said.

Hélène smiled. She had made a special effort tonight and was glad it was appreciated. She had even gone so far as to get a bottle of Château Hautecloque-de Léger from the wine cellar. She had opened it and then left it on the sideboard, letting it breathe. Now she picked up the dusty, mold-covered bottle and carefully strained the wine of sediment as she poured it into a silver-filigreed crystal decanter. She brought it over to the table and poured a little into Madame Dupré's glass. Then she stood back.

Madame Dupré brought the glass up to her nose and inhaled the fragrance of the grapes. She looked at Hélène with a smile of excitement. Then she took a sip. She put the glass back down and closed her eyes, savoring the taste. "Superb," she proclaimed finally.

Hélène looked pleased. She poured some more wine into the glass and sat down opposite Madame Dupré. After Marthe served the first course, Hélène dismissed her. She wanted to be alone with Madame Dupré. "Is the beef rib all right?" she asked.

Madame Dupré made a gesture with her fork. "Delicious. I've never tasted anything so fine."

"Marthe is quite accomplished," Hélène said.

They ate on in silence for a while. Then Madame Dupré laid down her cutlery. "Have you given your magazine any further thought?" she asked.

Hélène nodded and toyed with her meat. "Yes, but it's still too early to think about. To start a magazine takes a lot of money."

"How about the Comte? I mean . . . not as a gift," Madame Dupré added quickly, dropping her eyes. "As a loan or an investment." She looked across the table at Hélène. "Have you brought the subject up?"

Hélène smiled sadly. "Yes, but unfortunately he's very old-fashioned. He still believes that a woman's place is in the home. I'm afraid he has enough trouble trying to accept the fact that I'm working at Odile Joly's."

"Have you tried explaining to him that there's not much difference between working for someone else and working for yourself?"

"Yes." Hélène sighed. "He thinks women are not cut out for business."

"Indeed!" Madame Dupré's eyes flashed. "Have you pointed out to him that there are many women who are successful? Look at all the designers! Chanel, Schiaparelli, Madame Grès, Madame Vionnet."

"And Odile Joly," Hélène added with a smile.

"Above all, Odile Joly," Madame Dupré said. "They've all been enormously successful!"

"I'm afraid the Comte just doesn't see it that way. Actually, I think he's afraid that if I start a magazine, I wouldn't have enough time left over for him."

"Then what are you going to do?"

"I don't know. I do know that I'll never be able to start a magazine on my salary from modeling. It's simply not enough. Nor can I hope to start it with the Comte's help and blessing." She sighed helplessly. "Sometimes it just eats at me. It's as if my hands were tied."

Madame Dupré nodded. "It's very difficult to build up something from scratch. Twice as difficult if you're a woman."

"So what do I do?"

"You wait," Madame Dupré advised gently. "You wait patiently and bide your time until the opportunity comes. If nothing else, I've learned one thing from life: everyone has a time when his moment comes. The secret is for you to recognize it for what it is, and have the courage and stamina to let yourself be carried away with it. And follow through with it. When that times comes, you must not be afraid. I've had my opportunity, and I didn't take advantage of it. It's ironic, but I didn't even realize it was there until it was too late."

"So I wait," Hélène said slowly. "But how long?"

"You are young," Madame Dupré said. "So very young. Give yourself time." She smiled. "You perhaps don't realize it," she went on, "but in a way, you have already begun."

Hélène felt a ripple of excitement strumming through her body. "I don't think I understand," she said slowly.

Madame Dupré's dark eyes were gentle and wise. "Don't you see it? The magazine is your destiny. It's in your blood. And everything that has happened to you so far is another step toward it. The first time you set foot in my shop was the first step. The month at the château was the second. Now you are in the third stage. You are seeing the inside of the fashion industry. You are headed toward it steadily but surely. Mark my words, Hélène. You will make it. It is like the grapes that make the wine. They must be picked at the moment they are the ripest. Not before, not after. You are not yet ripe. But soon you will be."

Baghat Cheops smiled with self-importance as the slim young man led him into the private office. "Monsieur Bonnard will be with you shortly," the young man said smoothly.

Cheops nodded and smiled. "I am at his service," he said as he took a seat opposite the desk, which was cleared of everything but some high-intensity lamps. When the young man withdrew, he drummed his fingers on the briefcase on his lap and looked around the room.

The sparsely furnished office was on the second floor of number nine, Place Vendôme. In many ways it was like the other luxury shops on the square. The first floor was devoted to selling, the second to management and buying. On the ground floor, the gold script on the arched windows was duplicated on the scalloped white awnings. It read: "Claude Jassel."

Cheops lit one of his brown Egyptian cigarettes and inhaled the pungent smoke nervously. He put his briefcase down, rose to his feet, and started to pace the room. He never liked to be kept waiting. Even less by a snob like Bonnard. He was impatient to exchange the piece of jewelry he had brought along for a nice six-figure check. He glanced at his cigarette. The ash was long and cocked. He looked around the office, but as usual there was no ashtray in sight, and so he was forced to tap the ash into his trouser cuff. He made a mental note to brush it out once he got home. He always forgot, and his cuffs were filled with ash and cigarette butts.

A few minutes later a tall, distinguished-looking man dressed in an exquisite suit came into the office. "Bonjour, Monsieur Cheops," he said briskly.

Cheops stopped pacing and looked at him. "Bonjour, Monsieur Bonnard," he replied, his voice suddenly smooth as oil. He sat back down in the chair, carefully pinched the end of the cigarette between his fingers, and placed the butt in his trouser cuff.

Bonnard walked over behind the desk and sat down, folding his hands. "What may I do for you today, Monsieur Cheops?" he asked brusquely.

Cheops smiled nervously, his gold tooth catching the light flooding in through the window. He could feel the sweat breaking out on his face and he reached for his rumpled handkerchief. "I have another piece of jewelry which I would like to dispose of," he murmured, mopping his forehead. "Discreetly, of course."

"Of course." Bonnard permitted himself a slight smile. Cheops was anything but discreet. He had conveniently picked up the word that every society matron down on her luck used. The matrons, however, insisted that the stones of their jewelry be reset before being resold, so that their friends would not recognize the jewels and find out about their reduced circumstances. Cheops, however, used the word loosely; he never insisted on having anything reset. To him, "discreetly" merely meant not disclosing to whom the jewelry had belonged.

"It is the most magnificent item yet," Cheops said in a gushy voice. "The stones are of the highest quality. It is a necklace fit for an empress."

"May I see it, please?" Bonnard held out his hand.

"Of course," Cheops said, Hastily he released the catch on his briefcase and lifted the lid. He took out a long slim box and put it on the desktop, pushing it toward Bonnard. It slid halfway across the polished desk. The box was imprinted: "Van Cleef & Arpels."

Nonchalantly the jeweler lifted the lid. He took a velvet cloth out of a drawer and deftly spread the necklace out on it. The sapphires were smoldering blue, surrounded by icy white diamonds. Cheops sucked in his breath, but Bonnard barely glanced at them. He switched on the high-intensity lamps. His face was inscrutable as he took out his loupe. Then he studied the stones closely but impersonally. To him, the most beautiful gem was no different from the plainest wedding band. It was merely a piece of merchandise. Only when he showed it to prospective customers would his attitude change. Then he would become fawning, praising the necklace with sumptuous words.

Cheops watched him eagerly. "The best piece yet, eh?" he said with a grin.

Bonnard was silent. He studied each stone carefully.

Snob, Cheops thought to himself. He always thinks he's better than everyone else. But he consoled himself for the snub by doing some quick mental calculations. He'd probably be able to get about half of what the necklace was worth. He knew it had a retail value of at least 250,000 francs. He congratulated himself on what he'd paid for it; a mere 15,000 francs. He'd probably end up getting 125,000 from Bonnard. A 110,000-franc profit was not bad for making a single trip to the jeweler's. No, it was not bad at all. He only hoped that the woman who sold it to him would continue bringing him more pieces. She probably would, as long as she didn't stop by at the better jewelers. Because he wasn't selling them to tourists and foreigners as he had promised. Most of the jewels had been bought in shops around the Faubourg St.-Honoré. And most of them ended up no more than three blocks from where they'd been bought.

He mopped his forehead again. He hoped she wouldn't find out too soon. She was the goose who was laying his golden eggs. Twenty-four karat eggs, at that.

It was after two o'clock. The room was dark and the snow was coming down heavily as Hélène sat in the window seat. Her knees were drawn up to her chin and her head leaned back against the window frame. She had been sitting in that position ever since the snow started to fall. That was hours ago.

Her eyes stared out into the night. Through the thick lead glass, the world outside looked distorted. As if everything were either stretched out of shape or compressed, depending on the angle she looked at it. Sort of like funhouse mirrors, she thought. She pursed her lips. Only nothing was funny. It was all frightening. Too frightening.

Up until now everything had been going quite well. Even she had to admit it. She was a top model at Odile Joly and she enjoyed the advantages of the Comte's affections. From him she had gotten the closets full of fashionable clothes, the jewels she had been pawning to pay Häberle, the three fur coats. From him, too, she had gotten the use of the big town house on the Boulevard Maillot. She had managed to put a hundred thousand miles between herself and the grimy labyrinths of Montmartre and the horrors of Saint-Nazaire. There was no doubt about it. She was on her way up.

But now? She turned her head away from the window and stared wearily down at her hands. Now suddenly the tables had turned. She had missed her period. She was never late, but at first she had told herself that that was all it was. So she waited. Then she missed the second month. Then the third. Finally she had panicked and gone to see the doctor. He had confirmed her worst suspicions. She was three months pregnant. Biting down hard on her lip, she wondered what would happen to her now.

She was a fashion model. She didn't have to be told what happened to pregnant fashion models. There weren't any. She knew she was lucky to even have a job modeling. She knew, too, that there were hundreds, even thousands, of beautiful girls already lined up, ready to jump into her place. Ruthlessly awaiting their opportunity. And she had heard somewhere that giving birth left stretch marks. So what if they eventually went away? She couldn't just take a leave of absence and go off to have a baby. When she got back, her job would be gone. And without a job, how could she ever expect to support and feed the baby? She shook her head. It was a malicious cycle that fed on itself.

Then, there was the matter of the Comte. She no longer had any illusions left as far as he was concerned. To him she was nothing more than an exceptionally constructed toy in a lavish dollhouse. He would never tolerate a pregnant mistress. As soon as he found out about it, she would be kicked out, back into the cold. The most she would be able to expect from him would be a financial settlement of some sort. Along with a notice to vacate the town house and find her own place to live.

Finally, and most important of all, there was her dream. Her secret ambition. Her magazine. She had already picked out a name for it. *Les Modes.* And she knew that *Les Modes* was the only child she would ever really want to have. She shook her head in despair. The baby. The baby. It wasn't even born yet, but suddenly everything revolved around the baby.

On an impulse she stretched out her legs. Then with her fingers she felt her belly. It was still flat and hard. It didn't feel a bit different. Not yet. It wouldn't be noticeable for a couple of months, but it was there, all right, deep down inside her. She could almost feel it growing, that infinitesimal spark of life.

She closed her eyes and took a deep breath. Over the past few hours a vague plan had been hovering nearby. At first it had been an ugly, shapeless cloud and she kept pushing it away. But now she let it metamorphose into the ugly dark shape that it was. It was a way out.

TODAY

Friday, January 12

1

Hélène and Edmond got off the elevator on the twenty-first floor of the ManhattanBank Building. Hélène looked extremely elegant. She was wearing a sable coat, a sable hat, an ivory-colored Givenchy suit with a sable-colored blouse and a single strand of pearls. Her handbag and shoes matched: they were made of choice lizard skin. The attaché case she carried came from Botega Veneta on Madison Avenue and had cost two thousand dollars.

This morning, Hélène had dressed with special care. She had gone through her wardrobe and chosen each item piece by piece. The result was an outfit that made her look rich, and yet it had the elegant understatement and conservative style that was associated with "old money." It was a bit of camouflage, since her money certainly wasn't "old," but today some camouflage wouldn't hurt. The pearls, she decided, were a good touch. They were not too much; not too little. You could never go wrong with pearls, she thought. She decided that she must look cautiously conservative and extremely restrained. Even aloof. Appearances were all-important.

She looked at the familiar block letters on the wall above the reception desk: "International Commercial Banking Division." This part of ManhattanBank, as well as the personal banking division on the floor below, was a side of the banking world that most people never saw. Here the important clients were handled *by appointment only* in plush private offices. When millions of dollars were involved, there was no waiting in line for surly bank tellers or nasty "officers." Up here, everything was strictly first-class. Very professional. Very efficient. Very slick.

The receptionist looked up at Hélène and Edmond and smiled professionally. "May I help you?" she asked in a polite voice.

"We have an appointment with Mr. Rowen," Edmond said.

The receptionist reached for the call directory and lifted the receiver. "Who should I say would like to see him?"

"Miss Junot," he replied.

"One moment, please." The receptionist smiled apologetically, punched a four-digit number, and murmured softly into the receiver. A moment later she hung up and smiled again. "Room two-one-oh-seven," she said. She pointed down the hall. "It will be on your right. Mr. Rowen's expecting you."

"Thank you," Edmond said. He touched Hélène's sable sleeve and guided her down the blue-carpeted corridor. Framed color renderings of worldwide ManhattanBank branches hung on the white walls.

At room 2107 they found a young man sliding a brass nameplate into the metal slot on the door. Hélène looked at it curiously: "R. ROWEN, Vice-President." When the man finished, he noticed them and stepped aside. "I'm sorry," he apologized quickly. "I didn't realize . . ."

Hélène smiled automatically. "That's all right," she said. But her smile faded when she saw the old brass sign in his hand. It was engraved: "J. C. GORE III, Vice-President."

She shivered. How quickly the new replaces the old, she thought. Only a single day had passed since Gore's death, and already all evidence of his tenure was being obliterated. Suddenly the hallway was oppressive, stifling. She was glad when Edmond opened the door and they entered the office. A dead man's office.

Alice, Gore's middle-aged secretary, looked up from her desk. Her eyes were red and she looked like she'd been crying.

"Hello, Alice," Hélène said softly.

"Good morning, Miss Junot." Alice sniffed and wiped her nose with a Kleenex. "Mr. R-Rowen is expecting you."

"I'm sorry about Mr. Gore," Hélène said.

"Thank you, Miss Junot." Alice composed herself, rose to her feet, and walked with dignity toward the veneered door of the inner office. She knocked twice and opened it. "Miss Junot and Mr. Junot are here to see you, Mr. Rowen."

Alice stepped aside, waited for Hélène and Edmond to enter the office, and quietly closed the door behind them. Hélène started. The office seemed strangely dim: a huge plywood board covered one of the big expanses of window, blocking out some of the light and most of the view. She shuddered.

Mr. Rowen got to his feet and came around from behind the desk. He shook hands firmly with Hélène and Edmond. "I'm Robert Rowen," he said in a friendly, reassuring voice. He gestured for them to take a seat.

Hélène unbuttoned the sable and let it slip back on the chair as she sat down. Edmond took a seat beside her, and Rowen went back behind the desk. Hélène couldn't help noticing that with the plywood over the window, she could see Rowen's face clearly. It used to be difficult for her to read Gore's expressions with all the light coming in from behind him. She also found it a bit disconcerting that Gore's successor was so unlike his predecessor. She hadn't realized that she'd gotten quite used to Gore's obesity and wheezy self-importance. This man was in his mid-thirties, slim, and dark-haired. He was part of the new breed, one of the Bright Young Men who'd made it. For his age, he was somberly dressed. He wore the traditional pinstriped suit and Turnbull-and-Asser shirt indigenous to the banking profession.

Rowen pushed a stack of computer printout aside and cleared his throat. He chose his words carefully. "For the time being, I have been designated to act as Mr. Gore's replacement. I have no idea whether this is a permanent position. However, I will try to handle everything to your satisfaction." He looked at Hélène. "Hélène Junot International, Incorporated, seems to do the bulk of its American banking with ManhattanBank. I cannot pretend that you are anything but a highly valued client." He smiled, showing straight white teeth. "As well as my wife's favorite publisher, I might add."

Graciously Hélène smiled back. It was expected of her.

"At any rate," Rowen continued, "our only immediate concerns are to ensure a continued smooth relationship between yourself and ManhattanBank, and to come to a mutually satisfactory decision regarding your ten-million-dollar loan." He looked at Hélène. She nodded slowly. "In order to acquaint myself more fully with the circumstances involved, I do not want to make any decision concerning the loan until Monday."

Hélène nodded again, but she remained silent. Edmond had told her to let him do the talking. Now he spoke up.

"Mr. Rowen, I fully understand ManhattanBank's position. But as the head of HJII's international legal department, as well as Miss Junot's personal adviser and brother, I have requested this meeting in order to familiarize you with the urgent need for an extension.

"As you may know, HJII is the world's largest and most powerful fashion instrument. We have subscribers on six continents. One word in our magazines can make or break a major designer or manufacturer. We have helped push many of today's most successful couturiers into the forefront—Halston, d'Itri, Armani, Geoffrey Beene, to mention a few. Our faithful readers—we have a monthly circulation of over twenty-eight million copies—trust us implicitly and spend almost six hundred million dollars a year buying our magazines. Our advertising revenues—"

"You don't need to acquaint me with Hélène Junot International's success, Mr. Junot," Rowen said quietly. "The fact of the matter is, the ten-million-dollar loan was not made to the corporation but to *Miss* Junot."

Edmond shook his head. "Miss Junot *is* HJII," he said smoothly. "And since she used a portion of her HJII shares as collateral, you must admit that the loan does indeed affect the corporation. Especially since her control over the corporation hinges on your decision."

Rowen steepled his fingers. "I can appreciate that," he said carefully. "But I do not quite understand what it is you're trying to get at."

Edmond reached for his cigarettes. "May I?" he asked, holding up the flat eighteen-karat-gold Tiffany case.

"Certainly."

Edmond selected a cigarette, tapped it on the case, and slowly lit it. It was a device he had invented long ago in order to stall for time to think. Rowen was sharp, he realized. He would not be as easy to handle as Gore had been.

Edmond blew the smoke out through his nostrils. "All I'm trying to get at, Mr. Rowen, is that without Miss Junot's leadership, taste, and expertise, the corporation would be in extreme danger of losing its appeal. Without her, HJII would probably close its doors and go bankrupt within five years. Maybe less. It is therefore vital that the collateral shares held by ManhattanBank are *not* sold.

"Like any big institution or wealthy person, Miss Junot occasionally has cash-flow problems. I am sure that you can appreciate that. Much of her money is tied up in investments.

334

You can be assured that her cash-flow problems are very temporary.

"Also, I would like to reiterate what you yourself have stated—that the bulk of HJII's banking is done with ManhattanBank. That is due entirely to Miss Junot's discretion. Should her collateral shares be sold, she would lose control over HJII and you would have no guarantee that ManhattanBank would continue getting HJII's business. I don't think I need to tell you that more than one hundred and sixty million dollars a year flow through our ManhattanBank accounts. I'm sure you already know that."

Rowen nodded. "I do. And as I said to you over the telephone yesterday, I shall consider all these factors before coming to a decision."

Nonchalantly Edmond leaned forward and stabbed out his cigarette in the big ashtray. His eyes met Rowen's. "Mr. Gore . . . he was mainly in charge of our accounts, wasn't he?" he asked lightly.

"Yours and several others," Rowen replied carefully.

Edmond sat back. "I take it, though, that HJII was his single largest account?"

"I'm not certain. I would have to check that out. I can only presume so."

Edmond smiled agreeably. "Which means, of course, that if Mr. Gore did indeed 'borrow' money from various accounts, more money would be missing from HJII's accounts than any of the others?"

"Mr. Junot, let me assure you that this institution is fully insured and if—and I stress the word 'if'—this turns out to be the case, we would immediately be able to cover your losses."

"I understand that," Edmond said easily. "And I'll try to make Miss Junot understand that, too. But you must agree that it would be rather . . . unfair if we were the victims of having our accounts fraudulently mishandled, and at the same time be doing business with an unresponsive bank?"

"What exactly do you mean?"

"I'm certain most corporations would not look lightly upon their bankers 'borrowing' money from their accounts. But Miss Junot fully understands the problems of having many employees. She has hundreds of them herself, all around the world. Any corporation—even a bank—can have one rotten apple in a barrel of good ones."

Rowen leaned across the desk. "Mr. Junot," he said quietly, "you wouldn't by any chance be trying to blackmail ManhattanBank into giving Miss Junot an extension, would you?"

Edmond grinned suddenly. "Not at all, sir. I'm only saying that as far as HJII and ManhattanBank are concerned, we hope that our mutually successful business relationships in the past can be smoothly continued in the future. Miss Junot would hate having to take one hundred and sixty million dollars' worth of annual business elsewhere." Edmond rose to his feet and looked down at Hélène. She got up, and he helped her into the sable. Then he turned back to Rowen. "It was very kind of you to see us, Mr. Rowen. We know that you must be extremely busy, and we don't want to take up any more of your time."

Then they left the office. Only after they had gone did Rowen realize that Hélène had not spoken one word.

2

The snow was coming down in flurries when Robert Rowen climbed into the back of the Checker cab. He let out a sigh of relief. At last he was on his way home. He rubbed his eyes. They hurt fiercely. He had been straining them all day and far into the night going over the Junot accounts. Finally he had called it quits and telephoned for a cab. Then he waited in the lobby of the ManhattanBank Building for it to arrive. After business hours, Wall Street became a morgue and you couldn't find a cab if your life depended on it. Every time it snowed, it was the same old story.

Finally, after he'd waited more than forty-five minutes, the cab had pulled up in front of the building. He hurried out through the swirling flakes. "Park Avenue and Seventy-second," he told the driver.

During the ride uptown, he kept thinking about the Junot accounts. He hadn't realized just how mind-boggling they were until he'd really started going over them. There was no end to the number of accounts. There were some into which bank drafts and letters of credit were paid, there were separate accounts for each of the advertising agencies (twenty-seven in all), several for payroll, a few for taxes, one for the shareholders' dividends, one for billing, one for receiving, one for receiving funds from each overseas branch, one for each New York department, another for travel expenses, a miscellaneous account, a slush fund, a petty-cash fund, and no less than seven personal accounts for Hélène Junot. The list was endless.

His mind was still on the accounts when the cab pulled up in front of the prewar Park Avenue building. "Good evening, Mr. Rowen," the doorman said as he held the door of the cab open.

Rowen paid the driver through the little slot in the scratched-up Plexiglas divider and climbed out of the cab. "Good evening, Pedro," he said in an annoyed voice. He fished in his pocket for a quarter and silently cursed the doorman for running out and making a tip necessary.

Pedro held the lobby door open and Rowen hurried out of the cold and into the warmth. He crossed the lobby to the old elevator, punched the button, and waited an eternity for it to arrive. When it did, he stepped inside the varnished wooden cage and pressed the button marked 12.

When the elevator door slid open, he turned right, walked down the tiled hall, fished for his keys, and began to unlock the door of apartment 12C. It opened just as he was turning the key.

"Hi, honey," Jennifer said softly. She wrapped her arms around him, stood on tiptoe, and gave him a long, hard kiss. Then she drew back, smiling up at him. Her brown hair, with its preppy cut, shone softly in the light. "Have a tough day?"

He shrugged and nuzzled her ear. "How's my baby?"

She giggled. Then her face turned serious. "Honey, I missed you."

"I missed you, too."

"Martini?"

"You said it." He followed her into the living room. It was furnished with the heavy mahogany pieces she'd inherited from her mother. He watched as she took two glasses from the sideboard, then disappeared into the kitchen. She opened

337

the freezer and reached for the martinis they kept on ice in a glass shaker.

"Honey? Are you hungry?" she called out.

"I can wait," he called back.

She tossed an olive into her glass, *gently* lowered a grape into his, and poured the martinis. Carefully she carried them out to the living room.

He was loosening his tie. Wearily he sank onto the camel-back sofa. She handed him his drink and sat down beside him, curling her legs under her torso in that peculiar manner of hers. She watched him take a swallow of his martini.

"So tell me," she said finally. "How did your day go?"

"Well, come to think of it, I met a rather interesting person. A woman."

Her eyes narrowed teasingly. "Was she beautiful?"

He looked suddenly thoughtful. "Yes."

"More beautiful than me?"

He looked at Jennifer. This was an old game between them. Whenever he met a woman, she would always ask that. He would invariably hesitate, she would pretend to be cross, and finally he would say, "No, honey, you're the most beautiful woman in the world." Then she would be content and they would kiss happily.

"Well?" Jennifer demanded with mock petulance.

"She was . . . very beautiful," he said slowly.

She sat bolt upright. She looked suddenly cross. "You're serious, aren't you?"

He nodded.

"So she's that special," she said bitterly. She shook her head angrily, but her eyes were frozen.

Now he knew she was really upset. He sighed helplessly. He should have known better and stuck to the rules of the game.

"Well?" she demanded. "Who was this . . . this Helen of Troy?"

He couldn't help but smile at her unintentionally appropriate metaphor. "Hélène Junot," he said. "The publisher."

She tried to laugh lightly, but it came out sounding very ugly. He looked at her with surprise.

"So she got to you, too," she said accusingly.

He looked at her blankly. "What do you mean?"

"What do I mean! Really, Robert! Don't you know anything about her? According to the columnists, she leaves a path of destruction wherever she goes."

He looked at her angrily. "Come off it, Jennie. It's nothing personal. Hey . . ." He reached out to stroke her cheek, but she drew back coldly. "I didn't even speak to her. Her brother did all the talking." Once again he looked thoughtful. "You know what?" he said, thinking aloud. "They're a very slick pair of operators."

Despite her anger, she looked at him with deepening interest. "What do you mean?"

"Well . . ." He took another swallow of his drink. "It was strange. I got the idea she was there just as window dressing. You know what I mean?" She nodded. "He did all the talking. Come to think of it, she never even said 'hello' or 'good-bye.'" He shook his head. "Her brother's real sharp. Almost *too* sharp. And yet . . . she's the power behind it all. You can almost feel it. It's sort of . . " He paused, searching for the right word.

"Scary?" she offered.

"Hmmm . . . I guess you could call it that."

Suddenly the telephone rang. They glanced across the room at it.

"I'll get it," Jennifer said quickly. She uncurled her legs, got up, and crossed over to the round mahogany fern table that they used as a telephone stand. "Hello?" A moment later she put her hand over the mouthpiece and turned to Rowen. There was a peculiar look on her face. "Honey . . ."

"Who is it?"

"I don't know. A man, I think. He says he wants to talk to you."

"Well, find out who he is."

"Honey, he sounds kind of creepy. He's *whispering.*"

Rowen saw the expression on her face. He sighed, got up, and crossed the room. She handed him the receiver and then put her ear close to his, trying to eavesdrop.

"Robert Rowen here," he said.

For a moment there was silence. Then a whispering voice echoed in the telephone. "*Mr. Rowen,*" it said, "*how would you like to make a million dollars?*"

YESTERDAY

IV
ABORTION

1

Paris, 1955

The snow had stopped falling but the air was like a breath of ice as Hélène hesitated on the doorstep of the old building. For a moment, she couldn't move. It was as if the snow had frozen her feet to the sidewalk. She glanced up. The building looked like any of the countless ugly gray buildings which the tourists found so picturesque. Only there was nothing picturesque about what went on in this one.

Determinedly she bit down on her lip. It was a moment before she realized the force of the bite. Then she could taste the thick warm sweetness of her blood. Slowly she opened the door and began to climb the dark, steep flights of stairs which were illuminated by a single naked bulb. There was trash piled high on the landings, and the stench of urine and cat feces hung foul in the air. Halfway up, she stopped suddenly and gripped the banister. She could feel the fear in her heart hammering against her ribs. She closed her eyes. She was frightened and depressed and alone. She had been feeling like that ever since she had come to a decision and gone to see Angélique.

She hadn't known whether Angélique still danced in the revue at the Folies de Babylon, but she had hoped so. She had never forgotten her first day there. Angélique had been testy because she was pregnant and had to pay for her abortion herself. She smiled grimly. Angélique was the only person she had ever known who had gotten an abortion.

At six in the morning Hélène had waited outside the employee door of the Folies de Babylon. She had stayed awake all night long, and her exhaustion showed. Her eyelids were red and puffy from lack of sleep, and she had to wait in the snowy darkness for almost an hour; inside the nightclub, closing and cleanup were running late. Finally the door had opened and the girls poured out into the narrow street. She drew deeper into the shadows so that she would not need to speak to anyone she knew.

She recognized Angélique immediately, and a lump rose up in her throat. She waited while the tall showgirl stopped to light a cigarette. Then she watched her pull her coat tightly around her and hurry down the alley, the footsteps of her flat heels noiseless in the snow. Quickly Hélène slipped out of the shadows and fell in step behind her.

"Angélique?" she said in a small, timid voice, a band of fear suddenly constricting her chest.

The showgirl stopped and looked at Hélène in the dim light of a streetlamp. "Yes?"

Hélène pushed her hat back from her face. "Remember me? I used to work with Yvette in the hat-check."

Angélique looked at her blankly. "There's no job opening right now," she said in a bored voice and continued walking. "Look someplace else," she said over her shoulder.

Hélène ran after her and caught her arm. "I'm not looking for a job," she said quickly. "I need your advice."

Angélique laughed. "Listen, chérie. It's been a grueling night. My legs ache, I'm tired, and I want to go home."

"Please," Hélène begged. "I've just got one question."

Angélique stopped and faced Hélène wearily. "All right, what is it?"

"I remember you had to get an abortion—"

"Listen, young lady!" Angélique snapped. "What I do or don't do is none of your business!" She squinted and frowned. Then her eyes flickered with recognition. "Now I remember you," she said, giving a short laugh. "You're the wholesome one."

Hélène felt her cheeks stinging as if she'd been slapped. She looked down at her feet. "I need to know where I can get an abortion," she said quietly.

Angélique laughed. "Don't tell me! So you're not that wholesome after all!"

"No," Hélène said tightly. She looked back at Angélique. "Please," she whispered. "I need to know where I can go."

Angélique looked at her. Suddenly the girl's misery sank through. She thawed immediately. "All right," she said in a gentler voice. She put her arm around Hélène's shoulders. "Hey, you're crying!"

Hélène nodded and wiped her eyes.

"You really want to keep the baby, don't you?"

Hélène's voice trembled. "Yes. But I . . . I can't."

"Come on," Angélique said, smiling. "I'm suddenly not that tired after all. How about some breakfast?"

"I'm not hungry," Hélène said. "But I'll have a cup of coffee."

Angélique smiled. "Then I know just the place. Henri has the worst coffee in Paris, and nobody drinks it. But he keeps the best brandy under the counter."

The brandy was served in coffee cups. Hélène looked down at hers and smiled faintly.

"Henri can't get a liquor license," Angélique explained. "So in his typically sneaky fashion he circumvented the liquor laws by serving drinks in cups. Not that it's legal. It just looks aboveboard to the casual observer. Even the gendarmes on the beat drop in for a cup of his 'coffee' every now and then." Suddenly she reached across the table and took Hélène's hand. "Listen," she said softly, "how far gone are you?"

Hélène's lips twitched. "Three months," she whispered heavily.

Angélique was silent for a moment. "It'll be difficult," she said quietly. "Once you've carried a child for that long, it gets very tricky."

Hélène stared at her.

"You're sure you want to . . . get rid of it?"

Hélène winced at the expression. Slowly she nodded.

Angélique toyed with the cup. "I know this intern . . ." She smiled humorlessly and shrugged. "At least he says he's an intern. If you decide to go ahead with it, I'll have to call him and recommend you. Then he'll get in touch with you. Just think it over carefully first. If you do it, there's no going back, you know. Once it's done, it's done."

Hélène nodded. "I've thought it over already," she said. "I have to do it."

Now she felt a tightening in her throat as she knocked three times on the door on the top floor. A muffled voice came from inside. "Who is it?"

"Angélique's friend, Hélène. I . . . I have an appointment?"

There was the sound of a key turning in the lock and then the door jerked open. A sloppy, fat young man stood in front

345

of her, scratching his beard. Behind him, the room was dark and musty. He stared at her. "Well, don't just stand there! Quick! Come in."

Hélène quickly stepped past him. He glanced suspiciously out into the stairwell and lost no time in shutting the door and locking it behind her. She looked around, a nervous smile masking her disgust. There were newspapers spread out over the floor, and cats were everywhere. Licking their paws, sizing her up, slinking around.

The fat man shuffled over to her, the soles of his mules slapping against the newspapers. "Three thousand francs," he said, holding out his hand.

Hélène nodded. Nervously she reached into her coat pocket. "Don't take a purse," Angélique had advised her. "Don't take anything you'll have to carry. You'll feel very weak afterward." She peeled off some bills and handed them to him. Wordlessly he wet his finger and counted them. Then he grunted and stuffed them into his trouser pocket.

"Follow me," he said, gesturing with his hand.

Hélène hesitantly followed him into the kitchen. Here, too, the floor was covered up with newspaper. There was a pot of water boiling on the stove and dirty dishes in the enamel sink. In the center of the room was a large wooden table. The top was covered with a thick layer of newspapers.

"Take off your clothes and lie down on there," he said.

She stared at the table. "On . . . here?" she asked hesitantly, pointing at it.

"You don't see no other place, do you?"

She shook her head. "No," she said softly. Self-consciously she began to unbutton her blouse. Then she stepped out of her skirt. She glanced at him. He had his back to her, washing his hands in the kitchen sink. Quickly she stepped out of her slip and shrugged off her brassiere. She draped her clothes neatly over a chair. The room felt suddenly cold. She shivered and rubbed her arms with her hands.

He turned around and looked at her indifferently. Instinctively she tried to cover herself. "I told you to get on the table," he said.

Her face turned scarlet. She looked at him without replying. She took a deep breath and then climbed onto the table.

"Lie down on your back," he said. With his foot he pushed a metal trashcan over beside the table.

"What's that for?" she asked with a sudden fear.

"Let me worry about that."

She nodded hesitantly. Stiffly she lay back, her head hanging over the edge of the table.

"Slide farther down," he said. "And put your legs up. You know, like someone's going to shove something up your pussy."

She bit down on her lip and did as she was told. Then she watched him reach for a long, thin piece of wire with an ugly hook at the end. He tossed it into the pot of boiling water. A minute later he fished it back out, holding the end of it with a rag. Some water dripped down onto the burner and hissed.

Hélène closed her eyes. She hadn't had any idea that it would be like this. She had thought it would be nicer, somehow. Cleaner. More professional. Dignified.

"Spread your legs apart," he said. "And keep still."

She took a deep breath. Her legs were trembling as she splayed them. Then she felt his fingers brushing her pubic hair aside. She tensed, her hands gripping the sides of the table, her breasts rising and falling with her quiet breathing. A moment later he began to push the warm metal hook inside her. It felt foreign, like an object that didn't belong. Something deep within her made her want to cry out, but she fought against it, biting down on her lip. She felt the wire going in deeper. Deeper. Probing, moving around. Then the hook hit against something.

"No," she cried, hammering her head against the tabletop. "No!" she screamed as she felt the hook digging in. The pain shot through her belly as the something inside her was being poked and jabbed and jostled loose.

She knew what it was. Her baby. The spark of life which she and the Comte had produced and which her body had been nurturing for more than three months. The tears pushed out of her eyes, running down her cheeks.

Now the pain was gaining in strength. She forced herself to open her eyes and look down at the man. He was holding the end of the wire, moving it around within her, poking still farther in and then giving it short, swift tugs. Suddenly the pain burst through her like a flash of red-hot lightning. Her body convulsed and she screamed in agony as her baby was wrenched from her womb.

"Don't look," he advised grimly.

She opened her eyes and pushed herself forward into a sitting position. "I want to see," she whispered in an anguished voice. "I *have* to see."

Then she saw and she let out a cry of terror. The newspaper under her was soaked with thick, sticky blood. On it lay the motionless little fetus. It had an oversized pink head, short little limbs, and a network of fine blue veins crisscrossing the misshapen body. Its umbilical cord still snaked up inside her.

Now she knew what the trashcan was for. Her baby.

The door behind her crashed shut and then there was silence. It was the kind of unearthly silence you would experience if you were the only person alive on earth. She looked slowly up and down the alley. It was still daylight. What time was it? she wondered. Slowly she pulled back her sleeve and looked at the watch on her wrist. Could it be possible? she asked herself. She had been upstairs for less than half an hour. Yet she seemed to have aged a few years.

She stumbled along the sidewalk, veering like a drunkard. Her face was pale. She leaned against a wall and shut her eyes. There was a terrible pain within her; suddenly she felt hot. She wiped her sleeve across her forehead. It was wet and her hair was plastered against her head. But there was snow on the ground. Why should she feel so hot?

Then she slumped to the ground.

2

Hélène twisted her head to one side and a moan came through her lips. Slowly she opened her eyes and stared straight ahead, a puzzled look on her face. All she could see was one dark, unfocused blur and a vague vertical line of light that kept changing shape as it danced in front of her.

She frowned and blinked her eyes. Slowly her vision focused. The room was dark, but it was daylight outside; straight ahead there were chinks of light between the drapes.

The window was open, and the light kept shifting as the draperies moved. So that was the dancing, changing shape. She had imagined it to be many things. A whirling ballerina, a nightmare creature, a white horse prancing in front of her. But never draperies.

She tried to sit up in bed, but her body felt like lead and refused to obey. Frustrated, she sighed deeply and let her head sink back down on the pillow. What had happened? What was wrong with her?

Then she remembered. She wrinkled her nose in disgust. Still she could almost smell the offensive odor of urine and cat feces. She could almost see the dingy apartment covered with newspapers and the fat bearded man holding the long piece of wire that had the hook on the end. And now she also remembered the cats stalking around everywhere, and the . . . the fetus . . .

Nausea rose up within her. Quickly, as if it would chase away the demons in her memory, she turned her head sideways on the pillow. She frowned again as the curtains billowed and the room was flooded with sudden light. The pillow was white. So were the bedsheets. And they were starched, not soft like the Porthault sheets embroidered with violets that she had at home.

Wearily she moved her head from side to side, her violet eyes straining to get a better view of the room. It was a large room, but one in which she had never been before. That much she knew. But it was a clean room. There were no newspapers, no cats. She felt an immeasurable relief at that.

She tried to look up as she heard a door opening. A man came quietly into the room. He approached the bed and looked down into her face. "How are you feeling?" he asked gently.

She looked up at him with curiosity. "Who are you?"

He smiled and switched on a lamp. She could feel the mattress shifting as he sat down on the edge of the bed. "I was going to ask you the same question," he said, tucking the sheet around her chin. "But that can wait." He smiled reassuringly and reached into his pocket. Then he took a pair of thick wire-rimmed glasses out of an eyeglass case. Carefully he put them on. Then he picked up a thermometer off the nightstand and shook it with short, expert jerks of his wrist. He peered closely at it, gave a nod of approval, and stuck it in her mouth. Dutifully she closed her lips over it and looked up at him.

He was short and small-framed, with narrow shoulders that seemed to sag under an enormous invisible burden. His hair and beard were of various shades of black and gray, his nose was magnificent, almost noble in its size and shape, and seemed sadly out of place in a face so deeply engraved with sadness. Under the hooded lids his eyes were dark and heavy. They were eyes that had seen too much pain in the past and could foresee a future that was filled with no less suffering.

He waited patiently. After a while he reached for the thermometer, slipped it gently out of her mouth, and held it close to his eyes. He looked pleased. "Your temperature is stable, as I suspected it would be." He put the thermometer down on the nightstand. "You are out of danger. Your fever broke yesterday."

"Yesterday!" Hélène said in a small voice. A sudden intuition came into her eyes. "How long have I been here?"

"Four days."

"Four days!" She shook her head unbelievingly. "But I just woke up . . ."

The man nodded, "You were very weak," he explained to her. "And you lost a lot of blood. But that wasn't half as debilitating as the infection."

"Infection!" Hélène struggled to sit up, but he shook his head.

"Don't try to move," he warned. "You are still too weak. It will be a few days before your body recovers its strength."

Hélène nodded obediently and lay quietly back. "Where am I?" she asked.

"Don't worry, you are under good care. I am a doctor. My name is Simon Rosen."

She relaxed a little. "How did I get here?"

"I found you and carried you here. You had passed out."

She felt a sudden stab of guilt. "I put you through a lot of trouble," she apologized meekly.

"Don't worry yourself about that. I should have taken you to a hospital, but I thought it was better to bring you here. The hospital would have been forced to call the police. They would have asked many ugly questions."

Now she understood what it was like to owe a big debt. He had not only saved her life. He had kept her name clean as well.

"I don't know how I can ever thank you," she said solemnly.

He smiled. "Just concentrate on getting your strength back." He got to his feet. "I will bring you some food in a moment."

She nodded gratefully. Suddenly she felt very tired. He noticed it. He would wait with dinner and let her sleep. It would do her more good right now than eating. But first she needed to drink some water. He reached for the glass, placed one hand under the back of her head, and held her up as he put the glass to her lips. She drank slowly. When she had had enough, she nodded. Gently he let her head back down.

"I shall be right back," he promised.

She smiled weakly and closed her eyes. Already she could feel the mantle of sleep closing in around her.

"By the way," he said. "You never told me your name."

"Hélène Junot," she whispered so softly that he could barely hear it.

Her eyes were shut so she did not see the tears behind his glasses. He shook his head. God worked in strange ways. He had seen to it that his path crossed with another Junot's. Hélène Junot. He frowned and searched his memory. There were four children. She would be the second youngest.

He took off his glasses, wiped them carefully with his handkerchief, and placed them back in the case. He rubbed the tears from his eyes with his fingers. Then he just stood there looking over at her. Her face was lost in innocence, and the sounds of her breathing were slow and regular. She was fast asleep.

He shook his head sadly. "Sleep peacefully, little one," he murmured. "Gather up your strength, for you shall need it. You should never have had to hear the story I must tell you. But God would not have crossed our paths if he did not will you to hear it."

She slept through two days and two nights. When she awoke, her strength had returned enough so that she could eat, sit up, talk, and worry. Her biggest worry was over her job. "Please," she begged Dr. Rosen. "Could you call the Maison d'Odile Joly for me and tell them that I am sick? That I can't come in to work yet?"

"Odile Joly?" Dr. Rosen asked. "You mean the couturière?"

She nodded.

He looked at her strangely; then his face broke into a smile. "I shall call immediately."

He left to place the call. When he returned, she looked at him questioningly.

He smiled. "I spoke to Odile Joly herself. She was very worried about you. She hopes that you will get well soon."

Hélène looked suddenly troubled. "You didn't tell her . . . ?"

He looked genuinely upset. "Of course not!" he said, drawing himself up indignantly. "I am a doctor. A doctor keeps his patient's illness in confidence."

"I'm sorry," she said contritely. "I should have known better." But there was a look of relief in her eyes.

That afternoon, an enormous bouquet of roses arrived from the atelier. Dr. Rosen went to find a vase and made room on the nightstand for it. Hélène pulled the stiff card out of the small white envelope. The spidery handwriting was so elegant she could barely read it. Finally she made it out: "Feel better soon. Your job is waiting. So don't worry about that. Odile Joly and all the girls."

Hélène smiled suddenly and stared at the roses. They were long-stemmed and luxuriantly pink, just barely open. The delicate petals tightly cocooned the thick fat buds, promising huge blossoms to burst forth. She could smell their sweet fragrance in the air. Odile Joly could be hard as nails, but as far as her "girls" were concerned, she had a soft spot in her heart.

The next day, Dr. Rosen sat on the edge of the bed. He was reading to Hélène from a new book that was causing a sensation. It was called *Bonjour Tristesse* and was written by an unknown young writer named Françoise Sagan. Abruptly she reached out for his hand. She gripped it fiercely. He stopped reading, carefully placed a ribbon between the pages, and closed the book.

"Dr. Rosen?" she said in a small, frightened voice.

He shook his head and smiled. "You must call me Simon. We are friends, non?"

She smiled. "Yes, we are good friends, Simon."

He smiled slowly and looked pleased. Tenderly he brushed aside the hair that fell down over her forehead. Suddenly her violet eyes clouded over. He was startled to see them change color so rapidly. One instant they had been violet; now they were a dull amethyst. It was as if a cloud had pushed its way in front of the sun.

"I have to ask you something, Simon," she said in a quiet, heavy voice. "I need to know the truth."

He nodded in silence. He knew what she was going to ask. He had wondered how long it would be until she did. But he hadn't thought it would be so soon.

She stared at him, and her voice dropped to a whisper. "Simon? Will I . . . will I be able to bear any more children?"

He closed his eyes. He who had managed to comfort so many people all his life found that words failed him at this moment.

"Thank you, Simon," she said softly. "Thank you for not trying to deny it. For not giving me false hopes." She turned her head sideways on the pillow and stared at the wall. She felt an agony like she had never thought could exist. She didn't make a sound, but the tears streamed down her cheeks. Only now did she realize the true gravity of what she had done. Her lips trembled. As far as she was concerned, she was now only half a woman. She could never have another baby. Then her lips stopped trembling. Yes, she would! She would have a baby of the spirit. She would have *Les Modes!*

Now her recovery speeded up. There was no time to lose, she told herself. Time was a luxury she couldn't indulge in. Every day she spent in bed would be a day's delay for *Les Modes.* And the very next day, she was able to walk around the room. At first she felt wobbly on her feet, but she forced herself to exercise them. Dr. Rosen was surprised by this sudden willpower, but he said nothing. He was relieved. Now he knew that she was emotionally stronger. That night he carried a little table into the bedroom and spread a cloth over it. "We shall dine together," he said.

She smiled. "That will be very nice."

A little later, he helped her into a chair and she looked down at the table. It was simply set with inexpensive white china. She thought that these simple plates were far more beautiful than any of the gold-rimmed flower-patterned Limoges or Meissen plates she had been using in the town house. Somehow the plain white looked refreshingly honest and unpretentious.

When they finished dinner, she carefully laid her knife and fork in an X across the plate. "While you were out earlier, I went into the other room and used the telephone," she said slowly. She stared down at her plate. "I'm afraid I won't be able to stay here much longer. I am expected home tomorrow."

He nodded, thinking how peculiar it was that she had wanted him to contact only Odile Joly, and no one else. Was it because she had no friends? But surely a beautiful young woman had many friends. And what about the man who had made her pregnant? "I think you will be strong enough to go home tomorrow," he said. "You have a strong will and incredible recuperative powers. But you must take it very easy for the next few weeks. You must promise me that."

She nodded. "I promise."

"And no . . ." He made an agitated little gesture.

She smiled. "I know. No sex for a few weeks."

He nodded, his face reddening suddenly. Then he cleared his throat. "Also, I insist on escorting you home. You will find that even getting in and out of a taxi takes a lot of energy."

She looked at him gratefully. "Thank you. You've been so kind. I . . . I don't know how I can ever repay you."

He waved her to silence. "Someday you shall run across someone who is sick and in need of help," he said. "You can repay me by helping them."

"I will do that," she promised solemnly.

He leaned back in his chair and looked at her. His voice was filled with sadness. "I cannot help but feel sorrow that we must part."

"I, too," she said. "I will miss you. I hope we can visit each other."

He smiled. "I would like that very much." Then he looked at her intently. "Tell me," he said carefully. "Now that you are on your way to physical recovery, how do you feel . . . emotionally?"

Her eyes dropped. "How can I feel?" she asked softly. "Except ashamed and dirty?" She gave an ugly little laugh. "It's funny, isn't it? I thought I was doing the right thing. The *only* thing. But I realize now that I was wrong. I murdered my baby." She was silent for a moment. "I saw it, you know. It even *looked* like a baby." She shook her head. "I don't know if I'll ever really get over that."

He took out a pipe and looked at it thoughtfully, turning it over and over in his hands. "I think you have a right to know what I am about to tell you," he said, looking back up at her.

354

"I do not know whether you are emotionally ready to hear it now or not. But perhaps . . . yes, perhaps it will help you feel better about yourself. You see, we all suffer, Hélène. We suffer many times in our lives. Some of us suffer more, some of us suffer less. I don't want you to misconstrue what I am going to tell you. I am not trying to show you how little you have suffered. But that we all have suffered. And that, sometimes, exposure to immense suffering helps ease our own. Do you understand what I am trying to say?"

"I . . . I think so," she said haltingly.

He filled the pipe with tobacco and lit it carefully with a match. Then he smoked in silence for a long time. Finally he spoke. "Hélène, I am a Jew. We Jews have suffered for thousands of years." He smiled bitterly. "Sometimes I tend to think we have cornered the market on suffering." Then his face grew extremely sad. "But it is no joke. Every so often someone comes along who tries to wipe us off the face of the earth. So far, we have always managed to survive somehow. We have bled and been decimated, but all the pogroms could not get rid of us as a race. I don't think I need to point out to you the last time such a tragedy occurred."

She nodded quietly. Ever since she had been a little girl in Saint-Nazaire she had heard about the camps. About the unspeakable horrors that went on in those wholesale slaughterhouses of hell. About the millions who had been shot and starved and burned and gassed to death.

"It was my lot in life to endure the last such attack on my people," Dr. Rosen said. Slowly he unbuttoned his cuff and rolled the sleeve of his white shirt up to his elbow. Hélène stared at his arm. The dark blue numbers stood out clearly beneath the light matting of his hair. Her eyes were moist and fathomless. Slowly she reached out and traced her fingers across the numbers.

"It was hell on earth," Dr. Rosen said tightly. "And the devils were in uniform." He put down his pipe as if it left a bad taste in his mouth. "You cannot imagine the horrors unless you were there."

Hélène nodded. "The concentration camps were the shame of all mankind," she said gently.

"They were," Dr. Rosen said. He took a deep breath. "But you must remember that there were two types of camps. Concentration camps and extermination camps. They were all horrible, and people suffered and died in all of them. The concentration camps were in France, Holland, Germany, and Austria. But the extermination camps? They were in Poland. Their only function was to kill millions of people. Just the names of those places still fill me with dread. Names like Belzec and Treblinka and Stutthof and Auschwitz." His voice was trembling uncontrollably, and the muscles in his cheeks twitched. "I was in Auschwitz."

"Please stop," she said softly. "Haven't you suffered enough? Telling this will only make the pain so much worse."

He shook his head. "I have to tell you. You see, not only we Jews were sent to Auschwitz. There were Gypsies and homosexuals and 'enemies of the state.' " He stared at her sadly. "There were even members of the French Resistance."

Hélène suddenly went cold. She couldn't speak. Somehow she knew what he was going to say next.

His voice suddenly rose with a cry of anguish. "I met a woman there," he said, tears flooding from his eyes. "Her name was Jacqueline Junot."

Hélène closed her eyes. For a moment she sat in shocked silence. Then she leaned across the table, her face an expressionless mask. "Tell me!" she whispered. "Tell me everything! Please. I have to know!"

And so he told her.

Maman had been gassed in Auschwitz.

3

It was ten o'clock in the morning when the two taxis swung into the Avenue Fréderic Le Play and pulled to a halt alongside the curb. The girl dresser and the tall male hairstylist climbed out of the first car and watched as the driver lifted three suitcases out of the trunk. Hélène and Jacques emerged from the second cab. While he paid the drivers, she looked down the Champs de Mars toward the Eiffel Tower. It rose up from the intricately laid lawns and swirling paths of the formal gardens high into the clean winter sky. She cringed.

She was frightened. Something told her that she should never have agreed to this. But when Odile Joly had taken her aside, it had sounded like a good idea.

"There is a very fine photographer doing a spread for *Paris Vogue*," Odile Joly had said. "He will use seven pieces from my summer collection. He saw you on the catwalk and insists that you be the model."

Hélène had been flattered and excited. The magic word, of course, was *Vogue*. How often had she leafed through the slick pages of that magazine, hungrily staring at the models? But more important, she had kept in mind what Madame Dupré had said. That perhaps she had more steps to take in order to realize her ambition. Maybe this was yet another such step. Plus there was the matter of the photographer.

Jacques Renault had already made quite a name for himself as a free-lance photographer. His trademark was "daring." He posed his models on the unthinkable—on cliffs, cranes, precipices. One winter morning, he shot various models dangerously posed on the parapets and gargoyles of Notre Dame Cathedral. The pictures had turned out to be fantastic. They were everything Jacques Renault had hoped for. The models' faces were white with fear, as if they were trying to get away from Quasimodo himself. Their fear looked very genuine for one reason. They really were terrified.

There had been only one problem. Jacques had simply taken his models, gone inside the cathedral, and climbed the steps in the north tower up to the roof. There the models threw off their coats. Underneath, they were scantily clad in slips and brassieres. The ad was for Bonaparte Lingerie.

There had been a public outcry. The film had been confiscated, and Jacques retaliated by going to court. The case was lengthy, and Jacques became a kind of *cause célèbre*. After six months, the court ruled in his favor. Overnight he became a major celebrity, a martyr for art. He had made such a sensation that Condé Nast immediately offered him a lucrative contract. Jacques signed it and had worked for *Vogue* ever since.

When Hélène discovered that the photographer who wanted to use her for the spread was Jacques, she did not hesitate. Of course, she had known that his trademark was danger. But she had thought it had been overplayed by the press.

Now, looking toward the black pig-iron girders rising up

from the edge of the Seine, she felt sick. Ever since she was a tiny girl, she had been afraid of heights. And on top of it all, it was cold out. And up there, on the second platform of the Eiffel Tower, the wind would be much stronger yet. She looked at Jacques; he was watching her.

You mustn't think of the height, she told herself as she gritted her teeth. You mustn't think of the danger. You must think only of other things. Comforting things. She smiled wryly. She knew of nothing that could comfort her. The Comte? That was a laugh. Right after Dr. Rosen had taken her home, the Comte had arrived. He had been furious that she had been gone for over a week. She knew that he didn't believe that she had been ill, so she decided not to tell him about the abortion. She had a feeling that he wouldn't have understood.

Instead, she defied Dr. Rosen's orders and dutifully went to bed with the Comte. She had to get good and drunk in order to deaden the pain that tore through her abdomen. It was a terrible pain. The wounds inside her had not yet healed completely.

She thought back to how she had quietly climbed out of the bed and gone to the bathroom when the Comte had fallen asleep. Carefully she had washed the blood from her pubis. The Comte hadn't even noticed how he hurt her. Only in the morning, when he awoke to the bloodstained sheets, did he realize that something was wrong. He had slapped her awake. "Why didn't you tell me that you were having your period?" he demanded. "You know I can't stand making love to a bleeding woman!" He threw her arm loose. "Don't ever let that happen again!"

"All right, first we'll take some shots using the tower for the background," Jacques said swiftly. He shoved his hands deep into his trouser pockets and looked around, shoulders hunched, his young face twisted in concentration. "Merde! That grass looks all dried up. That's always the trouble with shooting summer clothes in winter." Irritably he signaled to the dresser and the hairdresser. "Lug that stuff down to the water fountain."

They picked up the suitcases and started walking. The oval fountain, halfway between the Eiffel Tower and the Coeur d'Honneur, was dry. When they got there, Jacques looked pleased. He turned to Hélène.

"Good. We'll take the first pictures down in there, with the tower rising above you from behind. After that, we'll take the rest of the shots up on the second platform."

Hélène glanced over at the tower. She closed her eyes. The second platform was a dizzying hundred and fifteen meters off the ground.

Half an hour later they were standing on the roof of the second platform. Hélène had changed into a simple pale evening dress that hugged her bosom and then flared to a full skirt below the waist. With a few expert flicks of his wrist, the hairstylist dusted her face with a powder puff; then, noticing the wetness around her eyes, he dabbed them carefully with a piece of tissue. The wind was powerful. It whipped at the carefully pinned-up hair, flogged the skin of her bare back like an icy whip, and forced the tears right up out of her eyes. The makeup had been carefully applied; tears would ruin it. Hélène narrowed her eyes, fighting to keep the tears back.

A few feet away, Jacques looked through the viewfinder of his Hasselblad. He grunted and fiddled with the lens. Without needing to be told, the dresser and the hairstylist quickly got out of the way. With one hand he signaled for Hélène to move sideways.

"Hold it!" he yelled above the noise of the wind. She froze and he grinned suddenly. "That's great! The sun's right behind you, and I can see straight through your dress. Your figure's good. Very good."

"Come *on*, Jacques!" she shouted, briskly rubbing her arms and doing a series of quick little hops. "My teeth are chattering and I'm freezing to death!"

Suddenly he started snapping away, his mouth twisted in a frown of concentration. She began to move fluidly, like a dancer swaying to some music only she could hear. Jacques picked up the rhythm of her dance and edged closer, backed up again, stalked around her, all the time clicking his shutter. He stopped a few times to reload the camera. Each time, the hairdresser hurried over to her and dabbed her eyes.

After a while Jacques stopped. Hélène looked across at him. His face was serious now. "Move to the edge of the platform, chérie. And careful. We don't want to have to scrape you off the Champs de Mars."

She tightened her lips across her teeth. Now came the famous Jacques Renault touch. The acrobatics. She knew just what the girls straddling the Notre Dame gargoyles must have felt like. She could feel it in her gut.

For a moment she couldn't move. Then she managed to turn around, lifted one foot slowly, and began taking half-steps toward the edge of the platform. Careful, she told herself, there's no railing. Easy does it. . . .

When she reached the corner girder, she grabbed hold of one of the pig-iron struts and clung to it for dear life. She closed her eyes. She couldn't bear looking down and seeing the distance between her and the ground. It was a long drop. Forty stories.

Jacques's voice was harsh. "Come on, we're not in a church. Turn around and open your eyes, for God's sake!"

Slowly she opened them. Then she twisted around awkwardly and faced Jacques. He was crouching low, once again studying her through the camera. Suddenly he grinned. "That wasn't so bad, was it?" he shouted.

"Not bad for you, you bastard!" she called out in a frightened, wavering voice. "You're nice and safe!"

"Come on, give me a smile."

She bared her teeth.

"That's the girl. Now, step right to the edge."

She took a deep breath, loosened one hand from the strut, and cautiously backed up a few centimeters until her heels hung out over space and only the toes of her shoes were balanced on the riveted platform. With her free hand she reached down and grabbed hold of the hem of the dress. She lifted it and held it up at arm's length like one shimmering unfolded butterfly wing. The light fabric caught the wind like a sail and began to billow. She held tighter to the strut. It seemed as if the wind delighted at her vulnerability and suddenly flung even angrier gusts at her. Her teeth were chattering. All too easily an unexpectedly powerful gust could propel her backward and cause her to lose her balance.

Jacques pointed. "Look down at Paris!" he shouted. "And hang out over the edge a little!"

Her face went even whiter. Almost paralyzed, she tightened her grip, let her body angle out sideways into space until her arm was stretched stiff, and slowly lowered her head. The city sprawled beneath her like an endless sea of stone divided by the gray, snakelike S-curve of the Seine. She forced her face to assume an unafraid, blasé expression. As if hanging off the girder was the most natural thing in the world.

Finally Jacques grinned widely. "All right," he shouted. "Wrap it up!" He came close and held out his hand. She tottered forward. A few steps later, she felt him grab hold of her, and she collapsed into his arms. He caught her and held her close. She was sobbing uncontrollably. "Hey, it's all right," he said soothingly into her ear. "It's finished."

She nodded weakly, letting him push her away so that the dresser could throw a chinchilla wrap over her. Suddenly she shivered. Until now, she had only been afraid. She had forgotten how cold it was.

"Why didn't you tell me you're frightened of heights?" he asked her.

She looked at him, and a shroud seemed to fall down over her eyes. How could she explain to a virtual stranger about her ambition? That this was just a necessary step toward it?

"I'd like to use you again," he said as they took the elevator back down to the ground.

She smiled bleakly. "What's next? Hanging off the wing of an airplane in flight?"

He laughed. "Don't plant any seeds in my mind that you will be sorry for later."

"I won't be sorry," she said, "because I have no intention of becoming a stunt woman." The elevator came to a halt and she started out the door.

He described his ideas for the next layout in detail while they waited for a taxi on the Avenue Gustave Eiffel. He seemed pleased at the opportunity of having an attentive audience, and as he talked, his eyes shone and he made animated gestures. "What I have in mind is the reconstruction of a murder. A crime of passion. It will be a photo essay of five or six pictures. In the first one I'll have a woman and her lover in bed. In the second picture, the husband arrives and they quarrel. Then she shoots him. The next-to-last picture will have him lying in a pool of blood and she'll be standing over him, smoke trailing from the barrel of her revolver. And in the last picture I'll have her back in the arms of her lover."

Hélène found herself laughing. The idea sounded contrived and absurd. It was a farce. "Those are supposed to be fashion pictures?" she asked incredulously.

He looked at her with such a hurt expression that the

laughter died in her throat. "Of course," he said seriously. "They'll be a sensation. Will you model for them?"

She thought for a moment. "On one condition."

"And that is?"

"That this 'crime' takes place on terra firma."

He grinned. "You have my word." He paused for a moment. "But I need to have your word, also."

She looked surprised. "What for?"

"You know that I'm on the staff of *Vogue*?"

She nodded.

"Well, the crime pictures will be for *L'Officiel*. Sometimes I moonlight as a free-lance photographer. *Vogue* winks at it as long as my credit doesn't appear with the pictures. Of course, everyone who knows my style can immediately pick up on who did them. Just don't advertise that I did the pictures."

"You can trust me," she said, fighting to keep her face serious. "I won't tell a soul."

By the time she came home from the atelier a week after the shooting, it was, as usual, a quarter to six. She closed the front door wearily, crossed to the telephone table, put her purse down, and began to pull off her gloves. She sniffled. She hoped she wasn't coming down with a cold. She started as the telephone began to ring. Quickly she reached down and picked up the receiver.

"Hélène? It's Jacques."

"Jacques," she said, "this is a surprise."

"Listen, I called to tell you that the proof sheets are printed. The photos turned out even better than I'd expected! You're naturally photogenic. Anyway, what do you say I pop over and show them to you?"

"Now?"

"Why not?"

"I appreciate your calling, Jacques, but I'm afraid I'm tied up tonight." That was the truth. The Comte was in town and he'd be spending the night. Just thinking about it made her grimace. She'd be up half the night. What she really wanted to do was crawl under the covers and sleep for thirteen or fourteen hours. Maybe then this cold would work out of her system.

"Christ," he mumbled with bitchy disappointment. "Well, I suppose there's plenty of time for you to see them." Then his voice took on a brighter tone. "Before I forget, what do you say we take the *L'Officiel* shots on Saturday?"

"So soon?"

"Sure. Don't forget, it takes months before the issues hit the stands. The sooner they're taken, the sooner you'll be a star."

She smiled. "Saturday it is. I'll call you on Friday to confirm?"

"Fine. Talk to you then," he said. " 'Bye."

She said good-bye, and when she heard the click at his end, she dropped the receiver back down on the cradle. At the same moment she noticed a letter propped up against the vase. She recognized the envelope immediately. It was from the Karl Häberle Agency. Her heart pounded as she snatched it up. The first thought that entered her mind was that Häberle had found Schmidt and the white-faced one.

She tore open the envelope, took out the letter, and unfolded it. The type was thick, black, and smudgy, as if the typewriter it had been pounded out on was a piece of antiquity. As she read, her excitement faded. It was nothing more than a progress report—a report of no progress at all.

Hélène balled up the paper angrily and tossed it into the wastebasket. What was it with Häberle? Did she have to pound him over the head for him to realize that she was dead serious? She would have time to draft a quick letter to him. The Comte wouldn't be here for another hour.

She went into the salon, sat down behind the leather-covered desk, and took a sheet of vellum from the box in the top drawer. She dipped the pen into the inkwell, hesitated for a moment, and then swiftly scrawled the reply:

Dear Herr Häberle,

I have received your letter. I think I have made it quite clear that no matter how long or expensive the task, I am totally dedicated to finding the men who have perpetrated such evil. I shall not rest until then. Please continue and let me know if there is any progress.

Sincerely,
Hélène Junot

She read it through, wrote out an envelope and affixed a stamp on it. Then she rang for the maid. When she came,

Hélène handed her the letter. "Marthe, post this immediately, please."

"Oui, mademoiselle." The maid gave a little curtsy and hurried back out.

Hélène rose to her feet and went upstairs. After taking a quick bath, she slipped into a rose-colored peignoir and went back downstairs to the salon. Efficiently she set about arranging things just the way the Comte liked them. It was Marthe's job, but she insisted on doing it herself. That was the way she knew things would be perfect. Not that Marthe couldn't be trusted. It was just that the Comte was fussy. He insisted that everything had to be just the way he wanted it. Eggs, three minutes to the dot. Bathwater, forty-one degrees. Drinking glasses, polished.

Finally everything was ready. The big ashtray and the humidor on the cocktail table, the soft lighting, the low mood music, the iced champagne.

She turned around as the door chimes tinkled. The Comte never rang. He had his own key. She shrugged her shoulders. Perhaps he had misplaced it. She could hear Marthe's footsteps in the hall.

"That's all right, Marthe." she called out. "I'll get it."

"Oui, mademoiselle." Marthe's footsteps immediately receded.

Hélène went out into the foyer. By reflex, she ran her hands over her hair and rearranged the front of her peignoir so that her breasts appeared to push up out of her décolletage. Then she pulled the door open.

Hubert de Léger was standing there, dressed in evening clothes. He didn't say a word. He simply pushed the door wide, staggered inside, and slammed it shut behind him.

She stared directly into his eyes, her pupils completely encircled with white edges. She sensed his drunkenness even before she smelled it.

Quickly she tried to block his way. "Hubert, please. This is not the time to visit," she said.

He began to laugh and pushed her aside. "I wanted to pay my respects," he said gruffly. "Besides, this house does belong to my family, in case you've forgotten."

"It belongs to your father," she corrected him in an icy tone.

He started toward the salon. "Speaking of my father, where is he? Upstairs asleep already?"

"Hubert!" she said sharply. "I won't have you talking about your father like that!"

He gave a low laugh. "You're one to talk! I suspect I'll get a lecture on virtue next. Ah. The salon is nice and cozy. We can have a little chat." He rubbed his hands together and crossed the Savonnerie to the sideboard, where he poured himself a slug of Armagnac. Then he walked toward the couch, picked an ice cube out of the champagne bucket, and tossed it into the glass. He looked down at the drink as he sloshed it around in the glass. "The Americans drink everything with ice," he mumbled. "I learned it from some of the students at the university. There are a lot of Americans there, you know?" He looked at her.

"I didn't know," she said quietly.

He tossed his head back and downed the drink in one big swallow. Then he grimaced and his eyes flicked around again. "*Very* cozy, yes." He nodded slowly. "A fire roaring in the grate. Mood music. Champagne . . ." He reached for the bottle and pulled it out of its nest of ice. "Dom Perignon. Good, good." He leered at her.

She felt the heat in his eyes and pulled the peignoir tighter around her. "Hurry up and finish your drink," she said. "Your father will be here at any moment."

He grinned. "You mean you're not going to sit with me?"

She sniffed. "No, I will not." She crossed over to the window, parted the curtains nervously, and looked out. Somehow she would have to get rid of Hubert before the Comte arrived. The question was how to do it without him making a scene,

He came up behind her and caught her arm and without any preamble said, "I want you." He spun her around, his hand pulling her toward him.

She struggled to push him away. "Leave me alone!" she hissed, breathing deeply. Her eyes flashed fire.

Suddenly he let go of her arm and stepped back. "My, aren't you the coy one," he said nastily. "I'll comfort myself with the idea that I don't take hand-me-downs." He went to pour himself another drink, and she watched him toss it down. Her contempt for him was growing stronger by the minute.

He slammed the glass down on the sideboard and looked at her for a long moment. "I'll let you off the hook. I'm leaving," he said sullenly.

She didn't answer, but a breath of relief escaped her lips. She followed him out into the foyer. When he reached the front door he turned around and looked back at her. "Just remember, I turned you down," he said pointedly in an ugly voice. "You've got the distinction of being the only whore in the city who's been rejected."

She could feel a searing blush rising up her face and looked away.

He flung open the door and then drew back. The Comte was standing outside, key in hand. Hubert stared at him for a moment, then regained his unseemly composure and grinned nastily. "Don't worry, *Father*. I didn't touch her." He gave a jerky shrug of his shoulders and glared at Hélène. "Funny how the French will cheat on their wives but insist that their whores remain faithful." Then he pushed past the Comte and stumbled down the steps.

The Comte stared impassively after his son. Then he came inside and closed the door quietly. He looked across at Hélène. "You shouldn't have let him in," he said softly.

"I didn't," she said, twisting her fingers in agitation. "The chimes rang and I thought it was you. When I opened the door, he pushed his way in."

"All right," the Comte said wearily. He followed her into the salon, shrugged off his coat, and threw it over the back of a chair. He looked thoughtfully down at his feet. "Sit down. I think it's time we had a little talk."

She stared at him. "I'm sorry that you don't believe me, Philippe. He really did push his way in."

"That's not what I wanted to talk to you about."

Hélène looked surprised. "Then what is it?"

"Sit down."

She was startled by his sharp command. Slowly she took a seat, folded her hands in her lap, and looked at him curiously. She had no idea what this was about. She knew that he had many business interests in Paris. But business problems or no, he shouldn't be taking them out on her.

Idly he paced the carpet. "I've always trusted you, haven't I?"

"Yes," she said cautiously.

Unexpectedly he took one hand out of his pocket and came up with a tangle of jewels. She recognized them instantly. They were the ones she had sold to Cheops. Almost

366

casually he dropped them down on the sideboard. "Then how do you explain this?"

Her face had suddenly gone pale. Her eyes were riveted on the incriminating jewels. That slimy Cheops had lied, she thought angrily. She had been a fool ever to trust him. All along, he must have been selling the jewels to the major dealers and not to transient tourists as he'd assured her. And these dealers kept careful records of every item they sold, and to whom. They must have contacted the Comte.

"I bought them back, but what I want to know is . . . why?"

She tore her eyes away from the jewels and looked at him. "I needed the money," she replied.

"What for?"

Suddenly she looked weary. "It's a long story, Philippe."

"Tell me. I have all night."

For a moment she sat in thoughtful silence; then she looked into his face and shook her head. Her vow to destroy those who had destroyed her family was something she had to do alone. It couldn't be shared with anyone, least of all him. She was only beginning to realize that her past was her weakness but that it was also her greatest strength. From it stemmed her ambition, her indomitable will to survive. It did not seem right to have to bare her vulnerability for him to see. "No," she said slowly. "It's something I don't want to discuss."

"All right, you leave me no choice," the Comte replied. "It is over. As soon as possible, I want you to find another place to live."

"So it's over," Hélène said softly. "Just like that."

He smiled grimly. "I demand total honesty from everyone I deal with. I feel I can no longer trust you."

Hélène made a thoughtful face and nodded slowly. "All right," she said slowly, rising to her feet. "I shall go upstairs and pack my things immediately. It will take me half an hour. Then I shall call a taxi and go to a hotel."

"Don't forget these. They're yours." He picked up the jewels and threw them at her. Some of them hit her, others scattered on the carpet around her feet. She stared stoically first at him, then down at them. On principle, she started to turn around and walk away. But she was a practical woman. You've earned those jewels, a little voice inside her asserted. You've been at his beck and call for over a year now. You let him own you. You've even carried his baby and let it be torn out of your womb. Because of it, you'll never be able to bear children again. If you've ever worked for anything, you've worked for these. As if in slow motion, she fell to her knees and began picking them up. When she reached for the last earring, she lifted her eyes. The Comte was watching her. She got to her feet, drew herself up with dignity, and went upstairs to pack.

The next day she took all the jewels to Van Cleef and Arpels, where she sold them for an excellent price. She deposited the check in her savings account and then found a small apartment on the highly respectable rue Paul Valery, just off the Avenue Foch.

4

A week later, Jacques was set to shoot the photos for *L'Officiel*. He had borrowed an apartment on the Avenue Foch to use as a location. Besides Hélène, there were two men dressed in custom-tailored tuxedos that were clearly British. Even the French, world-renowned geniuses when it came to designing women's clothing, had to acknowledge that when it came to men's garments, the English were without peer. One of the men would pose as Hélène's lover, the other as her husband.

Hélène came out of the study which they used as a dressing room and stopped in the doorway of the salon. Jacques was sitting in an armchair; her "lover" and her "husband" were forced to stand so that they wouldn't wrinkle their tuxedos. They stared at her. She wore the latest gown from Odile Joly. It had a strapless top that encased her breasts, a narrow, form-fitting skirt that went to the calf, and was entirely encrusted with sequins and colored rhinestones shimmering in the intricate swirls of an arabesque.

Jacques got to his feet slowly and motioned for Hélène to come closer. When she was in the center of the room, he gestured for her to stop. She stood there silently, watching him. His face was expressionless. Then he walked around her in circles. Finally he stopped, frowned, and put his hand on his chin. "It's a beautiful gown," he admitted slowly.

She tilted her head forward and looked down at herself. It was one of the most exquisite creations anyone could ever have imagined. Costly, too. A house in the suburbs carried the same price tag as these few meters of fabric.

"Odile Joly calls this a gown fit for a Persian princess," she said, frowning, and slowly walking over to the pier glass between the two tall windows. She watched herself critically. Each time she moved, her body flashed with brilliance. It was as if a million gems were glued right onto her body. She turned around. "You don't like it." It was a statement.

"Go and take it off," Jacques told her. "You look like a samuri warrior. Then we'll put on our thinking caps and see how we can remedy this situation."

Hélène was disappointed, but it was obvious that Jacques had made up his mind. She shrugged her shoulders and obediently returned to the study. She let the dresser undo the back of the gown and wearily stepped out of it. She pulled on a white silk robe, tied the sash around the wrist, and went back out to the salon.

Jacques looked at her and nodded. "That's much more becoming."

"You're not going to take her picture in *that!*" one of the male models squeaked incredulously.

Suddenly Jacques snapped his fingers excitedly. "That's it! Why didn't I think of it before!" His face broke into a smile. Casually he sat back, then stretched out his legs and clasped his hands behind his head.

Hélène placed her hands on her hips. "Well?" she demanded imperiously.

"We'll do the unheard-of," Jacques said. "Instead of dressing *you*, we'll dress them. It'll be a new angle. You know, the way women would like their men to dress. We'll get them a few more tuxedos. A different one for each picture, but similar enough so they won't detract from the overall theme."

Hélène stared at him for a moment, then paced the room. "What do I tell Odile Joly?" she wailed. "She did me a personal favor by getting that gown out in time for the photos!"

369

Jacques grinned. "Tell her anything, but make sure it's diplomatic. Now, what are you doing tonight?"

Hélène sniffed. "What I do tonight is my business."

"Well said, but my intentions are honorable. I have a party to attend, and I want you to come with me."

The house was seventeenth-century, Hélène thought, and most of the guests could probably trace their lineage much farther back than that. There were ambassadors, film stars, politicians, industrialists, artists, and financiers. The guests spilled from the foyer and the salon into the music and sun rooms.

"Jacques," an elegant middle-aged woman with angular cheekbones said as they politely pushed their way through the throng clustered in the foyer.

Jacques stopped and smiled at her. She lifted her bony, jewel-studded hand grandly and he bent over and kissed it gallantly.

"You've been hiding, you naughty boy," she said with a reproachful pout.

He smiled. "May I introduce my newest model, Hélène Junot? Hélène, our gracious hostess, the Vicomtesse de Sévigné."

"How do you do?" Hélène said politely. She stared at the woman in fascination. She had read of the de Sévignés in all the society columns. They were among the richest people in France. The reclusive old Vicomte was a financier; the Vicomtesse was a partygoer, a party-giver, and the owner of a chic costume-jewelry boutique. She was also an interior designer, for friends; a hairdresser, her own; and a couturière of sorts, by insisting that the designers of the hallowed houses alter their great creations to her own specifications. They obliged, but only because they recognized the Vicomtesse's innate good taste.

"Jacques is a terribly talented young man," the Vicomtesse said to Hélène. "His photographs are works of art. And he is so handsome. He could sweep half the women in Paris off their feet." She sipped her champagne delicately.

"Unfortunately, he prefers to go to the pissoirs to pick up his bed partners," a slurry male voice said from behind.

The Vicomtesse paled beneath her carefully applied makeup. Abruptly the conversation around them ground to a stop. People began to stare; a few started to move away in embarrassment. A deep flush rose up Jacques's face and the Vicomtesse and Hélène turned around slowly. Hubert de Léger was smiling innocently at them.

Hélène felt sick with disgust. She couldn't believe that Hubert was here. Even worse, that he had just said what he had, and so loudly.

"Did I say something wrong?" Hubert asked in a charming voice.

"You bastard," Jacques said quietly. "One of these days I'll knock your filthy teeth out." He clenched his fists threateningly.

Quickly Hélène grabbed his wrists and restrained him.

"Fancy a cream puff being so brave," Hubert said with a faint smile. He turned to the Vicomtesse and gave a little shrug. "I suppose if one invites so many people, one pervert will be bound to slip in. You are forgiven, madame."

Without answering, the Vicomtesse swiftly hooked one arm through Hélène's, the other through Jacques's. "I think we should pay our respects to the guest of honor," she said quickly. "Come."

As she marched them across the salon, she apologized for Hubert's behavior. "He is worse than a peasant," she said derisively. The words were bitter, but Hélène noticed that a careful smile masked her face. Anyone looking at her would have thought that she was chatting amiably.

Halfway across the room, the Vicomtesse drew to a halt. "Ah, here is our guest of honor." She extricated herself elegantly from their arms and gently pulled an old white-haired man out of a crowd of people. "Stanislaw, chéri," she said, kissing him on the cheek.

Hélène stared at the old man. She had seen the world-famous pianist once before. It had been at the opera. While she and the Comte had been in the box, Stanislaw Kowalsky had been sitting in the front row.

The Vicomtesse made a sweeping gesture. "Stanislaw, I would like you to meet two of my friends. Hélène Junot and Jacques Renault."

The old man smiled pleasantly and bowed to both of them. "I am enchanted to meet you, mademoiselle," he said to Hélène. He took her hand and kissed it, his breath barely brushing her flesh.

Hélène was speechless. He looks so small and shrunken, she thought. Strange, that such a little man could take the

371

world by storm. She couldn't help noticing that his arms were long, his fingers slender, flat, and elongated, the small pink fingernails clipped down to the quick. But in his own way he was impressive-looking; even the unruly tufts of white hair on his head were worn like a regal crown. His eyebrows were gray and bushy; his dark eyes beneath them twinkled with merriment.

The Vicomtesse smiled. "Mademoiselle Junot is a model. She has just done a spread for *Vogue*. Monsieur Renault took the pictures."

The old man smiled. "I am certain they will turn out to be fine pictures. With a model so lovely, who could fail to take a beautiful picture? Unless, of course, Monsieur Renault forgot to put film in the camera."

"I hope not." Hélène laughed. "He had me hanging off the second platform of the Eiffel Tower."

"Jacques!" The Vicomtesse looked horrified. "Haven't you learned enough from that Notre Dame incident!" Mystified, the Vicomtesse looked at Hélène and shook her head. "I don't know how you did it. You must be very brave. Myself, I find it difficult even to climb a flight of stairs. I'm afraid I'm a terrible coward."

"Hardly, my dear," Kowalsky said to the Vicomtesse. "You are the bravest woman I have ever met."

"Please," she protested.

He held up a liver-spotted hand to silence her. "During the war, she hid thirteen downed American fliers and two Jewish families in her château. And imagine—at the same time, the Nazis occupied another wing of the same building! She hid us right under their noses for three whole years!"

"She hid *you?*" Hélène asked in surprise.

"My family and another. She is very brave, non?"

Hélène looked at the Vicomtesse with new respect. She seemed so frail and delicate, hardly the stuff of which heroes were made. But the eyes told otherwise. If you looked deep into them you could tell that they were eyes that had lived. They were unwavering, strong, and filled with character. Still, it took courage for a woman of such social standing and wealth to put her life on the line for others. She had so much to lose.

"But what about the piano?" Hélène asked Kowalsky. "I've heard that pianists have to practice for hours every day. You must have had to start over from scratch after the war."

The old man smiled. "No, I played throughout the three years. But I played for ghosts. You see, the Vicomtesse was good enough to dismantle the keyboard of the Bechstein in her salon. She brought it to me during the middle of the night, and I was able to practice and play without anyone being able to hear it."

"It was such a pity," the Vicomtesse said. "Just think! I had the world's finest concert pianist under my roof and I wasn't able to hear a single note that he was playing! Sometimes I think it was crueler to me than anyone else, I love his music so."

Hélène nodded. She smiled gently at Kowalsky. "It must have been sad for you, too, not to be able to hear what you were playing."

He smiled. "Ah, but you see, I *did* hear it. I could imagine the sound of every note. Don't forget, Beethoven composed music when he was deaf. I think I could play even if I were. To lose one's hearing is bad, but to lose one's faculties is disastrous. Thank God, I still have them."

"Come, come. Let us not be so maudlin. This is a party," the Vicomtesse chided them. "What would people think if all we did was to discuss such weighty subjects?"

Kowalsky nodded. "Of course." Then his eyes glittered. "Is your piano tuned?"

The Vicomtesse drew a deep breath. She looked at him with surprise to see if he was serious. "Really, Stanislaw, there's no need . . ."

He patted her hand. "I would love to play a few pieces."

She was delighted. Hubert's outburst had nearly ruined the party. Having Stanislaw Kowalsky play would not only overshadow that but also make her the hostess of the season. "You really don't have to, you know," she said without meaning it.

"And that is why I shall," Kowalsky said. "For you, I would do anything."

The Vicomtesse clapped her hands. Immediately the room fell silent. All eyes were on her.

"As you know, Monsieur Kowalsky is our guest of honor," she announced in a clear, melodious voice. "I don't need to tell you that his charity concert at the opéra tomorrow has been sold out since two months ago. But tonight he has decided to honor *us*." She paused dramatically. "If you will follow us to the music room . . ."

An excited murmur rose from the guests. Kowalsky bowed to the Vicomtesse and Hélène. "Could I have the pleasure of being escorted to the music room by both of you?"

"We'd be delighted," the Vicomtesse said without hesitation.

Hélène turned to flash Jacques an apologetic look as Kowalsky hooked one arm through hers, the other through the Vicomtesse's. Then they led the crowd into the big, high-ceilinged music room overlooking La Cité and the floodlit rump of the cathedral. Quietly the guests pressed around the big grand piano as Kowalsky took his seat on the bench. He smiled at Hélène, stretched out his arms as if to push back his cuffs, carefully poised his hands above the keyboard, and then brought them crashing down in Chopin's "Ballade in G Minor." The resonant beginning notes gave way to a light airiness, the tune wafting effortlessly from the piano, always the clear, sweetly melodious notes mingling with the richness of the lower ones.

Hélène watched in fascination as his fingers flew effortlessly up and down the keyboard, sometimes slowing deliberately, then skipping quickly across the keys again. Behind the piano he seemed so big, so lively, so much in command. He was like a lion tamer and the piano was his lion. For him, it performed to perfection. The music swirled and flew and quickened until it reached the last deep chords. He didn't stop there. Immediately he moved into a piece by Schubert.

The guests listened intently, but none with as much rapture as Hélène. The beautiful notes climbed and fell and swirled and danced around her, finally working up to a crescendo.

For a moment the guests stood in stunned silence. Then they forgot where they were and burst into wild applause.

Kowalsky smiled and gave a little bow of his head. Then he began playing Debussy's "Serenade for the Doll." As he played, he smiled up at Hélène. She stood there mesmerized, her breath caught in her throat, her arms breaking out in gooseflesh. She had never known music to do this to her, not at the opéra or at the ballet. It was as if he were playing to her alone. When he finished the piece, he rose to his feet. The applause was like thunder. He made a courtly bow and took the Vicomtesse's hand.

"How can I ever thank you for this precious gift, Stanislaw?" she asked softly.

"Please," he said politely. "The pleasure was entirely

mine." He gave a little smile. "I think I am a bit tired. I have the concert tomorrow and I'm afraid I shall need my rest. You will excuse me?"

The Vicomtesse smiled graciously. "Of course, Stanislaw. And thank you again for the recital. My guests will be talking about it for years to come."

"I am always only too happy to accommodate you," he said gallantly. Then he turned to Hélène. "It has been a pleasure meeting you, mademoiselle."

Hélène smiled. "Not as much as mine."

"Would it be forward of me to ask you to attend my performance tomorrow? As my guest, of course."

"But . . . I thought it was sold out."

"A seat shall be found for you."

Hélène smiled at him. "I would be honored."

Once again he bowed formally. "Good night."

The Vicomtesse watched him leave. "He is such a kind man," she said softly. "I wish he did not feel so indebted to me."

"He plays beautifully!" Hélène said. "It was magic."

The Vicomtesse allowed herself a smile. "He always plays beautifully. But the 'Serenade for the Doll'? It was plain as day. He was playing that to you."

Hélène found herself blushing and turned away.

The Vicomtesse touched her arm gently. "Stanislaw is an old man," she said wisely. "He is old because of his years. But inside, he is a youth trapped in a frail body. He is seventy-two, would you believe?"

Hélène shook her head. "He certainly doesn't act it."

The Vicomtesse smiled. "He has a son and a daughter, both much older than you. They have lived in America since after the war."

"Did you hide them, also?" Hélène asked.

The Vicomtesse had a faraway look in her eyes. "Yes, but unfortunately the war drew them apart. Being cramped together in a tiny attic room for so long was not good for them. They grew to hate each other."

Hélène nodded. "You have been a good friend to him," she said softly. "I can see how much he appreciates it."

"He 'appreciates' you, also," the Vicomtesse said suddenly.

"Me? What do you mean?"

"Can't you tell? He's in love with you."

"No." Hélène looked at the Vicomtesse to see if she was

serious. The dark eyes and elegant lips held an expression of truth. "But . . . he doesn't even know me!" Hélène stuttered.

"He knows you better than you think," the Vicomtesse said. "Stanislaw has good instincts when it comes to people. Besides, the last time he played the 'Serenade to the Doll' was when he met his late wife."

Hélène shook her head and looked away. She did not know what to say. The Vicomtesse's revelation dumbfounded her. But it went deeper than that. Even if Stanislaw Kowalsky had fallen for her, he wouldn't want her. Not only was she too young for him but also there was her past to consider. Her miserable tenure with the Comte.

But she was wrong. After the concert, Stanislaw listened to her story quietly over a simple peasant dinner in a Hungarian restaurant and then smiled. He reached across the checkered tablecloth and covered her hand. "We have all done things we are not proud of," he said simply. "Sometimes we did not have much choice."

"But don't you see? I did!" Hélène told him vehemently. "I knew exactly what I was doing!"

But it did not matter to him. Three weeks later, he asked her to marry him.

For the first time in months, Hubert felt really good. He hadn't realized what a bad turn his life had taken until he'd smashed up Le Bon Coin, a little bistro near the university. Almost before the gendarmes threw him in jail, the family's slippery lawyer, Maurice Hugo, had everything under control. Before the night was out, the proprietor of the bistro had received three envelopes containing money. One for damages incurred during the brawl, one for the loss of customers during the necessary renovation, and one because he was a forgiving man of the world and could surely see that there had been a mistake, that there hadn't been a melee, merely a boisterous celebration. A fourth envelope had ended up in the hands of the gendarmes. Like magic, Hubert de Léger's name disappeared from the police files.

Any harm this incident might have produced had been quickly averted, but the Comte's face had been white with anger. Hubert's behavior had cost a great deal of money, but more important, a family branching out into politics and diplomacy did not need the black mark of a barroom brawl against it. It was not enough to just sweep such an incident under the rug. There would perhaps be another one, and then another. Somewhere along the line, one of them could spark off a major scandal and cause irreparable damage to the de Léger name. The Comte realized that his son was, in effect, a walking time bomb. The cure was not to whitewash the harm caused by his disastrous behavior, but to wipe out the cause of it. Hubert needed to be dried out and get professional counseling. Without hesitation, the Comte had him signed into an exclusive clinique near Deauville that specialized in treating alcoholism and its related emotional problems.

At first, it had been hell for Hubert. He was moody and struck out at anyone and anything. He battled constantly with the doctors and nurses, and started fights with fellow patients. Once he managed to run away and was picked up at a local bar, hardly able to stand, and taken back to the clinique. It was there, while he was drying out for the second time, that he saw the picture in *Ici Paris*. Hélène's familiar face was smiling reluctantly into the camera, and beside her was a withered old man. Hubert had to reread the headline five times before he could begin to believe it: "WORLD-FAMOUS PIANIST TO WED FASHION MODEL."

At that moment, Hubert knew what he had to do. He wouldn't say a word to anyone. He would fool the doctors with his best behavior. Then maybe they would release him from this prison in record time. He hoped that it wouldn't be too late to stop this revolting marriage from taking place. If it was, he'd just have to find a way to break it up.

His lips curled into a tight smile. At least he now knew where to find her.

Hélène looked up at the train as it labored slowly into the Gare Montparnasse. Most of the windows were down and the passengers were leaning out with expressions of expectancy. She recognized Jeanne and Edmond immediately. They were in the fourth coach from the front. Her face broke into a smile and she began waving her hand. Suddenly Jeanne caught sight of her and nudged Edmond. They waved back excitedly. Hélène hurried along the platform beside the second-class coach until the train hissed and jolted to a stop.

As soon as they stepped off the train, she flew toward them and threw herself into their arms. "I'm so happy to see you!" she cried, her voice husky with emotion.

Their embrace was long and emotional. For a moment,

none of them said anything more. They were content just to hold each other. Edmond gently stroked her hair.

Hélène looked at Jeanne. She hadn't changed much. Still the mousy hair and pale skin, the soulful but strong dark eyes, the sturdy provincial clothes. But Edmond had changed; she could see that right away. Somehow he looked thinner, and there were tight lines of tension around his mouth. He must be working himself hard, she thought. He had three mouths to feed. Suddenly she felt a tinge of guilt. Things were not going nearly as well for them as Jeanne had written. They were probably struggling to make ends meet in Saint-Nazaire while she was living it up in Paris.

"Hey, how's my Little French Girl?" he asked softly.

She burrowed her head in his chest. "How's my big brother?" Her voice sounded muffled.

He shrugged. "Getting old, I guess." He pulled her away and studied her. "You're looking good."

She smiled, stood on tiptoe, and kissed his cheek. "Maybe it's because life is finally agreeing with me."

"I'm glad to hear that."

Hélène turned to Jeanne and held both her hands. "Good, sweet Jeanne. You haven't changed a bit."

Jeanne laughed. "You should have seen me when I was pregnant. You would have thought I was carrying a whale!"

"How *is* Petite Hélène?"

"It's too bad we couldn't bring her along, but she's being well taken care of," Jeanne said as Edmond picked up the battered suitcase and began to lug it toward the exit.

"I can't wait to meet her," Hélène said with a smile. "When you write, I read the letters over and over. I've kept each one. They cheer me up to no end." Then her voice was serious. "How is Madame Dupré? I sent her an invitation but she wrote that she is ill and couldn't come."

Jeanne nodded. "She's been feeling bad for quite some time now. I'm not sure what's wrong with her, because she won't talk about it. But she doesn't look well."

"I hope it's nothing serious," Hélène said in a worried voice.

When they were out on the Boulevard de Vaugirard, Hélène signaled for a taxi.

"Why don't we take a bus or the métro?" Edmond suggested. "Taxis are so expensive."

Hélène allowed herself a laugh and shook his arm. "Don't

worry about money," she said lightly. "I'm about to become a very rich woman." She gestured at the taxi. "Hop in."

Jeanne exchanged glances with Edmond. He nodded imperceptibly and she climbed stiffly into the cab. Hélène climbed in after her and Edmond sat up front next to the driver. The driver looked at him questioningly. "Where to?" he grunted.

"The Georges V," Hélène said.

"Oui, mademoiselle." The driver sounded impressed. He put the car in gear and they swung out into the traffic. Edmond kept staring out through the windshield, his eyes thoughtful.

"It looks so different," he said, twisting around to look at Hélène. "There are so many people, so much traffic. All I've remembered were empty streets, vélo-taxis, and wood-burning trucks."

Hélène smiled at him. "Funny that you should say that. I'll never forget the day I first arrived. I thought exactly the same thing."

He turned back around to gaze out the windshield some more.

Jeanne took Hélène's hand and shook it excitedly. "Tell me about your fiancé." She gave a lively little shrug. "Is he handsome?"

Hélène smiled slowly. "No, but he is beautiful. I wrote to you that he is a pianist."

Jeanne nodded. "And that can make a man rich?" she asked.

Hélène nodded. "He performs all around the world. He has played for General de Gaulle and Queen Elizabeth."

Jeanne shook her head in wonder. "He sounds very important."

"He *is* important." Hélène turned to look out the window for a moment. Much as she hated to, she would have to warn them that Stanislaw was not a young man. Otherwise, when they met him, their shock might be too evident. But she wouldn't tell them here in the taxi. It could wait until they got to the hotel.

Jeanne looked wide-eyed around the suite. "This hotel must be very expensive," she said. "Did you see the lobby? And the way the clerk looked at us? It's our clothes, Hélène. Don't you think it would be better if we went to another hotel? One more suitable to . . . to our station? We're not elegant like you."

"Nonsense," Hélène said firmly. "A little luxury never hurt anybody. Believe me, you'll get used to it very quickly. You are going to stay here, and tomorrow I will take you shopping."

Edmond paced the big room, his hands in his pockets. He looked thoughtfully down at the thick carpet. Then he squashed his cigarette out in an ashtray. He came over to Hélène, put his hands on her shoulders, and held her at arm's length. His voice was flat. "You don't have to go through all this trouble and expense for us, Little French Girl. We're not used to living like this."

She met his eyes evenly. "Please, Edmond. Let me do things my way. I'm going to become the wife of a very prominent man. This is the way we will have to live."

"Madame Dupré said you lived in a house. Can't we stay there?"

"No," Hélène said quickly. "I don't live there anymore."

"Where do you live?" Jeanne asked curiously.

Hélène smiled. "I had an apartment, but I've just given it up. For the past few days I've lived here, in the hotel. After the wedding, I'll move in with Stanislaw. He has a house."

Edmond smiled good-naturedly. "All right," he said. "We'll be good relatives. We'll do as we're told and try not to embarrass you."

Hélène looked at him gratefully. "I . . . I have to tell you something," she said.

"I'm listening."

Nervously she clasped her hands in front of her and began to pace the room. "I want you to know that I love Stanislaw. Maybe you won't be able to understand that. It's not like the love you both share. That's something I can only hope for, but I don't think it will ever happen to me."

Jeanne looked confused. "What do you mean? Maybe if you . . ."

Hélène shook her head. "Please," she said. She looked out the window at the traffic down on the Avenue Georges V. "Let me finish. You see, Stanislaw and I respect each other. We'll be good for each other. Don't ask me to explain. I just know it."

"Why don't you just let us meet him?" Edmond said straightforwardly. "We can form our own opinion."

Swiftly she turned around to face him. Her voice was guarded. "I just want you to know something before you meet him. You see, you'll think that we can't possibly have anything in common. I just wanted to tell you that we *do*."

Jeanne and Edmond exchanged glances. Finally Jeanne came toward her and put an arm around her shoulder. "What is it?" she asked softly. "What's worrying you?"

Hélène's face was impassive. "Your reactions. You see, Stanislaw is not a young man."

Jeanne smiled and tried to put Hélène at ease. "It's not like you're marrying your grandfather!" she joked.

Hélène paled and threw Jeanne's arm off her shoulder. Her face was agonized. "Yes, it is. You see, Stanislaw is seventy-two years old."

Hélène read through the telegram and sank slowly down onto the edge of the bed. For a moment she just sat there shocked. It can't be true, she thought dully. There must be a mistake. Slowly she read the concise message again. There was no mistake.

REGRET TO INFORM YOU MADELEINE DUPRE DIED OF CANCER AT NANTES HOSPITAL THIS MORNING.

There was a quick knock on the door. Hélène didn't look up. "Yes?" she said weakly.

The door opened and Jeanne sailed into the room. "You're not even dressed yet!" she scolded. "We're due at the chapel in half an hour!" She smiled. "Hey, you're not nervous, are you? Edmond and I both think that Stanislaw is a fine man."

Hélène wiped her eyes and looked up at Jeanne. "No, I'm not nervous," she said in a small voice.

"Then what is it?"

Wordlessly Hélène handed her the telegram. Jeanne read it through and paled. "How terrible! Who would have thought that Madame Dupré had cancer?"

Hélène sniffed. "She died on the day I'm getting married." She thought for a moment and looked at Jeanne. "She was . . . my savior. I think I should postpone the wedding."

Jeanne sat down beside Hélène. "No," she said firmly. "She wouldn't want that. Otherwise she would have let us know what was wrong. She was brave, can't you see that? She didn't want you to worry."

Hélène sighed and reached for a handkerchief. "I suppose you're right, but all the same . . ."

Jeanne patted her on the back. "Come on, dry your eyes and get dressed. I'm responsible for getting you to the chapel on time."

5

The white clifftop villa Stanislaw had taken on Cap Ferrat for their honeymoon was magnificent. Palladian in style, it consisted of a two-story fifteen-room main house and a connecting six-car garage. The roofs were terra-cotta tiles and all the windows were elegant glass arches. Tucked away among a Mediterranean forest of dark cypresses, umbrella pines, and overgrown hedges, it looked like a castle in the midst of a jungle. But that was only from the road. Within, it was a whole different story. Planted like a garden, the entire estate consisted of formal rose beds, expertly pruned topiary, and oleander-filled urns. It even boasted a climatically controlled greenhouse for orchids.

In addition, there was an enormous pool pavilion set a hundred meters back from the house. Like the villa, the pavilion was Palladian. Outside it, terra-cotta greyhounds sat gracefully in niches built into the walls. Inside, it had a generously scaled living room decorated with detailed moldings and sleek dark wicker furniture,

The pool, poised near the edge of the cliff, was enormous, with rounded edges and a water fountain at each end. Its clever design presented the viewer with an optical illusion: surrounded by a raised marble coping on all sides except for the seaside, it appeared far calmer than the sea below but seemed to be a part of it.

Between the pool and the pavilion stood a relic of antiquity, a giant marble head of Apollo. From his pedestal he gazed out to the distant cliffs at the other side of the bay.

The house came with a staff of five. There were the

Gaudets—a housekeeper/gardener couple—two maids, and a cook.

Madame Gaudet welcomed Hélène and Stanislaw when they arrived. She was a stern elderly Breton dressed in somber gray and white. Hélène immediately got the impression that she ruled the house with an iron hand. The first thing Madame Gaudet did was to show them around. Throughout the tour Hélène was busy making mental notes.

She grasped the layout of the house immediately. There were two identical hallways on both floors. These were located off one central circular staircase that divided the house into symmetrical halves. The staircase was located under a large frescoed rotunda.

The public rooms were on the ground floor. One look told Hélène that the living room was perfectly suited for Stanislaw. It had two huge black Bechstein grand pianos and plenty of shelf space for his music library and recording equipment. The tall, arched French doors opened out to both the front and back gardens. No matter how hot it got, the room would always remain cool and comfortable. It had good cross ventilation and would catch the breezes coming in off the sea. Like sentinels, rows of potted palms were lined up between the doors.

The room next to it was the formal dining room—huge, marble-floored, and liberally hung with crystal chandeliers. The table would seat thirty. Fine for a banquet, Hélène decided, but hopeless for an intimate dinner for two. Depending on the weather, they would take their meals either in the greenhouselike breakfast room or out on the terrace.

All the bedrooms were on the top floor. Hélène noticed at once that their luggage had already been brought upstairs and deposited in their rooms, the suitcases serving as discreet announcements of who would sleep where. She wondered whether it was Stanislaw or Madame Gaudet who had been responsible for that. Or was it that rich people slept in separate bedrooms?

The bedroom staked out with Stanislaw's suitcase, to the left of the rotunda, was cool beige decorated with overstuffed suede furniture. French doors led to a large balustraded balcony overlooking the pool pavilion and the sea and cliffs beyond.

Hélène's suitcases were in an even more luxurious bedroom directly across the hall. It was the biggest bedroom she had ever been in, and it was entirely pink. The walls were covered in pink silk and the carpeting underfoot was thick and soft and pink. The enormous bed was canopied with miles of pink silk, and so was the silk-skirted vanity. A crystal chandelier gleamed overhead, and there were two down-filled pink couches with matching armchairs.

Hélène walked over to the windows. The curtains were pink, and even the view of the front garden was—what else could she have expected? she asked herself—pink: a massive round bed of roses in bloom. Vases of these same roses stood on the nightstands that flanked the bed.

Madame Gaudet threw open four white doors set in the pink walls. Hélène inspected them. Three opened into walk-in closets, the fourth into a pink marble bathroom. It was the most lavish bathroom Hélène had ever seen.

Overcome, she sank down into one of the pink sofas.

"Like it?" Stanislaw asked eagerly.

Hélène sighed and nodded. He wanted so desperately to please her.

She got to her feet and signaled for Madame Gaudet to leave. The housekeeper nodded and silently left the room. When the door closed behind her, Hélène stepped toward Stanislaw. "Separate bedrooms?" she asked gently.

He looked away. "I thought you'd want that."

She reached up, touched his chin, and turned his face toward hers. "I want us to share the same bedroom," she said softly. "I want to sleep with you."

"I am an old man," he whispered uncomfortably. "I . . . I no longer need to . . ." He made a quick gesture with his hands. "To do that."

Hélène looked deep into his eyes. "Why do you think I married you?" she asked. "I want to be your wife in every way."

"But I am old."

"That doesn't matter. You are my husband."

Tears welled up in his eyes. "My dear Hélène," he whispered, "you are a good woman. I do not deserve you." Gently he squeezed her hand. Her skin felt soft and young between his old, wrinkled fingers. It made him feel the difference in their ages and it saddened him.

Hélène disengaged herself from him, reached down, picked up her suitcases, and marched across the hall with them. He followed her. One of the uniformed maids was already in his bedroom unpacking his luggage. She gave a curtsy.

Hélène shook her head. "No, thank you," she told the maid. "I prefer to do it myself."

"Very well, madame."

When the maid had gone and Hélène was in the middle of unpacking, she said suddenly, "Stanislaw, what do you say we give the servants an extended paid vacation? I want you all to myself. Let's just be us two here. Alone. On a *real* honeymoon."

He thought about it for a moment. Unpacking suitcases was one thing; running a fifteen-room villa without help was another. "It's a big house," he said at last. "And the grounds are tremendous. Are you certain you can handle it?"

She smiled with eagerness. "The weeds may grow and dust may collect on the chandeliers, but I want to give it a try. Please."

He shook his head. He wondered if he would ever get to understand her; every other woman he had ever known could not be pampered enough.

He took her in his arms and looked into her eyes. They caught the light coming in through the French doors and shone like polished amethysts. She wanted so much to please, he thought. And those eyes—how could he refuse those eyes anything? Well, if taking care of him was what she wanted, then that's what she would get. He smiled. "Tell them to take a vacation."

She stood on tiptoe and gave him a quick kiss on the cheek. Then, like a delighted child who had been given a toy, she was off to dismiss the staff.

An hour later they watched from the living room as the staff piled into two black taxis. The maids were chattering happily, but Madame Gaudet gave one last disapproving look toward the house. This was her domain, her stern eyes seemed to say. God only knew what condition the place would be in when she returned.

As the cars disappeared around the circular drive, Hélène looked at Stanislaw and let out a breath of relief. "Now I finally feel like I'm at home."

He laughed. "Me, too. I'm glad they're gone. To tell you the truth, there was too much help buzzing around all over the place. I would never have been able to concentrate on my music."

Her eyes flashed mischievously. "Today *I* won't let you concentrate on it," she said. "In another few hours it will be dark. In the meantime, I'll go prepare us a light supper. Then we'll drink champagne. And afterward . . ."

Hélène tugged gently at Stanislaw's hand as she led him through the garden to the pool pavilion. Both of them had changed to belted bathrobes. The temperature had dropped and the wind had picked up. The air was scented with roses, oleanders, and pine. In the pavilion niches, the greyhounds were in deep shadow.

Holding hands, they stood wordlessly by the edge of the pool, watching as the sun set. The water fountains were turned off and silent, and the sky overhead was red and orange as the sun dropped down the burnished horizon like a blazing fireball. Far below, a lone sailboat raced across the bay.

Hélène slowly released Stanislaw's hand. She untied her robe, letting it fall around her ankles. She was completely nude, her firm breasts silhouetted against the sky. Proudly she threw back her shoulders and felt the wind rushing against her nakedness. A strange new strength coursed through her.

Stanislaw stared at her. She could hear him breathing heavily as she undid his robe. The champagne had done its bit. It had softened the edge of his inhibitions.

She took a deep breath. In the sunset his naked body did not look old at all. In fact, it glowed with vitality, and even his snow-white hair seemed golden blond.

She reached out to touch him. There was a look of anguish in his eyes. "I . . . I don't know if I still can," he said quietly.

Intuitively she understood. He was afraid. Afraid of being rejected; afraid of being humilated. And above all, afraid of not being able to function as a man any longer.

She looked deep into his eyes. "Sssssh," she whispered solemnly. She reached up and strummed a gentle finger across his lips. "Don't say a word, my husband. Don't say anything."

Tenderly she began to run her fingertips across his back. He began to tremble. Without looking, she could sense the beginnings of passion rise up within him. Now was the moment, she knew.

6

The weeks on Cap Ferrat flew. Hélène learned a great deal about Stanislaw, and he about her. At first they were slightly nervous, but realized that this was only natural and accepted it. For a while their politeness to each other verged on awkwardness, but slowly they dropped their guard and began to enjoy each other's company.

Hélène found herself slipping quickly and easily into Stanislaw's life-style and routine. Since he rose late in the mornings, so did she. But she would wake up first and hurry downstairs to prepare him a light breakfast. Then she would run outside, cut the most perfect rose she could find, stick it into a bud vase, arrange everything on a linen-draped wooden tray, and serve him breakfast in bed. It was several weeks before she realized the truth: all along, he had been awake long before her. But he enjoyed both his breakfasts in bed and the pleasure she got from preparing them so much that he pretended sleep. When she discovered this, she served him breakfast in bed every morning whether he was asleep or not.

After getting out of bed, Stanislaw would quickly shower, dress, and go downstairs. Immediately he would sit at one of the Bechsteins and begin practicing scales and études. This would continue into the afternoon. She spent this time shopping in the Vieux Village or in Beaulieu, going to the Ile de France Museum, walking along the promenade Maurice-Rouvier and enjoying the beautiful view of the coast, or just simply working in the garden.

Every afternoon she made a lunch of fruit and salads. They ate outside on the terrace while watching the sailboats tacking into the wind in the bay below. Then he would take a nap in the pool pavilion and she would sunbathe on a chaise or swim in the pool. Sometimes she tired of the tranquil water and had a reckless craving for the sea. Then she would go to the edge of the cliff and descend the seventy-six steps carved out of the rock to the shingle beach twenty meters below. She loved swimming in the cold and powerful sea.

After an hour and a half, Stanislaw would wake up and go back inside the house to play his piano. At this time Hélène would stay close to the house so that she could enjoy the music that wafted out through the open French doors. Her favorite piece was no longer the "Serenade for the Doll," but Chopin's Mazurka in C-sharp Minor ("Opus thirty, number four," Stanislaw told her later). And when he found out that it was her favorite, he made a point of playing it over and over again. Sometimes she would tiptoe into the living room and just stand there watching him play. He always sat stiffly erect, his small body dwarfed by the big black piano while his nimble fingers flew over the "teeth," as he jokingly called the keyboard. A few hours later, they would eat a light snack (he disliked big dinners), and then he would begin working on his pet project: transcribing *Clytemnestra*. It was a "lost" opera that had recently been found, and the ancient score had to be translated note by note for modern instruments. Hélène was especially fascinated with this process, since he used his antique instruments to play through a portion of the notes before translating them. After a few hours, they would either go upstairs or outside and make love before going to bed. Always she was gentle, not only guiding him along but also encouraging experimentation. But she always managed to make him think it was his own idea. Actually, he understood what she was doing, but he never let on: he didn't want to spoil her pleasure in pleasing him.

One day, although Hélène didn't tell Stanislaw the reason why, she put an abrupt halt to their outdoor lovemaking. She missed it immediately, because it had been her favorite place for sex. She loved the feel of the elements all around her— the caressing freshness of the wind, the smell of the earth, and the cushiony softness of the grass against her skin. She loved the romance of the gorgeous sunsets and the stars overhead and the sound of the water. She stopped it because she had the feeling that they were being watched.

She had felt it for the first time when she was swimming in the pool. She told herself that she was being ridiculous. But later, when she was sunbathing, she had the feeling again. She looked up suddenly and frowned. She could swear she saw some of the thick bushes at the end of the property moving. Quietly she slipped into her heavy terry-cloth robe and went over to investigate. At first, there was no sign of anyone. But upon closer inspection she found footprints in the dirt around the bushes, and the grass was crushed.

When she looked around and discovered an overgrown path nearby, she decided to follow it. It led along the very edge of the cliff and connected their villa with the one next door, an Italianate U-shaped structure with a loggia overlooking a terra-cotta terrace. The blue shutters were closed.

She walked around the property and called out a few times, but no one answered. Finally she shrugged her shoulders and returned the way she had come.

She had just been imagining things, she tried to tell herself. But deep inside she knew better. She had seen the footprints.

The next week, Hélène discovered who was spying on her. While Stanislaw was practicing his études, she walked to the Vieux Village to get some shopping done. The day was perfect Côte d'Azur weather: sunny, cloudless, hot, but breezy. She wore one of the bright print dresses from Odile Joly.

First she ran some errands and then she stopped at the salon de coiffure. She would surprise Stanislaw with a new hairstyle she had been thinking about getting. Carefully she instructed the hairdresser to cut it into short, boyish bangs instead of giving her the wavy permanent that was so fashionable at the moment. When she finally left the salon, she stopped at a greengrocery. Once again, that peculiar feeling of being watched came over her.

Quickly she turned around and saw a fleeting shadow darting into a doorway. She lost no time going to investigate, but whoever it was had disappeared. With a weary sigh she returned to the greengrocer and finished her shopping. On the way back to the villa she walked past the secluded houses lining the boulevard. Suddenly she heard rapid footsteps behind her.

She whirled around. "What are you doing here!" she said angrily.

"I decided to be near my love," Hubert de Léger said fervently. His eyes looked glassy and they shone like a puppy's, eager to please.

She recoiled. She could smell his breath; he had been drinking. "Leave me alone!" she said coldly.

"After all the trouble I went through to be near you?"

She looked at him with distaste. "Hubert," she said softly, "I love Stanislaw and I am his wife. I have no intention of seeing any other man. Especially you!"

She started to leave, but he caught her arm. "Not so quickly, my sweet," he whispered. "It wasn't easy to get the house next door at such short notice. I expect some reward for my effort."

She stared at him. "So it is *you* who have been spying on me!" She shook her head. "I should have known!"

Suddenly she felt sick. Was there no getting away from him? Would he follow her everywhere she went? Why couldn't he just leave her alone?

"Hubert," she said quietly, "I think that from now on you'd better stay away from me. My husband won't like it when he hears about this."

He laughed silently. "Your husband! That old crow? He's old enough to be your grandfather!"

Her hand flashed out and slapped him.

He grinned. "Did I hit a nerve, love?"

She turned her back on him and started walking quickly. After a moment he caught up with her and took her by the arm.

She shook off his hand and angrily whirled around. Her voice was quietly menacing. "Leave me alone, Hubert. If you don't, I'll call the police!"

Suddenly he was angry. "Then call the police, you bitch!" he yelled. Then he laughed softly. "See if it keeps me away!"

She shuddered. Hurriedly she started walking again. Only after she'd gone a quarter of a kilometer did she dare look back over her shoulder. She let out a sigh of relief. He wasn't following.

When she got back to the villa, Stanislaw was still at the piano, and she could hear the sounds of a polonaise. He must have heard her come in, for he instantly switched to the Chopin mazurka. In spite of the harrowing incident with Hubert, she couldn't help but smile.

She left her shopping bags by the staircase under the rotunda and went into the living room. She approached Stanislaw soundlessly and kissed the back of his neck. With a flourish, his fingers swept the length of the Bechstein's "teeth." He pounded a few deep chords and then raised his hands dramatically in midair and held them there. He slid around on the bench to face her.

He raised his eyebrows. "What a lovely hairstyle," he said with an approving smile. "It becomes you."

She looked pleased. "It's not exactly what everyone's wearing. Even the hairdresser tried to get me to change my mind, but I was adamant."

"Good girl. You have more taste than all of them combined. What else did you do?"

She shrugged. "A little shopping. Errands. The usual."

She was ashamed of herself for not telling him about Hubert. But she didn't want to worry him, especially with the upcoming world tour his agent had just booked. It was her job to keep everything running smoothly.

He looked at her closely. "Is something the matter?"

She detected the note of worry in his voice. She wanted to kick herself. There, I've really done it now, she thought.

Quickly she shook her head. She forced her facial muscles to relax and tried to laugh. "No, nothing's the matter. I was just thinking about what I would wear on the tour. I *am* going with you, you know."

He took her hand and pulled her down onto his lap. "It will be the happiest tour of my life," he predicted. "Every night, I shall forget the audience is even there. I will play my heart out to you alone, as if you are the only person in the concert hall."

Suddenly she hugged him tightly. "And I shall sit in the crowds," she whispered. "And I, too, will forget that any of them are there. For me, you will be the only one in the concert hall."

7

Stanislaw waved. "Hélène!" he called out. "We have a visitor!"

"Just a moment!" She pulled off the thick gardening gloves, took off the big straw hat, and struggled to her feet. She ran a hand through her hair and saw Stanislaw and someone else walking toward her. Suddenly she stared at the visitor. She knew only one person who wore sport coats and ascots.

"Jacques!" she exclaimed with delight. Then she ran toward him and flung herself into his arms. He lifted her off the ground and whirled her around in the air a few times. Then he spun dizzily to a halt, and they laughed and embraced. He drew back and held her at arm's length.

"Let me look at you," he said with a smile. "Good God!" He glanced over his shoulder at Stanislaw. "Married life certainly seems to agree with her. I've never seen her this radiant before. You must be doing something right."

Stanislaw looked pleased.

"Well?" Hélène demanded. "What are you doing here? Don't tell me you've decided to chaperon us."

"Not at all," Jacques replied lightly. "I just had a mad impulse to see you, that's all." He grinned. "So I grabbed a cab, told the cabbie to drive me to the Gare Lyon, hopped on board the Train Bleu, and bribed the conductor into giving me a berth. And here I am on the beautiful, sunny Côte d'Azur!" His face fell. "But just until tomorrow."

"I'll get one of the guest rooms ready," Hélène said firmly. "There are plenty of empty bedrooms." She waved at the house. "Just look at this place. It's big enough to sleep an army!"

He shook his head. "No, thanks. I've already got a room at the Voile d'Or."

She was visibly disappointed. "If you insist . . ." Then she brightened. "Anyway, what brings you here?"

"Actually, I only came to drop off something. I wanted to deliver it in person."

"But . . . you've already given us a wedding present."

He smiled secretively and wagged a finger at her. "Ah, but this is not a wedding present. Come to the terrace."

Hélène looked at Jacques, then at Stanislaw. Suddenly her eyes shone with excitement. "It . . . it isn't . . ."

"It *is*!" Jacques said. "Advance copies of *Vogue* and *L'Officiel*. I didn't think you could wait to see them. They're up there on a chaise."

"Well, come *on*, then!" Hélène cried impatiently. She took each of them by the hand and pulled them toward the house. When they reached the terrace, she let their hands drop and raced up the steps. On the chaise lay the two magazines. She sucked in her breath. Her face was staring up at her from the cover of *Paris Vogue*. Slowly, as if it might be a mirage that would disappear when she touched it, she reached down and picked it up. Then she studied it intently. "Why, it's fantastic!" she said at last. She glanced at Jacques, who nodded in agreement. Then she flipped through the magazine. On page fifty-four, there she was again, dizzily hanging off the girder of the Eiffel Tower, with Paris far below her feet and the pale evening dress billowing in the wind like an enormous spinnaker. Quickly she put *Vogue* back down and snatched up *L'Officiel.*

And there she was again, this time in a five-page four-color spread. She stared at the pages silently for a moment. These were the smoking-gun photos. At first she couldn't believe that the beautiful model in the slip was her. But it was. She—Hélène Junot—was standing arrogantly over the body of a man, her legs in a defiant stance, one high heel poking the tuxedoed body, her face glaring into the camera. The barrel of the revolver was smoking. They were more than just photographs. They were works of art. She remembered laughing at Jacques, thinking the idea ridiculous. Soberly she realized that he had been right.

She shook her head, wondering if all this was indeed real. It was. And she felt strangely light-headed at seeing herself for the first time in a magazine.

Finally she turned to the men. "I . . . I simply can't believe it! They're beautiful! Stanislaw, did you see them?"

Her husband smiled warmly. "Jacques showed them to me the moment he arrived."

"These call for champagne!" she announced. She started to go inside the house.

"Oh . . . there is one more thing," Jacques said.

She looked back at him questioningly. "What?"

He reached into his sport coat and produced a long slim envelope. Puzzled, she retraced her steps and took it. Slowly she tore it open. One glance was enough. She knew what it was. A modeling contract from the most prestigious agency in Paris. Slowly she sank down onto the chaise.

Jacques grinned. "Well?" he asked. "What do you say to that?"

Wordlessly she put the contract down in her lap.

Jacques was looking at her strangely. "Is something wrong?"

She shook her head. "No, Jacques. I appreciate it. I really do . . ."

"Then what is it?"

She looked up at him and met his gaze. "I don't think I want to model anymore," she said quietly.

"Are you crazy!" He looked like someone who had just discovered a charge of dynamite in his pocket. Openmouthed, he turned to Stanislaw. "But . . . I don't get it!" he sputtered.

Hélène smiled gently. "Jacques, you wouldn't understand. And please, don't be angry or hurt." She reached out and touched his arm. "All I want right now is to be a good wife for Stanislaw. And then, if there's time . . ." She made a vague gesture. "Never mind. It's still too early to plan that."

"But the money! And the terms!" Jacques snatched the contract off her lap and waved it in front of her face. "Look what they're offering you!" He jabbed the paper with a finger. "It's astronomical! You'll be the highest-paid model in France! And next year, they're even planning to send you to New York!"

She smiled gently. "Jacques, please don't think I'm ungrateful. I appreciate everything you've done. It's just that I've already made up my mind. I know what I want to do."

He stared at her in exasperation. "Oh, Jesus! Women!"

An hour later, Jacques returned to his hotel. Hélène walked him to the taxi. When she came back inside, Stanislaw looked at her. "Is he coming back for dinner?" he asked.

Hélène shook her head. "No. He's returning to Paris tonight."

"He feels hurt," Stanislaw said with wisdom. "He was certain you'd be delighted."

"But I *was!*" Hélène protested.

"Sit down, my darling," Stanislaw said. "I think it's time we had a little talk."

Hélène raised her eyebrows questioningly, but she crossed the room and obediently sat down on the couch. The down-filled cushions were soft, and she sank deeply into them. He sat down beside her and reached for her hand and covered it with his. His eyes were sad. "You don't have to sacrifice anything for me," he told her gently. "That includes modeling."

"But I'm not!" she protested earnestly.

"Hush! Keep quiet and listen to the ramblings of an old

man for a minute!" He cleared his throat and chose his words carefully. "You are young, Hélène. Too young to sit around being bored. You must have something to keep yourself occupied. Especially since you're saddled with an old husband like me who locks himself away for hours on end transcribing old manuscripts and practicing the 'teeth.'" Again she started to protest, but he motioned her to silence. "You must have a life of your own, too. A hobby. A career. Something worthwhile."

Hélène smiled. "I'm not trying to play the martyr. Please believe me. It's just that modeling isn't for me. Of course, I would have jumped at the chance when I first came to Paris. No," she corrected herself, "I would have *killed* for the chance! But now, I'm glad I tried it. I found out that I'm not really crazy about modeling. I can't seem to get any satisfaction out of just looking pretty. Once in a while, yes. But not for a career." Suddenly she clutched him. "I want to *do* things, Stanislaw. I want to create something." She looked at him earnestly. The short haircut made her violet eyes look huge. "I want to start my own fashion magazine. I know I would be good at that. And I would *enjoy* it."

"Then that is what you must do," he said simply.

"It takes a lot of money to start a magazine," she said.

He shrugged. "I have a lot of money. Besides, what good does it do, just sitting in the bank? It's your money, too."

Her eyes were suddenly moist. He understood what she wanted to do . . . what she *needed* to do. Not like the Comte, who was afraid it would take up all her time and leave none for him. Stanislaw was secure. He just wanted her to be happy.

"Perhaps I will do it once the concert tour is over," she said thoughtfully. "I only hope that Jacques will understand the way I feel. I would hate to lose his friendship. But to create a new magazine—a new voice for couture—yes!" Her eyes shone with excitement. "I would like that!"

He smiled. "Good. Then as soon as the honeymoon is over, you shall get to work and start planning it."

She smiled back at him. "But let's not cut our honeymoon short. After all, this is the first vacation I've ever had." On an impulse, she leaned over and kissed him, then toyed with his white hair. "You know," she whispered, "I really love you. You're the first person who has ever understood me. You can't know how happy that makes me."

* * *

The following morning, Hélène helped Stanislaw set up his bulky reel-to-reel tape recorder in the living room.

"I'm going to record some of my playing," he announced. "Come up to the bedroom. I'll need your help carrying the tapes down."

She nodded and followed him upstairs. The trunks that he'd shipped there the day before the wedding were in one of the big walk-in closets. Fortunately the one with the tapes was right inside the door. They pulled it out and slid it across the carpet. Inside, it was filled to the rim with boxes of recording tape.

"Good Lord!" she exclaimed. "I've never seen so many tapes in my life! We're not going to carry this whole thing downstairs by ourselves, are we?"

He shook his head. "No, it's too heavy. We'll just take some of the boxes." He bent over, lifted out a stack, and piled them high in Hélène's arms. "You can take these downstairs," he said. "They're blanks."

At the door, she stopped and poked her head around them. "What are you going to carry?"

"Some of the recorded ones. I'll just be a minute selecting them."

A little while later, she helped him get everything ready. She tore the wrappers off the new tapes and laid the reels out on a table. Carefully he threaded one of them through the machine and tested it. She noticed that the reels he had brought down were carefully labeled and dated. They were all Chopin or Scriabin. She picked up one and peered closely at the handwritten date. He had recorded this particular one nearly fifteen years earlier. She put it back down. "What are you going to record?" she asked.

He pointed at the blank reels. "Everything I've transcribed so far on *Clytemnestra*. Then I'm going to listen to some of the old recordings I made years ago, just to compare my style with today's."

She shook her head. "That sounds like an awful lot of work." She brightened suddenly. "Maybe I can help you change the reels?"

"No, my dear. You go and do whatever you want."

"But I want—"

He gestured her to silence. "I'll need total peace and quiet for this." He kissed her gently. "I know you'd be as quiet as a mouse, but I need to *concentrate*." He smiled. "You're so pretty, I'd get distracted. Out you go." He put his hands in the small of her back and propelled her toward the door.

"Do you want me to call you for lunch or dinner?" she asked.

"No, *I'll* call *you*."

She sighed helplessly. "All right, if you say so."

"I do," he said with finality.

She spent the day in the garden. First she took a swim in the pool. Then she placed her hands on her hips and surveyed the lawn. She frowned. It was beginning to look disgraceful, but it would have to wait. Instead, she weeded some of the flowerbeds, trimmed around them with clippers, and snipped away dead blossoms. As she worked, she could hear the piano. She recognized the overture from *Clytemnestra*.

In the afternoon, Stanislaw came out onto the terrace. "I'm taking a break," he called out.

Quickly she prepared lunch. Then he took his nap and she sunbathed and swam. When he went back inside the house, she kept her bathing suit on. She'd gotten used to the sun; a little more tan wouldn't hurt.

For hours, until the sun set, she could hear him playing, often the same passages over and over. At first some of them sounded awkward and laborious, but finally they were pure magic.

Clytemnestra.

Hélène shut her eyes for a moment. The music was hauntingly beautiful and she could imagine the drama unfolding onstage. She could almost see the beautiful Clytemnestra join her lover Aegisthus in murdering her husband upon his return from the Trojan War, and then being herself killed by their son, Orestes.

"Pretty music."

Hélène jumped. Her eyes flew open and she stared at Hubert standing there in front of her. "Go away," she whispered coldly.

He reached for her hand and held it. "I've loved you," he said, "ever since that first day I saw you. I'd do anything for you. I'd even help you get rid of that old man!"

She felt a sudden chill and her eyes flashed in the sunset. She tried to pull her hand away, but he was clutching it tightly. Suddenly she was frightened. "Let me go!" she said quietly.

"Uh-uh. Not until you tell me the truth," he persisted. "That you love me and that you only married him for his money!"

She glared at him. Her voice was flat. "Hubert, there is nothing to tell. I love Stanislaw. Now, I think—"

"Aren't you at least going to admit that you love me?"

"No, Hubert," she said wearily. "I'll never admit that. You see, I *don't* love you."

Suddenly his face clouded over. Savagely he pulled her up from the chair and pressed his face against hers. His cheeks scratched her as she fought to turn away. His mouth found hers, and suddenly he pushed his tongue between her lips. She tried to shove him away. Clumsily he thrust a hand inside her bathing-suit halter and squeezed one of her nipples. She let out a cry of pain.

The music had come to a crescendo and then stopped abruptly.

"Stanislaw!" Hélène screamed. "Stanislaw!"

A moment later, Stanislaw came running out to the terrace. Hélène turned her head and looked up at him. His face went purple. She pushed away from Hubert and ran toward her husband.

"Go inside," he said in a quiet voice.

She nodded wordlessly and ran into the house. She watched from the French doors as Stanislaw approached Hubert. They were both silhouetted against the spectacular bloodred sunset. She could hear their voices raised in anger. As she watched, Stanislaw grabbed Hubert by the collar and shoved him backward. Then he raised a trembling finger and pointed to the edge of the property.

Hubert did not move. Hélène could hear his ugly, taunting laugh. Suddenly Stanislaw struck him across the face. Hubert recoiled.

Hélène shut her eyes. When she opened them, Hubert was flinging himself at Stanislaw. They began fighting with their fists.

"*Stop it!*" Hélène screamed. "*Stop it!*" She pounded her hands on the frame of the French door. The panes of glass rattled in their mullions.

The men continued grappling. They fell to the ground and started rolling around. Hélène's face had turned white.

Hubert was young and strong and Stanislaw was old and weak. And there were his hands to consider. His *piano* fingers. If only one got broken, it would be enough to put an end to his concert career. Suddenly she sucked in her breath. The cliff, she thought. Oh, God! She hadn't given it a thought, and now they were nearly at the edge!

Abruptly she ran out of the house, across the terrace, past the pool pavilion toward the cliff. When she was almost there, one of the silhouettes lost his balance and vanished, abruptly dropping out of sight.

The last thing Hélène saw were two clawing hands desperately clutching at air. Then a drawn-out, fading scream pierced the dusk, blending with her own.

And suddenly there was silence.

8

The Place Vendôme was very quiet at night. Even during the day, it had a kind of peaceful, secluded elegance. But it was by lamplight that one got the real ambience of the place, the illusion of what it must have been like when it was first built in the 1700's. It wasn't just the expensive shops, or the fact that it was closed off from the world by the majestic pilastered buildings on all sides, or that there were only two openings into this most exclusive enclave—one the rue de la Paix, the other the rue de Castiglione. The quiet came from the staid smell of money. It seemed to seep out through the doors and windows of the mighty Banque Rothschild; it somehow managed to escape the well-sealed vaults filled with millions of dollars' worth of gold and gems in the jewelry emporiums. It hung over the Ritz at number 15 like a sterling-silver cloud. And why not? Its wealthy international clientele were those who crossed borders with true carte blanche. These borders were not defined on maps; they were carefully surveyed and charted in the minute-by-minute fluctuations of multimillions, the dizzying plunges and peaks of power.

Hélène smiled as they got out of the taxi. For a moment she paused in front of one of the pedimented gray buildings that melted into other identical buildings that made up this side of the square. Her delicate nostrils flared as she tried to pinpoint the exact source of the elusive, quiet scent. It seemed to come from all around. There were few other places where it hit you with this impact. Palm Beach, parts of New York, Beverly Hills, Zurich, and the French Riviera.

"I used to dream of this place when I was a kid," she said, looking around with a proprietary expression. "Only then I knew I didn't belong here. I belonged in the slums of Montmartre."

"You've come a long way," Jacques said.

She sighed and looked down at her hand-sewn shoes. Then she looked back up. "Sometimes I wonder. You know, the older I get, the more I realize that distance isn't measured in kilometers. It's measured in francs and dollars and deutsche marks. Montmartre's not so far away from here. Just a little bit beyond the Opera. So how far have I really come in all these years? Three kilometers, maybe. That's not far, is it?" Suddenly she touched his arm. "I'm getting maudlin. Come, I want to show you something."

With a sigh of anticipation she led him to a recessed doorway in the arcade. On one side of the door, the lamp caught the sheen of a new brass plaque. Jacques looked closely at it. It was engraved with simple block letters:

LES ÉDITIONS HÉLÈNE JUNOT S.A.
Les Modes

He looked at her strangely and swept his finger along the lettering. "What's this?"

She reached out and touched the plaque. The brass was cold and lifeless. "I suppose it could be called the culmination of a dream," she said softly. "Ever since I was a young schoolgirl I've waited for this moment." She got the keys out of her purse and unlocked the door. "In a minute I'll tell you all about it."

He glanced at the sign once more and followed her inside. She turned on the lights and closed the door. The big rooms

400

were empty and silent. For a moment they stood there without speaking.

She spoke finally. "I just signed the lease yesterday. The plaque went up this afternoon. You're the first person to see it."

"I'm honored," Jacques said in a puzzled voice.

She led him from one tremendous room to the next, then up a broad staircase. On the second floor she switched on another light. "This will be my office. Look," she said. She crossed the room, each hollow footstep echoing around the bare white walls. She threw open one of the six tall windows. He came up beside her.

Across the huge square, most of the buildings were dark. Except number 15. Lights were blazing at the Ritz.

She went over to a corner, bent down, and picked up a bottle of Château Mouton-Rothschild and two glasses that were sitting on the floor.

"Wine?" he asked in surprise.

She glanced at him as she poured it into the glasses. "This is a celebration. I would have had champagne, but the icebox hasn't been installed yet."

He took his glass. "You still haven't told me what exactly you're celebrating."

"My new business. Hélène Junot is now a publisher." She gave a little laugh. "Or rather, will be soon. After Stanislaw died, I found I was a rather rich young woman with a lot of free time on my hands. I had to do something."

"You could have retired in youthful splendor."

"Not me. I have to keep busy."

He raised his glass. "Congratulations." He drank the wine. "Now, tell me about this publishing company."

She stood with her back to the window, her hands resting on the sill. She chose to keep her words and voice light. "You've heard of *Elle,* you've heard of *Vogue* and *L'Officiel.*" She paused. "I intend to take them down a peg or two."

He looked to see if she was joking; her violet eyes were dead serious. "That's a big ambition," he said carefully.

"Not really. I have the money to pump into it. What I need now is a staff."

"I think I'd better have some more wine," he said. Quickly he refilled his glass and drank it down. The Mouton was warm and smooth as liquid velvet. "Shoot."

401

"I'm offering you a job, Jacques."

"I already have a job."

"I know that. You're a photographer, and a damn fine one,"

"I'm at *Vogue*. That's top of the line."

"*Les Modes* will surpass *Vogue*," she said with a certainty he had never heard in her voice. "Give me a year and you'll see."

"You haven't even set up yet. It'll be six to eight months before the first issue is ready to go out."

"It'll be out in four months. What I need now is a staff. The best people I can find. I'll need your help hiring them."

"Where are you going to get them?"

She grinned. "I'm going to pull off the biggest heist French publishing has ever seen. I intend to steal the best talent that *Vogue, Elle, L'Officiel, Marie Claire,* and *Harper's* has to offer."

He shook his head. "Why do you think *you'll* be able to do it?"

"I'm going to offer them big francs. Everyone likes to get a raise. Plus there's the matter of ego. The chance to have a hand in shaping something new."

"You seem to have it all worked out."

She shrugged. "It's one way to get things done quickly. The sooner the ball gets rolling, the sooner *Les Modes* is out. What do you say? Will you consider coming in with me?"

He looked at her cautiously. "How big are those francs you were talking about?"

"What are you making now?"

"This," he said. He took a check from Condé Nast out of his pocket. "I don't usually carry these around with me. I just got paid today and haven't been able to get to the bank."

She took the check and looked at it. It was for twenty-eight hundred francs. She handed it back. "You don't do badly taking pictures."

"As you said, I'm a damn fine photographer."

"All right, I'm prepared to offer you thirty-five hundred a month."

"That's not bad," he said slowly. He thought for a minute. Then he nodded. "I'll give notice at *Vogue*. Two weeks from tomorrow, I'm yours."

She narrowed her eyes shrewdly. "I'll make it four thousand a month and you start tomorrow. Plus, there's no moonlighting around here. God help you if you smuggle pictures to *Vogue* or *L'Officiel,* byline or none."

Suddenly he grinned. "Boss," he said, "you've got yourself a deal." He extended his hand and they shook on it. "Where do I report in the morning? Here?"

"Right here." She smiled and looked around the empty room again. Their voices sounded as if they were bouncing off the walls of a cavern. But soon that would change. She could already envision what it would look like. A thick carpet on the floor would deaden the hollow sounds. So would the furniture. Her desk would be placed diagonally in front of the window. That way, she would be able to swivel her comfortable chair around and look down at the Place Vendôme whenever she felt like it. The chairs for her visitors were another matter. They would be stiffly uncomfortable; anyone coming to see her would immediately be put on the defensive. There must never be any doubt of who was in command. There would be filing cabinets and bookcases around the office, and the only decoration on the walls would be covers from *Les Modes.* A sudden idea hit her. She would change the covers each month so that only the most recent one would hang there. She made a mental note and filed it away among the hundreds of other details that had occurred to her.

"Where *are* you?" Jacques asked. He was watching her with an amused expression on his face.

She gave an apologetic little smile. "In the future."

"That's as good a place as any, I suppose."

"Yes, it is." She nodded slowly. The future would be a good place, she thought. At any rate, it couldn't be any worse than the past.

It seemed unbelievable that her dream was beginning to take shape at long last. She frowned suddenly. Something was missing. Then she knew what it was. She should be feeling elation. Triumph. There should be excitement and electricity crackling through the air. But there wasn't. The only thing she felt was a levelheaded determination to work hard and succeed. It was as if her childish sense of wonder and joy had deserted her when she had stood over Stanislaw's crumpled body on the rocks below the cliff on Cap Ferrat. That had been the final step she had had to take toward her ambition. Strangely enough, it had endowed her with that which she needed to become successful. A new sense of awareness and maturity. The willingness to take the worst kind of situation and turn it around to her advantage.

She was breathing heavily from the exertion of the climb, but she barely noticed. The windows of the villa were red with fire. For a moment she stared at the house dumbly, her hands at her side. Then she realized that it was not on fire. The windows were merely reflecting the sunset. Slowly she held out her blood-covered hands and looked at them with a blurred expression. "He's dead," she whispered. "He's dead!"

Quickly Hubert came over to her and put his hands on her arms. His eyes were wild. He seemed to have aged thirty years. "I didn't mean for this to happen!" he said softly. "It was an accident! You have to believe that."

In a daze she pushed him away and started walking toward the house. She couldn't even feel the ground beneath her feet. It was as if she were walking on air. She could not even feel any pain. Only a dull numbness. The pain would come later.

Solicitously Hubert helped her toward the house. "Maybe you're wrong," he said quickly. "Maybe it we call a doctor he'll be able to do something. Patch him up . . ."

Hélène stopped in her tracks and pushed him away. She shook her head vehemently. "He's dead! He landed on the rocks." She turned away from him in time to see the red sun dropping into the sea. She shuddered. "It . . . it's terrible. He's all crushed, and there's blood everywhere."

"Hélène, why don't you lie down and rest? I'll take care of everything."

"No!" Her voice took on the high pitch of hysteria. "Haven't you done enough! You've killed my husband!"

"Please, Hélène . . ." He stepped toward her.

Her eyes were wide with fear. "Stay away from me, Hubert!" she warned. "Don't come near me!" Suddenly she turned and ran to the terrace.

He watched her disappear into the house. He sighed heavily. Then he ran after her. At the French doors he stopped and paled. She was on the telephone.

He rushed into the living room and snatched the receiver out of her hand. Quickly he slammed it down on the cradle. "What are you doing?" he hissed.

"I'm calling the police."

"What are you going to tell them?"

She flashed him a nasty look and reached out for the telephone. Swiftly he blocked her way. He was almost childlike. "Don't tell them," he pleaded. "Please. I'll do anything for you. Give you anything . . ."

Her voice sounded weary as she held out her hand demandingly. "Hubert, just give me the receiver."

"Will you listen to me for a moment!" His usually deep voice, now high-pitched and whining, sounded grotesque. "Do you think I wanted this to happen? It was an accident!"

She flashed him a contemptuous look. "How old are you, Hubert?"

He looked at her quizzically. "Twenty-five."

She gave a mirthless laugh and slapped her thigh. "Twenty-five! To think that you fought with a man of seventy-two! A pianist whose fingers were his life, who couldn't defend himself. And you hurled him off the cliff!"

He turned away from her. "I told you it was an accident! He lost his balance!"

"I don't believe you," she said dully.

"All right, then don't!" He whirled around savagely, his narrowed eyes blazing. "I wanted to kill him!" he spit out wildly. "You're right. Ever since the day you two first met. He was too old for you! Too damned old and too damned ugly! I'm glad I killed him!"

"Do you know what you're saying?" Her words were scarcely audible.

"Of course I know what I'm saying!" he snapped angrily. "And if you tell the police that I had any part in it, I'll deny it. I'll call you a liar! He was a frail old man." He made a disgusted gesture. "Even a woman could have tossed him down that cliff!"

She started to laugh and flung her arms out unbelievingly. "I can't believe this! You would tell the police a lie like *that*?"

"If you tell them I did it, yes! I will even say I witnessed *you* doing it. That he was just standing there admiring the sunset and that you gave him a push. You had the perfect motive. After all, you married him for his money!"

"How dare you!"

"Go on—call the police." He laughed tauntingly and started for the French doors. Halfway there, he turned around. "Come on, let's see if you have any guts."

She looked into his dark eyes to see if he was serious. For

a moment she could see straight through them into his soul. It was a dark soul, mangled and decayed, festering with venom. She closed her eyes to wipe out the terrible sight.

He's crazy, she thought. Not just drunk; this time it went much deeper than that. Somewhere along the line, the blue blood had curdled. As much as the young Hubert de Léger had once charmed her, he now repulsed her.

"Get out of here," she said quietly.

He left without a word.

Slowly she lifted up the telephone. Her fingers trembled as she dialed the police. They answered immediately.

She took a deep breath and fought to keep her voice under control. "There's been an accident!" she whispered hoarsely. "My husband is dead. Please . . . come quickly!"

While she was waiting for the police, she looked around the big airy room. There was the big black Bechstein Stanislaw had been playing, the one nearest the terrace doors. The sheet music was still leaning against it. She walked over and stared at the carefully penned score. Slowly she picked it up and leafed through it. Then she closed it. On the first page was scrawled in his precise handwriting:

CLYTEMNESTRA
An Opera by Jean Baptiste Lully
Translated and Arranged by Stanislaw Jastrow Kowalsky

And under that, newly scribbled words caught her eye:

This translation is dedicated to my darling wife, who makes me feel like a young man again.

She stared at the words, and then she pressed the paper against her breast. The heat of her tears burned her eyes. It was at this moment that the true tragedy sank in. The numbness wore off; the pain began. Quickly she replaced the score on the piano, but that didn't alleviate the anguish she felt.

Snap! A noise startled her in the silence. She jumped and spun around, her eyes darting from door to door. Then she glanced over at the table on the other side of the piano. The tape recorder had just turned itself off; a piece of the flesh-colored tape was still fluttering against the big machine as the reels did a few last spins. She let out a breath of relief. It was only the tape recorder. Funny how a little noise like that could set you off when you were all wound up. She hadn't even realized that it had been running all this time.

She caught her breath. No, not only running. *Recording*. Stanislaw had been making a tape of *Clytemnestra* when her screams had interrupted him.

Suddenly the enormity of this discovery flashed through her mind. Momentarily it even isolated the pain in a small, unimportant corner of her body. On that tape was not only *Clytemnestra* but also Hubert's incriminating confession. She had enough evidence to incriminate Hubert de Léger for the murder of her husband, regardless of what tales he'd tell the police. Stanislaw had inadvertently trapped his own killer by leaving the machine running.

Hélène's mind began to race. With this confession, she could put Hubert behind bars. There was only one problem. The de Légers were powerful. They had connections. Exactly how far-flung these connections were she could not know. But as a de Léger, Hubert would probably get off with a light sentence. Perhaps even a mere slap on the wrist. After all, his family was one of the ten most powerful in France. One didn't just throw a de Léger into a jail packed with hoodlums, common thieves, and butchers.

She took the reel off the machine and tapped it in the palm of her hand. It did not weigh much, but somehow it felt very heavy. And no wonder. As long as it was in her possession, *she* would be in a position to punish Hubert. For as long as he lived, she could make his life miserable. For a moment she hesitated. Wasn't this called blackmail? Who was she to dispense justice? She pursed her lips thoughtfully and came to a swift decision. Better she than no one.

She thrust the spool into the box labeled "Clytemnestra" and put it in a drawer of the bureau.

Then the police arrived.

Inspector Rème found her sitting on one of the soft beige couches in the living room, her lips compressed into a thin twisted line, her face chalk white. One of the lights under the palm pots threw the shadow of a knifelike frond across her face. She was a beautiful woman, he thought to himself, but like most beautiful women, grief did not agree with her. In his thirty-one years on the force, Inspector Rème had learned to tell when grief was genuine. But grief itself proved

407

nothing. He knew of several cold-blooded women who had thought nothing of killing their husbands; afterward they had been genuinely grief-stricken for having done it.

"Inspector . . ." Her voice was barely a whisper as she began to tell him about the accident.

9

Hubert stood at the bedroom window looking out at the sea. The wind was brisk and the waves were capped with foam. He tapped his foot impatiently. What was the matter? He'd finally been able to trace her to the Grand Hotel. Why wasn't she answering?

Finally he heard a click and her voice came on the line. It sounded small and weary. "Hello?"

"Hélène? It's Hubert."

"Yes, Hubert. What do *you* want?"

"How are you?"

For a moment she was silent. When she spoke, it was as if every word were frozen. "My husband is dead and I've been questioned by the police. I don't think they believed my story. How do you think I am?"

"What did you tell them?" he asked curiously.

"I don't think this is the time to discuss that," she snapped, and then he heard a click.

He stared dumbly at the receiver. She had hung up on him. Angrily he banged it down and cursed. The worst thing was, she wouldn't even tell him what she'd told the police. If they came to question him, how was he to be sure that their stories matched?

But they hadn't come to see him, he thought suddenly. That at least indicated that she'd been wise enough not to mention him.

The press had a field day. As soon as the news of Stanislaw Kowalsky's death leaked out, reporters descended on

408

Cap Ferrat in swarms. Most of them were from sensational journals like *Ici Paris;* a few even came from as far away as Germany, Italy, and England. Stanislaw Kowalsky was news. In death as much as in life.

Jacques didn't bother with trains. He hopped on the first Air-Inter flight to Nice. There he hired a car to take him to the isolated, exclusive Grand Hotel du Cap-Ferrat. Hélène was in a suite consisting of two connecting bedrooms, each with its own door out into the corridor. That way, if any reporters managed to slip past the alert staff downstairs, Jacques would at least be able to come and go from his room without being harassed.

The bellboy put down his suitcase and thanked him profusely for the tip. Jacques grinned good-naturedly and looked around the room. When he heard the door close, his face grew serious. "Hélène?" he called out softly.

She opened the connecting door a crack, peered out suspiciously, and then flung it open. She rushed into his arms. For a moment he held her tightly. Her small voice was muffled in his chest. "Thanks for coming, Jacques. You don't know how much I appreciate it." She looked up at him and tried to smile.

He leaned down and kissed her cheek. Then he looked at her silently for a moment, shocked by her appearance. Her face was white and drawn, her eyes lackluster. He felt helpless. All he could do was try to comfort her. And that he did, as they talked long into the night. Finally he convinced her to try to rest. The hotel doctor had given her some pills, but she hadn't take any, not wanting to miss Jacques's arrival. Now, as Jacques handed them to her, she accepted them gratefully. After a few minutes she did what she had believed to be the impossible. She slept.

Whether it was the pills, the tiredness, or the emotional strain, something knocked her out completely. She even slept through the jangling of the phone. Finally Jacques shook her awake. She looked at him groggily.

He held his hand over the receiver. "It's Inspector What's-his-name," he said. "He wants to talk to you right away."

She moaned and struggled up. What was it with the police? Didn't they sleep like normal human beings? Or did somebody wind them up with a key like one of those mechanical toys?

She glanced at the alarm clock on the nightstand. It was still light out, but the clock said eleven-thirty. She sat up straight. Was it possible that she'd slept fifteen hours straight through? She shook her head to clear it of the fog and took the receiver.

"Madame Kowalsky? This is Inspector Rème. I hope I'm not disturbing you."

"No, not at all," she lied. "If I sound a little groggy, it's because of the pills the doctor prescribed. What can I do for you?"

Jacques stood there looking at her questioningly. She caught his look. "Coffee," she mouthed soundlessly. He nodded and quickly slipped out of the room.

"I'm all right, Inspector," she said into the phone. "Please, go ahead."

"Perhaps you will feel better once I tell you what we've discovered," Inspector Rème said. "A witness who saw the accident take place has just come forward."

She felt a sudden chill and drew the sheet higher around her neck. So someone had seen Stanislaw and Hubert fighting, she thought with dismay. How could that have been? Had someone across the bay accidentally focused binoculars their way? Had a sailboat been going by, and a member of the crew looked up as the body fell? It could have been any of a dozen things. A hundred things.

"Yes . . . ?" she said cautiously.

"It seems that the villa next to yours was rented to a certain Hubert de Léger."

Whatever sleep was still in her body shot out of her like a bullet. "I see," she said. She had to fight to keep her voice calm.

"Monsieur de Léger was in his garden, also admiring the sunset, when your husband lost his balance. He said that he saw you rushing toward him, trying to save his life."

"I didn't succeed, Inspector."

"But you tried." He paused for a moment. "I've called to let you know that you're free to leave Cap Ferrat whenever you like. The case is closed."

She forced herself not to show her relief in her voice. "Thank you, Inspector. Do you have any idea why this person did not come forward sooner?"

"It seems that he is from a prominent family and didn't want its name involved. He said he came forward after much deliberation because it was his duty as a citizen."

"I see," she said dryly.

"If you need any help leaving," Inspector Rème said, "I am glad to be of service. I can have my men try to get you past the reporters. Also, your husband's body is still in the morgue in Nice. Do you wish to have it shipped to Paris?"

"Please."

"I will be happy to arrange it."

"Thank you, Inspector. Au revoir."

Slowly she replaced the receiver. For the first time she noticed the persistent ticking of the alarm clock. Almost angrily she snatched it off the nightstand and buried it under the pillows. It didn't do any good. She could still hear the *tick-tick-tock, tick-tick-tock*. But at least it wasn't so loud that she couldn't think. Her eyes were thoughtful. Trust Hubert to be a slippery fish. He had managed to squirm out of this mess nicely, even clearing her in the process. He would probably expect her to be eternally grateful.

She smiled grimly. But he *had* done her one favor without even knowing it. He'd left himself wide open to be punished for his crime. By her.

She reached for the telephone and waited for the hotel operator to come on. "Bonjour, madame."

"Bonjour," she replied. "Connect me with the desk, please."

"Right away." There was a clicking sound; then the unctuous voice of the head desk clerk came on.

"Please prepare my bill," she said. "I'm checking out. Also, reserve two seats on the next flight to Paris." She tossed down the receiver and swung her legs over the side of the bed. She pulled on her robe. Then she got her suitcase and threw it on the bed and began to pack.

"What's the hurry?" Jacques looked at her questioningly as he came in with a steaming cup of black coffee."

"Pack your things," she said without looking up. "We're leaving."

He stared at her incredulously and slowly put the cup down. "What! Leaving! Where to?"

"Back to Paris, of course."

At the airport in Nice, they passed a newsstand in the

411

lobby. Hélène stopped in her tracks. A grayish color came over her skin as she stared speechlessly at a tabloid on display.

Jacques looked over at it too. He winced. It was one of the weekly scandal rags. It was enough to knot your stomach. The bold red banner read: "LUCKLESS MARRIAGE ENDS ON THE ROCKS." There was a big black-and-white paparazzo shot of Stanislaw and a half-page blowup of Hélène. It was the "smoking-gun" photo. The one from *L'Officiel.*

"Jacques, it's your photo!" she said in a tight voice. She furrowed her brow. "You didn't . . . give them permission to use it?"

He caught the look in her eyes. "No, of course I didn't. They must have pirated it from *L'Officiel. Le Monde Internationale* is always pulling stunts like that," he said angrily.

"But it's so . . . so out of context," she whispered.

"Forget it. There's nothing you or I can do about it. More important personalities than you have tried to stop them. *LMI* always wins. Your best bet is to forget about it. Let it die a quiet death. Don't even demand a retraction."

She felt a terrible surge of anger because she knew that he was right. But it wasn't fair. A person shouldn't have to take such slander. It wasn't right to have to feel so impotent. Then she had a sudden brainstorm. "Can't *L'Officiel* sue them for ripping off the photo?"

He nodded. "But it would cost them a fortune and could take forever. Years, maybe. Even then, there's no way to be sure of the outcome. *Le Monde Internationale* could get just a slap on the wrist. Listen, take my advice and forget you ever saw it."

She stared at him. "But how can I? 'Marriage Ends on the Rocks.' That's despicable!"

"Keep busy for a while," he advised her gently. "Stay out of the public eye. Do nothing, say nothing. In a few weeks, you'll be yesterday's news. In a month, no one will even remember who you are or what you look like."

But Jacques was wrong. For the rest of her life, the reporters would always be there to haunt her. She would not only be in the news. She would create constant news.

Stanislaw Kowalsky was buried on the silent slopes of the Père-Lachaise Cemetery in Paris. The grave was off the Avenue Transversale Number Three, a few graves away from

412

Modigliani's. It was a short, private ceremony. Besides Hélène and Jacques, the only other friend of Stanislaw there was the Vicomtesse de Sévigné. She sniffed ceremoniously into a lace-edged handkerchief, her huge black picture hat with the big black satin bow flapping perilously in the wind. The Vicomtesse was a very elegant mourner, Hélène thought, but a genuine one. The eyes that had seen so much were red-rimmed and puffy from crying.

Also at the grave were Ada and Herbert, Stanislaw's estranged children. Neither had come from New York for the wedding, but both had turned up for the funeral. Before the service, Hélène had tried to speak to them, but they had turned away. They made it clear that they did not regard her as a member of the family, and that even the Vicomtesse was a barely tolerated friend of their father's. During the service, Hélène looked over at them. They stood together at the far side of the grave, Ada with her face hidden behind the thick veil of what looked like a black beekeeper's bonnet. Her long black skirt reached almost to her swollen ankles, which were encased in black nylon stockings. Herbert, pear-shaped and wearing heavy glasses, studiously kept his eyes on the grave like an engineer studying a blueprint.

At the end of the service, Hélène picked up the tiny shovel and scooped a little symbolic earth out of the big mound beside the grave. She took a deep breath and looked stoically down at the gleaming coffin. Then she flicked her wrist awkwardly and the pebbles rained noisily down on the curved mahogany lid and slid off it into the sides of the grave. Quickly she turned away and began to walk to the exit. Jacques fell into step beside her and put his hand under her elbow. Behind her she could hear the Vicomtesse weeping as she threw her shovel of earth. "Au revoir, mon ami," she heard her cry thickly.

At the cemetery gate, the Vicomtesse caught up with Hélène. She put a hand on her arm and drew her aside. "I want to tell you that Stanislaw was very fortunate," she said, carefully dabbing her eyes with a corner of her handkerchief. "His last few weeks were the happiest of his life."

Hélène looked away, her eyes distant. "No," she said firmly. "If he hadn't married me, he'd still be alive."

The Vicomtesse put a gloved hand on Hélène's chin and twisted her face around. "Even in grief you have no right to say such a thing," she said coldly. "Stanislaw wrote me a letter the day before he died. I received it only yesterday. I've memorized every word. He wrote: 'I only regret that I did not meet her years before. She is strong and sweet, my Hélène, sensual and caring, passionate and maternal. If she had been the mother of my children, I am sure I would have had a close-knit, loving family instead of one that fell apart at the seams.' "

Suddenly Hélène's eyes filled with tears. She didn't answer. She gave her a little hug, pulled herself away, and hurried to her waiting Citroën limousine.

That afternoon, in Monsieur Duchamps's stuffy, paneled law office on the Avenue de L'Opéra, she found out just how much Stanislaw cared for her. He had made her the sole beneficiary of a single rare Stradivarius violin, a house in the sixteenth arrondissement, all his recording royalties, bank accounts, and stocks and bonds worth in excess of two and a half million dollars. He had left Ada and Herbert with a paltry twenty-five-thousand-dollar a year trust fund each.

10

Hélène sat beside Karl Häberle, the private detective, in the front seat of his battered Opel Rekord. Her posture was tensely erect, her violet eyes keen and hard, her nostrils flaring with anticipation. She ducked down again and looked out the dirty windshield at the plain four-story apartment house. The first part of her long-vowed search had ended here on the Berliner Strasse in a small town in Germany. Not even in her wildest dreams had she considered that it would end anywhere but in some dark, seedy, furtive place. The Hamburg waterfront, perhaps. Even a secluded village on the pampas of Argentina. But Seulberg sprang up from the slopes of the Taunus Mountains just north of Frankfurt. It was a new community being built from scratch. Quiet suburbs like this one were popping up all over. The postwar boom was in its heyday.

Hélène studied the building closely. It looked like a big rectangular box. There was something almost antiseptic about the sharp Bauhaus angles, the immaculate white stucco, the big plate-glass windows with gauze curtains behind them. There was no personality, no grace. No style. Only function, and in postwar Germany, form followed function as B followed A. Only one thing seemed to be more important, and that was C. Cleanliness. Neatness. Order. It was as if after the rubble of the war had been cleared away, neatness was the most strictly enforced requirement of them all. She looked over at Häberle. He was watching her curiously. "Well?" he asked. "Are you ready?"

She didn't speak. After having waited so many years for this moment, her body felt somehow leaden. She thought she had been emotionally prepared. Now she knew she was not. Slowly she reached for the door handle, pushed down on it, and swung the door open. When she stood on the sidewalk, she looked up and down the new street. The asphalt gleamed blue-black in the bright sun. On top of the hill, the bulldozers were grading more land. She nodded to herself. The air out here was country air. It smelled fresh and clean. Even the birds swooped happily in the skies above the nearby fields. The recent war was way in the past.

Häberle took her arm and led her along the concrete path to the entrance. When they reached it, she looked at the row of doorbells. Each tiny black button had a small metal slot beside it. In each was a slip of cardboard with a carefully printed name. The third one from the button jumped at her. Schmidt. A shiver of revulsion ran through her.

Häberle turned to her and raised his eyebrows questioningly.

She forced herself to smile. As soon as he wasn't looking, she bit down on her lip. She watched him push on the doorbell with his finger.

A few seconds later, a crackling voice came on over the squawk box. "Wer ist da?"

He didn't answer, just pushed the button again and again. Finally the door buzzer that released the catch sounded noisily and he pushed on the door. He held it open for her and they found themselves in an anonymous corridor with a staircase in the back. They headed toward it.

"Third floor," he said.

She nodded as they climbed the stairs. They were clean

and spotless. The smell of antiseptic was everywhere in the air.

"It smells like a hospital," she whispered.

He didn't reply. On the third floor, a door opened and a woman looked out at them just as they reached the landing. "Wer sind Sie?" she demanded in a shrill Bavarian dialect that echoed hollowly in the stairwell.

Hélène looked at her. She was tired-looking and thickset, her size accentuated by her shapeless gray housecoat. Her mangled grayish-blond hair was in the remains of a long-past permanent and a tired wave hung down over her forehead. She brushed it aside irritably with her hand.

Häberle gave a little bow and stepped forward. "Verzeihung. Mein Name ist Karl Häberle. Das ist meine Frau. Sind Sie Frau Schmidt?"

The woman looked at him suspiciously, drew back inside, and closed the door a little farther. "Ja?"

Häberle came right to the point. "Ich war in der Wehrmacht mit Hans. Ist Er zuhause?"

Hélène knew what he was saying. He had explained his tactics to her in the car. If Schmidt himself didn't answer the door, they would gain access by Häberle posing as an old army buddy.

"*Ach so.*" Some of the woman's suspicions faded and she smiled tentatively. She opened the door wide and invited them inside. "Guten Tag," she told Hélène.

Hélène smiled automatically but kept quiet. Häberle had told her not to open her mouth, her speaking French might create suspicion.

"Mein Mann ist in der Küche. Kommen Sie." The woman led the way down a narrow hallway and through a stiffly furnished parlor that looked like it was never used. Hélène looked around with curiosity. The chairs, tables, and wall unit all had long, tapered, blond wood legs. There were no pictures, no flowers, no personal knickknacks of any kind. They went into the kitchen.

Hélène let out a gasp and drew back. Her mouth was suddenly dry. There was no mistaking the man seated at the table. It *was* Schmidt. The same Schmidt who had been with the white-faced one. The Schmidt who had unbuttoned Marie's little suit and burned her on the belly with a cigarette. Now he was sitting with his back to the wall, contentedly munching on Belegte Brote. A half-full stein of beer was on the table in front of him.

Silently Hélène's eyes traveled up the wall beside the table. She stared at it in morbid fascination. It was covered with memorabilia from the war. There were medals, pictures, photographs; an Iron Cross, ribbons with swastikas. It was a long time since she had seen items such as these. She couldn't believe that anyone had the gall to display them. Then out of the corner of her eye she noticed that the man no longer had legs. She could see the scarred, rounded ends of his fleshy stumps protruding from his shorts. She looked at Häberle with a curious expression. With his eyes he motioned for her to remain silent. She tightened her lips across her teeth and nodded imperceptibly.

The woman leaned down over her husband. "Hans, Du hast besuch!" she shouted as one does to a person who is hard of hearing.

"Was? Besuch? Wer den?" Schmidt looked up, squinted, and reached for the thick wire-rimmed glasses on the table. Carefully he looped them over his ears. He frowned as he looked from Häberle to Hélène and then back at his wife. "Wer sind diese Leute? Ich kenne Niemand."

The woman frowned and looked at Häberle sharply. "Soll das ein Witz sein?" she demanded angrily. "Lassen Die doch mein Mann in Ruhe!" Protectively she put her thick arms around her husband's shoulders and pulled his head into her bosom.

Häberle turned to Hélène. "Wait in the parlor," he told her firmly in French.

She nodded gratefully and fled the stifling kitchen, the mutilated sadistic man, the evil memorabilia staring down from the wall. She sat on one of the hard upholstered chairs. From the kitchen she could hear voices raised in anger. After a while she got up, went over to the window, and parted the filmy curtains. She looked out thoughtfully. The view was uphill, and she could see bulldozers pushing at mounds of earth. She wondered what the arguing in the kitchen was all about. She thought it peculiar that the Schmidts were so violently defensive. She hadn't expected that. She had expected sincere apologies, begging for forgiveness. Anything but such a noisy battle. Weren't they sorry about what had happened? The answer now came to her. Obviously not. Otherwise, what would all those horrible medals and photographs be doing on the wall?

Ten minutes later, Häberle came out of the kitchen, Frau Schmidt at his heels. Hélène let the curtains fall back in place and slowly turned around. Frau Schmidt's eyes flashed with hatred. When she spoke, it was in badly accented, venomous French. She had obviously learned the language long ago. It was very rusty and grating, the naturally melodious pronunciations curdled by her thick, guttural Bavarian dialect.

"Do you sink ve vant the vor?" she shouted suddenly, flinging her arms around. "Ve are peaceful citizens! Vhy you come here and accuse my Hans of dese terrible sings?"

Hélène could only stare at her.

The woman made an indignant gesture toward the kitchen. "Don't my Hans suffer enough? He give his legs, almost his life! Not that he vant to! He vas . . ." She looked questioningly at Häberle.

"Conscripted," he said quietly.

"Conscripted!" she repeated almost triumphantly, rolling the word on her tongue. "Do you understand? He has no choice!"

Hélène looked at her steadily. She could no longer remain silent. She was tired of being intimidated, of being made to feel that she was the one who had done something wrong. "No, I don't understand," she said quietly.

Frau Schmidt had a challenging look on her face, "Even I—a vuman—have to vork for Hitler. Not that ve liked him. Ve had no choice! I vas in the Arbeitsdienst. Vorking on a farm to grow foods so that people don't starve. Am *I* a bad person vor doing this? For growing foods?"

Hélène looked at Häberle. "Did you find out about the other one?"

He nodded.

"Let's talk in the car." She shot a contemptuous glance at Frau Schmidt. "I can't stand the air in here."

"You . . . you sink you know everysing!" Frau Schmidt screamed. "How vould you like a man with no legs? I even have to stretch our government stipend by being a Hausmeisterin!"

Hélène looked puzzled.

"Sort of a concierge," Häberle explained.

Hélène whirled around and glared at the woman. She had taken just about as much of this as she could. "I had a mother, Frau Schmidt," she said disgustedly between her teeth. "She was pregnant. The Nazis punched her in the belly until her baby ran down her legs. My mother ended up in Auschwitz and was burned. My older sister? God only knows what happened to her. Probably gassed and burned. And my baby sister?" She pointed a trembling finger toward the kitchen. "That husband—that *Hans* of yours—burned her! A baby! That's right, a *baby*. Right in the belly. Here." Hélène yanked her blouse out of her skirt and jabbed at her navel. "And how do I know this?" She glared at Frau Schmidt. "*Because I saw that monster doing it with my own eyes!*" Hélène turned on her heels, marched through the hallway, flung open the front door, and stomped down the stairs. She could hear the venomous tirade coming from the landing above. "You young vons! You sink you know everysing. You alvays have a quick answer. Sure, you know everysing. How do you know vat it is like? Ve don't *like* Hitler! Every time the radio says there is a victory, we have to hang flags out the vindows. Do you sink ve like that?"

Häberle rolled down the window of the Opel and lit a cigarette. He inhaled noisily, drawing the smoke deep into his lungs. His face was pale and drawn. Hélène was shaking. Her eyes were expressionless as she stared blankly out the windshield. For a long time they sat in intense silence. Then without turning to him she asked, "What did they tell you?"

He looked at her. "Do you want to stop at a Gasthaus? You look like you could use a drink."

She twisted around in the seat and faced him. "No!" she said sharply. "Tell me here."

He tapped his fingers on the steering wheel. "All right," he said quietly, "I'll tell you. But I think the man in the kitchen speaks for himself. He is desperate and beaten."

"And all that . . . that junk on the wall? What about that?"

Häberle smiled grimly. "Don't you see? He has nothing left but the past. That is where he now lives. That was where he was a man."

She laughed. "A man? What kind of a man tortures a baby?"

"I'm not talking about that," he said irritably. "I'm talking about his physical condition."

"I know that he hasn't got any legs. I could see that for myself. I don't think that should alter anything."

Häberle laughed softly. "In the kitchen, the woman had him pull his shorts down. He doesn't have any genitals, either. He stepped on a mine in Russia."

Hélène closed her eyes. Somehow nothing was turning out the way she'd expected it to. She had imagined herself an avenging angel wielding a swift, clean sword. What kind of a sword could she lift against a legless man who was no longer a man? She shook her head. Nothing was going right. *Nothing.*

"Tell me about the other one!" she shouted, suddenly slamming her fist down on the dashboard. "The goddamn albino!"

Häberle took a drag on his cigarette. "I've got to warn you. You're opening a can of worms with that one. He's in the big leagues."

Her voice was soft. "I'm listening."

"His name is Karl von Eiderfeld and he's a pillar of respectability. About ten years ago he began to deal in oil and shipping. Since then, his company has become a behemoth; it's worth millions. It's called Von Eiderfeld Industrien, G.m.b.H. and it's based in Düsseldorf. I know nothing about von Eiderfeld himself, though. I'm pretty certain I've never come across a photograph or an article about him. Not in *Stern* or in *Der Spiegel*." He frowned thoughtfully. "Almost all of the industrialists have been written about in terms of the great postwar miracle, but never him. And he's certainly contributed to it. Yes, it is rather peculiar . . ."

Hélène ventured a guess. "His company was begun just after the war?"

"I'd have to research that, but I believe I can safely say yes."

"Then he must have had connections from the war. A huge industrial complex like that doesn't just start overnight. He's had help. Or knows things. Perhaps those who have helped him aren't even aware of it. There's got to be a shady beginning somewhere."

"It's supposed to be a very conservative company."

"I don't care." She clapped her hands together as if in prayer and inclined her head. "I want you to begin a discreet inquiry," she said slowly. "Look for anything connected with von Eiderfeld—especially from before the war. Get a dossier together. Include documents, passport photos, anything. Lie

420

in wait for him and snap his picture. I want to see it. But above all, dig for the dirt. I want his whole army career from A to Z. I want enough to charge him with to last five lifetimes. But it's got to stick. Every allegation must be documented. There has to be *proof*!" She turned to him, her eyes flashing with violent anticipation. She allowed herself a little breath of excitement. Somehow she felt—knew, she corrected herself—that she was now on the right track. Woman's intuition or no, it was a strange feeling. He was out there somewhere. Healthy and living it up.

"That's a tall order."

She allowed herself a smile. "I'm certain you're capable of it. Even if things haven't turned out well so far, you can't be faulted."

His expression became serious. "I have to warn you," he said gently. "Von Eiderfeld has more than just money. He has power."

Suddenly she smiled confidently. "So? Even Achilles had his weak spot. Von Eiderfeld will have one, too. Start digging!"

Daylight was beginning to fade as the big car finally turned into the poplar-lined drive that led up to Hautecloque. As it rolled through the gate, she caught a glimpse of the familiar crest of the de Légers chiseled into the stone. In the evening shadows, the lion and the salamander looked curiously weary and bored. She sat up straight. There in the distance Château Hautecloque-de Léger stood, its haughtiness worn like an implacably elegant mask. Against the velvet purple of the twilight, the lights shone yellow in the elongated windows and the air was very quiet. Somehow Hautecloque looked much smaller and less formidable than that first time she had seen it. For now she recognized the haughty coldness for what it really was. Simply a facade that both inflated the achievements of the early ancestors and hid the decadence of the present generation.

"Wait here," she instructed the chauffeur as she got out of the car, attaché case in hand.

He nodded courteously and closed the door behind her. When she was on top of the marble steps, she banged twice on the brass knocker. For a moment she turned and her eyes lingered on the car. The chauffeur was leaning against it, cupping his hands and lighting a cigarette against the wind.

Behind him, the green-and-black coachwork flashed snobbishly in the flickering glow of the gaslights. She smiled grimly to herself. She was facing the de Légers on their own terms. First-class.

A liveried footman opened the huge carved doors and a big square of corrugated light spilled out onto the steps. He made a production of clearing his throat. "Madame?" he said with the reserved air of self-importance that Hautecloque, by its very magnificence, seemed to demand even of its servants.

"I am Madame Kowalsky," she said formally. "I believe the Comte is expecting me."

He looked at her expressionlessly as she stepped into the big foyer. Then he slowly pushed the heavy doors shut. "Please wait here, madame. I shall inform monsieur le Comte that you have arrived."

She nodded her acquiescence. Then soundlessly he withdrew down a long corridor and disappeared. She smiled to herself. She didn't know whether it was a new rule in the house or not, but there was only one way a servant could walk so quietly. By wearing crepe-soled shoes.

As she waited, she looked around. She couldn't help remembering what a big deal it had seemed the time she had used the front door instead of the servants' entrance. In five years, some things had changed. At least for her.

A few minutes later, the footman came back into the foyer. "The Comte will see you now, madame," he announced. "He is in the Salon de la Rotonde. Please follow me."

Hélène nodded and followed him down the hall and through a succession of rooms. When they reached the salon, he opened the double doors, stepped aside so she could enter, and slowly drew the doors closed behind her. She looked around the room. It was exactly the way it had been the night she had dined with the de Légers, the night Hubert had taken her to dance in Saint-Médard and she had refused to go to bed with him. Only the pale blue moiré-covered walls seemed a shade paler. That was par for the course; fabric faded in five years. The fine old paintings all around were cast in soft pools of light coming from the brass arc lamps bowed down over the carved gilt frames. She noticed the Raphael she had admired so much. Then she saw the Comte.

He was standing motionless at one of the windows, one hand tucked in the small of his back as he gazed thoughtfully down at Le Nôtre's dark park. For a moment she thought he did not know that she was here. Then he turned around and looked at her with an expression of disapproval.

"Hello, Philippe," she said softly.

He crossed the big Savonnerie toward her. "I thought I made it quite clear that I did not wish to see you again," he said coldly.

She gave a little laugh. "It seems I have the habit of popping up like a bad penny."

"Indeed. What is it you want?"

She stared at him. "Why this brusqueness, Philippe? Are we such strangers?"

He did not reply. With his hand he made a familiar elegant gesture. She looked at the nearest settee and sank down into it. It was the same one on which she had sat with the Comtesse while the Comte and Hubert had been at the far side of the room discussing politics and business. Was it really possible that all that had been five years ago? Slowly she set the attaché case down on the floor beside her.

For a moment she was silent. She had been so awed by the de Légers, had been so easily blinded. But now she knew better. They were involved only in themselves, their own business, their own pleasure. They took and they took and they never gave. They thought everyone had a price. Dangle a bauble in front of a girl and watch her melt. The Comtesse was just as bad. Why else would she have used Madame Dupré to copy the great couturiers' creations? They played sick little games, the de Légers. To them, everyone was a pawn who could be kicked off the board without a moment's notice. Maybe they had done that with enough people to believe they really were invincible. But she could be as hard and unforgiving as they were. She smiled coolly at the Comte. If that was the way he wanted to play it, then she was willing to go along with it. She held all the aces and he didn't even know it. Her voice was suddenly brisk and businesslike. "The reason my solicitor contacted you was that I have a business proposition."

His blue eyes clouded over and he took a seat opposite her. So that was it, he thought. She was like all the others who had been jilted. He had wondered how long it would take for her greed to rise to the surface. Sooner or later it always did. They were stupid, these girls, to think that all they had to do was to keep coming around and demanding more money. He knew their ploys well enough by now. They came to see him under all sorts of pretexts. They would begin with charming small talk, casually bait the hook, and then try to pull him in. He was used to it. Not once had he given in to their offensive tactics.

"I'm in a bit of a hurry," he said wearily. "If it isn't too inconvenient, I'd appreciate it if this didn't take too long."

"Very well," Hélène said. "I don't know whether or not you are aware that I am now a widow?"

He offered no condolences. "I think I heard mention of it somewhere," he replied dryly. "It seems you've become a rather wealthy young woman."

"Wealthy, perhaps. Terribly rich, no. But I'm finding myself with a lot of time on my hands. I think that during times of mourning it is best to keep busy, non?"

He started to rise to his feet. "I don't know what it is you're getting at," he said irritably, "but I'm a very busy man. Now, if you'll please excuse me . . ."

Her voice was suddenly icy. "*Sit down!*"

He started, and met her eyes. There was something challenging in them that he'd never seen before. It was as if the soft amethyst had been suddenly cut into brilliant facets. Slowly he took his seat again.

She folded her small-boned hands in her lap. The hardness in her eyes faded as quickly as it had come, and once again her voice was low and controlled. "As you might recall, Philippe, I once made some mention of having ambitions of becoming a magazine publisher."

"Yes," he said noncommittally. "So?"

"Well, the corporation is now set up," she answered. "My solicitor has requested this meeting so that I might make you more aware of the company. You see, I'm selling stock in it."

"I'm afraid you've come to the wrong person."

She gave a low laugh. "No, Philippe. I've come to the *right* person. You are going to buy ten percent of Les Éditions Hélène Junot, S.A."

He sat back and began to relax. He looked at her with good humor. "You have a lot of nerve, I'll credit you with that."

"Don't give me credit for that which you know nothing of," she said pointedly. "Do you have a tape recorder?"

He looked at her curiously. "A tape recorder? What on earth for?"

She reached down for the attaché case, swung it onto her knee, and flipped it open. She took out a reel of recording tape and held it up. "I think you should hear this," she said in a level voice.

At first his mouth fell open. Then he began to laugh. "Why, of all the cheap tricks!" His voice took on a taunting edge. "I'm afraid that's not very original. It's been tried before by one of your predecessors."

She looked at him innocently. "What has?"

"Taping our lovemaking and then making an ultimatum."

"An ultimatum such as what?"

"Don't play the innocent," he snapped angrily. "Demanding a financial settlement . . . or the tape will be sent to my wife. I know that routine and you should be smart enough to realize that it won't work. As I told you once, I demand total honesty from everyone. Not only that. I reciprocate. You see, blackmail is not possible because the Comtesse knows all about the house on the Boulevard Maillot and what goes on there."

Hélène's eyes fell and her voice was quiet. "Don't make it sound so cheap, Philippe."

"You're the one who's being cheap," he said. "Now, I'm afraid you've taken up all the time I can spare."

"You'd better listen to this tape," she said quietly. "It's the only chance you'll get. If you haven't got a recorder, I brought one with me. It's outside in the car."

He made an impatient gesture. "I have a recorder in the library. I'll listen to the tape there."

She got to her feet and followed him into the richly furnished two-story library. He gestured at a round baize-covered table at one end. She went over to it. On it stood a radio, a record player, and a tape recorder. Her face was expressionless as she placed the reel on the recorder, carefully threaded the tape through the machine, and then turned to him. "Bear in mind, Philippe, that this is only a copy. The original is in a lawyer's vault. Need I say that it's not the same lawyer who arranged this meeting?"

"You make it sound very ominous. Go on, turn the damn thing on. Let's get it over with."

She inclined her head, smiled pleasantly, and brought a finger down on the green plastic button.

At first there was only a hissing noise. Then came the sound of footsteps and a chair scraping against a floor. Finally the first elegantly baroque notes of the overture from *Clytemnestra* filled the library.

She took a chair near the Comte's and scraped it closer. "As you know, my late husband was a concert pianist. One of the greatest in the world."

"If you say so," the Comte said dryly. "Myself, I've always preferred Horowitz."

She shrugged. "To each his own. Let's listen, shall we?"

She settled back silently as the familiar piano notes rose and fell, swirled and banged, went through all the moods and emotions that could possibly be lured out of an instrument, and then some. Suddenly the music stopped, there was an abrupt scraping sound, quick footsteps, and then silence.

"Really, Hélène—"

She held up a hand. "There's more. Be patient, Philippe."

The sudden sound of footsteps—this is where it started, when she had run through the French doors into the living room.

She watched the Comte closely. His face was an impenetrable mask.

Then there was the unmistakable sound of a telephone being dialed. Suddenly a second set of footsteps echoed loudly, and the receiver was slammed down.

"What are you doing?" a voice hissed.

Despite himself, the Comte leaned forward as he recognized his son's voice. She nodded to herself. He was starting to show signs of curiosity. Then she forgot all about him. She could feel herself starting to tremble as she slipped back in time.

"I'm calling the police."

"What are you going to tell them?" The sound of a scuffle, then Hubert's voice, humble and desperate: *"Don't tell them. Please. I'll do anything for you. Give you anything."*

"Hubert, just give me the receiver."

His voice started to whine. *"Will you listen to me for a moment! Do you think I wanted this to happen? It was an accident!"*

"How old are you, Hubert?"

"Twenty-five."

Her little laugh was strained and humorless. Then there was the sound of a slap. *"Twenty-five! To think that you fought with a man of seventy-two! A pianist whose fingers*

426

were his life, who couldn't defend himself. And you hurled him off the cliff!"

She caught the Comte's eyes flashing for a moment. Then he got to his feet and faced a wall of books so that she couldn't see his face. But she could see the sag of his shoulders as his hands fell to his sides.

"I told you it was an accident!" Hubert shouted. *"He lost his balance!"*

"I don't believe you." Her voice sounded dull and lifeless.

"All right, then don't!" Hubert screamed. *"I wanted to kill him! You're right. Ever since the day you two first met. He was too old for you! Too damned old and too damned ugly! I'm glad I killed him!"*

There was a pause. Then: *"Do you know what you're saying?"*

"Of course I know what I'm saying! And if you tell the police that I had any part in it, I'll deny it. I'll call you a liar! He was a frail old man. Even a woman could have tossed him down that cliff!"

The Comte suddenly lunged at the recorder and snatched the reel off the machine. Angrily, he threw the reel against the wall. Then he slumped over the table and grabbed hold of it. His hands were shaking. Suddenly he looked very old and defeated.

Her voice was soft. "Philippe, at the time all this happened, I didn't even know that the machine was running. Stanislaw had been recording the piece you heard and left the machine on when Hubert attacked me in the garden."

Slowly the Comte straightened and turned to face her. His eyes were pained but unwavering. "Hubert's behavior cannot be excused."

"Don't you think 'inexcusable behavior' is rather too casual a term for murder?"

He ignored her. "I don't care what you want to call it, but I will not let myself be blackmailed," he said with dignity. "Not by anyone or for any reason."

She looked at him levelly and rose to her feet. "I'm leaving now. You may keep that tape. As I told you, I have another. More copies can easily be made. I can send them to the police, to the newspapers, even to *Ici Paris* or *Le Monde Internationale.*"

His mouth hung open. "You wouldn't do that!"

427

"No?" Her lips were grim. "Try me, Philippe."

He looked at her in silence.

"I have brought along all the documents you need for buying into Les Éditions Hélène Junot, S.A.," she continued. "I should mention that they are made out in Hubert's name and require *his* signature, not yours. The contract specifically states that he cannot under any circumstances sell his shares and that he must attend any and all board meetings as scheduled by me. He must stay in constant touch with me and let me know all his movements. That is to make certain that in case of emergencies he will always be available. Need I state that if he fails to do all this, the tape will fall into rather . . . well, into rather unsavory hands?"

He still did not speak.

"Furthermore, ten percent of Les Éditions Hélène Junot, S.A., will cost one million francs. That is the fair market price. I own ninety percent of the corporation and have put up nine million francs as required. So you see, it's not blackmail at all. You're simply being coerced into making a small investment. I should mention that dividends shall be paid quarterly."

His voice was bitter. "You've got it all figured out, haven't you?"

"I like to think so. As I said, I shall leave the documents here. You can have your lawyers go through them. I believe they will find everything in order. I will give you seven days to consider this option. If at the end of that time I do not receive the signed documents and one million francs deposited in the company account at the Banque Rothschild—" She shrugged helplessly.

The Comte slammed his fist down on the table. "I won't have it!" he roared. "I won't let myself be blackmailed!"

When she left the room, he dropped down into a chair. Suddenly he was very tired. He closed his eyes and sat there in silence.

Three days later, when Hélène returned to Paris, the documents were waiting for her. She went over them carefully. Each copy had been signed by Hubert de Léger and witnessed by one of the de Léger lawyers. She called the Banque Rothschild. One million francs had been deposited in her account. She tapped the documents in her hand. *Les*

Modes was finally on its way. But it was a way she had never expected. She was using it as an instrument of justice.

At least that was what she liked to think. But sometimes, when she lay awake at night, she wondered about it. Was it really justice? Or was it vengeance? Sometimes there seemed so little difference between the two, and then, after a while, she could no longer even tell what that difference was.

11

After she left Hautecloque, Hélène had headed for Saint-Nazaire. She had the chauffeur put in at the Hotel Soubise in Rochefort for the night. By noon the next day they reached Nantes. Then once again she was riding along the Loire. The day was overcast and gray, the clouds low and threatening, and the meandering river in its huge, sandy bed picked up the charcoal tones of the sky. At a little past one o'clock they arrived on the outskirts of Saint-Nazaire.

As soon as she saw the road sign with the name of the town on it, she felt a peculiar sensation. At first it began with a buzzing in her temples and she felt the heat of a blush coming on. The strange thing was, the blush wouldn't leave. It took her a while to realize what caused this. Self-consciousness and fright. There was something about this place that could do that to her. It wasn't just the fear of running into Tante Janine. That was part of it, but it went deeper than that. It was the fear of being recognized by *anyone*. Schoolmates, shopkeepers, customers who had come to the nursery. In Paris, she was becoming a somebody. Here she was plain Hélène Junot, the gawky kid who lived with the crazy old woman who ran the nursery. Here she would always be remembered for that. It made her feel a deep sense of shame and resentment. It was difficult to put her finger on what it stemmed from. It was simply there. When you left a place, you could never go back. Not as yourself.

She sighed. All the pain of her childhood seemed to be

429

capsulized in this one small, unimportant town. She felt pain in Paris sometimes, but nothing like here. She had lived here for years and still felt like an outcast. It was when she returned to Paris that she felt she was coming home.

She looked out the window. In many ways, the town had changed. A lot of construction was going on, especially on the outskirts. It reminded her somehow of Seulberg. The new houses here had the same boxy shape, the same kind of cold neatness and sharp angles and stuccoed walls. Was that what the war had done? she wondered. Was all the individual character of a place wiped out and replaced with the unimaginativeness of the new? Why was style just swept aside like antiquated dirt and forgotten? Didn't beauty count for anything anymore?

She pushed the button that lowered the glass partition between her and the chauffeur. "Drive to the church," she instructed.

She pushed the button again and the glass slid silently back up out of the seat. She stared out the window again. She should never have come here. She knew that now. She should have had Edmond, Jeanne, and Petite Hélène come straight to Paris. Saint-Nazaire was a torture.

The chauffeur had no trouble finding the church. He drove around the walled-in churchyard until they reached the main gate. Then he pulled the car expertly up alongside the curb, jumped out, and held the rear door open. Hélène climbed out slowly and looked around. On the other side of the street was the stonemason who specialized in tombstones and statues. A winged angel sculptured out of marble stood outside in the yard, keeping guard over gravestones and what looked like short marble and granite railroad ties. There were other angels, too. Some were weeping, some had their hands over their faces. Next door was a florist. That would be Herriot's. She was surprised. The familiar old stone building had been torn down and a new one had gone up in its place. Progress and prosperity had finally come to Saint-Nazaire.

She started across the street toward "Herriot's." Then she stopped. The sign over the door didn't read "Herriot." It read "Janine Péguy." So the old lady was doing all right for herself, she thought grudgingly. She had expanded all the way into town.

She retraced her steps to the Rolls. The chauffeur was

stretching his legs and smoking a cigarette. As soon as he saw her, he made as if to toss it into the gutter.

"Don't bother," she said quickly. "I was wondering if you could do me a favor."

"Oui, madame?" He inclined his head, took a few quick puffs, tossed the cigarette down, and ground it out under his boot.

She snapped open her purse and took out some crisp bills and handed them to him. "Go across the street and buy some flowers." She frowned suddenly. "On second thought, make that a potted plant."

"Any preferences?"

She shook her head. "Anything, as long as it's something nice."

He gave a little bow, waited for a Simca to pass by, and hurried across the street. A few minutes later he returned carrying a big potted plant wrapped up in dark green tissue. She took the plant into her arms. "Merci. I'll be back soon," she said.

He nodded and watched her go through the gate and disappear into the cemetery that surrounded the church. He reached for his pack of cigarettes, fished one out, and lit it. Vaguely he wondered about a person who left Paris to visit a château in Bordeaux for an hour and a cemetery in the boondocks the next day. Then he gave a typically Gallic shrug. Chacun à son goût. To each his own.

Hélène looked around at the neat rows of crosses and stone memorials. The cemetery was laid out like a precisely surveyed town, the paths straight and defined, the rectangular plots marked off by thick borders of marble or granite. The earth inside each perimeter was covered with chalky white gravel. Centered in it were either minuscule flowerbeds or big stone planters. She shifted the plant around in her arms and gave a sigh of bewilderment. She had forgotten that there would be so many graves.

She turned as she heard a scraping noise. Not far off, a wizened old gravedigger was standing knee-deep in a rectangular hole. She watched as he grunted while stomping on his shovel, trying to dig it into the hard-packed soil. She walked over to him and cleared her throat. "Excuse me, monsieur," she said politely.

He stopped digging, leaned on his shovel, and looked up at her. Then he turned his face away, hawked noisily, and spit the soil up out of his lungs. He wiped the sweat off his forehead with his dirty sleeve and gave a toothless smile.

"Tell me, would you happen to know where the grave of Madeleine Dupré is?"

He screwed up his face thoughtfully for a moment, rubbing his unshaved chin as if that would help him remember. Then his eyes brightened and he pointed across the cemetery. "Over there, on the other side of the church. Third row from the wall, about in the center. It's got a small gray marker with a black plaque. I remember it because the stone was put in before the earth had a chance to settle."

She smiled her thanks and followed his directions. After a while she found the grave. She stood very still and looked down at it. The gravedigger had been right. Both the tombstone and the stone edging had been installed far too soon; they were sagging and the granite had cracked in three places as the earth underneath it had shifted. The little flowerbed in the center of the dirty gravel was sadly neglected. The weeds were even pushing up through the gravel. She looked at the graves on either side of it. They were both neatly tended, but the one on the right was big and lavishly planted. She set the pot down on the granite edging of Madame Dupré's grave and looked over at the neighboring one. The right side of the expensive, shiny headstone was blank, meaning that one of the spouses was still living. The left was inscribed in chiseled, gilt-filled letters:

PIERRE PÉGUY
1918–1955

Hélène's face clouded over and her eyes glittered. So he was dead. Of course the grave was well-tended, she thought resentfully. And she knew by whom. Tante Janine. Who else's devotion could be so blind? To her, Pierre had been some kind of saint. She shook her head slowly and looked back at Madame Dupré's sagging, overgrown grave. Then she hiked up the skirt of her Odile Joly suit, got to her knees, and began to tug at the weeds that grew from her friend's grave. Later, after she had finished and the earthenware pot of pink hydrangea was sunk halfway into the ground, she clapped the dirt off her hands and got to her feet. She surveyed her work. It helped somewhat, but it wasn't enough. Immediately she came to a decision. Before leaving, she would see the stonemason across the street about putting in a new border and a new headstone. Something nice and solid. And marble. Madame Dupré had appreciated quality.

Deftly Jeanne made shallow cuts on both sides of the small turbot. She sprinkled it with salt and pepper, dipped her fingers into the cup of congealed grease, and rubbed some sparingly on the fish. Then she carefully picked up the turbot by the head and the tail and laid it flat in the heavy iron baking pan, white side down. She opened the oven door and shoved the pan inside. There. At least there would be food to eat.

Things hadn't been going well since Petite Hélène had been born. She had fought Edmond and kept working at Au Petit Caporal right up until she was ready to give birth. Then a new girl had temporarily taken her place. Monsieur Boivin, the fat proprietor, had promised that her job would be waiting for her. When Petite Hélène was six months old, she had gone back to the restaurant to reclaim her job. Monsieur Boivin had hemmed and hawed and squirmed uncomfortably. Finally he had stammered that he couldn't fire the new girl. Her husband had just died and she was now the breadwinner of her family. Jeanne had nodded quietly and made the rounds looking for another job. There were none to be had.

Now she shrugged philosophically and turned around as she heard movement behind her. Petite Hélène was sitting in a corner, her little hands cautiously pawing through the pile of laundry. Her pink face was screwed up in deep wonder and curiosity as she inspected the colors and textures of the fabrics.

Jeanne cocked her head and studied her for a moment. There was something about watching your child that made you realize you were watching a little part of yourself. Strange, how quickly the little ones grew. It seemed only yesterday that she had pushed the child out of her womb and the midwife had held it up in the air by the legs and given it a resounding smack. She would never forget the joy she had felt when she had heard Petite Hélène's first angry cry. And now, more than ever, Petite Hélène was her pride and her joy. She was just at that age where they are getting into everything. Exploring, discovering, trying to grasp the feel of life, her tiny lips glum when the mysteries were too big to comprehend, the smiles wide with delight every time one was solved. She was such a beautiful child, Jeanne thought. An angel, really. Her hair was neither brown nor golden, but aggressively red; yet each curly strand was as delicate as spun copper. Her eyes were big and blue and naturally wide with curiosity. Jeanne envied her. It would be years before she would find out what her lot would be—that she was poor, that the smell of fish in the walls of her home was not in homes everywhere.

More than three months ago, Edmond had left the fishing fleet and had gone to work at one of the new shipyards. The pay was much better, and they had both been happy about the job. Then, a month ago, the company went bankrupt. Ever since, something had gone out of Edmond. He seemed to be spending all his time at the taverns. There was no money for anything, but he always seemed to come up with enough for a drink. It wasn't until last week that she found out how. The wife of one of his friends had come to her, demanding that his loan be repaid.

There was a sudden hissing sound behind her. Quickly she spun around, the reality of the chore at hand forcing the thoughts out of her mind. The pot on top of the stove was boiling over. Instinctively she grabbed a rag and used it to lift the lid off. She picked up a fork and gently prodded a potato. It was soft and perfect. "Now, if only Edmond comes home on time," she said aloud, wiping her hands on her apron.

From out in the hallway she could hear someone knocking on the door. She felt a sudden chill. She listened carefully. The knocking came again. Quickly her mind raced over the possibilities of who it might be. Not Edmond; he always let himself in. No, it must be someone to whom they owed money. Not the landlady; Jeanne had already run into her earlier that morning, promising that it wouldn't be long. She wrung her hands in despair. There were so many people to whom they owed money. She sighed, went over to Petite Hélène, and picked her up. She tiptoed out into the hallway, put one hand over the child's mouth, and silently approached the door. Soundlessly she moved aside the hinged piece of metal that hung over the peephole. She blinked to make sure she wasn't dreaming. Then she let out a cry, threw aside the bolt, and flung the door open.

"Hélène!" she gasped.

"Jeanne!" Hélène stepped forward, wrapped her arms warmly around her sister-in-law, and kissed her. Then she stepped back to study Petite Hélène.

Jeanne smiled proudly and handed Petite Hélène over. "Look who's here, ma petite," she whispered. "Your aunt. See . . ."

Hélène took the child in her arms and held her tightly, swaying her back and forth. The tiny pink face broke out into an enormous smile.

"Come in, come in," Jeanne said quickly.

Hélène stepped inside and Jeanne closed the door, carefully locking it behind her. She led the way to the kitchen. "Make yourself comfortable," she said timidly. "I'm afraid everything's in a mess."

Hélène laughed. "Don't worry about it. It's my fault. I should have given you some notice instead of arriving on the spur of the moment."

"Nonsense!" Jeanne took Petite Hélène and sat her down on the dinette.

The tiny girl picked up a spoon and started tapping the table with it. "Tante Hélène! Tante Hélène! Tante Hélène!"

Jeanne and Hélène both began to laugh. "She knows my name," Hélène said.

"She'd better. I've been teaching it to her since the day she was born." Jeanne quickly slipped out of her apron and patted her hair. "She already knows more than thirty different words. She's a prodigy!" Then she took Hélène's hands in hers and her voice became suddenly sober. "I'm sorry about Stanislaw. I got your letter and heard the news. Even people here were talking about it."

"I can imagine," Hélène said dryly.

"I'm sorry we didn't send flowers." Jeanne looked away, her face suddenly red with shame. "But I wrote you a letter."

Hélène frowned. "That's strange. I never got it."

"I couldn't send it," Jeanne confessed in a quiet voice.

Hélène pulled Jeanne toward her in an embrace of understanding. "Are things that bad?" she asked softly.

Jeanne nodded miserably. "Things haven't been going well. In fact . . ." Suddenly she burst into tears.

435

Gently Hélène patted the back of Jeanne's head. "Do you want to talk about it?"

Jeanne nodded and wiped her eyes. "Au Petit Caporal . . . well, they wouldn't give me my job back after Petite Hélène was born. And Edmond quit the fishing fleet to work for a new shipbuilder. They went broke right away and ended up owing him three weeks pay."

Hélène listened in silence. "But why didn't you let me know?" she asked finally. "I would have sent you money."

"Edmond's stubborn, Hélène. He's so proud."

"That's ridiculous!" Hélène said angrily. "We're *family*. He should know that better than anyone! But don't you worry. You can stop crying now."

"Please . . . don't tell Edmond I told you," Jeanne begged.

"I promise I won't." Hélène smiled. "Come, now, your troubles are over."

"No." Jeanne sniffled and wiped her nose with her finger. "We're so far in the hole that we'll never be able to dig ourselves back out."

"Don't worry about that. I want you to make a list of all your creditors and give it to me. I'll take care of it. You won't even have to see them. And by the way . . ." She propelled Jeanne toward a chair, reached into her purse, and took out two thick envelopes. She handed one to Jeanne.

Jeanne looked up at her. "What's this?"

"You'll need to buy tickets, new clothes, new furniture. New *everything*."

Jeanne looked confused. "But . . . what are you talking about?"

Hélène gave her the second envelope. "And here's Edmond's tuition for the University of Paris."

"The . . . University of Paris?" Jeanne stared dumbly at the envelope.

"Did I forget to tell you?" Hélène said lightly. "There's an apartment waiting for you. It's just across the street from the Bois de Boulogne."

"But . . ." Jeanne could say no more, only stare at Hélène.

"Of course, there's a catch," Hélène said. "I've just started my own business."

"The magazine?" Jeanne asked in an awed voice.

"The magazine. When Edmond's finished with his schooling—it'll be a few years, of course—he has to help me.

436

I'll need a bright international lawyer I can trust." She looked around. "By the way, where *is* Edmond?"

Jeanne looked down at her hands. "Probably at the tavern," she said quietly.

"Good," Hélène said with finality. "Go and get dressed. We'll join him and a buy a round for everybody in the place."

TODAY

Saturday, January 13

1

Spruce Point was located on the Hudson a few miles upriver from West Point. It was set in a magnificent old park that sloped gently down to the railroad tracks along the river's edge. From uphill you could see the river. When you stood near the tracks, you couldn't. That was because a high stone wall separated them from the manicured lawns of Spruce Point.

From the road, Spruce Point Manor, set behind the stately blue spruces from which it took its name, looked just like it had for the past hundred-and-some years since a tin-can tycoon had erected the neoclassical folly. After his death and a much-contested will the white elephant had been sold and turned into an institution for special people. It was still a beautiful place, but there was something stifling about it. There were uniformed guards in the gatehouse, an electronic surveillance system, and the walls surrounding the property—once necessary to keep people out, now to keep them in—were high and in good repair. In a posher era, the residents of Spruce Point had dressed in furs and fabulous jewels, and the staff wore black-and-white uniforms. Now the residents looked neat but far from elegant, and the staff wore the smocks and uniforms of doctors and nurses.

At the entrance, one of the brown-uniformed guards hurried out of the gatehouse. He bent down to look through the passenger window of the long chauffeur-driven black limousine that had just pulled up. The tinted window lowered silently.

Z.Z. looked up at the guard through her dark sunglasses. "Mrs. Bavier," she said coldly. Nervously she flicked the ash from her cigarette into the ashtray. It missed and she brushed it off the seat with her fingers.

The guard consulted his clipboard. "Mrs. Bavier . . . yes, ma'am, you're expected." He signaled the second guard to open the gate. Quietly the iron doors swung open electronically. Then the Cadillac started to roll and drove past the gate and along the gravel drive between the blue spruces. The trees made the drive look dark and depressing. On an impulse, Z.Z. twisted around in her seat and looked out the rear window. Behind them, the gates were swinging shut again. She shuddered involuntarily. This place was a prison. The prison into which she had locked her . . . her *baby*.

Nervously she lit another cigarette with the butt of the old one. Her hands were shaking. What would Wilfred look like? she wondered. She had never seen him since that day in the hospital, ten years ago. The day he had been born.

Suddenly she felt a chill. Maybe he would recognize her. Maybe there would be a scene. Maybe he would go out of his mind and try to attack her. Maybe . . .

The limousine pulled to a halt in front of the colonnaded building and the chauffeur held the back door open. Flustered, Z.Z. reached for her black leather purse, pulled her mink collar closer around her neck and held it there as she got out.

A middle-aged woman with short brown bangs and large baby-blue eyes came down the portico steps. She wore a stiffly starched white smock and black leather pumps. "Mrs. Bavier?" she asked in a reassuring, friendly voice.

Z.Z. looked at her. "Yes," she replied hoarsely.

"The gate called and said that you were on your way. I'm Dr. Rogers. You had requested to see your son's doctor." She smiled and extended her hand. "I am she."

Limply Z.Z. shook the hand. For once, her self-assurance deserted her. "My . . ." She swallowed. "My . . . son's. . . . Yes."

"Won't you come in, Mrs. Bavier? We can talk in my office."

Z.Z. followed her up the stone steps and into the building. From outside, the mansion had looked neoclassical. Inside, the main hall was strictly Gothic. There were thick stone pillars, heavy dark paneling, and an oppressive vaulted ceiling. Suddenly she froze. A young nurse was leading a little boy down a corridor that branched off the main hall. Even through her sunglasses, Z.Z. could see him all too clearly. He was a boy, but close up he didn't really *look* like a boy. She winced and felt a tightness within her. He was short and

442

overweight. His eyes were close-set and slanted, his forehead flattened. His tongue was hanging out.

Dr. Rogers turned to Z.Z. "Could you please excuse me for a moment?"

Z.Z. couldn't speak. She nodded dumbly and watched her approach the child.

"Hello, Stephen," Dr. Rogers said in a friendly voice. She squatted down so that her face was level with his. "Where are you going?"

He stared at her. When he spoke, his words sounded thick and labored, and his mouth twisted into a kind of smile. "I'm going to the craft shop."

Z.Z. forced herself to shut her eyes. What kind of monsters did they keep in this place? Oh, God, why had she come? Why hadn't she just let sleeping dogs lie? Why?

But she knew why. It was because the battle for HJII—for the destruction of Hélène Junot—reopened all the old wounds. It was because she had to *see* what Hélène had put her through. What she had made her suffer alone, without Sigi.

". . . and you be a good boy." Dr. Rogers tousled the child's straight black hair. Then she came back to Z.Z. "I'm sorry to have kept you waiting." She smiled. "But Stephen needs a little love every now and then."

Z.Z. nodded wordlessly.

Dr. Roger's office was off the main hall. It was a small low-ceilinged room with an enormous stone fireplace and more dark paneling. The metal filing cabinets and the teak-and-chrome desk looked out-of-place.

Dr. Rogers gestured for Z.Z. to take a seat in an armchair. Then she went behind her desk and sat in the swivel chair. "I must admit that your appointment to see Wilfred came as a surprise, Mrs. Bavier. Wilfred has been here for ten years, and this is your first visit." Dr. Rogers paused.

Wordlessly Z.Z. snapped open her purse and lit a cigarette. Her hands were shaking.

Dr. Rogers continued. "Your request for a visit specifically stated that you do not wish your son to know your identity. We will respect that wish." She looked at Z.Z. rather queerly. "You know, in a way, he rather looks like you."

Z.Z. stiffened. Rigidly she put her splayed fingers on the arms of her chair and started to rise.

"Please, Mrs. Bavier," Dr. Rogers said. "Do stay. I assure

you that Wilfred is quite normal physically. Except for the unfortunate fact that his brain is damaged, he is quite like any other boy his age. It would be unfortunate if you did not at least see him."

Slowly Z.Z. nodded. "Where is he right now?"

"In the craft shop."

"You mean with that . . . that . . ." Z.Z.'s voice cracked.

Dr. Rogers folded her hands on the desktop. "You mean, with Stephen?" she asked in a soothing voice.

Z.Z. nodded.

"Yes, with Stephen and quite a few of our other residents. Crafts are very popular here at Spruce Point. Stephen and Wilfred are good friends, actually. There is nothing wrong with Stephen except that he had the misfortune to be born a mongoloid."

Z.Z. smoked in silence.

"Do not worry about the residents intermingling. They do so constantly. Indeed, we encourage it. However, there is always a member of our trained staff on hand. You see, the residents are all quite harmless. To them, Spruce Point is not only their home, it is their *world*. Very few of them have ever been to the 'outside' as we call it. Their world consists entirely of the fifteen acres that comprise Spruce Point. Most of our residents have no desire to leave here. They feel safe inside these walls. In fact, the majority of them would be terrified at the prospect of going 'outside.' "

"And Wilfred?" Z.Z.'s voice was a whisper.

"Wilfred is slow but quite normal," Dr. Rogers said carefully. "He has expressed a desire for adventure."

Z.Z. leaned forward and stubbed out her cigarette. "I think I'd just better—"

"Please, Mrs. Bavier. I am not trying to put you on the spot. Just because you have expressed a desire to see your son doesn't obligate you to take him home with you."

"Does he . . . know who he is?"

"He knows nothing about his family," Dr. Rogers said gently.

"Has he . . . ?"

"Asked? Yes. Many of our residents are naturally curious. But your instructions were to keep his identity a secret." Dr. Rogers smiled warmly. "Shall we go and see him?"

Z.Z. nodded and slowly rose. She was glad that she was wearing sunglasses. They hid the moistness in her eyes.

Dr. Rogers led the way to the craft shop. When they got there, she opened the door and motioned for one of the supervisors to come out into the hall. A pretty young woman with fair hair appeared. She was wearing a smock. Z.Z took off her sunglasses and tried to see past her into the room, but the door closed quickly.

Dr. Rogers introduced the pretty young woman as Janet Kovacs, the arts-and-crafts teacher. As soon as she saw Z.Z., a flicker of recognition showed in her eyes. Z.Z. noticed it. "Is something the matter?" she asked.

Quickly Janet Kovacs recovered. She shook her head. "No, it's nothing," she said softly. "I'm sorry."

On an impulse, Z.Z. put her sunglasses back on. For some reason, Dr. Rogers seemed to view this gesture with approval. Then she cleared her throat and turned to the teacher. "Would it be possible for us to observe the class without attracting undue attention?"

Janet Kovacs glanced at Z.Z. and thought for a moment. "I don't see why not," she said finally. "The residents are quite wrapped up in their projects. I doubt they'll pay much attention to you other than showing natural signs of curiosity. I do suggest that you stay near the door. That way, they'll be less likely to be distracted."

Dr. Rogers nodded. "Very well." Then she turned to Z.Z. and gave her a reassuring smile. "Let's go in."

Janet Kovacs opened the door and they followed her inside. Z.Z. looked around the noisy room in horror. She was suddenly dizzy. To her, this room looked like the devil's workshop. Painting, needlecraft, macrame, pottery; arts and crafts of every sort were being worked on. But it was not the projects that made her feel faint. It was the people doing them.

They were of all sizes and ages. Some were mentally retarded, some were mongoloids, some had birth defects, others had been struck down by accidents or disease. One small girl in a corner had no arms or legs, only a head and torso. Studiously she was drawing with a felt-tipped pen clenched between her teeth. Next to her, Stephen was sitting at the potter's wheel laboriously working on a piece of clay, and his already contorted face was screwed up even more in concentration. By the window overlooking the Hudson sat an old man in a wheelchair. He had multiple sclerosis. His body was as twisted out of shape as the wreckage of an automobile. For a moment Z.Z. could only stare at him.

These were some of the nameless residents of Spruce Point. They all went by their first names; their surnames were kept secret even from themselves. Only the older ones who had been struck down by disease knew who they were. The rest did not. Neither did Z.Z. She only knew that they all came from the "best" families. Their last names were those of people who moved in lofty circles, people listed in the *Social Register* or the *Celebrity Register*. People who owned Fortune 500 corporations or who made it big in politics or in the performing arts. It was ironic that the residents of Spruce Point were the would-be heirs to some of the largest fortunes in America. But they would never claim these fortunes. Spruce Point was their prison.

Suddenly Z.Z. noticed that the man in the wheelchair was modeling for a painting. She glanced over at the canvas and winced. For a long time she couldn't take her eyes off it. It was a horrible painting and yet it was beautiful. Its depiction of the twisted, crumpled body looked abstract in its very realism. Somehow it managed to convey raw power in the useless, tortured limbs. But more than just power; there was a fierce anger, and compassion, too. Tears sprang to her eyes. Then she caught her breath. She saw the artist.

He had his back to her. In his right hand he held a paintbrush. His hair was honey-colored—just like hers! My God! she thought. Wilfred! For a moment she felt a surge of maternal love. She wanted to rush toward him and throw her arms around him. Beg for his forgiveness. Promise to take him home. But she was frozen.

Suddenly he turned around. For an instant she felt the floor beginning to spin. She caught herself on the door frame.

Wilfred's retardation wasn't the worst part. The worst was his perfect face. Now she understood why Janet Kovacs had been so startled, why Dr. Rogers thought her wearing sunglasses was a good idea.

Dr. Rogers had been right. Wilfred looked absolutely normal. But the cruelest irony of all was that he looked like Z.Z. She had been prepared to come face-to-face with a horribly misshapen mutant like Stephen, or someone contorted like the man in the wheelchair. But instead, it seemed that nature had compensated for Wilfred's brain damage by giving him an extraordinarily beautiful face. He was by far the most handsome boy she had ever seen.

For a moment he stared at her. The sudden pain in his intelligent eyes seemed to burn straight through her.

Z.Z. clutched Dr. Rogers. "Get me out of here!" she whispered hoarsely. "For God's sake, get me *out*!"

2

The Chameleon had no trouble finding the place he was looking for. It was located in Westchester County, just a short drive north from Mount Kisco. When he reached it, he pulled his rented black Ford over on the shoulder, rolled down the window, and looked out. Here a narrow private drive branched off from the road. It led up to a white house set a quarter of a mile back behind some bare old oaks. At the entrance to the drive stood a big painted sign: "PAUL ROEBUCK, Master Trainer/Kennels."

A twisted smile crossed the Chameleon's lips. Yes, this was the place. Expertly he put the car in reverse, then made a left turn, forward into the drive, and drove up to the house. It was one of those colonial-style wooden buildings with a porch running all the way around it. Parked up front were a station wagon and a white van with the legend "PAUL ROEBUCK KENNELS" painted on the side. He pulled in behind the van, got out, and approached the house. When he stepped up on the porch, he found a huge German shepherd guarding the front door. Its watchful dark eyes were oddly hostile. It didn't move, but it let out a low, menacing growl. It smelled danger.

The Chameleon smiled with contempt. He never could understand what people saw in dogs. They were noisy and dumb and dirty. Still, they had their uses, he supposed. Just like he had a use for one now.

Giving the dog no more than a cursory glance, the Chameleon lit a cigarette and pressed the bell. Melodious chimes tinkled somewhere inside the house.

A tall, heavy set blond man opened the door. "Mr. Samuels?" he said easily.

The Chameleon smiled and nodded as they shook hands.

As he had expected, the man's grip was strong and firm. "I'm Erik Roebuck," he said.

The Chameleon still smiled, but he was silent for a moment. Erik Roebuck? This was something his research had overlooked. He felt like kicking himself for being so sloppy. Not that it made any difference. But in the future he'd have to be more careful. One silly mistake like that, and in the wrong situation, could mean curtains. He laughed softly. "I'm sorry," he said apologetically. "You just threw me. I was under the impression you were Paul Roebuck."

"So are many people. Paul Roebuck is my father. He founded this place twenty-five years ago. Last spring he decided to retire, and I took over for him. I hope you're not disappointed."

The Chameleon puckered his lips thoughtfully. "I was counting on getting one of his dogs."

Roebuck smiled warmly, showing straight white teeth. "Have no fears, Mr. Samuels," he said reassuringly. "My father did not restrict his training to canines. He personally trained every man who works here. That includes me."

The Chameleon smiled. "Good. Your word is enough. Now, let me explain a few things to you, if I may."

"Certainly," Roebuck said as he went behind the desk. "Won't you have a seat?"

The Chameleon sat down in the vinyl chair and made himself comfortable. He took out another cigarette and lit it. Then he looked Roebuck straight in the eye and began to recite the cover story he had come up with. "Let me be frank with you, Mr. Roebuck. My wife and I recently moved here from California, and we live near Port Washington. In a rather secluded neighborhood, I might add. I'm a businessman, and unfortunately, my work requires that I travel a great deal of the time. Sometimes for weeks on end. And my wife is frightened when she's left alone." He smiled sadly and spread his hands apart. "So I'm here."

"And you want a watchdog?"

"Precisely. Something that has both a bark and a bite."

Roebuck folded his hands and looked down at his cuticles.

"Tell me something, Mr. Samuels," he said. "Do you like dogs?"

Better to play this one straight, the Chameleon decided. The animal would instinctively sense his dislike and give him away. He shook his head. "I'm afraid I really don't care much for them."

Roebuck nodded. "You'd be surprised to find out how many people lie when I ask that question." He smiled. "Exactly what kind of dog is it that you're looking for?"

The Chameleon shrugged and pretended to think. He wanted a black Great Dane, or maybe a Doberman, but he wasn't about to say so. Let Roebuck suggest the breed, and he would think it was his own idea. "Oh . . . just something mean-looking and big. Size is no problem, since the dog will have a lot of running-around space. We have a large property, fenced in I might add. Probably short-haired . . . yes, Amanda would like that." Good touch, that "Amanda." Now his wife had a name.

Roebuck frowned. "We have quite a few short-haired breeds to choose from." He waved at the pictures on the wall. "Why don't you take a look and tell me what appeals to you?"

The Chameleon got to his feet and made a pretense of studying the photos. Finally he smiled helplessly. "It's really not my line. What do you suggest?"

"Either a Doberman or a Great Dane. Both are short-haired and fast." Roebuck smiled and got to his feet. "Would you like to go down to the kennels and see one in action? Then I'll let you decide."

A moment later they left the house and went outside. In silence Roebuck led the way and they started down a frozen dirt path to the base of the hill where the kennels were located. As they approached, the wind brought their scent toward the dogs, and suddenly they all jumped up and began to claw excitedly at the fences. The cacophony of howling and barking filled the air.

"They can smell us coming," Roebuck explained.

When they reached the nearest building, a man was there waiting for them, smiling brightly. "This is Edward," Roebuck told the Chameleon. "He's the best trainer here." Then he looked at Edward. "Bring Rufus out into the pen."

Edward's smile faded. "Rufus?"

Roebuck nodded curtly. There was no mistaking the authority in that gesture.

Edward shook his head and shrugged. Without another word he went inside the building.

Roebuck put his hands in his pockets and smiled at the Chameleon. "The pen is on the other side of the building." He led the way around the corner to the far side of the kennels. Here was the huge three-sided pen. One side of it was actually the wall of the building; the other three sides were ten-foot-high, heavy-duty mesh wire attached to sturdy steel posts. Roebuck opened a gate and they went in.

"It won't take Edward but a minute," Roebuck promised.

The Chameleon nodded patiently. He looked at Roebuck with interest. "This Rufus," he said slowly. "What's so special about him?"

Roebuck's voice was soft. "Rufus is no ordinary dog, Mr. Samuels. He's quite intelligent. He's also big and well-trained. Depending on what you instruct, he can either be gentle or mean." He paused. "He's also capable of killing a man."

The Chameleon stared at him. He was digesting this welcome piece of news in silence when Edward came out of the building leading a black Great Dane. The Chameleon studied the animal closely. Little as he knew about dogs, he could tell that this one was exceptional. Rufus looked as big as a horse but moved with the lithe grace of a swan. His bulging, taut muscles stood out clearly under gleaming short hair.

Roebuck reached into his pocket and took out a small object.

The Chameleon glanced at it. "What's that?"

Roebuck held it out. "This is a sonic dog whistle," he explained. "You and I can't hear it because our ears can't catch certain high-pitched decibels. But Rufus can. When I give two short blows, Rufus attacks. When I give a long, drawn-out one, he retreats. Watch closely." He raised the whistle to his lips, inflated his cheeks, and blew.

Rufus suddenly perked up. For a split second his ears quivered; then he trotted complacently over to them, his tail wagging.

"Sit!" Roebuck commanded in a stern voice.

The dog immediately sat, looking up at Roebuck with a questioning look in his shiny black eyes. He was an alert dog,

450

all right, the Chameleon noticed. Then he looked over at Edward. The trainer was going back inside the building. A few minutes later, he came out again, thick, bulky padding strapped around his arms, chest, and legs. Suddenly Rufus was emitting a low, steady growl, his alert eyes concentrated on Edward, but he remained obediently seated.

"Ready?" Roebuck called out.

"Ready!" Edward shouted back.

With quickening interest the Chameleon watched the dog as Roebuck blew twice into the silent whistle. Then it happened. Rufus sprang forward and went flying down the length of the pen toward Edward. Instinctively the trainer held up his padded arms to cover his face. Seconds later, the beast collided with him, attacking in a frenzy and knocking him to the ground. The fierce snarls were carried away by the wind and sounded strangely distant, almost too quiet. For a moment the Chameleon winced. The Great Dane was sinking its teeth into the trainer's padding. Edward went rolling around, trying to protect himself, but it was impossible. Rufus was a powerful brute. He was trying to rip the padding to shreds.

The Chameleon shook his head. God help that dog's victims, he thought with new respect. Even a pro wrestler would be no match for him. And a woman? A woman would be finished off in a minute. Maybe less.

Once again Roebuck raised the whistle to his lips and blew deeply. Rufus immediately froze in his tracks. Then he looked in their direction and came trotting obediently back to them, his tail wagging. His mouth was lolling open and he was panting from the exertion, his breath making clouds of vapor as saliva dripped to the ground. For an instant the Chameleon caught sight of long white fangs.

"Sit!" Roebuck commanded. The dog sat, and he scratched it behind the ears. "Good boy, Rufus," he said gently. "Good boy."

The Chameleon's eyes wandered down toward the end of the pen. Edward was getting nimbly to his feet, unbuckling the padding.

Roebuck turned to the Chameleon. "Satisfied, Mr. Samuels?"

The Chameleon suppressed a smile. Was he satisfied! That

dog was perfect! It was a walking time bomb. It would tear Hélène Junot to shreds.

His voice soft, the Chameleon looked Roebuck deep in the eyes and said, "Sure thing, Mr. Roebuck. I'll take Rufus—he's exactly what I want."

YESTERDAY

V

BLACKMAIL

1

Paris, 1958

Lubov Tcherina, editor-in-chief of *Les Modes*, knocked on the door with her characteristic impatience, flung it open, stalked briskly into Hélène's office, and shut the door behind her with a decidedly firm *snap*. Hélène smiled up at her and put aside the marketing report she had been studying. She folded her hands on the desktop. "You wanted to see me, Luba?"

Luba's cracked-plaster face, with its apple-red rouged cheeks and most determined of determined chins thrust indignantly forward, was set into the haughtily ominous expression that Hélène knew could only mean she was on the warpath. With a quick motion of her hand, Luba snatched her shocking pink framed glasses off her regal nose. She threw the layouts she was carrying under her arm down on Hélène's desk.

"Yes!" Luba's voice was shrilly dramatic. She waved a quivering red-lacquered finger at the layouts. "These . . . these *things*!" she said, her red cheeks getting even redder under the flush of her outrage. "You're not really serious about printing them!"

Hélène smiled at her and picked up the artboards. Quickly she glanced through them. They were for the June-July issue and showed the summer collections. The photos were crisp and clear, the vacant-eyed models in starkly dramatic poses. Jacques had them wading around in the Neptune basin at Versailles, hiking their chic dresses and skirts up above their knees.

"Yes," Hélène said. "I think they're very good."

Luba vented a volcanic sigh. "Don't you *see*?"

Hélène looked at her with a puzzled expression. "See what?"

455

"They're so . . . so *ordinary*." Luba rolled the distasteful word on her tongue as if it were poison.

Hélène couldn't help smiling at Luba's overdramatizations. Everything about the woman was bigger than life. Her voice, her gestures, her looks. A White Russian refugee, whose voice was a strangely exotic mixture of mispronunciations and foreign dialects, Luba possessed a face and figure that were one of a kind. Ordinarily she would have been a tall, bone-thin woman with a long neck like all other tall, bone-thin women with long necks. But Luba was not content with that. She *worked* at her looks. She dyed her hair so pitch black that it gleamed like shoe polish, she painted her eyes with an astonishing amount of mascara, shadow, and eyeliner, and she used rouge like it was going out of style. Most important, she knew how to look vibrant, and that was what made the ugly duckling into a swan. She could never be a beautiful swan, but she settled for second best by becoming an exceptional swan. She shone like ten layers of lacquer, dressed herself in the most unusual finery—Japanese kimonos, Persian robes, Prussian boots trimmed with gold lace, scarlet dresses with purple furs—and could command the attention of an auditorium full of people. If Luba ever went to an auditorium, that is. She went to theaters, fancy-dress balls, important openings. People might have laughed at her, but her style was so deadly serious, so highly original, so indisputably tasteful despite the costumy effects, that she created new trends and styles wherever she went. One word from Luba could make or break a designer's collection.

Being editor-in-chief of a fashion magazine was a natural for Luba. The only pity was that the world lost a potentially great couturière or costume designer in the process. Still, she was already a legend in her own time. In the trade, she was reverently nicknamed "The Czarina." She had been editor-in-chief at *Marie Claire Elle*, and *L'Officiel* for years at a time. She had charted bold new courses in fashion reporting with the same inimitable flair she used in transforming herself.

A little over a year ago, Lubov Tcherina had been fired from her last job—legend had it she had been vacationing at a posh villa in Costa Smeralda when one of the houseboys brought a telephone to the poolside. She swam over and picked up the receiver. It was her magazine. It had just undergone a change in management. "You're fired," she was told, and Luba promptly sank to the bottom of the pool and nearly drowned. Hélène considered herself lucky on two counts. The houseboy was alarmed by the bubbles rising from the bottom of the pool and dived in. The Czarina was saved by mouth-to-mouth resuscitation and joined the staff at *Les Modes*.

Now Hélène carefully studied the artboards Luba had brought in. "I don't see anything wrong with them," she said carefully.

Luba threw her hands up in the air in frustration. "Summer dresses in the Neptune basin? No no, *no!* They should be on a *glacier*. On a mountain peak. An *ice* floe. In a refrigerator. This is too ordinary. Too *trite*."

Hélène slowly nodded and pursed her lips thoughtfully. She could see what Luba was getting at. More drama was called for. These photos were good, but they were staid. Almost benign. *Elle* and *L'Officiel* might have done them. And if that was the case, then *Les Modes* was certainly not going to become the leader of the world's fashion magazines.

Still, these boards had already been laid out, the copy written. Everything was ready to go to the printer in two days' time. Already the August *Les Modes* was being worked on. Each issue was completed six months before the public ever saw it. Hélène gestured for Luba to stay put. She thought for a moment, frowned and quickly pressed down on her intercom buzzer.

Her secretary's efficient voice came over the wire like a distorted squawk. "Oui, mademoiselle?"

Hélène was now going by her maiden name and insisted on being called mademoiselle instead of madame. She leaned forward and spoke directly into the box. "Eleonora, call up the travel agency. Make arrangements for . . . ten?" She glanced at Luba, who nodded pontifically. "For ten to . . ." She thought quickly.

"Chamonix," Luba said in a stage whisper. "I've already checked. They have plenty of glaciers and *cable* cars." Her dark eyes glittered wickedly.

"To Chamonix, Eleonora. Leaving tonight, returning the day after tomorrow. Make overnight arrangements at a decent hotel."

"Oui, mademoiselle."

"And, Eleonora?"

"Oui?"

"Order me a new intercom," Hélène said irritably. "One of

the new American ones. I like to be able to hear what you're saying."

"Oui, mademoiselle." Eleonora buzzed off.

Hélène looked up at Luba sternly. "Now, about those cable cars and Jacques. I want *no* accidents. *No* scandals. *No* broken bones. And *no* hysterical models marching in here in tears. I know the way Jacques works only too well."

Luba smiled malevolently and picked up the artboards.

"You may throw those away," Hélène said.

Luba sniffed the air disdainfully. *"Gladly,"* she announced, as if it were her moral duty to march straight to the nearest trashcan.

Hélène watched her leave. She knew that Luba's taste was unerring, as inbred as a champion's pedigree. Still, she couldn't get over the feeling that the older woman was constantly testing her. Almost challenging her power to see how far she could go. Hélène sighed. As far as her work was concerned, she trusted Luba explicitly. The only thing Luba would have to learn was how to descend from her lofty heights every once in a while and show a little more respect for those she worked for.

Hélène pushed her chair back and got to her feet. She came around from behind her desk and walked over to the wall where a blowup of this month's *Les Modes* cover was carefully spotlighted. She stared up at it. She had now seen it hundreds of times. During production, on the printer's proofs, on every kiosk she passed in the streets. It was the twelfth issue. Could that be possible? she wondered. Had *Les Modes* already been going strong for over a year? They put out ten issues annually; June-July and December-January were counted as one each. That meant they had been covering the French fashion scene for fourteen months already.

She studied the oversized cover as critically as she had studied all the others. She liked seeing them this big. It was easier to recognize the flaws and make certain they did not recur in the future. This particular enlargement was from the December-January issue. The glossy logo had been specially done to look like clear ice. It read:

LES MODES®
Paris

Decembre-Janvier

Centered at the bottom were more ice-cube block letters:

Spécial
Pour une nuit d'hiver

For a winter's night. She liked the theme. She herself had come up with the idea. The glossy close-up photo showed a model from the neck up. The huge stand-up collar of a Max Reby Chat lynx framed her leonine face. Her dark hair was like a mane speckled with glistening snowflakes, and her makeup was frosty, the lipstick almost pinkish-white, the Lancôme eye shadow glistening frost against the rich bronzé makeup cream. The combination was tawny; the model looked like an aggressive tigress ready to stalk the night.

Hélène congratulated herself. It was the best cover to date. Much better than the current *Vogue*. Quickly she crossed over to her desk and pushed down on the intercom again. "Eleonora?"

"Oui, mademoiselle?"

"Call the art department. Tell them to put a hold on the June-July cover."

"Consider it done."

Hélène smiled to herself. She could count on Jacques and Luba coming back from Chamonix with a spectacular new cover shot. On an impulse, she lifted a current copy of *Les Modes* off the stack beside her desk. She opened it, and as her eyes skimmed the masthead, she felt a rush of proprietorial authority and pride.

Decembre 1957/Janvier 1958   *No. 12*

LES MODES

est publié par Les Éditions Hélène Junot S.A.
Président-Directeur Général: HÉLÈNE JUNOT
Directeur des Éditions: NICOLAS DUCOUT
Rédactrice en Chef: LUBOV TCHERINA

She smiled. No matter what anyone tried to tell you, there was nothing like seeing your name in print. Slowly she flipped through the 168 pages. Even now, she could still feel a surge of electricity every time she turned a page.

To date, each issue of *Les Modes* had sold out before the first half of the month was over. Not a single copy had ever been returned from the newsstands. In fact, there was such a demand for *Les Modes* that the distributor was pressing Hélène for an increased run each printing. But Hélène was playing it cautiously. When they'd begun, it had been with a small first run of thirty thousand copies. Even then, she'd kept her fingers crossed. Now they were printing and selling out almost seven times that number. She knew that it was better to have people clamoring for more copies than being stuck with a warehouse full of unsalables. She was cautious, but she shrewdly coupled caution with daring. It was paying off. The first ten issues had been in the red, issue eleven had broken even, and now *Les Modes* was truly in the black for the very first time. Hélène knew that that wasn't bad for a magazine starting off from scratch. In fact, it wasn't bad for any new business. Sometimes it took three to five years before they showed a significant profit. She was very pleased. *Les Modes* was turning out to be a good investment.

Hélène nodded to herself. All in all, it was a magazine to be proud of. And slowly the monopoly of fashion publishers—*Vogue, L'Officiel, Elle,* and *Marie Claire*—who in the beginning had sneered contemptuously at her, were now starting to sit up and take notice. And well they should. A good number of their previously ardent readers were deserting them for *Les Modes*. Already they were feeling the bite.

The intercom sounded noisily. "Yes, Eleonora?"

"Monsieur Ducout is here. And there's a message from a Karl Häberle. He said to tell you that he's here in Paris and staying at the Sèze."

Karl Häberle was in Paris? That took Hélène completely by surprise. Suddenly she stiffened. He had found something. Why else would he have come? She knew of the Sèze. It was one of the moderately priced tourist hotels. She thought quickly.

The man awaiting her was Nicolas Ducout, her managing editor. Excepting herself, he was the most important person on the staff. Even more important than the Czarina. Because when it came down to brass tacks, it was circulation, money, and power that really counted. The first-rate quality, art, and layout were important, but the salesmanship had to come first. She had set up this meeting with him in order to discuss foreign distribution of *Les Modes* and the possibility of planning an Italian-language edition within a year.

460

She came to a swift decision. "Eleonora, tell Nicolas to have a seat and wait. I won't be long. Then call the Sèze and get hold of Karl Häberle. I need to talk to him right away!"

2

"I don't know what to do," Hélène said quietly. She got to her feet and paced the room restlessly. "At first, I thought it would be clear-cut and simple. But now?" She clenched one of her fists and smacked it into the palm of her other hand. "Now, I just don't *know*."

Dr. Rosen took a deep breath as he looked down at the papers scattered across the scarred desktop. He was sitting stock-still on one of the cane-backed chairs in his book-lined study. From the distance came the muffled sounds of traffic. Behind him, the curtains drawn across the window shifted slowly as they caught an elusive draft. Outside, it was dark already. Night came early in winter.

Hélène stopped pacing and watched him in silence. Behind his wire-rimmed glasses, his heavily hooded eyes were wide in horror. For the first time, she was aware of how old he really was, how truly overburdened his narrow, stooped shoulders must be. Perhaps she had been wrong in coming to him, she thought suddenly. He had already suffered so much. She should never have added to it with this. Right in front of her eyes, he seemed to have aged ten years. Even his black-and-gray hair and beard now looked much more gray than before, and the deeply furrowed skin of his face seemed to be stretched tightly across his bones. The muscles in his temples did a series of twitches.

For a moment Dr. Rosen could not speak. It was as if keeping himself under control was all he could hope to do. When he looked back up at her, she could see the tears glistening in the corners of his eyes. Once again he looked down at the papers. Everything blurred. He couldn't even see the papers on the desk clearly. Slowly he reached up and lifted his glasses off the bridge of his nose, wiped the tears from his eyes with his fingertips, and let the glasses sit back down on their prominent Roman perch. Then with a trembling hand he somehow summoned the courage to reach out and shuffle through the papers.

Hélène had never expected Häberle to come up with what he had. She had seen to it that the two hundred thousand deutsche marks she had deposited in the Dresdener Bank in Cologne had been released to him. He well deserved the reward. She wondered how he had ever managed to dig up this much dirt.

There were several photos. One had been taken recently with a telephoto lens. It showed a man in a business suit stepping into a late-model Mercedes-Benz limousine. Despite the graininess of the blowup, she had no doubt who it was. The colorless skin, the skull-shaped head, the bloodless cruel lips spoke for themselves. He was the white-faced one. Karl von Eiderfeld. The one who had ordered Schmidt to burn Marie. The one she herself had seen through the knothole of the dumbwaiter as he had ordered Maman to be "punished."

There were three other photos. Older photos, with dog-eared corners and ragged edges. All of them showed von Eiderfeld in the sleek black uniform with the silver piping. In one, he was standing among a group of men posing for the camera. Written on the back in neat Gothic script was the legend: *(Links zu Rechts): Goebbels, von Eiderfeld, Göring, Hitler, Himmler.* The photo was dated 1935 and von Eiderfeld looked almost youthful. In another, he was standing in an open SS staff car parked by a roadside, watching as an SS unit went by in single file. The men had rifles slung over their shoulders and were pushing bicycles. The third photo showed him with two other officers inspecting a platoon of rigid infantrymen. That one was taken in 1944, and he looked considerably older.

Just seeing those photographs was enough to make Hélène feel a terrible rage. It was poetic justice, she thought, that another German with the same first name as his should have come up with all this evidence.

But there was much more than just the photos. Häberle's search had turned up nineteen different documents, which he had painstakingly translated into French. Most of them were Nazi reports and requisition forms, but one was a copy of Karl von Eiderfeld's military record. Hélène had studied it closely. Karl Jürgen von Eiderfeld had been born in Rüdesheim on the Rhine in 1915. His father had been a general in the Kaiser's army and his mother had been the daughter of a Viennese merchant. In 1932 Karl von Eiderfeld had joined the SS. Almost immediately, the organization had been officially disbanded by the Weimar government. Three months later, when the SS was reinstated, Karl von Eiderfeld had joined once again. He started off on the right foot. Hitler had tried to gain an aura of respectability for the SS by recruiting members of the aristocracy, church dignitaries, and former generals to hold honorary rank. Von Eiderfeld's long-retired father had taken one such rank and had thereby managed to pull enough strings that his son rose quickly within the rigid hierarchy of this army which had been built upon a bastardization of the principles of the Order of the Jesuits. Karl von Eiderfeld had everything going for him. He was considered an outstanding officer and had been decorated numerous times. Then, in 1944, his promotions stopped abruptly and he had been transferred to the Belzec Concentration Camp in Poland. The new job was punishment for having failed what had been considered a simple mission: despite all the resources available to him, he had been unable to find two of four French children who had fled a house in Paris after wounding one German soldier and killing another.

Hélène had closed her eyes. She didn't have to see the names listed. She knew very well who those two French children had been. But there they were on the document, jumping out at her from the German type.

Edmond Junot . . . Hélène Junot. There was something obscene about their being listed in this hellish document.

Von Eiderfeld's short career at Belzec was well-documented by the other papers. He had been the deputy military liaison between the death camp and private industry. There were requisition forms and correspondence signed by him. A receipt for a trainload of Zyclon B crystals from I. G. Farben. Approval for new, fast-burning incinerator devices from Topf and Sohn in Wiesbaden. The crystals had been used for gassing victims in the chambers, the oven to burn their bodies. The last order for a new consignment of Zyclon B had been signed a scant three weeks before Belzec was liberated. That was the most terrible thing of all. Even when it was clear that everything was lost, the Germans had done nothing to stop the senseless horrors. Almost everywhere, the wheels of destruction kept on turning until the very end.

Dr. Rosen sighed painfully and pushed the papers away. The tears came into his eyes again. "This is a powder keg," he said at last. He took off his glasses and slowly put them back in their case.

Hélène nodded slowly. "I know," she whispered. "Even I had no idea there'd be all this."

He looked up at her. "What are you going to do?"

She came closer, sat down again, and looked across the desk at him. "I don't know," she said honestly. "I'll have to think about it." She glanced down at the papers and twisted her lips. "I've thought of going to the Israeli authorities."

He lifted his eyebrows. "And?"

"I'm afraid they wouldn't punish him enough. I mean, there's bound to be a big trial and a lot of publicity. But the worst he'd get is to be hung or electrocuted or shot." She gave a bitter shrug. "I don't know if that's enough."

Dr. Rosen's voice was gentle. "What would be enough as far as you're concerned?"

She reached suddenly across the table and dug her hand into his wrist. Her eyes were hard and relentless. "I want him to suffer," she whispered vehemently. "I want him to live in constant fear. He keeps himself well-hidden. When he leaves his house, he's driven directly to the garage of his office building in Düsseldorf. From there, a private elevator whisks him upstairs to his penthouse office. Few people have ever even seen him. He allows no pictures to be taken. Karl Häberle told me he posed as a reporter wanting to do an article on him for *Der Spiegel*. Not only could he not get near him, but he was warned off. Von Eiderfeld's scared, Simon. But I want him to run even *more* scared." She grabbed some of the papers, held them up, and shook them angrily. "I want to let him know I have *these*. I want to make certain he won't be able to sleep nights. I want him to worry himself sick for as long as he lives!"

Dr. Rosen heaved a big sigh. His face wore a fixed expression of sadness. "The dispensation of justice is a heavy burden," he said simply, "and vengeance an even heavier one. It exacts more from the judge than the judged."

She looked at him and nodded. He was right. The hold she had over Hubert proved that. Was it punishment enough just to dangle a constant threat over someone? The last time she'd forced Hubert to attend a meeting at Les Editions Hélène Junot, S.A., it seemed she had been more miserable than he. In fact, he had constantly challenged and taunted her to see just how far he could go.

Dr. Rosen patted her hand. "Think it over well," he advised in a gentle voice. "Don't rush into anything."

"I won't," she promised. "I'll wait until I've managed to get over some of my immediate anger. But somewhere, somehow, he's got to be made to pay!"

3

She looked out the window of the taxi as it swung onto the quiet elegance of the Boulevard Maillot. In front of the Comte's town house, she saw the familiar Rolls-Royce parked under the streetlamp.

She twisted around in her seat and looked back at the house. The lights shone in all the windows. That meant the Comte was in town.

For a moment she wished she had found Edmond a different apartment than the one on the Boulevard Maurice Barrès. The trouble was, she always had to pass the Boulevard Maillot in order to get there, because the two short streets were actually part of the same long one that ran across the top of the Bois de Boulogne. There was only one way to get around it. In the future, she'd instruct her taxi driver to make a wide detour and come down along the Ancien Cimetière de Neuilly.

It was she who had decided that Edmond should live on the Boulevard Maurice Barrès. The location had seemed only natural. Petite Hélène would be practically across the street from the Jardin d'Acclimatation with its small zoo, amusement park, ponds, Enchanted River, and the Bois de Boulogne. It was the perfect place for a child to grow up. Where else was there the same enchanting mixture of city, nature, and fantasy? She had figured—rightly—that the chances of her ever running into the Comte were almost non-existent. He was not the type of man who wasted time walking around the Bois. If he wasn't working, he was either at Hautecloque with the Comtesse or in the town house or a restaurant with his mistress. The only thing she hadn't figured on was the way she'd feel each time she passed by the town house.

When the cab pulled up in front of the big mansion which had been converted into apartments, she got out and paid the driver. As he meshed the gears and drove off, she tucked the gift-wrapped box under her right arm and went up the balustraded steps. In the lobby, she greeted the concierge and then took the little elevator to the third floor.

When it bobbed to a halt, she pushed the metal gate to one side and stepped out into the hall. Her heels clicked on the polished stone floor as she walked to the far end and rapped on the varnished-wood door.

A moment later she heard a click and the heavy door swung slowly open. Hélène looked down. Petite Hélène was standing there, bathed by the bright light from inside. Hélène caught her breath. The girl was gazing up at her almost shyly. Her eyes seemed bigger and bluer than the last time she'd seen her, her cheeks were the color of pale, ripening strawberries, and her delicate copper hair was like a fuzzy halo fashioned out of the softest down. In the back, it was gathered and tied with a dark blue silk ribbon. Her matching dress, styled along the lines of a painter's smock, was the one Hélène had given her on her last birthday, the dark blue wool trimmed with a Peter Pan collar of beautifully crocheted lace.

Petite Hélène showed off her manners to perfection and dropped a curtsy like a little princess. "Bonsoir, Tante Hélène," she sang formally.

Hélène smiled. "Bonsoir, Petite Hélène."

Suddenly the girl's cherubic face broke out in the most dazzling of smiles and her stiff manners dropped away like a veil off a painting. She flung her arms around Hélène's thighs and squeezed them. "Tante Hélène! I'm so glad you've come," she cried happily, her voice muffled as she buried her face in Hélène's skirt. "I've waited for *hours*."

Hélène reached down with her free hand and held her niece close. Then gently she began to stroke the copper hair. It felt even softer than it looked. Suddenly her eyes dimmed over. Was this what her baby would have been like? So delicate, so fragile.

Then Jeanne bustled into the foyer and by reflex wiped her hands on her apron. "You're late!" she reprimanded.

Hélène looked up and smiled apologetically. She handed Jeanne the bottle of red wine she had tucked under her arm along with the big package. "Peace?" she asked in a small voice.

Jeanne looked at the wine and made a pretense of frowning. Finally she had to laugh. "Peace," she returned, leaning forward and kissing Hélène affectionately on the cheek.

Hélène returned the kiss. Every time she was around Jeanne, she could feel the flow of warmth and love in the air. It was in every corner of this house.

Jeanne took her by the arm and pulled her into the foyer. Hélène squatted down so that her face was level with Petite Hélène's. "And this is for you, young lady," she said in a solemn voice. She handed over the gift-wrapped package.

Petite Hélène's eyes got big as she took the box. She could barely contain her excitement. "Merci beaucoup, Tante Hélène," she managed to spurt out politely. Quickly she pecked Hélène on the lips and then staggered into the living room with the box.

"You're spoiling her," Jeanne said disapprovingly as Hélène got back to her feet.

Hélène gave a little shrug. "At her age you deserve to be spoiled a little. I want her to have everything I could never have."

Jeanne smiled. "We'll see if you change that tune once you have children of your own."

Hélène felt her stomach beginning to cramp. She looked quickly away.

As they walked into the living room, Edmond looked up. He was sitting behind the big desk, his nose poked in a thick law book. He flashed a dazzlingly white grin across the room.

The dentist had done a good job, Hélène thought. Edmond hadn't wanted to go, but she had worked on him until he had finally gotten fed up with her nagging. It had been well worth it. A thousand francs was little enough to pay for replacing what the recoil of a Boche rifle had ruined when he was eleven. Somehow, she had never been able to get used to the gap when he smiled. Now she was satisfied. Edmond looked more handsome than ever. And no longer did he have that hungry look he'd had in Saint-Nazaire. He held himself with a confidence she had not seen before. The incidents with the Nazis and Tante Janine might never have happened. But she knew better.

Carefully Edmond marked his place and closed the book. Then he rose to his feet and quickly strode across the room. They embraced warmly. "How are you, Little French Girl?" he asked softly, his breath warm in her ear.

"Fine, I suppose. Busy, at any rate," she said, relishing the warm strength of his arms. For a moment she felt a foolish pang of jealousy toward Jeanne for holding title to his strength. She could remember what it had been like when they were children. How strong and protective he had been. You felt safe when you were in his arms, like nothing in the world could harm you. She wondered if she would ever find a man of her own who would be able to make her feel this way. As suddenly as they had come, the feelings of jealousy and yearning dropped away. Self-consciously she slipped out of his arms and stepped back. "And . . . and you?" she asked awkwardly. "How's school?"

"Some days are better than others."

Jeanne came over to him and punched him good-naturedly. "Nonsense," she said proudly. "Don't believe a word of it! My Edmond's at the head of his class."

Hélène looked pleased; Edmond, perpetually ill-at-ease when hearing words of praise, flushed and studied his feet.

"Come and sit down," Jeanne said. "I'll uncork the wine. It's only a few minutes until we eat. Is there anything I can get you in the meantime?"

Hélène shook her head and obediently took a seat as Jeanne headed toward the kitchen. She tried her best to avoid looking around. That way her face wouldn't register the disappointment she felt whenever she saw the apartment. Quickly she amended her thoughts. It wasn't really disappointment. Disillusionment, perhaps. It was the sort of feeling a magician must have if his rabbit crawled out of his sleeve at the wrong moment. She had tried her hand at magic and failed. She had tried to get Jeanne to spend the money necessary to buy the appropriate furnishings for this elegant apartment, but it was no use. Jeanne would purchase only fourth-rate items, insisting they would one day repay Hélène. Only Petite Hélène's little room at the far end of the hallway was lavishly decorated. This was because Hélène was determined that her niece was going to turn out to be a lady of taste and means. For her, only the best would do. She had seen to it that the bed which replaced the crib she had outgrown was fit for a princess. It was huge and soft, replete with a silken canopy, mountains of satin and lace pillows, and a shimmering white silk spread. This oasis of luxury vied for attention with the miniature French chairs she'd found in an antiques shop on the Left Bank, the small Venetian chandelier which looked like cake frosting. In one corner stood Petite Hélène's favorite item, a miniature vanity complete with neatly lined-up atomizers filled with yellow play perfume. Without Hélène's realizing it, Petite Hélène had become her surrogate child.

Now she smiled to herself as Petite Hélène knelt on the living room floor, her hands tugging impatiently at the bow of the satin ribbon tied around the package. Finally she got it off and handed it over to Jeanne, who had just come back out from the kitchen. Expertly Jeanne coiled the ribbon around her index finger, then went over to the desk and placed it in a cubbyhole. Petite Hélène started attacking the wrapping paper.

"Careful," Jeanne warned her.

"Oui, Maman," she said in a frustrated voice. What she really wanted was to rip the box apart. But obediently she unwrapped the tissue paper, smoothed it out on the floor, and folded it so that, like the ribbon, it too could be used over again.

Finally, with mounting suspense, she lifted the lid off the glossy white cardboard box. Then she held her breath as she reached in and dramatically parted the cover of white tissue paper. A cry of delight escaped unbidden from her lips.

For a long moment she could only stare at the doll that lay in a lavish nest of yet more tissue paper. Then slowly she lifted her out. It was one of the new dolls, the kind with jointed arms and legs that could be moved, soft and realistic plastic skin, and thickly lashed eyes that opened and shut. Her straight hair was so pale blond that it was almost white, and long enough to be combed and styled. Petite Hélène stroked it gently with her fingers. Each strand felt smooth and satiny, like real hair. This was more than just a doll, she was thinking. This was a beautiful little girl of her own. She was far more beautiful than any of the other dolls she had.

469

This one would have the place of honor. She would always keep her right on top of the bed.

But what fascinated her most was the way the doll was dressed. For it was not a frothy concoction of lace over crinoline, but a perfectly tailored replica of the suit Hélène was wearing—a pale pink Odile Joly out of raw silk with a rich smattering of tiny nubs. Pinned to the lapel was a tiny brooch. It, too, was the same as the one Hélène wore, a gold circle encrusted with diamonds, but in miniature.

Petite Hélène struggled to her feet and hugged the doll. "Ooooh! Je l'aime bien! Maman! Look, Maman!" Proudly she held the doll out.

Jeanne looked at it and shook her head. "My word . . ." she began. Then she inspected the brooch closely, and suddenly a dark expression crossed her face. She shot Hélène a knowing look. The diamonds were real. They were not carats in weight but mere points; yet each one was fully faceted and cut.

Hélène shrugged. To stave off any further lectures on spoiling the child, she jumped to her feet and sniffed the air. "Something smells like it's burning! It must be the food! And just when I'm starving!"

Jeanne had no choice now but to hurry back to the kitchen.

Hélène caught Petite Hélène's eye. They winked at each other. Then the girl studied the doll's eyes as they opened when she stood the doll up, and slowly floated shut as she was laid back down. Up again, and the eyes opened, unblinking and deep blue. Down again, and the lashes rested on the rosy cheeks.

Petite Hélène looked up. "I already know what I'm going to name her," she declared.

Hélène smiled. "Are you going to tell me?"

The little girl nodded and went over to her. "Can you keep a secret?" she asked in a semiwhisper.

Hélène nodded solemnly.

Petite Hélène's eyes were fixed on Hélène's. "There's only one name that's elegant enough for her."

"Oh? And what's that?"

"She's going to be named after a queen," Petite Hélène gestured for her aunt to bend down. Then she stood on tiptoe, placed her lips next to Hélène's ear, and whispered softly. The little girl's breath was like an icy chill. *"Antoi-nette!"*

Hélène froze. Her eyes were focused on another dimension. There was no way Petite Hélène could have known of her own doll, Antoinette.

"Don't you think that's a pretty name?"

"Yes, it's . . . it's a very pretty name," Hélène managed to say.

4

After Petite Hélène had gone to bed, the adults sat around the living room as they had once sat around the kitchen in Saint-Nazaire. Jeanne took out her sewing and Edmond stoked the fire in the fireplace. He smoked and drank peacefully, his feet up on a hassock. Hélène was content just to sit there, sipping her wine and soaking up the warm family atmosphere. They spoke of bygone days and caught up on the latest news. Inevitably their talk got around to *Les Modes.*

"I'll never forget the night of the publication party," Hélène said, "when the first issue came off the press. Strangely enough, no one was in a good mood that night. I guess they were all overworked. And to think that I rented the ballroom in the Georges V for the occasion! Finally I couldn't take any more of it and I just left. Well, Jacques knew where to find me. He came to the office at three in the morning, and there I was, wandering around like a lost soul, wondering where all the thrills and excitement had gone." She smiled at the memory. "I'll never forget it. He had a big paper bag, and in it was a chilled bottle of Dom Perignon and two Baccarat glasses. We sat and drank champagne till everyone came to work in the morning. Then we went home." She shook her head and smiled again. "The glasses are now on the shelf in my office."

Jeanne glanced up from the sock she was darning. "You

mean the ones engraved 'Les Modes, Volume 1, Number 1'?"
she asked.

Hélène looked somewhat embarrassed. "I'd forgotten that I
must have told you that story already. Anyway enough of all
this," she said firmly, changing the subject. "Tell me what's
happening with you."

Jeanne glanced questioningly at Edmond. He nodded.

Hélène looked from one of them to the other. "Well?" she
demanded finally. "What's the matter now?"

"I'm pregnant again!"

"Pregnant!" For a moment Hélène stared at her with big
eyes. Then her face broke into a huge smile. "Oh, Jeanne!"
she cried. "That's *wonderful!*" She jumped to her feet and
crossed over to her. Then she bent down and her arms went
around her sister-in-law's neck as she hugged her happily.

Edmond lifted his feet off the hassock. "What about me?"
he asked with mock hurt in his voice. "Doesn't the father get
any credit?"

5

Luba Tcherina flung open the door to Hélène's office and
marched in, her pomegranate-lacquered fingernails sweeping
through the air. Jacques was at her heels. He closed the door
softly behind him.

Hélène was perched on her desk, one delicate shoe resting
on a chair, the telephone receiver tucked between her ear and
her shoulder as she consulted a sheaf of papers on her lap.
She glanced up, motioned for them to wait. The Czarina
sighed impatiently, her elongated fingers tapping her folded
arms. Jacques just nodded. Quickly Hélène finished her conversation and replaced the receiver. Today the Czarina was
dressed in elegant head-to-toe black. "Tartar black," she
would have called it. Black breeches, black high-heeled silver-trimmed boots, and a beautiful black wool tunic embroidered with silver thread that had an enormous monk's

cowl framing her face. On this occasion, to match her outfit, Luba wore black-framed glasses; legend had it she collected drawers full of different colored glasses to match her wardrobe. Her cheeks, like her nails, were pomegranate: two big circles liberally smeared into the wrinkled skin. Hélène couldn't help wondering if the Czarina had her own cosmetics lab at home. How else could she manage to get hold of all the long-out-of-date colors? Not only that, but make them appear the height of fashion.

The Czarina's dark eyes flashed. "I think," she exclaimed, "I've gone *blind*! I never want to see snow again for as long as I live! And I never, *ever* want to set foot in a darkroom again! You know, don't you, that the red light in there *only* makes it look like a *cheap* whore's bedroom?" She shivered with revulsion and slumped into one of the chairs, the back of one elegant hand dramatically resting across her brow.

Hélène hopped off the desk. Jacques stepped forward, gave a sweeping bow, and handed her the manila envelope he was carrying.

She looked at it curiously. "What's this?"

"Proof sheets, princess."

"Proof sheets!" Hélène parroted. Her voice was incredulous. "Already! But you must have gotten back from Chamonix in the wee hours!"

"That we did." The Czarina heaved a weary sigh, her gaunt bosom rising and falling beneath the voluminous folds of her tunic. "As soon as we got back, Jacques simply insisted that we lock ourselves in the darkroom and work all night through!"

Jacques grinned at Hélène. "I figured you'd want to see the results right away."

Luba's black eyes flashed with mischief. "The results are that when this issue comes out, the editors-in-chief at *Vogue, Harper's,* and *L'Officiel* are going to tear their hair out!"

Quickly Hélène began to unravel the figure-8 string that held the envelope shut. She slid out the proof sheets and lined them up neatly, sat down and took her tortoiseshell magnifying glass out of the top drawer. Silently she gave each print a cursory first glance. She nodded to herself. She had been right in allowing Luba and Jacques to go to Chamonix. Even on these miniature prints, Jacques' genius came through, as did the Czarina's dramatic posing of the models. They were a good team, Jacques and Luba.

When she finished scanning the shots, she went over them again, this time scrutinizing each one closely. She was pleased. There was something about the juxtaposing of summer couture and winter backgrounds that gave the photos the elusive "something special" she'd been after all this time. Up to now, everything *Les Modes* had done had been superb. But these? These were sublime.

She picked up a black grease pencil and began circling the ones that most appealed to her. Like the one with the giant yellow snow remover. The plow was raised high in the air and the models were posed in the giant scoop as if they'd just been bulldozed off the snow and trapped there. Or the ones where the models, in their delicate print dresses, were standing knee-deep in snow, their beautiful long legs red with cold. And . . . She felt a sudden chill and closed her eyes for a moment. There it was. The unmistakable Jacques Renault daredevil trademark. The cable car.

It was not far off the ground as far as cable cars went; it had obviously been stopped just after leaving the ground station. But still it must have been at least fifteen meters up. And any way you looked at it, a four-story drop was a long way. But it was a spectacular shot. All that could be seen was the shiny red car and the athletic models clinging to its sides for dear life. The backdrop was a pristine blue sky cut in half by thick cables.

Hélène chose the shot she'd use for the cover without hesitation. Even in its tiny state, she could see that it was perfection itself. And blown up and cropped, it would be a sensation. It showed the typical *Les Modes* cover girl, tawny and leonine, stretched out on a carpet of crystalized snow. In front of her, delicate snowdrops, like miniature lilies, had pushed their way up through the snow, each hardy bloom bowed over its pale waxy leaves like miniature bells. The model had her nose poked right in them, her chin aggressively thrust in the snow and her Cleopatra-like eyes glaring up into the camera. Her glossy red lips were barely visible behind the flowers.

"They're fantastic!" Hélène said finally. She looked up at Jacques and Luba. "Just make certain the competition doesn't hear about them until we're on the stands."

"Have no fear," Jacques said. "We went so far as to have

the models sign agreements that if they shoot their mouths off, they'll be docked and held legally liable."

"Good." Hélène looked at Luba. "Why don't you go home now and get some shut eye? You look like you could use it."

"I do, do I? Well, just this *once*, I'll let that slide." The Czarina of haut goût rose haughtily to her feet.

"Oh, and one more thing," Hélène said quickly. "Have you gone through the American *Harper's* recently?"

The Czarina nodded. Part of any editor-in-chief's job was to keep a keen eye on the competition.

Hélène picked up a sheaf of papers. "I've just gotten a translation of some of the columns. I like Diana Vreeland's column, 'Why Don't You . . .' Have you read it?"

The Czarina's eyes narrowed. She didn't favor any comparisons, no matter how exalted. "No. Is there any reason why I should?"

"I think so," Hélène said. "It's very funny and positively chic. You know, like: 'Why don't you turn your old ermine coat into a bathrobe?' That kind of thing. There are no end of possibilities with something like that."

"Indeed not." The Czarina's nostrils flared distastefully as she ticked off some quick titles on her fingers. "Why don't you . . . let's see . . . turn your old Porthault sheets into new terrace awnings? Why don't you . . . use your old diamonds to stud your bolero jacket? Why don't you turn your old gold bracelets into napkin rings? Why don't—"

"All right," Hélène said testily, "I get the idea. You don't like it."

"On the contrary," the Czarina said. "I like it. Only it's been done. We'll have to be more original than that."

"I agree. But let's try to think up a column along those lines. It's got to be something terribly useless, though, otherwise it won't be chic. When you come up with some ideas, we'll have a powwow. Now, off you go."

The Czarina rose, offered her cheek for Jacques to kiss, and then swept out of the office. When she was gone, Jacques started to gather up the proof sheets. "I'll blow up the ones you've marked after I've gotten my forty winks."

"Fine," Hélène said. "But I'd like you to do something for me first."

"Sure. What is it?"

Hélène went over to the big floor safe, knelt down and spun the combination. After a moment of fiddling, she swung the heavy door open and took out a manila envelope. She snapped the safe shut again and spun the dial around for good measure. "Let's go to the lab," she said. "I need you to take some pictures right away."

It took two hours for Jacques to finish. He snapped all the von Eiderfeld documents, developed the film, blew it up to eight-by-tens, and printed one copy of each. While it was being done, Hélène stayed in the darkroom. She wasn't about to let those precious documents out of her sight. Not after all the trouble she'd gone through to get them.

When everything was finished, they went back to her office. She studied the prints. Jacques had done a fine job. He had photographed each document carefully and they were eminently readable. Even the photos of von Eiderfeld looked better than the originals had, since he had played around some with the lighting.

She put the copies in one envelope, the originals in another, and both of them in her attaché case. She placed the negatives separately in her purse. Later, she would destroy them. There was no point in having too many copies of something this volatile floating around.

"Thanks, Jacques," she said. "I really do appreciate it. I know you're overworked and tired."

He grinned. "Anytime, princess." He paused. His voice was suddenly very serious. "That's heavy stuff." He gestured at her attaché case.

"I know that." She forced her voice to remain light. "Now, you'd better go home and get your forty winks."

"I'll do that." He started for the door. When he reached it, he turned around. "See you tomorrow. I'll be in the darkroom all morning. By afternoon, you'll have the Chamonix blowups."

She smiled. "Tomorrow, then."

As soon as he was gone, she drummed her fingers thoughtfully on the attaché case. She hadn't wanted to get Jacques involved in this. There was no need for him to know anything about it. But she needed a set of copies, and he was the only person she could trust to make them. She shrugged. Some things just couldn't be helped.

Quickly she made three telephone calls. The first was to her personal lawyer, Émile Mauriac. It was he who had the original of the *Clytemnestra* tape locked away in his vault.

She would put the von Eiderfeld originals in there along with it. And the same instructions would apply: if she didn't contact him regularly, he was to go promptly to the police. She smiled grimly to herself. She wondered what Hubert and von Eiderfeld would think if they knew what dangerous ground they were treading upon. If one of them succeeded in harming her, the other would suffer the consequences as well. She thought it rather poetic.

She had made an appointment to drop by Monsieur Mauriac's office at eleven o'clock. She glanced at her wristwatch. It was after ten already. She'd have to hurry.

Next she called Paul Clermont. He was the lawyer whose offices handled all the legal ends for Les Éditions Hélène Junot. She would meet with him after lunch. He would help her gain entrance to see the reclusive Karl von Eiderfeld. She had mapped out her strategy very carefully. She would have him send the von Eiderfeld lawyers in Düsseldorf a tiny portion of one of the documents. A cryptic portion only von Eiderfeld himself would be able to recognize. That should flush the fox out of hiding, she thought. And to keep him dangling, she would use the name Madame Kowalsky. That wouldn't set off any warning bells. And using the Clermont offices to make contact was a good idea. She'd done the same thing when she'd gone to see the Comte. This way, neither of them had any idea where the documents were.

Finally she called Edmond.

"Hey, Little French Girl," he said in surprise. "What's up?"

"Not much. Are you doing anything exciting?"

His laugh was warm. "I'm afraid not. Just cramming for exams, as usual."

"Oh, I should have known better." She hesitated, then decided that she was being a fool. Family was family. When something important came up, you just had to drop what you were doing. "Listen, would it be a great inconvenience if you took a break and met me for lunch?"

"That's no inconvenience." Then a note of worry crept into his voice. "Is anything the matter?"

"No," she assured him hastily. "It's just that I need your opinion on something. It's . . . well, it's rather important."

Hélène hung up thoughtfully after they arranged to meet. She had never meant to discuss von Eiderfeld's "punishment" with Edmond. But he had a right to know. He had been victimized by that horrid albino as much as she had. And sooner or later, when he finished school and joined *Les Modes*, he was bound to find out. Better that he knew now.

After leaving Monsieur Mauriac's office, Hélène walked to Fouquet's. It was only a few blocks down the Champs-Élysées. The attaché case in her left hand felt much lighter now; the originals of the von Eiderfeld documents were safely locked away. No matter what von Eiderfeld threatened, he wouldn't dare lift a finger against her. Not now. She had all the bases covered.

She would talk it over with Edmond and ask his advice. The only trouble was, she thought she knew what he would say. That since it was she who had set the wheels in motion, it was up to her, and her alone, to decide von Eiderfeld's fate.

She crossed the rue de Bassano and passed the TWA office without giving it as much as a glance, At the Avenue Georges V she stopped for the red light. She waved to Edmond. He was standing on the far corner, waiting for her outside the café's glass-enclosed terrace. He smiled and waved back.

The light changed and the automobiles stopped behind the zebra-striped crosswalk. As she stepped off the curb, she heard the high-pitched, clucking whine of a moped. Instinctively she stopped in her tracks and whirled around. The moped was shooting recklessly forward from the narrow space between two cars, the driver and passenger both wearing bowllike white helmets with big gray goggles. Her heart gave a leap. For a moment she was certain they were going to run her down. Then she let out a slow sigh of relief. The driver had swerved to a sudden halt. She shook her head angrily. Just as she started walking again, the passenger's leather-jacketed arm shot out, a gloved hand grabbed her purse, and the moped went roaring off in a blue cloud of exhaust.

It took a second for what had happened to register. Then Hélène let out a scream and frantically began chasing after the bike. "Thief! Stop him, somebody!" she cried. "My purse! My purse!"

But she wasn't fast enough. They burned the red light, made a sharp right turn onto the Champs-Élysées, and swiftly merged into the heavy traffic. For a moment she could see the passenger twisting around to look back at her. But all she could see was a pair of goggles.

Hélène stopped running and slowed to a halt. It was useless. She would never catch up with them. Not on foot, nor in a car. Besides, one of the heels of her shoes was coming loose.

The last thing she saw was the moped weaving in and out of the traffic. A few seconds later, it disappeared out of sight. She made an angry, futile gesture with her arm. Then Edmond was beside her and held her tightly. He, too, was out of breath. Like her, he had started to give chase on foot. Silently she let him lead her up onto the sidewalk and into Fouquet's. They were quickly shown to a sidewalk table and she sank down into a chair. She sat there motionless for a moment. Blankly she stared out the glassed-in terrace. Then she covered her face with her hands as the enormity of the situation hit her. She had not yet had a chance to destroy the negatives. They were still in her purse. Her stolen purse.

Edmond twisted around and motioned for a waiter. "Quick —a glass of brandy!"

"Oui, monsieur." The waiter hurried off.

Edmond leaned solicitously across the table. "Do you think you can remember anything about either one of those punks?"

She shook her head dumbly.

"Did you catch the license plate?"

"No," she whispered. She still stared out the window. "It . . . it all happened so fast."

He sighed and slumped back wearily. "I didn't either." Then he started to get up. "I'll be back in a moment."

She looked up suddenly. "Where are you going?"

"To call the gendarmes. It won't hurt to report this."

"No!" She gripped his arm so fiercely that he looked at her in surprise. For a brief moment he half-sat, half-stood.

"But . . . your money . . . your ID papers?"

"I don't want to go to the police," she said flatly.

He stared at her. "But . . . you can't allow them to get away with it!"

"They already have," she pointed out. Her usual practicality was quickly returning. "Besides, it's not the money that worries me." She leaned across the table and clenched her fists. "It's the film."

479

"The film?" He looked at her blankly and settled back in his seat. "What are you talking about?"

Her brandy arrived and she took a quick swallow. Her hands were still shaking, but not as badly as they had been. She was starting to regain her calm. She set the glass down and looked around quickly to make certain she couldn't be overheard. "Just hear me out, Edmond," she said in a low voice. "Then you'll understand."

She cleared her throat and started telling him about her search for von Eiderfeld. While she talked, she couldn't help wondering about the coincidence of her purse being snatched while the negatives were in it. She'd never had anything stolen before. She'd read of women's purses being snatched by thieves on mopeds. The papers were full of such stories. But that it should happen now? And to her? Long ago, she had stopped believing in coincidences. They were too pat an answer. And. . . . She paled suddenly. If it was really more than just a coincidence, then who could it have been? The hairs at the back of her neck prickled. Only one person knew that she'd put the negatives in her purse.

She tried to push the creeping thoughts out of her mind. No, she thought quickly. She was overdramatizing things. He would never do anything to hurt her. Jacques was a friend.

6

Hélène looked out the round porthole of the Lufthansa DC-7 as it neared its destination. Outside, on the starboard wing, she could see the twin propellers spinning in a silver blur. She could hear a muffled roar as the motors changed pitch.

The hostess came down the aisle. "Please fasten your seat belt, Fräulein," she said, leaning forward. "We're approaching Köln-Bonn airport."

Hélène turned away from the window, fastened her seat belt, and stared straight ahead. Once again, she was returning to Cologne. But this time it was different. The other trips were merely to make the arrangements that would culminate in this one visit for which she had waited so long. The moment she would face Karl von Eiderfeld. The destroyer. The butcher. The white-faced one who had filled her with such terror that sometimes she still had nightmares about him. It had been more than fourteen years since she had first laid eyes on his hideous face. Fourteen years was a long time to wait for anything, but now she was ready.

She rolled her head to one side of the headrest. She had chosen a most exquisite and fitting form of punishment. He, too, would have to buy into Les Éditions Hélène Junot; just as Hubert had had to. But this time the terms would be different. When Paul Clermont drew up the papers, he had thought the terms bizarre. But he hadn't known what she was up to.

Hélène smiled slowly. Von Eiderfeld's punishment was going to suit his crimes. She was going to prey on his greatest fear. The fear of discovery. The fear of having an accusing finger pointed at him. Well, she wouldn't be the one who'd point that finger. She would allow him to remain burrowed in his paranoid seclusion. Except, that is, for four times each year. Once every three months he would have to attend a board meeting. Otherwise, he could come and go as he wanted. But for her board meetings, the rules were stringent. She stipulated in writing (and he would have no choice but to agree to her terms, unless he wanted her to go to the Israeli authorities) that he must use second-class public transportation to get there. He could use his choice of scheduled airlines, scheduled railroads, scheduled buses. But he could not go by private or rented car, could not, in fact, charter anything—plane or bus—not even hide in a wagon-lit on a train, nor even use a taxi. Ship's travel, too, was strictly forbidden, for ships were like floating hotels. It was too easy to lock yourself up in your cabin. No, for her meetings Karl von Eiderfeld would have to travel openly with that which he feared most: crowds. She had even mapped out his airplane routes carefully. Frankfurt–Tel Aviv–Paris. Paris–Tel Aviv–Frankfurt. It was a big detour, but it wouldn't hurt him to have to set foot on Israeli soil and deal with Jewish officials every now and then, she thought. In fact, that would probably frighten him the most. Customs officials were enough to unnerve anybody. Especially somebody with something to hide.

Yes, the danger of discovery would be an all-consuming threat. Albinos were a rarity. They attracted attention and weren't easily forgotten. And somewhere, sometime, a survivor of his brutalities would put the finger on him. If not in Paris, then perhaps in Tel Aviv. Sooner or later it was bound to happen.

She nodded to herself. The more she thought about it, the more sense it made. She didn't feel proud of what she was doing, but she didn't feel ashamed of herself, either. She believed that this time, what she was doing was truly the right thing. And this time, the severity of the punishment she meted out verged on genius. Von Eiderfeld wouldn't be able to slide through with a splashy, quick trial and then feel the hangman's noose around his neck. For then, all his suffering would cease. Dead men didn't feel anything.

No, she would make certain that before that happened, he would suffer first. Slowly. Painfully. For as long as it took his past to catch up with him. Especially with such stipulations as the one which specifically stated that he could not undergo cosmetic surgery of any kind. Or the one that forbade travel under any name but his own. There was even a clause that he could not wear hats of any kind during his trips, and only those eyeglasses which were absolutely necessary and whose lenses were each no larger than six and a half square centimeters. This way, disguises of any kind were out of the question.

A grim smile tightened across her teeth. Four times a year, the fear-ridden fox would be flushed from his hole. Four times a year was enough. Between each meeting, he would have ninety days to worry about the next one.

She started as the wheels of the plane touched down on the tarmac and the fuselage gave a shudder. She straightened in her seat and looked out again. The flaps on the wings were in a vertical position. And in the distance was the terminal, surrounded by planes like a mother nursing her litter. They were already taxiing toward it. She could see the black-yellow-and-red-striped German flag that had replaced the ominous swastika banner of the war years. It was surrounded by smaller flags of many nations fluttering festively in the breeze. Now it wouldn't be long. The showdown was at hand. Only a short drive away waited Düsseldorf and Karl von Eiderfeld.

Karl Häberle was waiting for her inside the terminal.

"Welcome back to Germany," he said in French, raising his voice above the noise of the crowds and the echoes of the loudspeaker system.

She smiled. "I hope I'm not imposing," she said carefully in German. "It's just that I don't know anyone else here."

"You're not imposing at all," he assured her politely, also in German. "I hope you'll forgive me, but I didn't arrange for a car and driver as you requested. If you don't mind, I'd like the pleasure of being at your service."

She smiled gratefully and slipped her arm through his. "Thank you, I like that. Now we'd better switch back to French." She laughed as she changed languages. "I'm afraid I still have much to learn."

"On the contrary. You speak it very well. And your pronunciation is excellent."

She was pleased. She didn't bother to tell him that she was simultaneously learning English and Italian as well. She had figured that it was high time. Now that *Les Modes* had foreign distribution channels—if not foreign editions themselves, yet—it wouldn't hurt to be multilingual. Surprisingly, learning all the languages at the same time posed no problem for her. Instinctively she grasped the meanings of words and mastered the syntax and grammar of each language. She never once mixed Italian words into an English conversation, or French ones into German.

"I've got a new car," Häberle said offhandedly as they walked to the parking lot. "Thanks to your generosity, my tired little Opel could finally be retired."

She looked at him. "And you bought a Mercedes," she said slyly.

He laughed. "And I bought a Mercedes."

Hélène held her breath and hesitated. Slowly she swung her legs out of the silver-gray car and stepped out, staring thoughtfully up at the tall building that threw its shadow full force across the parking lot. Absently she pushed the car door shut. The parking lot was in the midst of an expanse of hardened, frost-touched earth that had been graded but not yet landscaped. Only the building, the road, and the parking lots had been completed. The rest looked like a lunar landscape, ugly, barren, and brown. There was an enormous industrial complex a kilometer away; like an expanding, misshapen hydra that had spawned a mind-boggling array of offspring, it sprawled hideous, twisted, and complicated beyond belief. Behind it were the huge chemical tanks, like bloated silver bellies, and from the midst of it all rose the tall chimneys that spewed forth eternal flames. As if the fires of hell had burst through the earth, she thought. A grotesque place, perfectly suited to the man she had come to see.

Karl von Eiderfeld turned away from the expanse of tinted windows and went back behind his desk. Wearily he lowered himself into the teak-and-leather chair. Several minutes ago the guards at the main gate had called to notify him that Madame Kowalsky had arrived. He had made it a point to watch her car pull up in the parking lot below. From fifteen stories up, all he could see was a man and what appeared to be a slim, attractive woman. Nothing more. Not that he had hoped to recognize her from this distance. He knew better than that. But he prided himself on his photographic memory. He could remember faces from years ago, even connect them with names.

A knifelike pain shot through his chest. His lips tightened as he touched his ribs with his hand. He knew what that pain was. His heart.

He reached into his desk drawer and took out a gold-and-enamel pillbox that had once belonged to the Czar of Russia. He didn't give the exquisite Fabergé workmanship a single glance. Quickly his fingers sought the catch and snapped it open. Inside were several minuscule pills. He popped one into his mouth and dry-swallowed it. Then he put the box away.

His heart had been acting up regularly ever since the afternoon his lawyers had forwarded the cryptic portion of an old document. Even before he opened it, he had had a terrible premonition of what was inside. The power to destroy him and all that which was his. Just when he had almost begun to believe that he had finally left his past entirely behind him. That there was nothing now that would surface. And why should it? During the war, he had been careful. Unlike most Germans, he had been a realist. He had accepted the fact that either side could win the war. And before 1943 was over, it was obvious to him that the Germans were losing. That was when he had begun rerouting shipments of propane to his secret depots and destroying the shipping forms. That was when he had seen to it that anyone who had witnessed him giving orders that he might later regret had been promptly shipped to the camps. Could anyone have survived that fate? In the beginning he had doubted it. But when the war was over, it became clear that unthinkable blunders had been made. Survivors had begun to straggle to the surface, picking out one war "criminal" after another, many of them men he had once known and marched beside. Most of them were brought to trial; a few had managed to commit suicide first. The newspapers had been full of their stories in the beginning; then they steadily dwindled, until after a while it was only a few highly publicized cases a year. Finally the public grew weary of them.

As the years passed, he had begun to sleep better. Whatever ax had descended upon the others had missed him, and for a good reason. Unlike them, he had covered his tracks well. At least that was what he liked to believe. Nor had he ever flaunted himself. Not during the war and not after. Even now, hardly anyone had ever seen or heard of him, and no one questioned his seclusion or connected it to "atrocities." All people ever heard of was Von Eiderfeld Industrien, G.m.b.H; never anything about Karl von Eiderfeld himself. Millionaire recluses never raised suspicions.

After receiving the cryptic portion of the document, he had spent whole days and nights racking his brain. He had tried to remember who might have escaped the execution he had planned, who might have gotten hold of the incriminating document. Who was this mysterious Madame Kowalsky, and why had she sent that message? To gain access to see him, of course. But that was strange, too. For she herself was coming, not the police or the Israelis. Was it blackmail she was after?

He buried his bloodless face in his white hands. For so long now, everything had been going well. He had prospered more than he had ever hoped. He had climbed to unimaginable heights of wealth and power. Yearly, six million barrels of crude oil passed through his refineries. Millions of tons of steel were being poured in his mills. His coal and iron mines were thriving. And his shipyard in Kiel was already producing seven new tankers every fifteen months. Now, all this was threatened. Everything he had built could fall like a house of cards if Madame Kowalsky took a deep breath and blew on it.

He pushed down on a white button recessed in his lacquered desk. Ahead of him, a portion of the highly polished teak wall slid soundlessly aside, exposing a large television screen.

He pushed down on the blue button and a bluish light came on within the gray screen. A moment later he had a flickering view of the inside of the elevator. There were a man and a woman. The man was German; that much he could tell. His lips, his hairstyle, his facial structure, and the cut of his clothes gave him away. But the woman was young and beautiful, expensively dressed. Her clothes were obviously Paris couture. He had never seen her before. And if he had, she must have been a child at the time. She could only be in her early twenties.

A child. He froze, cursing his stupidity. The blue face on the screen seemed to be mocking him. Angrily he pushed down on the third button. The red one. The picture faded slowly and the wall slid shut again.

His eyes narrowed in memory. He had slipped up only once—when he had let those two French children go. He should have had them killed.

Now he knew who she was.

Hélène had noticed the camera lens in the elevator the moment they stepped inside. But it was only after the car began to move that she had the feeling they were being watched. She glanced up into the thick glass lens that was focused on them. She could *feel* him now. Von Eiderfeld was watching. Waiting.

When she was shown into the hushed silence of his office, von Eiderfeld looked up slowly. His hands were folded on the desktop and his hooded pink eyes were guarded. She turned her face and smiled automatically at the secretary. The instant the door closed, her smile dropped away. She turned back around and for a long moment locked eyes with von Eiderfeld.

She shuddered and tightened her grip on the attaché case. He looked older than she'd imagined.

He waved his thin hand elegantly, his voice soft and emotionless. "Be seated, Fräulein Junot."

How could he possibly have known who Madame Kowalsky was? she wondered. Then she threw the thought away. It really didn't matter. "I prefer to stand," she replied coldly.

"As you wish."

Her eyes moved slowly around the elegant but sterile office. She forced her face to remain impassive as she took in the nightmarish Max Ernst canvases. They were very appropriate. Only a truly twisted mind could appreciate them.

"You have built quite an impressive empire," she said quietly.

He gave a modest shrug of his narrow shoulders. "It is not that difficult when one works hard."

"Or when one has no distractions and can do nothing *but* lock oneself away and work."

He looked at her calmly. The fire within his eyes seemed to dim. "What is it you want of me?"

She put her attaché case down on one of the modular units and snapped it open. "I, too, have begun an empire of sorts," she said, taking out several issues of *Les Modes*. She handed them to him.

He glanced quickly at them, and then, looking slightly puzzled, put them down on his desk. "I am afraid that fashion holds little appeal for me," he said. He folded his hands again, waiting for her to continue.

"It should," she said after a moment. "You see, I am selling stock in my corporation, Herr von Eiderfeld. Ten percent of that stock will cost you one million francs."

Von Eiderfeld looked relieved. Blackmail, by whatever name, was something he could understand. "Your company is in financial difficulties, then?"

She permitted herself a low laugh. "Quite the opposite."

"Then why is it you are selling stock?"

Hélène was silent. She reached for a thick envelope, undid the flap, and dumped the contents out on the desktop. His face was still expressionless as he looked down at the glossy black-and-white photographs, but his mind was racing. He had thought that she had somehow managed to get hold of one document. But these! There were so many. Gott im Himmel! Was so much incriminating evidence still floating around? Silently he cursed the Reich. No wonder they had lost the war! The bungling idiots in Berlin hadn't even had the sense to burn the archives.

But he betrayed none of these thoughts. His face was a studious mask. "One million francs is a small price for these," he said softly.

She shrugged. "It's not a small price," she said, "it's the fair market price."

His pink eyes narrowed suspiciously; this was no ordinary

blackmailer he was dealing with. She wanted something else besides money.

She reached into the attaché case again and took out a thick document bound in a light blue folder. "Here it is. Your copy of the stock offering. I suggest you read it through very carefully before you sign."

Something in her voice set off warning bells. He gave her a sharp look but said nothing as he took it from her.

She continued. "Need I mention that the lawyer who contacted you for this meeting is not the same one who has the originals of your documents? Or what will happen if any harm comes to me?"

He tapped the folder in his hand. "Let me ask you a hypothetical question."

She said nothing.

"If I were to purchase these . . . these shares. Then would I get the originals of the documents?"

Hélène shook her head. "I'm afraid not, Herr von Eiderfeld. You see, they are my insurance for a long and healthy lifespan. Do go ahead and read the contract."

"It's a long document," he said. "It will take time to read."

"I have time." She indulged herself in a smile and took a seat in front of his desk.

He sighed, opened the folder to the first page, and began to read. It was not long before he sat up straight. His white face seemed even whiter than before. "Th-this is preposterous!" he sputtered suddenly. "You don't really expect me to agree to such ludicrous terms!" Disgustedly he flung the document across the room.

Hélène looked over at it, then back at him. Patiently she got up, retrieved it, and placed it on his desk. She sat down again. "Yes, Herr von Eiderfeld," she said softly between clenched teeth. "I expect you to agree to all these terms. And no, this is not preposterous. What happened to my family was preposterous. Four children fleeing Paris with the Nazis on their tail was preposterous. A baby burned in the belly—that was preposterous. My mother gassed at Auschwitz—that, too, Herr von Eiderfeld, was preposterous."

He made an irritable gesture. "How would you know where she was sent?" he mumbled halfheartedly. "You were not even there."

"My mother told another survivor, who in turn told me. The camps were one giant grapevine—you should know that.

Many people told others their stories in the hopes that when it was all over, the world would hear the truth."

"The truth!" he spat out venomously. "Speculation and hearsay, that's all it is!"

Hélène shook her head. "No, it's not. You see, Herr von Eiderfeld, my mother lived almost to the very end. I have an eyewitness who was with her, a Jewish doctor. He is willing to come forward and testify. Now about those papers . . ."

His eyes met hers. "And if I decide not to sign. What happens then?"

"Then I shall not go to the German authorities." She paused. "I shall go to the Israelis."

For a moment he closed his eyes.

Her voice lowered to a whisper as she began hammering his alternatives home. "Not only will you be tried and convicted. Something even worse will happen. Let's not fool ourselves, Herr von Eiderfeld. I am a businesswoman and you are a businessman. We both know what it is that is most important to us. Our empires. Von Eiderfeld Industrien is what you live for. That, above all else. You have no shareholders. You own one hundred percent of the corporation, which would make it one of the biggest fortunes ever to be seized by the German government. You know what they would use it for, don't you?" She smiled as he winced. "To pay Israel reparations. To pay Jews who have claims against Germany for restitution." She leaned toward him. "Every asset your companies have would end up in Israel!"

He made no comment.

"Think of all the orange groves it would plant! Think of all the desert irrigation it could provide! Think of how the harbor at Haifa could be dredged and expanded!"

He looked totally defeated now, but he made one last, desperate attempt. "You forgot one thing, Fräulein," he said with weak dignity. "I am a powerful man."

"Are you?" She shook her head. "You *used* to be powerful. But that is all over. In ninety days I shall expect you in Paris for the first board meeting. You remember, don't you, what a beautiful city Paris is in the spring?"

"Why are you doing this?" he said. "*Why?*"

She shook her head unbelievingly. Had he no inkling of the difference between right and wrong? Had he no conscience beneath that hideous white skin? She wanted to grab him and shake some humanity into him, but that would have been useless. His soul was dead.

"The young man who is waiting outside for me will be the one who escorts you to and from the board meetings," she said impassively. "I suggest you start getting your passport and visas in order. As specified, you will take a bus or train from your home to the airport. Then you will fly to Tel Aviv, second class. You will remain there overnight. The next day, you will proceed on to Paris and take public transportation from the airport into the city. Just one slipup, Herr von Eiderfeld, and Israeli agents will have in their possession every original of the documents you have before you. And I know you won't try to flee to South America or some other sympathetic haven. Not after all you've built. But I'm cautious and distrusting, so I shall see to it that this company is under constant scrutiny. I advise you not to try to sell it. Before you even approached a buyer, it would be all over for you."

He looked at her with a grudging respect. "You drive a hard bargain," he said quietly.

She got up, went back to her attaché case, and snapped it shut. She looked over at him with disdain. "I don't make bargains, Herr von Eiderfeld."

She turned and started to leave. When she reached the door, she spun around. "By the way, Herr von Eiderfeld. You wouldn't know what happened to my two sisters, would you?"

"They were sent to the camps."

"And . . . ?"

He looked down at his desk. "Children were the first to be . . ." His words trailed off.

Hélène tightened her lips. "You have forty-eight hours to get those papers back to me." She glanced at her watch. "Forty-eight hours from *now*."

His eyes instinctively dropped to his wristwatch.

Thirty-six hours after her meeting with von Eiderfeld, her lawyers in Paris received the signed stock documents, and one million francs was deposited in the Les Éditions Hélène Junot account in the Banque Rothschild.

Von Eiderfeld had met her ultimatum with twelve hours to spare.

Hélène felt like a member of the Chinese acrobatic circus as she tried to contort her body every which way in front of the tall beveled mirror. She thought that this way she just might possibly be able to reach back far enough with her hands to hook together the back of the pale satin evening gown. After a minute of fumbling she let her hands drop in exhaustion.

"Merde!" she cursed uncharacteristically under her breath as the top hook, located in that elusive area between the shoulder blades and the nape of the neck, somehow still evaded her dexterous fingers. It was infuriating! She made a gesture of frustration and stared at herself in the mirror. Already she felt sweaty from all the effort, and in a minute her carefully coiffed hair would go limp. She reached for a tissue and gently dabbed the beads of perspiration from her forehead. Now her makeup, too, was in danger.

She scowled restlessly into the mirror at the gown. Then, holding it up by placing a hand flat against her bosom, she half-tripped over the hem as she stumbled to the telephone. Impatiently she lifted the receiver. As soon as the switchboard picked up, she said, "Jacques Renault, please."

"Un moment, mademoiselle," the operator sang. And a moment later, Jacques came on the line.

"Yes, boss?" he said good-humoredly.

"Jacques, get the hell up here. Right away."

"Sure, princess," he said with guarded caution. "You know I'm only downstairs. What's the problem?"

"The problem is . . ." She took a deep breath to try to calm herself. "The problem is this goddamn gown!" she said between her teeth. "I can't get it hooked up!"

He chuckled. "I'll be right up. Just let me get my pants on!"

Hélène slammed the receiver down, whirled around, and stalked across the room to the open window. The perfume of flowers was strong in the air, the lingering sweetness mixed with the tangy salt breeze from the sea. For a moment she looked out without appreciating the view.

How had she gotten into this anyway? She should never have let Jacques and Luba talk her into coming along. She'd much rather have stayed in Paris. That was where the power of Les Éditions Hélène Junot pulsed like a loud-and-clear heartbeat. On location with the models, she felt helpless. This was Jacques and Luba's territory. All she could do was stand around and get in the way.

But she thought that only now. Forever afterward, it would seem it was fate which had drawn her to the Côte d'Azur. For after the pain of Cap Ferrat, she had sworn to herself that she would never set foot in the South of France again. Added proof of fate's drawing power was the fact that this was the only time she had ever accompanied Jacques, Luba, and the models anywhere.

They had wrapped up the two-day shoot early that afternoon. The models had departed to their rooms at the less expensive Helvetia Hotel while she, Luba, and Jacques went back to the lavish Hôtel de Paris. Even after less than forty-eight hours here, the distinction was clear. There was Monaco and then there was Monte Carlo. The Hôtel de Paris was in Monte Carlo.

It was more than just a hotel. It was a spun-sugar dream imagined somewhere out of this world and set down amid a garden of paradise. Almost every hotel in the world made you feel you didn't belong, but at the Hôtel de Paris they made you feel like royalty. Upon arriving, the first thnig the worldly Luba had done was to seek out the chief concierge. He had given her a polite bow and smiled. "Madame Tcherina," he said. "I trust that everything is to your liking."

Luba had drawn herself up, her imperiousness worn like a titular crown as she demanded that the furniture in their rooms be changed to suit their tastes. And a half-hour later, after they sipped a cooling wine on the flowcring terrace, their rooms had indeed been refurnished. They now looked like sumptuous palace salons filled with the best of antiques. At first, Hélène had been embarrassed by the Czarina's demands; already she was taking them for granted. The management hadn't raised an eyebrow. It was a customary request at the Hôtel de Paris, and they were only too happy to oblige. Life here was different, she thought. It was richer, more comfortable; one's every whim was magically catered to. It was easy to get spoiled.

The famous Hôtel de Paris was located diagonally across from the equally or even more famous casino with its green weathered-copper domes, twin towers, and elegant arches. The hotel's pool and sauna, like the windows of Hélène's suite, looked down to the port below. It was early evening, and despite her irritation with the gown, her anger slowly seeped out of her. There was no way you could look out and not let the view affect you. The warm Mediterranean air was slowly cooling off, the faint, fragrant breezes like gentle caresses. The expensive yachts were lined up with military precision inside the calm, sparkling breakwater. Behind the town that sloped up the hillsides rose the rocky Maritime Alps, towering and magnificent above the deep blue of the sea. It was August, and August was to see the principality in its fullest glory.

Like a dowager empress, Monaco had bedecked herself in floral jewels. Everywhere, the majestic palaces, villas, and high-rise condominiums were surrounded by fine flowering terraces, rare exotic plants, cacti, and palms whose fronds rustled in the breezes. Hélène had learned to differentiate between the stately date palms with their tall, smooth trunks and the shorter, more squat Canary palms, which had rough and scaly trunks. Lining the avenues and clustered in the parks, magnificent eucalyptus trees grew to a great height and perfumed the air with their distinctive, almost medicinal aroma.

She couldn't help feeling glad now that she had come. This was by far the most beautiful place she had ever seen. More beautiful even that Cap Ferrat, because everything wasn't walled up behind gates or hedges. And there was even a little bit of Paris here, as if to squelch any homesickness a visitor might have. The same man who had designed the Paris Opéra had had a hand in designing the casino.

A smile pushed through her frown as she thought of how Luba and Jacques had persuaded her to accompany them to the casino tonight.

"Really, I'm not one for gambling," Hélène had tried to beg off as the models had gotten dressed on the imported white stones that comprised the manmade beach.

The Czarina's coal-black eyebrows seemed to lift right off her patrician brow. "Indeed!" she snorted disdainfully. "You know, don't you, that the casino is *only* the most glamorous spot in Monte Carlo? Propriety, if nothing else, requires you to go."

"Propriety?" Hélène sputtered. "I don't see how—"

Swiftly Jacques had cut her off. "Where's your sense of adventure, princess?"

"My sense of—"

"Adventure. We shall knock on your door at seven-thirty sharp, have dinner down in the Grill, and go on to the Casino from there."

"But what a—"

Jacques placed a restraining finger on her lips. "Live, for once, princess," he coaxed with a glint of amusement in his eyes. "And don't look so indignant, for God's sake! Casinos aren't exactly low-life fleshpots. They're respectable haunts of high society."

"Take one of the models. Really, Jacques. I don't *want* to go!"

Suddenly he reached out, caught her in a tight bear hug that made it impossible for her to argue any further, and lifted her off her feet. "Say you'll go and I'll release you," he whispered.

She stared down at him. Her face was getting red, but she shook her head emphatically.

He appeared not to notice. "Oh, and don't forget to dress. You don't want to look like a yokel or an American, do you?"

"Put me down! You're hurting me!" Her voice was sharp with anger.

He grinned. "I'll let you go as soon as you agree to come. Just nod your pretty head."

She glanced up at him out of the corner of one eye. Finally she lifted her head and nodded. Then he set her down, unwrapping his arms slowly and gently.

She took a swallow of air. "You . . . you brute!" she spit out, trying to catch her breath and smooth her clothes at the same time. "That was blackmail!" She looked at him, her eyes flashing. "You forced me into agreeing! It doesn't count!" She turned her back on him.

He took her arm gently and twisted her around. "Come on, princess," he said. "A deal's a deal."

"Some fine deal," she snapped. "It was coercion, nothing more and nothing else!"

The casino. Now she thought about it again. Just having to go there filled her with a certain trepidation. She had never been inside a gambling palace before. As far as Monte Carlo went, she knew only what Luba and Jacques had told her, and what every schoolchild in France knew. That it was the queen of all casinos.

About gambling itself, she knew nothing. It had never interested her in the least. The lure of breaking the bank was for others, for those who still dreamed of the impossible. She didn't believe in luck, and any investment she undertook was gamble enough. But a casino, where one just threw money away? It was an obscenity that she couldn't comprehend. She'd worked too hard to get where she was; she'd done without too much in the past even to consider that such waste could be fun. And when the Czarina had reeled off the staggering array of games that could be played at the casino—baccarat, roulette, chemin-de-fer, boule, craps, blackjack, and trente-et-quarante—none of which she knew anything about, her terror only grew. But as with everything else she had tackled, she kept that terror well under control. Her quick mind had immediately seen through Monte Carlo. Like Hautecloque, it was nothing more than an elegant facade. And elegance was the one thing she knew plenty about.

That afternoon, while Jacques and Luba had taken their naps, she left her room. She took the elevator downstairs and walked through the lobby to the conciergerie.

Enlisting the aid of the chief concierge, who was familiar with the problems that could face the hotel's guests, an appointment was made at the best coiffeur in Monte Carlo—the best in the South of France. Étienne's was located just a few meters from the quay. When she got there, an indignant middle-aged woman was just leaving. She pushed stiffly past Hélène and slammed the door behind her in no uncertain terms. Hélène turned and stared after her. Then she looked around the salon. It was empty but for Étienne himself, a male assistant, and two young girls in crisp white smocks.

Étienne stepped forward. He was a tall, bearded, virile-looking man. His white silk shirt was unbuttoned halfway to the waist. His chest was hairy, and he wore a heavy gold chain around his neck, "Mademoiselle Junot?"

Hélène nodded and gestured at the door. "That woman—why was she so upset?"

He laughed as the pixie-faced girl hurried to pick up a magazine off the floor. "Madame Laprade is always upset," he said with a shrug. "I simply told her that it was impossible for me to do her today."

"But why?" Hélène asked. "Didn't she have an appointment?"

He remained discreetly silent, and Hélène felt a stab of guilt. Now it was clear. The woman's appointment had been cancelled at the last minute because of her. The chief concierge must have impressed upon Étienne how important she was when he had made the appointment. Perhaps he had even hinted that it was to his advantage to drop everything to take care of her. That he might even get exposure in *Les Modes*. It wasn't fair to Étienne, Madame Laprade, or herself, and she knew it. But it was too late to worry about that now. "Really, I . . . I should have been told," she said miserably. "I didn't mean to push my way in—"

He interrupted her. "Please, Mademoiselle Junot," he said smoothly, putting her fears to rest, "don't worry yourself about it. Madame Laprade is not going anywhere tonight. She has her hair done for the same reason that she goes shopping. To relieve her boredom. Please . . ." He gestured to the serious-faced girl. "Just follow Roxanne into the changing booth. Besides, it is not always that we have such an important client as you. See?" He nodded at the girl who was replacing the magazine that had been lying on the floor. She saw now that it was the August *Les Modes*, and it was going on top of the stack of past issues. He looked at her. "Your magazine is my clients' favorite," he announced.

"It seems that it's also their favorite weapon to fling at you," she observed archly, following Roxanne to the changing booth. Roxanne stayed outside and pulled the curtain shut with a well-practiced flick of her wrist.

He laughed and kept on talking while she changed. "In this business, one learns to take the lumps." He lowered his voice. "You've heard of Pauline Monnier?"

Hélène stuck her head out from behind the curtain and nodded. Pauline was the society reporter for *Couture Magazine*. Occasionally she'd run into her in Paris. She could still remember the first time she had ever seen her. It was from the catwalk when she'd first begun modeling at Odile Joly's. She knew, too, that the witty, unscrupulous Pauline was so often seen with Daphne Epaminondas that nasty tongues wagered they were carrying on a lesbian affair.

"The Epaminondas yacht was in the harbor all last week," Étienne was saying as Hélène pulled aside the curtain and stepped out wearing a starched white smock. She turned around and let the pixie-faced girl tie a plastic bib around her neck. Then she took a seat while Roxanne spun the taps on the sink and tested the water with her hand.

Étienne wasn't finished with his story. "Poor Pauline came in only the day before yesterday and demanded that I cut her hair in a style which I warned her was totally unsuitable," he said sadly. "Afterward, she decided I'd ruined her looks. She actually picked up a pair of shears and tried to attack me! Can you imagine that?"

Hélène suppressed a smile. She could well imagine the minuscule Pauline in a rage. She could also imagine how quickly and easily she must have been subdued. Nevertheless, she clucked her tongue sympathetically, cautioning herself to refrain from telling Étienne a thing. He might look like a masculine sailor, she thought, but he seemed a terrible gossip.

"Well, the Epaminondas yacht was here up until yesterday morning. Then, as soon as the Skouri yacht came in through the breakwater, they hauled in anchor and sailed straight out. You know that Madame Epaminondas was once Madame Skouri, don't you?"

Hélène started to nod, but he didn't wait for a reply.

"Ex-husbands and ex-wives can either be great friends or terrible enemies," he philosophized in an aggrieved voice. Then he sighed and was silent for a moment. He shook his head. "Unfortunately, they're archenemies. I've even heard it said that the casino won't allow her in while he's there. Not just because they have such public rows, but because Monsieur Skouri is powerful enough to keep her out. He's one of the directors of the SBM."

Hélène nodded. She knew what the SBM was. The Société des Bains de Mer et Cercle des Etrangers. It was the organization which controlled or owned a good portion of Monte Carlo, including the Hôtel de Paris, the casino, and the magnificently planted gardens.

"Anyway, the way I see it, Madame Epaminondas doesn't have anything to gripe about. She's come a long way, you know. Greek peasant girl makes good, that sort of thing. She got a settlement of fifteen million dollars from Monsieur Skouri, and as soon as the divorce was final what did she do? Turned around and skipped off with Monsieur Epaminondas, that's what! They say he's good for at least a hundred million. Of course, Monsieur Skouri's worth three times that, but she doesn't have anything to worry about really, now, does she?" He stopped short suddenly, "How much time have you got?"

Hélène was thrown by the sudden change of subject. "I . . . I should be back at the hotel by six-thirty."

He frowned and glanced at his wristwatch. "That gives us a little more than three hours. Nina!"

The pixie-faced girl looked up and caught his nod. Obediently she went over to the door, quickly turned the key in the lock, and flipped the "Fermé" sign around to face the sidewalk outside.

Étienne was now all business. "It will take us all of three hours," he said, clapping his hands. "Now, then, have you given any thought to the kind of hairstyle you want?"

Hélène shook her head. "Not really. But I want something very elegant." She gave a faint smile. "Even showy."

"Ah." He stepped back, strummed his lips, and frowned thoughtfully for a moment. "I take it you're going to the casino?"

She nodded.

"What are you going to wear?"

"A Marcel Manet," she answered, adding: "He's a new designer. The gown's of pale blue satin, almost white, actually, and looks sort of like a Grecian toga."

"Sounds lovely." He looked thoughtful. "Jewelry?"

"I'm not certain. Aquamarines or coral."

He came close and placed his fingers lightly on her head. While he felt her hair, her eyes went to the big round mirror. She watched him closely.

"I think we should stick with an overall Greek look, then," he suggested. "What do you say we part your hair right here in the middle and have it sprout tiny, delicate curls all the way back to here? Then, here on the back, we'll pin on a fabulous fall."

She thought for a moment; there was an unsure look in her eyes. What he was suggesting was elaborate and extremely

498

formal. She wondered whether it was too formal for the casino.

He sensed her indecision. "It'll look spectacular," he assured her. "But I'll show you what I mean, and you can make up your own mind." He turned around. "Ambrose!"

His male assistant perked up.

"The Grecian curls. Bring out all the dark shades."

Ambrose nodded and hurried to the back of the salon. A moment later he came back out with a stack of boxes. Étienne frowned as he went through all of them. Finally he selected a thick black fall and pinned it expertly to the back of Hélène's head. "It's a fantastic look," he said. "Sort of à la Elizabeth Taylor. You could even wear a jewel on the hairpiece."

Roxanne and Nina held up hand mirrors so that Hélène could see herself from all angles. Slowly she nodded. Étienne was right. The elaborate hairdo would set off the classic simplicity of the gown sensationally. He had good taste, she thought, even if he did borrow liberally from Alexandre. But what the hell, she thought. If you had to borrow, just make sure you borrowed from the best. And she liked his idea about wearing a jewel in her hair. She knew exactly which one. The large pearshaped pearl mounted in white gold and surrounded by a spray of aquamarines. Any other jewels were out of the question. They would only detract. Her arms, neck, and ears would have to be bare. For a wrap, there was the thin satin stole that was an integral part of the gown. For footwear there were the delicate silver evening sandals. The matching white-gold-mesh clutch purse with her aquamarine initial on the clasp would be the crowning touch. There was no doubt in her mind but that she would make heads turn. And long ago, that first night when she had set foot in Maxim's, she had learned that elegant dress made a world of difference. It closed the social gulf a bit and made you feel you were at the top of the world. Yes, she would be stunning. The only thing that still bothered her were the games. Suddenly she had an idea. She knew that Étienne liked to gossip, but she decided to take that risk. Better that a few stories circulated about her than that she made a fool of herself tonight. Just as Roxanne was about to rinse her hair, she turned to Étienne. "You wouldn't happen to know how to gamble, would you?" she asked huskily.

He looked at her sympathetically. "Like everyone else, I know enough to get by."

"What's the easiest game to learn?"

He didn't hesitate. "Roulette."

Her face took on an enthusiastic expression. "I need a crash course," she said. "To tell you the truth, I've never been to a casino in my life."

"That's no problem. By the time your hair is done, you'll know everything there is to know about roulette, and then some."

Hélène looked around the roulette table as the bets were placed. The multicolor chips rose like neat clusters of miniature skyscrapers from the green baize. Each chip represented anywhere from five francs on up. She estimated that a fortune lay on that table.

Almost furtively she leaned forward to place her lone chip on the black, and then quickly withdrew her hand and stood back. She had been watching the game carefully. Étienne had taught her just enough so that she wouldn't get confused. "Bet on the red or the black," he'd said. "Forget about the numbers." So far, the wheel had run to the red. She reasoned it was time for the black to come up.

The croupier spun the wheel, and the dressed-up crowd quickly placed their last bets.

"Rien ne va plus," the croupier announced.

No more bets could now be placed, and the gamblers watched intently as the ball that was to decide the fate of their money was tossed into the wheel. It did a few hops and then began to do a wide roll.

The tension around the table was tangible. The society matrons' hooded eyes were like those of eagles, their pupils darting and flashing like the diamonds around their necks. One young blond, on the arm of a fat old German who kept mopping his brow with a handkerchief, was almost jumping with excitement. A tall, elderly gentleman watched the ball with a studiously expressionless face, but his fingers ticked nervously against his trouser seams. A younger, shorter man beside Hélène glanced at her and smiled nervously.

She smiled back at him and then watched the ball as the wheel began to slow down. The gamblers held their breath; the ladies pressed their red lips more firmly together and clutched their mink stoles tighter. Then the wheel came to a stop. The ball did a final, almost lazy roll. Hélène watched it without breathing. She was going to win! It would land in the black!

But it only looked that way. The elusive ball hesitated and then dropped neatly into the red compartment labeled thirty-four. The croupier expertly raked in the chips.

Hélène sighed and turned away. Her lone chip was being scraped away along with the others. Not that she'd really thought she'd had a chance at winning. It was just that controlled though she was, she *had* been excited during that last half-second interval when the ball had nearly dropped into the black.

She felt Jacques pull her aside as the next batch of chips was placed. "Are you winning?" he asked.

She shook her head morosely, her Grecian curls doing a little dance. "I've played five games and lost all five," she said wearily, opening her palm to show some chips. "These are all I have left."

He made a face and clucked his tongue in mock sympathy. "Poor princess. Lose much?"

"Twenty-five francs."

He laughed. "I should have known you'd be placing the unité de mise. Shame on you!" He wagged a finger at her. "A rich girl like you should be reckless. You shouldn't be in the public rooms. You should be in the Salles Privées, where the stakes are respectable."

"Is that where the Czarina is?"

He shook his head and grinned. "She's in the Salle des Amériques playing blackjack, cursing in Russian, and losing her shirt!"

Hélène smiled. "She must be a sight."

He nodded. "I'm going to try my hand at craps. Want to join me?"

She shook her head. "I think I'll stay right here."

He lifted his hand and crossed his fingers. "Good luck."

Now she looked around the roulette table again. While she and Jacques had been talking, she'd missed placing her new bet. The sharp eyes of the gamblers were already on the spinning wheel.

She shrugged, turned away from the table, cashed in the remainder of her chips, and started out of the room. When she reached the magnificent staircase, she descended to the Ganne Room. She hesitated in front of the nightclub, then decided against it and went into the tearoom instead. She was shown to the best table immediately.

"I'll have a mint tea," she told the waiter. When he brought it, he carefully poured a cupful from the pot. The spicy aroma of the mint was sweet to her nostrils, and the steam curled lazily out of the thin white china cup. She had no inkling of it yet, but luck was indeed at the casino this night. It had brought her down here to the tearoom, and it was smiling benevolently upon her.

8

"You've been sitting here for over an hour now," the man said politely.

Hélène set her third cup of tea down in the saucer and looked over at him. Vaguely she had wondered whether he was a gigolo. She had heard that that type of man hung out in the casinos and preyed on lonely women. Then, realizing how foolish this thought was, she saw that he was too refined-looking, too understated. She wondered where she had seen him before. He looked vaguely familiar, but she couldn't place him. He was British, probably. Only the English could cut a tuxedo so superbly. And now that he spoke, she realized her guess had been right. His French was excellent, but the accent was unmistakably upper-crust British.

She inclined her head and smiled. "I'm not terribly keen on gambling, I'm afraid."

He smiled back at her. "Neither am I," he admitted. "I came in with a group of people and managed to sneak away. What about you?"

She laughed. "I came here with friends also. They're gambling away upstairs."

"You are very wise," he observed.

"So are you," she replied.

"Would it be terribly forward of me if I joined you?"

Hélène brightened at the prospect of having company.

Luba and Jacques were both preoccupied with the games, and they were the only people she knew. Sitting alone for so long was a bore. "Not at all. I'd be delighted. Please . . ." She gestured to the empty chair opposite her.

Delicately balancing the cup, he lifted his saucer and slipped over into the chair. It was only now that she realized how tall he was, and she could smell the faint scent of his eau de cologne. His hair was brown and thick, carefully combed back, and his features were very fine. But it was his eyes which she found so fascinating. They were brown and warm, speckled with little flecks of gold.

It was then that she realized where she had met him. Years ago, at the Lichtenstein Gallery, after Odile Joly had "discovered" her. His name was Nigel Somerset and it seemed he was far more handsome than she had remembered him to be.

For the next half-hour they talked and got reacquainted with one another. She knew little about English society, but his manners, like his dress, hinted at a cultured, perhaps titled background. Still, he might be merely upper-middle-class with a good education. The rigid system of structured society was slowly changing, even in England. She learned that he lived in London and in the English countryside and sometimes spent holidays and vacations on the continent. He talked so casually, and without pretense, that she could easily envision his country home. She had seen enough pictures of quaint English cottages with thatched roofs and ancient beams and stucco to be able to do that.

She found out, too, that he worked for a living in the family business, a subject about which he was rather vague. That killed off any notion she had that he was one of the idle rich, but this revelation didn't disappoint her at all. A working person of quality was someone she could understand and identify with. Even appreciate. After all, she was a working woman. It hadn't hurt her any. If anything, she honestly believed it had only made her more interesting.

She couldn't help wondering about his personal life. He made no mention of having a wife or children, so she took it for granted that he was unmarried. When she glanced—discreetly—at his ring finger, she saw that it was bare. The only family he mentioned were his parents. They were both alive, and he would say no more except that he was here in Monte Carlo with friends; he had been invited to cruise on board their yacht.

She found out this much in the first twenty minutes; what he didn't put into words she saw in her mind's eye. Then, adroitly, so that she hardly knew what was happening, he turned the subject around and began asking questions about her. She was frank and talkative. It had been a long time since she had talked seriously with anyone. It felt good to do it now. Nigel Somerset, she had to admit, was a good listener, and good listeners were a rarity. She opened up easily. There was something about him that made her feel comfortable. He ordered another pot of tea, this time a strange blend she had never heard of; but then, he was English, she reminded herself, and the English were great tea drinkers. When he gently probed and asked if she had a husband, she told him that she was Stanislaw Kowalsky's widow. He didn't raise an eyebrow. If he thought it strange that the old pianist had had such a young wife he concealed it behind that implacably expressionless quality that was so much a part of the British. He simply nodded and said that he had met Stanislaw twice when he had performed at Royal Albert Hall. He thought very highly of him, both as a man and as an artist. Then he prodded some more, and she found herself telling him about *Les Modes*. Although at first she was certain she must be boring him, she realized after a while that he was genuinely interested. Then she became suspicious.

"You're sure you don't work for the competition?" she asked good-naturedly.

He grinned. "I'm afraid not."

She took a sip of tea. "You still haven't told me what you do."

He started to tell her, but at that moment Jacques appeared in the doorway, and motioned to her. She set down her cup and pushed her chair back. "Could you excuse me for a moment? It seems that one of my friends is looking for me."

"Of course." Nigel got up, gallantly held out her chair, and watched her make her way through the tables toward the door.

Jacques held the door open for her, and she went outside with him. "What is it?" she asked.

"I think I'm going to leave." He glanced impatiently down the hall, and her eyes followed his. Étienne, her hairdresser, was standing a discreet distance away. His eyes met hers and he gave a little bow in her direction.

She took Jacques by the arm and pulled him into a corner. "So you dragged me here and now you want to run off and play!"

"Have a heart, princess."

"All right, go on," she said, affecting a weary tone. She was anxious to get back to Nigel. "But when I got my hair done at Étienne's, I tipped lavishly. Now, don't you go promising him exposure in *Les Modes* in return for any . . . any favors," she warned dryly.

He shook his head. "Really, princess, when you think things like that, you disappoint me."

"Just make certain you keep business and pleasure separate."

"I always do." He sniffed. "Now, I'd better run off before he gets impatient. You just go back to Nigel Somerset and enjoy yourself." He started to turn and leave.

"Whoa." She grabbed his arm. "Not so fast. How do you know Nigel's name?"

"Everybody knows who Nigel Somerset is." He looked at her in surprise. "Don't you?"

"No, but he's a very nice man."

"He's a very nice *rich* man," Jacques corrected her. "He's the future sixteenth Duke of Farquharshire and heir to the Somerset fortune. I suppose you'll tell me next that you didn't know that his father, the fifteenth duke, just happens to be the third-richest man in England?"

The Monte Carlo Beach is in French territory. It was there that Jacques had shot the models on the imported white stones. Now Hélène glanced around the darkness as she and Nigel cautiously picked their way down the beach. It was after midnight, and the big pool was deserted, the parasols around it closed. The casino crowd, which sunned here during the day, was still at the gaming tables, and here on the beach in the middle of the night, everything was quiet, even the tiny bungalows where the rich and famous held their private beach parties. Except for one, and it was there that they were headed. About a hundred meters down the beach, the glow of fires and the sounds of a band marked where the Skouri crowd was having a Mediterranean-style luau. Nigel had insisted she accompany him to the party. When they neared it, Hélène saw that it was complete with calypso band, fiery torches stuck in the ground, and a buffet table laden with bowls of caviar stuck in ice and with all the delicacies the Mediterranean could provide. The music was nearly ear-splitting, and the flickering torches cast shadows that gave everyone an eerie reddish-bronzed hue. There must have been at least thirty or forty people there, none of whom she knew. But Nigel had been right about one thing. They were all in evening clothes. Some of the men had begun to strip to the waist as they danced to the frenetic beat of the calypso; the women had prudently taken off their delicate evening slippers.

Hélène stopped, quickly slipped out of her sandals, and carried them in her hand.

"Niggle!" a deep voice boomed out above the party sounds.

Startled, Hélène looked around. A short heavyset man with white hair and thick black-rimmed glasses was hurrying toward them. He was wearing baggy trousers and a white shirt open to the waist. He flung his arms around Nigel. Then he glanced at Hélène.

"I knew it, Niggle!" he cried excitedly. "Sooner or later, the charms of a beautiful young woman were bound to affect you!"

Hélène glanced at Nigel. He was smiling. "You think she's beautiful, Zeno?" he asked.

Zeno studied Hélène closely. Then he laughed. "I would say she's very beautiful!" Suddenly he stepped forward, embraced Hélène tightly, kissed her once on each cheek, and stepped back. "I'm Zeno Skouri," he said, not waiting for an introduction.

"I'm Hélène Junot."

"Enchanté," he said, making a production of kissing her hand as well. Then he hooked one arm through hers, the other through Nigel's. They started to walk. "Come, let us drink some champagne. We have fifty magnums on hand. It would be a pity to let it go to waste." He looked at Hélène. "You like Dom Perignon?"

She smiled. "Yes, but only a little. I'm afraid I have to be fit for travel tomorrow. I'm returning to Paris in the morning."

Skouri frowned. "A beautiful woman like you must return to the city? I thought all beautiful people left Paris for the summer."

She laughed. "I'm afraid I'm a working girl."

He looked at her shrewdly. "A model or an actress?"

"Neither. She owns a fashion magazine," Nigel explained. "Perhaps you've heard of it. It's called *Les Modes*."

Skouri beamed. "I've seen it," he said enthusiastically. "Ariadne swears it's the only decent one on the market."

Hélène looked pleased. Ariadne Cosindas was the world's most magnificent ballerina. She had also been Skouri's long-time mistress. Still, it was strange to hear the revered La Cosindas referred to as simply "Ariadne."

"Since you're self-employed and presumably have a capable staff, I insist that you join us for the next two weeks," Skouri stated flatly.

Hélène stared at him. "I . . . I don't think I understand," she stammered.

"The cruise. We started in Barcelona and are going to work our way around the boot of Italy and up to Venice." Skouri stopped walking and looked at Hélène. "What do you say? You'll honor us with your company?"

For a moment, Hélène looked confused. She had never before received such a spur-of-the-moment invitation. Nor had she ever had a real vacation. The chances of being invited on the legendary Skouri yacht some other time were slim. It would be nice to go, she thought. Besides, any excuse to wheedle out of it would sound skimpy. Zeno Skouri was right. Why else did she have a staff if they couldn't get work done in her absence? She could always put the Czarina in charge. Quickly she made up her mind. She leaned forward and glanced sideways at Nigel. He was smiling enthusiastically.

"Do *you* want me to go?" she asked softly.

He nodded wordlessly.

Skouri caught the nod. "See?" he boomed exuberantly. "Niggle says you must go, so you must go. It is set, then. The day after tomorrow, we sail on. I'll send a car to pick you up. Where are you staying?"

"The Hôtel de Paris."

"It's my favorite place in the world," Skouri said proudly. "That's the only reason I bought into the SBM. Because I liked the Salle Empire so much." He shot her a challenging look. "You like it?"

Hélène nodded. "It's a masterpiece of Belle Epoque," she said seriously, thinking of the big room and the opulent mural of the busty women. "I have a weakness for the period."

"Then we'll hit it off well. The salon of the *Evangelia* is all original Belle Epoque." They had reached the bar. "Now, for the champagne. And don't worry, if you get a hangover, you have all day tomorrow to recover."

Nigel patted Skouri's broad back and cleared his throat. Skouri turned around, then heaved his shoulders and sighed. "Just my luck," he said with mock resignation. "The most beautiful woman here, and spoken for." He assumed a morose expression and made his way toward a tall, smoothly exotic woman in a silver sarong.

Nigel and Hélène watched Skouri's instant jovial smile as he put a hand in the small of the woman's back, propelling her toward the beach.

Nigel grinned, hooked his arm through Hélène's. "Dance?" he asked.

She smiled at him, her face radiant and flickering in the torchlight. "Dance," she said huskily.

Till dawn lit the beach, Hélène danced and drank with Nigel, both of them losing their reserve, until dance after dance and drink after drink melted into countless others. She didn't mind at all that he wanted to keep her all to himself rather than share her with the rest of the party. And when he took her back to the hotel, the sun was already streaking the pale sky in a fan shape, and she realized only then that she had been introduced to no one but Zeno Skouri.

Nigel, she thought with a peculiar stirring, was enough. More than enough.

The next day Hélène awoke to find the bedroom dim, but afternoon sunlight shone in the bright chinks between the curtains. She looked up at Jacques, who was sitting on the edge of her bed. "I had a great time!" he said happily. "That Étienne's really something, you know that? He's not like all those fairies in Paris. He's a real man. And what he can do with his tongue!"

Hélène tried to lift her head up off the pillow. "Please," she said weakly. "Spare me the gruesome details." Gingerly she touched her forehead with the back of her hand and let her head drop back down on the pillow. She tried to swallow. Her mouth tasted stale and sour.

Jacques watched her with an expression of amusement. "What's the matter, princess? Got a hangover?"

"Please," she begged, "lower your voice. It's pounding in my temples."

He shook his head. "Poor princess." He got up, and she could feel the mattress shifting under her. He crossed over to the telephone table and picked up the receiver. He had his back to her and she could hear snatches of his conversation. "Room service . . . a tomato juice with ice, Tabasco sauce, and salt . . . and a jigger of vodka." He turned around and glanced over at Hélène.

She made a face. "Now I know I'm going to be sick."

He hung up the phone and grinned. "All I sent for was the American cure for a hangover." He clapped his hands and she winced. "Come on, princess, there's a lot we have to do today! We're leaving in three hours, remember?"

"Leaving?" Her voice was tiny. She shook her head slowly. "I can't go anywhere."

"Sure you can. It won't be long till you'll feel fit as a fiddle." He crossed the room and went from window to window, swiftly yanking aside the curtains. Sunlight poured in.

Hélène let out a gasp and covered her face with a pillow. Her voice was muffled. "Close those damn things!"

"We've got to get up, princess," he said in a hearty voice. "The trains won't wait for us. The Czarina's already packed and brunching downstairs."

She peered out from under the pillow. "What time is it, anyway?"

He pulled back his cuff to glance at his Baume and Mercier. "Five past three," he said mildly.

"Three o'clock!" she moaned. Small wonder that she was feeling so lousy. She'd come in at five-thirty, high as a kite and giggling hysterically. The last thing she remembered was Nigel bringing her up here, putting her to bed, and kissing her gently on the forehead. Could there have been more? Perhaps he . . . No, she'd have remembered if they had done anything. And how could she think such horrible thoughts, anyway? Nigel was a gentleman. Through and through. He wouldn't take advantage of a lady in distress.

Suddenly she sat bolt upright. Then she cursed herself for the sudden move as flashes of pain shot through her skull. She placed her thumb and index finger firmly on her forehead. The cruise! Good God, she'd have to let the chief concierge know that she'd be staying an extra day. And she'd have to get Luba in here and give her instructions on running the office in her absence. Or . . . An ugly thought managed to worm its way into her mind. Had the invitation for the cruise been a hallucination? No, she hadn't even started drinking when Zeno Skouri had invited her. She let her head drop to the pillow again.

"Jacques . . ."

"Yes, princess?" He came toward the bed and looked down at her.

"Call the chief concierge. Tell him I'm staying another day. Then get Luba up here."

"You're staying?"

"Just do as I say," she said wearily, closing her eyes.

"Sure, princess." He gave her a curious look and went back to the telephone table. A moment later he had the chief concierge on the wire. When he finished the call, he looked across at her, an incredulous expression on his face. "The chief concierge already knew," he said in a disbelieving voice. "You move in mighty exalted circles, princess. It seems that Zeno Skouri himself called up to extend your reservation."

Hélène opened her eyes and stared at him.

"Not only that, but I'm supposed to tell you that you're to consider yourself a *guest* of the Hôtel de Paris."

Hélène let out a sigh of relief. So the invitation hadn't been a dream. She could feel some of her energy returning. "Good," she said. "Now get the Czarina up here."

"Will do. But you still haven't told me why you're staying."

She kept her face carefully expressionless. "I've decided to take a two-week vacation, that's all. Boss's prerogative."

"Good for you! Where are you going?"

"On the Skouri yacht."

"The Skouri yacht!" He let out a low whistle. "Good Lord, a few days here, and you set Monte Carlo on fire!" He looked thoughtful. "Princess?" he said hesitantly.

"Hmmmm?"

"You wouldn't mind terribly if I stayed on here for one more day also, would you?"

"What about the pictures?" she pointed out. "They've got to be developed."

"That can wait a day. I'll get to them the instant I get back, cross my heart. Besides, we're a month ahead of schedule."

Before she could answer, there was a discreet knock on the door.

"Come in!" Jacques called out, hurrying across the room.

It was room service with the tomato-juice concoction and a perfect red rose in a bud vase. Jacques took the tray and brought it over to the bedside and held it out to her.

She grimaced.

"It works, princess. Just be a good girl and drink up."

"À votre santé," she mumbled, slowly bringing the glass up to her lips. She looked at him over the rim as she took a tentative sip.

When Luba came into the room, Hélène looked over at her from the settee. She put down the buttered croissant she had been nibbling. Luba was carrying the new *Paris Vogue* under her arm. The life-sized cover girl was glaring out at her with a spiteful expression.

"I hope I haven't inconvenienced you," Hélène said apologetically.

"Not at all," Luba said quietly. "In fact, I was going to come and see you."

Hélène nodded. "I just wanted to let you know that I'm not returning to Paris with you. I've decided to take a two-week vacation. You'll be in charge in my absence."

Luba nodded. "Before you turn the responsibilities over to me, there's something you might first like to take care of yourself," she said with gravity.

"Oh?" Hélène raised her eyebrows. "And what's that?"

"Before lunch, I noticed that the new *Vogue* was already out," Luba explained. Despite the fact that they were alone, she lowered her voice confidentially. "So I bought a copy." She glanced down at it. "Only to keep tabs on what the competition's doing, you understand," she added unnecessarily.

Hélène smiled, but her eyes looked at Luba with concern. The Czarina wasn't her usual dramatic self. Something serious was up. She nodded to a chair. "Won't you have a seat, Luba?" she said gently.

Stiffly Luba pulled the chair closer and sat down. She handed over the *Vogue*. "Pages eighty-four through eighty-nine."

Hélène glanced at her, but Luba's dark eyes were carefully veiled. Then wordlessly she opened the magazine and flipped to page eighty-four. Suddenly a horrified look crossed her face. Quickly she thumbed through the following pages. Still clutching the *Vogue*, she sprang to her feet, regretting it the instant her headache started again. She began pacing the room, her lips set in a grim line. Against her specific orders, Jacques had been moonlighting. Taking pictures for the competition while he was *Les Modes*'s staff photographer. That in itself might have deserved a severe dressing-down. But he had gone further than that. A blatant credit was printed alongside each picture. It was a direct stab in the back.

After a while she stopped pacing and turned to Luba. "Thank you for showing this to me," she said.

The Czarina got to her feet. "I wasn't trying to get anyone into trouble," she said uncomfortably.

Hélène forced a smile "Of course not. I realize that, in many ways, *Les Modes* is even more important to you than to me. Don't worry, I won't tell Jacques that you brought this to my attention."

Luba smiled gratefully and started to leave the room.

"You don't mind if I keep this for a little while?" Hélène asked, holding up the *Vogue*.

Luba shook her head and went quietly out.

Quickly Hélène changed from her peignoir into a dress, ran a comb through her hair, and went in search of Jacques. He wasn't in his room. Finally she found him out on the terrace, eating under a tilted parasol. He looked up as her shadow fell across him.

He grinned. "So you're already up, princess. I told you that vodka and tomato juice work wonders. Here . . ." He leaned sideways and pulled out a chair for her. "Have a seat and we'll order you an early dinner."

She remained standing, a dark expression on her face. "No, thank you," she said quietly. She plopped the *Vogue* down on the table. "Your contract specifically reads that you may not publish pictures in any magazine but *Les Modes*."

He shrugged and looked away. "So the shit has hit the fan," he mumbled. "Surely you're not serious about binding me to that contract?"

"I not only stipulated it orally, but in writing as well. Is that binding enough for you?"

"Come on, princess—"

"Don't you 'princess' me!" she said sharply. "As of this moment, you're fired! I expect your resignation in writing immediately."

512

He looked dumbfounded. Then he burst out laughing. "Fired? This is Jacques, your loyal employee, remember? I helped you put that magazine together from scratch."

"I repeat, you're fired. I'm being kind enough to let you resign," she said quietly. "I suggest you give Luba all the film you've shot here."

He looked at her tauntingly. "And if I don't?"

"I'll sue, and then you're finished. Word spreads. You'll be tagged as 'unreliable.' Not one fashion publisher in the Western world will as much as look at one of your snapshots."

He picked up his napkin from his lap and tossed it on his plate. He pushed his chair back and got to his feet. "Fine. Then I won't show my face in the office until you're back. But I want us to have a talk."

She tensed. "What's there to talk about?" she asked curtly.

"My severance pay." He patted her cheek. "But that can wait. I wouldn't want to spoil your vacation, princess."

She started to reply, but he was already on his way back into the hotel, leaving her seething on the terrace. Angrily she turned away from the table. She had both liked and trusted him but he had broken the bond between them. For a moment she considered calling Skouri and canceling the cruise. Then she decided against it. The copy and pictures for *Les Modes* were ahead of schedule. Luba would find someone to develop the shots. In the meantime, they would use a freelance photographer. Maybe Cecil Beaton, William Klein, or Hiro was available. Why should she suffer because of Jacques?

9

It was midmorning and the sun was already high and white and baking, but the breezes swept in from the sea as they always did to rustle the palm fronds and cool the air. Inside the breakwater, the white yachts did a little bob in the wake of a speedboat heading out between the twin stone towers that guarded the entrance to the port.

Jacques was standing in the shade on the rue des Remparts. A pair of Zeiss binoculars hung from around his neck and there was a magnificent view of the harbor from up here on the bluff. But he hadn't come to enjoy the view. He was waiting for someone.

Meanwhile, he thought back to last night. He had seen Étienne twice now. All night, they had drunk a lot and smoked some opium which Étienne had gotten hold of. As a result, Jacques hadn't gotten nearly enough sleep. There was plenty of time for that later, he told himself. Besides, now that he had been fired, and Hélène wouldn't be back in Paris for two weeks, he really had nothing to do. He might even stay longer here. At least until the good things wore off.

Someone was approaching. Jacques turned around, his eyes fixed steadily on Hubert de Léger. Suddenly he had to smile. Hubert was headed toward him on foot, his face florid and his chest heaving from the exertion of the climb. In Monaco, no matter where you walked, it was either up- or downhill. Twice Hubert had to stop to wipe the perspiration off his face with a rumpled handkerchief. Jacques waited until he was near. "You're late," he said.

"What's so important?" Hubert asked in a surly voice. "What did you have me fly down here for at such short notice?"

"It would be well for you to learn some patience." Jacques dug his hands into his trouser pockets and nodded down to the harbor. "Nice view, don't you agree?"

Hubert was silent.

"Recognize any of the yachts?"

Hubert looked at him. His voice was belligerent. "Should I?"

"Take a look at the prime berth." Jacques took his hands out of his pockets, unlooped the binoculars from around his neck, and held them out to Hubert.

For a moment Hubert hesitated. Then he took them and squinted through the lenses. The prime berth was just inside the breakwater on this side of the port. A four-decked yacht was moored there, Mediterranean fashion, stern to the quay. He studied it for a moment. There was no doubt but that it was the biggest yacht in the harbor, long and sleek, the blinding white throwing off a dazzling glare. It was the size of a small ocean liner, three hundred and thirty feet long. The bow was rakish and sloped gracefully downward to the stern, which was gentle and rounded. The funnel was painted navy blue, and so were the two amphibious Piaggio airplanes behind the on-deck crane. Also navy blue were the canvas covers on the speedboats and the big awning stretched over the aft deck.

"Whose yacht is that?" Hubert asked.

"The *Evangelia*," Jacques replied. "The Skouri yacht. It's big, isn't it?"

Hubert lifted the binoculars again. As he watched, five Rolls-Royces pulled to a halt behind the Skouri yacht and the chauffeurs got out to hold the rear doors open. He counted twelve people getting out. He focused in on each one of them. Suddenly his face went pale and ashen. He had recognized one of the passengers. A woman wearing cork-soled sandals, a checkered dress, large round sunglasses, and a big straw hat. His eyes narrowed as he lowered the binoculars. He did not notice the way Jacques was looking at him. All he could think of was the woman he'd just seen. It was Hélène.

His hands started to shake. The desperate longing he'd once felt for her had long since curdled into something quite different and more powerful.

Hate.

After the *Evangelia* was a white speck halfway to Menton, Jacques and Hubert headed to the Ariston Bar. It was cool inside and the place was filled with tourists nursing their drinks.

They got a table in a quiet corner. They didn't speak until after the drinks arrived.

Hubert's face held a hostile expression. "I know there's no love lost between us," he said suspiciously. "Why the sudden interest?"

"Because it's to our mutual benefit to call a truce and join forces," Jacques replied smoothly. He took a swallow of his Campari. It tasted deliciously bitter and refreshing. "I know you don't like me, Hubert," he said. "You've bad-mouthed me in public once too often. But *I've* been discreet. *I* haven't told anyone a thing about you."

Hubert's florid face reddened even more. It looked like his blood vessels were about to burst. "What's there to tell?" he asked angrily.

Jacques laughed thinly. "Come off it, Hubert. You know very well."

Hubert looked down into his drink. "I was very drunk at the time," he said quickly. "It was a set-up."

Jacques stared at him steadily. "Was it?" His voice was flat. "Sure, you were only a kid of fifteen spending the weekend in Paris with his parents. But you did sneak out of the hotel and come into the *pouf* bar, didn't you? You did go home with Maurice and me. And you did suck on our pricks. Remember?"

Hubert grabbed Jacques by the collar and pulled him close. Instantly, Jacques's face reddened and he began gasping for breath. His hands flew up to his throat, tugging at Hubert's fingers. "Let me go," he rasped. "You'll be sorry."

Hubert twisted the collar in his hand, tightening the stranglehold. "Listen, you slimy queer," he snarled into Jacques's face. "I'll kill you if you say that again!"

Suddenly the conversations around them had stopped and Hubert could feel eyes upon them. He looked around. Contemptuously he released his grip and threw Jacques backward into his chair. Jacques swallowed and loosened his collar. For a moment he stared at Hubert.

"Everyone tries something like that once in his life!" Hubert hissed in a half-whisper. "I'm not a queer. It was part of growing up. All adolescents do that sort of thing."

Jacques recovered quickly. "What about the pictures, Hubert?" he asked tauntingly. "I've still got copies of them, you know. Sure, they're not exactly sex pictures. But you're naked in them. Masturbating, remember? At the time you thought posing was a great turn-on."

"It was a mistake! Can't you get that through your perverted skull? I was a kid." He brought the brandy up to his lips and took a swallow.

Jacques gave a low laugh. "Who'd believe it? The pictures speak for themselves. Me, I'll never forget that day. I had to take a cab home, remember? Because you rode home on the back of Maurice's moped. Playing with him the whole way, I might add."

"What is it you want? Money? Here." He reached for his wallet and started counting out thousand-franc bills.

Jacques shook his head and pushed the money away. "I don't want your money. I want to make a deal."

516

Hubert stared at him. "I don't think I like your deals," he said quietly.

Jacques now leaned across the table, his confidence fully restored. "But you liked *her*, didn't you? And she left you cold. I know how much you must hate her. Don't you want to get even?"

Hubert drew himself up and finished his drink. He put the glass down. "Just say what you have to and let's get this over with," he said irritably.

"All right." Jacques frowned into his Campari and toyed deliberately with the stem of the glass. "If I'm not mistaken, there are three shareholders in Les Editions Hélène Junot." he said calculatingly. "Hélène, you, and a certain German. Joining forces, you and the German hold twenty percent of the shares."

"Why would you care about that?" Hubert mumbled. "You're the one who's chummy with her."

Jacques looked at him. "And what would you say if I were to tell you that I was going to become a shareholder? That would give us thirty, maybe forty percent if we stuck together. Enough to throw some wrenches into the publishing machinery."

Hubert sat up straight now. "*You* hold shares!" he said incredulously. "How? What has she got on you?"

Jacques looked puzzled, wondering what this was supposed to mean. "Got on me? My dear boy, what on earth are you talking about?" His eyes widened suddenly as everything fell into place. "So *that's* it!" he exclaimed in triumph, answering his own question. "Now I get it!" He burst out laughing. The world had gone crazy. Jacques was crazy. Even Hélène was crazy.

Hubert looked at him sharply. "*What* do you get?"

"Why you are a shareholder. I always thought it strange. She's hated you for as long as I've known her. And she was rich enough not to need your money." Delicately Jacques sipped his Campari. When he spoke again, his voice was a whisper. "What did you do, Hubert, that she could force you into investing?"

"Nothing," Hubert answered quickly.

"Come on, I'm not a fool." Jacques looked at him shrewdly across the table. "You said you would kill me—I wonder if that would be new to you?" he said softly. "That's the key to everything, isn't it?"

Hubert said nothing. He just looked at Jacques. What he saw was a hungry, ambitious look in his eyes which he had never seen there before.

"Who would you have killed, Hubert? Let me see, now . . ." Jacques pretended to be deep in thought as he made a production of drumming the table with spiderlike fingertips.

Hubert watched the fingers in morbid fascination. They looked like they were moving slowly up and down the keyboard of a piano.

Jacques smiled widely and looked at him. "Kowalsky," he stated softly.

The decks vibrated pleasantly as the big diesels pushed the *Evangelia* through the water. Monaco was slowly slipping away behind them like just another cluster of white houses on the Côte d'Azur. When you looked away from the coast, all you could see was water, deep blue and undulating gently. The horizon was blurry. It was difficult to tell just where the sea ended and the sky began.

Hélène turned around as Zeno Skouri came up beside her. "Are you ready for the grand tour?" he asked. "Everyone's had it but you."

She laughed. "That's because I didn't know you when the cruise began in Barcelona."

"Come, I give you your tour now." He looked around. "Where's Niggle?"

"He went inside," Hélène replied. "He told me he'd be right back."

"Then we shall wait." The old Greek smiled as he planted himself against the railing. "I don't want him to think I'd kidnap you." He looked at her shrewdly. "He thinks very highly of you, our friend does."

Hélène felt a blush coming on.

"Ah, here comes Niggle now."

She turned around. The salon doors were sliding apart and Nigel came out on deck. He had changed into white shorts, a polo shirt, white knee socks, and deck shoes. She was conscious of his slim but muscular physique, his lithe, easy movements, the curls of hair on his tanned legs and arms. He grinned and walked straight toward her and Zeno. He seemed to catch her stare, and she blinked suddenly and looked away. As if she had been caught looking at something she shouldn't have.

"She is getting the grand tour," Skouri announced proudly. "You're welcome to come along, if you think you can bear to indulge an old man's whim."

"I'd be honored," Nigel said gallantly, taking Hélène by the hand.

A pleasant thrill ran through her as he wrapped his fingers around hers. His grip felt good. It was firm, yet also gentle. She raised her head. For a moment she found herself looking into his eyes. They were warm and smiling and unblinking. There was a sensual quality in his touch, and she felt herself trembling.

The grand tour lasted over an hour. The *Evangelia* was Skouri's pride and joy. Once started, it was difficult for him to stop talking. He delighted in having an attentive audience. Born into poverty on Thera, he had made a career out of wooing the rich, the famous, the accomplished. It was quite natural that his yacht should serve as public evidence of his social status in international society. The guests who had already cruised aboard were like a list lifted from *Who's Who*, the *Social Register*, and the *Celebrity Register* combined.

The *Evangelia* had been a 2,500-ton American frigate which had seen undistinguished service during World War II. Skouri had bought her in 1953, dilapidated and in mothballs, for forty thousand dollars. He then spent millions converting her into a yacht. This had been done at the von Eiderfeld shipyard in Kiel, Germany. This news distressed Hélène, but she tried her best to leave her personal feelings out of it. Probably even Skouri had not met the reclusive Karl von Eiderfeld; his shipyard had simply gained a reputation for its fine German craftsmanship.

The yacht was more than just a floating palace. From the beginning, Skouri had intended it to be his home, and he personally followed every phase of the conversion. Anxious as he had been to move aboard immediately, he had had to wait for a year and a half until the conversion was complete. In the end, it had been worth it.

Like an expectant father, Skouri descended on the shipyard without warning to inspect the work as it progressed. When he didn't like the location of the air-conditioning ducts, whole bulkheads had to be torn out and the air-conditioning shafts rerouted. His endless demands nearly drove the designers and workmen out of their minds. And then there were the special touches. Like the sunken bathtubs, which meant

519

that the deck floors had to be raised. Or how to have a dance floor as well as a swimming pool on the aft deck. The engineer cleverly solved that particular problem by creating a hydraulic pool floor. The pool could then be drained and the floor raised and danced upon. There was even a special device that kept the seawater that was pumped into the pool several degrees below air temperature so that swimming in it would be refreshing.

Hélène marveled at all these luxurious touches. When she was finished with the tour, she was quite taken aback. And to think that she had been impressed when she was first shown to her stateroom! The door had an engraved, gold-plated plaque on it that read: "Pissarro Suite." At first she had been puzzled; then, being led down the corridor, she had noticed other doors marked "Rembrandt Suite," "Van Gogh Suite," "Picasso Suite," "Goya Suite," "El Greco Suite," "Dürer Suite," "Raphael Suite," "Dali Suite," "Matisse Suite," and "Renoir Suite." Only after she was inside her suite did she realize the significance of the name. Above a sofa in the little sitting room hung a framed, hermetically sealed Pissarro. There was another in the bedroom. She half-expected to see one in the bath as well, but there she was disappointed. It was plain marble, albeit with gleaming gold fixtures, embroidered Porthault towels, and a staggering array of soaps, perfumes, and toilet waters. By the sunken tub there was a reading lamp and a pillow so that you could soak in comfort. Never in her life had she seen such shameless luxury.

And the guests! So many socialites and celebrities. There were Magda Mond, a reclusive Hungarian film star; Sir George Broyhill, an ancient British statesman who had helped the Allies win World War II; Blanche Benois, the French sex-kitten film star who had once been the subject of a *Les Modes* article; Elena and Evangelia, Skouri's attractive twin daughters; Nikos, his son; Ariadne Cosindas, the world-famous ballerina who was also Skouri's long-time mistress and had survived his two marriages; Giorgio Marioni, an Italian menswear designer; and Paolo Ralli, a Grand Prix circuit driver for Ferrari. Conspicuous by her absence was Skouri's beautiful American wife, Cynthia.

The cruise was all mapped out. The *Evangelia* was steered on a steady course along the French and Italian Rivieras. Just past Portofino, she turned and cut straight down to Corsica.

Stops after that were to be Sardinia; Capri and Naples; Corfu; Elena, Skouri's lavish private island in the Ionian Sea; and finally Venice, where the cruise would end and all the guests would attend the event of the season, the Black-and-White Ball in an ancient palazzo on the Grand Canal.

Hélène enjoyed herself from the moment she came aboard. She managed to push Jacques's backstabbing into the farthest corner of her mind. The days were too beautiful and sun-drenched to harp on something like that; the nights were too cool and romantic. The *Evangelia* was the perfect ship to cruise aboard. It was large enough so that no one got in any-one else's hair, and yet it had the feel of an intimate vessel. Activities could either be joined or ignored. Onboard there were the usual deck games, nightly Magda Mond movies, and daily swims, either in the pool or in the sea. When they were in port, Skouri had arranged for cars ahead of time, and there were plenty of sights to see and restaurants to visit. On Corsica, Hélène and Nigel went off on their own to the chalky cliffs at Bonifacio, where in the fifteenth century the inhabitants had resisted a lengthy Spanish siege. Hélène mar-veled at the strong scent of the maquis, the dense under-growth growing all over the island, a combination of the rich perfumes of myrtle, lavender, eucalyptus, wild mint, and cyclamen.

"Napoleon once said, 'I would recognize Corsica, eyes closed, only because of its perfume,' " Nigel quoted.

On Capri, they went off by themselves again. They climbed to the top of the island, drank wine on a fragrant terrace, and later hired a boat and rowed through the Blue Grotto. It was the stuff of which romances were made.

One evening, some of the *Evangelia*'s crew played bouzouki music and everyone danced on deck and broke piles of plates. Hélène continued to be astounded by the una-bashed luxury that surrounded her. Daily, fresh bread was flown in by seaplane from Skouri's favorite bakery in Paris, and when Ariadne demanded fresh Greek lamb, it, too, ar-rived by special plane from Crete. The *Evangelia* had two chefs, one Greek and one French. To top it all off, there was even a completely stocked wine "cellar" and a sommelier. In-variably, Hélène chose to eat Greek food, and Skouri was delighted by her choice. Like him, she drank ouzo during the cocktail hour, champagne with her meal, and a sip of Cour-voisier after dinner.

"You are a Greek in soul!" Skouri cried one afternoon. "If you like, I let you send a writer and photographer onboard and they can do a big article on the *Evangelia!*"

Hélène was flattered. "I'll make sure you stick by that, Zeno," she warned.

He laughed heartily. They were sitting on the bar stools which were covered with the skin of whale testicles, and he wrote on a napkin: "I the undersigned do hereby permit Hélène Junot to send any and all photographers and writers of *Les Modes* to do a feature article on the *Evangelia*. The entire yacht is at their disposal. (signed) Zeno Callicrates Skouri." It was a memento she was to treasure forever.

The cruise was the first real vacation Hélène had ever had, and it worked wonders. She had never felt so relaxed in her life. She had vowed that she wouldn't spend a minute thinking of business, and she nearly kept that vow. Only twice was *Les Modes* mentioned, and both times the subject was brought up by someone else. The first time had been Skouri, and she had arranged with him for Luba to work on the *Evangelia* article. She knew that the Czarina would be forever grateful for the opportunity. The second mention was by Giorgio Marioni. He wanted to know why Hélène didn't create an edition of *Les Modes* for menswear. She promised to think about it.

From every place they dropped anchor, she wrote post-cards to Edmond, Jeanne, and Petite Hélène.

Skouri, forever the perfect host, seemed to find time for everyone. He had that rare gift of making sure that neither Ariadne, his mistress, nor Magda Mond, his most cherished friend, was lacking in attention. But most important he gave Hélène the opportunity to get to know Nigel.

She stood on deck with him one fine evening. The lights from shore were like the stars above, twinkling and bright and moving slowly in the night. The moon was full, flooding the deck with half-light. She never remembered what they had been discussing, but suddenly he took her in his arms and pressed her against him. His lips sought hers, and she gave herself up to his kisses. They were deep and demanding. Then he held her face to his chest. "Hélène . . ." His voice was a whisper, half-carried away by the breeze.

She looked up and could see his eyes shining down at her in the moonlight. "Nigel . . ." she said huskily. "Oh, Nigel . . ."

"I love you," he said.

She closed her eyes and smiled up at him. "I love you, too," she whispered.

"Darling!" He held her tighter. She made no move to get out of his arms. She was willing to stay in them forever, enveloped and protected, loved and cherished. She could smell the powerful masculinity of him, feel the strength of his body. He needed her; she could feel that, too. And she needed him. She needed his strength.

His murmur was a caress in the moonlight, his lips a thrill of warmth as he nuzzled the nape of her neck, his breath a stir in her ear. "Is my suite all right?"

She could not trust herself to speak, but her eyes flashed her answer in the light spilling out from the open door, her pupils dark wide jewels of desire.

The off-white carpet was deep and velvety and her bare feet made no sound as she crossed over to the bed. He was stretched out naked, slim and tanned, watching her approach in the dim light.

He felt a sudden dryness come up in his throat. She had pulled the pins out of her hair, which flowed long, black, and silken down her naked back. Her skin was tanned and taut, smooth as polished alabaster, and her belly was so flat that her navel seemed to protrude. Her breasts, small but firm and perfectly shaped, rode high and proud above her taut rib cage. Her nipples were already erect, dark and hard with longing.

He moved lithely off the bed, his motions fluid as he got to his feet and reached for her hands.

Quickly her eyes moved over his body, downward past his chest and slim hips to his groin.

For a moment she stood transfixed as he held her hands and looked deep into her eyes. She could feel her heart fluttering as he brought her slim, tapered fingers up to his lips and kissed them seductively, looking directly over at her through those sparkling, gold-flecked eyes. Then he let go of her hands and moved one of his to the small of her back, tracing small circles on her flesh with his forefinger. The rousing scent of her musk was in his nostrils. "You're beautiful," he said softly. "Beautiful." His lips sought hers now. As his fingers glided smoothly up and down the ridge of her back, he felt her responding to his touch. He pressed her

523

toward him so that she sucked in her breath as she felt the wetness seeping from within her.

Before Helene could ask him to wait, Nigel had lifted her effortlessly off her feet, and without interrupting their kiss, carried her the rest of the way to the bed.

His searching tongue parted the soft dark curls of her pubic hair. She widened her legs and thrust her hips forward and could feel his face snuggling close, his moist tongue parting her and probing inside. It was a soft and rousing sensation, and it brought a tingling warmth spreading throughout her.

Gently he rolled her over on her stomach. Obediently she complied. He continued to tease her with his tongue. Her anticipation was unbearable. She had waited too long to sleep with him. She begged him to come inside her, but he continued to touch another part of her. The inside of her thigh, the back of her knee.

Suddenly she let out a cry. "Nigel!"

He knew she was ready for him, and with a thrust of his hips he quickly slid himself up inside her. He could feel her strong muscles contracting around him, trapping him inside.

Slowly he began to thrust in and out until her breath came in gasps and she surrendered herself completely to him. Neither one had to say a thing. Never had Hélène been loved like this. Her life would never be complete without him.

Blanche Benois felt trapped. She could feel the familiar ache swelling up inside her. For the past week, it had been unbearable, but nothing compared to this. It felt as if her pubis were about to explode.

Frantically she began pacing up and down the stateroom, but it didn't do any good. Her pink lips were set in an angry pout and her huge gray eyes with the long lashes were wide with boredom. Her tight white jeans and the straining bikini top which barely covered her full breasts looked strangely out of place in the quiet luxury of the stateroom.

For a moment she stopped pacing. On an impulse she pushed aside the curtains and unlatched the porthole. She stuck her head out into the night. The air was cool and clear. She could hear the muffled throb of the diesels and the sounds of another Magda Mond movie coming from the deck above. She cursed, drew her head back in, and slammed the porthole shut again. Everyone seemed to be having a good time but her.

At first she'd thought the cruise might be fun. And it would have been, too, if that sexy American athlete hadn't had to cancel at the last minute. Only after she had boarded in Barcelona did she learn that the handsome black boxer had sustained injuries in the ring and had been hospitalized. She had wanted to get off right then and there, but she didn't. You couldn't just board Skouri's yacht, find out that a guest was unable to make it, and then pack your bags and get right off again. Skouri's empire was too far-flung. He owned a film-production company, International Artists. It was I.A. that held the option for her next three films. No, she couldn't walk out on Skouri. Not without feeling the full force of his wrath.

Who else was there to have fun with? No one. Sir George was too ancient, Elena and Evangelia had Giorgio and Paolo tied around their little fingers, Hélène had Nigel falling all over her, Ariadne had Skouri, and Nikos Skouri liked nothing better than to consort with the engineers and tinker with the engines of the Piaggio seaplanes or one of the many speed-boats.

With a frustrated sigh she plopped herself down on the king-size bed and stared up at the padded-leather ceiling. What a bore this was turning out to be! And there were six more days of it. The way things were going, she'd probably be a raving lunatic by the time the cruise was over.

Blanche Benois could be characterized as a vampire. She lived on men and took from them. On screen, her sex-hungry quality reflected her sexuality, which was all-consuming. When she worked on a film, she retired to her trailer and had sex with whoever was available before she would stand in front of the cameras. That way, the film was certain to capture her torrid appeal. She knew that only a woman who had just had satisfying sex radiated a certain animal quality.

But much as she threw herself into sex, she only took from men. She sucked all the sweet juices out of their loins and never gave of herself in return. She usually only had to lie there and moan while they did all the work. And they never noticed that she did nothing, the fools! They were always too concerned with their precious penises to realize that as long as they were humping her, there was a triumphant gleam in

525

her eyes. They thought they were showing off their prowess, when actually it was she who controlled them.

She let out another sigh and arched her body off the bed so that only her head, shoulders, and feet were firmly planted on the mattress. She undid the buttons of her white jeans and peeled them down around her ankles. When she was out of them, she shrugged off the bikini top and lay naked on her back. Deliberately she let her fingers brush across her nipples until she felt the fine, tingling sensation starting up within them. She moaned and looked down at them. They were large and plum-colored against the deep bronzed tan of her breasts. Million-dollar tetons, they were. That was what they were insured for by Lloyd's of London. They had always been perfectly shaped and big, but now they were even better since she'd had the silicone implants.

She felt her fever rising. Hundreds of thousands of men who went to see her movies hungered after those tetons, could imagine the sweetness of them between their lips. Hundreds of thousands—perhaps even millions—of men would have given anything to jump into bed with her and show her how they could make those tetons feel. And yet . . . and yet she was alone, dammit! Nobody wanted her, and her body demanded that she have a man!

She took a deep breath as she felt the moistness starting up between her legs. It was like Sister Magdalene at the Catholic boarding school had told her: she would suffer. But Sister had been wrong. Blanche's suffering was not the kind she had been warned about. She smiled now, thinking back to that time in the dormitory.

She had just turned fourteen. Sister had come into her tiny room unexpectedly, finding her naked on the iron-framed bed with both hands half-buried inside her. Blanche hadn't even realized she was there until she'd heard the gasp. Then suddenly she sat bolt upright in embarrassment. The pink face framed by the white wimple and black veil looked at her with shock.

"Blanche!" Sister Magdalene hissed harshly, trying to control her voice. "What are you doing!"

Blanche laughed now. What the hell had that old virgin thought she'd been doing? Praying?

Sister's voice had risen righteously. "Get decent immediately and then come down to the office!" Swiftly she turned on her heel, her black robes rustling and the rosary beads around her waist clicking faintly against one another as she marched back out.

Ten minutes later, Blanche was bent over the big scarred desk as Sister Magdalene brought the wooden cane down upon her bare buttocks again and again. Blanche strained her ass muscles, tightening them to lessen the sting. At first the pain had been exquisite; then it began to burn fiercely, like fire. Blanche hadn't been able to contain herself. The pain, plus the picture of a crucified Jesus being flogged by the Romans staring down at her from the wall, brought on the strongest orgasm she was ever to know.

Strange that she should think about Sister Magdalene now. She hadn't thought about her for years.

She rolled over on the bed. But that was long in the past. She needed a man now, today, and there was none.

Suddenly a calculating glint came into her eyes. She couldn't steal Giorgio or Paolo from Elena and Evangelia. Skouri wouldn't have it. But there was always Nigel.

She smiled now. All she had to do was wait a little while till they all went to bed. Till Hélène slipped out of his suite in the wee hours of the morning. She had never known a man who could say no after she'd sneaked into his room and wakened him up by flicking her tongue over his balls.

An hour and a half later, the movie ended; everyone congratulated Magda Mond on her performance and then headed to the bar or to bed. Hélène and Nigel went up on the sundeck and stood beneath the stars. They were the only ones there, and the sounds of soft music drifted up from the bar below. Hélène stood there listening to it. She was watching Nigel closely. His face was illuminated by the pale wash of moonglow. She wanted him to take her in his arms.

Instead, he said, "It was a wonderful movie. They don't make them like that anymore."

She was surprised by his small talk. It took a moment for her to find her voice. "No, they don't."

He shook his head. "It must be terrible to be a star. One's aging never shows so much as on film. It's a sad reminder of how quickly one grows old."

She nodded slowly.

Suddenly he reached out and took her hands in his. "Oh, Hélène, I know this is sudden and rash. But I want to . . . Could you . . . I mean, will you marry me?"

527

She drew in her breath and stared at him. The proposal had been sprung on her so suddenly that she was momentarily speechless. Then her heart gave a joyous leap and her eyes shone. "Are you sure?" she stammered. "You know so little about—"

He didn't wait for her to finish. "Just say yes," he said earnestly, squeezing her hands. "Darling, please say yes!"

Her eyes stared down to the deck below. She looked back up at him. "I will give you your answer tomorrow," she said in a trembling voice.

Much later, after they made love and he lay asleep, she brushed her lips against his, slipped out of his bed and back to her own suite. He said he loved her. And she was certain she loved him. Or was it only physical attraction which drew them together? No, it was more, she decided. Much more.

It took a long time for her to get to sleep. Back in her own bed, she stared up at the dark ceiling for what seemed like hours. The night was quiet save for the sounds of water slapping against the hull. She missed the warmth of his body, the steady sounds of his breathing. She could only lie there thinking of Nigel and his proposal. When she finally fell asleep, it was into a pleasant, dreamless black depth, totally at peace.

She was brought out of it by the ringing of the telephone. She opened her eyes and looked groggily at her Hermès travel alarm clock. The luminous green dial read two o'clock.

Bewildered, she reached for the receiver. "You have a call from Paris," the yacht's operator said. "Please hold." Then she could hear the ship-to-shore operator making the connection through the *Evangelia*'s radiotelephone system. A moment later a voice came on over the air, crackly and far away.

"Edmond!" she said.

"I wouldn't call you if it weren't an emergency," he said quickly in a distraught voice.

"What's the matter?" Hélène demanded, suddenly frightened. She sat up straight in bed, sleep falling away in brittle shards.

The words spilled out of him. "It's Jeanne. She's in the hospital."

"The hospital!" Hélène's voice was disbelieving. A sudden chill seized her heart. "Edmond, what *is* it?"

"The baby. There are complications."

She didn't hesitate. "I'll be there on the next plane!" she promised.

"Please hurry." He tried to say more, but his voice cracked suddenly. It took a moment for him to recover. "I . . . I don't know how much time she's got left . . ."

"I'm leaving, Edmond. Straightaway. Please tell her I'll be there!"

"I will, if she . . . if she's conscious long enough. Thanks, Little French Girl."

She hung up and sat there in the dark, stunned. The stateroom was quiet except for the low hum of the air conditioning. She covered her face with her hands. She couldn't believe it. Something wrong with Jeanne? The best friend she had? It couldn't be true. Then tears were pouring down her face. She wiped them away with her fingertips and switched on the lamp. The yellow glow spilled out over the nightstand.

She stared at the telephone. Then, without losing another second, she dialed the bridge. A moment later she got hold of the captain. Almost immediately the *Evangelia*'s diesels changed pitch and the yacht slowed to a halt. The crane on deck swung one of the Piaggio seaplanes overboard. Quickly Hélène threw on some clothes, took a sheet of the engraved *Evangelia* stationery out of the desk and hastily scribbled a note to Nigel. When she was through, she quickly read it over. It would have to do.

My darling,
    A family emergency requires me to leave at once. I'll get in touch with you as soon as possible. In the meantime, my answer to your proposal is: Yes! Yes!! Yes!!!

All my love,
Hélène

By the time she folded it, the telephone rang again. It was the Captain. The Piaggio was ready for takeoff, the pilot standing by. She hurried into the corridor and stuck the note in the door of the Rembrandt Suite. Then she went up on deck. A Riva speedboat had already been lowered from the davits. A sailor was waiting for her and helped her down the portable stairs to the floating platform. Another sailor helped her into the Riva. The line was untied and he let out the clutch. The boat began to nose slowly toward the seaplane.

529

She could just make out its dark shape bobbing on the water a short distance away.

She didn't see Blanche Benois tiptoe to the Rembrandt Suite, take her note, read it, and tear it into tiny shreds. As Nigel awakened from his sleep to a moist tongue licking at his scrotum, the faint drone of a plane overhead hummed away into the distance.

10

The receptionist looked up at her with annoyance. "Visiting hours are from one to four," she said sternly.

Hélène stared at her. She was worried and bushed. She had tried to doze on the planes, but it had been impossible. For the four hours it had taken her to get to Paris, she'd been able to do nothing but worry. Now she had to fight to keep her temper under control as well. In a split second she sized up the receptionist. Long ago she had learned that those on the low end of a bureaucratic totem pole tended to try to exercise their power the most. There was only one way to deal with them.

She drew herself up imperiously. "Do I get to see my sister-in-law, or must I have words with whoever is in charge of this place?" Hélène turned her back on the receptionist and looked around, trying to spot a supervisor.

"I'm sorry," the receptionist said apologetically. "I didn't realize you were a relative. What did you say the patient's name is again?"

Hélène turned back around. "Jeanne Junot."

The receptionist consulted a ledger on the desk and ran her finger down a long list. Finally she looked up. "Room three-oh-nine." She leaned forward and pointed. "Make a right turn at the end of the waiting room and follow the corridor to the St.-Gatien wing. Take the second bank of elevators."

Hélène nodded her thanks, turned again, and went briskly in search of the elevators.

On the third floor, she found Edmond pacing outside

Jeanne's room, his expression blank. Hélène could feel her heart dropping. His face was pale and white. It was a face that had lost all hope.

Taking a deep breath, she hurried toward him. Her deck shoes made no sound, but he sensed her approaching. He looked up. "Little French Girl," he said in a tight voice.

She put out her hands and embraced him. Then she held him at arm's length. "How is she?" she demanded, looking up at him.

He avoided her eyes. "I don't know." There was hopelessness in his voice, too. "The doctors keep using medical terms I can't understand."

She bit down on her lip. "Can I see her?"

He shook his head. "The doctors are in there now. We have to wait."

She let go of his arms, turned away, and began to pace the corridor. Suddenly she had an idea. She stopped and whirled around. "Wait a moment! I'm going to make a telephone call."

He looked at her curiously. "To whom?"

"A friend who's a doctor. He's helped me before. He'll at least be able to unravel the mysteries of the jargon and let us know what's going on. I'll be right back." Quickly she started down the hall to find a telephone.

Dr. Rosen arrived long before the doctors were finished with Jeanne. From the corner of her eye, Hélène caught sight of him approaching. He was wearing a worn gray cardigan and his eyes were red-rimmed from interrupted sleep. Hélène felt bad at having awakened him, but she looked at him gratefully. She kissed his cheek. "Thank you for coming." She took his gnarled old hands into hers and held them silently for a moment. There was something about his quiet strength that made her feel better almost instantly.

She introduced him to Edmond and the two men shook hands. "What have the doctors told you?" he asked immediately.

Edmond made a futile gesture and looked down at his feet. "Not much. Something about fluid retention and renal failure."

Dr. Rosen was silent for a moment. "Hélène told me your wife is pregnant. What month is she in?"

"The eighth."

"The eighth." Dr. Rosen shook his head. It was the old story, he thought miserably. The wife probably knew all along that something was wrong but was afraid to tell the husband. Even without seeing her, he could guess what was the matter. Fluid retention was bad enough in itself, but renal failure probably meant toxemia. Poisoning of her body by her own fluids. "And how long has she been having the problems?" he asked.

Edmond shrugged painfully and looked away. His face was an expression of self-contempt. "I'm not certain. She didn't want to worry me, so she kept quiet. Finally I knew that something was wrong and insisted . . ." With shaking fingers he reached for a rumpled pack of cigarettes.

The door to Jeanne's room opened suddenly. A nun in flowing black robes and a starched winged hat came out. She was carrying a tray expertly balanced against her hip while she silently pulled the heavy door closed behind her.

Hélène hurried over to her. "How is she, Sister?"

The nun frowned disapprovingly and shook her head. "I cannot say. The doctors will be out shortly, I believe. They will be able to tell you more accurately than I." The nun looked past Hélène and eyed Edmond severely. "I'm sorry, monsieur, but smoking is strictly forbidden!" she announced in sepulchral tones.

Edmond took a quick last puff and looked around helplessly. Finally he dropped the cigarette on the stone floor and ground it out under his heel, shredding the tobacco. The nun said nothing, but gave him a stern look before she swept away down the corridor.

A team of doctors came out of Jeanne's room shortly after nine o'clock. By then Hélène had been waiting nearly three hours. She, Edmond, and Dr. Rosen quickly surrounded the doctors.

Edmond recognized one of them. "Dr. Dufaut, can we go in now?"

The doctor cleared his throat and held up his hands. "Yes, but only for a moment. Your wife is quite weak. She needs rest."

"How is she, doctor?" Hélène asked. "I mean, will she—"

"It's still too early to tell," the doctor cut in smoothly, sidestepping the question before it was fully formed. This was familiar territory for him. No matter how badly a patient was doing, you never admitted it. You had to leave the relatives with hope. He smiled tightly now. "Let me assure you, we're doing everything for her that we possibly can."

532

Dr. Rosen stepped forward. By habit, he took off his glasses and began polishing them with a handkerchief. "What, exactly, is wrong with Madame Junot?" he asked.

Dr. Dufaut frowned and looked at him closely. "Who are you?"

Dr. Rosen smiled agreeably. "I'm Simon Rosen. I'm a doctor and a close friend of the family's. I am here at their request."

The doctor took a deep breath and turned around. "You may go in now," he told Hélène and Edmond, "but the nurse won't let you stay long." Then he took Dr. Rosen aside.

The sickroom was dim and Hélène was not prepared for the sight of Jeanne lying on her pillow, breathing heavily. She didn't move. Perhaps she hadn't heard them come in.

Hélène took a deep breath and stifled her tears. This was not the Jeanne she knew and loved. The Jeanne who had waited on tables in Saint-Nazaire, who had given her the guidance and love of an older sister, who had married Edmond, who had given birth to Petite Hélène. This woman was a stranger. Her face was beet red and swollen. She was staring vacantly up at the ceiling. For a moment Hélène found herself looking up too. But there was nothing to be seen there.

"Jeanne . . ." Edmond said tentatively.

Slowly Jeanne turned her head on the pillow to face him. Her eyes were glazed. Trying hard to focus. "Edmond?" she mumbled thickly through swollen lips. "Edmond, I'm . . . I'm sorry." Her eyes brimmed over with tears. Her voice was tiny. "Edmond . . ."

He was beside her now, searching for one of her hands and holding it tightly. "You'll be all right in no time," he said, sitting down on the edge of the bed. With his free hand he stroked her forehead. "The doctors said you're making fine progress. Just keep it up, and in no time we'll have you back home."

"If things are going so well, then why are you looking away?" Jeanne asked calmly. She stared at him, and there was a sure look in her eyes as she shook her head. "No," she whispered. "I'm not going to go home. Never again."

Hélène stepped forward. "Jeanne!" she said in a choked voice. "I won't have you talking like that! You mustn't give up! You have everything to live for. You have me, Edmond, Petite Hélène, the new baby . . ."

533

"Hélène, dear sweet Hélène," Jeanne said gently, looking up at her gratefully. "You came. Edmond said you would, but I thought he was only saying that to placate me." Jeanne shook her head from side to side. "I know I won't get better. Just . . . just promise me one thing."

Hélène and Edmond nodded.

"Don't let Petite Hélène see me like this. Don't make her . . ." Jeanne twisted her face away from them and looked out over the side of the bed.

"Don't make her do what?" Edmond asked gently.

Jeanne closed her eyes wearily. "Don't make her . . . kiss me when I'm dead. I want the coffin closed. She's too young to have to see such . . . ugliness." With an immense effort, Jeanne fought to open her eyes. They were clear of tears. Her other hand found Hélène's, and the icy fingers closed over it like a vise. Her voice was growing fainter. "Hélène . . ." Jeanne swallowed and lifted her head. Her eyes were unwavering. "You'll . . . take care of Petite Hélène? Like your own daughter?" she asked in a small voice. "Can you promise me that?"

Hélène nodded solemnly and squeezed Jeanne's hand. "I promise," she said huskily.

Jeanne smiled and slowly let her head sink back down on the pillow. She let go of Helene's hand, the fingers unwrapping slowly.

A nurse came into the room. "Please, you'll have to wait outside for a while," she said sternly. "The patient is tired."

"Don't make them go!" Jeanne's face was suddenly contorted with fear. "Please," she begged. "Let them stay! I don't want to die alone!"

11

Jeanne did not die alone. The terrible thing was, she needn't have died at all.

When Hélène and Edmond went back out into the corridor after visiting with her, Dr. Rosen quickly slipped inside to examine Jeanne for himself. It was not long before he returned, but the wait seemed interminable. Hélène looked at him hopefully, but his face was grim. He drew her and Edmond aside and glanced around to make sure they couldn't be overheard. When he spoke, his voice was low. "We've got to move Madame Junot to another hospital."

Hélène stared at him. "But why?" she asked in surprise. "I don't—"

Dr. Rosen didn't let her finish. "Because this is a Catholic hospital," he explained, "run by nuns and priests, following the doctrine of the Church. Listen carefully, for we don't have the time to run through this twice. There isn't a moment to lose."

He turned to Edmond and looked up at him from above the glasses which were slowly slipping down his nose. He jabbed them back in place with his thumb.

"Your wife is diagnosed as having acute toxemia. That diagnosis is, unfortunately, correct. The illness was brought about by difficulties arising from her pregnancy. It is a dangerous condition, often fatal. In her case, assuredly so. The toxemia can cause"—he ticked the complications off on his fingers—"renal failure, that is, failure of the kidneys to function, which has already occurred; pneumonia, which is also beginning to set in; and pulmonary edema and cardiac failure could follow. In other words, the chances of heart failure are now great. While you were visiting her, I had a discussion with Dr. Dufaut. It is my opinion"—Dr. Rosen glanced from Hélène to Edmond—"that what Madame Junot needs is an immediate abortion!"

The word cut through Hélène's heart like a searing knife. Instantly a terrible nausea rose as a flood of memories engulfed her. Visions of her own baby that she had had cut out of her flashed before her eyes. She tried to swallow.

Edmond was visibly shaken. Somehow he found his voice. "An abortion!" He turned away suddenly. "My God, *no!*"

Dr. Rosen placed a hand on his arm. "Have courage, young man." He turned to include Hélène. "An abortion is the only thing that will spare Madame Junot her life. To do that, we've got to get her out of here. Catholic hospitals forbid abortion under any circumstances, and this one is especially strict. We must get her to a private clinic immediately."

Hélène wiped her eyes. "Where do we . . . find one?" she whispered.

"There's a good private hospital in Passy. Please, don't misunderstand me. I'm not in favor of taking a life. In this case, it is the only way in which we can save Madame Junot's life. Otherwise, both she and the child are doomed to die. Even Dr. Dufaut admitted that to me."

Sudden anger pushed through Hélène's shock. "And yet he won't perform it?" she asked incredulously.

Dr. Rosen shrugged helplessly. "He is a devout Catholic."

Edmond was silent. Hélène looked at him levelly, waiting for a moment. "Edmond," she prodded quietly, "there isn't much time."

His face was white with anguish. Then his eyes fell. "Please, Hélène," he begged huskily. "I . . . I can't make that kind of decision."

For a moment she could only stare at him. A fleeting realization came to her. Her stalwart Edmond, who as a child had bravely killed the Boche and led her on that impossibly treacherous journey halfway across France, was now hunched over in pain, indecisive and afraid.

But Hélène's mind was working swiftly. Tenderly she wrapped her arms around her brother. His body was locked in stiff tension, the muscles frozen. "I trust Dr. Rosen," she said softly. "Now's not the time to go into it, but he saved my life once. If he says an abortion is necessary, then it is."

Edmond could only nod. "It isn't me, it's Jeanne. She's so devout. She'd never allow it."

"I'll talk to her," Hélène declared briskly. "She'll listen to me."

After giving Edmond quick orders to prepare for Jeanne's transfer, she went back into the sickroom, got rid of the nurse, and went over to Jeanne and sat down on the edge of the bed. She reached for the wet sponge, wrung it out, and gently began dabbing Jeanne's forehead. Jeanne lay still. For a moment Hélène was afraid she was dead. Then slowly Jeanne's eyes fluttered open. She smiled thinly. "You came back!" she whispered. "I knew you wouldn't let me die alone."

"I won't let you die, period," Hélène said grimly. She looked down at Jeanne. "Edmond and I are transferring you to a different hospital."

"A different . . ." Jeanne looked suddenly confused. "But . . . they're so good to me here."

"I know that," Hélène said gently, "but another hospital can make you well again. Think of Petite Hélène and Edmond. Don't you want to live for them?"

A glimmer of hope pushed its way through Jeanne's dull eyes as she struggled to sit up. "What must I do?"

"We shall take you to a private clinic. You'll probably have to stay there for a few weeks. Then you will be as good as new."

Suddenly a look of understanding crossed Jeanne's face. She snatched her hand away and her eyes moved down the length of her body to where her swollen belly distended the blanket. After a prolonged moment her gaze moved back up to Hélène. Her eyes were penetrating. "And my baby?" she asked softly.

Hélène looked away. It was useless to lie. Her expression would give her away. "The baby must die," she whispered.

"No!" Jeanne croaked sharply. She shook her head stubbornly. "I know what it is you want them to do to me! I won't let that happen."

"But you must!" Hélène pleaded. "Your life . . . and what about Edmond and Petite Hélène! What about them? They love you, Jeanne. Edmond needs a wife. And Petite Hélène needs a mother."

"Not one who is disgraced in the eyes of God. Please, Hélène . . ." Jeanne sought Hélène's hand again and squeezed it with the little strength she had left. "Forgive me, but I cannot."

Jeanne's last request was to die in the chapel, and she was wheeled there on a rolling stretcher to spend her last minutes lying in front of the altar rail, the stained-glass windows throwing their kaleidoscopic splotches of color everywhere. The last earthly sight she saw was the gleaming crucifix the priest held over her as he said Last Rites.

537

im-
nol-
of
let-

12

This house is dead, Hélène thought as she watched Petite Hélène getting dressed in a somber black dress. It was like the villa on Cap Ferrat after Stanislaw died. Something that had lived and breathed had gone out of it. Overnight, the house that had been such a happy home had become nothing more than an empty shell.

Petite Hélène finished dressing. She came toward Hélène and turned around solemnly. "How do I look, Tante Hélène?" she asked quietly.

It has already affected her, too, Hélène thought. She was more mature, more serious and grown-up. She had taken the news of her mother's death very soberly, almost without emotion. Even that morning at the funeral, she had been dry-eyed. Of course, Hélène hadn't really expected her to understand what death was. Not yet. Often it took a while for the tragedy to sink in. Especially with children.

"You look lovely," Hélène said automatically, retying the black satin ribbon in the girl's fiercely orange hair.

"Where are we going?" Petite Hélène asked.

"I thought it would be nice to walk in the Bois for a while," she answered. She forced a smile. "Afterward, we can stop somewhere and have an ice cream."

"I don't think I want an ice cream."

Hélène shrugged. "In that case, we shall just walk. Hurry, or we'll miss the sunshine."

When they got outside, the day was still bright and fresh. Aimlessly they wandered along the less-used paths in the Bois. Hélène couldn't help looking around constantly. It was as if Jeanne's soul could be found here floating somewhere among the thickly leafed chestnut trees, dancing among the fragile flowers that bent in the breezes, even soaring elusively overhead alongside the birds that swooped in the puffball skies. After an hour, they sat on a bench in the Jardin d'Acclimatation and watched the children at play. Petite Hélène was five years old, but she was in no mood for the animals and the rides. It was as if she had suddenly shed the Renoir-girl quality and outgrown the laughter and games. Instead of mingling with the children as she usually did, she sat quietly beside Hélène, her short legs not quite reaching the ground. After a long silence, she turned to Hélène with that curious, adult wisdom that some children tend to have. "Tante Hélène . . . ?"

Hélène looked at her silently.

"Maman's gone, Tante Hélène. We'll just have to keep on living, won't we?" She turned her head slightly and looked vacantly at the noisy playground. A crowd of screaming children was hanging on to the whirling merry-go-round. "Just sitting here waiting won't bring her back."

Suddenly Hélène found herself crying. She drew the girl against her, wrapping her in her arms and holding her close. The tears were streaming unchecked down her cheeks. Petite Hélène was right, she thought. Jeanne was gone. Her soul wasn't here in the Bois. It was in this girl she was holding in her arms. A soul was passed from mother to daughter, from father to son. Only, her own soul could never be passed on, for she could never have children.

Silently she let Petite Hélène go and wiped away the tears that shone on her cheeks. Petite Hélène was watching curiously. "Can I get you something, Tante Hélène?" she asked in a small voice, embarrassed at having caused the outburst.

"No," Hélène said huskily. There was a distant look in her eyes. "I . . . I'm fine." Suddenly she changed her mind and unsnapped her purse. She took out a few twenty-franc bills. "Here, go to the kiosk and buy some newspapers and magazines."

"Any particular ones?"

Hélène shook her head and nodded with her chin. "You pick them out."

Petite Hélène looked at her, quietly palmed the money and left. Thoughtfully Hélène watched her going down the path. Even the girl's walk had changed. It no longer had that awkward childish bounce. She was still many years from puberty; she was also many years from being a mere baby. The painful years were yet to come. Or were they already upon her?

When Petite Hélène returned, she carried a big stack of

newspapers and magazines. Wearily she dropped them on the bench and then plopped down beside them.

Hélène looked blankly at the publications. *Ici Paris* was on the top. She made it a point never to buy it, but she didn't want to disappoint Petite Hélène. Slowly she picked it up. For a moment she could only stare at the cover. It took a moment for it to sink in. The big color photo showed a pouting Blanche Benois on the arm of Nigel Somerset, scion of a dukedom, at the Black-and-White Ball in Venice. It was the very ball to which Zeno Skouri had invited her. Only now did she realize that things had been so topsy-turvy that she hadn't given much thought to Nigel.

Wearily she closed her eyes and let the paper drop unread onto her lap. She felt very, very alone.

Hélène drew a deep breath as she climbed out of the taxi in front of Fouquet's. For a moment, she couldn't help but stop and glance around at the pulse of the city. For the first time since Jeanne had died, she felt a little something stir inside her. The late-summer weather was on its best Parisian behavior. The café owners were jubilant; everywhere, the outdoor tables were doing a brisk business. The chestnut trees lining the avenues were deep dark green, not the lush, fresh green of spring, but that perfectly mature green when they are at their ripest.

Hélène clutched her purse more tightly now. The brilliant day had soured suddenly as harsh reality grabbed hold of her. Quickly, without another glance around, she entered the terrace of Fouquet's. At the far end, she saw Jacques already sitting at one of the sidewalk tables. He waved at her as the maître d' led her to the table and helped her into her seat.

She put her purse on the table and started to pull off her gloves. "Hello, princess," Jacques said quietly.

Hélène nodded curtly. The packed tables and the traffic beyond the sidewalk seemed suddenly to fade into the distance. Her voice was low but clear. "Well?" she asked, getting right down to business. "Why not the office? Why Fouquet's?"

"Because it's appropriate," he replied. "But all in good time. Besides, I vaguely recall your warning me never to set foot in the office again." He sat back and studied her. He made a production of frowning. "You're not looking very well," he said in a reprimanding voice. "You're all pale and

540

washed out. Black does not suit you. You of all people should know better."

She shrugged. She no longer cared what he thought about the way she looked or anything else. Nor was she about to tell him that it was a miracle she didn't look worse after all she'd been through the past week.

"The cruise didn't seem to do you a bit of good," he continued in a bitchy tone. His eyes narrowed shrewdly. "By the way, did you happen to see the latest issue of *Ici Paris?*"

She noticed now that he had a copy beside him. He unfolded it and held it up. Nigel's face stared mockingly at her.

"His Lordship, it seems, is quite smitten with Blanche Benois." Jacques smiled smugly.

"Get to the point," she said wearily.

She knew perfectly well why he had arranged this meeting—and why Fouquet's. In Monte Carlo, he had mentioned something about severance pay. That could only mean that he had the von Eiderfeld pictures and was going to blackmail her with them. Her purse with the negatives in it had been snatched right outside here, on the crosswalk not four meters away. At the time, she had suspected he was involved. But as time had passed, and he'd made no move, her suspicions had died down.

A waiter approached. "A white wine, s'il vous plaît," she said. When he was gone, she turned back to Jacques. The best defense was an offense. "You have the photos?" she asked brusquely.

He looked at her in surprise, momentarily thrown. There was a drawn-out, uneasy pause. "So you've known all along."

She kept her voice flat. "I've had my suspicions."

"You're clever," he said with grudging respect. "I didn't think you were onto me."

She remained silent as the waiter brought her wine. She pushed it aside and looked at Jacques. "How much do you want?"

"Always to the point, aren't you?" he asked dryly.

"I find that it saves time."

He shook his head and smiled. "Still watching those precious minutes."

She didn't reply.

"I'm afraid you won't like my terms," he said.

"Go ahead, state them."

"You've got two shareholders in Les Éditions Hélène

Junot," he said slowly. "The first, of course, is Hubert de Léger. For a while I was mystified as to why he should be one. But that's cleared up now. He told me what it is you've got on him."

"And what's that?"

Jacques smiled knowingly. "He killed Stanislaw."

Hélène's face was impassive. "Go on."

"He says you had him do it. So you could inherit."

She couldn't help laughing. "To think I've always given you more credit than you deserved!"

"You told Inspector What's-his-name that it was an accident."

She shrugged. "It was simpler in the long run."

"All right, I'll take your word for it. But it doesn't add up."

"There's proof."

He smiled thinly. "I'm sure there is. Now, to the second shareholder. A certain German industrialist. Karl von Eiderfeld."

"What about him?" she asked cautiously.

"Come, come. We both know what you've got on him."

"You've got the negatives," she said frankly, "and my name's on one of the documents. It's all there for you to see."

He gave a tight little smile. "Those negatives are worth a lot, princess," he said slowly. "They're damaging enough to put a noose around his neck. Yet he's walking around scot-free. Anyone who has information like that would take it to the authorities. Obviously you haven't. Then I asked myself why. And do you know what I concluded?"

She said nothing.

"You're blackmailing him." He smiled triumphantly. "Only I still can't figure out one thing. Why? You've got plenty of money. You don't need his."

She stared at him. It was her business, not his. He had no right to know why. She would never tell him.

He sighed. "Well, then, don't tell me. But we both know that *Les Modes* is the darling of the French fashion scene," he continued. "And you know what the French think of the Germans. It's as if no time at all has passed since the war ended. As a nation, we still hate them with a passion. Sure, we let German tourists invade our cities and crowd our beaches. We want their money. Why should Spain get it all? But there isn't a Frenchman alive who wants anything to do

with a *known war criminal*. The wounds are still too fresh."
He paused again, choosing his words carefully. "What if I
were to leak the von Eiderfeld documents to . . . oh, let's say
Le Monde Internationale? Along with a copy of von Eiderfeld's last year's dividend statement which I lifted from your
files and copied some time ago. Do you have any idea of
what would happen then?"

She sat stiffly, not moving.

"After the war, the French shaved the heads of women
collaborators," he said softly. "They don't do that now. But
Les Modes would be finished, and so would you. You
wouldn't be able to walk down the Champs-Élysées without
being spit upon."

Her eyes narrowed. "How much do you want? Ten thousand francs?"

"Ten thousand francs!" His laughter echoed crazily.
"That's chicken feed. Each share of Les Éditions Hélène
Junot is worth two hundred thousand." He lowered his voice
to a whisper. "I want a percentage of the company, princess."
He looked at her confidently. "I want, say, twenty percent?"

13

In the months that followed Jeanne's death, Hélène threw
herself into her work with an almost superhuman vengeance
that surprised even herself. She pushed herself beyond the
boundaries of her almost limitless energy until she was exhausted. She realized, of course, why she was forcing this
grueling regimen upon herself. It was to cover up the deep
pain she felt. Yet despite all her efforts, the thoughts somehow kept on coming. Busy as she kept herself, they always
managed to worm their way into her mind: Jeanne had been
the best friend and only confidante she had ever enjoyed. She
missed her terribly.

There was another hurt Hélène couldn't get over. Nigel.
Before they'd met for the second time, she had never even

heard about him. Of course, because Zeno Skouri surrounded himself with successful, brilliant people, she had known that Nigel was prominent. But she had never suspected the magnitude of his importance. Now, suddenly, it seemed that he was everywhere. Whatever he did was news. The sensational press linked him to a dozen speculative romances ranging from film stars to a certain young English noblewoman, Lady Amelia Ayers. But it was primarily his career that catapulted him into the limelight.

One morning in November, when the chestnut trees in the Bois were barren of leaves, Eleonora brought the latest bundle of magazines into Hélène's office and left them in their usual spot on the sideboard. Hélène glanced over at them but waited until the late afternoon before getting to them.

First she glanced at the covers. Suddenly she sat bolt upright. The third one from the top was the latest issue of *Time*. The yellow corner banner read: "Britain's New Breed of Leader." From within the red border Nigel stared out at her.

She looked at the picture for a long time. The lean, square jaw, the aristocratic forehead, the intense eyes—they were all the way she remembered him. Especially the eyes, flecked with tiny specks of gold, that had looked at her in the moonlight as he had proposed to her. She sat back and sighed painfully. Proposed . . . and not been heard from since.

She stared at the cover for a long time. She wasn't able to take her eyes off him. She ran her hand over the glossy paper to feel his face. But it was flat. Lifeless. No amount of imagining would bring it to life.

How long had it been now since Jeanne had died, since Hélène had left the *Evangelia* in the early hours of the morning and left the note at his door? Almost three months now.

She felt an ache stir within her. She knew that the best thing she could do for herself was to throw away the magazine unread. Nigel was part of her past, a part that had disappeared forever. But she couldn't. The way she felt about him was still there. Would probably always be there. She still loved him.

She found herself opening the magazine to a picture of Nigel sitting behind his desk.

For a moment she put down the magazine, then took a black case out of her top drawer and flipped it open. She picked her tortoiseshell magnifying glass out of its nest of baize and studied the photo closely. Nigel's desk was an ancient one, all mahogany and centuries of polish. Behind it, on the gleaming paneled wall, hung an oil portrait of a frowning, distinguished old gentleman with white hair. Was that Nigel's father, the Duke? Or was it his grandfather?

The next photo showed Nigel stepping out of a Bentley in a shipyard in Ireland. Yet another, with his back turned to the camera and his hands clasped behind his back, showed him gazing out a big window. Below him was the Thames, wide and sluggish, and in the distance, the object of his view. The Houses of Parliament.

After studying the pictures, Hélène began to read the article. Clearly Nigel was a part of the political winds of the English future. A powerful part. More than ever now, she was fascinated with this man about whom she knew so little.

She tossed the magazine down on her desk and sat back. Thoughtfully she brought her right hand to her lips and sucked on the knuckle of her forefinger. She began to see Nigel in a new light. He was more than just the charming man who drank tea at the casino and scrambled among the rocks of Corsica with her.

Suddenly she was angry with herself. On impulse she reached for the intercom. She had made up her mind. Perhaps it was up to her to make the next move. After all, it was she who had left the *Evangelia* as if she were fleeing from a fire. For her, an emergency had arisen. Perhaps the same thing had happened to him. Perhaps he didn't get her note. Perhaps . . .

Her secretary's voice came over the wire.

"Eleonora, place a call to England immediately. To Somerset Holdings, Limited. I believe they're located in London. I want to speak with Nigel Somerset."

"Right away, mademoiselle."

The call seemed to take forever.

Irritably Hélène sprang to her feet and started walking around the office. For a moment she stopped at the windows and stared down at her beloved Place Vendôme. For once, she couldn't appreciate the elegance of the square. All that appeared before her eyes was Nigel.

"Why didn't you try to contact me?" she whispered to herself, her face drawn in pain. "You know who I am. Where to find me. I've waited and waited for you."

The one person she *had* heard from was Zeno Skouri. She had sent him a thank-you note and an apology for having left so suddenly. He, at least, had taken it for granted that an emergency had arisen and forgiven her sudden departure. True to his word, he had left the yacht at *Les Modes*'s disposal for an entire week so that the article he had promised her could be done. Hélène had been tempted to go along with Luba and the photographer. But she hadn't gone. She had known only too well that the *Evangelia* would only have served as a painful reminder of Nigel.

Now, suddenly, she turned away from the window and went back to her desk. She pressed down on the intercom button again. "Eleonora?"

"Oui, mademoiselle?"

"Cancel the call to Somerset Holdings."

Wearily Hélène lowered herself into her chair. He'd had time enough to get in touch with her. He just hadn't wanted to.

She had never felt this way about any man, ever.

TODAY

Sunday, January 14

1

The Chameleon drove slowly past the rural Connecticut house in his black Hertz car. On the backseat, the huge Great Dane named Rufus sat quietly alert, his ears cocked, his shiny black eyes staring benignly out the window.

The Chameleon studied the house. It was set far back from the road in a yard of bare old maples. It had been built in the first half of the nineteenth century, was sided with gray clapboard, and stood two stories high. From the front it looked L-shaped, with a gable facing the road. The open shutters were painted black, and smoke was rising from one of the chimneys. The silvery mailbox by the driveway was neatly stenciled "E. Junot."

Satisfied, the Chameleon turned the car around and drove back in the direction from which he had come. After he'd driven a quarter of a mile, he backed into a dirt road and parked behind a screen of evergreen bushes. He looked at the quartz chronometer on his wrist. It was three-forty-five. There was time for a quick reconnaissance of the Junot property before dark. The voice on the telephone had informed him that Hélène Junot would probably be spending the weekend at her brother's. He wondered if the information was correct. Well, now he would find out.

The Chameleon left Rufus in the car and pulled the collar of his unobtrusive brown, wool jacket high around his neck. Then he got out of the car and made his way back to the house on foot. He had no desire to be seen, so he stayed well in the woods, walking soundlessly on crepe-soled shoes. It was quiet out here in the country. A little noise could travel a long way. Not like in the city, where sounds were blanketed by an ever-present cacophony.

When he reached the house, smoke was still trailing from the chimney and already the lights were turned on. For a while he stood still and listened intently. He could hear no sound of anyone outside. They must be in the house, he thought. So far, so good. He just wished it weren't winter. Winter in the country was a special bitch. It was too easy to be seen when most of the trees were bare. At least it would be a lot safer once night fell. He was an expert at working in the dark.

But night had not yet fallen, so he would have to take special care while finding out everything he needed to know.

Behind the house was the big clapboard garage. It had two windows along each side. Cautiously he approached one of them and peered in. He could see an orange BMW coupé and a black Lincoln Continental. No white Rolls-Royce, though. Still, that didn't prove anything. She could have been driven out here in the Rolls and then had the chauffeur take it back to the city. Or maybe her brother had driven her out here in one of his cars. Or she might even have come by Conrail or bus. Even wealthy people commuted between New York and Connecticut on public transportation.

He shrugged. There was no end of possibilities. He continued his stealthy reconnaissance.

To the left of the garage was the rectangular swimming pool, covered over with heavy-duty canvas. A flagstone path ran along the side of the pool, connecting the house with a big barn set thirty yards farther back. The barn was covered with weathered cedar siding. It had big picture windows, and the lights were on inside.

He approached it stealthily and looked in through one of the Thermopane windows. He suppressed a whistle. This was no ordinary barn. It had been converted into a swanky guesthouse. He could see teak-paneled walls, a beamed ceiling, plush carpeting, and expensive furniture. The hand of an interior designer was evident, as was the fact that this was a woman's domain. He saw a handbag on the coffee table. He guessed that the voice over the telephone had been right after all. Hélène Junot must indeed be here. She was probably using the guesthouse instead of staying in the big house. Unless, of course, the handbag belonged to another woman altogether. Well, he'd just have to be careful and wait and see.

He made his way back to the car by the same route he'd come. Then he let Rufus out to sniff around and do his business. He lit a cigarette and watched the big, obedient dog

550

lift his leg against a rhododendron. Rufus didn't stray; he stayed close by, always watching for instructions.

The Chameleon smiled. Soon now, it would be dark. In a half-hour he would return to the house.

This time with Rufus.

Hélène smiled at Edmond. He was standing over the big Jenn-Air range, apron tied around his waist. She watched as he expertly forked the two steaks onto the grill. Immediately they started to sizzle. Then he put the fork down, picked up the tongs, and opened the oven door. He took out two giant baked potatoes.

"It smells good," Hélène said in French, bending down to shut the oven door.

He turned around and grinned. "Wait until dessert. I spent all morning on it."

"What is it? *Boule de neige? Profiteroles?*"

"You'll have to wait to find out," he said mysteriously. "Where do you want to eat? Dining room, den, or here in the kitchen?"

"How about right here? I still can't seem to get kitchens out of my blood. Remember when we were kids? We always seemed to live in kitchens. Looking back, I've grown rather fond of them. They always smelled so good."

He grinned at her. "You've still got the peasant in you, you know that, Little French Girl?"

She laughed. "Please, keep it a secret. You wouldn't want the world to know that the queen of high fashion is nothing but a homespun kitchen slut, would you?"

He chuckled, "Cross my heart, I won't ever tell." He picked up the fork again and expertly flipped the steaks over. "What do you want to drink? Champagne or red wine?"

The Chameleon glanced at his watch. The half-hour had passed. He got out of the car and held the rear door open. "Come on, Rufus," he said quietly. The dog's ears instantly cocked. Then he got to his feet and leaped neatly to the ground. He stopped and gazed questioningly up at the Chameleon, the slack pink skin of his jaw making him look deceptively benign.

The Chameleon smiled crookedly. "Come on, dog. It's time you earned your supper."

* * *

"That was good," Hélène said.

She took a last sip of wine, delicately patted her lips with the pink linen napkin, and got to her feet. She started clearing away the dishes, slipping them into the slots in the dishwasher.

Edmond pushed his chair back. "I suppose I'm becoming very Americanized. Steak and potatoes are my favorite foods now."

She looked over her shoulder. "Mine, too."

"But you didn't finish your potato."

She laughed and touched her flat stomach. "I don't want to get fat," she replied. "If I do, you'll have to call me *Big* French Girl."

He chuckled and shook his head. "And you didn't even touch your apple pie," he said admonishingly.

She made a face. "Really, Edmond. Building up a dessert that took you all morning to fix! So you went into Roxbury and bought a Sara Lee to heat up in the oven." She placed her hands on her hips in mock anger. "I suppose the trip into town took you all morning?"

"Almost," he admitted. He got to his feet and stretched. "Ready to go through the financial reports?"

She nodded. "Fine, but I've got to go back to the barn first. I left my figures there."

"All right, I'll be waiting upstairs in the library."

She nodded and closed the dishwasher door, then turned the machine on. "I won't be long," she promised.

Edmond went upstairs and she took her quilted, down-filled coat from the hall closet, slipped it on, and went back into the kitchen. She snapped a switch, and the path between the house and the barn was suddenly flooded with light from fixtures hidden in the trees.

She opened the door and stepped outside. The Connecticut night felt crisp and cold against her face. She put her hands in her coat pockets and stood on the porch for a moment, taking a deep breath. The air smelled good; clean and fresh. Somehow innocent. She looked up. The skies were clear and the stars were winking brightly on a peaceful sea of black velvet. And above all, it was quiet. Very quiet. That was what she liked best about the weekends out here. The solitude. It gave her time to think. Somehow you couldn't do that in Manhattan.

She started across the flagstones toward the barn.

The moment the outside lights clicked on, the Chameleon drew deeper into the shadows. The beginnings of a tense excitement stirred within him. It was an almost sexual excitement. He always felt it when he was about to face his prey. It was the excitement of the hunt. But no matter how strongly he felt it, he always kept it under control. He never let it overstep its bounds. His first priority was—and always would be—extreme caution. In this line of business, only the fools took chances. And fools died.

An instant after the lights went on, he saw the door opening and a woman coming out of the house. For a moment she just stood there looking around. He nodded to himself. He guessed that she was on her way to the barn. But he would wait patiently until she came closer. He had to make certain that it was Hélène Junot.

With growing anticipation he watched as she came down from the porch and started walking toward the barn. Her heels echoed on the flagstones. Beside him, Rufus stiffened and emitted a low growl.

The Chameleon looked down at the dog. The canine's eyes were caught in the floodlights and gleamed yellow. "Quiet!" he whispered.

Instantly the growl died in the dog's throat. But the Chameleon could still sense the animal's tension. That was good, he thought. The dog was as excited as he was.

He smiled to himself. Anticipation wouldn't hurt. It would propel the dog to special fury.

Slowly he reached into his pocket and took out the sonic whistle. He remembered the trainer's instructions. Two short blows for attack. One long one for retreat.

The Chameleon kept his eyes glued on Hélène. He watched her with appreciation. She moved elegantly and sensually, but without any overt suggestiveness. This was one classy dame, he thought to himself. That is, if it was her. . . .

When she was halfway between the house and the barn, he caught his breath. One of the lights in the trees bathed her face and he could see her clearly. The photo hadn't done her justice. He no longer had any doubts. It *was* her.

Hélène suddenly stopped in her tracks. She stiffened as she felt a sudden prickling of her spine.

Something was wrong.

Danger lurked nearby. She didn't know what it was, but she'd experienced this feeling before. Long ago, in Paris. Before the Boche came, when she had been playing with Antoinette in the little park. Only this time, the warning was even stronger. It swept over her like a persistently pounding surf. As if this time the danger was closer.

Her eyes darted as she looked around, but she couldn't see beyond the shadows; the lights in the trees bathed only the path.

For a moment she stopped breathing and listened carefully. She couldn't hear anything, but still the feeling persisted.

She shivered, briskly rubbing her chill arms with her hands, but it was not a shiver from the cold. Then she tried to swallow her fears. "You're just being silly," she told herself. "There is nothing here to hurt you."

Nevertheless she gauged the distance between where she stood and the house and the barn. The barn was closer.

She started to run toward it.

The Chameleon frowned. What was that crazy bitch doing? Why was she running? Had she seen them? But that was impossible. They were too well hidden. And they had been quiet, so she couldn't have heard them, either.

He didn't hesitate. Swiftly he raised the sonic whistle to his lips and blew into it twice. The night remained quiet; not a sound was made that could be heard by human ears.

But Rufus' ears weren't human. They picked up the high-decibel whistle. The dog tensed, and then, with the speed of lightning, emitted a low growl and shot to his feet.

He flew silently out of the shadows toward Hélène.

The richly paneled upstairs library was warm. Far too warm and stuffy with the fire crackling in the grate, Edmond decided. He and Hélène were likely to fall asleep before they got past the first page of the financial report.

He crossed between the twin chamois-upholstered Chesterfield sofas which faced each other across the shimmering silk Tabriz rug. Four windows, burgundy velvet draperies drawn tightly across them, punctuated the wall of books. He parted one set of draperies and leaned down, slid the mullioned window open. Then he released the catch of the storm window and slid it up, too. He stuck his head out.

554

The blast of night air felt good. He looked down. The tree lights were on and Hélène was standing between the house and the barn, spotlit as if onstage. He frowned. She was oddly posed, all her weight on the ball of one foot, the toes of the other hesitantly poised as she looked around slowly. Suddenly she started to run for the barn.

Even before Edmond saw the black blur lunging out of the darkness, long-buried instinct took over. His heart crashed against his rib cage, and for a moment he couldn't breathe.

Danger, he thought automatically. *She's in danger.*

He jumped back from the window, cold fear sweeping over him as he lunged across the nearest Chesterfield. He reached across it to the desk and seized a letter opener. It was like a miniature scimitar, with a sharp, sturdy, paper-thin blade. It would be a lethal weapon as long as the porcelain handle did not break.

He weighed it in his hand for a split second. It would have to do.

He thrust it between his lips and clamped his teeth down on the handle, at the same time rushing back to the window.

He did not have to think. He was governed by reflex alone.

Got to protect her. No time to take the stairs, run through hallways and rooms. The window is the most direct way down.

He clutched the top of the window molding between both hands and like an acrobat lifted himself off the floor. He swung his buttocks backward, bringing his knees up under his chin, and then swiftly flung his legs forward and out, loosening his grip as his body caught the momentum. He ducked his head as he shot feetfirst through the open window. Mentally he blessed his workouts at the Athletic Club. He was no longer young and spry, but still sinewy, still in good shape.

He slid down the steep roof of the back porch, bumpy and abrasive and cold under him. The edge was coming up. Careful, he cautioned himself. Timing was everything. Careful . . .

He shot past the drainpipe, off the roof, and out into the open air. He brought his knees neatly under his chin and crouched forward, ready for the impact.

It came, and with a jar, the pain shooting like fire through his ankles and up his legs. He somersaulted over, sprang to his feet, and began to run across the frozen ground toward Hélène. Her screams pierced the night, and on top of them he could hear the vicious snarls of a dog gone mad. Yards ahead, he could see her struggling with it, both of them rolling around, the dog huge, its short black hair glistening in the lights. He glanced up at the tree lights as he ran. They would be on for only two minutes. Then the timer would automatically shut them off again. He wondered how many seconds of light were left.

He grabbed the letter opener from between his teeth and let out a yell.

Hélène had heard the dog before she saw it. At first there had been a heavy crashing in the underbrush. Then a menacing snarl. She could sense the muscular body racing toward her. She glanced backward and saw the flashing yellow eyes and the black sinewy blur in the glare of the floodlights. She let out a scream and began to run faster, knowing in the back of her mind that running would not be enough. The dog was faster. Much faster.

Suddenly the beast lunged at her. She dived sideways, instinctively tightening the muscles in her arms as she threw them up behind her. She could feel the rush of cold air as he missed her by inches. She rolled over on the hard ground and quickly scrambled back to her feet, continuing to run toward the barn. To safety.

In front of her, the dog, confused by the miss, skidded to a halt. Only as he turned around to attack again did Hélène realize the magnitude of her mistake. The dog was to one side of her, to be sure, but he was between her and the barn, cutting off her escape.

Fractionally she hesitated, wanting to turn and run toward the house instead. But then the dog would be behind her, and she would be blind to his tactics.

For a moment she stopped running, her pulse racing, the cold air raw in her throat. Perhaps she should have stayed near the path, keeping a tree between the beast and herself. A tree. She glanced desperately behind her. The nearest one was seven yards away. She glanced back at the dog. It was growling menacingly, already on its haunches, ready to put all its weight into another spring.

Her mind raced. It was a Great Dane; she could see that clearly now. And it was enormous; it probably weighed as much as she. Probably outweighed her, in fact. Its jaws were enormous. And she had no weapon with which to defend herself. No protection of any sort.

No, she was wrong, she realized suddenly. She did have protection of sorts. Her coat. Her down-filled coat. It was thickly padded. If she rolled herself into a ball, tucked her head down against her chest, hid her hands, and curled her legs up under her, she would be afforded some protection. Not much. But maybe enough. . . .

The dog hesitated, his eyes glittering like iridescent headlamps. For a drawn-out second he seemed to crouch there, indecisive. Then the second was over and he lunged.

For one long frozen moment the dog seemed to be suspended in midair. Its razor teeth flashed whitely in the light from the trees, its enormous lean body, tapered as a greyhound's, showing the defined masses of hard muscle under the short gleaming hair.

Hélène ducked and dropped to the ground, readying herself for the swift maneuver of rolling herself into a ball. But the dog was too fast. He loomed larger and larger in front of her, and when she was least ready, the impact came.

Stabbing daggers of pain shot through her as the dog collided into her. She had had no idea the beast was this heavy or powerful. He had caught her on the chest, just as she had let her legs crumple and had felt herself starting to fall. She felt sleek black hair against her face, smelled the hot stench of his breath. The wind was knocked out of her lungs with a noisy *whoosh!* and her breasts were suddenly heavy and bruised as she fell backward, choking for air as any remaining wind was knocked out of her a second time as her back hit the frozen ground. But she could not wait to regain it. The air in her lungs would return. More important that she curl herself up, that she give the animal no outstretched limbs for his crazed jaws, that at all costs she keep her neck down. Dobermans went for the neck. Did Great Danes? She was taking no chances.

For the moment, the dog was not upon her. She had sensed him somersaulting over her, and the collision had stunned him momentarily. Wasting no precious seconds, she curled her knees up against her chest, wrapped her arms protectively around her, careful to keep her hands tucked far up her sleeves. She hunched her shoulders, trying to tuck her neck as far into her collar as possible, like a tortoise retracting into its shell at the first scent of danger. As the dog snarled and struggled to his feet, she quickly rolled over on her belly and pressed her face into the ground. It was hard and icy and scratchy, but she knew that her face was the most vulnerable, the most easily injured part of her body. She must keep it turned away from the dog at all costs.

The Chameleon watched in excitement. Tension welled up within him until it became almost unbearable. His penis hardened and strained against the fabric of his trousers. Rufus looked as big and powerful as a horse, yet was so light on his feet that his movements had the grace of a panther's. The woman had the same fluid grace. There was something peculiarly sensual about her.

The Chameleon's eyes glittered as he fingered his penis. He was witnessing a battle to the death—a battle between a superior brain and a superior body. A pity that they were so unevenly matched. The woman had no chance. The dog would win.

He congratulated himself for using the dog instead of his hands or a gun. There was something primordial about a duel between a human and a beast. But best of all, once the woman's body was found, her death would be blamed on a crazed animal. It would be a neat killing. A superior killing. One for which no man, however unknown, would ever be blamed. There was no chance that anyone would connect him or Rufus to the "accident." Both of them would be long gone. He on his way back to Chicago, the final installment for the murder in his pocket. The dog buried in a pit somewhere. Dead, like the woman.

All traces would be neatly obliterated. Once again, he had created a masterpiece. The perfect murder.

He raised the sonic whistle to his lips and blew into it again to egg the dog on. Not that Rufus needed any egging. He was onto the scent of blood. Any second now, and he would taste it.

The thought was almost enough to release the Chameleon's passion. Already he could sense his seminal emission surfacing. Instantly, he stopped stroking himself and willed his orgasm to die. He did not want to be racked by the splendid passion until the final moment was at hand.

Suddenly a yell rent the air. Rufus stopped in mid-attack, and turned toward the house. The Chameleon's eyes shifted. For the first time, he became aware of Edmond, head bent forward, blade in hand, racing across the yard.

Again Edmond's yell rang out clearly. This time the Chameleon could hear the word distinctly.

"*Sit!*"

The Chameleon's erection died, and he felt a cold paralysis coming on. His eyes were wide and unbelieving. The stupid dog—his goddamn killing machine—was actually backing off! Obediently starting to sit down!

The Chameleon quickly lifted the whistle again, giving two more short blows.

"Sit!"

Confused, the dog sprang to his feet, then sat hesitantly back down again. His head twisted first in the direction of the silent whistle, then to the man verbally commanding him to sit.

"Motherfuck!" the Chameleon cursed under his breath. He blew into the whistle again. The short hair stood up on Rufus' back; then the dog sprang gracefully to his feet, fangs bared.

"*Sit!*"

The dog sat obediently.

Edmond stopped running. As he slowly approached Hélène, Rufus let out a low, menacing growl.

"Sit!" Edmond commanded.

The growl died in the dog's throat, and he remained seated.

"Get up slowly, Little French Girl," Edmond cautioned softly. "Don't make any sudden moves."

Hélène raised her head slowly. The dog began to move again.

"Sit!"

The Chameleon cursed under his breath. Of all the stupid things to have happen! Why did those trainers teach a dog to obey common commands like "Sit"? They should have used code words. And he should have been more alert and noticed that yesterday.

It was too late now. He didn't even have a gun to finish the woman off himself. Nor could he rush out of the bushes and use his lethal hands or his knife. The element of surprise was gone. And now there was the man to contend with, too. He had a blade on him. No, better to retreat and try again some other time.

He whistled one last time—a single, long, drawn-out blow

559

to recall the dog. Rufus got to his feet, backed off slowly, and then retreated into the darkness.

Hélène took a wobbly step toward Edmond. She felt suddenly drained and collapsed limply in his arms, closing her eyes.

"It's over," he said softly, pocketing the letter opener. He held her tightly. "The dog is gone." He rocked her gently in his arms. "Are you hurt?"

She shook her head. "No," she said huskily. "But that dog—"

"Forget it," he whispered. "It's over now." He pressed her face against his chest and stared out over her head. At that moment, the tree lights clicked off. Two minutes were over. Had it lasted only that long? he asked himself. It had seemed a lifetime.

"It's over," Hélène repeated to herself, trembling. But her tremors were dying down. Edmond's presence was warm and comforting. "Thank God, it's over."

But was it? Edmond frowned into the darkness, his body still tensed. He did not have the heart to worry her by telling her otherwise.

He had heard not just the dog crashing through the bushes. He had heard something else. Something that moved with greater stealth.

A man.

2

Karl von Eiderfeld sat in thoughtful silence behind his big desk. The silk-shaded ormolu lamp cast a warm pool of light on the highly polished wood. He looked at the silver-framed photographs of his family. First there was Helga, his beautiful blond wife.

The oval photograph had been taken right after they were married. She was forty-four now and her hair had grayed, but she was still an extremely attractive woman. He hoped that this Hélène Junot business would soon be cleared up. He had just spoken to Helga long distance. She had told him that Düsseldorf was grim this winter and she wanted to fly to Marrakesh for a few weeks' vacation. He had promised that as soon as his business in New York was finished, they would fly to Morocco together.

Personally, he despised the north of Africa—all of Africa, for that matter. It was too filthy. There were too many ver-dammte flies. Worse, the whole continent was filled with an inferior race. As if that wasn't bad enough in itself, half the natives seemed to be missing something. Eyes. Ears. Noses. Limbs. He shook his head. Nor could his sensitive eyes take the harsh desert sun, the blinding glare of the whitewashed houses. He always stayed indoors in Marrakesh, never venturing farther during daylight hours than the cool, shady loggia.

But Helga liked the hot North African winters. She loved the Olympic-size swimming pool she had persuaded him to build at the villa.

He shook his head fondly and his white face broke into an unaccustomed smile. When he had met Helga Recknagel, she was a minor legend in Germany. She had brought a feeling of national pride to the degrading postwar years. At the 1956 Olympics in Melbourne, she had won a silver medal for the 400-meter freestyle swim event. She had clocked in at 4:55.9. Her face had been plastered in all the German newspapers and on the magazine covers. On her return from Australia, she had been met at the Bonn-Köln airport by a weeping mob. *Die Heilige Helga*, they called her. The Saintly Helga.

Unknown to everyone but him, Helga Recknagel had been born in 1936 in the first of the Lebensborn maternity homes. These were Heinrich Himmler's pet project, institutions he had set up in order to increase Germany's birth rate. Helga's mother was one of many women encouraged by the state to have an illegitimate child by an SS officer. Dutifully she had spread her legs for the Reich, let pure Aryan seed enter into her, and nine months later pushed an Aryan child out of her womb. At the Lebensborn home, with its large picture of the Führer in the lobby, both mother and daughter led a comfortable life.

Three weeks after they met, Karl von Eiderfeld married Helga Recknagel. In her he found everything he was looking for in a woman. She was a pure-blooded Aryan. Her father had been an SS officer. She was sturdy, strong, and had brought honor to her country. They honeymooned briefly on the Chiemsee in Bavaria and then he had begun building their family.

He glanced at the two smaller silver frames flanking Helga's oval portrait. Rolf and Otto. His sons.

Helga had wanted to have children, but he had refused. It had been the only major fight they had ever had. He had been afraid that the children would be born albino. He still believed in the pure Aryan ideal, and he despised himself for his own lack of physical perfection. So they had compromised. He and Helga had scoured the adoption agencies for a nice blond boy.

What they found were two boys, orphaned brothers. Actually, they had wanted a much younger child, but the boys had looked like Aryan ideals. Rolf was now twenty-three, Otto twenty-eight. They had been good-looking boys when they had been adopted, and they still were.

Otto had always been tough and unsmiling. He was very fair, with pale eyes, sensual lips, and a stern, almost judicious expression. Already Otto was embarked on a promising political career. The Christian Democrats were beginning to take notice of him as one of their future strengths, the Social Democrats as a formidable future opponent. A high position in the Bundestag was not out of the question. Who knew? In time, perhaps, Otto von Eiderfeld might even become chancellor.

Rolf had always been the prankster, the one with the sense of humor. But suddenly, almost overnight, the boy inside him had disappeared and a hardness had taken its place. Von Eiderfeld had been surprised but pleased by this change in his son. He could pinpoint the exact moment when it had occurred. The day of Rolf's first job in the family business . . . with the knowledge that he was being groomed as the heir to Von Eiderfeld Industrien G.m.b.H. Already he was surprising von Eiderfeld with his keen business acumen. His toughness when it came to dealing with hardened competitors. His German efficiency. Von Eiderfeld Industrien was assured of its future with Rolf at the helm.

The only thing that rankled von Eiderfeld about the boys was that they were not of his flesh. Not of his *blood*. But he never mentioned this. He consoled himself that with the boys, everything he had built would continue to prosper. At least the von Eiderfeld name would continue on for generations. Rolf's young wife, Monika, was already pregnant.

He sighed sadly, folded his old white hands, and looked down at them. There was no doubt but that the boys were going to surpass the parent. Of course, they had a head start. Von Eiderfeld Industrien had already been a very powerful corporation by the time they arrived on the scene. But the boys were brilliant. They would go far. In fact, either one of them was probably far better equipped for dealing with Hélène Junot than he was. But he couldn't divulge his past to them. Even Helga didn't know about it. She suspected, yes, but she never said a word. She loved him. She was devoted to him. She was German. *She understood.*

He sighed again. The incriminating evidence Hélène Junot had collected was burned. But was there more? If one person could get hold of such documents, couldn't someone else dig some up also? After all, the Reich had been one massive bureaucracy. Many documents had been destroyed, but far too many had survived. And what about human survivors? Millions had died in the camps—he alone had sent hundreds of thousands there—but some of them had returned alive. All it took was one person who might recognize him, blow the whistle on him. He took precautions, yes. He shunned publicity. He led a quiet life. He always traveled by private car, private plane, private boat. Photographers were never allowed near him. But always he walked around with a death sentence hanging over his head. *Someone might recognize him.*

The worst had happened the day Hélène Junot arrived at his office, slapping copies of the incriminating documents down on his desk. He shuddered, remembering that day. Still, was it enough that the documents were destroyed?

He pushed a weary hand through his thinning white hair. She was a witness. She had seen the documents. She could still make him stand trial for war crimes.

She was alive.

3

Jennifer Rowen rolled over in the bed and gently shook her husband awake. Her voice finally pushed through the thick blanket of his sleep. "Honey . . . wake up, honey."

He moaned and opened his eyes, looking up at her. Then he blinked and shaded his eyes with his hand against the glare of the nightstand light. He struggled to sit up. "What is it?" he asked irritably.

She held up one hand to show him. She was holding the ivory receiver of the bedroom extension phone, the cupped palm of her hand wrapped around the mouthpiece. "Honey, it's that person again," she whispered in a frightened voice. "You know who I mean."

"The whisperer?" he asked sleepily.

She nodded and handed the receiver over to him, ducking the cord. He took it and cleared his throat. "Robert Rowen speaking."

"Mr. Rowen?" The whisper over the wire was thin and reedy. For some reason, it sent a chill up his spine. Perhaps it was because the voice sounded so disembodied and he couldn't connect it with a face.

"Are you there, Mr. Rowen?"

"Yes, yes, of course."

"Have you given any more thought to our proposition?"

For a moment, Rowen hesitated. He glanced over at Jennifer. She was watching him with open curiosity. He wished she would take some kind of cue and leave the room, but he couldn't ask her to do that. She would get too suspicious. He kept his voice noncommittal. "Yes," he said carefully, "I've given it thorough thought."

"And what conclusion have you arrived at?"

Rowen didn't hesitate now. "You have yourself a deal," he said. "That is, unless she comes up with the money by five o'clock tomorrow afternoon." He glanced at the alarm clock on the nightstand. "I mean, *this* afternoon," he corrected himself. "If she doesn't, the bank will confiscate the collateral and I'll make certain that we sell it as you see fit."

"A very wise decision, if I say so myself, Mr. Rowen." The voice gave a low, whispery laugh. *"She can never come up with eleven million dollars, believe me!"*

There was a pause. Rowen waited for the caller to continue.

"Say we meet in the morning? An attaché case filled with five hundred thousand dollars will be exchanged for your word. You'll receive the other half-million once the transaction is completed and the shares are in our hands. We warn you, though . . ." The whisper took on the sharp, harsh tones of a hiss. *"Do not try to double-cross us!"*

Rowen smiled into the receiver. "I wouldn't dream of doing that."

"Another wise decision, to be sure, Mr. Rowen. To show our goodwill, we shall deliver the money to you at eight a.m."

"Where shall we meet?"

"Is the Staten Island ferry terminal convenient?"

"That would be very convenient," Rowen agreed. "How will I recognize you?"

"It is I who shall recognize you, Mr. Rowen. You do have a trench coat?"

"Yes," Rowen said curiously, thinking of the London Fog raincoat Jennifer had given him last Christmas.

"Then wear it. And please, do be trite and put a red carnation in your left lapel buttonhole. I will recognize you by that. We shall meet in the men's room. Good night, Mr. Rowen."

"Good night—"

But the phone had already clicked; the caller had hung up. Rowen stared at the receiver for a moment, shrugged, and then slowly handed it back to Jennifer.

She took it and dropped it on the nightstand extension. She turned to him. "Honey . . ." She looked at him anxiously. "What's wrong?"

He forced a smile. "Nothing's wrong. It was just business." He leaned over and planted a kiss on her lips.

She stiffened and refused to respond. "At two in the morning?" she asked suspiciously. She shook her head. "By the look on your face, I know that something's up. Why can't you tell me?"

"All right, Jennie," he said wearily, "after tomorrow morning, we're going to be rich."

"Rich! Now I know you're pulling my leg!" She turned away.

"I'm serious," he said quietly.

Something in his voice caught her. "But how?" Her eyes narrowed suspiciously. "You're . . . you're not thinking of *stealing*!"

"Bite your tongue." He smiled tightly. "No, I'm not going to steal. Who do you think you married, a fool? Just trust me, Jennie." He took her hand in his and squeezed it. "You wait and see. We'll have money to burn!"

YESTERDAY

VI

DIVORCE

1

Paris 1960

Edmond stepped aside to let Hélène into the apartment.
Her eyes swept down the hall to the living room. It was stuffy
and hot in here. Despite the fragrant spring weather, all the
windows were shut and most of the curtains were drawn
against the sunlight. She shuddered. There was something dismal about it. As if he was trying to shut the world out. "I'm
glad I caught you at home," she said. "I'm not disturbing
you, am I?"

He smiled weakly as he closed the door and led the way
into the living room. "I'm just studying." He waved helplessly
toward the desk. Open volumes were illuminated by a single
arc desk lamp with a weak bulb. "Can I get you something?"

"No, thanks," she said, putting her purse down on the
couch and smoothing her skirt behind her before she carefully took a seat, avoiding one of the lethal exposed sofa
springs. She had to fight to keep from wrinkling her nostrils.
The apartment wasn't only dim, it was dirty and dusty as
well. Already she could feel it irritating her nostrils. Long
gone were the sounds of laughter, the smiles of contentment,
the delicious smells of cooking hovering in the air.

"I just came by to have a little talk," she explained in what
she hoped was an offhand voice. It took an effort for her to
smile at him. She quickly forgot her own emotional disap-
pointments when she saw him. He looked haggard and so
terribly beaten. His threadbare red cardigan had holes in the
elbows. If Jeanne were alive, she would have seen to it that
they were mended.

"What do you want to talk about?" he asked.

"In a minute," she said, suddenly uncomfortable. "I think
I'll have something to drink after all. Do you have any
chilled white wine?"

569

He nodded. "I think so. I'll be right back."

She watched him walk toward the kitchen. Slowly, she shook her head. Why doesn't he snap out of it? she asked herself. Why doesn't he come back to life instead of burying his nose in his books? You can mourn for only so long. Then you have to go on living. She knew, too, that the person who suffered most was Petite Hélène. Young and resilient though she was, she had lost her mother, and now, Hélène realized she had lost her father also, albeit to the university. Only Hélène herself had profited psychologically from having to shoulder some of the responsibility for her niece. It had given her yet another task to undertake, one which filled up the last remaining gaps left by Jeanne's death and Nigel's desertion. Even more important, it had opened up a whole new vista of the future. A future so dazzling she dared not breathe a word of it to anyone.

She had given careful thought as to how Petite Hélène was to be raised. She had made her promise to Jeanne, and she was determined to stick to it. Not only for Jeanne's sake but also because it suited her own ambitious ends. Already she had carefully begun to plot Petite Hélène's future, inextricably tying it to Les Éditions Hélène Junot. Since her abortion had made it impossible for her to have children, it was only natural that Petite Hélène would be her link to the future, her insurance that *Les Modes* would be kept in the family.

It was a long way off, but that was the strength of the plan. Grooming an heir was a painstaking process that takes time, and there was sufficient time to do it correctly. Time to supervise the complicated process and make sure that it was done step by step. Petite Hélène would have everything she herself had ever lacked. The way was already paved; the wherewithal was there. Now it was only a matter of careful guidance. Petite Hélène would go to the best schools, meet the right people, attend the best Swiss finishing school, become a social item, an expert businesswoman. Hélène had it all worked out. Never once did she give a passing thought to the fact that the girl might not be cut out for a business career or that her plan might somehow fail. She thought about only one thing. It had to be done.

Since it was so far in the future, she kept her strategy to herself. She did not even tell Edmond about it. Meanwhile, she would start the process, but she wouldn't go overboard, either. Petite Hélène had to be raised like other children. She must not be deprived of a normal childhood as she herself had been. Yet the fires of long-term ambition had to be constantly fed and kept alive. After all, Petite Hélène was already six. It wasn't premature to breed a little bit of the lady into her. As far as that was concerned, one could never start too soon. Hélène knew from her own life how impressionable she had been at Petite Hélène's age. All her adult strengths had their roots there.

The only thing that took time was planning how to go about her plan. It had to be done in the best possible way for all the parties concerned. First, she had to have more control over Petite Hélène, but she couldn't just take the child and raise her by herself. Petite Hélène was Edmond's daughter. Despite the fact that he didn't see enough of her, Hélène knew that he loved her above everything else in the world. She was all that was left of his union with Jeanne. It would be cruel and terribly unfair of her to tear his daughter away from him.

For a while, Hélène entertained the idea of getting a huge apartment and living together with them. That way, she would be close to Petite Hélène. It would give her a thousand opportunities to give her niece constant guidance. But eventually she discarded this idea, also. It wouldn't do for a brother and sister, no matter how close the relationship or how big the apartment, to be living together. Not that it would raise any eyebrows. Besides, she had long ago stopped caring about what people thought. It just wouldn't have been fair. Not to Petite Hélène or to Jeanne's memory. Jeanne had been her mother; Petite Hélène must never be confused about that.

But finally Hélène had come to a decision.

Edmond came from the kitchen, careful not to spill any wine from the glass. He handed it to her.

"Aren't you having any?" she asked.

He shook his head and sat down beside her.

She took a sip and set the glass down on the table beside her. She folded her hands in her lap and watched him light a cigarette. Then he looked at her through the cloud of smoke. "I take it this is not a social call?"

She smiled uncomfortably. "I'm afraid not. And I hope you won't think I'm trying to barge in on something that's none of my business."

He smiled grimly and smoked in silence.

571

"Edmond, we've always been close. You know that."

He nodded his head slowly.

"Far closer than most brothers and sisters. But ever since Jeanne . . ." Hélène sighed and quickly looked down at her hands. "Ever since Jeanne died, things haven't been the same between us, and that's been a long time now."

He turned away and faced the far wall as he felt the tears springing to his eyes.

Hélène glanced sadly at him. It was said that time heals all wounds. Yet it seemed as if his were as open and bleeding as the day they were inflicted.

"If you'd rather not talk about it, I'll understand," she said quietly. "I didn't drop by to cause you any more pain."

She saw the back of his head nodding. "I know that," he said huskily.

She bit down on her lower lip and wondered how to continue. Perhaps she should just wait and broach the subject some other time? Then she took a quick swallow of wine. No, this couldn't wait. It was too important.

She shifted around on the couch and touched his arm, gently pulling him back around to face her. There was sorrow in her eyes. "Edmond, it's Petite Hélène I'm worried about. Can't you see what this is doing to her? You're never around, and if you are, your nose is buried in your books."

He nodded dumbly and stared straight through her. "What do you want me to do?"

She pressed his hand between both of hers. "To give her more attention. Get someone to cook for her. To keep her company."

"Madame Courbet is taking good care of her."

Hélène sighed and jumped to her feet. Angrily she started to pace the room. "Madame Courbet is the concierge, and she's busy. Perhaps she's adequate, but she can't focus all her attention on Petite Hélène. She's a growing child, Edmond!" She stopped pacing suddenly. "She needs company. Guidance. A family."

He jerked his hand suddenly. His cigarette had burned itself down to the filter and scorched his fingers. Quickly he half got up and tossed the butt into the fireplace. Then he sat back down.

"Edmond, Petite Hélène needs a nanny."

His lips tightened. "Nannies are for babies."

But she kept pressing him until he would finally admit that

572

none of the arrangements he had come up with thus far had worked out. At first, there had been an irresponsible au-pair girl; then a woman who came in every day while he was gone, took Petite Hélène to school and picked her up again in the afternoon. Hélène discovered after a while that the woman drank heavily. Several times she had even had blackouts and couldn't remember a thing that had happened. And Madame Courbet just wasn't suited for the job.

"I'd be no good at picking out a nanny," Edmond said lamely. "I don't know the first thing about it!" He looked at her beseechingly. "I know you're awfully busy, Little French Girl, but . . ."

Hélène nodded. "I'll see to it," she said with satisfaction.

Now that it was settled, she didn't waste another moment. She took a week off from work during Petite Hélène's Easter vacation and flew to England with her. After all, nannies were one thing the British were famous for, so what made more sense than trying to find one in London? After the histories of the au-pair girl and the drunk, Hélène wasn't about to compromise. Of course, the thought that she might run into Nigel while in London did enter her mind.

They stayed at Claridge's, where Hélène had booked a suite. It had a quietly luxurious living room, two bedrooms, and two baths. For once, Hélène was content to do nothing but play tourist and enjoy Petite Hélène's company. The girl's energy was boundless, her excitement infectious, her quick intelligence stimulating. Sometimes Hélène just stood back and watched her niece as she approached something new with a cautious, almost adult curiosity. Together they explored London from top to bottom, holding hands and skipping along the Thames esplanade through the fine-mist fogs and marveling at the patience of the polite English as they queued up for the double-decker buses or the Underground. They attended a performance of *Der Rosenkavalier* in the sweetly gaudy Covent Garden opera house, visited Tower Bridge, the Houses of Parliament, and saw the crown jewels guarded by the Yeomen of the Guard in their colorful uniforms in the Tower of London. They marveled at the Egyptian antiquities in the British Museum, shopped Regent Street and Harrods, visited the Old Curiosity Shop immortalized by Charles Dickens, and shuddered when they saw the wax figures at Madame Tussaud's. One afternoon, Hélène hired a chauffeured car and they drove out to the country to see Windsor Castle. On the way back, they stopped in a delightful old country inn and ate sliced roast beef and Yorkshire pudding and drank Earl Grey tea.

They were in England to look for a nanny, and every day before they went out exploring, Hélène patiently interviewed the various potential nannies the services sent over.

It seemed to Hélène that she would never find one both she and Petite Hélène could get along with. Some were dour, some patronizing, some overly sweet.

But if she had hoped to run into Nigel, it was in vain, even though the week stretched into two. She never saw Nigel, but she did finally find a nanny who was satisfactory.

Her name was Elizabeth Stewart and she was a stout Scottish woman in her late forties. She had a natural way with children—that much was obvious from the start. She and Petite Hélène immediately took to each other—something that stirred up irrational jealousies in Hélène. It was she who had insisted on getting a nanny, but at the same time, she wanted all of Petite Hélène's affections for herself.

With the nanny engaged, there were no more excuses to keep them in England, so they flew back to Paris. However, Hélène was not content with just having found a nanny. Every family needed a home, a constant refuge to go back to in times of joy and crisis, a place where they could spend the holidays together. The old house with the canary-yellow door in Montmartre would have been her home had Maman been alive. She missed not having had it. She knew, instinctively, that Petite Hélène needed such a place, too. But not in the city. It would have to be out in the country; as far as Hélène was concerned, they all spent too much time in the city. And it would have to be a secluded place. A private place.

When she found what she wanted, she signed the papers, bought it for just over a million francs cash, and took Edmond and Petite Hélène to see it one Saturday afternoon. She had kept the purchase a secret. She didn't even tell them where they were headed.

Two hours after they left Paris, Hélène rapped on the glass partition of the Citroën limousine. The chauffeur glanced back through the rearview mirror. Hélène pointed to the left, and he nodded. As soon as the next intersection came up, he slowed down and made a left turn into a bumpy, rutfilled road that branched off into a forest.

574

"Where are you taking us?" Petite Hélène asked with growing excitement.

Hélène smiled secretively. "I've just bought a little cottage in the country. I thought we should have a refuge to escape the bustle of Paris." She leaned forward, looked around Petite Hélène, and smiled at Edmond. "You don't mind my not telling you? I wanted to keep it a surprise."

Edmond smiled. "I don't mind it at all as long as you'll agree to take some time off every now and then, too."

"And likewise," she said. "Look who's telling me."

But she was pleased. Ever since Nanny had joined the household, even Edmond was starting to come back to normal. The curtains were drawn aside each morning, the rooms aired out, the cooking done. Nanny's influence even showed in their family relationship. Once again they had become close-knit.

Edmond sat up straight as the car came into a clearing. "A cottage, did you say?"

"Well . . ." Hélène shrugged and made a helpless little gesture with her hands. Petite Hélène was suddenly trying to crawl across her lap, "ooohing" and "aaahing" excitedly as she pressed her nose against the window.

Hélène couldn't help but smile as she looked out. The sun was high in the sky and bathed the clearing. The grass and moss were moist and lushly green, and the sunlight between the cathedrallike trees was like flashes of silver. The château was a brownstone island with corner turrets, a central cobblestoned courtyard, and a moat that emptied into a big green pond which had ducks and swans gliding gracefully across their own reflections.

As soon as the car came to a halt, Petite Hélène jumped out and ran over to the pond.

It was a beautifully proportioned house, Hélène thought as she looked up at it, her hands in her pockets. It wasn't nearly as lavish as Hautecloque, but it had an unpretentious charm of its own. It was neither haughty nor majestic. It was simply a manageable country château 160 kilometers south of Paris. And it was steeped in history, parts of it dating from the sixteenth century. Originally the château had been owned by Diane de Poitiers; then it had undergone various changes in family ownership. It had a caretaker's cottage, a guest house, stables, and a livable three-story stone tower on the far side of the pond.

Hélène had decided to keep on the old caretaker couple, Monsieur and Madame Greuze, to run the place. And she had bought Petite Hélène a pony of her own.

Jeanne was gone, never to be part of them except in their memories, but Hélène couldn't help thinking that Jeanne would have been pleased. Petite Hélène now had a house she could come home to, that would eventually be her own.

2

The Banco di Milano was located on the ground floor of a thirty-story office tower that rose out of the ancient pedimented buildings of old-town Milan. An inverted black cone, it dominated the skyline like a huge, uncircumcised phallus. When Hélène came out of the building, she squinted in the bright sunlight, put on her sunglasses, and took the flight of low, curving steps down to the sidewalk. There she skirted the crashing water fountains that split up the concrete piazza like an enormous ultramodern cupcake pan. The warm May breeze carried the shroudlike mist from the fountains over to her. It felt cool and refreshing.

A slight smile of satisfaction played across Hélène's lips. Things were going well. It was the second month since she had officially become a millionairess in her own right—not counting her inheritance from Stanislaw, and not in worthless lire or in so many, many francs, but from *Les Modes*, and in the currency that counted. Dollars. Not bad, everything considered. The first issue of *La Moda*, *Les Modes*'s Italian counterpart, had already hit the newsstands.

She smiled, thinking of how Signor Piarotto, the bank president, was becoming increasingly ingratiating every time she entered the bank. He was beginning to realize her worth and saw to it that he always took care of her personally, a fawning smile on his face. How different things were now from a few years earlier, she thought, when she hadn't had as much as a sou in her pocket. When she'd arrived "fifth-class" on the Right Bank of Paris and couldn't afford to eat anything but old bread and scavanged fruit—and only when she was lucky.

She glanced at her gold watch. It was nearly ten o'clock; she'd have to hurry. She had meetings scheduled with paper suppliers and advertisers, and at noon there was a working lunch with the Czarina.

She turned right on the via Montenapoleone and headed for the offices of Edizioni Hélène Junot S.p.a. They were located several blocks away in an enormous old Medici palazzo that had been carved up into high-class commercial space. The building was shared by several fashion designers, three giftware wholesalers, a parfumerie, and *La Moda.*

On the way, she passed the newsstand where she always bought her morning paper. It was run by a wrinkled old widow. Hélène paused; something had caught her eye. There it was. A stack of *La Moda.* She watched as two blond women hesitated between it and *Vogue.* Finally curiosity won out over habit. They picked up *La Moda* and flipped rapidly through it. The expressions on their faces immediately changed: they were transported from their drab, humdrum lives into the exciting world of couture and makeup and fine jewelry, a Cinderella world where anything was possible, where a slickly photographed pair of seventy-thousand-lire Ferragamo shoes replaced the traditional glass slipper.

Hélène felt a wave of pride coursing through her. She was sharing her taste and knowledge—indeed the entire fashion world—with these women, perhaps making their lives more beautiful, more worthwhile. At any rate, bringing their dreams into perspective and putting them down on paper where they couldn't evaporate. Perhaps even giving them ideas to apply to themselves, to make them feel more beautiful and secure, desired. How well she could still remember how the magazines at Madame Dupré's had changed her life.

Without another glance at *Vogue,* both women reached into their purses and snatched up *La Moda.* Happily they began to chatter and walked off.

Hélène smiled. It was only the first issue, but already she had witnessed two tiny victories—two minor miracles—two women reaching for *La Moda* instead of *Vogue.* On an impulse she walked over to the newsstand. The old woman knew her already, but she didn't know who she was. So much the better.

577

"Good morning, signorina," the old woman said.

"Good morning." Hélène looked down at the stack of *La Moda*. "A new magazine?"

"Yes, signorina, but finally one that is bellissimo!" For emphasis the old woman made a circle with her thumb and forefinger and kissed it noisily.

Hélène reached into her purse, took out a thousand-lire note, and picked up a copy. It was thick and heavy.

Thanking the old woman, she left the newsstand and strode down the street, the magazine tucked proudly under her arm. When she came across a sidewalk café she took a seat under the striped canvas awning and ordered a cup of espresso; the meetings would have to wait. Then she laid the magazine faceup on the table, took off her sunglasses, leaned her elbows on the table, and proudly stared at the cover.

The block letters "LA MODA" were huge and white and dazzling.

As Hélène flipped through the magazine, she found it hard to believe how much had happened in the last two years. *Les Modes* was here to stay, a growing giant that was a power to be reckoned with. The Italian edition, *La Moda Uomo*, was out only a month behind schedule. And, most important, men's editions of both magazines—*Les Modes Homme* and *La Moda Uomo*—were in the planning stages. But that was only a fraction of what she had up her sleeve—the visible fraction. Like a deceptive iceberg, she chose to keep her ambitions and future plans well hidden. She knew—instinctively, and from experience with Stanislaw's inheritance—that it took money to make money. And she knew perfectly well that having money, like owning art, was an awesome responsibility. Once you had it, you had to make sure that it was constantly working for you, increasing steadily. What good did it do you otherwise? By simply banking it, you lost it steadily but surely. Nothing shrank as fast as idle money.

She put this knowledge to good use by expanding her empire and thinking of starting another, entirely different but related business. But as always, she combined caution with just the right amount of shrewd daring. Instinctively she sensed when to wait and when to go all-out. Her instincts had served her well in the past, and she relied upon them completely. For her, Paris and *Les Modes* had only been the jumping-off point. Italy was where her fortune would skyrocket. She knew that as surely as she knew that Thursday followed Wednesday, and she was already planning for it. She saw things happening in Italy that were not happening elsewhere. Design was new and bursting and alive; the young designers were branching out, freed from the shackles of conservatism to forge ahead and create exciting new styles previously unheard-of.

Yes, a lot was happening. And she planned to be where it was happening.

Hélène entered the building, crossed the hollow-sounding lobby, and hurried past the glass cases filled with expensive giftware. She didn't bother to glance at them. She had seen that same display a hundred times already. The air in here smelled expensive. It was the fragrance of perfume.

The glass cases belonged to the giftware wholesaler who occupied the ground floor; the scent drifted down from the parfumerie on the third. Quickly she ascended the wide balustraded staircase to the second floor and crossed the marble landing to the carved double doors. She glanced at the engraved brass plaque:

"EDIZIONI HÉLÈNE JUNOT S.p.a."

She pulled open the door on the right and went inside.

For a moment, she paused. As usual, the offices were humming with the activity of the business day. She could feel the cogs turning, could almost reach out and touch the creativity that crackled visibly in the frenetic atmosphere. The persistently ringing telephones, the clattering of typewriters and telex machines, and the fragments of raised voices coming from the conference room, where she knew a "creative meeting" was in progress, were music to her ears. The big office space reminded her of the Place Vendôme headquarters. The language here was Italian, but the flavor—for a moment she closed her eyes—the *flavor* of the Milan offices was exactly like that of the Paris headquarters. The business of reporting on and predicting style and elegance, of "making" promising new designers or sending established, staid ones to their death—not through spectacular battle, but by simply ignoring them—here the *power* of fashion pulsed strong and loud.

Hélène hurried down the plush-carpeted corridor to her private office. She was sorry to have missed the meetings scheduled for that morning and the working lunch with Luba, but she had been too involved with her plans to notice how much time had passed. It was already two o'clock.

She crossed over to her chrome-and-glass desk and put down her purse and her copy of her magazine. A pink note under the small Jean Arp bronze she used as a paperweight caught her eye. Carefully she slid the note out from under it. The writing, she could tell from a glance, was Luba's. It was as elegant and spidery as the woman herself. True to the Czarina's fashion, it was both cryptic and dramatic: "*I've found him! L.*"

Hélène crumpled it up into a ball and tossed it into the wastebasket. Then she picked up her telephone and summoned the Czarina to her office. While she waited, she sat down in her upholstered swivel chair, swung around to the molded filing cabinet to her left, pulled open a drawer and took out a report. The light blue cover was stamped in red ink: CONFIDENTIAL.

She sat back, opened the report to the first page and started to read. Within a moment she was as immersed in it as a housewife reading the latest blockbuster novel.

La Moda
Projections

Issue:	November
Start Production:	June 1
Advertising Deadline:	July 1
Projected Advertising Pages:	230
Advertising Pages Sold to Date:	223
Projected Article Pages:	70

Monthly Features

Editorial:	*La Moda*'s Point of View: ?
Guest Speaker:	?
Society:	Bonacossi-Peretti wedding in June
	Charity ball in Florence (send Luba and photographer)
Cuisine:	Heartwarming Soups
	Eating with Flair: Tureens
Travel:	Sun in the Alps—Switzerland, France, and Austria
	Sun on the Beach—the Great Barrier Reef, Tunisia, and Malibu
Interiors:	John Fowler
Health:	Avoiding Skin Cancer on the Slopes and Beaches

Beauty:	New Skin Tones for Winter
	Interviews with Six Plastic Surgeons
	New Colors for Eyes and Lips

She pursed her lips thoughtfully and drummed her nails on the glass desktop. So far, everything was too predictable. Too much like the first issue. Like the others that were in production right now. What was needed was a new approach.

She had a sudden inspiration, picked up her pen, and wrote a note in the margin: *"For lipstick features, focus close up on lips and mouths. Tongues with caviar on them, lips with straws sipping Coca-Cola, etc."*

Satisfied, she laid down her pen and continued reading:

Arts:	Film—Fellini
Architecture:	Palladio
Art:	Sculptures by Marino Marini and Eduardo Paolozzi
Theater:	London This Season
Fashion:	Focus on—Valentino
La Moda's Boutique:	Our Choices for Winter
Around the World:	Finnish Leather to Alaskan Parkas
Haute Couture:	Paris, Milan, and New York
Ready-to-Wear:	This Season's Top Designers—Milan
Accessories:	Skis and Skates—New Designs for the Sixties
Jewelry:	Colombian Emeralds, Peruvian Gold, Celtic Jewelry from Ireland, Navajo Turquoise, New Pop-Art Plastics
Special Features:	Visit with Picasso at La Californie
	What's New for Winter—Paris, New York, Milan
	Furs for All Seasons (*Note: Max Reby bought 6 pages of ads!*)
	Dressing Up by Dressing Down
	Revlon's Cosmetics—a Retrospective (1932 through present)

Hélène was startled when Luba knocked on her door. She looked up. "Come in!"

Luba approached the desk with her usual purposeful pace. Hélène noticed she held a typed sheet of paper in her hand.

Hélène closed the report, put it aside, and folded her hands. "Luba," she said with a smile.

The Czarina stood confidently gaunt in a black knit shift belted at the waist with the thickest black leather strap and the biggest silver buckle Hélène had ever laid eyes on. Her black pumps had identical but slightly smaller buckles. As usual her pitch-black hair was gathered on the right side of her head and plaited into a single long, thick braid that hung aggressively down to nearly her waist.

Luba's tangerine nails slashed through the air. "I've found the patsy!" she announced in a dramatic stage whisper.

Hélène looked at her in embarrassment. "Please, Luba. You know I don't like to use that word."

Luba's black eyes flashed from within her thick sable eyelashes. "A patsy is what best describes what you're looking for."

Hélène sighed. "Patsy it is, then." She waved to a chair.

Luba made a production of consulting the paper in her hand. "His name is Marcello d'Itri. Born in Sicily, current resident of Milan. Studied fashion here while apprenticed to Missoni as a weaver. Left for New York and spent two years studying at the Fashion Institute of Technology. Came back, spent a year as a laborer in a ready-to-wear garment factory. Was one of the assistants to a fabric designer at T. and J. Vestor. That lasted six months. Tried to open his own boutique two years ago, failed miserably, and has been knocking on the doors of every designer in this city since then. He's a bachelor and a heterosexual, and that's it in a nutshell." Luba dropped the paper on Hélène's desk.

Hélène looked thoughtful. "And you think he's the one we're looking for?"

"I've kept my eyes wide open," the Czarina said. "He's the perfect patsy."

Hélène winced. She wished Luba would stop using that word. But the Czarina was right; what she wanted *was* a patsy. A handsome ladies' man, preferably Italian, who had a fashion background but was a miserable failure. She wanted someone with enough intelligence to face that fact, yet someone who wasn't so independent that he wouldn't do as he was told. He had to be someone who could never become successful on his own. Someone who was . . . weak.

Hélène glanced down at the paper that summed up one man's life in such terse, unfeeling terms. Could that really be all there was to a life? she asked herself. Was the rest just padding? Could her own life be outlined just as concisely, with only one difference—success substituting for failure?

In a way, she felt sorry for Marcello d'Itri without even having met him. Getting a start in the fashion business was like swimming in an ocean full of sharks. It didn't matter whether you were good or bad. You were a potential competitor, and as such, the others ganged up on you and cut you swiftly down to size before you even had a chance to start swimming. It was Darwinism, pure and simple. The survival of the fittest. You had to be a shark to survive.

Yet as much as she felt sorry for him, the fact that he had had such miserable luck was a plus. For her. She had been searching for someone like him for months, but until now none of the candidates met all the qualifications. And for what she wanted (as usual, she knew *exactly* what she wanted), each qualification was important. For she, Hélène Junot, was going into the fashion business. Not just reporting on fashion as she had been doing all along, but having an atelier of her own. She knew that she and Luba had an abundance of taste and foresight—and that *Les Modes* and *La Moda* were powerful enough—to assure the atelier's success. Only for once, her magazines stood in her way: she couldn't open an atelier in her own name. That would be a blatant conflict of interests. What she had to do was to own an atelier but remain a silent partner. She had to set up someone else as a figurehead. Someone who would listen to her and Luba and pretend that he was in charge. Someone who would take orders from them. Someone who had little or no talent.

Of course, an atelier needed talent, but that would remain as silently in the background as she herself would. She would simply get a design team together. Just as she had begun *Les Modes* by robbing *Vogue, Harper's Bazaar,* and *L'Officiel* of their talent, so she would snare the best design talent for her atelier. Of talent there was always a plentiful crop. It was the figurehead who was more difficult to find. And Hélène knew one thing better than even the established couturiers who gambled on the Look of the season. *She knew the exact direction in which the winds of fashion were blowing, be-*

cause she helped them blow that way. Her atelier wouldn't be a gamble. Nor would it cajole customers into buying beautiful, expensive things by relying on their own good taste. No, she would cleverly cater to them from the beginning, playing on their ingrained tastes and snobbishness. Her atelier would sell exactly what people wanted. Nothing else.

Hélène did not realize it, but she had stumbled across what was to become a trend that would continue for years. Creating a figurehead and making his name a household word, or using a figurehead to carry on a name, would become an intrinsic part of the fashion world on both sides of the Atlantic. It was coincidental whether the figurehead could design or not, although some of them could. What was important was that people would pay for the name.

Marcello d'Itri.

Hélène rolled the name on her tongue. It sounded good. Now, if only he was what she was looking for. She winced as Luba's words came back to her.

The perfect patsy.

Hélène forced herself to push the word out of her mind. She rose to her feet and smiled. "Thank you, Luba," she said.

The Czarina rose also. "Do you want me to schedule a meeting with d'Itri?"

"Please. I've got to return to Paris on Friday, so make it as soon as possible."

"Is tomorrow soon enough?"

Hélène nodded. "Tomorrow will be fine."

"Good. I'll send for him."

"No," Hélène said slowly. "I tell you what. I'll go to him instead. I want you to accompany me, of course."

The Czarina looked baffled, but she knew better than to ask why the mountains were going to visit Muhammad. She nodded.

After she was gone, Hélène thought about her decision to go and visit d'Itri. She knew instinctively that it was a good idea. You could always tell more about a person from his surroundings than if you summoned him to your office. Of course, in the office he was more vulnerable, more ill-at-ease and nervous. But she didn't want d'Itri to be any of these things. She wanted to find out the little things about him that only a shelf of books or the throw on a chair could reveal.

That was far better than seeing him disguised in his best suit.

The next day Hélène and Luba sat in the back of the company's tiny chauffeur-driven Fiat, negotiating the narrow, ancient streets of Milan.

Marcello d'Itri was sweating. He was not usually prone to sweat, but he couldn't help it now. Not with the two elegant women he faced. The tall, gaunt, aggressive one and the expensively dressed younger one. They looked so different—like an elegant old lizard and a poised gazelle. Yet undeniably they both had chic—an instinctive, intimidating chic such as he had never been exposed to before. And they wore it so naturally, so comfortably! Most people he knew felt that way only in worn sweaters and old bathrobes. Yet here they were, dressed to kill, and totally at ease. The old lizard in a turtleneck sweater and a skirt—both of black silk interwoven with cashmere—a long gold-mesh chain knotted around her neck, and an Hermès belt around her waist; the young gazelle in a pale apricot Chanel suit with dark piping, an off-white silk blouse, and a straw hat. Her ear clips were unmistakably Bulgari—an emerald-cut diamond surrounded by baguettes and set in white gold.

But chic was not all they were. He felt something menacing under their beautiful veneers. They were powerful. He could see that in their eyes, in their self-assured poise. He knew they weren't the type to be taken in by overt displays of masculinity or suave, effusive compliments. There was something hard and businesslike about both of them. Especially the younger one.

Marcello d'Itri was slender and good-looking. His skin was olive and his eyes and hair were dark and glossy. He looked a little unkempt, Hélène thought, but it was clear that that was a matter of finances. He'd obviously done all he could to make himself presentable, even getting a haircut. Not a very good one, but probably all he could afford. His suit, though of a good fabric and cut, was worn and more than a little frayed. It had had a last-minute pressing. It was either the best suit he owned, or the only one. It was made of wool and he was wearing it in May. His white shirt was of good-quality cotton, but there, too, wear and tear showed. But she knew better than to judge him by his immediate appearance. What

585

mattered was how he *could* look. And she instinctively realized that with a little flair and some money, he could look highly presentable. His skin tone was just slightly exotic, his full lips could be construed as sensual. He was good-looking enough for any woman, and yet not perfect enough to instill an instant dislike in men. His tiny dark apartment was shabby. In one corner stood a large loom with an unfinished design woven on the hundreds of vertical strings. Hélène glanced at it disapprovingly and then caught Luba's eye. They both recognized the design instantly. Missoni.

Marcello d'Itri clearly copied from whoever was in vogue.

D'Itri fidgeted nervously with his hands, waiting for one of the women to speak. He wondered what they could possibly want from him.

"I've taken the liberty of ordering a rundown on your personal history," Hélène was saying. She smiled apologetically, looking directly into his eyes. "I hope you don't mind. However, I like to make certain I know whom I'm dealing with whenever I anticipate throwing money in any direction."

D'Itri nodded in bewilderment. He squirmed nervously in his chair. He looked as if he were facing a firing squad.

"You have an interesting background." Hélène smiled, trying to put him at ease. "Not a spectacular background, but one I'll accept. Signor d'Itri, time is my most precious asset and I don't like to waste it, so I'll come right to the point. How would you like to become a fashion designer?"

"I've already tried that route." He smiled sadly, relaxing a little.

"Unsuccessfully."

"Yes." His voice was small.

"How would you like to become famous, Signor d'Itri?" Hélène asked softly.

He gave a short, nervous laugh. Now he knew she was crazy. There was a time when he had thought he was talented. It had taken him years to find out he wasn't. Surely a woman as important and powerful as she was, a woman who was constantly tuned in to fashion, knew it even better than he.

Hélène continued. "Within a short period of time I could make you as well known as Valentino, as successful as Dior. Would you like that?"

"I'd be a liar if I said I wouldn't."

586

"Fine. At least you're honest. I appreciate honesty. I also appreciate the fact that on your own, you'll never make it in this business."

D'Itri sat frozen now, flushing under the sudden onslaught. It had come so suddenly that he broke out in a fresh sweat. Quickly he began dabbing his forehead with the balled-up handkerchief clutched in his fist. "Then why are you here?" he found himself saying. He seemed startled to hear his own voice.

Hélène stared levelly into his liquid eyes. They were dark and confused, as if he'd awakened to find himself in a place he'd never seen before. Quickly she told him about her plans to open an atelier. He heard her out in silence.

"You don't want a designer, then. You want a . . ." He struggled to find the right word.

"A figurehead, Signor d'Itri," Hélène said smoothly, avoiding Luba's narrowed eyes. She knew what the Czarina was thinking. *Patsy.* Quickly she continued. "The design team will do everything. But that's not to say you won't have work to do also. You'll have to work very hard. Acquiring polish, meeting people, wooing clients. Believe me, that is a job in itself."

D'Itri couldn't believe his ears. Out of the blue, just as he was at the lowest ebb of his life, came *this*! He couldn't understand it, but he was smart enough not to try to. Obviously the two women were either crazy or they knew exactly what they wanted. If they were telling the truth, all he had to do was go along with them and he'd be living like a king.

He listened as Hélène went on, his mind rapidly seizing upon the possibilities. With the power of *Les Modes* and *La Moda* behind him, he could live in a villa, travel around the world, get his picture in the papers. Sure, he'd know he wasn't doing anything. But no one else would.

"It would be like selling my soul to the devil," he told Hélène bleakly. But his mind raced. Airplanes, expensive cars, yachts . . . Suddenly all the things he had dreamed of, and some he hadn't, were possible. And a social position! The poor boy from Sicily could make good. Very good.

He forced himself to remain subdued. "What would I get out of this arrangement?" he asked, trying to appear businesslike.

"As I said, you'd become one of the foremost designers in the world. You'd get fame. Respect." Hélène paused, and when she spoke again, it was a whisper. "Fortune."

His dark eyes flashed greedily. "How much fortune?"

Hélène shrugged. "That depends on how the business fares. You'd own a small percentage of the company."

"How small?"

"Fifteen percent."

He looked disappointed. "That means I wouldn't have any say in it."

"That's right. The company would be run by projections of the market. We'd sell only what's guaranteed to sell. My policy is not to go out on a creative limb. However, you can rest assured of three things." Slowly Hélène ticked them off on her tapered fingers. "First, your name would be the name of the atelier. Second, it would be based here in Milan and have a branch in Rome before we'd branch out further. And third, *it would be the most expensive store in the world.*"

He stared at her in silence for a moment. "And fifteen percent . . . that would make me rich?"

"Very rich, Signor d'Itri. For the time being, until we begin production, I also plan to pay you a salary, which will eventually be deducted from your earnings. A salary of . . ." She paused, pretending to think it over. "Say, one and a half million lire a month?" She raised her eyebrows.

He held his breath, suddenly feeling giddy. One and a half million lire! Mamma mia! Three thousand dollars. And every month! Was it possible? Oh, sweet Blessed Mother, let it be true, he prayed.

He grinned now, suddenly feeling more sure of himself. "It sounds interesting," he said reflectively. He looked down at his lap, his mind spinning. When he looked back up at her, he said shrewdly, "I'd want twenty-five percent, though."

Hélène had expected this; she had purposely offered him fifteen percent, planning all along to let him have as much as thirty. Twenty-five suited her even better. But she didn't want to seem too eager.

"Twenty," she said firmly.

He hesitated, once again finding himself wading around in foreign territory. He felt he should demand more, but how much more? If he got too greedy, there was the danger that he would frighten her off. Then he'd lose out completely. He looked at her. She was sitting there quietly. "Twenty-two?" he asked.

"Twenty."

He looked offended. "Twenty," he agreed meekly.

Hélène smiled. "It's a deal," she said, not believing her good luck. She would own eighty percent of the atelier outright.

She and Luba rose to their feet.

"Come to the offices next Tuesday," Hélène told d'Itri. "My lawyers will have all the papers prepared."

"I'll be there," he promised. Already he was planning to stop by the Alfa Romeo showroom on the way.

When Hélène reached the door, she turned around and shook his hand. "Good-bye, Signor d'Itri."

He unexpectedly bent down over her hand and kissed it. "Good-bye, signorina." He looked up at her over her hand, his dark eyes shining. "Together, we shall be rich."

3

On an overcast day in June, Hélène attended a party held by Odile Joly. The invitation had come as a total surprise, since she knew that Odile Joly wasn't one to throw parties. The old designer had spent a good part of her life guarding her privacy as jealously as the secret to her success. But then Hélène understood. It was her eightieth birthday—which happened to coincide with the sixty-third anniversary of the Maison d'Odile Joly, which she had begun in September 1898 as a millinery shop. It was for that occasion that she threw the doors to her apartment in the Plaza Athénée open to everyone she had ever known. Or, as sharp Parisian tongues had it, to everyone she was still on speaking terms with. It was a party which lasted for half a day and far into the night. The wealthy and the famous came to crowd the apartment and pay homage to the greatest couturière of all time.

Photographers were everywhere, including a team from *Les Modes*.

Like a queen, Odile Joly received each guest individually. When the guests entered the apartment, a servant took their coats and had them line up; another servant took them, one by one, to see Odile Joly. Never one to do things by halves, she sat in lonely splendor on a mountain of cushions and Oriental rugs inside a silken tent specially erected for this occasion. The tent was lit by lanterns and lined with pots of bushy areca palms. Sandalwood incense burned in a brass brazier, and an Indian singer sat cross-legged in a corner strumming a harplike instrument and singing in a high-pitched voice. For this occasion, Odile Joly had gone all-out. She wore a sheer veil, an elegant silk sari she had bought on a recent trip to India, and gleaming gold jewelry. She allowed each guest to do two things: congratulate her on her success and longevity and pick her mind for a single pearl of wisdom by asking one, and only one, truly important question.

Odile Joly enjoyed herself immensely. She knew how everyone seized upon her every word as if it were gospel, and she made a game of it. When a model asked her for the secret to beauty, she replied elusively, "Beauty is that elusive gift that no one can find."

When a man asked her for the secret to success, Odile Joly looked thoughtful for a moment and mused, "Hmmm . . . success." She placed a finger across her lips, apparently deep in thought. Then she looked up, her dark eyes sparkling with sudden knowledge. "Success is either there or it isn't."

When asked what was the most important thing in the world, she succinctly explained, "Economy of motion."

"When should I get my first face lift?" someone else asked.

"Face lift! Non, non, non, non! Never get a face lift. Add wrinkles!" Odile Joly cried. Then with a look of self-satisfaction she settled back on her mountains of cushions. "Wrinkles," she sighed happily, "add character."

Hélène was nearly overcome by the sumptuousness of Odile Joly's apartment. She had never before been there. Though it was an apartment in a hotel that was known for its luxury, she had expected something Spartan like the workrooms in the maison where the cutting and designing went on, or at the most, a comfortable but uninspired suite of hotel rooms. She was mistaken on both counts.

The enormous suite had been decorated by Odile Joly herself, "with a little help" from the great English decorator John Fowler. Along one wall of the formal living room were built-in black-lacquered bookcases, and in front of them was a long couch filled with goosedown and upholstered in rich bone-colored suede. The two end walls were completely mirrored except for the delicately carved marble fireplaces. The coffee tables and the chairs were genuine Empire, the carpeting was a thick wool pile that looked like velvet, and life-size bronze deer stood around looking as if they were grazing upon it. There were coromandel screens, ormolu clocks, furniture inlaid with mother-of-pearl, paintings by Turner and Renoir, a pair of tiny Titians, and a collection of Kang H'si porcelains. As if all this were not enough, even the ceiling was mirrored.

As Hélène awaited her turn to see Odile Joly, she kept thinking back to how much her former employer had been responsible for her own success. For it had been Odile Joly who had sought her out so many years ago at the André Lichenstein Gallery and offered her a job as a model. It was she who had recommended her to Jacques to pose for the sensational Eiffel Tower pictures. Then, when she had begun *Les Modes,* Odile Joly had once again given her all the support humanly possible, even breaking with the High Fashion Association in order that *Les Modes* might have the jump on covering her collections. Perhaps without Odile Joly, *Les Modes* would never have become a success. Perhaps would never have come into being at all. Or would it have anyway? Were some things in life just destined to happen? Would Hélène have found another way to do it? They were questions to which she would never find the answers. All she knew was what Madame Dupré had once told her: things happened when you were ripe for them to happen.

But of one thing she was absolutely certain. Three people had helped her get to where she was today. Madame Dupré, Odile Joly, and Stanislaw. They had been her guardian angels.

At seven-thirty-three a footman came over to Hélène and bowed. "If you'd please come with me, mademoiselle? Odile Joly will see you now."

They walked down a long corridor and stopped at a door at the end. The footman opened it, stood aside, and then followed her inside.

Hélène stared curiously at the huge tent. Then the foot-

591

man held the flap open and she ducked inside. She caught her breath. The tent was so beautifully exotic that for a moment she forgot she was in Paris. The singsong wail of the Indian singer, the incense, and the jungle of green palms mixed with the arabesque of the rugs and cushions were part of another world.

Instinctively she took a step backward. In one corner she had noticed movement and then heard a menacing growl. It was an ocelot, sleek and alert and sitting on its haunches. Its yellow eyes seemed to glitter hungrily.

"Don't worry, Sheba doesn't bite," a chuckling, throaty voice said.

Hélène turned her face to the left. Like a venerable guru, Odile Joly was sitting on a pile of pillows, her back as ramrod straight as a young girl's. The light from the lanterns threw a soft glow on her wrinkled face. Her deep-set eyes lit up and her face crinkled into a sudden smile. "Hélène!" She held out a gnarled hand. "Come over here and let me have a good look at you. It has been a long time."

Hélène glanced hesitantly at the big cat and noticed it was chained to a post. She smiled nervously and gave it a wide berth as she slowly walked over to Odile Joly. She looked down at her. "Yes, it has been a long time. Happy birthday, and many happy returns."

Odile Joly made a weary gesture. "I've had so many birthdays I stopped counting them half a century ago. Here, sit down beside me." Odile Joly patted the cushions.

Hélène knew what an honor this was. Everyone else had been whisked in and out within a minute. She looked around hesitantly. Then she smiled. "Are there any snakes in here?"

Odile Joly narrowed her eyes. "In here, none. But I'm sure the rest of the apartment is *filled* with vipers." She waited until Hélène had taken a seat. "You've done very well for yourself, chérie. You're one of the few people I've learned to respect—did you know that?"

Hélène blushed at the compliment. It was the last thing she had expected. "*Les Modes* would never have gotten to where it is without your help," she said.

"You've worked like a maniac. It is only too bad that your personal life did not work out as beautifully. I adored Stanislaw."

Hélène felt a sudden lump in her throat. "Yes, so did I," she said softly. "He was an exceptional man."

Odile Joly nodded. Then she looked at Hélène shrewdly. "A few minutes ago, a man asked me for the secret to success. Do you know what I should have told him?"

Hélène shook her head.

"I should have said, 'Ask Hélène Junot. She has found it.' "

"I think that's overstating it a bit."

For a while, neither of them spoke. "Well, aren't you going to ask for the answer to one important question?" Odile Joly asked finally.

Hélène laughed helplessly. "I'm afraid I wouldn't know where to begin."

"Good girl." Odile Joly paused. "You know that I don't give parties very often?"

Hélène nodded, wondering what she was leading up to.

"People are racking their brains trying to figure out why I broke down and gave this one, although they don't dare come right out and ask me. They think it's my farewell to life."

"That's ridiculous," Hélène said. To her, Odile Joly always was and always would be.

Odile Joly smiled ruefully, held her hands out, and looked at them. She shook her head. The fingernails were perfectly lacquered, but the skin was ancient and age-spotted. "I'm eighty years old now. Perhaps I'll live for another ten years, perhaps not." She shrugged philosophically. "Why do you think all these people came? To wish me many happy returns?" She laughed dryly. "No, they wanted to see how much life an eighty-year-old woman has left. They wanted to see how much I've slowed down." She leaned forward and reached down to a round brass box at her feet. She lifted the cover and took out a chunk of raw, bloody meat. She tossed it over at the ocelot, which sprang to its feet. A second later, its teeth were embedded in the meat as it started to chew.

"They came to see how life has eaten me up after all these years." Odile Joly nodded in the cat's direction. "Just like Sheba devouring the meat." She sighed and met Hélène's gaze. "I'm a dinosaur, a leftover from the last century. There are a hundred new designers out there waiting to take my place. And it's funny. I really am getting tired, you know. I can feel that deep inside my bones."

Hélène felt sorry for the old woman. She knew how hard it must be for her to have to slow down. Mentally she was so active; she'd always had the energy of the hyperactive. It seemed strange that her body could be slowly wearing down. And yet, Hélène had always thought Odile Joly to be as indestructible as a French monument. It seemed peculiar to see her in another light. As just another mortal.

Suddenly Odile Joly seized Hélène's hand and held it tightly. "Make sure your photographers cover this party thoroughly!"

Hélène did not speak. A worried expression crossed her face.

"Don't look at me that way!" Odile Joly said. "There's nothing wrong with me. Tell me, what issues of *La Moda* and *Les Modes* are you preparing right now?"

"November."

"Oh." Odile Joly sounded disappointed.

"What's the matter?" Hélène asked.

Odile Joly smiled. "I was wondering if it was possible for you to stick a few extra pages into an earlier issue . . ." Her voice trailed off.

Hélène thought quickly. She knew Odile Joly well enough to realize she was sounding her out about giving her another scoop. "I could kill an article in the September issue," she said without hesitation. "That's still in page proofs. I'm afraid the others are already at the printer's or in the warehouses."

"September is fine." Odile Joly nodded and smiled in relief. "Use the party photos from tonight. And when you leave, send your photographers in here to do some nice big portraits of me. You see, chérie"—she lowered her voice confidentially—"I'm finally ready to retire."

Hélène couldn't believe her ears. "R-retire!"

"Yes, once you're eighty, I think it's high time. After all, it's important that one knows when to retire." Odile Joly smiled. "I wouldn't want people to say, 'At last.' However, I'll wait to make the public announcement. I'll wait until . . ." Her dark eyes flashed mischievously. "Until the day the September *Les Modes* and *La Moda* come out."

Hélène took both the woman's hands and squeezed them affectionately. "Thank you," she said, her voice suddenly husky. She knew at that moment how much the old woman loved her. Even as she was retiring, she was seeing to it that *Les Modes* would benefit by it.

"Now, go out and party," Odile Joly said gruffly. "The people waiting to get in here are probably lined up for kilometers!"

594

She smiled as Hélène left. Her former mannequin had done well. She hadn't let that turn her into a fool, either. Odile Joly had watched her closely, following *Les Modes*'s steady climb to the dizzying heights of power. Just as there would never be another Odile Joly, she thought, there would never be another Hélène Junot.

After leaving the tent, Hélène had a few words with her photographers and then she left the party. It was early evening, but her business hours didn't stop at five. There were still many things she had to do. Like approving the architect's renderings for the two d'Itri boutiques. The mock-Egyptian interiors needed a few changes. But they would have to wait. First she would call Luba and together they would start mapping out the layouts for Odile Joly's farewell from the fashion world.

As Hélène came out of the Plaza Athénée, she saw a limousine plowing through the sudden deluge and watched it roll to a halt in front of the hotel. Probably another guest coming to honor Odile Joly, she thought. She watched the doorman hurry down the steps, holding up an oversized black umbrella. Only when the passenger ducked out of the limousine did Hélène freeze.

It was Nigel Somerset.

Her knees went suddenly weak and she felt her body starting to sag. She caught hold of the balustrade and clung to it. For a moment she just stared down at him. Then, as he hurried up the steps, she averted her face so that he wouldn't see her. She tried to stem the waves of longing washing over her.

"*Hélène!*" The word was almost a whisper, low and filled with a thousand memories and promises.

He *had* seen her. He had spoken to her.

Her heart sang loudly, joyously, triumphantly. Slowly she turned around.

"Nigel!" The voice was choked and husky, a voice belonging to someone else.

Then she quickly turned away again as a woman came out of the revolving brass doors to meet him.

The voice *had* belonged to someone else. To Hélène Giraudoux.

4

Forty thousand spectators crammed the tribunes at Auteuil
to watch the horse race. Two hundred thousand others surrounded the racecourse; many people had camped out there
for two days. It was the first of November, the traditional
date of the autumn Grand Prix. This last race of the season
always drew a good crowd, but never before had a race been
known to virtually stop the wheels of industry. All over the
country, factories and businesses reported that fifty percent of
their work forces had called in sick. The bookmakers in
Montmartre were doing business as never before. Not only
had the racing buffs tuned in to the race, but all of Paris was
out in its finery, buzzing with low-keyed excitement. It was
the same all over France. Those who couldn't be there were
glued to their radios.

This season, for the first time, five horses were running
neck and neck. The horses were so evenly matched that no
one could even guess the odds. The way it turned out, the
race had become a showdown between five of the leading
families of France. Running were the de Rothschilds' Baron,
the de Sévignés' Très Jolie, the de Gides' Mylène, the
d'Ermos' Piper, and the de Légers' L'Afrique.

The excitement had begun on Palm Sunday and built up
steadily all summer long. On Palm Sunday, the de
Rothschilds' Baron won the President of the Republic Stakes.

On Whit Monday on the St. Cloud racecourse, the de
Gides' Mylène placed first.

On the last Sunday in June, the same horses had run again,
this time at Longchamps for the Paris Grand Prix. The de
Légers' L'Afrique had come out the winner.

In Vincennes in September, the d'Ermos' Piper had won
the summer Grand Prix.

At Longchamps on the first Sunday in October, the de

596

Sévignés' Très Jolie came in ahead of the others in the Arc de Triomphe Grand Prix.

Steadily, with each race, excitement had risen until it verged on feverish hysteria. All five winners of the season's previous races were present again for this last big race. It was clear that one of these five would be running away with the prize.

Hélène took Petite Hélène to watch. "After all," she'd explained to the nanny, "she must be exposed to all facets of society. I know she's young. But she should have some idea of what is going on in the world."

A hush had now fallen over the crowd at Auteuil as the horses shot down the racetrack. Their hooves threw up clumps of earth as the cadence of their run beat out a staccato drumbeat. Right from the start, five horses pushed ahead of all the others. Baron was in the lead. No more than half a neck behind him, L'Afrique, Très Jolie, Mylène, and Piper were already inching ahead.

Petite Hélène craned her neck and lifted the binoculars to her eyes, but the horses were past the grandstand now and it was difficult to tell just which one was in the lead. They seemed so close together.

The crowds began yelling and screaming.

When the horses turned the corner of the oval and were opposite the grandstand, L'Afrique was clearly in the lead, but not by much. The others were not far behind. It would be a very close race.

Edgardo Jiménez, the jockey hunched over L'Afrique, turned his head and glanced backward at the others. He could see Très Jolie gaining on his right, Piper on his left. He could not see the bent-over jockeys, just the horses' heads. The air roared with the sound of hooves. His face tightened with determination.

Hubert de Léger had warned him what he would do if L'Afrique placed anything other than first. He would be fired; ruined. Hubert de Léger had told him he would see to it that he never rode again. That he would be deported back to Argentina.

Jiménez dug in his knees, screamed at his horse, and beat its rump furiously with his riding crop, forcing it to fly even faster.

The others must not catch up.

Ermanno Foggi, the Italian jockey astride Mylène, smiled grimly to himself. He was at the rear, a neck behind Baron, two lengths from L'Afrique. He had let himself slow down purposely, waiting for the moment that would now soon come. It was his style always to stay near the front, but never to push his horse to its absolute limit until the last quarter stretch. Then he would summon all its remaining strength and shoot ahead, squeezing between the others and with a final burst of speed dash across the finish line first.

Ermanno Foggi needed to win. His young daughter needed expensive surgery and the de Gides family had promised him a hundred thousand francs extra if he won.

As if one, the screaming people in the grandstands rose to their feet as the horses reached the last quarter of the oval track. Piper and Très Jolie had gained on L'Afrique; now the three horses were running neck and neck.

Ermanno Foggi shot ahead now. He and Mylène were one and the same. He didn't even look sideways as he passed Baron. His eyes were focused straight ahead as he skillfully cut in front of Baron, blocking him. Now in front of him were L'Afrique, Piper, and Très Jolie. They were tightly knit. He cursed. He needed an opening.

Edgardo Jiménez was panicking. On his right, he could see the blurry chestnut form of Très Jolie. *Gaining.* Already Très Jolie was inching ahead. He must not let that happen. Très Jolie must be stopped at all costs.

Jiménez knew that the time to make his move was now or never. He had pushed L'Afrique to his limits since the start and the horse was tiring. If he didn't act swiftly, he would be deported.

Without thinking of the consequences, Jiménez raised his riding crop in the air and slashed out at Très Jolie's face. It came down so fast that none of the spectators in the tribunes could tell what had happened. All they saw was Très Jolie rearing suddenly and her jockey fighting to keep her under control. Then he was thrown from the horse. He landed on the track, and the thundering hooves of Baron and Mylène instantly crushed him.

A sudden hush filled the tribunes.

Ermanno Foggi felt rather than saw what had happened. For an instant Mylène's hooves had not touched earth. What they had touched was soft and pliable. Yet this was a race. He couldn't stop to give assistance. He had to keep on going.

598

Expertly he skirted Mylène around the rearing Très Jolie and came up alongside L'Afrique and started to pass him. For a moment he looked to his left and caught a glimpse of Jiménez's dark eyes flashing behind his goggles. Then he saw a riding crop raised high in the air. Instinctively he ducked his head. It was too late. He felt a burning slash across the back of his neck and a white fireball burst in front of his eyes. Then the world blacked out. Jiménez had whipped him unconscious. Mylène collided into L'Afrique and the two horses went tumbling.

The crowd screamed in a frenzy as Piper burst across the finish line.

After the race, Hubert de Léger and Edgardo Jiménez were standing outside the stables. Hubert's face was red with rage. Jiménez had his head wrapped in a bandage and there was a terrified look in his eyes. Behind them they could hear the sudden crack of a gunshot. Both men had been prepared for it; still, they both jumped.

A moment later the stable door creaked open and the Comte de Léger came out with stiff dignity, his face white. He stopped in front of Jiménez, towering over the tiny jockey. "Why?" he asked in a whisper, fighting to control his anger. "*Why?*"

Suddenly Jiménez went to pieces. The terror of Hubert's temper and the threat of deportation loomed like a specter in front of him. "Is not my fault!" he screamed in fright. "I had to do! *He* made me!" The jockey wiped away his tears and pointed a trembling finger at Hubert.

The Comte jerked as if he'd been struck. He turned slowly and stared at his son without speaking. Hubert lowered his head and studied his feet.

The Comte took a deep breath. What he had feared the most had finally happened. Hubert had done something which all the power and money of the de Légers could not undo. A hopeless sadness welled up inside him. Didn't the fool know that never again would any member of the family be able to hold up his head in public? Didn't he realize the disgrace he had brought down on the house of the de Légers?

Wordlessly the Comte drew himself up and walked stiffly back into the stables. Hubert glared menacingly at Jiménez. His eyes bore right through the jockey's. The little man shrank back in fear.

At that moment a second gunshot cracked the air at Auteuil.

Hubert had become the new Comte de Léger.

Nigel Somerset had sat with the d'Ermos in their private box. He did not normally go to horse races if he could help it, and for one simple reason. Just as he did not get caught up in the gambling fever in the casinos, neither could he get caught up in the spirited excitement of watching some horses flying around a track. The only reason he was here was that he had come to Paris for business dealings with the Marquis. It was he who had invited him.

"You must come," the Marquis had said. "Our Piper is racing at Auteuil. It will be the race of the year."

Nigel was no stranger when it came to horses. He had ridden all his life. The proper social upbringing of any upper-class Englishman from a wealthy family included learning to ride, attending private boarding schools, and playing polo. Nigel had been a polo player, mostly because it had been expected of him. He had had a string of polo ponies, and though he found the game diverting, he found that his mind was far better equipped for business and politics than sports. As far as races went, his social station required that he appear regularly at Ascot. Especially when the royal family—*his* family—was out in full force. He found Ascot bearable because of its pomp. Everyone dressed in stylish finery and the Royal Box was festooned with purplish-blue hydrangeas and white lilies. The Queen, a distant cousin, always sat in her place of honor under a scalloped canopy. Although Auteuil was crowded with the rich and the titled, it just wasn't the same. No one knew how to stage an extravaganza like the English. But the chief reason he did not like to attend races was that he preferred to ride horses himself rather than watch others doing it.

Until this particular race he had almost forgotten how uncivilized other countries were. The behavior of the de Légers' jockey had been deplorable. No Englishman from the lowliest cockney to the stiffest upper crust would tolerate such scandalous foul play. But sportsmanship was one thing, murder another entirely. The jockey who had been trampled was dead. Any accident casts a pall on a sporting event. This one, done so deliberately, left a foul smell in the air.

He had congratulated the Marquise on her heavy gold trophy and then turned around, making room for the other well-wishers who had swarmed to the box.

Suddenly he froze as he found himself face to face with a beautiful woman and a child with a freckled nose and bright orange hair. His heart began hammering. For a moment, neither he nor the woman could speak. Then he found his voice and said softly, "Hélène . . . ?"

For an instant Hélène's violet eyes widened in confusion. Then she forced herself to smile politely, but it was a sad smile. "Nigel," she said stiffly, "it has been a long time."

The moment the words were out, she realized how reproachful they sounded. She had wanted to be cold and aloof. Like a stranger, not a wronged wife. What was wrong with her?

"Yes, it has been a long time," he said quietly. "Much *too* long."

5

Hélène had loved her château from the moment she'd first laid eyes on it. Now, with Nigel, it took on a special characteristic it had never had before. She banished Monsieur and Madame Greuze, the caretakers, to their cottage and wouldn't allow them to enter the château once all week long.

Madame Greuze placed her hands on her big hips and sniffed disapprovingly. "Just make sure you're in the kitchen at six each morning," she admonished. "The barrel next to the door is filled with stale bread and rolls."

Hélène nodded. She didn't know what Madame Greuze was talking about, but as she propelled her out into the hall, she assured her that everything would be well taken care of.

Madame Greuze looked at her with indignation and heaved a sigh, her big bosom rising and falling. But obediently she untied her starched white apron, hung it neatly in the cupboard under the stairs, and left without arguing any further.

Hélène shared her bedroom with Nigel. It was her favorite room, on the second floor of one of the corner turrets overlooking the pond. It had been newly wallpapered a lovely deep blue with a continuous pattern of miniature white ovals in which blue urns sprouted thistle-like flowers. The bed was wide enough for two, in a sleeping alcove, half-hidden behind draperies. They matched the wallpaper and were lined with heavy white cotton in order to cut any drafts. The ceiling, too, was blue, and so was the wainscoting. A faded Oriental rug covered the rough-hewn reddish stone floor; the table, which doubled as a desk, was draped with another, smaller Oriental carpet. The ancient French chairs grouped around it had white-painted frames and gold velvet upholstery, and the pictures on the walls were inexpensive but charming small landscapes in simple gold frames.

They stayed up late into the night. Nigel built a birch log fire in the huge fireplace in the salon and turned off the lights. They spread cushions out on the rug and lay on them, enjoying their closeness as they talked in the snug air and drank brandy from balloon snifters.

"We have a lot to catch up on," Nigel said softly.

Yes, we have, she silently agreed. The cushions were soft and warm, and his closeness, or the brandy, or both, made her feel heady. Deliriously happy. She snuggled against his warmth, and he held her close, comforting and smelling of freshness. Now that he had come back into her life, she needed him more than she needed anyone or anything else, and she knew that he needed her in the same way. He tightened his arms around her and kissed her, his lips warm and moist and demanding, hers not at all submissive, but just as demanding as his.

Suddenly she pulled away from him. There was something she had to ask him before they made love.

"Nigel?"

He saw the anxious expression on her face, the fear and the hesitation. "Yes, darling? Is something wrong?"

"No," she said slowly, her eyes locked into his. "I just have to know . . ." Her words trailed off, and she shook her head miserably, afraid of the question she had to ask; even more afraid of his answer.

He reached for her hands and held them gently. "Tell me," he said.

She nodded and swallowed. "Why . . ." she whispered miserably, "why didn't you contact me after you got my note?"

He looked perplexed. "Note? What are you talking about, darling? What note?"

She heard the honest bewilderment in his voice, and her heart ached for both of them and that which they had almost lost. She told him about Jeanne's sudden illness and the note she'd slipped in his door aboard the *Evangelia*. They both came to the same conclusion: Blanche Benois had destroyed it.

"She told me she ran into you as you were leaving," Nigel said. "She explained that you two had a woman-to-woman talk. That you were running away because you didn't want to get any more deeply involved with me than you were." The anguish showed in his face. "I was tempted to call you a thousand times, but each time I started to call, I hung up." He smiled sadly. "What a fool I was! I thought you didn't want me."

Oh, if she'd only called him!

He wrapped her in his arms and she gave herself up to his gentle kiss. "But now we're together again, darling," he said softly, nipping her lips. He smiled down into her eyes. "And this time I won't let you slip through my fingers. I've missed you terribly."

And then she felt him urgently but gently unbuttoning her blouse. She turned as she felt the pull of silk, as it slid smoothly off her. His warm lips played on the nape of her neck, rippling the tendrils of hair, stirring her. A tingling warmth moved down her back and through her breasts, then gathered force deep within her. Yes, hers was a need that had been dormant and unsatisfied for too long. His fingers unzipped her skirt, removed her slip, pulled off her stockings. She lay on her back, the cushions warm and soft beneath her, and looked up at him, her eyes blazing with intense hunger, her lips unsmiling as he hurriedly started to unbutton his shirt.

"No!" she whispered. "Let me . . ." And she reached up. Her fingers nimbly undid his shirt front and sleeves. Finally he let it fall away from his body and carefully lay down beside her. She sat up and untied his shoes. Putting her hands on his hips, she gently pulled off his pants.

Hélène took a deep breath, running an index finger down the stiff bulge in his shorts, carefully moving to the softness of his scrotum, fondling, exploring, teasing. Mesmerized, she watched the penis tense at her touch. Then, slowly, reverently, she pulled the trunks down and his cock sprang free.

She could feel the warmth within her melting to wetness as he rolled on top of her. His hands and lips were everywhere at once, stroking, kissing, licking, caressing. His entire body felt hard against her own tight softness. Helene shuddered in expectation.

"Please. Now." Her voice was eager and tight in her chest, the words coming in whispered gasps.

"No," he whispered, his breath and tongue in her ear. "Not yet."

And then he was on his hands and knees, his lips moving down over her satiny skin, gently nipping, inexorably moving downward from her shoulders to her soft breasts, twirling his tongue around her stiff, erect nipples, moving downward still . . .

"Don't stop!" she moaned.

He paused for one endlessly suspended moment, his gold-flecked eyes looking up at her; then slowly he moved back up, finally flicking his tongue over each nipple in turn. She arched her back with a lissome feline grace as he mastered her, making her wait. Nigel teased her, drawing her on and out of herself. Suddenly he drove into her, finding her smooth, warm, and welcoming. His hips thrust against hers, as their wet bodies danced a high-precision ballet. Breaking the frantic rhythms, he abruptly threw his head back while pinning the twisting, driven woman underneath him, his orgasm melting into the ecstatic pulses of her own.

When at last they fell against each other in an exhausted sleep, oblivious of the bed awaiting them upstairs, the embers in the fireplace had long since lost their glow. They slept naked on their sides, his arms wrapped protectively around her, his body curled into hers, the back of her head contured in his neck. It was a gloriously sated, peaceful, and dreamless sleep for both of them.

In the morning, just as daylight broke, Hélène awakened to the sound of banging on the kitchen door. She rubbed her eyes, flipped a coil of loose hair from her forehead, and turned to look at her alarm clock. It was not beside her. Nor was she in bed. She was still on the cushions in the salon, beside Nigel, who was snoring softly, a smile of content on his face. She fell back on the cushions and snuggled deliciously against him, feeling the warm comfort and glow of his flesh. His arm wound sleepily around her, and she shut her eyes.

But the rude, insistent banging continued. Finally she extricated herself from his embrace, got up, slipped into her skirt, and held her blouse against her breasts as she tiptoed into the kitchen to investigate. A moment later she felt Nigel's presence behind her.

"What's going on?" he asked, mystified.

She turned and covered her mouth as she yawned. "I don't know," she said sleepily. "But I aim to find out."

She opened the back door and they burst out laughing. The swans, ducks, and geese had marched over from the pond and were clustered at the door, pecking it impatiently with their bills as they demanded their breakfast.

Hélène remembered Madame Greuze's instructions, and they took the old bread and rolls from the barrel and tossed some of them outside. With a squabble, the birds instantly attacked the food.

Every morning after breakfast, Hélène and Nigel took long walks through the autumn woods, breathing the fresh moistness of the air and feeling the cushion of fallen leaves beneath their feet. Once they wandered off the property and walked through the orchards to the fields surrounding the nearby village. The farmers were burning the cut weeds and grass, readying the land to plow in the spring. The smell of fire and roasting potatoes was in the air, and the farmers greeted Hélène and Nigel with solemn respect and offered them potatoes they had roasted under the fires. She and Nigel thanked them politely and peeled the charred skins back with their fingers. They ate the potatoes as they walked on. Neither had ever eaten anything so delicious. You could almost taste the sweetness and the strength of the land, she thought.

Determined to show off her cooking skills, one afternoon Hélène scoured the second-floor library that the previous owner had left behind. After searching for a while, she found a cookbook and proceeded to prepare an elaborate meal. She followed the laborious instructions to the letter, slaving for hours in the high-ceilinged turquoise kitchen with its solid wooden worktables, black fireplaces and stoves, tile ovens, and white enamel sinks. For a moment she couldn't help comparing herself to Marie Antoinette. Only, instead of playing shepherdess, she was playing housewife. Then her lips tightened and she shoved that thought out of her mind. She wasn't playing housewife. She was simply spending a week alone with Nigel.

The meal turned out to be delicious, and she was content. While she was preparing it, Nigel kept her company. He sat at one of the worktables reading a book he had found in the library. She felt a heady glow of euphoria just because he was so near. She thought: This is what a honeymoon must be like.

"You're going to an awful lot of trouble," he said.

She thought: I'd go through anything as long as you're beside me.

On Saturday night Nigel asked if he could use the telephone to call England.

"Of course," she said with forced lightness. "Just don't call Singapore." But the call was a painful reminder that they had less than a day left. Tomorrow evening they would drive back to Paris. And Monday morning . . . She didn't want to think of Monday morning. Monday morning would come soon enough.

She watched him heading for the telephone in the salon. Could a whole week have flown by already? she wondered. Was it possible? It seemed as if they had spent only minutes together. How much longer would she have to wait before she could once again taste his kisses and feel his strong arms around her?

When Nigel came back from making the call, he smiled apologetically. "I forgot something in England. They're sending it over by messenger tomorrow."

"But we're going back to Paris tomorrow night."

"It will get here on time," he said.

The last day began, as had the others, with the feeding of the birds. But the magic was missing. After breakfast they went to the stables and saddled the horses. Wordlessly they rode through the woods, where they had to duck the low, scratchy branches, up the crest of a hill which looked out over the fields and the village. When they got back to the château they had a subdued lunch, interrupted by the arrival of Nigel's messenger, who seemed to signal loud and clear

606

that only a scant few hours were left. Four more. And then they would have to drive back to Paris. The minutes were racing faster and faster, and Hélène could find no way to stop the clock.

"Let's take a walk," Nigel said when they had finished their lunch.

She nodded, forced herself to smile, and changed into slacks and an old corduroy coat. They walked for an hour, followed by the Greuzes' dog. They threw sticks for him to retrieve. Hélène picked up a fallen branch and lackadaisically strummed it along the trunks of trees. She couldn't remember a time when she'd felt so miserable.

On their way back to the château, Nigel stopped in a clearing and pulled her towards him. "Hélène . . ."

She looked up at him, her eyes wide and frightened. "Nigel . . ."

As he looked down at her, he noticed the sadness in her eyes. For a long moment he held her close without speaking. He knew how she felt. He could never forget the numbness that had come over him after Blanche Benois told him that Hélène had fled the yacht. It was the kind of pain that was difficult to work out of your system.

"I can't tell you how much I've enjoyed this past week," he said softly.

Enjoyed it? *She* had *loved* it. Every last minute of it, but most of all the hours they had spent in bed. "I . . . enjoyed it also," she said under her breath.

He smiled sheepishly. "I'm afraid I don't want to leave without you."

"We'll see each other again," she said.

"I'm counting on that." He reached into his jacket pocket and took out a cubelike velvet case. For a moment he hesitated and looked down at it. "The messenger brought this," he said, holding it out to her.

She looked at him, took the case, and lifted the lid carefully.

She caught her breath. Glittering on a tiny cushion of velvet was a round diamond. It was the most enormous, most uniformly yellow stone she had ever seen.

"It's canary yellow!" she whispered, holding it up in the sunlight. She stared at it incredulously. It must weigh thirty carats.

He seemed to read her mind. "Twenty-eight."

She shook her head adamantly. "Really, Nigel. I . . . I can't possibly accept this," she protested. "It's . . . it's far too valuable." Quickly she shoved it back in the case, snapped it shut, and pushed it into his hands.

He opened the case ceremoniously, fished the ring back out, and carefully slipped it on her finger. "Yes, it's very valuable," he said slowly. "It's been in my family for centuries. It's called the Somerset Sun."

"Yes, but—"

He placed a finger on her lips. "Let me try to explain. There are certain traditions in my family. The Somerset Sun happens to be one of them." He paused and then continued. "For three centuries now, it has graced the finger of every woman in line to be the Duchess of Farquharshire."

As if paralyzed, she stared at him.

Suddenly he threw his arms around her and gave a joyous laugh. The gold flecks in his brown eyes shone brightly. "Don't you see? Darling, I'm *proposing* to you! When I'm duke, you'll be my duchess!"

She dared not believe her ears. She had hungered to hear these very words for so long. They soared and sang and she could find no words to reply.

"I love you," Nigel said. "I've loved you ever since that night in Monte Carlo. I've loved you . . . Say yes, my darling!" His voice was anguished. "Please say yes. God knows, I don't deserve you. Not after letting you down the way I have. I know I've hurt you, but I promise I'll spend a lifetime making it up to you."

This time it was she who placed a finger on his lips. "Yes!" she whispered. "Oh, Nigel, *yes!*"

They embraced again. Her heart beat wildly against her chest. They would be together. Eternally together.

It seemed too good to be true.

6

The de Havilland Comet belonging to Somerset Holdings, Ltd., flew them from Paris to England. The interior of the jet was like a house. There were a living room, two bedrooms, a kitchen, and a bath.

"I've never seen anything like it," Hélène marveled as she boarded at Orly. The living room was subdued in its luxury, with thick carpeting, polished tables, and crimson-upholstered easy chairs, even a desk.

They drank champagne, and the chef served a superb lunch which they ate over the English Channel.

"It was delicious," Hélène told the chef when she had finished.

Then they moved to one of the curtained windows as the engines changed pitch and the jet started its descent. Nigel pointed out the sights. "As far as your eye can see, up to the horizon, is Farquharshire."

She stared out at the endless fields and forests and toylike villages. She glanced at him. "You mean your family owns it all?"

He grinned. "I'm afraid not. We do own a lot of property, though. Coal and zinc mines, textile mills, farms, dairies, real estate, electrical-machinery plants, six newspapers—"

"Six!"

He nodded. "Three in England, two in Australia, and one in New York."

"So *you're* in publishing too."

Then her smile faded. She gazed back out at the checkerboard fields, the precisely surveyed property boundaries marked with hairline walls, and the thin gray ribbons of roads that seemed to float past below them. So she knew even less about him than she had thought. She wondered at the trifling things she did know, the things she'd read about him and the things she'd learned while they'd been on the Skouri

609

yacht and during the past week they'd spent together. The thought suddenly crossed her mind that perhaps she should have waited awhile instead of accepting his proposal so quickly. After all, it was only by spending a lot of time together that people really got to know each other. And what did she know about him, anyway? That he was rich, that she loved him, that he was titled? A man like Nigel was very complex. Now she knew that it would take a lifetime to get to know him completely.

Yet he wasn't like any man she had ever met. He made her and everything around him seem to come alive. And he seemed to know so much about everything. Business, international politics, many languages, the arts. There wasn't a thing that seemed to baffle him. In a way, he overpowered her. But that was one of the things she loved about him. And yet she couldn't help feeling that perhaps she wasn't quite right for him. After all, she was a power within her own field. Perhaps a man like Nigel needed someone who had no responsibilities to anything except him. Who could be at his beck and call at any hour of the day or night. Someone dedicated to his political ambitions. A wife who had the time to entertain constantly and graciously, who could put people at ease, who could campaign for him, who knew just how to run the staggering array of residences he'd reeled off to her: Fallsworth in the autumn; the house in Mayfair when they were in London; Winthrow Abbey, the castle in Ireland, during spring; Craigmore, the lodge in Scotland; and on Mustique, the pink gingerbread house . . . Was she the kind of woman who could handle all that? Would she be a credit to him or an embarrassment?

These misgivings weighed heavily on her mind. After all, they had never even discussed how they would run both the Somerset businesses and Les Éditions Hélène Junot. Well, they had plenty of time to discuss that, she told herself. They weren't even married yet. No, not yet. But soon would be. And they would have to come to some decision regarding the businesses before then.

She glanced down at the Somerset Sun. It felt heavy and demanding, a prophecy of a thousand responsibilities that were to come. For the first time in many years she felt a real terror. Did all women who were about to be introduced to their future parents-in-law and yearned for their blessings— did they all feel this panic-stricken? Or was the fact that

Nigel's parents were the Duke and Duchess of Farquharshire, and she a commoner, only reinforcing her dread? Would the fact that she was a foreigner be a black mark against her?

Worst of all, she knew so little about the English aristocracy. She wondered if she was dressed right for the noble society she was about to mingle with. The classically demure Odile Joly suit, the high-necked silk blouse buttoned to the collar with a big bow under her chin, the wide-brimmed felt hat, and the low-heeled slippers—were they the right, understated look? She had called Luba in a panic, not trusting her own instincts for this important meeting.

"Look fashionably staid," the Czarina had specified. "And very, very modest. You know, don't you, that those kinds of people lead the most boring type of life?"

Hélène had followed Luba's instructions to the letter. Her only jewelry was gold earrings, a thin gold watch, and the Somerset Sun.

Nigel interrupted her gloomy thoughts. "We're almost there."

She turned to him and forced a smile.

"Are you nervous?"

She nodded.

"Don't be. They won't eat you alive, you know."

She wasn't so sure. The misgivings were brewing like somber dark storm clouds. She didn't know what would happen if for some reason the Somersets should reject her. She had already been through so much anguish during Nigel's long absence. How much pain would she feel if something went wrong now?

She scolded herself angrily: Get a hold on yourself!

But it was difficult. The last time she had felt this way was long ago at Hautecloque, when Hubert had proposed to her. She had felt a boundless social gulf then. Now she felt it again.

The jet made a smooth three-point landing on a long private airstrip. Hélène was surprised. She had expected that they would put down at some commercial airport.

As soon as the plane rolled to a halt, an old-fashioned boxy-looking Rolls-Royce pulled up alongside. "Good day, Master Nigel," the ancient chauffeur said, respectfully touching the visor of his cap.

"Good day, Stirling."

"Did you have a nice trip, sir?"

"Yes, thank you, Stirling."

Stirling looked at Hélène impassively. "Let me help you with that, mum."

She surrendered her cosmetics case.

As soon as their luggage was transferred, they were driven north on a winding country road to Fallsworth, the Somersets' ancestral home. It was a pleasant-enough drive, but the closer they got to Fallsworth, the more agitated Hélène became. Everything went past in a blur. The charming villages, the neat fields, the sudden forests. Everything looked civilized and well-tended.

"It's beautiful," she said.

"Not as beautiful as you, darling." Nigel took her hand. "Now, relax."

She was trying to.

Half an hour later they approached the gates of Fallsworth. The car came to a stop and they had to wait for the old gatekeeper to come out from the gatehouse. He bowed effusively and pushed the big iron gates open.

"That's Mackie," Nigel said. "He's a little slow, and although we'd gladly pension him, he loves his job. He's been in the family's service for over sixty years now, and he won't hear of retirement. That's why we don't mind waiting for him."

Hélène nodded. Hearing that, she felt a little better. At least the Duke and Duchess sounded human.

The Rolls began to move again. Hélène stared out at the tree-lined drive as they picked up speed. The road was asphalt and narrow, just wide enough for one car. The trees were big and ancient, with massive trunks and thick, powerful branches. It must look beautiful in the spring, she thought, when the leaves would be thick. Now they were all dried up, a layer of brown mulch raked high around the trunks.

"Here we are," Nigel said.

The road made a curve, they crested a hill, and the Silver Lady hood ornament dipped. Below them was Fallsworth. Any courage Hélène had left evaporated completely. Fallsworth was a sprawling stately home. By comparison, her own pitifully small château seemed to be nothing more than an inconsequential farmhouse. Fallsworth was big and elegant, but not haughty like Hautecloque. It seemed to belong

on the estate, imposing and solid, its buttery sandstone walls
fortified by powerful pilasters, its copper roofs green and
aged, its elegant windows tall and slim. Like a colossus the
house rose up from the formal gardens of clipped golden
yews, the temple-style pediment ornamented with the Somerset coat of arms.

"Do you like it?"

Hélène looked at Nigel. "It's . . . impressive," she said in
a shaky voice.

He shrugged. "A house is a house." Then, as if he could
read her mind, he quickly added, "I much prefer your
château."

She turned and stared doubtfully out at Fallsworth.

7

"Another cup of tea, my dear?"

Hélène looked at the thin, regal woman. The Duchess of
Farquharshire was the kind of dignified, flawless-skinned
woman the British aristocracy had been churning out for centuries. Other people in other countries changed with time, but
the upper-crust British had withstood the test of wars, disease,
and democracy. Hélène thought the Duchess would have
looked perfectly at home on the walls lined with ancestral
portraits. Someday hers would indeed hang there for poster-
ity, looking unsmilingly down at anyone who chanced to look
up into her hooded liquid brown eyes.

Fallsworth was the perfect setting for the Duchess. The
gilded, high-ceilinged rooms contrasted with the comfortable
no-nonsense floral slipcovers, the red-draped tables, and the
ancient carpets and turned what could have been a sterile,
palatial interior into understated luxury at its best.

"Please," Hélène said politely. "It's delicious tea." She
handed the Duchess her cup.

The Duchess nodded and with her small, smooth hands
picked up the sterling Georgian teapot. She smiled as she

handed the replenished cup back to Hélène. "I subscribe to *Les Modes*," she said, smiling. "I prefer it even to *Vogue*."

"You're very kind," Hélène said. She looked over at Nigel, who smiled encouragingly. Hélène had to stifle a laugh. Beside Nigel, the frail old Duke, seated in a big armchair, looked as if the cabbage-rose upholstery had swallowed him up. He was snoring gently.

"I think you should start an English version of *Les Modes* next," Nigel said. "After all, *Vogue* is here. And there's a ready market waiting."

The Duchess nodded. "That *is* a good idea," she said.

Hélène felt her hopes rising. Unconsciously her eyes strayed down to the Somerset Sun on her finger.

A quarter of an hour later, Nigel rose to his feet. He looked at his mother. "I'd like to show Hélène around before it gets dark."

The Duchess nodded. "Don't forget the aviary." She smiled at Hélène.

Hélène rose also. "I'll make sure that Nigel shows it to me. Thank you for the tea. It was lovely."

Nigel led her from the Green Salon through the quiet, lofty marble corridors to the front entrance. They passed the great Francesco Guardi paintings, which rivaled those in the world's greatest museums and made anyone who gazed upon them feel like an inconsequential midget. Hélène realized that Fallsworth housed collections worth fortunes. Not just the fortunes of one lifetime, but the accumulation of centuries.

Nigel looked at Hélène and smiled. "Well, they *didn't* eat you alive, did they?"

She shook her head. "They're very kind."

"But formal." He grinned goodnaturedly. "That's civilized British blood. In time you'll get used to it. Come."

He took her hand and gave her the grand tour of the gardens. In the back of the house, a wide gravel path split up the park. This path came to an end at a large oval fountain where glistening bronze figures frolicked under thin arcs of water. He showed her the topiary garden, where the trees and shrubbery had been clipped to look like figures, and then to the aviary. It was a long glass-roofed building, a series of wrought-iron pavilions linked by elaborate corridors alive with the shifting colors of rainbow plumage and the cries of exotic birds.

Hélène was very impressed. "Fallsworth is like a country in itself," she said when they finished the tour.

He laughed. "Not a country. City, maybe. You haven't seen a fraction of it yet. We have an indoor staff of thirty-nine servants and an outdoor staff of fifteen gardeners and twenty handymen. Let's see if I can remember everything correctly." He pretended to have to frown thoughtfully. "The house has almost eight thousand panes of glass, twenty-two bathrooms, three acres of copper on the roofs, seventy-nine clocks, all of which have to be wound—"

"You're joking!"

He shook his head. "I'm dead serious." And he told her the long, complex history of Fallsworth. The story was one of restlessness and constant achievements. It began in the early sixteenth century when Sir Arthur Somerset took over the estate which was to become the ancestral home of the Somersets. He began building a small Elizabethan manor, which was now consolidated into the far wing. His firstborn son was made Earl of Farquharshire in 1573. In 1693 the fifth Earl began rebuilding the house and sheathed it with a new exterior. His son became the first Duke. Slowly Fallsworth as it looked now began to take shape, each subsequent duke and duchess building onto the original house. Gardens were uprooted and planted anew, and whole forests were imported. Even the nearby riverbed was changed and a new channel built so that it passed by in front of the house. By the time the ninth Duke came along, all the various wings were consolidated into one solid classical building. Then came even more alterations, more great wings. Famous gardeners were called in, and the greatest architects of each century found work at Fallsworth.

But each duke and duchess did more than just add onto Fallsworth. If much care was taken with the exterior, then even more love went into the interior. The notable art collections were continuously added to and upgraded: Gainsboroughs, Bouchers, Fragonards, and Reynoldses; royal Savonnerie and Aubusson rugs; Meissen and Sèvres porcelains; Limoges enamels; Beauvais tapestries, fine French cabinets. All these treasures were cared for in the most befitting manner. Blinds shielded the rooms from the harsh sunlight. The canvases were regularly cleaned and restored. Daily, the precious porcelains received light dustings only. To date, not one single item had ever been broken.

Charlotte Somerset, the fourteenth Duchess, suffered ill health and had to spend winters in the South of France. During this time, each treasure was wrapped in made-to-measure chamois pouches and packed in specially constructed boxes and crates and stored. Each spring, when the Duchess returned from France, every item was unpacked again and put in its proper place. During World War II, Fallsworth had housed three hundred children so that they might avoid the bombs falling on London. The present Duke and Duchess saw to it that Charlotte Somerset's chamois pouches, boxes, and crates were again put to use. For the first time in nearly sixty years, the treasures were once again packed and stored in the vast cellars of Fallsworth. Not one item was damaged.

Hélène listened to the history with great interest, but she felt new misgivings. Clearly Fallsworth was not a home. It was a national treasure that required the full attention, love, and dedication of each duke and duchess.

"I've never seen Nigel look so happy," the Duke said. "She's a fine young lady." He lowered the newspaper he was reading. It was the royal edition of the *Times,* which, like the edition delivered to Buckingham Palace, was specially printed on rag paper.

The Duchess got to her feet and walked over to one of the windows. She held aside the heavy curtains. For a long time she stared out at the two people walking hand in hand toward the house. Then she turned around. Her eyes were veiled. "Yes," she said slowly. "She's a rather . . . remarkable young woman."

Dinner was held in the Private Dining Room. By now Hélène had been exposed to enough of Fallsworth not to be overly impressed by this room. The walls were paneled in white and the moldings were gilded. The heavy red curtains were velvet, the marble fireplace seven feet tall. There were antique Chinese screens and large paintings by Rubens. The stemware was Waterford, the cutlery heavy Georgian silver, the candelabra gold, the prominent centerpieces on the polished Georgian table two antique Ascot gold cups won by Somerset horses in the nineteenth century.

Hélène was glad when dinner was finally over. They retired to a salon for coffee, and after a suitable amount of time she and Nigel went for another walk. It was dark out, and she breathed deeply. The air was clean, rich country air, alive with the noise of the crickets and the humming insects of the night. When they came to a wrought-iron pavilion, they sat down on the stone garden bench inside it. For a while, they were both silent.

"You're not comfortable here," Nigel said finally.

Hélène pursed her lips thoughtfully as she looked across the lawn to the multitude of yellow windows. "It's not you, Nigel. It's Fallsworth. It's like . . ." She sighed. ". . . a museum."

"I agree with you."

"You do?" She looked at him in surprise. His face was dark, but she could feel the warmth of his eyes.

He nodded. "I wasn't planning for us to live here." He sought her hand and squeezed it. "I was thinking we'd get a house of our own in London. A place we both feel at home in. I've lived my entire life in museums. What I want now," he said emphatically, "is a home."

She smiled in relief. "You don't know how happy that makes me."

He hugged her and smiled. His teeth gleamed faintly from the lights in the distant house. "Darling, I want to marry *you*, not a curator."

She laughed. "I don't want a big house," she warned him. "I want something small and manageable—"

"Without servants crawling all over it—"

"And airy and modern. I mean, we're in the 1960's. I don't want to have to live like we're part of the last few centuries—"

"Indeed not. But it must be cozy—"

"Yes! With a nice garden—"

"Where we can raise our children."

She froze. Slowly she turned and stared numbly at the huge house—the house that demanded a continuous dynasty. A dynasty which her body could not provide.

She slipped her hand from his. "No, Nigel," she said flatly.

"What is it?" he asked. "I mean . . . did I say something wrong?"

Hélène closed her eyes. A fierce pain burned inside her. Her voice was a whisper. "Nigel, I don't know why I never told you. It's just that it didn't seem important." She gave a low laugh. "I was a fool. I thought it was us that mattered."

617

His voice was worried. "Of course it's us that matters. Darling, what on earth are you talking about?"

"Children."

"What about children?"

"I can never have any."

"I'm sorry, darling. I didn't know." He drew her toward him and held her in silence. Finally he spoke. "It doesn't matter," he said gently. "If we want children, we can adopt some. A whole brood, if you like."

"It's not right," she said heatedly, extricating herself from his arms. "Your family's endured for centuries. If you don't have children, you'll be the end of the line."

"And you think that's so important? Doesn't our love count for anything?"

"It counts," she said frowning. "I just don't think it would be fair! Not to your parents, not to your ancestors—"

"Why are you worried about my ancestors and my family?"

"Perhaps because the war claimed most of mine," she said quietly. "Maybe that's how I know having a family is so important. Why else would you work so hard to build and achieve, if it's not going to endure beyond your own lifetime?"

"And you?" he asked gently. "Why do you push yourself so hard if you can't leave your empire to anyone?"

A note of pride crept into her voice. "There *is* someone I can leave it to, Nigel. My niece. She's like my own daughter."

"And what's wrong if she's left Fallsworth also?"

Her voice was shaky. "Do you mean that, Nigel?"

"Of course I mean that, darling. If I can't have you . . ." His voice was filled with pain. "Then what's the point of going on living?"

She knew when he kissed her that he meant every word. And she had never known such happiness to exist.

It was late at night and Hélène stood at the window of her bedroom. She had switched the lights off, and the night outside was black as only a night in the country could be. She was filled with a sense of well-being. Ever since coming to Fallsworth, she had dreaded that something unexpected would tear to shreds what she and Nigel shared. Now she felt certain that that would not happen.

There was a discreet knock on the door. Nigel was coming to share her bed! She tried to keep the excitement out of her voice as she said, "Just a moment!"

Quickly she switched on one of the silk-shaded lamps, hurried over to the bed, and picked up her peignoir. She slipped into it and ran a hand through her hair. Joyfully she hurried to the door and swiftly pulled it open.

Standing in front of her was the Duchess of Farquharshire. Hélène's smile froze.

"I'm sorry to bother you, my dear," the Duchess said. She made an embarrassed gesture with her slender fingers. "May I come in? I was wondering if we might have a little talk."

Hélène stepped aside. "Please . . . come in."

The Duchess stepped inside and Hélène closed the door.

8

When Nigel awoke he flung aside the covers, jumped out of bed, and went over to the windows. He opened the holland blinds. The sunlight was already bright on the outside of the window frames.

Impulsively he flung the windows wide, letting the sunshine and chilly morning air wash over his bedroom in the East Wing. For once he was oblivious of the rule of shutting out the daylight from the valuables of Fallsworth. He wanted to revel in the sunshine. To let its life-giving brightness soak into his skin. Ever since the day before yesterday, when Hélène's eyes had shone as she had cried, "Yes! Oh, Nigel, *yes!*" he had been filled with the warm, satisfied glow of love. What he and Hélène shared was a treasure that surpassed anything at Fallsworth.

As Nigel was opening the windows in his bedroom, Hélène was staring out of another window. Twenty thousand feet above England, the BOAC Comet dipped its silver port wing and she could see the English coast far below. The distant breakers looked like a smooth line of motionless white along the beaches. Then the coastline slipped out of sight and all she could see was an uneven, monotonous gray. Once again she was flying over the English Channel.

She turned her face away as the morning sun glared into her eyes. There was a numbness in her body that made it feel heavy and lifeless.

"Would you like a drink, miss?" a voice asked.

Hélène looked up at the stewardess bending solicitously toward her. She shook her head and wearily turned away again. "No, thank you," she murmured. She tilted her head sideways to avoid the sun. She looked as if she was staring out at the bank of clouds they had headed into, but what she was seeing was her bedroom at Fallsworth and the Duchess of Farquharshire standing in front of her. She could see herself, too. Staring at the imperious woman with a sudden fear. "Please," she had said, "come in."

The Duchess inclined her head and entered. Her aristocratic eyes were veiled and heavily lidded.

Hélène closed the door. "Won't you sit down?"

The Duchess sat regally on one of the petit-point-upholstered chairs. With a feeling of dread, Hélène slowly took the seat opposite her. "What can I do for you?" she asked hesitantly. But she needn't have asked. Her intuition told her why the Duchess had come.

The Duchess looked at her for a lingering moment. Then she sighed and folded her smooth hands in her lap. For a moment she looked down at them and then back up at Hélène. "My son," she said carefully in her cultured voice, "has expressed the desire to marry you."

"Yes," Hélène said in a tight voice, "we love one another."

The Duchess smiled thinly. "That is an admirable sentiment. I'm sure you love him very much." She made an agitated gesture with her hands. "We Somersets are an old family. I'm sure you realize that."

Hélène didn't answer. She nodded cautiously and waited for the Duchess to continue.

Victoria Hollingsworth Somerset, the fifteenth Duchess of Farquharshire, had been named after a queen and born of an earl. From childhood she had been groomed to make a good marriage. She had not married the Duke as much for love as for the fact that his title was better than her own. That was reason enough for matrimony. One didn't go in search of love. That was for the lower classes. Although love had not been an integral part of her own marriage in the beginning, she was an excellent chatelaine for Fallsworth. Indeed, she now shared a sincere affection with the old Duke. She also genuinely liked Hélène Junot. She respected anyone who worked hard and achieved so much, and she did not like what she had to do now. But she was the guardian of Fallsworth and she knew her responsibilities. The Somerset name had to be guarded as jealously as any of the treasures in the great house. It had to be kept within the narrow confines of the aristocracy as it had been for centuries. Not once had the Somerset strain of the blood royal ever been diluted by a commoner. It was up to the Duchess to see that it did not happen now.

The Duchess inclined her head thoughtfully. "Tell me, my dear. Has my son discussed his future with you at all?"

Hélène kept her face impassive. *His* future. Not *their* future. The implication was clear. "I'm not quite sure what you're trying to get at."

The Duchess sighed. This was difficult enough without having to do battle. "Well, let me put it this way. My son has political ambitions."

"Yes," Hélène said carefully, fearing a trap somewhere.

"And I'm sure you realize that for a future duke, the correct wife is one of the most important assets in his life."

Hélène smelled the trap and adroitly sidestepped it. "Every man needs a woman he loves," she said. "A stable marriage is important under any circumstance."

"And would your marrying him be a sign of stability?"

Hélène frowned. "I'm not sure I understand."

"Then let me try to explain. Nigel's social position is secure." The Duchess paused. "At least for the time being. But, my dear . . . a wife like you?"

"You don't like the fact that I'm a businesswoman?" Hélène asked.

"It isn't that *I* don't like it," the Duchess said smoothly. "It's the public. The average Englishman, I'm afraid, is rather ordinary and set in his ways. A man running for election who has a wife who runs her own business . . . well, the people can't be expected to accept that. It's so . . . common." She rolled the word on her tongue as if it were something dirty. "Not that I personally have anything against it, you under-

stand. But the public looks up to us. They expect us to be
. . . noble."

Hélène's intuition had borne her out. "You don't want me
to marry Nigel," she said flatly.

The Duchess smiled sadly. "I want what's best for him,"
she said gently.

"And you think you know what that is?"

For a moment the Duchess did not speak. "I know what's
best for the family."

Hélène sat there white-faced and quiet. So her worst fears
had turned into stark reality. She wouldn't be welcome in the
Somerset fold. She was a commoner, a foreigner. Her eyes
fell to her hand. The Somerset Sun seemed to wink mockingly at her.

After a while the Duchess spoke again. "Don't you want
what's best for my son? If you love him—"

"I *do* love him!" Hélène said stubbornly.

There was another silence and the two women's eyes met.
Each one sized up the other. Finally the Duchess spoke
again. "Don't you want Nigel to have the future that is his
birthright?" she asked softly.

Hélène didn't reply.

The Duchess looked down at her lap. "Everything will
have been for nothing," she said. "Everything will be over before it even begins."

Hélène leaned forward. "Nigel will have a future!" she
said vehemently.

The Duchess shook her head. "Not with you, I'm afraid."

"I'll be a credit to him!"

The Duchess got to her feet. She looked down at Hélène.
"If you love him as much as you say you do, for God's sake,
let him go!"

Hélène stared at her. "I can't!"

The aristocratic eyes were hooded. "Then I'm afraid you
leave me no alternative. I cannot let this marriage take
place."

Hélène felt as if she was being smothered by an invisible
pillow. Suddenly the luxurious bedroom took on a new personality. The poppies on the turned-down sheets looked like
bloodstains and the sphinx heads on the Empire dressing
table seemed to smile carnivorously. "What . . . are you going to do?" she whispered haltingly.

"I shall have to consult our solicitors about that. But I can assure you of one thing. Nigel will not inherit a penny. Fallsworth will be forever closed to him."

"I have enough money," Hélène said defiantly. "We can live on that."

The Duchess smiled faintly. "Yes, but can Nigel live with the fact that he has been ostracized from his own family? That the doors to every noble house in Great Britain will be closed to him?"

"You wouldn't do that!" Hélène said sharply.

"I would. And eventually this love which you now share would be soured. The marriage would not have a chance of lasting." The Duchess laughed a thin, brittle laugh. "Do you think my son could conceive of living off his wife?"

Hélène looked defeated. Her face was pale and her lips were trembling. "What is it you want?"

"Leave him!" the Duchess implored. "He belongs in the aristocracy. Leave him among his own kind!"

Hélène rose with dignity. For a moment she looked down at her hand. Then she worked the Somerset Sun off her finger. She handed it to the Duchess. "I would not want to become a member of such an unloving family," she said in a quivering voice. "You are not worthy of your son. Please believe me when I say I much prefer being Hélène Junot to Hélène Somerset." She took a deep breath and fought to retain her composure. "If you'll be so kind as to send your chauffeur around, I'll have my bags packed within a few minutes."

"I'll telephone the airfield to have the airplane in readiness," the Duchess said.

This time it was Hélène who smiled thinly. "I think I'd prefer a commercial airliner," she said.

"As you wish." The Duchess looked down at her feet. "What should I tell Nigel?" she asked quietly.

Hélène looked at her, but she wouldn't meet her eyes. "The truth, perhaps?"

The Duchess was silent.

Hélène's laugh sounded like a hysterical cry. "I expect you would like me to write him a note and have *me* break off the engagement?"

"If it's not asking too much."

"It is," Hélène said, "but I love Nigel too much to make him hate you for the rest of his life." Her voice dropped to a whisper. "I'd much prefer for him to hate me."

9

As it had been so often in the past, Les Éditions Hélène Junot continued to be a barometer of Hélène's personal life. When she looked back at the progress of the company, its growth and achievements seemed to leap sporadically each time she suffered a personal crisis. Ironically, what was an enemy to Hélène turned out to be a friend to the company. Although she was never consciously aware of that fact until the crisis was behind her, she worked herself mercilessly during those times, building and expanding and pushing all those around her to a level of achievement that was almost superhuman. Now that she knew she could never share Nigel's name and love, she banished him completely from her life. She refused his calls and returned his letters unopened. Once he even arrived unexpectedly at the Place Vendôme office, refusing to leave until he could at least see her. Warned by her secretary, Hélène slipped quietly out the back way, fleeing down the stairs to the delivery entrance. She could fight many things, she thought bitterly as she flagged a taxi, but not the loss of Nigel's birthright. If she became responsible for that, she knew that she would never be able to live with herself.

This crisis continued for six months. As time passed, Nigel's letters and calls got fewer and fewer, until they stopped coming completely. And then, just as she was starting to recover, the crisis peaked. She was leafing through a copy of *Paris Match* one evening when she suddenly froze. The title of the article was "A Society Wedding." And the color photo showed a young bride named Lady Pamela Grey leaning against the groom's shoulder. The groom was Nigel, and in the background loomed the unmistakable glorious elegance that was Fallsworth.

Hélène knew from the terrible pain she felt that she still loved Nigel. That for her the feelings they had shared were not over. Would never be. It was impossible simply to shut

Nigel from her life and then expect the feelings to vanish, too.

She stared at the picture for a long time. She tried to console herself with the fact that at least now Nigel would no longer be trying to get to her. But this was a defensive reaction, and she knew it. He hadn't even tried to get in touch with her for over two months now. She had wanted Nigel to find out by himself why she had cut him off so suddenly. She had hoped he would somehow manage to straighten things out. But these wedding pictures were irrefutable proof that it was too late. That everything they had shared, everything she had hoped so desperately for, was over. She was no longer even left with hope. It was clear that she was no longer a part of Nigel's life. Lady Pamela was.

Hélène narrowed her eyes as she inspected Lady Pamela's picture closely. Lady Pamela was not a beauty by any standards, although she was pretty enough in a quiet, wholesome way. The first thing Hélène noticed about her was her skin. It was flawless pink English skin. She had blond hair, conservatively coiffed under the Belgian-lace bridal veil, large dark eyes, and a ready smile. Her wedding dress matched the veil and came to a puritanically high collar. She wore no jewelry except for the ring on her finger. Her hand was casually but intentionally poised against her collarbone so that the Somerset Sun was shown to its fullest advantage.

Hélène felt physically ill. The Somerset Sun, which had graced her very own finger, and which was to announce to the world that she would become the sixteenth Duchess of Farquharshire. And beside the bride, cutting a handsome figure in his black tuxedo, Nigel seemed tall and stoic, looking expressionlessly into the camera.

He's staring at me, Hélène thought, catching her breath. She could almost feel the heat of his eyes, the warmth of his breath. She was pleased about one thing only. Nigel, who was supposed to be the happy groom, was not smiling on this, his wedding day. She couldn't help wondering if he were unhappy. If the Duchess hadn't arranged everything.

What a silly thought! she told herself. Of course she had. She had chased Hélène from Fallsworth and Nigel. That was arrangement enough.

In an uncharacteristic rage, Hélène suddenly ripped the page out of the magazine. Her fingers were shaking as she tore it into tiny shreds, letting the pieces flutter down to the floor. She looked down at them, her breasts heaving, and she could see one of Nigel's familiar eyes gazing up at her. She kicked at the scrap of paper until it turned over.

This time, the pain was so intense that she plunged into her work with a vengeance so fierce that all her other work binges paled by comparison. And while she herself looked unchanged, Les Édition Hélène Junot was reflecting the effects.

There was no stopping her now.

Les Éditions Hélène Junot began growing like a mushroom after a rainfall. Between Paris and Milan, the staff numbered close to two hundred. The Place Vendôme headquarters was expanded. The building next door had become vacant, and Hélène readily signed a twelve-year lease. Soon even that additional space was not enough and she had to rent yet another building on the nearby rue des Capucines. The building in which she had started her empire now housed only the administrative offices—the accounting department, the advertising offices, the circulation managers, and the legal section. The connecting building housed the creative staff— the various editors and writers and the art director and his artists. The photography studio, with its sets and darkrooms, was moved to the rue des Capucines. It was like a small film-production studio and boasted the latest in photographic equipment. It was no longer necessary to send photographers and models to a tropical beach or to the mountains. Everything but the most important layouts could be shot right in the studio. The sets were constructed in the workshop in the back of the building.

The Paris office and showroom of Marcello d'Itri were on the rue Cambon. Hélène was pleased that everything was within a few minutes' walking distance, but she was waiting for another space on the Place Vendôme to become available. She wanted to have the d'Itri office and showroom conveniently next door to Les Éditions Hélène Junot. Especially now that she lived in a suite in the Hotel Ritz, just across the square. Living at the Ritz provided her not only with unsurpassed luxury but also with the added convenience of hotel services. This way she could dedicate every waking hour to her work.

Hélène Junot was big business.

More magazines had been added to *Les Modes* and *La*

Moda. The roster now included *Les Modes Homme,* the definitive men's fashion magazine, and *Beauté,* a smaller version of *Les Modes* that was geared to younger women. *Beauté* was filled with makeup and fashion tips and with more ready-to-wear than haute couture. It was for women on a budget and it outsold even *Les Modes. Les Modes,* however, remained the top of the line. It gave the empire its prestige.

The progress was not confined to Paris. In Milan, *La Moda* gave birth to *La Moda Uomo,* the Italian equivalent of *Les Modes Homme.*

In June 1963 Edmond joined the Paris staff as a full-fledged corporate lawyer. For nine months Hélène had him do nothing but learn the ropes. When she thought he was ready, she promptly moved him up in the legal staff. In a few years he would be in charge of the empire's entire legal department. He was learning fast and becoming an expert at delegating authority. What he lacked in experience he more than made up for in intelligence and dedication.

Luba, too, was promoted. Officially, she became vice-president of Les Éditions Hélène Junot, S.A. Unofficially she also became vice-president of Marcello d'Itri, but this particular position was kept very quiet so that there would be no visible connection between the ateliers and the magazines. Hélène was afraid that if the readers put two and two together, it might stir up a conflict of interest in their minds. Although *Les Modes*'s and *La Moda*'s backing of the ateliers had been responsible for their success, for practical purposes it was important to make it appear that the magazines were unbiased and owed no allegiances.

Hélène was gratified that the ateliers in Milan, Rome, and Paris were thriving so soundly.

She had conquered France and Italy. But still she was not satisfied. If anything, she was more restless than ever. Deep inside, her craving for Nigel was raging out of control. She barely managed to keep her emotions in check by ever increasing her workload. Determinedly she saw to it that Petite Hélène's grooming followed her careful planning to the letter. Even more doggedly she plotted the course her magazines and ateliers would take. There was still one place she had to conquer in order to prove her magazines' prowess. Once you had made it there, you'd made it everywhere.

Paris and Milan were not enough. She liked the battle for

success far more than the success itself. She knew where her fashion tentacles had to reach next.

New York.

10

New York in the 1960's was a tough place to crack. The city beat with the very pulse of fashion. Odile Joly's prediction of many years earlier had become reality. *Women's Wear Daily* was now the Bible not only of Seventh Avenue but also of much of the international fashion world. Bitchy, gossipy, and all-powerful, *WWD* was read as much for its snide comments as for its fashion news. The paper had come a long way since 1954 when John Fairchild, in charge of the Paris bureau, found himself in a humiliating rear seat during the couturiers' showings.

No less powerful was *Vogue*. After twenty-seven years at *Harper's Bazaar*, Diana Vreeland moved over to the competition and reigned from *Vogue*'s lofty throne like a Wise Lady scattering crumbs of chic to a drab populace. It was Diana Vreeland who sent her photographers into the desert to shoot models wrapped in nothing but clear plastic. Everything that had never been done before was being done by Diana Vreeland. She became a thorn in both Hélène's and Luba's sides. It seemed that "the Empress," as the indefatigable Mrs. Vreeland was deferentially nicknamed, had a limitless imagination. For once, even the Czarina had met her match. For the eight years that Diana Vreeland would be at *Vogue*, American *Les Modes* and *Vogue* would run neck and neck in a constant race. This friendly running battle between the Czarina and the Empress brought about some of the most dramatic and creative concepts in fashion photography and reporting the world was ever to see.

Hélène was fascinated by New York. She knew better than anyone how a camera could be used to overdramatize anything, so she was ready to meet the challenge of the spectacular skyline that rose into the sky as the SS *United States* steamed into New York harbor. But she had not been prepared for what had happened on board the ship. She took it as an omen that New York would become *her* city. For during the transatlantic crossing, she fell in love. For the first time, she had met a man who was not overshadowed by the image of Nigel Somerset.

His name was Siegfried Bavier and he didn't look like a night in shining armor. In fact, he was everything that Nigel was not, and perhaps that was what attracted her to him in the first place. From the start, she knew that he was married because he came right out and told her. He didn't try to hide things. He was as shrewd and toughly honest with himself as she was.

They met in the cocktail lounge during one of the fiercest storms at sea the liner had ever encountered. Ninety-five-foot waves were crashing over the bow, and had she or Siegfried been afflicted with weak stomachs, chances were they never would have met. As it was, they had been the only people in the first-class lounge. At first, she had been the only one. She was seated at one of the little tables, holding on to her glass so that it wouldn't slide off and crash to the floor. Oddly, she had been aware that he was behind her even before he spoke.

She turned around slowly and looked up at him. Their eyes met. His shoulders were wide and he was powerfully built. He held a drink in his hand. His dark hair was cropped short and he looked more like a stevedore or a prizefighter than a first-class passenger. She sensed that he was ill-at-ease in his dinner suit. But there was a look in his piercing blue eyes that she recognized instantly, that drew her to him like a magnet. It was the confident look of success, and he wore it better than he wore his clothes.

"Can I buy you a drink?" he asked in English. He had a surprisingly deep, resonant voice.

"No, thank you," she said. She smiled and showed him her glass. "I have one."

"Mind if I join you? Company is kind of scarce tonight. Everyone seems to have disappeared."

"Not at all," she answered quickly. "Please . . ." She gestured to the banquette at the other side of the table. As he slipped into it, the liner suddenly listed to starboard and the deck sloped precariously. The man was caught off guard. For a moment he teetered almost drunkenly and then was unceremoniously thrown onto the banquette. Under the impact, the bourbon shot out from his glass.

Hélène burst out laughing. Then she saw his scowl and covered her lips with her fingers. She forced herself to look serious. "I'm sorry," she said contritely, removing her hand from her lips. She looked suddenly concerned. "You didn't hurt yourself, did you?"

He shook his head. "Only my pride's wounded." He looked darkly into his glass. "Hell of a waste of good bourbon, though." Then he noticed the bodice of her dress. A dark stain was spreading slowly across it. "I'm terribly sorry," he apologized embarrassedly. "It seems I've ruined your dress."

She glanced down at herself and then looked back across the table at him. "The cleaner's will get it out," she said confidently.

"You're sure?"

She nodded. "I'm sure."

She studied him more closely. He looked no more than forty years old, she thought, and there was something about him that was incredibly vibrant. He seemed more alive than many men half his age. She felt a strange and powerful feeling well up inside her. It was a feeling that had been dormant for far too long.

She watched as he settled comfortably on the banquette and took a cigar from the inside pocket of his jacket. He struck a match, carefully held it to the end of the cigar, and inhaled deeply several times. Finally he waved the match out. He leaned sideways so he could see past Hélène and signaled to get the bartender's attention. "Another bourbon!" he called out. He leaned toward Hélène. "You're positive I can't buy you a drink?"

She shook her head. "I'm positive, thank you. I've had two of these already."

He frowned at her glass. "Vodka?"

She laughed and shook her head. "Club soda."

He grimaced. "Don't see how you can drink that stuff. It gives me gas." He grinned, showing strong, even white teeth. "By the way, my name's Siegfried Bavier," he said easily. "My friends call me Sigi."

She flushed. Over the years she had met quite a few Americans, but she had yet to become accustomed to their easy familiarity. As soon as they met you, they insisted on being on a first-name basis. Europeans weren't like that at all.

"How do you do?" she said. "I'm Hélène Junot." She paused and added with an embarrassed smile: "My friends call me Hélène."

The bartender came over with the bourbon. Bavier signaled him to wait. He downed the drink in one swallow and handed the empty glass back. He laughed when he saw the intrigued look on Hélène's face. "Best cure in the world for seasickness," he explained.

"Is it?"

"Sure. When you drink too much, everything reels around you, right?"

She nodded doubtfully.

"Well, the way I figure it is this. Once you're good and drunk, everything's topsy-turvy anyway, so how are you going to notice the motions of the ship on top of it?"

She laughed. "You have made your point . . . Sigi." She looked at him closely. "But don't you like to feel the sea?" she asked. "The power of the wind and water?"

"Sure, I like it. I'm a born sailor. I sailed around the world alone on a forty-foot sailboat a few years back. Even hit a bad typhoon in Micronesia. Nothing like this . . ." He made a condescending gesture. "This is nothing compared to that. The waves must have been a hundred and twenty feet high and the sky was a solid black wall of water."

Hélène shivered. "Weren't you frightened?"

He made a face and was tempted to brag, but when he saw her serious expression, he decided against it. "To tell you the truth, Hélène"— he grinned sheepishly—"it scared the living shit out of me."

And that broke any ice that was left between them. Suddenly she felt completely relaxed in his presence, even on a first-name basis. His language was salty, to be sure, but to her knowledge, most Americans were crude. They lacked the cultured refinement and breeding of the Europeans. Yet there was something about Bavier which attracted her to him in spite of that. Perhaps it was that he had an almost French joie de vivre, which, coupled with his confident bearing, clinched her feelings toward him. He was honest and good-natured, yet there was something untamed about him. She felt secure in his company.

It was then that she saw the flash of gold on his finger.

"Your wife isn't weathering this storm well?" she asked.

His face went suddenly sad as he glanced down at his wedding band. He had been in Europe for more than a month and he realized now that he hadn't once thought of her.

Hélène dropped her eyes. Her own question had caught her by surprise. She had never asked a strange man about his wife before. "I'm sorry," she said softly. "I had no right to ask."

"Of course you did." His face creased into a warm smile. "When a strange man comes up to you and invites himself to join you, you have every right."

She smiled gratefully.

"My wife is in New York," he said quietly. He looked down at the ring and twisted it around on his finger. "I'm afraid we don't get along well."

"Oh. I'm sorry."

He smiled weakly. "Sometimes it just takes a while to find out that you're not suited to each other. It took us a few years. At first, I used to think it was all my fault. That I wasn't giving her enough of myself. Then I used to blame her." He shook his head slowly. "I've gotten wiser now. When a marriage doesn't work, you can't lay the blame on either of you. It's both your faults or neither of you is to blame. It took me a long time to realize that." He looked at her and smiled sadly. "What about you?"

Hélène shrugged her shoulders expressively. "I'm widowed. Then I was engaged again, but it turned out his family didn't like me."

The truth was, the Duchess had been downright hostile. But it was close enough. What had transpired at Fallsworth was her own business, and no one else's.

"His family are fools, then," Bavier said. "Didn't he at least put up a fight?"

It was her turn to sigh.

He shook his head. "He must be a fool too. I can't see any man not fighting for you."

She was suddenly angry at him. He hadn't said anything nasty, but she resented his attitude all the same. For some strange reason, she felt compelled to come to Nigel's defense. Her voice went cold as she said, "It wasn't his fault. I didn't give him half a chance. You see, it was I who broke it off."

He looked at her curiously. "But you still love him."

632

"It's over," she said sharply. Then her voice fell. "Besides, he married someone else." She gave a sad little smile. "So you see, it really is over."

He nodded. "I didn't mean to pry."

"That's all right."

"Good. Let's change the subject. What's bringing you to New York?"

"Business."

"Which do you do? Act? Model?"

"Neither." She laughed and toyed with her glass. "Whatever gave you those ideas?"

"You're beautiful. I thought most beautiful women were either actresses or models."

She glanced up at him, her eyes serious. "I'm a magazine publisher."

He looked at her with deepening respect. "Have I seen your magazines around?"

She smiled. "I don't know. They're mostly women's magazines. *Les Modes* and *La Moda*."

"Hey!" He grinned. "They're fashion magazines."

She nodded. "How did you know?"

"My wife always buys *Les Modes*," he explained. "In fact, she swears by it. But she always curses because she can only get it at Hotaling's on Times Square."

"That's going to change soon," Hélène said. "I'm setting up an American edition, and seeing to it that the European editions get better distribution outlets in the major cities across the United States."

He nodded approvingly. "You'll do well in New York."

"I hope so. It will be a challenge."

He shook his head knowingly. "Not for you. I have good instincts about people. You'll turn the city inside out in no time." He glanced at his cigar appreciatively. "You're a fighter."

She could feel her face flushing. "And you?"

"I'm a fighter too," he said. "It takes one to know one."

She looked at him and laughed. She saw the solemnity in his blue eyes.

"I'd like to see more of you when you're settled in New York," he said quietly.

"I would like that too," she said quietly.

She looked at him and then rose unsteadily to her feet. He

got up also. The deck lurched and she suddenly found herself in his arms.

"I've got you," he said, holding her gently.

A warmth seemed to seep from her insides as she looked into his eyes. They were bright and intense, filled with an ocean of promises.

"I think I know a good way to weather this storm," he said softly.

Hélène sank into the pale blue quilted satin spread. She rolled on her side and then settled on her back, feeling the sleek, sensual fabric beneath her. The cabin was lit by the glow coming from the sitting room and a single dim bedside lamp. The big square windows looked out onto the promenade deck. Chances were that nobody ventured out on deck in this weather, but the curtains were nevertheless drawn, ensuring full privacy and somewhat muting the lashings of the rain and the sea.

She could hear Siegfried's movements in the sitting room. There was a click as the light went out, and finally the whisper of his feet moving across the carpet. Slowly he entered, pulling the bedroom door shut behind him.

Hélène was stretched full length on the bed, the light casting shadows across the firm contours of her body. She had let her hair fall free from the chignon. It hung down her back, and would have seemed to be a single sheet of black silk in the dim light if it hadn't been for the one renegade tendril that caught on her breast.

He hesitated momentarily at the sight, and then moved toward her, unable to see her eyes until he stood a foot away. She raised her head and stared up at him, meeting his gaze. Her violet eyes moved down his tanned, muscular body. His chest was covered with small spirals of dark hair, his hips flat and narrow. From the thicket of hair at his groin, his penis pushed out, the veins sculptured in bold relief.

She reached out and took his hand, guiding it toward one of her breasts. Closing her eyes, she felt his gentle fingers kneading one nipple and his moist tongue flicking against the other. His free hand began slowly to stroke her perfumed flesh, gradually increasing momentum as it moved down to her navel and then found its way to her clitoris, one finger probing its wet, radiating warmth.

Hélène began to shudder as the pleasure began culminating toward pain. Just as she thought his stroking would overwhelm her, he stopped and moved over her. Straddling her gently, he pressed his lean hips down against hers. Her arms reached up, encircling his neck, and drew him fiercely downward. Siegfried's face was an inch from hers when suddenly he halted, and in that one silent moment Hélène's world stopped. Urgently her eyes flicked up to meet his, and there she saw a stare so determined, yet at the same time so unreadable. There was something fearful in the intense power she saw in those features, something that seemed to have gathered force like a dam ready to burst.

His face never moved, but she could feel his hips slowly, steadily lifting from hers. Up they rose until they stopped, seeming to hover, ready, yet hesitant. And then he drove down hard, plunging through her slick, wet walls. Hélène's body arched with the impact, as he reached her deepest recesses in that one, long-awaited drive. He then pulled away from her and began to quickly enter and withdraw, enter and withdraw in shallow, rapid thrusts.

She writhed beneath him, her legs firmly clasped around his waist, while her head moved back and forth. Hélène felt his pace slow, as if he feared he would hurt her.

"Don't slow down! Please . . ." she whispered, anxiety betraying her.

"Sssssssh."

He pulled out gradually, and in a panic she felt he was abandoning her. But then he slowly entered her again, and the joys of relief and pure physical sensation brought breathless sounds from her. Over and over he repeated the maneuver, sometimes quickening his thrusts, then easing them. Hélène's body shuddered as she climaxed again and again, each orgasm rushing over her until he, too, finally cried out, slapping into her with all his force, bringing her to still another orgasm. Siegfried came, his muscles quivering with the release of vibrant liquid energy.

She lay back as his body collapsed against her, the still-muted sea now a comforting wash of sound in the air.

Siegfried Bavier and Hélène had many things in common, but of all their shared qualities there was one which stood out above the others. Their beginnings. Both of them had begun life penniless and worked their way up from the depths of poverty and despair. As a result, each recognized and respected the restless hunger which drove the other. In Bavier, Hélène saw a mind that was a mirror image of her own. He was cunning and ambitious and enjoyed his wealth and status. Yet it hadn't gone to his head. On the contrary, during his climb to success and power he had never lost touch with his simple beginnings. He liked the whole process of making money—the work and the struggle and the skill he had to employ in order to get it. There was no reason for him to continue working. Years ago, he could easily have retired in splendor for the rest of his life. But he kept adding to his riches. Mainly because he enjoyed exercising the skill and the gambling it involved. Had he possessed a different, less creative mind, Bavier might have spent his life playing cards or gambling on horses or numbers. But he recognized these as children's games. To him, the gambles that went on daily in big business were the Big Leagues. And the winning wasn't nearly as important as the Game. He was a gambler like no others. Forty-one years old, he had been a millionaire three times, and twice in between he had gone bankrupt.

"A man who can make a fortune once, lose it all, and make it all over again from scratch has nothing to worry about," he was once quoted as saying. "If success isn't a fluke, it can be repeated a hundred times over."

And he proved it. Each time he lost a fortune, he not only regained it but also ended up with more than he had before. When Hélène met him, he was worth in the vicinity of twenty-two million dollars, was playing the stock market and investing heavily in futures and commodities. Wisely enough, he kept five million tied up in tax-free municipal bonds. The rest he used to play with.

His financial ups and downs had their roots during the war, when he had been an eighteen-year-old infantryman marching from France deep into Germany. By the time he was shipped stateside he was in one of the last waves of returning GI's. The first waves had gotten the heroes' welcomes and the ticker-tape parades. Victory had then been fresh in people's minds. But by the time he got back, there were no more parades. There were no more heroes' welcomes. There was a housing shortage and all the jobs were taken. Giancarlo Iacono, his old employer in Brooklyn, had slapped him on the back before he had been shipped off to Europe. "Just remember, Sigi-boy, you a got friends here," Iacono had promised expansively. "Your job will be a waiting for you when you a get back."

But when Bavier got back, his job was held by one of Iacono's many nephews, and his girl had married someone else. His future had never looked bleaker. When he had boarded the Liberty Ship in France, he had been ready to grab the future by the balls. He had had twenty thousand dollars tucked inside his boots. By the time he got off the ship at the Brooklyn Naval Yard, he was dead broke.

For as long as he lived, Bavier would never forget the hellish march through Germany. Day after day, he and the other GI's in his platoon were met by the same ugly sights, smells, and sounds. Nothing but death, destruction, misery, hunger, and despair. As the march progressed, Bavier had watched as half his platoon was steadily decimated, either shot to pieces or blown up by land mines or falling bombs. Somehow, almost through sheer willpower, he managed to survive. He did his duty to the best of his ability, and tried to blot out all the ugliness. But that was difficult. For the GI's, there was no such thing as even a semblance of normalcy, even for a few hours. And no recreation of any sort. There was only the promise of more fighting, the constant specter of death, tasteless cold rations, and perhaps a little much-needed sleep. But never enough. It was hard to sleep when bombs were falling all around you.

Bavier recognized the need for recreation better than anyone else, perhaps because he himself needed it so badly. More important, he recognized this as an *opportunity*.

It did not take long for him to begin the recreational program. When a pimply young boy from Idaho was shot down beside him, he lifted the deck of cards the boy carried and pocketed it. He traded his cigarettes and rations for more decks of cards. Soon he was the only person within miles who had them. Then he made a small portable roulette wheel out of junk he stumbled across. At first everyone laughed at him, but he knew that they would come around. And he was right. In the wet foxholes and the icy, windblown tents, the card games and gambling parties he organized became so popular that he had them solidly booked for a week in advance. The "recreation" was, in fact, a traveling casino, and one of the best-kept secrets in the division.

Bavier was well aware that in gambling you had to make sure people paid their debts. He couldn't let anyone slide by owing him. Especially not if the debtor could be blown to bits that very night. So before he even started the enterprise, he got together with Hector Carras, a husky fellow soldier who also hailed from Brooklyn and who, before he was inducted, used to be a minor collector for the notorious Zanmatti family. Together, splitting the proceeds fifty-fifty, Bavier and Carras had the games in the division organized to an astonishingly sophisticated degree. By the time his tour of duty was over, Bavier's share of the loot amounted to over twenty thousand dollars, which he kept carefully stashed in a plastic bag tucked safely inside his boots.

When the war was over, Bavier and Carras found themselves steaming back to New York on the same troop ship. The passengers were a restless, impatient mass of GI's. The ship was cramped and everyone was anxious to get home; the trip would take nearly a week and a half. Everyone was boasting about the women who were waiting. And as the men lay in their swinging hammocks in the dark, the sounds of their restless hands and the moans of their self-induced orgasms filled the nights.

Once again Bavier recognized the opportunity for organizing some lucrative recreation. After all, the men had nothing but daydreams to occupy themselves. Together he and Carras came up with the idea for making one last killing.

There was a big GI aboard named Luis Gonzales who kept bragging how he had been a professional prizefighter before he was inducted. Carras, too, had fought quite a few rounds professionally before he joined up with the Zanmattis. He and Bavier approached Gonzales. The ex-prizefighter agreed to a match. Then they talked to the platoon sergeant, who in turn went to see the company commander, who welcomed the fight as a way to entertain the bored men. There was only one hitch. The company commander was adamant about allowing no betting.

That didn't deter Carras or Bavier. They simply did it quietly and in a roundabout way. They bought the services of four privates, and it was they who went around making book. Betting was rampant and everyone went at it feverishly. Bavier decided to bet his entire twenty thousand dollars on Carras. It was a gamble, but if Carras won . . .

The fight was held on deck and lasted more than an hour. In the last round, Carras knocked Gonzales unconscious. Carras came out of the fight with a broken nose, some minor contusions, and forty thousand dollars on top of his twenty. Bavier also came out with sixty thousand. As was his habit, he kept his money hidden in his boots, each bill carefully marked in the right-hand corner with a tiny inverted B. He slept with his boots and socks on and took every precaution safeguarding his loot. When he had to shower, he had Carras watch over it. If Carras was on duty elsewhere on the ship, Bavier hid the money in the air duct. That was where he had hidden it when, two nights from New York, he returned from showering only to find his money missing. And Gonzales, who hadn't had a penny to his name after losing the fight, was sitting in the smoke-filled hold playing cards and betting heavily with hundreds of dollars. Bavier recognized the money instantly. It was his. His unmistakable trademark was scrawled on the corner of each bill.

The men sitting around watching the game fell suddenly silent. It was as if a gust of danger had blown through the hold, and everyone was aware of it.

Bavier grabbed Gonzales roughly by the collar and yanked him to his feet. "You stole my dough," he accused belligerently, spinning the bigger man around. "I want it back."

Gonzales looked down at him, his black eyes flashing. "I didn't steal nothing. I won it." He pushed Bavier away, turned around, and casually sat back down.

Stubbornly Bavier stayed put. He was filled with a murderous rage. Gonzales was the thief. The marked bills proved that. And he wasn't about to let him get away with it. It had taken him two years to get the sixty thousand together, and he wasn't going to let anyone walk away with it now.

He clenched his fists, and when he spoke again, his voice trembled with rage. "Come on, you thieving spic," he challenged, raising his voice a little louder. "I aim to get my dough back."

The others stared at Bavier. Slowly they shuffled to their feet and drew silently back in a circle.

Only Gonzales didn't move. He didn't even bother turning around. "I would watch who I called a spic if I was you," he warned softly.

Bavier's eyes bore into the prizefighter's back. Then he suddenly threw himself at him. Both men went crashing to the floor, rolling over and over.

The other men drew back even farther, giving the two room to fight. Normally Gonzales would have had the advantage. He was by far the bigger man, and much more experienced as a fighter. But he was caught off guard and he was still weakened from the punches he'd taken in the fight with Carras two days ago. Bavier caught him around the throat, dug his hands into the flesh, and watched his swarthy face go purple.

"Where is it?" he screamed. He clamped his fingers even tighter and shook Gonzales by the neck so that the back of his head kept banging on the steel decking. "God damn you! Where's my dough?"

At first Gonzales tried to push Bavier's face away with his hands. Then he attempted to rake his fingers across Bavier's eyes. Bavier saw what was happening and instinctively averted his face. Finally the big man felt himself weakening. In a desperate, last-ditch attempt to free himself, he tried to tear Bavier's hand loose, but to no avail. Bavier's hands were as steely as vise grips. All of his overwhelming rage was behind the choking hold.

Gonzales' frightened eyes flashed as he gasped uselessly for air, his throat making harsh noises.

Suddenly Bavier felt a pair of powerful arms around him, pulling him off Gonzales. He spun around angrily. It was Hector Carras.

Bavier's lungs were burning from the exertion of the fight and he swallowed huge mouthfuls of air. "What in hell did you go and do that for?" he demanded in a surly voice. He pointed a trembling finger at Gonzales. "That son-of-a-bitch spic stoled my dough."

Carras looked at Bavier calmly and slapped him affectionately on the arm. "Cool it," he said quietly. "The CO's on his way down here. Let's split."

The other men heard it and studiously began busying themselves as if nothing had happened. Bavier glared at Gonzales, who was still sprawled on the floor. He was trying to sit up, his hands tenderly touching his swollen neck. He looked up at Bavier.

"I'm gonna kill you, you yellow-bellied thief," Bavier spat from between his teeth.

"Shut up," Carras said sharply. He pushed Bavier ahead of him through the watertight bulkhead door. "Let's get outta here before we find ourselves in hot water."

Reluctantly Bavier allowed himself to be led away. "I'll kill that son of a bitch if it's the last thing I do," he threatened.

" 'Tenshun!" Carras barked.

Both he and Bavier snapped smartly to attention and saluted as the company commander walked past. The CO returned the salute negligibly and continued walking.

Carras relaxed when they were out of earshot. He pulled Bavier into a corner. "Listen, you dumb-fuck," he hissed angrily. "Don't ever go around spouting your mouth off like that. It ain't healthy, you know? If you want to do something, just go ahead and do it. But quietly. The way things stand now, if something happened to the guy tonight, you'd be the leading suspect."

Bavier stared at Carras. His friend was right. And smart, too. It was "CYA" all over again. That was how the army was run. By making sure you Covered Your Ass. Well, in the future he'd be wiser.

But it turned out that his resolution didn't help much for the time being. The guard-duty roster put Gonzales up on deck for the night shift. When his relief came, he wasn't at his station. Nor did he show up for roll call in the morning. The entire ship was turned inside out, but there was neither hide nor hair to be found of him. The lifeboats and life preservers were counted, but none of them was missing. The dreaded alarm was sounded throughout the ship: Man Overboard! The captain promptly turned the ship around and steamed back in the direction from which they had come. He put the vessel into a pattern of ever-narrowing concentric circles. The sea was searched for four days, and a searchlight played upon the black waters for four nights, but not a trace was found of Luis Gonzales.

Bavier looked upon these four extra days as a blessing. It gave him the opportunity to search everywhere he could think of for his money. A ship of this size had a million crannies where you could hide things. If you didn't know where to start looking, chances were you'd never find it. Sixty thousand dollars can be rolled into a small bundle. And to make matters even worse, the company commander got wind of the fight between him and Gonzales and his threat to kill him. The CO decided to investigate the incident. Luckily for Bavier, it fizzled out almost before it began. He had never been out of sight that fateful night, and he was cleared of any suspicion of wrongdoing. He breathed a sigh of relief. Military justice wasn't at all like civilian justice. You weren't automatically considered innocent until proved guilty. He should have been pleased by the outcome, but he wasn't. By the time the ship docked at the Brooklyn Naval Yard, he still hadn't found his money.

Service friendships aren't long-lasting. When a tour of duty is over, everyone goes his own way. Bavier and Carras said their good-byes and made the usual well-meant promises to look each other up. Both men knew they wouldn't. And unknown to Bavier, Carras got off the ship with a hundred and twenty thousand dollars in his pocket and blood on his hands. No one had even suspected him, least of all Siegfried Bavier. While Carras got himself a suite in the Waldorf-Astoria and renewed his contacts with the Zanmattis, Bavier was wearing out his boot soles searching Brooklyn for a job. Any job.

Finally he managed to find one unloading fish from the trawlers at Sheepshead Bay. He didn't like the job one bit. It was beneath him, and would take him nowhere, but he had no choice. He had to eat.

There were times when he thought he'd never be able to get the stench of fish out of his nostrils. It seemed to follow him wherever he went. And it was grueling, demanding work which sapped a man's energies and paid miserably.

Right before Christmas, he came down with pneumonia. When he was released from the charity ward, he made up his mind. He'd never eat fish again as long as he lived. He wouldn't even set foot in a restaurant that served fish. But more important, he was through with Brooklyn. It was a dead-end place, and no one knew it better than he. He wanted to be in the real New York. In the picture-postcard New York of skyscrapers and clogged streets and noise and lights and excitement. He didn't even return to the rooming house where he'd been living to pick up his clothes and precious few belongings. If he returned, he'd have to pay the back rent. Besides, a new beginning was better done completely from scratch. He bought the only thing he needed to pursue his dream. A subway token. Then he took the BMT across the East River into Manhattan and never looked back.

Manhattan was a whole different world from Brooklyn. A world with a distinctly different set of rules. Bavier's instincts immediately told him that here opportunities awaited those with foresight, intelligence, and ambition. There was an excitement in the air which you couldn't find in Brooklyn. You could feel it wherever you went, uptown or downtown, East Side or West Side.

The first thing Bavier did when he got into Manhattan was to walk all day and all night long. He listened, he watched, he smelled, he learned, and he absorbed. When he couldn't stay awake any longer, he boarded the subway and slept sitting upright, riding around within the bowels of the city. After he woke up, he made it his first order of business to look for a place to live. The Lower East Side was cheap, so he went there first. He found a two-room cold-water tenement apartment on Rivington Street.

There were four apartments to each floor, and they shared a common toilet in the hall. The bathtubs were in the kitchens. The stairwell was dimly lit with naked low-wattage bulbs which threw bizarre shadows onto the walls. There was one overpowering smell here which, like the fish at Sheepshead Bay, Bavier could never seem to get out of his nostrils. It was the smell of boiled cabbage and boiling laundry. Then, too, there were the sounds in the building. Not that he minded them, for they covered up the creaking of the building and gave it its mantle of life and dignity. There were the cries of babies and the sounds of families which proved that, despite all the poverty, the cycle of life went on. The languages he heard around him were a strangely exotic mixture of German, Polish, and Yiddish.

He wasn't at all intimidated by the bleak surroundings or the foreign flavor. He looked upon them for what they were —the first rung up the ladder toward success. He was in *Manhattan*, he kept telling himself. It was here, and only here, that opportunity upon opportunity beckoned. And Rivington Street was a symbol. Not only for him, but for all the thousands of others who had flocked here. Many years later when Bavier was rich and living on Sutton Place, he would look fondly back upon Rivington Street as the place where it had all begun. Even as his millions accumulated, he never once lost sight of those humble beginnings. He took an immeasurable pride in having started at the bottom and having made it to the top.

For quite a few years he played with his wealth as a child tends to play with his favorite toys, making and losing several fortunes in the process. Finally he decided that it was time to stop taking chances and put everything on an even financial keel. He bought the penthouse co-op on Sutton Place and tried to break into high society. Even with his wealth, it wasn't easy. You needed a social background as well as money, or at least good manners and a quick wit. Bavier lacked all the social graces, and he was looked upon as being brash and somewhat vulgar. He'd never had the time to acquire polish. He had been too busy working. Now he tried to make up for it. When he bought the penthouse, he hired the services of an interior decorator. He went to an expensive art gallery on Madison Avenue and let them pick out the paintings to hang on his walls. To his untrained eye they looked crude and baffling, as if a demented child had randomly splashed paint on canvas. But he thought that they gave him an instant veneer. It took him a while to discover that they didn't.

With the same misguided intent, he started haunting the best restaurants and nightclubs, only to discover how much he still had to learn. He had bought an off-the-rack tuxedo, and had gone, proud as a peacock, to El Morocco. Since he hadn't known that it was customary to tip the maître d', he had been seated at the worst table in the house. And to add to the insult, he had actually been mistaken for a headwaiter in his store-bought tuxedo. The next day, his lesson learned, he ordered tailor-made suits and tuxedos.

And then he met Z.Z.

Up until he met her, Bavier had very little contact with women. Not that he disliked them. On the contrary, he worshiped them and put them on a pedestal. Quite simply he'd never had the time for them. As a result, most of his relationships so far had been with prostitutes, for he had deemed sex to be as necessary as bathing or eating or brushing his teeth. For him, prostitutes were a convenience: he didn't have to waste any precious time on a relationship. He got what he wanted, and so did they. Then slowly he began to find that these sexual acts just weren't enough. That something vital was lacking. He thought about it and came to the realization that prostitutes mechanically did what was required of them, but no more. And that he now needed more. He was a rich man and it was time he had a woman he could call his own. No, not just a woman. A wife. But one with an acceptable society background, a credit to his wealth. One who could open all those doors that were still locked to him.

He met Z.Z. at a party given by a business associate. As soon as he saw her, he knew he had to have her. His unfailing instincts told him that she was special. That she was unlike any of the women he had ever met so far. He put her on an even higher pedestal than he had put any other. She was beautiful, with shimmering blond hair, a husky, cultured voice, and a graceful way of moving that brought an excitement to his loins such as he had never felt before. She had an aloof coolness about her, and yet he felt he could detect the smoldering passions which lay beneath the surface of her flawless skin. When she brushed against him, he felt a shiver tingling down his spine. Several days later, he proposed to her. She lowered her green eyes demurely and told him that she was flattered but needed time to think.

Had Bavier known more about the complicated workings of a scheming woman's mind, he would have realized that it was not he who had proposed to Z.Z., but she who had proposed to him. Without his even knowing it, she had baited the hook, dangled it in front of him, and then made him sweat it out before she reeled him in. Bavier took his having to wait as the sure sign of her being a lady. The truth was, Z.Z., who was in her early twenties, had been waiting to get married until she found a man who was rich enough to supply her with what she needed. Then she played her game. As far as sex and love were concerned, they were luxuries she never considered indulging in. What drove her was wealth, which translated into power. And she knew how to play her game. It was one which Bavier didn't even know existed.

In the beginning, theirs seemed a marriage made in heaven. The moment they left St. Patrick's Cathedral as husband and wife, with Z.Z. resplendent in a white gown and veil and both of them ducking to avoid the showers of rice as they sprinted down the steps to the waiting limousine, Bavier was as light-headed as a sweepstakes winner. For the first time in his life, he had someone to shower his affection upon. He was a dutiful husband and he generously let Z.Z. have anything she wanted. A beautiful woman, he rationalized, was born to be spoiled. Besides, she was opening doors to a society he hadn't even known existed. And he was grateful.

It took him a year to discover that the society he had entered was one he would gladly have done without. He didn't like the cocktail parties where he had to stand around talking about the stock market. He preferred to play it. He couldn't stand the interminable, boring dinners, or the Monday nights at the opera. He couldn't care less about Thoroughbred horses or the Kentucky Derby, the Preakness, or polo matches in Palm Beach. He didn't like talking about sailing. He preferred to sail. Slowly his disdain for Z.Z.'s crowd grew deeper and deeper. He despised the shallowness of these people. The constant snide social chitchat. The petty backstabbing and scheming. The gossip. The spiteful glee whenever misery struck someone they knew. And he discovered, to his dismay, that Z.Z. thrived on all these things. She was the most backstabbing, scheming gossiper of them all, and as venomous as the queen of the cobras. When someone wronged her, she inevitably got her revenge tenfold, even if she had to spend months weaving her web. When it came to that, she had the patience of a spider. Bavier became as disenchanted with her as he had with her whole social scene. If it had been possible, he would have washed his hands of the whole affair, but he was trapped. Slowly at first, and then with gathering momentum, he looked for escape whenever he could. He drifted into affairs with other women. He knew that Z.Z. knew. He also knew that as long as Z.Z. thought he was being discreet enough, she didn't care what he did. He could do anything with her blessing as long as it would not compromise her social position or cause her fellow vipers to turn their tongues on her. She even helped push him into his affairs. She found them to be agreeably convenient. As her maids freed her time around the house, so Bavier's mistresses relieved her from certain domestic duties she found distasteful. Slowly Bavier came to the conclusion that his wife hated sex. Not only with him, but with anyone. He got no comfort from the fact that she didn't sleep around. The truth was, he would have preferred that to a libido which had given up the ghost. At first her lack of desire confounded him. In time, he discovered the answer. When he did, he didn't know whether to laugh or cry. Z.Z. was terrified that having sex would leave her looking dissipated and give her hollows around the eyes.

When Bavier took his various mistresses out on the town, they always went to out-of-the-way places. For Z.Z.'s sake, he kept them out of her way.

As far as Z.Z. was concerned, her husband would always come crawling back to her, no matter how far he strayed. And whenever she realized that the gap between herself and her husband had grown a little too wide for comfort, she would play her old game, the one she had snared him with. She would fling out the bait, reel him back in, and devote herself exclusively to him. She would even give herself up to him in bed and pretend to enjoy it. If she thought these little bouts were strengthening their relationship, she was sorely

646

mistaken. On the contrary, these moments of contrition were so predictable that Bavier could even forecast their longevity to the day. They never lasted longer than a week. After that, Z.Z. would be climbing the walls and things would invariably return to the way they had been.

Had Z.Z. taken the time to analyze their relationship more carefully, she would have been aware of how truly precarious it had become. But she honestly had no idea how weary her husband had actually grown of her. She would never have believed that he needed someone more stimulating than herself.

In Hélène he found everything that was missing in Z.Z., and much more. Hélène possessed the exact qualities for which he had been unconsciously searching in a woman. She was entirely feminine, but in matters of business she was practical and thought like a man. Whereas his occasional crude manners and salty figures of speech embarrassed Z.Z., Hélène just naturally accepted them. She saw Bavier for what he was. A giant among men, but a kind giant. In many ways, he reminded her of Edmond. She felt she could rely on him in any circumstance. And he totally protected. But even more important, she truly loved Siegfried Bavier. In business, he was feared, and his lack of compassion toward anyone's interests except his own was legend. Hélène knew that that side of him existed, but she never saw it. Her Siegfried was kind and gentle, lusty, earthy, and spirited.

After the tugboats nudged the SS *United States* against the West Side pier, Hélène and Bavier parted company, but not for long. They ended up seeing each other nearly every day, even if they could snatch only a few precious minutes at a time out of their busy schedules. Neither of them minded this inconvenience. They respected each other's priorities and needs. Just having met each other seemed to have spurred them both on to new ambitions. Bavier was putting together a diversified investment package while Hélène rented two floors high up in the RCA Building in Rockefeller Center. She was setting up the American edition of *Les Modes*. Not only that, but she had come to a major decision which was to change her life. She loved New York. She loved its vitality, its larger-than-life glamour. She loved the frenzied creativity. But above all, she loved Bavier, and he loved her. Under the circumstances, it only made sense to stay here and move her headquarters over from Paris. The European editions would be put under a new umbrella: Hélène Junot International, Inc.

HJII was born.

For the first time in ages, Bavier felt like his old self. The weariness that had come over him after being saddled with Z.Z. had suddenly dropped away. Just knowing that Hélène was around seemed to be enough. It caused him to thrive as never before. For some strange reason, he and Hélène gave each other even more drive than either of them had ever had on their own. He sent his mistresses packing and worked himself to a frenzy.

Two months later, he met with Z.Z. and her lawyers to arrange for a quick divorce. Z.Z. took the news quietly, without undue concern. She didn't even try to put up a fight. She was certain that Bavier and Hélène were doomed. She began getting concerned only after he and Hélène got married in a quiet civil ceremony. Still, her concern was limited. Sigi would come crawling back. She was sure of it. All she had to do was reel him back in.

Edmond and Petite Hélène flew in from Paris for the marriage ceremony. Afterward Hélène and Bavier moved into the twelve-room co-op apartment they'd bought. It was on Fifth Avenue at Sixty-sixth Street and overlooked Central Park. Bavier never told her what getting his freedom from Z.Z. had cost him. Seven million dollars, the house in the Hamptons, the Sutton Place penthouse, the four-million-dollar art collection, and the priceless antiques. He thought the exchange well worth it. After all, he had a knack for making money. He'd make up for the losses in no time.

Nor did he tell Hélène that Z.Z. was pregnant. That news had caught him totally unawares, but he didn't let it influence his decision. Nor had he wanted it to influence Hélène's. Besides, the baby would pose no problem because Z.Z. had sworn she would get an abortion. Under the circumstances, it was the best solution.

What Bavier never knew was that Z.Z. decided against having the abortion. She was going to have the baby and try to use it for leverage to win him back. Not for himself, but so that no one else would have him.

And Z.Z. had made up her mind about one more thing. Already she was patiently beginning to spin her web.

Given time, she would destroy Hélène Junot.

11

Bavier and Hélène honeymooned in Acapulco for a week. The days flew by so fast that it seemed as if they had just arrived when they had to pack their bags and leave again. Like it or not, they had to get back to New York. Both of them had pressing business awaiting. But even after they returned, Bavier made certain that the honeymoon did not come to an end. He constantly showered Hélène with gifts. The first week after their return he gave her a small but exquisite Utrillo painting depicting a Parisian street scene. The next week came the square-cut eighteen-carat emerald from Harry Winston, which she refused to take off her finger even when she went to sleep. And finally, in the third week there was the pièce de résistance. The gleaming white 135-foot Feadship motor yacht which they christened the *Petite H*. It had cost six million dollars and carried a permanent crew of ten. It boasted three salons, a small discotheque, two speedboats, a master suite on deck, and four guest staterooms below. Bavier had had the yacht brought up from the broker's in Fort Lauderdale to the Seventy-ninth Street marina. After he and Hélène cruised around Manhattan on it in the moonlight, he instructed the captain to sail it on to Spain without them. They decided to keep it moored in Barcelona, planning to use it for vacations.

Unfortunately, there were to be no vacations. Fate played a cruel trick, and within weeks of their marriage, Siegfried Bavier dropped dead on the floor of the New York Stock Exchange. The doctor said it was caused by an aneurysm in the brain. Hélène was too numb to understand any of it, and she took little comfort in the fact that it could never have been detected in a checkup. Once again, it seemed that her happiness had reached its peak only to be flung back down into the ashes.

Bavier's death made headlines in *The Wall Street Journal*

and in the business section of the New York *Times*. The funeral was held at Campbell's on Madison Avenue. The chapel was packed with businessmen who had come to pay their last respects. When Bavier died, so had one of the last great gamblers on Wall Street. Hélène wished she knew who some of these people were, but most of them were strangers. She sat through the eulogy with a stony expression. The tears would come later. She didn't want to have to share them with strangers. Least of all with Z. Z. Bavier, who sat in the row behind her. It was Z.Z., she thought bitterly, who seemed to know everyone present. And who was receiving the condolences meant for the wife.

In his best boardroom voice, the president of a Fortune 500 corporation droned on and on about Bavier's merits and achievements. Hélène listened raptly, but not a single word penetrated her shroud of pain. All she could think about was the morning Bavier left to go to work for the last time. She had never seem him healthier or happier.

When the service concluded, she walked slowly out of the chapel, every step a special effort. She probably would never have made it past the third aisle if it hadn't been for Edmond and Petite Hélène. Holding her arms tightly, they somehow managed to propel her forward. Then suddenly her step faltered as she found herself unexpectedly face to face with Nigel Somerset. He had stepped quickly out from one of the aisles and was standing in front of her. She stopped walking and returned his stare. Her knees went weak and she could feel them shaking. Somehow she managed to keep her face composed. She didn't want to see Nigel. Not at a time like this. Or at any other, for that matter. What had once been between them was over, and she had no desire to start any relationship anew. But she couldn't turn her back on him, either. He had flown all the way from England for the funeral, and propriety, if nothing else, demanded she exchange a few words.

She turned to Edmond and Petite Hélène. "I'll see you outside," she said awkwardly.

"Will you be all right?" Edmond asked.

She nodded wordlessly and watched them leave. Then she turned back to Nigel. She was unaware of the businessmen filing out into the sunshine. All she could do was stare into Nigel's gold-flecked eyes. She felt the way she had at Auteuil when she had unexpectedly run into him. As had happened then, words seemed to fail her now.

"I'm terribly sorry about your husband," Nigel said.

"Thank you, Nigel," she said in a stiff, husky voice. "I'm so glad you came."

But she wished he hadn't. Just seeing him only seemed to reopen all the old wounds. Was it possible that they had never healed completely?

She looked down, and her face contorted in a pained expression, but when she looked back up at him, it was once again serene. Only she knew what an emotional toll that stoic mask cost her.

"I too am sorry, Nigel," she said politely. "I read about your mother's death last month. I'm afraid I didn't send any flowers . . ."

He looked at her gently. "I can't say that I blame you. On her deathbed she told me how she chased you from Fallsworth. You must believe me . . . I never knew."

"I believe you."

"I know you'll find little comfort in it, but in the end Mother realized she had done the wrong thing by forcing me to marry Pamela. She admitted it. She didn't often admit to her mistakes."

Hélène nodded numbly. Pamela. She remembered the pictures she had seen of Lady Pamela Grey, the woman who, instead of her, had become the sixteenth Duchess of Farquharshire. So she had been right. Nigel's mother had arranged it all. But that came as no surprise. In her heart, she had known it all along. Now the Duchess was dead, but the deed lived on after her.

"I should never have married Pamela," Nigel was saying softly. "I never loved her. Nor she me. Her parents forced her into it. And now . . ." His voice trailed off.

Hélène looked at him pityingly.

Nigel turned away. "Neither of us loves the other," he murmured. "The marriage is a sham." He took a deep breath and she could feel the pain that emanated from within him. "Unfortunately, a divorce is out of the question." He smiled grimly. "Social situation and all, you know."

Hélène reached out and touched the side of his face with her fingertips. "I'm sorry Nigel. It must be very hard on you."

He sighed and placed his hand atop hers, pressing it firmly

to his cheek. "Darling, I know this isn't the time or the place." He quickly looked around, lowered his voice to a discreet whisper, and stared into her eyes. "But I'd like to see you—"

Hélène took a step back. She had to look away so she wouldn't be drawn to his eyes. "I . . . I don't know, Nigel," she stammered, unsure of herself. "I'm sorry. It's just too soon. I need time to think about it . . ." Her voice cracked. And without another word, she turned on her heel and fled Nigel and the chapel and the stifling smell of chrysanthemums.

Two days later, unknown to Hélène, Jacques sold his HJII shares to Z. Z. Bavier and Marcello d'Itri.

12

The saying is true: time heals all wounds. And in time, although it seemed to her a very long time, Hélène's life returned to normal. Unquestionably she felt the unfairness of fate, the unfairness which gave her so much but relentlessly took from her its purest joys. However, she knew that with the help of Edmond and Petite Hélène, her family, she would be able to continue on, nourishing her dream. And now her dream had brought her to Venice,

It was after eleven o'clock at night by the time the last workman picked up his toolbox and left. Hélène saw him to the door and watched him getting into the waiting motorboat. As it surged away down the moonlit Grand Canal, she pushed on the massive carved double doors of the palazzo. Slowly they clanged shut with an echo of finality. Then everything was quiet save for the water lapping against the doorstep outside.

For a long moment she closed her eyes and leaned wearily back against one of the doors. She was dressed in a man's plaid shirt which she hadn't bothered to tuck into her faded

Levi's, her hair was pulled back from her face by a white silk bandanna, and on her feet were white tennis shoes.

With the back of her wrist she wiped the perspiration off her forehead. She heaved a sigh of relief. Little by little, she could feel her body starting to relax as her adrenaline slowed down. At last, everything was finished. And not a moment too soon, either. The party was tomorrow.

Had she anticipated at the outset what she was up against, she would gladly have left everything to the Czarina. But for once she'd insisted on organizing a party by herself. She had thought the occasion too important to trust to anyone. Even Luba. She laughed softly to herself. To date, except for holding intimate dinner parties, the biggest problem had always been what to wear to someone else's party, and then standing for hours in the stuffy ateliers while the couturiers and fitters tugged here, tucked there, pinned, stitched, hemmed, and re-hemmed in order to get her gown just right. While she had been a model, she hadn't minded all that standing around: it had been part of the job. Now she found it tedious and nerve-racking. But that was nothing compared to the two months of planning and hard work she'd just been through.

Once again she shook her head in disbelief. The biggest, most ambitious party she'd ever planned, and she'd expected to do it all herself! What a fool she had been. But who would have thought so much work was involved? Even trying to locate the help—florists, waiters, butlers, caterers, cleanup crews, orchestra, rock band, kitchen help . . . the list seemed endless—had been a mind-boggling job. Hiring those who seemed the most capable and then trying to explain to them just what was needed had been a nightmare. If one of her experienced friends hadn't come to the rescue, she would have had no choice but to cancel the affair. Well, she'd learned one lesson from this that she would never forget. In the future, she would spare herself these headaches and hire a professional coordinator. Even her fluent Italian, which she had been relying on so heavily, hadn't done her a bit of good. Venice was different from Milan, she'd discovered almost too late. Things were slower here. Less cosmopolitan, less efficient. Knowing the language just wasn't enough. You had to know the mentality of the locals you dealt with as well.

The problems had begun with the location, hunting for the appropriate—and available—palace in which to hold the party. Party, hell, she corrected herself. The ball. The Golden Ball.

From the beginning, she had envisioned it being held in Venice. As far as she was concerned, no place else could come close. Not for the splendor she had in mind.

Fine.

And at first it had all seemed so effortless. Even Peggy Guggenheim, when she'd heard that Hélène was in town searching for a palace, had generously stepped forward and offered her the loan of her own massive Palazzo Venier dei Leoni. This extraordinary palace was on the prestigious Grand Canal. An additional wing had been built on one side of the garden to house Peggy's world-famous collection of modern art. The Palazzo Venier dei Leoni was indeed one of the cultural highlights of Venice, but Hélène had politely refused the kind offer. Somehow, just the idea of a modern-art collection reposing under the same roof where the Golden Ball was being held took away from the magic of the ancient Venice that she was trying to recapture. Not only that, but she didn't want to be responsible for a magnificent home filled with millions of dollars' worth of museum-quality treasures while three thousand guests milled around in it. Besides, the type of place she wanted for the ball was one of those huge crumbling old palazzos whose rooms looked like gilded bird cages. Inside and out, except for the plumbing, it had to be unchanged since the time of Canaletto. She had discovered, to her delight, that many of those were available. So far, so good. An old, dilapidated palazzo should pose no problems. They were white elephants as far as everyone was concerned; many of them were up for sale. But for rent?

"Yes, for rent also," the real-estate brokers had assured her smoothly.

Then, when they had heard her out: "But surely not for such a short time, signorina!" they wailed, throwing up their hands in despair. "And certainly not for one party! Please, be *reasonable!*"

Finally she found an agent who was willing to accede to her terms. He showed her one palazzo after another. After inspecting nine of them, she found one she was crazy about.

It was enormous, situated halfway between the Rialto Bridge and the mouth of the Grand Canal. It had everything she had hoped for, and more. There were several tall, skinny pillars at the entrance where gondolas and speedboats could tie up by the marble threshold. Once inside, there was a baronial hallway with a sweeping staircase and decaying but splendid sixteenth-century murals attributed to Tintoretto. And when the agent had pushed open a pair of heroically scaled doors, Hélène caught her breath.

In front of her stretched the biggest ballroom she'd ever imagined. She entered slowly, hardly daring to trust her eyes. That one damp room alone was two stories high and took up almost the entire first floor. Between the marble pilasters, the walls were painted with peeling Byzantine-style murals. She leaned her head way back and stared up at the groin-vaulted ceiling. It was a heaven of rich, patinaed blue liberally sprinkled with gold-leaf stars. Her heart began to pound with the heady thrill of the discovery. This was *it*! This huge, forgotten room was the perfect setting for her Golden Ball. She could already visualize it. With the chandeliers lit, the gleaming gold stars would pick up the glow and actually look as if they were winking in the night above. With an orchestra in one corner and a discotheque set up in one of the other rooms, with buffet tables laden with feasts, with real gold dust captured in carved ice sculptures, with hundreds of magnums of Dom Perignon flowing freely, with three thousand guests resplendent in gold costumes, with all this, and more, the hollow emptiness of the palazzo would come to life as never before in its five-hundred-year history.

The agent watched Hélène as she walked slowly around the dim room, studying, absorbing, calculating, inspecting, and planning, the little wheels in her mind turning swiftly and clicking with the speed of an automatic shutter. Finally she marched determinedly over to him. Her voice was businesslike and brusque. "Whom do I see about signing a short-term lease?" she asked. "You or the owners?"

A week later, the gold-engraved invitations went out. Around the world their destinations were the international jet-setters, film stars, celebrities, and the socialites who set the trends for the times. The ball was scheduled to be held in six weeks. Hélène figured that would give everyone just enough time to rush to Paris, knocking each other down in their scramble to be the first one at the couturiers'. It was always that way whenever there was a theme party.

Yes, Paris was going to be humming, Hélène thought with satisfaction. There would be a run on gold fabric, on gold

655

lamé, on gold lace, and on gold thread. Tempers were going to fray and Givenchy would rake in a fortune. Ilias Lalaounis, more than anyone, was going to do a brisk business selling jewelry, since they specialized in gold. Because for the Golden Ball, gold costumes were de rigueur. Without one, it wouldn't matter who you were: invitation in hand or not, entrance to the palazzo would be strictly forbidden.

Hélène smiled to herself. Yves St. Laurent had finished Hélène's own gold costume over two months ago. She, the hostess, had the jump on everyone. Including the press coverage of her ball. At this very moment, Luba was carefully leaking news of the ball to selected reporters and paparazzi, but only a handful were actually being invited to cover the occasion from within.

Now came the second step. Hélène realized that it was already high time to start decorating the ballroom, that what she had in mind would take weeks. The palazzo was bare. Furniture would have to be found and brought in. And above all, the ballroom would have to be turned into the most festive, gilded fairyland imaginable. She envisioned everything in gold. Gold festoons, gold buffet tables, gold chairs. What she needed now was someone who could interpret her ideas and make them into a happy reality. The Golden Ball had to be one of those elusive fantasies that never would, never could, ever be repeated. She needed someone who was more than just an interior decorator or a stage designer. She needed, in short, a magician.

She sat down behind the ornate desk in her suite at the Hotel Danieli and scooted her chair forward. From the top drawer she took out a blank sheet of the hotel's stationery and put it down in front of her. Thoughtfully she picked up her pen and started to draw up a list of the best interior decorators she knew of in both Europe and America. Of course, whoever she picked would be exorbitantly expensive for one fleeting night only. But for this occasion, monumental extravagance was called for. Besides, what was more extravagant than the new product she was about to launch? A perfume worth its exact weight in gold. That was why she was throwing this ball in the first place. To draw attention to d'Or. The more lavish the ball, the more talked and written about d'Or would be. Word that a new, instant status symbol was available would swiftly spread down from the socialites and media to the uninvited masses. It was all perfectly timed with the massive, coordinated advertising blitz which was in readiness. The day after the ball, the ads would flood the market.

D'Or.

Hélène knew that whatever she spent now would be well spent. Would help seal d'Or's success. There were some things you couldn't scrimp on.

When she finished making her list of decorators, she went over each name carefully.

Impatiently she drummed her lacquered fingernails on the desk as her eyes scanned the list. Each had his or her own trademark, but none seemed to match d'Or. Could there really be so *many* designers? Would none of them do?

She let out a sigh, placed her elbows on the desk, and wearily rested her chin on her balled-up hands. For a moment she just sat hunched there like that. Then suddenly the idea surged up inside her from out of the blue.

Of course! Why hadn't she thought of it before? Her friend Yvette, with whom she'd worked the hat-check at the Folies de Babylon so many years ago, had become an enormously successful restaurateur and nightclub owner. Hélène had been as surprised by Yvette's success as Yvette had been by Hélène's.

Yes! Yvette was the perfect person to organize the ball! Hands down, she was acknowledged to be the world's most gifted party-giver. She would know exactly who was capable of decorating the ballroom. Who was the best caterer. What needed organizing and what didn't. Just hearing the magic name "Yvette" would be enough to set a fire under the locals. Especially if they thought there was a possibility that an Yvette's club might open in Venice. That would mean long and steady employment at good wages. Hélène wouldn't tell them that, of course. The name alone would be enough to get them jumping to conclusions. What they chose to believe wouldn't hurt her.

There was only one foreseeable problem. Would Yvette be able to spare the time to help her? After all, she was an extremely busy woman with all those worldwide clubs to run. Hélène stared at the telephone. There was only one way to find out. She reached for the telephone and placed a call to Yvette's International in Paris. That particular luxurious club on the rue Princesse had been the first of the clubs and had since become the headquarters of the entire chain.

An hour later, Hélène was chiding herself; she should have known better than to think it would be this simple. Yvette wasn't to be found at the Paris club. Nor in Monte Carlo, London, Rio de Janeiro, New York, Berlin, Sydney, Hong Kong, or Singapore. In fact, nobody had the least idea where she might be reached. At first Hélène was baffled by this discovery, but then she quickly saw the wisdom of it. By keeping everyone uninformed as to her schedule, Yvette could swoop down on any one of her clubs without advance warning, thereby forcing her employees to stay constantly on their toes. All Hélène was able to do was to leave a message for her at each of the clubs.

Finally at eight o'clock Venice time it was Yvette who called Hélène from Singapore, where it was the middle of the night. Yvette did not waste her nights sleeping. It was during the days while her clubs were closed that she slept on airplanes while flying from one of them to the next. She was a true night owl, and wide-awake now.

Her breathless, throaty voice bubbled in Hélène's ear. "Oh chérie, of *course* I'd be only too happy to help you out! Together we will see to it that it's the party of the year. No, not the year. The *decade*. Oh, it'll be *sublime*. I can't wait to get started on it. . . . Don't be foolish, I wouldn't dream of accepting a sou. I have enough money, and whatever are friends for, anyway? We'll get along splendidly, I just know it. We always did." From the depths of her throat came the laughter of the memories they had shared. "For as long as I live, I'll never be able to forget that time you blew the whistle on Jocelyne. You were the only person who ever had the guts to do anything about that bitch! Oh, by the way, did you know she's working the *streets* now as a twenty-franc hooker? I ran into her in the Pigalle last year and I almost didn't recognize her. All ugly and bloated like you wouldn't believe. Real down and out, let me tell you. It's really hilarious, though. She actually propositioned me. Took me for a dyke! Can you believe it? Me? A dyke?" More throaty laughter. "Anyway . . . *What? A Golden* Ball? Ooooh, I can see it already. How delicious! And the waiters and bouncers—at an affair like that you've simply *got* to have a squad of bouncers, believe me. . . . Why? There are bound to be party crashers and paparazzi and horrible drunks, that's why. Well, as I was saying, the waiters and the bouncers can be half *naked* and wear nothing but gold paint and bull's masks.

Isn't that marvelous? Oh, loincloths too, it goes without saying. We wouldn't want to get raided, would we? Listen, I repeat, you're *not* imposing. It's the most exciting thing I've heard about in ages! Why didn't *I* think of a Golden Ball? Never mind. . . . No, I haven't gotten my invitation yet. You sent it where? To Paris? Then *that* explains it. I've been traveling for nearly two solid weeks now and nobody in Paris knows where I am. . . . Oh, don't thank *me*. *You're* the one who saved *my* life. I can't wait to hop on the next flight out of here. It's so steamy, and the mosquitoes are deadly. I think they diet while I'm gone and lie in wait to feast on me when I return. . . . I'll call you the moment I get to Venice, I promise! A bientôt!"

Now the palazzo was silent as Hélène pushed open the massive carved doors to the ballroom. Suddenly the glare of all that gold hit her in the eyes. Instinctively she threw up a hand to shield herself against it. Except for the candles, which would be lit tomorrow evening, all the lights were on.

As in a daze, she walked slowly around the room. It was unbelievable—Yvette had truly outdone herself. The ancient ballroom was everything she herself had envisioned, and more. Much more.

With military precision, carved gilt ballroom chairs lined the walls. They were upholstered in a dark blue muslin which, like the ceiling above, was hand-painted with gold stars. The Byzantine murals on the walls were completely hidden by gold-veined mirrors that reflected—and refracted—everything over and over to minuscule infinity. The cold, dark marble floor was covered with a thick sea of tiny wafer-thin gold-foil stars that scattered and danced and swirled around your feet as you walked through them.

Hélène could feel a powerful surge of satisfaction, of having set a goal and then having surpassed it beyond even her own wildest imaginings. It would indeed be the party of the decade, she thought. And it was tax-deductible, for it was heralding the new d'Itri perfume. The perfume which she and Luba had helped the chemists in Grasse to create, and which would be sold only through the d'Itri boutiques and a select number of the world's most exclusive shops starting the day after tomorrow. Already, each of these shops had a special booth set up in the cosmetics departments. Each booth was hooked up to a central computer. Day by day and hour by hour, d'Or's price per ounce, per precious fraction of a fluid ounce, would fluctuate with the price of gold on the international market.

Her eyes rested now on the tall Lucite pedestal which stood in the very center of the room. On top of it was the enormous thirty-gallon crystal bottle of d'Or. Tomorrow, at the height of the ball, Marcello d'Itri would unveil it to a fanfare accompaniment. Each guest would receive one of the half-ounce sizes as a gift. Precious contents aside, even the bottles themselves were valuable and bound to become collectors' items. They were made of hand-cut Lalique crystal. The caps were miniature bars of bullion imprinted with the d'Or logo and the exact fraction of a gram of the real gold used in the plating.

Hélène sank down onto one of the ballroom chairs. Was it possible that all the work was finally finished? That everything for the twenty-eight hundred guests who had accepted was in readiness? Yes, it was possible, she told herself firmly. All the fatigue she now felt told her so. But worn out though she was, she'd take a Dalmane before she went to bed. Tonight, a sleeping pill wouldn't hurt. She needed to get a good night's rest. She'd have to be up early and look her absolute best. This was one occasion when having hollow circles around the eyes just wouldn't do.

She sighed. Morning would begin a gruelingly long day and an endless night. It would start at ten A.M. when a seamstress from Yves St. Laurent was arriving by train, just in case her gown needed some last-minute adjustments or she'd happened to put on a few pounds.

Wearily she closed her eyes. The seamstress wasn't all she had to contend with tomorrow. Alexandre himself would be flying in from Paris at one-thirty to do her hair. And at five, Pablo was arriving from Elizabeth Arden's in New York. He was going to paint her eyes to look like an African butterfly in flight, with ostrich-feather antennae as eyebrows and tiny glued-on canary-diamond tears. And she had to have a last-minute talk with Scavullo. She had hired him to take pictures of the ball for *Les Modes*.

Hélène let out a deep breath. She opened her eyes and shook her head as the staggering schedule sank in. There wasn't a moment to waste.

Before the Golden Ball was even in full swing, word had it that Venice would never see another occasion quite like it. It eclipsed even the Black-and-White Ball that had caused such a furor a few years earlier. Throughout the evening Hélène was everywhere, seeing to it that everyone was greeted, that each guest got just the right amount of personal attention, and that the proper introductions were made. She knew that ultimately it was up to her, the hostess, to see that it would indeed turn out to be the party of the season. She noted, with some satisfaction, that it was certainly beginning to look that way.

Never a big partygoer herself, she suddenly found herself enjoying this one immensely. Without a doubt, she was its star. Her shimmering gown was almost translucent except for its molded gold breast plates. The floor-length hand-painted African butterfly sleeves matched her extraordinarily made-up eyes to perfection. Each time she spread her arms, it was as if she were spreading her wings, ready to take flight. It was clear that of all the costumes, it was hers that was the most original, the most photographed, and the most envied. Yet it never failed to amaze her to what extraordinary lengths the celebrities she had invited had gone to when it came to their costumes. Each one had tried to outdo the other. There were gleaming belts of clinking gold coins, several knights in gold-sprayed armor, necklaces of nuggets, gowns of mesh and coins. The Vicomtesse de Sévigné stole the show as far as arriving in style went. Dressed as an Aztec idol, she had come floating lazily down the Grand Canal on a golden barge she had commandeered from somewhere, no one knew quite where. Not to be outdone, the Czarina wore an antique Florentine ball gown that had once belonged to one of the Medicis. It was sewn and embroidered with gold thread and trimmed with layers of soft gold lace. The train was so long and heavy that it required the services of two gold-clad midgets to hold it up all evening. A gold-costumed monkey (rented from some enterprising organ-grinder, Hélène thought) perched on Luba's shoulder, fascinated with the Czarina's latest trademark—gold Yves Tanguy earrings she had taken to wearing constantly.

As Hélène went past the buffet tables lining the hallway, she slowed down and paused for a moment to appreciate the scene. Gold-liveried servants stood behind the tables serving the hungry guests who were lined up, gold plates in hand. She managed to get a glimpse of the food. It looked even more delicious than it smelled. Once again, she mentally gave thanks to Yvette, at the same time marveling at how it had all been achieved in time, and how the platters of food could be so fresh. Even with the heat generated by the lights and the guests, all the food down to the last sprig of parsley looked bright and unwilted.

She made a left turn and glanced toward the front doors and the floodlit waters of the Grand Canal outside. The entrance was well guarded by the four gold-painted bodyguards hired by Yvette. Past them, outside the open doors, she could see more guests arriving. The armada of paparazzi was so thick that it was practically impossible for the guests to pull up in their gondolas and speedboats. Incessant flashbulbs popped blinding white lightning as the guests' boats carefully maneuvered to the floodlit palazzo entrance.

Hélène lifted her wrist and glanced at her gold watch. Nearly eleven o'clock. In half an hour, Nigel was due to arrive. She permitted herself a smile of eager anticipation. Nigel. It was comforting to know that he would soon be here beside her, dancing, laughing, holding her in his arms. Just his presence would be enough to make everything else about the ball pale. When he arrived, she would be waiting for him here, near the entrance. But in the meantime, she would make a few more rounds to make sure that everything was in order.

14

At eleven-twenty Hélène decided to go back out to the entrance hall and wait there for Nigel. It wouldn't be long now, she told herself with growing excitement, and then he'd be standing here beside her. Ten minutes at the most, if he was punctual.

She had nearly reached the ballroom doors when she caught her breath. Nigel was already standing in the doorway. Dressed in a gold satin tunic and matching breeches, he looked like a grown-up Gainsborough that had just stepped out of its massive gold frame. A breeze swept through the hallway behind him and caught his hair, fluttering through it as he looked around at the mass of golden people. His eyes were searching.

For her, she knew. She straightened. She could almost reach out and feel his anticipation, his disappointment that she wasn't there at the door waiting for him. She felt a surge of pride. He looked so dashing, so handsome.

He was about to step forward; then he checked himself. She realized at once why. He was afraid he'd get lost in the crowds. With this many people, chances were they could pass each other a dozen times without realizing it.

Hélène balanced herself on tiptoe, lifted her arm, and waved. After a moment she caught Nigel's eye. He smiled and swiftly strode toward her.

She threaded her way around some waltzing couples and then ran toward Nigel, throwing herself into his arms.

"For a moment I was afraid I wouldn't find you," he said. "You should have exercised the hostess's prerogative and worn red or white so that you'd stand out."

Z. Z. Bavier couldn't remember just how it had happened, but she and Hubert de Léger had become friends. Well, if not exactly friends, then at least fast comrades-in-arms. It didn't really surprise her. After all, they had a mutual bond. Both of them hated Hélène Junot, although neither would divulge his reasons to the other. And both of them shared the same goal: to destroy her. Yet Z.Z. found herself enjoying every moment she spent with Hubert. With her, he was always polite, always the perfect, charming gentleman, the worldly Comte de Léger. His title was ancient, his manners continental. She had never had a chance to see that other, terrible, childish side of him. But Z.Z. sensed a turmoil boiling within him that he kept well to himself. It always seemed to be lurking just beneath the surface, ready to erupt without warning. She knew that it had something to do with Hélène Junot, and it fascinated her. She only wished she knew what it was.

Hubert had never given Z.Z. much serious thought, but he, too, was surprised. He liked being in her company. He appreciated her biting wit, her sharply honed razor tongue, her ever-ready sense of adventure. It was as if the two of them had been made for each other. But they both instinctively knew that they were too much alike ever to sustain any deep relationship. That was their strength. They did not get emotionally involved with each other. Instead, they kept their mutual goal well in sight.

In silence now they floated down the Grand Canal in the gondola. They sat side by side on the red velvet seat, each immersed in his own thoughts, oblivious of the gondolier at the rear, who expertly paddled the thin, sleek craft through the water.

Z.Z. leaned forward and fished the single red tea rose out of the crystal bud vase attached to the gunwales. She sat back and brought the rose up to her face until her nose was buried in the petals. Then languidly she began tearing the petals off one by one and tossing them into the canal. Another hundred yards to go and they would reach the Palazzo Daniela Donatella, she thought with satisfaction. Another hundred yards . . .

Suddenly she felt the sharp sting of a thorn in her flesh. Angrily she tossed the remainder of the rose overboard and licked the blood off her finger. She stared fixedly ahead through her narrowed eyes and focused her thoughts on Hélène. On the woman who had stolen her husband and left her to deal with her son, Wilfred, alone. She wondered how Hélène would react to her and Hubert appearing at the ball, since they hadn't been invited. She smiled, thanking God that

664

her friend Betty Lindenbaum had come down sick and had let herself be talked into giving Z.Z. her invitation. Poor Betty. After tonight, she probably wouldn't receive another invitation from Hélène Junot for as long as she lived.

With rising anticipation, Z.Z. glanced now at the ancient palazzos as they drifted slowly past. Most of them were dark, their windows shuttered. It was close to midnight.

Suddenly she was aware of Hubert's eyes on her and she turned to him. He nudged her and pointed straight ahead. She sat forward and caught her breath. The Palazzo Daniela Donatella was just coming into view beyond the curve, floodlighted like something out of a Hollywood premiere. Z.Z. couldn't believe her eyes. Every window and cornice caught the light; even the outside had been decorated with festive garlands of gold. And the paparazzi—they must number at least a hundred! she thought as she saw the masses of little craft bobbing dangerously in the water in front of the palazzo.

She took a deep breath. "We're almost there," she said, settling back in the seat. Her long tapered fingers impatiently tapped the legs of her gold-lamé tuxedo. She turned to Hubert, her eyes challenging. "How do you think she'll react to your costume?"

He shrugged. "With Hélène, you can never tell."

"I think I can." Z.Z. smiled wickedly. "I can't *wait* to see her face when you take off your coat!" She let out a hoarse laugh of satisfaction as she reached over and traced a gold-lacquered fingertip down the side of his gilded leather coat. "This is one thing the imperturbable Hélène Junot hasn't bargained for!"

At exactly midnight, the lights in the ballroom flickered and then went out. For a moment there was total darkness. As if someone had thrown a master switch, the music, talking, and laughter subsided.

Suddenly there was a dramatic roll of drums and a single spotlight clicked on overhead. Marcello d'Itri, in a woven gold tuxedo, was standing at the foot of the draped pedestal beside Hélène. Slowly the guests drew closer around them.

Hélène looked around at the shadows of the people encircling her and Marcello. She could sense their curiosity. They were waiting expectantly.

She clasped her hands in front of her, cleared her throat,

and smiled. "My dear friends," she announced in a loud voice that rang out clearly and echoed from the vaulted ceiling. "Surely you are all aware that the theme of this ball is 'Gold.' This theme has not been chosen on a whim. There is a purpose behind it. It gives me pleasure to announce that my friend Marcello d'Itri"—she turned and curtsied graciously to him, and he returned it with a solemn bow— "has created a new and lavish addition to his already superb line of clothing and accessories. This new addition to the line is far more ethereal, and appeals far more to the senses than anything his genius has created thus far." She stopped and looked at Marcello. Their eyes met again. She smiled and nodded.

Marcello d'Itri took a step backward and reached for a corner of the gold cloth that draped the pedestal.

"Ladies and gentlemen!" d'Itri announced. "May I present . . . d'Or!"

There was another drumroll and Marcello tugged on the cloth. In fluid slow motion it began to glide to the floor. All eyes were raised to the enormous cut-crystal bottle with the gold-bullion cap. The facets of the crystal caught the spotlight and flashed fire in all directions, the liquid inside it glowing a deep rich gold. There was a roar of applause.

Marcello stepped forward. "Ladies and gentlemen. In a moment, the waiters will circulate to give each of you a half-ounce bottle. Need I say this is not such a small token?" He paused. "For the price of d'Or, ounce by ounce, is the price of gold on the international market!"

He stopped and bowed again. There was more enthusiastic applause and the spotlight went out. Immediately the chandeliers clicked back on and the music and excited talk started up as before. As quickly as the first notes of the fox trot had begun, they now faded, and the conversation died quickly until the ballroom was silent. People began turning around, craning their necks and standing on tiptoe to see what was happening.

Hélène had been heading toward Nigel. Now she looked around with a puzzled expression. Something was wrong. She could feel the tension in the air. But what was it? What could have happened?

Not losing a moment, she fought her way through the crowd, Nigel following behind her.

When she neared the doors, Hélène's steps faltered. She

came to a standstill, her face white with shock, and she began to tremble.

Hubert de Léger and Z.Z. Bavier stood there smiling, facing everyone. Their eyes were challenging.

It was not the fact that they had crashed the ball which caused the anger to constrict Hélène's heart. It was Hubert's costume.

Slung casually over his arm was a gilded leather coat, and set on his head at a jaunty angle was a visored golden cap. An SS cap. *He was in head-to-toe uniform. A golden Nazi uniform that flashed and gleamed obscenely beautiful.*

As if she had been struck, Hélène caught the nearest person's arm and grabbed hold of it as the ballroom suddenly reeled around her. She closed her eyes. Then she felt firm fingers pushing her into yet someone else's arms. She had been clutching Luba.

Hélène opened her eyes and shook her head like a dazed prizefighter. She barely realized that she was now in Nigel's arms.

She was shaking like a leaf. How dare Hubert come in that getup! Didn't he know that nothing repulsed her more? That nothing repulsed any of the people gathered here more? It was clear that he was trying to ruin the ball. Ruin her.

But that wasn't the worst of it. The worst were the memories that suddenly sprang up in front of her. The terrible things she'd suffered as a child at the hands of the Nazis.

Suddenly a set of footsteps rang out clearly. She lifted her head and turned slightly to the right. Luba was marching up to Hubert, the midgets holding up her heavy train hurrying bowleggedly to keep up.

Luba came to a stop in front of Hubert. For a long tense moment she stared daggers through him. Then wordlessly she flung one arm backward and brought it forward so fast that at first no one even realized what was happening. Only when the sound of flesh slapping against flesh rang out clearly was it obvious.

She hit him again with her open hand. This time Hubert anticipated her move and tried to duck. It was a mistake. Luba's hand missed his cheek and hit him squarely on the nose. Blood began to drip from it, and the monkey on Luba's shoulder screeched shrilly, clapping its tiny black hands together in delight.

Quickly recovering, Hélène signaled for two of the gold-

667

painted bodyguards. Silently they approached the unsuspecting Hubert from behind, grabbed hold of him under the armpits, and effortlessly lifted him up and carried him outside.

Hubert's legs futilely kicked the air. He glanced back over his shoulder, the sweat suddenly pouring down his face as he realized what they were going to do. Indignantly he shouted protests. "No! Somebody make them stop it!" he cried. "Put me down!"

At the entrance to the palazzo, the bodyguards paused. They looked out at the canal, then faced each other. Their eyes gleamed inside the narrow slits of their masks. They nodded and counted aloud.

Hubert started to scream as they grabbed his feet and swung him through the air in an arc. Once. Twice. On the count of three they let go and tossed him far out into the cold, black waters of the Grand Canal.

Hubert hit the water like a cannonball. The paparazzi in their boats quickly snapped pictures and then turned away, protecting their cameras from the sudden splash of water. When Hubert surfaced, he screamed in terror, his arms flailing the water. "I can't swim!" he screeched. "Help me! I'm drowning!"

The Grand Canal closed in over him as he submerged again.

"For God's sake!" Z.Z. screamed from the stoop. "Help him, somebody!" She turned to the two bodyguards who had tossed him in. "Help him!" She clenched her fists and beat one of them uselessly on the chest.

Then flashbulbs popped like lightning and the paparazzi went wild as Z.Z. dived in after Hubert.

Their pictures would make all the papers.

It was dawn by the time the last of the guests departed. Wearily Hélène sat down in the chair next to Nigel's and let out a deep breath. Besides them, only Luba was still there. For a long time Hélène surveyed the chaotic mess with a stern eye. There was nothing more dismal than the remains of a party.

She rubbed her eyes with her fingertips. "I'm exhausted!"

The Czarina smiled. She could move about unimpeded now. The midgets and the monkey had long since been sent home; the train had been unhooked from her gown and was

668

folded neatly over the back of a chair. She sat down opposite Hélène. "But was it worth it! You mark my words," she prophesied. "Within a week, not an ounce of d'Or will be left in any of our outlets." Her coal-black eyes glittered. "We'd better step up production right away."

"Tomorrow," Hélène said weakly, waving away the business talk. "All I want to do right now is to go to bed." She stiffened and clenched her fists angrily. "Hubert de Léger! How dared he crash the ball in a costume like that!"

The Czarina sniffed. "The blood of the de Légers has run bad. Too much intermarriage through the centuries, if you ask me. But don't worry." She leaned forward, patted Hélène's hand, and smiled, her pomegranate lips wide and knowing. "He may not realize it yet, but he's done you an enormous favor."

"Favor!" Hélène looked at her wide-eyed.

"The publicity, of course! You can't buy publicity like that."

Hélène shook her head. "Really, Luba," she said reproachfully, "is that all you can think of? Sales?"

Three days later the telephones in the d'Itri offices were ringing off the hook and the telex kept up a constant chatter day and night. The Czarina's prediction had been correct. The newspapers had been full of Hubert's rescue by Z.Z. from the Grand Canal. There was no way d'Or could not be mentioned, since everything had occurred at the Golden Ball.

As a result, d'Or had taken off, selling out instantly. Hélène quickly called up the factory in Grasse to speed up production tenfold. And as soon as the shelves were restocked, they emptied again. D'Or was the hottest-selling fragrance ever.

To Hélène, it suddenly seemed as if the world was paved with gold. It was difficult for her to imagine that she had ever been poor. Even the newspapers began referring to her as "Mademoiselle Midas."

She had laughed at the articles, but deep down inside, she was secretly pleased. She had always been well-known, even before she started *Les Modes*. Her fame and social position had been assured when she had become Madame Kowalsky. But now she suddenly found herself as famous as only a handful of women in the world. She couldn't believe it. Never had anything gone so right.

But things weren't quite as good as she thought. She realized that the instant she got the call from New York in the middle of the night. Once again it was Edmond, with bad news.

"Come back immediately!" he told her. "De Léger and the others have stirred up trouble!"

"What kind of trouble?" she asked. She couldn't seriously believe they could do anything that warranted a call at this hour.

But they had. Z.Z. and Hubert were taking her to court. They claimed she had misappropriated HJII funds for personal use. A subpoena would be awaiting her the moment she set foot in the United States.

Worse, in the morning the IRS was going to descend upon HJII.

15

The warrant was served on her the moment she came through customs. Even while she had been on the plane, IRS agents were already at the accounting department of HJII, throwing everything into chaos. Hélène wanted to drop by and see if there was anything she could do, but Edmond advised against it.

"There isn't enough time, Little French Girl. We have to be at the courthouse within the hour."

The case of *Z. Z. Bavier v. Hélène Junot* was due to begin.

Hélène nodded and stared out the window of the sleek limousine. In less than an hour, and for perhaps as long as the next few weeks, she would be faced with nothing but unpleasantness. She had never been taken to court before, and the prospect of being trapped in a courtroom was highly distasteful. Her only consolation was that she was innocent. There had been no misuse of funds.

By the time a week passed, the accountants, investigators, and lawyers realized it too. Everything began to fizzle out.

To their chagrin, the IRS men discovered that not only was everything tip-top in accounting, and all the taxes owed the government paid, but that the taxes had actually been *overpaid*. By nearly seven thousand dollars. HJII's account would be credited.

Not to be outdone by the IRS, Z.Z. and Hubert's accountants and lawyers had gone at it even more doggedly, but they, too, finally left with their tails tucked shamefully between their legs. Sheepishly they had to acknowledge that not a penny was unaccounted for or misused.

To top it off, the judge took Z.Z., Hubert, and their lawyers into her chambers and gave them a stern tongue-lashing on wasting the court's precious time and threatened them with contempt.

All charges were instantly dropped.

Instead of feeling elated, Hélène seethed with anger. The IRS and the accountants crawling all over the place had set work back by weeks. There hadn't been a single department of HJII that hadn't come under scrutiny. When it was over, she and Edmond met together in her lavishly appointed office high in the RCA Building.

"They're going to pay for this," she said, stalking restlessly back and forth. "But how? What can I legally do to get back at Z.Z. and Hubert?" Her face was flushed with anger and her violet eyes burned dangerously. She stopped at one of the windows, stuck her fingers between two slats of the venetian blinds, and looked down at Rockefeller Plaza. It was curiously empty. It was that in-between time when the Promenade Café cleared its outdoor tables away and the ice-skating rink was yet to be set up.

"You're looking for revenge?" Edmond asked cautiously.

She let the blinds snap back into place. Then she turned her back to the window, crossed over to him, and dropped into a chair. "I'm looking for legal options."

He lit a cigarette, sat back thoughtfully, and crossed his legs. "You could always countersue. For defamation or something along those lines."

"No," Hélène said firmly. "The judge was right. Enough of the court's time has already been wasted. I don't believe in making a mockery of justice . . ." Her voice trailed off as a sudden glint came into her eyes.

He caught her expression. "All right," he demanded

shrewdly, "I can feel your gears turning. Care to share your thoughts?"

She smiled. He could read her like a book.

"I think," she said slowly, "that I have come up with a way to get back at them. It won't make much of a difference to Hubert, of course. He's too rich. But Z.Z. . . ." She smiled. "Z.Z.'s life-style demands money. I happen to know that she overinvested in HJII."

"Oh? And pray tell, how did you happen to come across that information?"

She waved her hand deprecatingly. "I have ways. The important thing is, she's counting on her dividends. Do you think it would be legal if we shrank them?"

"Shrank them!"

"Yes."

"How?"

She leaned forward, the words tumbling from her mouth. "By expanding HJII, Edmond! I've wanted to do that for a while now anyway. This is the perfect opportunity. Let's see . . ." She was beginning to get caught up in her self-induced excitement. "We could start a British edition of *Les Modes*. Perhaps even a German one." She jumped to her feet. "And we could buy a piece of property right here in New York and erect our very own building. The Junot Building! God knows, the way we bounce back and forth across the Atlantic, the company could use a corporate jet, too. We could even get a few cars for the major executives, a Rolls for me . . ."

Edmond smiled suddenly, his teeth flashing. "Little French Girl, you're a blooming genius. Not only will you get what you want, but we'll be cutting our taxes way down in the process."

"It's legal, then?" she asked carefully.

"It's legal. Just don't go overboard," he cautioned. "Cutting the others' profits will cut yours in the process. Make sure you leave yourself enough so that you won't be caught short."

"I'll make do," she said with determination.

Once Hélène's mind was made up about something, she didn't waver. She put her plan into action immediately. She started by purchasing the property on Fifth Avenue and Twelfth Street. She liked the location. Lower Fifth Avenue appealed to her. It was quiet and sedate. The Washington

672

Square arch a few blocks down reminded her of Paris. Also, the property was already commercially zoned. But best of all, she liked it because she rubbed shoulders with that other fashion giant, Fairchild Publications. They were right next door.

Instead of simply razing the building, Hélène's architects suggested they gut it until it was just a shell. It was a sturdy building and would make a desirable framework for hers. Hélène hesitated, but once the firm came up with the plans for the renderings, she immediately saw their point and agreed.

When first the destruction and then the construction began, she watched over the process with an eagle eye. Not the smallest, most inconsequential detail escaped her. Every day she made it a point to drop by and watch the progress. She roamed endlessly through the shell of the empty building, poking into corners and asking countless questions. She even went so far as to don a hard hat and bravely walk the scaffolding that jutted out over the avenue. She supervised and suggested and egged on the workers so that, miraculously, the Junot Building was completed two months ahead of schedule.

As the inside was totally rebuilt, so the outside was slipcovered with a shell of crystalline mirror. It was one of the first truly face-lifted buildings in the city, and she had to admit that the architects had worked wonders. They had even angled the corners until the original shape of the building was no longer in evidence. It caught all the reflections of the traffic and the neighborhood and the pedestrians. It reflected all the life that went on around it and froze it for a fraction of a second. It mirrored everything, but nothing as gloriously as the changing moods of the weather.

The Grumman Gulfstream II luxury jet she had ordered was completed the same week as the building, and it was flown directly to Italy, whose coachwork is the finest in the world. The interior was being lavishly appointed under the supervision of an internationally renowned interior-design team. And at the Rolls-Royce factory in England, her specially designed Silver Cloud was undergoing the long process of receiving layer upon layer of lacquer.

Hélène should have been content. HJII had gotten its own headquarters—a building named after *her*—and its own corporate jet. Now she could wing around the world in total privacy without having to be inconvenienced by airline schedules. But much more important, both England and Germany had their own editions of *Les Modes*.

The empire had expanded some more.

But Hélène was not satisfied. All her successes so far had been a product of HJII's natural momentum. What she hungered for now was a new success. One which did not involve HJII. One which did not involve Z.Z., d'Itri, von Eiderfeld, or Hubert de Léger.

One which was totally separate from all the others.

A new magazine.

Her own.

Her very own.

16

"Why go out on a limb if you don't have to?" Edmond asked after the Sphinx left the office.

He and Hélène were sitting at the floor-to-ceiling windows where Julie had set up a folding table. It was draped with a crisp white cloth. The flaky croissants and brioches on the paper-thin white bone china were untouched. Far below their feet, the morning traffic on Fifth Avenue was picking up.

Hélène sipped her coffee slowly. "I'm restless, Edmond. I feel like everything's at a standstill."

He laughed. "Far from it. You're busier than ever."

Abruptly she set her cup down in her saucer and got to her feet, restlessly prowling back and forth. "Dammit!" She clenched her index finger and sucked on it. Suddenly she whirled around accusingly, her eyes flashing. "I want a success that's mine. That's mine alone!"

He looked surprised. "Little French Girl. You don't think HJII is yours? Or the d'Itri boutiques, for that matter? Your name is practically a household word. On two continents."

"Sure it is. Maybe that's the trouble. Any magazine I add to HJII's roster is almost certain to be a hit. Not because of me. Because of Luba and the whole staff. *Because* of HJII."

"Everybody should be so lucky. You have everything you've ever wanted."

She vented a deep sigh and slipped into her chair. She reached out and covered his hands with hers, her violet eyes shining earnestly across the table. "I want another success, Edmond. Everything's running fairly smoothly, sure. But I want a new magazine! One that's a challenge. One that's all mine!"

He let out a low whistle. "You're asking for a lot. A whole new publishing company—"

"Damn right. With no one sitting on the board but me." She gave a tentative smile and with a mango-lacquered fingernail toyed with the rim of her cup. "You know, it's funny. There was a time when I would have given anything—*anything*—to be where I am today. And now?" She gave a low husky laugh. "Now it seems like . . . like it was *too* easy." She frowned suddenly. "Like I've cut too many corners to get where I am."

He looked at her steadily. "Are you sure that's it? That that's what your restlessness is really all about?"

She eyed him sharply. "What do you mean?"

"Little French Girl," he said with patent patience, "remember, it's me you're talking to. Edmond."

She gave him a little smile.

"You're sure you're not restless because of . . ." He paused, choosing his words carefully. ". . . because of personal reasons?"

She placed her elbows on the table, rested her chin heavily in her cupped hands, and stared down at the Forbes Building. "I take it you're referring to my love life."

"What else is there?"

"What indeed," she murmured.

"Work is no substitute," he warned with reproval in his voice.

"Edmond, Edmond, Edmond," she said flatly, turning to face him. "God knows I'm no virgin. Oh, don't look at me like that! I'm no nymphomaniac, either. But if I go to bed with a man, I have to feel *something* for him. And it just so happens that the only man I love is Nigel." She smiled sadly. "Fate's played a cruel trick on both of us. We can't help it if we've got to meet discreetly and snatch a few precious hours or nights every now and then. But in his position, a divorce is out of the question. There just isn't any other way. Nor is

675

there anyone else for me. Between our meetings, what else can I do but keep busy?"

"All right. Enough said." He cleared his throat, clearly relieved to be able to change the subject. "The meeting you wanted scheduled with Gore is at ten-thirty. You're sure you want to go ahead with it?"

"Absolutely. I intend to borrow ten million dollars."

"Ten million!" He was shocked. "Why, you started HJII with only—"

"Times have changed, Edmond. Money is no longer worth what it used to be. You should know that better than anyone. Plus nowadays there isn't any room for failure or flukes. I intend to do a heavy TV advertising blitz. Things like that. It'll take a lot of money."

"And this magazine?" He looked at her questioningly. "It will be like *Les Modes*?"

She shook her head. "No, no. One that American women will snatch up even faster. Lately I've been giving it quite a lot of thought. I think I want to emphasize today's working woman. She's supposed to be a new breed, you know."

Hélène couldn't help but smile. New breed, indeed! She and Luba had been working all their adult lives.

"And it would be a mass-market magazine," she added quickly. "Available everywhere, from newsstands to supermarket checkout counters. It would be printed on glossier paper than *Good Housekeeping*, *Redbook*, or *Woman's Day*. Not as slick as *Les Modes*. What I'd like to do is combine today's many-faceted woman—at work, at home, at play. Something like a hybrid between American *Vogue*, *Cosmo*, and *Family Circle*. But big. Hundreds of pages covering everything from thirty-minute recipes to household hints to office management. Features on both white- and blue-collar women. And lots of how-tos. How to apply makeup. How to handle a job interview. How to hire and fire employees. How to dress for success. How to make your husband happy. Or your lover. Plus a whole lot more. Like what to do with your kids while you're at work. The pros and cons of day-care centers, the costs of housekeepers, what psychiatrists have to say about the effects of working mothers on their children. Maybe we can even get some big-name experts to do monthly columns."

Edmond looked thoughtful. "You'll have to get a whole new staff together."

676

"I know that."

"And keep everything separate from HJII. That means every last bank account, bill, printer, distributor, office space . . ."

She smiled. "I intended on doing that all along."

He nodded, and despite his calm, she could sense that his interest was aroused. "Figure out a name for it yet?"

She grinned. *"You!"*

"You?"

"That's right. *You,* followed by an exclamation mark. That's the name of the new slick. What do you think?"

He took a cigarette out of his case and tapped it thoughtfully against the brushed gold. "If it succeeds right off the bat like everything else you've done, you'll make tons of money," he said cautiously. "If it doesn't . . ." He let the unfinished sentence hang ominously.

She nodded wordlessly. She knew what he meant. If the new magazine failed, she would be ten million in the hole. No, more than that. There was the interest to consider, too. It was a frightening prospect, to say the least. Especially since, with the HJII expansion, the construction of the building, the purchase of the cars and the plane, the profits had shrunk. Massively. Even for her.

Her violet eyes were steady and unwavering. "I'm willing to take the gamble," she said softly. "I feel lucky."

She wasn't lucky. She'd never had to swallow the bitterness of defeat before, and now its repugnant taste coated her mouth. From the moment *You!* hit the newsstands it was a miserable failure. She'd gone out on a limb, and the limb had given way under her. She had hoped against hope that perhaps by giving it a few months, *You!* would catch on. By the time the third issue was out, the bell was tolling loud and clear. It could be heard all the way from the newsstands to Madison Avenue and down to Wall Street.

She stood despondently at the floor-length windows looking down at the traffic crawling along Fifth. It was a miserable, windy day, and waves of rain lashed against the windows. Her thoughts were heavy and dark. The failure of *You!* could only be blamed on her, and she felt like kicking herself. For once she had broken her cardinal rule. For every other magazine she had ever created there had been a ready market waiting to snatch it up. *Les Modes*'s secret had been to follow

677

in the footsteps of *Vogue* and *L'Officiel* and *Harper's Bazaar*. They had done the testing on the proving ground, and she'd simply marched in behind them and outclassed them all. She realized now that had she done that this last time around, everything would have worked out fine. But America just wasn't ready for a magazine catering to the working woman. *You!* had two strikes against it. It lacked the slickness and gloss people had come to associate with her, and, unfortunately, it was ahead of its time.

She tightened her lips, walked over to her bookcase, and slid out the first edition of *You!* She stared down at it with a grim expression.

YOU! The tilted letters in the left-hand corner took up half the width of the cover, and they were long and white and sleek, followed by a fire-engine-red exclamation mark.

Directly beneath that was the tilted white legend "The Magazine for Today's Woman."

And under that, on the right and parallel to the logo, were the feature titles, each line decreasing in size from top to bottom.

Staring out at Hélène from the glossy cover was *You!*'s prototype of the new American working woman with her two children. Mommy wearing a chic man-tailored suit, navy-blue silk scarf, white, feminine blouse. Perfectly coiffed, expertly made-up, an arm around each child's shoulder. Junior, seven, blond, shaggy-haired, wearing a Yankees T-shirt. Daughter, red-haired, freckled, cute. Everyone laughing happily.

For a moment Hélène's eyelids felt very heavy. The HJII board members were winning. "The Magazine for Today's Woman" had been resoundingly rejected by today's woman. She wondered if they knew that.

The telephone jangled suddenly. She started, then slowly went over to her desk. She punched down on the button of her private extension and picked up the receiver. It was Edmond.

"Gore just called," he said. "ManhattanBank wants to set up a meeting with you."

She drew in a deep breath, puffed out her cheeks, and slowly let the air out. "What about? The loan isn't due for another few months."

"He didn't say. My guess is that maybe they're getting itchy feet. After *You!*'s disaster, they're probably worried about your ability to pay off the loan."

She tightened her lips in annoyance. In this town, the only thing that spread faster than success was failure. She looked down at the magazine in her hand. It seemed to be mocking her. "Can we stall?"

"I highly advise against it. We can't buy more than a few days at the outside, anyway."

Wearily she closed her eyes. "All right, call Gore. Schedule the meeting for tomorrow afternoon. Then get the comptroller in here. I want to be briefed as to where exactly we stand right now."

"Will do. Anything else?"

"Yes," she said slowly. "Go to Citibank and open an identical account for each account we currently have at ManhattanBank. That includes both our personal accounts. But deposit only the minimum amount required for opening them."

He let out a whistle. "You do play dirty, Little French Girl," he said with a note of admiration in his voice.

Slowly she replaced the receiver. She stared down at the copy of *You!* On an impulse, she tossed it into the wastebasket. Then she collected the other issues from the shelf and threw them away, too.

She had enough reminders of *You!*'s failure.

Yes, the vultures were winning.

Suddenly she slammed her hand down on her desk. "I won't have it!" she shouted, and made up her mind. She would fight to the end. And then, even if ManhattanBank foreclosed and sold her collateral shares of HJII—even then, she would continue to fight.

What was it Siegfried had once said? *If you've made it once, and it wasn't a fluke, you can make it again.*

She would do her damnedest to prove him right.

17

James Cortland Gore III was waiting for them in his office. She kept her face impassive. She had learned one thing about bankers. They're bad poker players. When you're at the top of the world, they fall all over themselves trying to please you. When things aren't going too well, they're polite but curt. And when your world is slowly collapsing around you, they can smell it as clearly as a hungry shark can smell blood from a mile away. And the fat banker was smelling blood. She could tell that the instant she walked into his office.

He rose politely from his leather swivel chair, but this time he didn't come around from behind his big desk. "Miss Junot." He nodded curtly in her direction. She nodded in return. Then he faced Edmond. "Mr. Junot."

Edmond nodded. "Mr. Gore."

The men exchanged handshakes. Then they waited politely until Hélène took a seat. Once she was seated, they sat down too.

Gore cleared his throat and came right to the point. "We had a . . . ah . . . board of directors' meeting yesterday morning, and the subject of your ten-million-dollar loan was raised." His beady gray eyes appraised Hélène from beneath his bushy black-and-white eyebrows. "The board is considering calling in your loan."

She felt as though she'd been shot, but she managed to keep her face impassive. "Mr. Gore, I'm sure you're aware that the loan is a nonrenewable note," she said smoothly. "It is due in four months' time. Surely ManhattanBank is not so desperately in need of ready cash that it is calling in its oustanding loans early?"

"Miss Junot." The bald banker folded his hands on his desk and leaned forward. "Please try to understand our position. The directors are only trying to look out for the bank's best interests." He sighed regretfully. "They are troubled be-

680

cause they think you may be in the midst of a severe financial crisis."

She raised her eyebrows. "Indeed," she said coldly. She turned to Edmond. "Would you like to brief Mr. Gore on my current financial situation?"

Edmond started to reach for his briefcase, but Gore gestured for him to put it away. "Miss Junot," he said solemnly, "the reason the directors are worried is that ManhattanBank takes care of all your banking needs. They have a good overview of your daily financial status, and they have come to the conclusion that there is no way you'll be able to repay the loan in four months' time."

Edmond had been quiet up until now. "Mr. Gore . . ." he said softly.

Gore turned to him.

Edmond took out his gold cigarette case, selected a cigarette, and bought time by lighting it slowly. He inhaled deeply and blew out a cloud of smoke. "Your directors are, of course, aware of all of Miss Junot's financial transactions?"

"I believe that's what I just got through saying," Gore said irritably. "We've been handling all of Miss Junot's accounts for several years now."

Edmond watched Gore carefully. "And just because she *has* been banking with you for so long, you believe that you have financial insight into *all* her accounts?"

"Yes."

"No, Mr. Gore," Edmond corrected him quietly. "You are not completely aware of Miss Junot's financial dealings."

Gore stared at him, then at Hélène. "I don't think I quite understand."

Hélène held her breath, but Edmond smiled easily. "You are aware that Miss Junot is a very wealthy woman?"

"Of course."

"And you're also aware that she has businesses overseas?"

"Of course," Gore said more irritably than the last time.

"Do you happen to know just where her businesses abroad are located?"

Gore sighed faintly, resigned to have to play cat and mouse. "England, Germany, Italy, and France," he said wearily.

Edmond smiled. "And what country do Germany, Italy, and France border on?"

"Switzerland." Gore stared at Edmond. Then he turned to Hélène. There was surprise in his voice. And something else, too. Respect. "You have Swiss bank accounts?" he asked softly.

She smiled mysteriously. "Really, Mr. Gore. I'm sure you understand that I must keep that a confidential matter between the Swiss and myself."

"Then you *do* have eleven million dollars?"

"Ten million, seven hundred and ninety-five," Edmond said quickly. "That is what ManhattanBank would be due if the loan is called in at this time."

Gore steepled his fingers and nodded thoughtfully. "Very well. I shall inform my directors that they have nothing to worry about. Of course . . ." He coughed in embarrassment. "Of course, I shall have to verify that your Swiss accounts can indeed cover the loan."

Hélène rose to her feet. "As you wish, Mr. Gore." She had to force herself to stay calm and collected. But her heart was racing. "Need I remind you that ManhattanBank is holding eleven million dollars' worth of HJII stock as collateral?" She smiled at Edmond. "It seems that Mr. Gore and his directors do not trust us. The checkbooks, please."

She saw Gore watching them nervously, but she chose to ignore him. Edmond put his cigarette out, slung his briefcase onto his lap, and snapped it open. He took out thirteen checkbooks and a sheaf of long-term certificates of deposit. He leaned forward and stacked them neatly on a corner of Gore's desk. Then he took out thirteen more checkbooks. These were from Citibank, and he placed them prominently in two different stacks beside the others. Solemnly he handed his gold pen over to Hélène. She took it from him and smiled wordlessly. Quickly she sat back down and pulled her chair closer to the desk. "Mr. Gore," she said in a clear voice, "I would like the following transactions put into effect immediately." She pushed the long-term certificates toward him. "I know that there is a large interest penalty on early withdrawal, but I would like to convert these into cash. Instantly."

Gore leafed through them, and his eyes widened perceptibly. "B-but . . . they're seven hundred thousand dollars' worth!" he stammered.

She smiled sweetly. "Yes, they are." Then she picked up

682

the top checkbook from the ManhattanBank stack, flipped it open, and started to write out a check. "Pay to the order of Hélène Junot. Six hundred thousand, three hundred and ninety-three dollars and forty-two cents," she read aloud. She picked up a Citibank deposit slip and filled it out for that exact amount. Then with a flourish she ripped out the check. She looked at Gore. "Would you happen to have a paper clip?"

Silently Gore rolled his chair back a ways, opened his top desk drawer, and handed her a clip. "Thank you," she said. She took it and clipped the check and the deposit slip together. She laid them aside. Then she opened the next ManhattanBank checkbook. "Eight hundred thousand and sixty-eight dollars—"

"Miss Junot!" Gore seemed to have found his voice. "May I ask what you are doing?"

She looked across the desk at him but kept the pen poised over the check. "I'm simply transferring all my business to Citibank, Mr. Gore." She saw his face go pale and quickly added, "Don't worry, I shall inform my Zurich bank immediately and have them transfer to you the outstanding loan plus interest."

Edmond sat back and nonchalantly started to light another cigarette. He smiled at Gore. "No offense intended, of course, but I trust that our comptroller and some of our accountants can meet with the ManhattanBank auditors and determine that everything is in order?"

The banker had broken out into a sudden sweat, and he was mopping his forehead with a handkerchief. "P-please don't be so hasty, M-Miss Junot," he stammered.

"Mr. Gore," Hélène said in a level voice, "a bank is only as good as the services it provides its clients. When these services can't meet one's needs, it is time to change banks. Surely you can understand that. I have nearly four million dollars in various accounts here, my brother has two hundred thousand, and nearly thirteen million a month flow through the HJII accounts. Citibank has assured me that they can handle that volume to my satisfaction." She continued making out the check. Then she tore it out of the checkbook, closed it, and filled out another deposit slip. "I'm sorry, but could I trouble you for some more paper clips?"

"Miss Junot, *please*," Gore pleaded in a small voice. "I will ensure you that your loan will not be called in early. I agree that the directors were acting hastily—"

"I'm afraid you don't trust me, Mr. Gore," Hélène said. "Banking must be based on mutual trust."

He nodded effusively. "Of course, of course. Please, won't you reconsider? We're aware that you're a valuable client. Of course we won't need to verify your Swiss accounts . . ."

She exchanged glances with Edmond. He nodded his head imperceptibly. For now, they had won a round. Gore hadn't realized they were bluffing.

Only when they left ManhattanBank did Hélène realize that she was wrong. Gore *had* known they were bluffing. He'd swallowed the story of the nonexistent Swiss accounts too readily. But why he'd chosen to do that didn't matter now. She suspected he had something to hide, something that an audit would have uncovered. Idly she wondered if his fingers had been in the till, but she really couldn't care less. Whatever it was, it was Gore's problem, and his alone. The bank would cover any losses.

But she didn't have much time to wonder about Gore. When she got back to the office, Julie handed her a message. Nigel had called. She placed a call to England immediately; a few minutes later, she had Nigel on the line. "Darling, is something wrong?" she asked.

His voice sounded tortured and far away. "It's Pamela. She's been in a car accident." There was a pause. "Hélène, she's dead."

"Oh, Nigel! I *am* sorry." Hélène stared at the receiver, then said, "Nigel, I'll be there tonight. Wait up for me, darling."

As soon as she hung up, she picked up the phone again and dialed the airport. The HJII jet was ready for takeoff. Her passport was in her desk. She'd worry about clothes once she got to England.

Five minutes later she was in the white Rolls with the HJII plates, heading toward the airport. Less than an hour later she was already well out over the Atlantic, headed for England.

And that was . . . yesterday.

TODAY

Monday, January 15

1

Hélène listened to the faint rise-and-fall breath of Nigel's sleep. She stared at him, her head resting in the palm of her hand, her elbow digging into the crisp softness of the Pratesi sheets. The thick cashmere blanket rose and fell with each breath he took. His head was turned toward her, lying sideways in the softness of the down pillows trimmed with satin ribbons and scallops of lace. She had watched him ever since he had fallen asleep. Now that the sky was beginning to lighten and let a soft, muted winter glow in through the windows, he was more than just a dark shape.

Nigel. She had waited for him for so long. Now the wait seemed worth it; it almost felt as if so many years had never passed. Nigel was hers, and hers alone.

She pulled her free hand out from under the covers and reached out as if to stroke him. She kept her fingers a bare fraction of an inch above him. Affectionately her extended index finger followed the noble shape of his forehead, down along the bridge of his nose, almost but not quite brushing across his lips. She let her hand linger there, loving the soft feel of the warm whispers of his breath.

"Sleep well, my love," she whispered softly, "sleep well."

That she was awake and he was cocooned in the soothing blanket of his sleep didn't seem to matter. She was content just to know that he was there beside her. That he would always be there. She enjoyed just being able to look at him. Even asleep, he seemed powerful. He slept on his side, his body relaxed.

She twisted slowly around in the bed, afraid that any sudden move might awaken him. She smiled to herself in the pale blue light as she reflected on their night of lovemaking. He had been so strong and demanding. His thrusts had been powerful as he stroked deep and hard within her. Moaning, she had felt herself heat up, and clasped him tightly, respond-

687

ing to his every move. She had experienced one exquisite orgasm after another. Then he had fallen asleep with his head buried between her breasts. Now she felt complete. She was going to be the Duchess of Farquaharshire.

She glanced at the alarm clock. It ticked softly on the nightstand in rhythm with his breathing. The faint green numbers glowed softly. It was a little past six.

They had been up almost all night, and still she couldn't go to sleep. In half an hour she would have to get up. But she didn't feel at all tired. She felt . . . yes—*satiated*. Rejuvenated. Awakened.

Gently she played the fingertips of her right hand across the finger on her left. Once again the massive yellow Somerset Sun was heavy on her finger, this time for good. In six hours they would be at City Hall and together climb the wide, sweeping steps to the marriage bureau. Nigel was hers. Hers alone. She felt better now than she had at any other time in her life.

She reached up to the nightstand and felt for the piece of paper that lay in front of the alarm clock. She wanted to touch it, to make certain it was still there. It was. Nigel had given it to her last night in the Café Carlyle. He had flown to New York to beg once again for her hand in marriage and to present her with the Somerset Sun. And this time, she hadn't refused him. Once she'd let him slip the big ring onto her finger, he had reached into his wallet and pushed the certified check drawn on his account at Morgan Guaranty Trust across the tablecloth toward her. She had stared down at it. It was made out to Hélène Junot for eleven million dollars. She didn't have to be told what it was for. To pay the bank loan and save HJII from the vultures.

She had pushed the light blue check back toward him. "No, Nigel," she said firmly. "This has got to stay out of it. You have your businesses and I have mine. They have nothing to do with our love."

He put his hand firmly over hers. The check was in the middle of the table, caught in a tug-of-war under her fingertips. He shook his head. "Our empires have everything to do with our love, darling," he said softly. "Don't you see? We're builders, you and I. We're both power-seekers. You in your way, I in mine. That's what brought us together in the first place. That's what's kept us together all this time. We share more than just love. We share ambitions and dreams.

Besides," he added quickly, "consider it a loan. You may repay it at your convenience."

"Don't be ridiculous," she said.

"I'm not, don't you be." He leaned back in his chair and studied her levelly. There was a proud, determined pout to her lips. He knew that she needed help. He had also known that she would refuse it. But just this once, he couldn't give in. There was too much at stake and she had too much pride. Much too much for her own damn good. He would have to make her see reason.

He chose his words carefully now and spoke hurriedly. "Hélène, if I'm to be your husband, you must trust me enough to let me help you. Don't always try so hard to be so bloody independent. There are times each of us needs a little help."

"This isn't why I agreed to marry you."

"I know that," he said gently. "It's the reason why you kept on saying no."

She nodded. Silently she looked down at the check, then over into his eyes.

"Go on, take it," he said. Then he grinned. "You accepted a three-million-dollar diamond without qualms. What's wrong with a check for eleven million?"

"It's not the same," she said with stubborn dignity. "You know that."

He reached across the table, clasped both his hands around hers, and pressed them. "Darling, I love you," he said softly. "And I know how important HJII is to you. Too important for you to let it go down the drain because of foolish pride." He looked steadily into her eyes. "Take it," he commanded her gently.

And she had taken it, promising to repay him with interest. And he had laughed. "Marriage is a partnership," he said, "or didn't you know that?"

"I know that," she said in a trembling voice.

He smiled. "Just don't ever forget who'll wear the pants in this family. You'll have your business, but I intend to take care of you. I'm very old-fashioned. Is that clear?"

Suddenly her knees felt weak. She was glad that she was sitting down. Her voice dropped to a whisper. "I . . . I'll be sure to remember that."

689

2

Robert Rowen got to the Staten Island ferry terminal about fifteen minutes early. He located the men's room but didn't go inside yet. Instead, he decided to kill time by walking around the terminal. He despised public rest rooms.

A foghorn cried out mournfully as a Staten Island ferry pulled up in the foggy semidarkness, its windows ghostly rows of yellow light. A moment later it thumped against the terminal, sending a tremor through it. As he watched, a mass of passengers hurried off. He shivered and dug his hands into his pockets. It was too cold for a trench coat, even with the heavy knit sweater and jacket underneath. Everyone else was well-bundled for winter. And he felt silly having to wear the red carnation in his buttonhole. It drew too much attention to him. This meeting had all the ingredients of a disagreeable thriller.

As eight o'clock came around, he knew it was time he went into the men's room. Once inside, he glanced around suspiciously. It was deserted. There was no one at the urinals, and all the cubicles were empty.

For a few minutes he waited impatiently for the whisperer to make contact. Then he felt foolish just standing there. He went and pretended to use the urinal. He glanced at his watch. Already it was five after eight.

A few more minutes passed. Then he heard the door behind him opening and banging shut. He held his breath as he sneaked a glance backward. A man in a business suit had come in. Rowen turned his face away as the man approached the urinal beside his and set his briefcase down on the floor. *Zip!* The faint but unmistakable sound of a zipper sounded loud and obscene. Then he heard the splash of urine.

He glanced toward the man out of the corners of his eyes. Already the man was preparing to leave. Again Rowen averted his head; the man was turning around. Then he heard his footsteps. A moment later, the door opened and banged shut. He was alone again.

He wondered now if the voice on the phone had just been playing some kind of sick joke on him. Thinking about it now, he saw how foolish he had been to fall for it. A million dollars! No one in his right mind gave away a million dollars. Not for any reason. Least of all not for ten million dollars' worth of shares in a publishing company. That was an extra ten percent on top of the market price. Whoever wanted them would have a chance to bid on them anyway. Yes, it was high time he screwed his head on right and saw reason. He'd simply forget all this nonsense and go to the office early and get caught up on some backlog. What a fool he had been! A million dollars!

As he turned to leave, something caught his eye. The man had forgotten his briefcase. It was still sitting beside the urinal. He'd have to run after him and tell him. No, he'd catch up with him *with* the briefcase. That was better.

Quickly he went to collect it. Suddenly he felt his skin starting to crawl. An engraved brass nameplate was screwed into the top of the case. The name was his.

Robert Rowen.

Slowly he bent down to pick it up. Was it for real? Maybe he was going crazy and imagining it? Once he had the handle in his hand, he knew it was no mirage. And it was heavy. A lot of money was heavy. But then, so was paper. Or lead. Or any of a dozen things.

He took the briefcase with him into one of the booths and locked the door. Then he sat down on the stained toilet seat and placed the briefcase on his lap. He stared at it in silent fascination.

"You're being a sucker," a miserable little voice warned him. "You're falling for the joke."

But he couldn't help himself. He found himself fiddling with the catches. With a loud snap, they sprang open. His heart started to hammer against his ribs. Slowly he lifted the lid.

He sucked in his breath. Neat bundles of twenty-dollar bills were stacked inside, each bundle held together by inch-wide strips of white paper stamped by the bank. Each package was stamped "$10,000." There were fifty such bundles.

He examined a few of the bills and shook his head. He

couldn't believe it! They weren't phoney. It was really money, all right.

It was no joke.

3

"Double-crossing bitches!" Hubert de Léger's face was white with rage, but the purple splotches on his cheeks that came from burst blood vessels stood out clearly. For a moment he glared at the telephone in his hand. Then he raised it up above his head and brought it crashing down. It let out a painfully weak ring as it hit the corner of his ormolu desk and then bounced to the floor, the expectant crash muffled by the lush, sculptured pile of the Edward Fields carpet. He kicked the offending instrument out of his way as he stomped to the door. Flinging it open, he rushed out of the book-lined library. His chest was heaving and his breaths were coming in short gasps. He didn't bother to take the suede-lined elevator; the stairs were quicker. He went running down them two at a time. Once in the foyer, he stopped and looked around wildly. The town house was quiet. There wasn't a sound to be heard.

"Eduard!" he roared.

A moment later his imperturbable butler opened the double doors from within the living room. "Oui, Monsieur le Comte?" he said calmly.

Hubert glared at him darkly. "My car! Have it brought around immediately!"

"Oui, Monsieur le Comte." The butler turned and started to leave.

"And hurry for once, you slothful, ass-dragging . . ." Fuming, Hubert broke off as he struggled in vain to find the expressive noun he was looking for. More frustrated than ever, he made a contemptuous gesture. His voice was now a high-pitched screech. "Move it!"

"Of course, Monsieur le Comte," the butler said with toneless dignity. His face remained an impassive mask. He was long since used to Hubert's tirades and suffered them in silence. But this was the worst one yet. Vaguely he wondered what had happened to trigger it, but then he swallowed his curiosity. It was none of a good butler's business. He withdrew with implacable calm and left Hubert to pace the foyer impatiently.

When the Mercedes finally rolled up in front of the brownstone, Hubert immediately rushed outside, not even bothering to throw on a coat. He didn't wait for the chauffeur to help him. He jumped right in and slammed the door shut. "The Pierre!" he screamed.

With a burst of speed, the Mercedes surged smoothly off across East Sixty-eighth Street.

A drink. Feeling somewhat better already, now that he had come to some sort of decisive and positive step, he leaned forward, yanked the door of the bar cabinet open, and reached inside. He grabbed a bottle of Armagnac by the neck and fished it out from its shelf. For a moment he turned the bottle in his hands, feeling the smoothness of the glass. He licked his lips. They felt suddenly dry and cracked. He hadn't realized how thirsty he was.

Quickly, without wasting another second, he wrestled with the cork. Then he heard the satisfyingly familiar *plop* and the faint hiss of escaped air. He smiled and lifted the bottle to his lips, drawing on it hungrily, his lips sucking noisily like a starving baby at its mother's breast.

He took a deep breath as the heat of the alcohol burned down his throat and then rushed soothingly throughout his body, bringing a pleasing numbness to his limbs. He sank back in the seat, his hand clutching the bottle by the neck as if someone might snatch it away from him. Clumsily he rested his left elbow on the padded armrest and stared blankly out the side window, his hand at his mouth. Without realizing it, he began gnawing on his fingernails.

She had done it! he thought miserably. Somehow, against all odds and right under his very nose, she had managed to marry herself off quietly—to one of the frigging *richest* men in the world, no less—*and* repay the bank loan! How? How how how how how *how* was that at all possible? How, without his knowing it? Had it all been settled when she'd stopped in England in the Lear jet on her way to New York a week ago? When he'd found out where she'd interrupted the flight, he hadn't attached any significance to it. He had been sure, so *damned* sure, that he and the others held all the cards. But now? Now it was clear that she'd kept something hidden up her sleeve. But why hadn't his detectives been on their toes? That's what he was paying them so handsomely for. And above all, *how had Nigel Somerset managed to leave England and sneak into New York without his even knowing it?* Somerset was supposed to be watched night and day.

Hubert's coal-black eyes flashed. All along, his detectives had assured him that Nigel Somerset was still at Fallsworth. Well, he wasn't. That much even *he* knew. And what a fool he'd made of himself! Just six and a half hours earlier, he'd made the five-hundred-thousand-dollar drop to Rowen. A half-million dollars! And for nothing!

He started to shake anew with fury, just thinking of the telephone calls. Until he'd been on the phone, he hadn't even had an inkling of what was up. Nobody had bothered to inform him about anything. And that Rowen! He took a savage swig of Armagnac. Driblets of the liquid ran down his chin from the corners of his mouth. He wiped them away with the back of his hand. That Rowen was a son of a bitch!

He could feel a fiery hatred burning within him. Rowen was enough to make him sick. But he'd get him! He'd *ruin* him! Somehow, somewhere, he'd see to it that his banking career came to an end.

Up until he'd talked to Rowen this afternoon, it had seemed that everything was well under control. He had just called him to have him verify that the briefcase indeed contained a half-million. Not that he'd suspected anything had gone wrong. After all, he himself had watched Rowen from a distance as he'd come out of the men's room carrying the briefcase. He didn't really know what it was that made him call. Instinct, perhaps. Just to make sure. To add a bit more pressure.

"Robert Rowen speaking," the man's deep, familiar voice had said over the wire after the secretary had made the connection.

"Is everything in order?" Hubert had used his whisper, the same whisper he'd used first on Gore, and now on Rowen. "Did you count the money?"

Rowen's voice was very clear and casual. "I beg your pardon?"

694

A sudden foreboding constricted Hubert's heart. "The money!" he hissed sharply. "Did you count it?"

"Who is this? What money are you talking about?" Rowen's voice was properly indignant.

Hubert stared at the receiver. It suddenly dawned on him that something had gone wrong. It wasn't as if Rowen didn't recognize his voice. It was something else.

"You know very well what money!" Hubert hissed harshly. "The money in the briefcase you picked up in the men's room!"

"I'm sorry, sir," Rowen had replied politely. "I believe you must have the wrong extension."

"Listen, you creep!" Hubert spit out venomously. "I warned you about what would happen if you tried to double-cross us!"

"I beg your pardon?" Rowen's voice was noncommittal.

"I'll ruin you!" Hubert was screaming now; the last vestiges of the whisper were gone.

"I'm sorry, sir," Rowen said calmly. "It is obvious that you have the wrong extension. I see absolutely no reason for continuing this conversation. Good day."

Hubert stared incredulously at his telephone receiver. Rowen had hung up on him. Hung up! His mind was flying. *What could have gone wrong?*

He could feel the sweat breaking out on his forehead as his fingers quickly dialed Hélène's office. While he waited, he jumped to his feet and stared out the window behind him. The curtains were drawn aside and there was a good view of his back garden. The trees and shrubbery were bare and skeletal, the ground around the flagstones frozen. He listened as the phone at the other end began to ring. It was picked up halfway through the third ring.

"Good afternoon, Miss Junot's office." The Sphinx's unmistakable voice was brisk and businesslike.

"This is the Comte de Léger. Is she in?"

"I'm sorry, sir. Miss Junot won't be back until two weeks from this coming Friday."

"Two weeks . . . *What*! B-but I don't understand," Hubert stuttered. He turned away from the window and sank back down into his chair. He reached for a handkerchief and mopped his forehead furiously. "There must be some mistake. There was a meeting scheduled for late this afternoon!"

"I was told to cancel it, sir. I just tried calling you, but your line was busy."

For a moment Hubert was silent as he tried to compose himself. Then he found his voice. "Where is she?" he asked softly.

He thought he could detect a gleeful laugh in her voice. "Actually, Miss Junot is no longer Miss Junot, sir. At twelve o'clock noon she officially became the Duchess of Farquharshire."

Hubert could feel the blood draining from his head. It wasn't possible! He closed his eyes. His library was suddenly reeling around him like the world from a merry-go-round. "And the bank loan?" he whispered.

"Which bank loan are you referring to, sir?"

"The one for ten million dollars!" he snapped irritably.

"I'm sorry, sir, but I don't know anything about that."

"Bitch!" Hubert slammed down the receiver. Didn't anybody know *anything*? He stared at the telephone. He'd make one last call. Much as he despised Edmond Junot, he, at least, might be able to shed some light on this mystery.

"Legal department," a woman's voice said hollowly.

"This is the Comte de Léger. Is Mr. Junot in?"

"Please hold, sir. I'll check and see." There was a click and he was put on hold. After a while there was another click.

"Edmond Junot speaking." Even the telephone lines found it difficult to make the resonance of his voice sound hollow.

A grimace distorted Hubert's lips. He didn't like Edmond Junot one bit. Never had, in fact. Although he wouldn't admit it even to himself, something about the man threatened him.

"This is Hubert de Léger," Hubert said, automatically slipping into French.

Edmond chose to speak English. "Actually, I'm in the middle of an important meeting . . ."

"Then I won't keep you long," Hubert assured him quickly. "I was just wondering about the status of the HJII shares. Has the ManhattanBank loan been repaid?"

"That is my sister's business, I believe," Edmond said stiffly.

"I know it is," Hubert said smoothly. "However, as you well know, the status of that loan affects all of Junot's shareholders, myself included. Believe me, I regret very much having to intrude on your time."

696

Edmond was silent for a moment. "Perhaps you are right," he said finally in an even voice. "The status of that loan does affect you and the others." He paused. "It was repaid at ten-thirty this morning."

Hubert's voice was a whisper. "You're . . . you're not joking?"

"Believe me, Mr. de Léger, I don't joke about such matters. At the request of my sister, I went down to Manhattan-Bank to take care of the matter personally."

"Th-thank you."

With trembling fingers Hubert replaced the receiver. He was shaking with fury. *Mr.* de Léger! That peasant knew very well that he was *Monsieur le Comte!*

He got to his feet and looked down at his desk. The telephone seemed to be mocking him, laughing at him with its shrill rings. He hadn't even realized that it had begun to ring. All he knew was that the jeering sounds reverberated crazily in his head. And they had stopped only after he'd smashed the damned instrument and it lay broken at his feet.

Just as the Mercedes limousine pulled up in front of the Pierre, the bottle of Armagnac was empty. Hubert shook it, glared at it, and then tossed it down beside him on the seat. He didn't wait for the chauffeur to come around and hold open his door for him or for the liveried doorman to rush over. He jerked open the door himself and leaped out, leaving it wide open in his hurry. He rushed into the lobby. Not bothering to announce himself at the desk, he marched straight up to the bank of elevators. A minute later he got off on Karl von Eiderfeld's floor.

Impatiently he banged on the door of the apartment. A maid in uniform opened it. He pushed past her into the dim foyer.

"I beg your pardon, sir," she said politely. "Is there someone you wish to see?"

Hubert looked wildly around the foyer. "Where is he?"

"He?"

"Von Eiderfeld!" Hubert said irritably.

"In the living room, sir."

"Get out!"

"Sir?" The woman looked at him as if she hadn't heard right.

Hubert drew himself up to his full height. "Are you going to get out or do I have to throw you out?"

Wide-eyed, the maid fled into the corridor. She glanced over her shoulder and then swiftly shut the door behind her.

Upon hearing the commotion, von Eiderfeld had come into the foyer. "My dear Comte, you look beside yourself," he said smoothly.

"She's done it!" Hubert screamed.

Von Eiderfeld drew back and stared at him. "Who has done what?"

"The bitch, who else?" Hubert made a wild gesture as he whirled around and stalked into the living room. He blinked in the darkness, trying to get his bearings. Then he headed straight over to the armoire, flung the doors open, grabbed the first bottle in sight, unscrewed the cap, and took a massive swig. He let out a heavy sigh and banged the bottle back down on the shelf.

Von Eiderfeld was watching him quietly from across the room. He had never seen anyone in such a dangerous rage. Hubert needed calming down; that he could see. But how to do it? Perhaps by just remaining silent. That was what the General Staff used to do when the Führer flew into his rages. Eventually they worked their way out of the system. For the time being, the best thing to do was to humor Hubert.

His whole body shaking, Hubert dropped into a fragile French chair and buried his face in his hands. After a moment, a bit of his composure returned. He looked up at von Eiderfeld with a drawn expression. "You owe me a quarter of a million," he said quietly.

This came as some surprise, to be sure. Slowly von Eiderfeld walked over to the fireplace. There was no fire in the hearth, but the logs were already neatly stacked on the grate. He stared up at the big dark canvas above the mantel, his back to Hubert. He was thinking rapidly. The quarter-million could mean only one thing: half the five hundred thousand Hubert had insisted on bribing Rowen with. He would go just so far in humoring Hubert. There had to be a cutoff point. "Why don't you tell me exactly what has happened?" he said calmly.

Hubert glared at him. "All right, I'll tell you. She's done it. She's gone off, married the Duke, and paid off the loan."

Von Eiderfeld looked thoughtful and rubbed his chin with his fist. "It doesn't really surprise me," he said. There was a note of respect in his voice. "She's a remarkable woman, you know. Survival is at her very core."

"What kind of shit are you mumbling now?" Hubert sprang to his feet. He raced from one window to the next, yanking aside the drawn curtains. The morning sun was gone; the sky was a uniform gray, several shades lighter than the graffiti-covered boulders sticking up out of Central Park. Either tonight or sometime tomorrow it would start to snow.

Von Eiderfeld shielded his sensitive eyes with one hand. "Why don't you compose yourself?" he said quietly, turning his back to the windows.

Hubert's chest heaved and fell. "Compose myself!" he said. "I want a check for a quarter of a million. *Now!*"

"You believe that I should pay for your mistakes?" von Eiderfeld asked softly without turning around. "For your miscalculations? I warned you to wait until five o'clock this afternoon."

"We had a deal to split the bribe fifty-fifty, remember?"

"We had a deal to wait until after the close of the business day," von Eiderfeld corrected him.

"So you want to renege! I should have known better than to trust you! You're just like everyone else! Well, you're through!" Hubert snarled suddenly. "I know all about you! I read those files she had on you!"

Von Eiderfeld turned to look at him. His voice quivered slightly. "So? They are now just a pile of ashes."

Hubert laughed bitterly. "I'll see to it that there's a full-scale investigation anyway. I remember what was in those files. I even copied some of it down. You know what I'll do with that? I'll call the Israeli authorities. You're through, you pink-eyed albino freak! I'll see that you're put on trial and executed!"

"Sit down and compose yourself!" von Eiderfeld commanded.

Hubert lunged at him, grabbed his lapels, and shook him. "Nobody stabs *me* in the back, do you hear? I'll fix you! It'll be like they did with Eichmann! They'll put you in a glass booth like a pheasant under glass!" Hubert began to laugh crazily. Savagely he pushed von Eiderfeld backward and let go of the lapels. Von Eiderfeld stumbled and fell into a chair. He said nothing, just stared. Hubert wasn't rational. He should have stayed as far away from him as possible.

Karl von Eiderfeld didn't doubt for an instant that

Hubert's threat was serious. An irrational mind like his was capable of destroying anything and anyone. Still, there was one tiny consolation. Hubert was wrong about the end being at hand for him. One phase of his life, perhaps. But not the end. Call it . . . a new beginning.

After Hubert stomped out and slammed the door, von Eiderfeld got up from the chair with a peculiar sort of dignity. He knew exactly what he had to do. He brushed his sleeves as he crossed over to the windows. One by one, he drew the curtains shut again. Then he stopped at the telephone table. He bent over, unlocked a shallow drawer, and pulled it open. He took out two leather folders. In one was his passport, in the other a wallet. This passport and wallet were always within reach in the event of just such an emergency. The passport was his ticket to a new life. The wallet would help him get there. It was thick with cash and traveler's checks.

Quickly he pocketed both. Then he dialed a telephone number that he had committed to memory long ago. It was to a helicopter service operating out of the heliport beside the Fifty-ninth Street Bridge. He told them to have a helicopter waiting for him in twenty minutes, rotors turning and ready for takeoff. Then he dialed another memorized number in New Jersey. Hélène had specifically forbidden him ever to use private transportation. Up until this moment, he had followed her instructions to the letter. Yet, unknown even to her, he had a private Lear jet in readiness wherever he went, even though he never used it. It was waiting now at Teterboro Airport. Once he boarded, he would give the pilot piecemeal instructions. First, he would fly to Dallas, refuel, and fly on to Mexico City. From there, it was down to Panama City and then over the Andes, jungles, and pampas to Uruguay. He had fifteen million dollars stashed away there. Two million was deposited in a bank, one million in cash was hidden, and twelve million in gold and flawless diamonds was buried in a spot only he and Helga knew of.

After calling Teterboro, he put down the receiver. He was glad that he had had the foresight to foresee an emergency like this. Now that the moment had come, he didn't have to panic. For years he had generously seen to it that the high officials in the governments of several countries were well taken care of financially. When the governments in power changed or fell, as they tended to do with geometric rapidity in South America, he had immediately made contact with the new leaders. Besides Uruguay, he had two other contingency plans open to him, one in nearby Paraguay, the other in Costa Rica. His only regrets were that he would no longer be sitting at the helm of Von Eiderfeld Industrien G.m.b.H. and that he would never be able to set foot on his beloved German soil again. He hated semitropical and tropical climates. He missed the changes of season, and the sun hurt his eyes and burned his skin. In South America, everything was turned around. Efficiency was lacking, and even the seasons, one almost indistinguishable from the next, came lazily at the wrong times of the year. But at least his home in Punta del Este stood in readiness. It had been designed with shady loggias and thick blinds which cut the glare of the sun to a minimum. And Helga would be content. There was an Olympic-size pool.

Another comfort were his sons, Rolf and Otto. On and off, they could perhaps visit with him. That way, he would at least be able to oversee the business from a distance. Even with him far away in the background, Von Eiderfeld Industrien would be able to expand. When Hubert blew the whistle, a scandal would touch the corporation and his sons, but it wouldn't do any of them much harm. The bulk of the corporation was involved in oil and refining; both were in desperate demand. Germany had no petroleum resources of her own. The German government would gladly see to it that nothing would stop the wheels of Von Eiderfeld Industrien from turning. As far as Rolf and Otto were concerned, both were adopted. For once, he was glad about that. They knew he was not their natural father, and the stigma of his past wouldn't devour them. And he had taught them both well. They knew how to survive. Hubert's threats were harmless. Mere irritants. Besides, it was high time he retired. He was old and tired. It was time he spent his remaining years quietly with Helga.

At three-fifteen Karl von Eiderfeld walked out of the Hotel Pierre without even a briefcase in his hand. The sky was getting darker. Already, lights were on everywhere, yellow and bright. He never once glanced backward. He pulled up his Persian-lamb collar, adjusted his hat, and thrust his hands in his topcoat pockets. He walked slowly toward Madison Avenue. Like any tourist or native New Yorker, he stopped at the expensive stores and gazed in at the enticing windows. There was nothing suspicious about his behavior. He didn't flee, he didn't run, he didn't have luggage. He wasn't even nervous. Unknown to everyone, he had in his breast pocket the only two things he would ever need. His wallet and his passport. Everything else could be left behind.

Slowly he continued walking until he reached the heliport at the East River. Only when he was hovering above the glittering canyons of Manhattan and the Bell Jet Ranger helicopter turned and nosed swiftly through the darkening skies toward New Jersey did he let out a sigh of relief.

He smiled grimly to himself. He and Hélène Junot had far more in common than either of them would have liked to admit.

They were both survivors.

4

The snow was beginning to come down in plump white flakes as Hélène's white Rolls-Royce pulled to a stop on the tarmac beside the waiting HJII jet. The chauffeur helped Hélène out of the car. She was cocooned in the soft lushness of a Max Reby Montana lynx coat. Nigel emerged behind her.

Hélène was radiant with happiness. For once in her life, even winter, which she had always dreaded, could not detract from her joy. She felt far too good. It was hard for her to believe that she and Nigel were finally married and headed for—at last—the honeymoon both had yearned for so long.

Above the Rolls, the oval portholes of the jet shone yellow in the night. Small red and white lights along the wingtips and atop the fuselage blinked on and off with mechanical precision. Everything was in readiness for instant takeoff.

Suddenly panic swept through her. Perhaps this was only a dream. Perhaps . . . She took a deep breath and glanced down at her hand. The twenty-eight-carat Somerset Sun flashed on her finger. It was real. This was no dream. A flood of relief flowed through her. She really was Hélène Somerset, the seventeenth Duchess of Farquharshire.

Nigel touched her lynx-clad elbow. "Your Grace . . ." he said teasingly, as if reading her thoughts, and bowed low.

She giggled happily and threw her arms around his neck. "You'd better watch it, silly man," she warned playfully. "As a duchess I demand respect." Suddenly her face became serious and she stroked his cheek. "Nigel," she whispered, "what in the world am I going to do with you?"

He smiled. "Everything, I hope." Then he pulled her close and looked down at her. Delicate snowflakes were caught in her blue-black hair, and in the floodlights they sparkled like multifaceted jewels. Her cheeks were flushed and her eyes were oddly luminous. He shook his head in disbelief. "My God, but you're beautiful," he said in a whisper.

She took a deep breath and looked up into his eyes. "So are you, my darling," she replied softly. As she spoke, a tremor ran through her.

He could feel it. Slowly he inclined his head closer, and she let out a little cry as she parted her lips to meet his. She tasted deliciously soft and warm. Greedily he found her tongue.

He opened his eyes. "Oh, my darling," he said with a smile. "If you could only know how happy you make me."

She smiled back at him. "Mmmmmm," she murmured. Then she kissed his lips again.

In the distance, a 747 lifted off. For a moment its flashing lights were visible as it climbed into the snowy sky. Then it disappeared. The passing rumble sounded like thunder.

Nigel glanced at the HJII jet beside them. "We'd better go inside," he suggested. "Otherwise our flying coach might turn into a pumpkin."

"Or worse yet, our flying coach's runway may get closed down due to the snow," she warned.

They laughed, untangled their arms, and boarded. She was the first one up the folding steps. Once inside the six-foot-high headroom of the jet, Nigel ducked his head. "One inch," he moaned. "Why do I seem to be the only person I know of who had the miserable luck to be born just one inch too tall to enjoy full headroom on private jets and cabin cruisers?"

"Punishment," she teased. "For a lifetime of making everyone look up at you."

She looked around the cabin. Everything was in position

for takeoff. The burnished burl tables were folded down for safety, the overhead lights gleamed, and the recessed cabin lights above the portholes were reflected in the smoked-Plexiglas-and-mirror bulkheads that divided the cabin. The leather-trimmed, limousine-cloth seats were in their upright positions. Up front, in the cockpit, the complicated instrument panels were lit up like a carnival: red, green, blue. Through the tinted windshield, the night looked eerie. Greenish-yellow.

Hélène frowned. The pilot's seat was empty. "Where is Hendricks?" she asked the copilot.

He turned around, and she frowned. He was a total stranger. Not very tall, with brown hair and generally nondescript features. The remarkable thing about his face was his eyes. Behind the silver-rimmed aviator glasses, they were icy blue. Even his crisply starched pale blue shirt held more warmth.

"Who are you?" Her voice was puzzled.

For an instant the Chameleon's eyes bore right through hers. Then he got up and stepped nimbly sideways between the two seats, turning to face her. Hélène's eyes dropped and then flared in disbelief, and her blood ran cold. She tried to swallow, but her throat was tight and dry.

She was staring into the barrel of a Browning revolver.

"Someone named Z.Z. sends you her regards," the Chameleon said evenly. And pressed the trigger.

5

Nine intermitable hours passed before Dr. Weiner finally pushed through the double doors. He pinched the bridge of his nose with his fingertips. He was bone-weary, as if he'd been fighting a losing battle, which was closer to the truth than he liked to admit. His eyes were encircled with the deep, dark smudges of fatigue.

"Dr. Weiner!" Edmond jumped from the plastic waiting-room chair and rushed forward, Petite Hélène at his heels.

"We're doing all we can, Mr. Junot," Dr. Weiner said simply. "If it's any consolation, this hospital is one of the finest in the country, and three of the most eminent surg—"

Petite Hélène reached forward and dug her fingers into the doctor's arm. Her face was drawn and pale, and her eyes were red and swollen from crying. "How soon until we . . ." She swallowed and looked away. "Until we know one way or another?" she finished softly, turning to face him again.

Dr. Weiner looked deep into her eyes, wishing there was some way to give her more hope. But there was so little hope. He and the battery of surgeons had raced against the clock. Against one of the most devastating and dangerous wounds a human being could suffer. The bullet had been fired at nearly point-blank range and had perforated the stomach before lodging in the liver.

Petite Hélène pressed herself against Edmond, her face buried in his chest. "Is there anything we can do?" she cried softly.

Dr. Weiner clapped a weary hand on her shoulder. "Pray," he suggested gently. "If you believe at all in the power of prayer, now's the time to pray."

Petite Hélène entered the hospital chapel and quietly shut the door behind her. Soundlessly she slipped down the aisle and into the front pew beside Hélène.

Hélène turned to her, a questioning look in her eyes.

"The operation is over," Petite Hélène said quietly. "Now all we can do is wait and pray."

Hélène followed her niece's eyes to the crucifix suspended above the altar. Her lips quivered and her shoulders slumped. She covered her haggard face with her hands. Pray, she thought numbly. For ten hours, she'd been trying hard, but the prayers weren't forthcoming. Each time she bowed her head and closed her eyes, the same nightmare vision sprang before her.

"Someone named Z.Z. sends you her regards."

Hélène stared down at the barrel of the revolver, unable to move as the Chameleon's index finger began to squeeze the trigger.

Then suddenly Nigel knocked her sideways with all the

force he could muster. She screamed as her body slammed into the hard plastic cabin wall behind the Plexiglas bulkhead. She caught a blur of movement as Nigel charged forward, his forearm deflecting the Chameleon's aim.

The sound of the shot was like thunder. The bullet slammed into the bulkhead in front of her, the Plexiglas quivering under the impact, the mirror strips adorning it cracking into intricate glass cobwebs.

She felt the blood surging to her temples as Nigel wrestled the Chameleon. Both men's faces were red, and their veins stood out on their foreheads as if sculptured in bold relief. In seemingly slow motion they struggled for control of the gun, their arms quivering as they exerted as much pressure against each other as they could possibly summon. Then, in horror, she watched the Chameleon's gun arm slowly coming down ... down ... down. Down into Nigel's body.

Ca-rack!

She let out a piercing shriek and covered her ears with her hands as Nigel staggered forward, staring at the Chameleon in surprise. Then, with a superhuman effort, he somehow managed to turn the gun against the Chameleon. A last blast shook the cabin, and the Chameleon froze. This time it was his turn to look surprised. Then he slid slowly down to the carpet. Nigel bent forward and grasped the bulkhead, gasping for air.

"Nigel?" Hélène's voice was a strangled cry. "Nigel?"

On hands and knees she crawled out from behind the bulkhead and got shakily to her feet. He started to turn. Then his legs gave out from under him, and she caught him as he sagged backward. Slowly she lowered him.

"Nigel ..." She shook him desperately. "*Nigel!*" Then she let out a cry and shrank back. His abdomen was soaked in blood.

"Oh, God, Nigel, *no!*" she screamed in panic, the tears streaming down her cheeks. "Not *now!* Don't die now!"

And then she cradled his head in her arms, staring as if mesmerized as his blood pumped out from his body, and all her hopes and dreams along with it.

She heard a chilling, high-pitched scream. At first she thought it was Nigel. It was several moments before she realized where it had actually come from—the depths of her own throat.

* * *

706

"Tante Hélène! Tante Hélène!" She felt Petite Hélène's arms around her, compassionately rocking her back into the present.

Both of them were crying, and they cried and cried for a long time.

Nigel lay motionless in the narrow bed, a network of clear plastic tubes coursing into his body. The television monitors on the table beside the bed registered low, painful bleeps and traced listless graphs. Hélène turned and looked at the doctor without speaking. She tried to smile bravely, and touched his arm.

He nodded reassuringly and left her alone in the room.

For a long moment she just stood there looking at Nigel in silence. Then she turned away to stare at the monitors. She saw the unsteady green lines becoming weak mounds before becoming lazy lines again. Then slowly she tore her eyes away from the screen and approached the bed. She sank to her knees and pressed her cheek against Nigel's hand. It felt cool and lifeless. Only the occasional bleeping of the monitors assured her that he was still showing signs of life. She remembered what Petite Hélène had told her—how many hours ago, now?—"Now all we can do is to wait and pray."

Did she know any prayers? she wondered. And could she pray? No, she *couldn't* pray—couldn't since that winter afternoon so long ago when Maman had been carted off by the Nazis; couldn't since Catherine and little Marie's torture and disappearance; couldn't since the day Jeanne had been snatched so brutally from life. She hadn't been able to worship God after he had abandoned all things dear to her. So how could she pray for his help now? It would be . . . two faced. Hypocritical. A desperate, last-ditch attempt just in case all else failed.

She looked up at Nigel, lying there so pale and motionless. He had put his life on the line to save her. She owed him a prayer. A thousand prayers.

She took a deep breath. For a moment she hesitated. Then she kissed his hand. "I'll start praying for you, my darling," she whispered. "I'll pray for both of us!"

Once again she stared back at the monitor. It seemed to have been silent for too long. The bleep, when it finally came, filled her with relief.

She tried to swallow, but there was an immense lump

707

blocking her throat. Her hands were clammy and trembled. Could she really remember the prayers she had not said since childhood? She had promised Nigel that she would pray for him, but could she summon the prayers up from the dead-letter box that was religion in her mind and begin chanting them? For both Nigel's sake and her own? Could she even begin to believe in the *comfort* of prayer, let alone its power?

She closed her eyes, and again the scene of horror sprang up before her. Nigel throwing her out of harm's way, sacrificing himself to save her.

God bless him, she thought, and those three words triggered it. The long-forgotten prayers began to surface from the depths of her soul. Almost without her knowing it, her lips began to move, and in a whisper she surrendered herself to God.

"Our Father, who art in heaven . . ."

Her heart leaped joyously. So she really *did* believe. She squeezed her eyes shut and bowed her head.

"Hallowed be thy name . . ."

She thought she heard a sound, a quickening of the monitors' bleeps, but she couldn't be sure. Vaguely she heard activity, a door opening, soft footsteps, excited low voices, but nothing could penetrate the invisible wall of prayer that she had erected around her.

". . . Thy kingdom come . . ."

The nurse who had come in ran back out; a moment later, Dr. Weiner came rushing in with her, his stiff white smock flapping around his legs. There was a buzz of conversation.

"The monitors are registering an increase in his pulse," the nurse said quietly.

Dr. Weiner bent down and watched one monitor, then another, nodding slowly. "Maybe," he murmured. "Just maybe . . ."

The nurse turned and noticed Hélène for the first time. "How did she get in here?" she whispered harshly. "No one's supposed to be—"

"Hush," the doctor said patiently, feeling his hopes rising as the monitors' pulses quickened and jumped. "I invited her in. Under the circumstances, I didn't think it could hurt."

". . . Thy will be done. On earth as it is in heaven . . ."

Hélène's eyes were still closed. She wasn't even hearing the doctor and the nurse. Nor was she hearing the jumping pulsebeats of the monitors. Instead, she felt a tightening in her throat. She slumped forward and began to tremble. All at once she was realizing what the prayer was doing. It was stripping away all the years of pain. Like a snake shedding its old skin for a new one, she began to feel lighter. Freer. Like a caged bird must feel after its sudden release. Finally she was stepping over the threshold of heaven after spending an eternity in hell. The demons that had haunted her for a lifetime had been cast back into the darkness.

She looked up and opened her eyes. Then she caught her breath. The doctor was standing there, smiling as though he'd witnessed a miracle. The nurse looked confused as the monitors bleeped happily. And slowly, ever so slowly, Nigel turned his head sideways, opened his gold-flecked eyes, and smiled at her.

"Hélène . . ." he whispered.

A sob caught in her throat. For a long moment she was silent. ". . . And . . . and forgive us our trespasses," she said in a fervent whisper, "as we forgive those who trespass against us."